A Flash of.
DIAMONDS

OTHER BOOKS BY CLARISSA MCNAIR

Garden of Tigers
Dancing With Thieves
The Hole in the Edge

BOOKS BY CICI MCNAIR

Never Flirt With a Femme Fatale
Detectives Don't Wear Seat Belts

A Flash of
DIAMONDS

CLARISSA McNAIR

FEDORA PRESS
Philadelphia

Reissued by Fedora Press in 2011

Originally published by St. Martin's Press

Cover Design by Scribe Freelance | www.scribefreelance.com

Visit the author online at: www.mcnairwrites.com

Library of Congress Cataloging-in-Publication Data

McNair, Clarissa.
    A Flash of Diamonds / Clarissa McNair

ISBN 978-1-936712-00-7

This book is dedicated to special friends who, as invaluable advisors and confidantes, played leading roles in making my time in Geneva the adventure it was:

Baroness Marie-Claire von Alvensleben
André Michel
Catherine Ortiz

I also dedicate it to Clarissa Walton McNair, who, with her great spirit, gave me endless encouragement.

Acknowledgments

I wish to thank Adler Jewellery, Ltd., of Geneva and London, Arthur Altschul, Baron Bodo von Alvensleben, Wendula and Stefano von Alvensleben, David M. Anderson, Christiane Bordier, Count and Countess François de Brie, Victor Ciardello, Ron Edens, Lucien and Michele Fischer, Heather Hanley, Perri Klass, Gerard Le Roux, Jean-Louis Pargade, Olivier Turrettini, and Larry Wolff.

A very special thanks to Baron Serge Fliegers de Wolf.

Merci beaucoup to the entire staff of the Beau Rivage, which proved the happiest of places to write my novel. Thank you to Catherine Nickbarte-Mayer, Snuggi Mayer, and Jacques Mayer for offering a waif such luxurious shelter!

A note to everyone in the Protestant Rome who tried to help me understand—I did my best, but the more I discovered the less I knew. I agree with Talleyrand, who wrote: "There are five continents—Europe, Asia, America, Africa, and Geneva."

CHAPTER ONE

Cynthia

August 1988 — Geneva

"Too much has happened," Cynthia said aloud. The elegant woman dressed in white stood alone on the balcony, thankful there was no one to hear her. *The past is running after me and I've always been afraid to stop running and turn around and face it.* She stared out at Lake Geneva, a streak of silvery blue in the fading light. The water seemed cool and touchable, just beyond the balcony railing, just past the green treetops of the square below.

"Madame?" Simone asked again. She wore a gray uniform and a short white starched apron.

"*Oui, oui,*" Cynthia murmured. "Tea, *s'il vous plait.*" She turned to watch the retreating maid thread her way through the French antiques, past an Egyptian sphinx of black granite, past a marble table covered with letter openers shaped like daggers, past another marble table displaying scarabs of faience and stone. The dark blue walls were hung with what appeared to be old maps or pieces of maps, faded and under glass, in heavy, carved frames of gold. The room was ornately furnished, crowded. The only light or sense of space came from behind Cynthia where the French doors were open onto the balcony.

Cynthia Colbert sat at her desk in silence and sipped the tea. Then, as if remembering something, she pulled a piece of paper from the pocket of her dress. "I did it," she whispered. "Now I wait."

The copy of the telegram was creased, but her printing was clear. It was addressed to Mark Falconi in Washington, D.C., and in capitals pleaded, CALL ME TOMORROW. She had signed it CYNTHIA KENDALL COLBERT in block letters. Cynthia read it one more time, checking the familiar telephone number, then leaned back in the chair and closed her eyes.

Late August. Just about the time of conception. A little boy, no, a young man, he would be nine months shy of a birthday. Cynthia remembered the night she had lost her virginity more vividly than anything that had happened to her in all the years since. The day of the baby's birth was a blur. Abruptly she opened her eyes and, taking the paper, she folded it, then tore it lengthwise, then methodically crosswise again and again. The tiny pieces were crushed into her pocket.

Cynthia felt tears come and told herself not to think, not to remember her mother's cold logic, her own long, sad days of weeping and solitary walks on the beach that summer afterwards. She had been convinced that she could never atone for all that had happened. Getting pregnant was an accident, but she had consented to give the child away. Her own flesh and blood. She wiped her wet cheeks. But I am a different person now. I have nothing to do with Boston or the girl I was. She felt like screaming inside. These last few days have been unreal, too much has happened. The only thing to do is get through the next act, go back to Les Colombiers and take care of all that awaits me there.

Cynthia drank the last of the tea, then stood and walked slowly back to the balcony. Dusk was falling on the city outside as she leaned on the iron railing and willed herself to take deep breaths. Simone cleared the tea things behind her. When I was young, Cynthia began to think. But no, I was never young. I was married and starting life in a new country, this strange little island in Europe called Switzerland, this strange little island of Geneva that isn't Swiss at all. Me. Nineteen and married. Trying, with every ounce of strength in me, to be happy. To convince myself I was. Trying to convince myself that so many things never happened. She tasted tears in the back of her throat. "Bad dreams," she said softly, and swallowed. She watched a sailboat heel over on the lake with a fluttering of clean white sails, and thought of Marco. She said aloud to no one, "Bad dreams and dreams."

August 1966 — Edgartown, Martha's Vineyard

"Cynthia!" She could hear his voice, urgent, pleading, as though it had been yesterday. "Cynthia! Come on!"

The young girl in white looked up from the punch cup she held, and saw him in the doorway. Always in the doorway, never quite inside, more outside than ever in, she thought. Outlined by darkness, tall, handsome, intense, his dark eyes bright. The room was full of music, a band from Boston played "Yesterday," and couples swayed back and forth, clutching one another, as a sprinkling of parents acting as chaperons looked on in a mixture of amusement and disapproval. Crosby Hyatt was her official escort, and Cynthia anxiously scanned the room for him before she moved. Nowhere in sight. Probably in the men's room, swigging Scotch out of his father's silver flask with Bruce and Harry. Big deal. "Cynthia!" She put the cup down and, outwardly calm as always, slowly walked toward the door, turning to smile and nod hello to Mrs. Vandevere, who was admiring her from a distance. Mother's dear friend watching her leave—great! But she kept walking, turning this way and that between the dancers.

Once away from the glow and the heat of the yacht club, once in the darkness scented with the ocean, Cynthia shivered. Immediately his arms went around her, and she put her face against his. "Come on. It's too risky here," he whispered. He took her hand and they ran over the dock to shore. "I have a place," Marco told her as he led her toward the Hyatts' house. She balked. "But it's—"

"I know. But it doesn't matter. No one's home."

Cynthia knew it would happen when she saw the blanket spread on the shed floor. No, she thought. Not in the Hyatts' toolshed, between the lawn mower and the life preservers. "Let's go to the beach," she insisted. Marco grabbed the red plaid blanket and they cut through the backyards of the looming, gray-shingled houses, away from the tree-lined streets of Edgartown. In three minutes they had reached the narrow, sandy paths bordered by tickling, knee-high beach grass; they proceeded single file, like a pair of Indians.

Shoes were tossed aside and the blanket was spread on the sand. The ocean was dark and shining before them; thousands of square miles of it gleamed in the starlight.

"Our last night," Marco sighed into her tan shoulder. He pulled the eyelet-covered straps away from her and kissed each breast tenderly. Cynthia lay back with closed eyes, her long blond hair splayed around her on the blanket. She reached up to touch his black-as-ink cowlick and thought how much she loved him.

"Marco," she said softly as he pulled the bodice of her dress down. He didn't answer, but suddenly she felt his fingers farther up her thighs than ever before. They had given each other backrubs until it almost hurt to have the hands leave their skin, they had kissed until they practically couldn't breathe, but this was more, this was different. Not once this summer had Marco ever touched her there.

"I want to make love. We should. We have to." His voice was husky with wanting. "You'll be in Boston tomorrow night, in your own bed, and I might as well be in China."

"But, Marco," she pulled his head up toward hers; the star-spattered sky surrounded his silhouette. The black brows were nearly straight over the deepest brown eyes Cynthia had ever seen; the cheekbones were pronounced in a nearly square face. He possessed a rugged look—much too rugged for his gentle hands, his soft voice, his mouth of velvet. "It's the last night here, but in a few weeks I'll be at Smith and you'll be in Vermont and there are so many ways we can get to each other . . ." She was insistent. "Without my parents, without behaving like little kids, without hiding from that idiot Crosby."

His fingers made her stop in surprise. The intensity of the feeling made her gasp, then his mouth was over hers, muffling all protests. "No more discussion," he whispered in his careful way as clothes were pulled aside. When she cried out in pain, Marco soothed her. "I'll be very slow. Shhhh. Very slowly. It's all right. See? Very slowly."

Cynthia bit her lip and tears welled up, blurring the brightness of the starry night.

"Am I hurting you?" He smoothed a strand of hair away from her flushed cheek.

"No," she breathed. "No. Not ever. Because I love you."

His face, his sweet mouth blotted out the bruise of a sky hung with summer stars, and she felt herself falling into a rhythm that was like the waves, like the sea.

"I love you. I love you. Will love you always," he sighed into her neck. Cynthia dug her fingers into his broad shoulders, into the muscles he had developed working at the boatyard every morning. Marco's breathing became ragged as he moved inside her more quickly. She watched his face contort with an agony she couldn't understand, watched his eyes squint shut with a wild desperation. His lean, tan body pumped life into hers. And then it was over. Something was over. Cynthia stroked his face and smiled almost maternally. "I love you," he whispered. "I love you for always."

· · ·

"A cottage! We call it a cottage!" her father would laugh. "Absurdly too big," Otis Kendall always said of the house, as he watched the suitcases being unloaded onto the front porch every July. As though the house would sigh in acquiescence and drop a wing here or there or just shrink obediently like a raisin in the sun.

Tonight, as Marco and Cynthia lingered under the willow-lined driveway, it seemed larger than ever. The wide, three-story white building was graced with a veranda that stretched its entire length. The mullioned windows were dark—which surprised Cynthia, for her mother usually read in bed until all hours. Grand and imposing, the structure was crowned with a tiara of a widow's walk so that the first Mrs. Kendall who had lived there in the 1700s could gaze out at the Atlantic, longing for the return of her seafaring husband. The property was bordered by sand dunes that reached down to the ocean.

Marco put his hands on either side of Cynthia's face. "We finally did it," he grinned. "I've thought of it all summer, every day, especially when I'd ask little Throckmorton to recite his Latin verbs to me. 'I love, you love, he loves . . .' "

Throckmorton was their pet name for Robby, the horribly spoiled and very fat younger brother of Crosby Hyatt III. Robby waddled around the village eating ice cream, a splatter of flavors across his bulging, T-shirted front.

Cynthia stifled a giggle by putting her face against Marco's shoulder. How she loved the smell of him. The taste of his mouth. And now, she thought as she felt the stickiness on her thigh, there was something more to love.

"I can't say good-bye," he was saying as Cynthia wondered if Dr. Harrison would help her with some kind of birth control. For Smith. For the next time she was with Marco. No. She decided she'd have to wait until she reached college. Maybe somebody would know how to find a doctor who would fit her with a diaphragm. "I can't say it," he whispered. "It's painful to think of not seeing you every day. I won't see you tomorrow or the next morning or the day after that."

Cynthia looked up into those big, dark eyes and stroked his sideburns, which she called his feathers. His skin smelled of the ocean and had been burnished a very dark olive. They held each other for a long time and then she broke away. "I have to go in now."

"What time are you driving back to Boston?"

"Around eight. We're all packed. Daddy went back yesterday morning."

Marco kissed her lightly, and then the spirit between them became urgent once more. His breath was warm on her face. "I want you again and again and again. I meant what I said before. I want you to marry me. I want you always with me." Sometimes when he pressed her to him, Cynthia felt his muscles were her own. His hard leanness mirrored her own slenderness, his mouth always welcomed hers.

"A few weeks, and then we can be together all night. All weekend. I can take a bus from Smith to you, or we can meet in Boston."

He nodded, and swallowed thickly. "I know. It's . . . not forever." He ran his fingers through the tangled masses of her pale hair. "Your feathers," he laughed softly. They kissed again for one long, last, lingering time, and then Cynthia turned away from him. She forced herself to pull away from his strong arms, away from that face that almost made her sing with the pleasure of loving him when she saw him every afternoon behind the Hyatts' house. She turned away from Marco Falconi and ran lightfooted up the sandy path toward her parents' big white house.

. . .

The front door was locked, which was confusing. How odd. Mother must think I'm home and in bed already. Well, maybe that's a good thing, Cynthia decided as she padded in bare feet, clutching her sandals by their straps, around to the kitchen door. Mrs. Partridge, the housekeeper, had already moved back to the Beacon Hill house, but the cook would come early tomorrow to clear out the refrigerator. She and the local day girl would help close the cottage. How unlike Mother to not be in bed reading, Cynthia thought as she tiptoed up the winding staircase past the closed door of her parents' bedroom.

"Aaaaaah!" came the strangled voice. Cynthia froze. She could see the gleam of the picture frames on the landing reflected from the moonlight outside. The Oriental rug was soft under her feet. There was another cry more like a groan.

"Mother! Mother?" She ran across the hall and burst into the big master bedroom. "Mother, are you all right?"

"Help me!"

Cynthia reached for the overhead light switch, then blinked in the sudden brightness. Her mother was under her father, who was naked. With shock, Cynthia realized they were making love. Clothes were strewn all over the room, and the top bedsheet had slid onto the floor, leaving her father facedown, with his bare bottom looking ridiculous. It was a stripe of white between his tan back and his long, hairy legs.

"Get him off of me," her mother groaned.

Cynthia was frozen, puzzled. "Daddy!" She touched his shoulder and screamed. He was dead. With one fist in her mouth, gasping with sobs, she pulled him aside. With the momentum of that movement he rolled entirely off the bed and, with an awful, stomach-lurching thump, fell onto the floor, where he gazed upward, unseeing. His mouth was open with either the pleasure of orgasm or the surprise of dying. Margaret Lake Kendall pulled the sheet over her nakedness as her daughter began to scream.

The man wasn't her father after all. It was her favorite uncle. Uncle Teddy.

. . .

Margaret Lake Kendall remained dry-eyed, was indeed almost perfunctory about the whole thing. It was Cynthia's tears that fell on her naked uncle. The second naked man she had seen within the hour. Her mother pulled on a white peignoir and ran to the hall telephone, for some peculiar reason ignoring the one on the bedside table. She picked up the receiver and then, in exasperation, put it down again and returned to the bedroom. Cynthia stood at the open window, crying softly, but turned when her mother said, "We have to get him dressed."

The two women stood over the dead man, not knowing where to begin. "Don't stand there like a ninny! Help me!" Margaret tossed his trousers at her daughter, who caught them with dismay and not a little repugnance. Cynthia turned them around, looking for the zipper; several quarters and an unopened foil packet labeled "Trojan" fell on the flowered carpet. She hurriedly jammed everything back into a pocket.

Margaret Kendall had managed to yank and pull Uncle Teddy into his white undershorts. Brooks Brothers white cotton boxer shorts, just like my father, Cynthia thought.

Together they knelt over the body on the floor. Edward Tabor Kendall seemed diminished in death, and Cynthia was reminded of pulling a sweater on a child as she forced one terribly cold hand through a shirt sleeve. They labored in silence except for Margaret's sighs, which were directly related to the effort of moving the one-hundred-eighty-pound form, and an occasional sniffle from the niece of the deceased.

They dragged him down the stairs with Cynthia's mother holding up his head and shoulders on the top step, as Cynthia timidly pulled at his feet. His ankles were curiously unbendable, and shoes were deemed impossible. "We'll put him in the living room with the *Boston Globe,*" instructed Margaret Kendall. With much pulling and panting, they were able to sit him up in the wing chair by the fireplace. Margaret turned on the reading lamp and then arranged the paper in his lap. First she folded it back to the sports page, then changed her mind and arranged it so that it would appear that Uncle Teddy's last thoughts were of American involvement in Vietnam.

"Something wrong here." She put her index finger to her lips and took a step backward. "Something not quite—" She strode from the room, her white silk bathrobe fluttering, and in a moment had come downstairs again. Cynthia held his head up as her mother pulled the black dicky and the white Roman collar around his neck. "My God," sighed Mrs. Kendall. "First he had to leave the Episcopal Church to become a Catholic, and then . . ."

She didn't have to finish the thought. How well Cynthia remembered the family scandal. People in Boston still alluded to it these ten years later. Margaret tried to close his mouth, but couldn't. He seemed to be turning to plaster, a cold statue, getting colder and more rigid with every minute. "Mother," Cynthia suddenly said, "I didn't even think you liked Uncle Teddy."

"Well, these things happen."

"You always said that he was nothing but a rebel without a—"

"Not now, Cynthia! Don't let's talk about it now!" she said sharply. "There are things to be done." She waved her arm straight out, the wide kimono sleeve flapping like a bird's wing. "The telephone. Call the operater and get the police. Tell them that someone here has—oh, no. We'd better call Dr. Sutton first. Yes. That would be more normal."

. . .

The two officers of the Martha's Vineyard police force wore sports shirts and khaki trousers. There was little crime on the island in the summer community, and even less in the wintertime. "I'm real sorry, ladies," one of the policemen was saying as the body of Uncle Teddy was taken down the long front path on a stretcher toward the waiting ambulance. The doctor followed them to his own car.

"Oh, darling!" sighed Margaret Kendall as she closed the front door and turned off the porch lights. It was nearly half past two, according to the brass ship's clock on the mantelpiece in the living room. The two Kendall women faced each other, listening to the ambulance and the cars drive away. "I think you and I should have a drink together, something very strong, and talk about what to tell your father." She put her arm around the girl's shoulders.

Theirs was not a demonstrative family, and Cynthia moved away, surprised by the gesture. So many surprises. "I won't tell him a thing. Don't worry." Cynthia's voice was cold. "And I won't have a drink with you." She walked up the stairs slowly, feeling suddenly old and very weary. Sand was stuck to the inside of her thighs under the white sundress, and she was reminded of Marco and of the sorority of which she had just become a member. Cynthia slammed her bedroom door as hard as she possibly could; the noise was like a gunshot in the still, dark house. Margaret Kendall, who stood on the back veranda gazing out to sea, jumped when she heard it and spilled a bit of Scotch on her hand. Cynthia crossed her shadowy room and flung herself facedown on the bed, weeping. It was the last night of summer.

. . .

The next morning, Cynthia and her mother drove to Boston in the chauffeured dark blue Cadillac; Uncle Teddy's body followed in a hearse. Otis Kendall was at home in Beacon Hill, awaiting the arrival of the sad little entourage.

The secret was out the day before the funeral. After that, mentioning the name Kendall prompted giggles and guffaws all over Massachusetts. At first, Margaret Lake Kendall, daughter of Stoddard Lake, heir to his father's and grandfather's fortune in Standard Oil stock, and a highly admired professor of European history at Harvard, thought she had got away with it. She almost had—until Father Edward Kendall was undressed at the funeral home and discovered to be wearing a quite soggy, pale yellow Trojan X.

1988—Geneva

The Colbert apartment occupied the third floor of a cream-colored building between the Hotel Beau Rivage and its closest rival, the Hotel Richemond.

The hotels were the settings for parties, fashion shows, lectures, and receptions; in the autumn the Richemond hosted the Christie's auctions and the Beau Rivage was home to Sotheby's sales. The rue Adhemar Fabri in front was always crowded with taxis and shining, expensive cars. Out of limousines spilled elegantly dressed women and their prosperous-looking, dignified men. As Cynthia looked down, she saw a white Rolls-Royce trimmed in gold instead of chrome pull up to the Richemond. The license plates were Monegasque, and she recognized the Arab who lived at the hotel being helped into the back by a chauffeur. She looked out over the little park, a memorial to Charles II of Brunswick, who had bequeathed his money to the city of Geneva. He was a German who had quarreled with his family and, someone told her, there was so much money that the interest on it still paid for the maintenance of all the city's streets. Cynthia raised her eyes to the opposite shoreline. Though it wouldn't be dark for a while yet, the red, green, blue, yellow, and white lights of various companies and banks had been lit, a garden of bright neon between the shining water of the lake and the shadowy spires of the cathedral in the center of the Old Town.

Cynthia turned and reentered the drawing room. "Simone!" she called, and the maid appeared almost instantly. "I have to leave now," she said as she pulled on the white linen suit jacket, "if I'm to be in Chambesy before Monsieur Colbert arrives." She opened the lizard bag and checked for the keys to the Ferrari. "I don't know if anyone will be in on Saturday, but perhaps you should make sure the two guest rooms are prepared. I never know if Michel will want to have friends here. And why don't we start using the new bath towels? The dark blue ones. The next time I'm here, remind me to take the old ones back to Les Colombiers."

"*Oui, oui, Madame,*" Simone said as she reached for a light switch. The Colbert family was in perpetual motion between its various residences in any one of five different automobiles. Simone was used to guests—for lunch, for dinner, for the weekend, for two weeks, for two months. Many were collectors and dealers, people involved with those Egyptian things Monsieur Colbert collected. Hell to dust and hell when he suspected they hadn't been.

"I ordered several cases of wine from Maison du Vin, and they'll be delivered before noon tomorrow. The receipt is on the hall table, and please, Simone, before the boy leaves . . ."

Simone smiled. "I will check the labels."

Cynthia smiled back. They both remembered the champagne that had not arrived for the dinner party and all that inferior rosé that had had to be sent back—with a very angry Monsieur Colbert storming around the kitchen he rarely entered. "I will call you in the morning." She stood at the front door. "*Au revoir.*"

With that, Cynthia was gone, and the four-bedroom apartment was empty again. Simone remained like a statue beside the blue-striped brocade love seat. I wish I understood what was happening with Madame, she thought. In the last few days, she seems restless, nervous, even upset. She holds everything inside. Simone walked across the room and closed the balcony doors and turned the lock. "Yes," she murmured. "Madame Colbert locks everything in."

. . .

Cynthia liked to drive, and she liked to drive fast. She felt as though she could erase all the well-ordered carefulness of her life once she grasped the wheel. Tonight she punched in a cassette of a trumpet concerto and pulled out into the traffic of Quai du Mont Blanc. The U-turn was executed expertly, but someone honked at her anyway. Cynthia's response was to turn up the volume, letting the orchestra blare forth in the little red Ferrari. She raced along Quai Wilson, named after the American president who had helped to found the League of Nations, and past the Palais Wilson, where the peace accords were signed after the First World War. In a few minutes she had passed the guarded entrance of the United Nations on the right and the sprawling International Red Cross mansion on the left. The car sped up the hills, banked by woods, toward the village of Pregny. Cynthia passed the curlicued wrought-iron gates of the Rothschild estate, a glimpse of lake, and then the village of Chambesy.

The Colbert gates, as high and every bit as ornate as the Rothschilds', were open. Cynthia floored the accelerator and the car sped up the gravel driveway toward the garages. The land had been in the family since the sixteenth century, when the first Colbert arrived, a Protestant refugee from France after the Reformation. The property held a twenty-four-room chateau built in the early eighteenth century, a rose garden, a kitchen garden, twenty-two hectares of vines, a poolhouse, a pool, a fish pond, tennis courts, three farm buildings, and L'Orangerie, which was rented to an artist whom Cynthia described as the perfect tenant, "since I never see him."

She looked at the main house and felt the heaviness that always accompanied the first glimpse of what she called "Colbert territory." There was always so much to be done to it, for it: preparing for winter, preparing for Christmas, before summer, at the end of summer. The seasons never stopped, and neither did the damned getting ready for them and cleaning up after them, Cynthia thought as she slammed the door of the Ferrari. She noticed green leaves that needed to be swept up; soon there would be the autumn ones. Cynthia frowned as she crossed the cobbled courtyard.

Babette materialized in the front hallway to ask her about dinner. In twenty years, maids had come and gone, but Babette, one of the first maids of Cynthia's married life, had stayed. Cynthia sighed, "I never know exactly when he'll arrive, so tell Marie to have everything ready and just call me when you hear the car." She took off the jacket as she started up the wide staircase, hoping not to bump into Charlie. "I'll be in my bedroom."

Suddenly Cynthia felt very tired; she was trembling as though she had been badly frightened. Weariness coupled with worry and the tension of the afternoon's decision made her walk very slowly upstairs and through the pale green bedroom to the bath.

The bathroom was entirely of mirror—great solid sheets of it on opposite walls, and little irregular pieces covering the ceiling and the other two walls like a mosaic of moving water. Cynthia dropped her clothes on the gray velvet stool and stood looking at the forty-year-old body reflected hundreds upon hundreds of times. It was lean and taut, a testament to the benefits of Cynthia's disciplined, nearly-daily runs. Bikini marks crossed her tan torso; her white breasts were small but firm and round. She swam every morning when there was a half hour she could call her own. Leaning down to turn off the hot water, Cynthia caught a glimpse of her face, hazily reflected in clouds of steam.

She lowered herself into the scented soapy water, then closed her eyes and leaned back against the edge of the tub. Jean-François. What would I tell him? She thought of all that had happened in the past few days. All that had suddenly come to light. She realized she didn't care what she had to tell her husband, or what his reaction might be. That realization made Cynthia feel at once sad and strong.

Slowly rubbing soap onto the washcloth, she remembered how she'd let Jean-François assume during their courtship—what an old-fashioned word! —that she'd never made love. That had appealed to him. Just because of an auspicious accident. Accidents. On beaches. Cynthia thought of that night with Marco again. Five minutes, was that how long it had taken? Five minutes, twenty years ago, on a red plaid blanket. She began, absentmindedly, to soap her feet. And after that, Mother had orchestrated everything in her own inimitable style. Cynthia grimaced. She hated any of her own traits that were like her mother's, and when she recognized them she immediately attempted to change them or at least to change direction. But she had noticed only the other day, while signing a check, that her signature grew more like her mother's every year. "So I went along with Mother," she said aloud. She leaned back into the suds once more and began to remember . . .

Her twin beds at the Beacon Hill house were littered with knee socks, underwear, sweaters, all name tagged, all folded carefully by Nora, the Irish maid. Starting Smith and the confusion of the dormitory, getting lost on the way to gym class, the bucktoothed roommate from Indiana . . .

And Marco. Marco promising to come that next weekend, but that had been the weekend she discovered she was two weeks late, and when she saw him, all she could do was cry. Crying in the rec room, trying not to let anyone see her, hiding her face to the side in one of the big, ugly, red vinyl armchairs. Marco had taken her hand and they had walked out the fire-exit door and far away from everyone. He'd been horrified. Yes. That was the word. But then he had immediately asked her to marry him. He did. He had asked.

Cynthia opened her eyes and stared at the jagged reflection of her face in the ceiling. Little pieces. Little pieces of me died when I was pregnant. She closed her eyes again. Her mother's voice came back to her. The voice of anger, and that from a woman whose departure from decorum had made the name Kendall a laughingstock. Mother's voice. If there was one reason to go and live with Kate Grayson in hiding in the Bahamas, Mother's voice was it. And Marco never answered her letters, never called, even though she begged him to, and gave him the phone number every single time she wrote. Kate had been instructed never to let her use the phone, and she had been caught twice trying to dial Vermont. Once she had actually reached his dorm, but Kate had silently entered the sunroom and simply pushed the button down. Without a word!

It stood to reason that if her mother had one good friend in the world, it would be a tough cookie like Kate Grayson. Her godmother was appalled to hear that Marco was on a scholarship, shocked to hear what she called his "ethnic" name, aghast that anything had happened between Cynthia Lake Kendall and a second-generation Italian who was tutoring for the summer. Of course she couldn't dream of marrying him! The two older women had called it "throwing your life away." That was a good phrase. "Even if he wanted to marry you, which he obviously doesn't." "But he asked me to marry him!" Cynthia shouted. They ignored her and went on. There was the talk about "breeding," which, if he'd been well brought up—in other words, white Anglo-Saxon Protestant Old Boston—he would possess, and that would mean he would offer to marry her. But of course he was Italian, so he would not make the gentlemanly offer, and of course if he did, she couldn't accept anyway because of his background.

Cynthia clenched her fists underwater. She had never been able to make herself hate him. But she had spent years never understanding how he could have ignored her letters! All those tear-stained declarations of love— desperate—pleading to hear from him. Not for marriage, just to know how he was . . . Cynthia held her breath until the urge to give in to tears passed. Yes. Me, the idiot. I actually went through a stage of thinking he had died. I couldn't believe that he didn't love me anymore, that he didn't care what happened to me. So he died. It was the only reasonable explanation for being so cut adrift, so achingly without someone, without the first person you'd ever loved, the person you had seen every day since you'd met him, the person who made your heart beat more quickly at the very idea of his materializing on his bicycle, in the drugstore, at the newsstand. The person you had decided you would die for. If it ever came to that. And he for me. Cynthia remembered lying in the sand dunes and deciding it together. When they were old. Maybe forty. Suicide pacts. Till death do us part. No. We would go on forever and forever. Cynthia's eyes stung. Romeo and Juliet. But in Beacon Hill the lovers don't die—just the love. She thought of her parents and of their truce.

She thought of Jean-François. Separate bedrooms. This marriage has been canceled due to lack of interest. No. Not true. We still make love. Not often. But it happens. Cynthia sighed as she stood up and reached for the gray bath towel.

Babette's voice came from the bedroom. "Madame! Monsieur Colbert just telephoned from the Bentley. He is on his way home."

"*Merci*, Babette. I will be down *tout de suite*." Her voice was pleasant, though she was thinking, Who cares that he's on his way home? Cynthia pulled on silk trousers and a silk blouse, spritzed on perfume, and stepped into open-toed sandals. As she descended the stairs she clipped on sapphire earrings.

So he was back. The perfectionist. His brown eyes took in everything. He had actually put on a white glove early in their marriage and run his finger across the tops of the lampshades in the study to explain to her how to handle servants.

Cynthia walked to the dining room and surveyed the twenty-foot-long table that seated fourteen. It was set for two. Now she remembered: Charlie, Yves, and Michel were in town for the tennis match. Wordlessly she began to move her place setting toward Jean-François's end of the table. Babette quickly picked up the silver and the wine goblet and followed her. "Can't sit like this, Babette. Make sure the new girl knows." Why, it's absurd, she thought, the two of us calling to each other down the entire length of an expanse of polished wood. Pink roses in a blue and white Dutch porcelain dish scented the air, as did the red wine that had been decanted at Jean-François's place. When Cynthia walked over to dim the Venetian chandelier, Babette reached to dim the silver sconces that lined the walls between the paintings. Jean-François had gone through a period of buying the Nabis school, and the pastel colors of Vallitton were lovely in the pale blue room.

Cynthia sat down, thinking of her husband's criticism of her moving the place setting herself. But it's simpler than always telling people. I have two hands. It isn't important who does it, just that it's done. His sharp tongue was always ready with scathing rebukes for the smallest things. She had only committed the most minor sins in her marriage. Charge cards left in a hotel room in Nice, three expensive accidents in this Ferrari or that one, hiring a maid who stole some of the family silver in a pillowcase.

Cynthia watched Jean-François stride into the dining room, still a very handsome man fifteen years her senior; gray-haired but giving the impression of strength, of youth. There was a quickness to his gestures, a light athletic stride—confident, even cocky. Cynthia suddenly thought of him with that woman. No. Don't. Too much has happened. One thing at a time. My careful, orderly world is coming apart.

A white-gloved servant poured wine into Jean-François's glass. He tasted it and nodded. They did not speak at dinner. Like strangers forced to share a table, they were silent, each alone. Cynthia, ever practical, stabbed a bit of the lake perch with her fork and hoped that someone in the kitchen had thought to make fish stock.

CHAPTER TWO

Iris

1988 — Geneva, a Suite at the Beau Rivage

"Madame! Madame!" Anna called timidly, opening the door.

"*Oui!*" Iris answered with irritation. The woman looked small in the enormous white marble tub, even as she rose a few inches out of the perfumed suds. Her blond hair was caught up in a lacy bouffant cap, but several tendrils had escaped and lay wet on her neck. Green eyes flashed in a heart-shaped face. She so hated to be disturbed in her bath. "What on earth is it?"

Anna stood over her in the steamy bathroom, extending the white envelope. "Madame! Another one! Joao saw it pushed under the door."

"Well, did he see who delivered it?"

"*Non.* He or she disappeared. Joao ran down the hall to the elevators, but there was nobody." Anna knew every single Portuguese porter in the hotel by name, though they'd only moved from Paris three months ago.

"He saw nothing?" Iris dried her fingers on the linen hand towel, and took the envelope. Identical to the others. Apparently she had not left this . . . this *nonsense* . . . behind her in Paris. Her throat felt tight as she pulled at the flap.

Anna left the room, closing the door carefully behind her. She busied herself in the bedroom, turning down the big double bed and precisely folding back the eyelet-trimmed sheet. She fluffed the large, square white pillows, all six of them, into place. Then she carefully sifted the rose-petal potpourri, stalling, awaiting her mistress's call.

It came. More angry than frightened, and very loud. *"Merde!"*

. . .

Iris brushed her nearly white blond hair one hundred times a night. It was the only thing, she had told someone once, that her mother had ever taught her. "It is your crowning glory." Iris remembered the words years later as perhaps the only compliment the woman had ever given her as a little girl.

When glimpsed from a distance, Iris seemed a diminutive pink-and-white blonde, perhaps Scandinavian. But when faced with her, the green-eyed gaze struck many men with the force of a stiff drink. She was delicate in her features, with the tiny, faintly upturned nose that so many New York women had instructed their surgeons to bestow upon them in the 1960s. She was as voluptuous as the first of the *Playboy* centerfolds in an age when Americans worshiped bone structure and lean limbs and jogging. Iris was a woman who reveled in eating and wore plunging necklines and figure-hugging dresses, totally secure in her well-rounded charms. An expatriate American who appeared to have found her happiness in another culture, she had arrived in France from New York an unspecified number of years ago, having been born somewhere between Arizona and Chicago, also an unspecified number of years ago. Her paintings were signed only "Iris." No one could remember her having a last name. Three of her maids had been bribed over the years to check her passport. Gossips were disappointed, for the birthdate on the document made her much younger than her apparent age, and there was simply no last name.

"She's obviously slept with someone at the consulate," sniped a Frenchwoman upon hearing this news. "Someone at the consulate, someone at the embassy . . . but which embassy?" asked someone else. "Any embassy you can think of," laughed another. "Start with A. Afghanistan? Now what would Iris want from the Afghan embassy?" they tittered.

In Paris the painter was described as a woman who got her way by using her wiles. Furthermore, Iris did not find her reputation in the least discouraging, which made her even more disliked. By women.

The white and gold Chaumet clock on her marble-topped dressing table said it was half past eleven. Jean-François had had it delivered only last week as a little present. Iris thought of him in Chambesy right now, summoning to mind the chateau called Les Colombiers, set back at the end of a tree-lined driveway. Its several dozen windows would be lit and golden. And beyond them the rooms would be bustling with servants and crowded with the expensive antiques she had watched him bid on here and there, on trips to London, at Drouaut right in Paris. How Iris loved going to buy paintings at Drouaut Montaigne, which was really the Théâtre de Champs-Elysées. The auctioneer actually stood onstage! Her thoughts returned to Jean-François. He would be in a book-lined library, poring over papers or perhaps an auction catalogue, wearing a maroon silk dressing gown, sipping a cognac. She smiled because he never wore a dressing gown with her. But he would with his wife. Iris yawned and put a delicate, pink-nailed hand to her lips. Jean-François. Only a few kilometers away, and there was tomorrow and tomorrow and tomorrow to be with him.

Iris reached for a jar of face cream and slowly began to massage it into her neck with long, feathery motions. Her skin was flawless white, and seemed translucent; at her wrists, the pulse was a pale blue. She looked at the clock again, and decided he would not call. Patting gel under her eyes, she suddenly peered sharply into the mirror.

Thirty-eight and no husband, went through her mind. Admirers by the dozen, any one of whom she could encourage toward a secure future. If not marriage, then an arrangement. Iris rolled her eyes. Anyone except that old goat from Liechtenstein with the breath of a cat's sandbox. Even if he were as rich as a king. Actually, he was richer than most kings. But no, he would not do. And Gaston could be ruled out. He was so boring until he was drunk, and then he was incapable of performing sexually. So dinner with Gaston was tedious, and bed a disappointment. One or the other Iris could handle if Gaston had enough money, a good enough name, but the two defects in tandem were tantamount to tragedy.

Jean-François came to mind again. He was never less than interesting. And had money to burn. A rather grand family history, too. Yes. Marriage. That would be fun. And that chateau she had supposedly only heard about. But Anna and she had taken one of their little trips and seen it from the outside through the trees. And Jean-François hadn't tired of her in two years. Nor had Iris tired of him. He was elusive enough to excite her. Do I want not only a good name, but a man I'm not sure I can have? she wondered.

Iris pulled at the pink satin ribbons of her peignoir and decided. Yes. I like the possibilities. How Iris loved that word. It made her world what it was. She got into bed, arranged the sheets and the little pink quilt, and then turned off the ormulu lamp on the bedside table. Iris smiled in the dark. Jean-François Colbert. Endless possibilities.

1956— Elliston, Illinois

"Ilsa! Ilsa! Supper!" The woman was annoyed. That girl was always out playing late after school, and never answered her call the first time or even the second. No sign of the scamp. She turned away from scanning the parking lot the neighborhood children used for kick-the-can, and back to the tiny kitchen.

The cabbage was boiling over, and with a mutter in German, she grabbed the handle without using the potholder. She swore loudly and ran cold water over her thick, fleshy fingers.

"Oh, Karl! You frightened me!" she cried out as her husband embraced her from behind. He had a difficult time getting his short arms around her bulk in the shapeless flowered housedress. "Kiss! Kiss! Kiss!" he cooed as she laughed and playfully pushed him away.

Karl Keller was the nicest man on the block; everyone thought so. How he could stay married to that shrew of a wife with the prematurely gray hair and the gray face and the thin-lipped grimace, no one understood. He, like her, was short, and had a barrel chest and short, stocky legs. But his face was pink from the outdoors and his dark eyes twinkled with fun. He was never unsmiling for more time than the moment it took him to sip a swallow of coffee.

"She here?" he asked as he took off his woolen cap and put it on the table. "I know! I know!" he laughed as he picked it up again. He always put his cap there, and she always told him not to. It had gone on for all twelve years of their married life.

"No. Of course she isn't." Hildemar Wirth Keller hurriedly dried her hands on the yellow checked dishcloth. "No telling where she is or what she's doing."

"Ah! You are too hard on our little one. She's a good girl. You know that." His voice took on such tenderness when he spoke of her. Ilsa was a gift from God after five childless years of marriage, and Karl thanked Him every time he bent over his last at the shoemaker's shop, every time he said his prayers in bed at night. He walked over to the door that opened onto the balcony, where Hilde grew a few herbs in pots, and pushed aside the damp dish towels on the clothesline. Leaning over, he called down, "Ilsa! Come home for supper!"

In seconds the voice came up to him. "Papa!" she shrieked with delight. "Papa!" A little figure in a red jacket waved frantically. Her long, skinny legs ended in white socks and scuffed brown tie shoes, and her white-blond hair cascaded halfway down her back. "I'm coming!"

He waved back, his broad face split like a jack-o'-lantern by his big toothy grin. His wife pinched her mouth tightly as she poured the water off the cabbage through the colander and the steam wafted in a cloud up into her florid face. "She answers *you*," she said with a grunt.

"Oh, Hildy, she didn't hear you. You know how kids are when they're playing . . ."

Clatter-clatter-clatter came the running feet, and then she was in his arms. "Papa!" She covered his face with kisses and he scratched her cheek with his growing beard and she squealed and giggled.

"Stop all that noise, Ilsa! You stop that screaming! Mama has a headache!"

Karl rolled his eyes, big and black, and put his fingers to his lips with a comically exaggerated gesture. Ilsa giggled softly and then slid from his lap to the floor.

"Go and wash your hands! Both of you!" came the command. Hildemar had her back to them as she spooned potatoes into a blue bowl.

It was always like that. Mama washed and ironed her clothes and gave Ilsa hot, nourishing food, but Papa gave her kisses and hugs and called her "my princess" and told her a bedtime story every night as she lay under the patchwork quilt from the old country and sucked her thumb. Mama told her what to do and was impatient with her, even more so when she was giggling with Papa, but Papa praised her and told her what a good girl she was. Ilsa decided in the second grade that everyone had two parents so that one could be stern and the other could be fun.

The Kellers were comfortable for Karl's parents had done well in America, and he owned his shoemaker's shop and a half-share in the bakery down the street. The apartment had six rooms for just the three of them, and was warm and full of the woodcarvings Karl whittled in the evening. Little crocheted doilies that Hildemar made, white like big snowflakes, were pinned to the chair backs.

They lived simply, as their parents had, but there was money in the bank, and Karl dreamed of a vacation in Minnesota someday. Someday in the summer when Ilsa didn't have school, when he could take time away from his shop, when Hildemar would come and not have an excuse about housework or headaches. Karl Keller imagined the three of them in a red canoe, wearing straw hats, laughing.

Ilsa was stared at on the street as she walked to school or nibbled a candy bar on the way home. Her hair was platinum, as pale as Kim Novak's. Her eyes were green—not gray-green, either, but as green as a river. When she walked hand in hand with her father, people would remark to one another, "She must have a beautiful mother," but when people saw her with her mother, they said, "She must look like her father." No one who knew the Kellers could understand how this couple could have produced this radiantly glorious child. It was as if there had been a mistake, a switch in the hospital, a mysterious adoption, or as if an angel had been born to very ordinary mortals.

Ilsa was oblivious to the attention; she cared only what her beloved Papa thought of her. She loved him more than anything—the way he smelled, the way his face felt against her cheek, his crooked grin, his shining black eyes, his laugh that jiggled his stomach when she sat on his lap. Ilsa especially loved his strong arms around her. Papa would always keep her safe.

When Ilsa Keller was ten, she came home for supper one evening and men in white coats were crowding the kitchen, putting a blanket over her father. She ran to where his arm stuck out, and grabbed him, screaming, "Papa! Papa! Wake up! I'm home!"

Hildemar pulled her away, but struggling, she fought to follow the stretcher down the hall and then tried in an agony of despair to throw herself over the railing of the kitchen balcony to where she saw him being loaded, like some strange bundle of mail, perhaps, or rags, into the ambulance with the red light going round and round on top.

The emptiness of the Keller apartment that night was as palpable as cold fog, as heavy with pain as the heartbeat that Ilsa could feel in her throat, as silent as the dark when you wake from a nightmare and stare into the void before reaching for the bedside lamp. Ilsa lay on her back, clutching the red and green and yellow old-country quilt, and tried to see his face again. All she could summon behind her stinging lids was that cherry-red light going round and round and round on top of the white truck that took him away.

· · ·

Ilsa literally bloomed into a young woman. Her hair was what people noticed first, pale sunlight, a cascade of silk around a sweet face. Tiny, strawberry-tipped breasts became larger and then large enough to embarrass her when she realized that boys had stopped looking into her eyes and that their gaze was riveted downward. She begged her mother for blouses two sizes too big, and pulled the fabric into a sort of blouson effect and then cinched a wide belt around her skirt, hoping to draw attention to her tiny waist. At five feet, she was destined never to grow a fraction taller; the idea of being forever "four foot twelve," as she called herself, was a disappointment. In her thirteenth summer she glimpsed herself in a shop window under a big umbrella, and decided she looked like a mushroom.

The Keller household was not a happy place. Since the death of Karl, Hildemar had developed a mania for order. She had never appeared to grieve, and Ilsa had seen no tears. Instead, the woman seemed to be possessed by a fanatical concern for the appearance of the apartment. Not that anyone came to sit in the big armchairs or on the horsehair love seat, or to drink a cup of coffee from a clean cup as they admired the freshly waxed floors. Karl had had friends, but had never invited them to come home with him, and after the obligatory calls on his widow, they had not returned. Hildemar had always claimed that she was busy cooking, and that visitors needed "tending."

Her daughter would remark bitterly, years later, "I was 'tended' the way you take care of a rabbit. Food, water, clean the cage."

"How's school?" and a few comments over steaming plates of cabbage were the extent of their conversation. Hildemar had no interests outside of her six-room kingdom. Ilsa was no trouble, for she never brought anyone home who might have muddy shoes or who would expect a glass of milk or a cookie after school. Ilsa knew to rinse the glass immediately to avoid the white ring, then to pull on the yellow rubber gloves that were kept under the sink. She had been taught to run the tap water until it was almost scalding, and then to squirt three drops of detergent into the glass and scrub it with the sponge Hildemar boiled for sterility every morning.

Rules covered all imaginable aspects of living. Ilsa was not allowed to wear her shoes in the house; she padded around in sock feet or in her pink corduroy bedroom slippers, which her mother encouraged her to wear. The little girl hated putting them on in the daytime, saying they made her feel as if she were sick. Suddenly that summer she had not been allowed to go barefoot either, for Hildemar had decided that the oil on the bottoms of human feet damaged the rug fibers.

The silent sprite at home became a giggler at Gretchen's house, where she and her best friend *oohe*d and *aah*ed over movie magazines and ate Hostess Twinkies on the frilly pink bedspread. Mostly they talked about boys, though Gretchen was still a stick and Ilsa had worn a brassiere for nearly two years. The gulf between the girls widened when Tommy Burke asked Ilsa to the movies and Gretchen warned her not to go. "But why not?" exclaimed Ilsa, shocked that her friend wasn't excitedly suggesting what she should wear.

"Because you're thirteen and he's sixteen and . . . well, Lisa Brown told me he's . . . he's *fast*." The last word was nearly whispered.

Ilsa laughed merrily. She liked the way he looked at her, as if she were wearing only a bathing suit. Her head came exactly to the breast pocket of his polo shirt and standing like that, she realized her face was so close to him that she could practically smell him. The discovery amazed and delighted her.

Ilsa lied to her mother about being at Gretchen Reimer's for the night, and pleaded with her friend for sanctuary after the date, but the difficult part was being pawed in the backseat of Tommy's best friend's Volkswagen for hours. The local lovers' lane was jammed with cars, and occasional squeals or deep masculine laughter could be heard from one to the other. Tommy Burke's kisses didn't feel the way kisses looked as if they felt on the movie screen.

"Stop it!" She pushed his hands away from her breasts. "Stop!" He was an octopus.

He sat up, surprise on his face in the pale green light of the radio dial. "Whaddaya mean?"

"Hey!" There was a face outside the open window. "Got a light?"

Ilsa recognized the rawboned features of Cutter Harrington. Everybody knew who he was—even the most tuned-out of seventh-graders. Cutter, at six feet one, was solid muscle and could have played football. He was bright enough to be an above-average student, and good looking enough to be effortlessly popular with girls. But he had slipped into the tough gang world of fistfights, shoplifting, and racing cars out on Morton's Road. Now he was labeled an underachiever and a troublemaker by his teachers, and a hood by the other students.

"Sure, Cutter." Tommy patted his pockets, grinning down at the bulge in his tight jeans.

"I want to go home," Ilsa said clearly as she pulled her blouse closed.

Tommy was embarrassed, angry. "Shut up!" he commanded.

Ilsa said it again, and this time Cutter walked around to her door. "I'll take you."

"Christ! What are you doing?" Tommy erupted, grabbing her arm.

"Going home." She felt calm now. Cutter Harrington was tougher than any other boy in school. Tommy would have to let her go. She never needed to see Tommy Burke again. At least not in the backseat of a Volkswagen. She was being taken care of by Cutter Harrington.

"Let go of her, Burke! Can't you see she's just a kid?" Ilsa winced at that.

"She doesn't look like any kid!" Tommy shouted at them as they crossed the dirt road to the tan Chevrolet.

"Get in back," he told her. Ilsa then saw the red bouffant hairdo of Wanda Kowalski.

"Hi," she said to the girl in the front seat. Wanda didn't answer.

The three drove back to the city without speaking; on the radio, the Everly Brothers crooned "Dream, Dream, Dream," and twanged their guitars in a state of acute melancholia. So great was the distance between Ilsa and the made-up redhead with her Dragon Lady fingernails and false eyelashes that Ilsa thought of herself almost as a child riding in the backseat with her parents up front. And Cutter was a man who dared to drive a car without a driver's license. Who shaved. Who probably even took off his clothes and did it. Had sex. With Wanda, maybe. She stared at the way his hair grew with keen interest. The sideburns and pompadour weren't "hoody" the way his friends' were, just because he was so good looking underneath the grease. Straight nose and kind of a mean mouth, Ilsa decided in the light of the oncoming headlights. She concluded that he was more handsome close up than he had been carrying his tray in the cafeteria.

"Drop me at the corner," was all she said, and in seconds she had murmured "Thanks," slammed the door, and the car was gone.

Ilsa walked through the wet grass to the Reimers' house and saw with relief that Gretchen had waited up for her. The front door was opened with a great deal of shushing from her friend, who was an apparition in a flannel granny gown; pink foam rollers the diameter of orange-juice cans covered her head, and her anxious face was dotted with brown smudges of Clearasil. "What happened?" she asked excitedly the moment the two were safe in her pink bedroom.

Ilsa grinned triumphantly. "Cutter Harrington brought me home." This revelation was greeted by a smothered scream from Gretchen. "Now, Gretchen," Ilsa continued, looking like a very satisfied little cat, "we have to find out everything we can about Wanda Kowalski."

· · ·

It wasn't difficult detective work. Everyone knew who Wanda Kowalski was: she and Cutter had been steadies since seventh grade; she, with two others, led the Clique. Linda Friedlander and Sarah Beck and Wanda referred to each other by their last names, smoked in the girls' room in blatant disregard for the rules, and thought of themselves as tough, cool, and worldly. They had nothing but disdain for those rewarded by the system: honors students, cheerleaders, football players. The Clique's followers were less tough, less cool, and entirely dependent upon their leaders' opinions of them. Their hairdos, the pale lipstick they applied frequently, the very weave of their bobby socks, were all under constant scrutiny. Push-up bras straining at tight sweaters and girdled young behinds straining just as futilely against painted-on black skirts constituted the uniform. Most of them smoked Salems or Kents, but Wanda preferred Camels, calling them her "super-strong coffin nails." No one smoked Lucky Strikes or Kools. It just wasn't done.

There seemed nothing else to know about Wanda Kowalski. She lived with her parents in an apartment house nearby. Her father sold Fuller brushes. She had an older sister who was married and lived in Kansas. A slim biography. She bought lots of her clothes at J.C. Penney, which was where most of the girls shopped, and her penny loafers came from Baker's. It was her habit to arrive at school early so that she could walk the halls with Cutter at her side, greeting their friends. After school they met at Carson's Drugstore and sat in the last booth together with Sarah Beck and at least six other Clique members.

Gretchen quickly fell into the role of acolyte, treasuring her nearness to the new Ilsa, but maintaining her own feelings toward boys and the world of dating and crushes and weekly infatuations. She lived vicariously on Ilsa's reports of this date or that one, of who had walked her down the hall and of which boy had whistled at her on the stairs. It was as though Ilsa Keller exuded a musk of attraction, or perhaps the story of Tommy Burke had gotten around. It had become a rape scene from which Ilsa had been dramatically rescued by the most notorious bad boy in school. Ilsa actually saw Cutter no more than twice a week in the school year, and then only from a distance.

"A kid," she said huffily to Gretchen, repeating his phrase.

"But to him you are one," said her solid, no-nonsense friend.

"How can I get him to change his mind?" insisted Ilsa.

Gretchen shrugged. She thought Ilsa should watch out, that she should stick with seventh-graders and stop entertaining dangerous fantasies of being alone with Cutter. "Wait a few years and you won't be a kid," she said.

Ilsa let her opinion be known by making a *brraaaak* noise with her Coke through the red and white striped straw. She felt so free away from her mother, had come to dread going home at dinner time. Gretchen's house, Gretchen's pink bedroom were more comfortable than her own apartment, her own spartan room would ever be. "A few years," murmured Ilsa.

She often told Gretchen she wouldn't stay in Elliston. Ilsa intended to marry someone from Chicago or even from New York. "How can people go on living in this town all their lives? My mother looks out over that parking lot as if she were gazing out to sea. As if it were some mountain range." Gretchen giggled. "And it's nothing! Nothing but a parking lot in a dumpy suburb of Chicago."

"Well, we're stuck here for now," said Gretchen in her commonsense manner. She herself couldn't imagine living anywhere else. "So, meanwhile, what about Cutter Harrington?"

"I've been thinking about him nonstop. I won't marry him, but . . ." She couldn't even tell Gretchen what she wanted from Cutter. "I want him to take me to the movies just once."

Gretchen shook her head at the audacity of it. "You might as well call up Elvis and ask him to help you with your geometry homework!"

. . .

The year passed, and then another. Gretchen timidly accepted a first date and accompanied Ilsa and Rick Havers to the drive-in. She knew Ilsa was still a virgin, but was unprepared for all that could be done to a virgin. Ilsa's giggles, interspersed with loud sighing, came from the front seat of the car and drowned out most of the dialogue of *The Sound of Music*.

Cutter Harrington had graduated from ninth grade and gone on to Morton High School, a few blocks away. Wanda, of course, was gone too, and there was a new Clique of the most worldly ninth-grade girls at Beidner. Ilsa was a ringleader; Gretchen was a sort of first lieutenant because of their special friendship, nearly equal in rank to Brenda, a very hard-looking blonde who chain-smoked Camels. They adopted the uniform of the older girls, but in 1965 skirts were short, and the amount of thigh exposed was a source of constant friction between the Clique and the principal's office.

Ilsa was a knockout, and she knew it. Her hair was back-combed like a halo around her face. She used a dark shade of pancake makeup, which gave her a flawless look, and dark brown, nearly black eyeliner around her green eyes. Her lips were the palest pink possible, very nearly white.

Hildemar had told her she looked ill. "That lipstick looks like medicine or suntan cream!" she had insisted. However, like Mrs. Reimer, she realized her nagging was comparable to talking to a wall. Ilsa left the room calmly, and lately had taken to leaving the house. Hildemar was afraid that Ilsa drank beer at the Shamrock, was afraid that she was in with a bad crowd. She had found a funny-looking cigarette in her stocking drawer. It smelled sweet and not like any tobacco she knew about.

Ilsa had taken to staying away from home all weekend. If she didn't sleep at Gretchen's, she stayed with Brenda. The girls had their own devices for getting in and out of the houses with no one to note the hour. Keys were copied—that was easy. The Reimers' first-floor bathroom window screen was left unlatched; Brenda's parents' apartment had a back door where they put out the garbage for the incinerator. It locked automatically when it slammed, until the girls thought of taping the bolt. The Keller apartment was never used, for Hildemar was ever vigilant.

Ilsa had developed an I-don't-care attitude toward her life. Boredom with her mother, with her schoolwork, with the boys her own age, had pushed her to shoplifting on Saturdays at the dime store, toward petty vandalism with spray cans at the bus station. She was often drunk, often laughed until Gretchen or Brenda shook her to stop. She was a minx, a flirt, a catch-me-if-you-can kind of party girl.

Still a virgin, though. She'd done everything else, she told Brenda, including going down on Mickey Fabio in the boys' john during homeroom. "I'm saving myself for Cutter Harrington," she confided drunkenly to Gretchen one night.

"You're nuts! He is *still* with Wanda Kowalski, and you are still three years younger, and even if we are in the same school again, he's a senior!"

Ilsa smiled crookedly. "Just wait. I've been waiting. Waiting for this year. Now I'm ready."

Cutter Harrington was better looking than ever. At nearly eighteen, he was narrow-hipped and broad-shouldered and walked like a hero in a western, complete with black high-heeled boots. His blue jeans were nearly as white as his T-shirts; he affected a jeans jacket in warm weather, and either a black leather jacket decorated with silver studs and zippers or a dark blue, fur-collared air force bomber jacket when the temperature dropped.

Ilsa had said hello to Cutter twice in the hall, and he had looked down at her with a smile of interest and then, both times, someone had called his name. Once it had been Wanda. Wanda had not improved in three years. Her skin was mottled under the thick makeup, and her eyes looked tired. "She looks twenty-five to me," Brenda insisted. "Really over the hill."

One Thursday became *the* day. Ilsa knew exactly to the minute when her quarry strode out of his mechanical-drawing class and headed across the football field toward Carson's. An ambush, she decided. She wore her tightest, shortest dark green skirt—praying all day not to be sent to the principal's office and then inevitably home to change. She wasn't, and at three-ten Ilsa took her books and went to the rest room. She repaired her eye makeup and back-combed her hair to new heights. Her green eyes were bright under the smudges of shadow. "I do look like her," she whispered in the empty, white-tiled room. "I *do*." Three different people had told her she reminded them of Brigitte Bardot, and it pleased her no end. She tiptoed down the hall and was nearly at the outside door as the three-fifteen bell sounded, releasing hundreds of teenagers from their classrooms. Ilsa hurried down the steps and out to the sidewalk, where the car-pool traffic was already jamming up.

She could practically feel him, fifty yards behind her and to her left. And he was alone. Ilsa knew she looked fantastic, but everything else worried her.

Sure, she was as confident as could be, totally cool around boys her own age and even around the older ones she'd dated. But Cutter was Cutter, and he was tougher and cooler and smoother than any of them. He looked a lot like James Dean, a strong version, she decided, without the hurt in the eyes. She walked faster and told herself to stop thinking. Just get to Carson's. Just get in position.

"Hi." Ilsa stepped towards Cutter as he ordered two cherry Cokes. He turned away from the soda jerk in surprise. Ilsa smiled slightly and looked up at him. "Do you remember me?"

"No." Then he laughed. "Should I?"

"No, I guess you shouldn't," she replied teasingly. "Maybe it's better that way. Will you buy me a Coke?"

Cutter was flustered. He held two in his hands, and he'd just tossed a dollar bill on the counter. He looked down at the glasses topped with crushed ice and henna-colored syrup, then at Ilsa. Her eyes were full of challenge. "Yeah, this is for you." He put them down on the counter and watched as she pulled herself up on the stool. The green skirt was amazingly short, and her legs were slender and pale and silky looking. "What's your name?"

Before she could answer, Wanda had answered for her. "Ilsa! Little Ilsa Keller, who's been following me for years! Staring at me! Tracking me! And now I know why!" She picked up the cherry Coke and poured it over Ilsa's head, then slammed it down on the counter and, with both hands outstretched, tried to push Cutter off the round red stool. He grabbed her by her wrists and slapped her once across the cheek. Wanda cried out and then, wrenching away, her shoulder-strap bag swinging wildly, ran through the crowd of football jackets and blue jeans and ponytails, and out of the drugstore.

Ilsa took a handful of paper napkins and mopped the sticky syrup off her face and then slid off the stool and walked to the bathroom in the back. There was a hush among the crowd. She put her head under the sink and then managed to pull a brush through the sodden mass of blond hair. So much for looking terrific, she thought as she dabbed at the ruined mascara and worked to repair the eyeliner. Her white sweater was spotted with reddish brown stains, but she thought, If I can only walk through everyone with my hair and my face looking all right, then I can feel less like an idiot. She dropped her comb, and when she bent down she saw a rubber band under the sink. In minutes she had twisted her hair atop her head loosely, and tucked under the ends. Two swipes with the sponge, and at least her face looked normal. The hair would do, she decided at last, as she opened the bathroom door with dread.

The place was packed, every red leather booth filled to overflowing. The laughter was loud but there was silence when she walked past them all and toward the front, where the soda fountain was. Cutter was still there, she saw with horror. Ilsa started to walk past without speaking, but he grabbed her arm and pulled her to him. She looked up into that handsome face she'd seen in daydreams for years.

"You're not going anywhere. Not yet." He practically pulled her atop the stool next to his. "I've ordered another cherry Coke." He grinned slowly and looked directly into her green eyes. "We're starting all over."

.   .   .

"I heard! I heard all about it! Susan called me at four o'clock!" Brenda was screaming into her baby blue Princess phone. "Jesus H. Christ! Wanda must have been out of her mind with jealousy. You know she's got an amazing temper. I heard that last week in art class she threw her ceramic ashtray against the wall when poor old Miss Crimmins told her it needed work. The whole class practically dove for cover when it made this crash noise. I mean, Ilsa, tell me everything!"

"I like him," Ilsa said simply. "I knew I would, and I do."

"Holy cow! Did he ask you out?" Brenda's voice had summoned her mother, who stood in the bedroom doorway and demanded, "What is the matter with you? I can hear every word down in the kitchen!" Then she dried her hands on her apron and turned and closed the door. Brenda made a face and tried to lower her voice. "Did he ask you for your phone number?"

"I'm going out with him on Saturday night," Ilsa said calmly. She didn't appear to be the least surprised.

Brenda could only gasp with excitement. Then she added ominously, "I hope Wanda Kowalski doesn't find out about that." She bit her thumbnail as she listened to Ilsa. "You know," she interjected, "a lot of girls at Beidner were afraid of her."

"Oh, Brenda! What could she possibly do to me?" Ilsa was on top of the world, as high as a kite with euphoria. "I think cherry Coke is a great conditioner. My hair has never looked this good." She twirled one still-wet, freshly shampooed lock around her finger. "See you tomorrow in homeroom." Ilsa hung up and smiled one of her little cat smiles. Cutter Harrington. After all this time.

.   .   .

Sarah Beck was the one who took her by the arm as she walked toward her locker after third period, and it was Linda Friedlander who pushed her from behind through the swinging door. But it was Wanda who faced her in the white-tiled bathroom, red hair wild and too bright, and fire in her eyes. "Okay, grab her arms," she told Lynn and Betsy.

They were all old members of the Clique so many years ago. All for one and one for all. Ilsa didn't speak, wondered what good it would do to scream.

Bells were ringing for the change of classes. The din was, as usual, deafening. She felt confusion as well as fear. What could she possibly do to me? she remembered saying to Brenda.

Then she knew. She was taken from behind and pushed into a booth and her head was pushed into the toilet. Coughing and gasping, she sputtered for air. Through the roar of water she heard Wanda say, "Let me do the honors!" as it flushed yet again, pouring horribly into Ilsa's mouth and nose and ears. She couldn't scream; she had no breath. She couldn't get away; the girls' fingers were pinching her wrists behind her waist. She felt her bra strap break as she struggled, and then yet another hand pushed her down still farther. Suddenly, when she was sure she would drown, she was released. It was over. Miss Pittman was standing over her with her mouth open forming an O. Nothing was coming out. Ilsa was coughing deeply, blood was pouring from her nose, and then, as she sat on the tile floor, she began to vomit.

· · ·

". . . everything we can to punish the perpetrators," Mr. Lipscomb was saying. "Everything we can to discover their identities."

"May I go now?" Ilsa requested wearily. She had been taken to the school nurse, who'd given her nose drops in lieu of anything else. As if I ever wanted anything else up my nose for as long as I live, thought Ilsa. Then she had been driven home by a young substitute teacher whose eyes brimmed with tears of sympathy whenever she glanced at the disheveled fifteen-year-old beside her. Ilsa had dried her hair and changed her clothes, and now she was being questioned by the principal.

"You could have died," Miss Pittman was saying. She thought she had recognized the redhead, but she couldn't be sure; she wanted the child to reveal exactly who had done this to her. And yet Ilsa Keller was a known rebel, a little tramp. Not as white as the driven snow. Not by a long shot. "Tell us who it was!"

Ilsa looked at the three faces staring at her. Mr. Lipscomb leaned forward, bracing his elbows on his desk, which was piled high with pink message slips. His nose was awfully red. Ilsa wondered if he kept a bottle in his top drawer. Miss Pittman crossed her poor, varicose-veined legs once more and pursed her chapped lips as if she were about to name names. The senior counselor, Miss Ames, was just out of college and seemed nervous. Perhaps she was nervous because she might have to take action against whomever Ilsa accused. Maybe she's worried she'll get dunked in a toilet, too, Ilsa thought.

Mr. Lipscomb cleared his throat. "Ilsa, we're waiting! Who were they?"

Ilsa blinked and then said clearly, "I didn't see their faces."

· · ·

From Saturday night on, Cutter Harrington belonged to Ilsa Keller. Of course, no one thought of it that way. It was more like "Ilsa is Cutter's property," but the truth was a little different. Her adoration was evident, but she pulled away when he reached for her, saying, "I want you, but not yet," or "I want you, but not as much as I *will* want you." For Cutter, who was used to Wanda routinely unhooking her bra when she slipped into the front seat of his car, the tease was exciting. Wanda took his hand in the movies and firmly placed it between her thighs. Ilsa held his big hand in her two small, silky ones, and when it moved she softly stroked his thumb as he imagined her stroking something else and tried not to squirm.

Ilsa told Gretchen that everyone else had been practice. "So all those little fish meant nothing?"

"Nothing. I was waiting for the swordfish."

CHAPTER THREE

Cynthia

"You've broken blood vessels in your eyes! You must stop crying!" Her mother's voice showed annoyance and not much concern over the sadness.

Cynthia reached for the Kleenex box on the white metal bedside table and blew her nose. "Why can't I even see the baby?" she asked for the tenth time.

"It's better not to. And don't ask me again if it was a boy or a girl, because I don't know, Cynthia. I don't *want* to know." Margaret Lake Kendall walked to the window that looked out over Central Park. Best room in the private hospital. Best room money could buy. Neither she nor Otis had wanted their daughter to give birth in the Bahamas. She pursed her lips when she heard the sounds of crying behind her, then smoothed the dark blue linen suit that had proved too warm for the weather. God. What an interminable year. Labor Day. Ha! Cynthia got pregnant just before Labor Day weekend, and here we are, nine months later, the shreds of a family. Otis's only brother dead the same weekend, and the Kendall name . . . well, never the same. And I have a daughter who may be headed for some sort of breakdown. Life is grand, she thought sourly.

"Cynthia, I think if you don't stop, we'll call someone to talk to you, or just pack up and drive you to Willow Hill."

The girl was aghast. Willow Hill was a clinic outside Boston. All of her mother's alcoholic friends had gone there at one point or another for a week or a month at a time. Then she closed her swollen eyes and thought, Another threat. Haven't I heard them all? Dear Mother. The idea that I was gaining weight was more upsetting than the idea of my being pregnant. Someone might see, might talk. And if Crosby Hyatt had done it, they'd be celebrating, but no. The Italian last name had been the payoff. You'd think I'd been raped by the gardener.

Her mother was still talking. "Maybe it would be a good idea. Just for a while. Not to come home just yet. Till you're feeling stronger." Margaret Lake Kendall stood at the foot of the tilted hospital bed. Her manicured nails were painted blood red. Cynthia knew what was coming next. "Until you can face people."

"I can face people, Mother. You can't, but I can." She reveled in the flash of anger that crossed her mother's face. They never discussed Uncle Teddy, but he often seemed to be in the room with them.

The older woman began to pull on white gloves, finger by finger, and when that project was completed, she turned to the table by the window and picked up her dark blue kid pocketbook. Only then did she face her only child, and she looked a child really, with dark circles under her green eyes, her blond hair splayed over the white pillows. "Try to feel better," Margaret said crisply. "And drink all the water you can."

Cynthia didn't respond. White gloves. My mother took more time to put on her gloves than to say good-bye. The tall woman in dark blue opened the door and was gone. The second she had disappeared, Cynthia grasped the water beaker with one hand and said aloud, "I should have thrown this at her."

. . .

Otis Kendall told Margaret he would pick Cynthia up at the hospital. It was a strange errand for him. He couldn't remember picking her up at school or after church or after a birthday party on a Saturday afternoon or . . . well, ever. Otis worked long hours. But that Tuesday morning he told Lydia to cancel his lunch date and postpone everything else. The shuttle took no time at all, and soon he was at La Guardia, slipping into the back of a limousine. He took off his suit jacket, for it was unseasonably warm, and closed his eyes, trying to gather his thoughts.

Cynthia. He remembered going to the hospital to see Margaret. He could see the white roses in green tissue paper. He could remember the white January snow swirling on the Boston street. The night Cynthia was born . . .

The oak-paneled library of the Corinthian Club was warm, gray with cigar smoke, and loud with men's voices. The brass chandelier above them glowed a dull gold and lit the leather volumes that lined the walls. "To the baby girl, the daughter of Otis Kendall!" The Mayor raised his champagne glass.

"Hear, hear!" echoed other voices.

Otis, fair-haired, as brawny as a linebacker, just turned thirty-two, glowed with both pleasure and the effects of the alcohol. He stood by the marble fireplace and nodded. The champagne tulip was dwarfed in his beefy hands. "I think we should drink a toast to my wife," he intoned.

They were on their feet now, a dozen of Boston's most important men, rising from the big, oxblood leather armchairs. All of them wore dark blue or gray vested suits, with the correct amount of handkerchief showing in their breast pockets.

"To Margaret, the lovely new mother," Sullivan Braden said solemnly.

"And here's to the father! The father of the bride, who'll be paying for the wedding in twenty years!" laughed another.

"Ah!" grinned Otis. "She's not getting near men until she's twenty-five, and then she'll have a strict curfew of nine o'clock!"

"Dreamer!" laughed Mayor Carston. "My Lillian's only twelve, and she talks about marrying the boy next door as if the wedding were next week!"

"She could well do worse," put in a lawyer who lived on the same tree-lined street.

"We'll match her up with my Tommy!" insisted one of the city's wealthiest bankers.

"No. She's perfect for my Harrison!" Tobias Barnes put in. "He's nearly two now, and think of the alliance between our families." He joked, "Blood as blue as the Atlantic!"

The others booed him soundly, and Otis motioned for silence. "What's her name? What are you calling her?" someone asked before the new father could speak.

Otis put out his glass for the white-coated waiter to fill yet again, and then spoke slowly. "Cynthia." Greek. The moon. "Cynthia Lake Kendall shall marry whomever she pleases . . ." He paused. "As long as *he* pleases me and Margaret!"

They all laughed, for they all knew it was true. The Kendall dynasty could be traced back to the Magna Carta, someone had once joked to Otis at Choate. The thirteen-year-old had shrugged as he pulled on his football shoulder pads and then retorted, "We didn't have a thing to do with signing it, though my dad would like you to think so."

Kendall, earlier known as Kendal and before that as Caindaile, which meant "from the clear river valley" or "from the bright valley," was easily one of the best-known families of southern England in the fourteenth century. Wealthy landowners for generations, one weak-chinned but clever second son persuaded his older brother to buy a ship. They became the owners of two, then three, then a fleet of oceangoing vessels.

The first Kendalls of the New World arrived three years after the Mayflower passengers. Of Puritan stock, they were proud and civic-minded. Equal to the

Adamses, the Gardners, the Lowells, the Cabots, the Saltonstalls, they were of the Boston Brahmins—who, like the highest caste of Hindus, from whom they took their sobriquet, set standards for all beneath them. The name Kendall was synonymous with business acumen. They built ships and made fat fortunes importing rum and spices from the Caribbean.

The Kendalls prospered. Their ships crisscrossed the Atlantic with cotton from the southern colonies bound for the mills of Birmingham; Kendall whaling ships set off from Nantucket. The family fell easily into the ranks of the new aristocracy, and members of the clan ran the new country—as governors, senators, cabinet members, and ambassadors.

A Kendall helped found Harvard College in 1636. The men went to Harvard and the women married well. They taught their children the proper way to do things, whether it was managing an estate with careful bookkeeping or fighting a duel with honor. Later generations would wince at any mention of their ancestors' involvement in the slave trade: New England rum was traded in West Africa for slaves; the human cargo was traded in the West Indies for sugar cane, and sugar was taken to New England to make more rum.

The population of Boston was swelled in the 1840s by the influx of Irish fleeing the Great Potato Famine, but the new arrivals were not to be accepted by Boston. It was the decade when the Corinthian, the Somerset, the Tavern, and the Union clubs were founded. Prominent men were allowed to join, but no Catholics, no Jews, no foreigners, and certainly no women.

Before the outbreak of the Civil War, when antislavery sentiment was growing in New England, the Brahmin answer was to found the American Colonization Society, which supervised the raising of money by wealthy Bostonians to purchase the freedom of Southern slaves. The Africans were not to be invited to live in Boston, though; they were to be sent back to Africa.

The men gathered together at the Corinthian Club on the night of Cynthia's birth were products of that heritage. A respect for the history of the Massachusetts colony and particularly for the city of Boston was bred into their very bones. The year was 1949, Truman was President, the stock market was sound, and the men were home from the war. The United States was surging forward in a spirit of optimism.

The waiter passed among the knots of joking men, tilting the green bottle into this and that extended glass. The Mayor was drinking Scotch, and several others had turned to gin and rye.

Another toast was made on behalf of little Cynthia, and Otis Livingston Kendall III thought of the petal-pink child he had been allowed to peek at through a glass partition. She would be a great beauty, he had decided. And that day, on her birthday, she had inherited both money and name with her first gulp of air.

Otis was jolted from his reverie by the swerving of the limousine in the

Manhattan traffic. He rubbed his eyes and sat up straight, feeling suddenly quite tired. All those toasts at the Club that night so long ago. He had been sure that his daughter would lead a charmed life.

Summer 1967 — Edgartown

The summer was endless. Cynthia woke in her same room of the cottage overlooking the same ocean as the year before, and felt overwhelmed with pain. Sometimes she slept until eleven, which had never been allowed in the Kendall household, and which infuriated her mother. Nora was sent up to wake her, then ten minutes later was sent up again to make sure she was actually out of bed, and then sometimes Mrs. Partridge would knock on the door to ask if she was coming downstairs.

Cynthia would sit in the dining room staring at her plate and the two English muffins for fifteen minutes at a time. She could usually swallow the orange juice, but couldn't seem to make any gesture toward lifting food to her mouth. "You look haggard, you look dried up," her mother told her, and she did actually weigh less than she had the summer before. After the ritual of sitting alone at the table, she excused herself and went upstairs to pull on a bathing suit under her shorts and bicycle to the beach. There she found a spot in the tall grass, always remembering exactly where she had lain with Marco, and spread the pink towel. Cynthia read any paperback she could find in the house, it didn't matter what it was, and stared at the ocean. She swam every day and always thought the cold water was the only thing that made her know she was actually alive.

He isn't here, she thought every time her bicycle whirred past the Hyatts' house. At least she knew that; hadn't her mother found out and told her? Yes, dear Mother. And dear Mother had told the Hyatts that she'd had mononucleosis and was still very worn out from it. And dear Mother had told Crosby to call her anytime. "She'd love to see you. Oh, she's longing to see you and catch up," her mother had gushed uncharacteristically on the hall phone.

Cynthia did go to a beach party with him one night, but found herself looking over his shoulder for Marco. Found herself waiting to go home. Actually trying to get a glimpse of Crosby's tank watch in the dim light of the bonfire. Her bedroom on the third floor, under the eaves, welcomed her that night. She tore off her clothes, then made her way up the outside steps to the widow's walk on the top of the house. There she stood naked in the cool night air, looking out to sea in the darkness, listening to the mournful groan of the foghorn.

. . .

What made it worse was there was no one to talk to. A plan. I'll make a plan and not be the ward of my mother in that big house. She thought of Sophie, her friend from Rosemary Hall. I'll call her and we'll just talk about normal everyday things, and I'll invite her here for the weekend. And once she's here, I can sound her out. Just talk. Find out what she thinks I should do. I have to do something, Cynthia thought as she lay back on the towel and stared up at the cloudless blue sky. Because I have to talk to him.

"Sophie? Oh, Mrs. Yates! It's Cynthia Kendall. You have the same voice!" She stood in the hall barefoot, in white shorts, and nervously twisted a strand of long blond hair around her forefinger. "In Europe? For how long?" She listened, disappointed. "You mean the twenty-seventh of *August*?" Cynthia started to scratch the date on the phone pad, and then didn't. "Oh, well, tell her I called. I wanted to invite her to the Vineyard for the weekend." She sighed and stood on the other leg. "Yes. Thank you. It's nice talking to you, too."

Cynthia replaced the receiver and thought, She knows. That's why she didn't ask about Smith or how I felt or what my plans are. Or maybe it's that thing with Mother and Uncle Teddy. She turned the corners of her mouth down. Beacon Hill. The infamous Kendalls of Beacon Hill.

Cynthia plopped down on the wicker chair and reached for the phone book, the skinniest one, for Rhode Island. She slowly flipped the tissue-paper-thin pages to Pawtucket, remembering her mother's horror. It wasn't Beacon Hill, it was a factory town for the have-nots, she had said. For the newly arrived. The way she'd said "newly arrived" was the way someone might say "syphilitic." Cynthia found Falconi, and the listing for Enrico, on Pearson Avenue. She swallowed and ran her finger over the line. Marco. He might be there. He might answer the phone. What would I say? Didn't you get my letters? That's perfect, she thought, frowning. Accuse him right away. That's attractive. She crossed her long legs and touched the line again.

"Did you talk to Sophie?" her mother called from the living room. She strode in carrying roses from the garden, her hands in gardening gloves. "Is she coming?"

Cynthia closed the phone book. "She's in Europe all summer. She should be in France right now, according to Mrs. Yates."

"Why don't you try Alison? Didn't you really like her?" Margaret Kendall was handing gloves, scissors, and basket over to Nora at the kitchen table.

"Okay, I will," Cynthia sighed, and reached for the black and red *Social Register*. She always looked up Kendall first, just to check. Amazing they hadn't been dropped since last year. The thing came out every year and dutifully reported births, graduations, new clubs, new addresses, new marriages. Divorce was no longer grounds for exile from the little five-by-seven-inch tome.

Five minutes later, Cynthia walked slowly into the kitchen and watched as Mrs. Partridge arranged the flowers. "Did you get your friend?" she asked.

Cynthia shook her head. "She's in Europe with Harriet."

"Small world," the housekeeper laughed.

"If Mother wonders where I am, tell her I've gone to the beach."

"But lunch is ready to go on the table, dear."

"I can't eat. I can't eat." Her voice sounded reedy and near tears. "Please." Cynthia turned and left the big kitchen quickly.

Mrs. Partridge walked after her through the coral dining room, through the long living room of wicker and flowered chintz, and then watched her leap on the bike and pedal down the driveway. "Poor child," she said aloud, holding the corners of her apron. "Poor child."

. . .

Cynthia lay facedown, arms folded under her, in the tall beach grass. She was a long, thin, tan figure in white shorts and green T-shirt. I'll call him, she said to herself. What do I have to lose? What else is there? Mother would say "self-respect." But Mother always runs her life being proud, being proper, pretending nothing is wrong, so that if you screw up, you pretend that's what you wanted all along. Mother never cries. Over spilt milk or Uncle Teddy or anything. She lifted her head, then sat up and pushed her hair back behind her ears. Cynthia had an oval, high-cheekboned face, but the first thing you noticed were her green eyes. Gray green, like a misty lake, they fastened upon a person and stared. They appeared all-seeing, all-understanding. She had her mother's straight nose and a lovely mouth with her mother's short upper lip. "Aristocratic," she was told when she complained she couldn't smile with her mouth closed. Cynthia rarely smiled at all.

A year ago, Marco and I were the closest possible two people in the world, on the whole planet, and you might think . . . She plucked a long piece of grass from the white sand. You might think that my being pregnant would draw us closer, would make him even more protective of me. Instead, he's disappeared. Well, he might as well have. I know he wanted to transfer to Harvard in his junior year, and maybe he did, maybe he'll be as close as all that, come September. And I'll bump into him on the subway or on the street and we'll say, "Hi, how are you?" and I'll go around the corner and slash my wrists quietly. No fuss. And bleed to death beside a gutter so I don't make a mess for anyone to clean up. She rubbed her nose when she felt the stinging that signaled more tears. And the baby. Should be three months old by now. *I didn't breastfeed you. I never even held you.*

Cynthia lay back in the sand again, and stared up at the sky. Marco's baby.

My baby. Marco. The three of us on the same planet, and we might as well have never known each other, for all it counts.

. . .

Cynthia tore the page that said "Falconi, Enrico," out of the Rhode Island directory and put it under her pillow. She touched it like a talisman so often that she even remembered to take it out and put it in her bureau drawer the day her sheets were changed.

She couldn't decide what she'd say if she ever actually got him on the phone. Odds are he has another job somewhere else, a job like last summer. Her eyes filled with tears. No, she wasn't up to hearing his voice. She might just sob and then have to hang up. She wiped her eyes on the sheet and then turned to look at the clock. God, two-fifteen. No wonder I look like hell, she decided as she turned over and pulled the pillow to her. I'll sleep, and then tomorrow I'll take a yellow legal pad to the beach and write exactly what to say. With commas and pauses and possible questions. And I'll walk up and down on the sand and practice being natural, like what's-his-name with the pebbles in his mouth. Yes, Cynthia yawned. It's a plan.

. . .

She didn't have to call him. The phone rang at ten in the morning, and Mrs. Partridge shouted to her from downstairs. Cynthia sprinted to the third-floor phone in the hall in her nightgown. She hadn't slept all night. "Hello." She tried to sound awake. A male voice.

"Cynthia, it's Marco. Please talk to me." His voice held an edge of desperation. "Don't hang up."

"Marco!" she nearly shouted. "Where are you?"

"I'm in a phone booth. New York City." He sighed. "How have you been?"

She felt a sob expanding in her throat. "Fine," she gasped.

Was this the person who never answered my letters? Was this the person who made love to me?

"But what happened to you? The baby . . . ?"

"The baby . . . the baby is gone—" She put her hand over the receiver so he wouldn't hear her crying.

"You mean—"

"The day it was born—" She began to cry. "They . . ."

"Oh, Cynthia! What can I do? What can I say?"

"Nothing." Her voice was slurred with tears. "It's too late."

"Can I see you? Can I come there?"

She was nodding, choking back sobs. A recording came on the line. "Please deposit another one dollar and seventy-five cents for the next three minutes."

"Don't hang up," he said, then Cynthia heard a clang clang of quarters going into the box. "Look, I'll call you back!" he shouted into the phone. "I need one more quarter."

"When will you call back?" she cried.

"Right away! Stay home! I'll call in two min—"

The line went dead. Cynthia hung up the phone and ran down the hall to her room. She'd have time to brush her teeth and pull on shorts before the phone rang.

Margaret Lake Kendall stood frozen at the foot of the stairs. Then she walked quickly into the study where her husband often worked on weekends. The big desk was littered with papers and files. It took her a moment even to see the phone. Then she took off the receiver and placed it beside the humidor. Not quite satisfied, she put a book in front of it, then strode from the room, closing the door behind her.

$$\cdot \quad \cdot \quad \cdot$$

"I think it'll be wonderful for you, darling," her mother was saying. "They'll all be at the airport to meet you. Alison's mother was delighted you could join them."

Cynthia was staring out the window at the trees of Central Park. Same view as the hospital. New York trees. Marco was somewhere in this city. Maybe only blocks away. "You know I don't care if I go or not." She'd never told her mother about the call. She didn't think Mrs. Partridge would, either. If Mrs. Partridge had even guessed who it was. No, she wouldn't. Cynthia had circles under her eyes from not sleeping. Two days had passed, and he had never called back. What could have happened? Had he just gotten the information he wanted, and decided not to go any further? Then why hadn't he just said he was sorry, and hung up? Why prolong the agony? *Can I see you?* and *I'll call you back!* She kept hearing his voice saying those two sentences. No, she hadn't imagined it. Was he a sadist? Not Marco. But nothing explained why he'd never answered her letters. God, those desperate letters from the Bahamas. "Mother, I'm going to take a walk."

"But we leave for Kennedy in half an hour! Are you—"

"I'm ready. Passport, ticket, traveler's checks. Everything is out of the bathroom." She glanced quickly around the St. Regis suite. Her suit jacket of peach linen was on a chair. "I just want some air." Cynthia grabbed her purse and was gone before her mother could object.

She thought of having the desk place the call, but there was a chance her mother would walk through the lobby and see her in the booth. So the moment the elevator doors opened, she nearly ran through the lobby and was out of the hotel and into the bright afternoon. She turned toward Madison and found a phone booth. Not working. She swore. So typically New York. Two blocks away was another. She pulled the telephone-book page out of her wallet, where it had been folded carefully, and read the number to the operator. Just like Marco, she winced when she realized she didn't have enough change. "All right! I'll be back!" She hung up and sprinted to the newsstand across the street. A newspaper and a *Harper's Bazaar* under her arm, and she was in the booth again. The day was sticky with humidity, and she kept pushing her hair back, feeling nearly feverish. The operator came on the line, and Cynthia told her to make it person-to-person to Marco Falconi. She hadn't said his name aloud for months. Her lips were dry.

"Please, please," she whispered as the phone rang in Pawtucket, Rhode Island. His mother will answer and she'll be very nice and tell me his number in New York and I'll call him and . . .

The phone rang eight times, and the operator twanged like a recording, "Miss, I'm afraid there's no answer. Do you have another number for the party you wish to speak to?"

"Oh, just let it ring four more times!"

It did. No one answered. "Thanks." Oh, why hadn't she thought of it before! She dropped in another dime and asked the operator for a listing for Marco Falconi. How she loved saying his name. "Wait. What about a new listing? I don't know how long he's been here." She clung to hope as she waited.

"No, miss. Got a Falconi in Queens named Gino . . ."

"Thanks anyway." Cynthia hung up the phone and walked slowly back to the St. Regis, to her angry mother who had all the luggage out front, to the waiting yellow taxi ready to take her to an airport, to a plane, to Paris.

· · ·

The first night in Paris, Cynthia waited until Alison was asleep, and then put her raincoat on over her nightgown and had the desk in the lobby try the Pawtucket number.

Still no answer. Well, it was a time when people were away. Then she made the concierge understand she wanted to talk to Gino Falconi in Queens. The man came on the line with a faint humming noise and said gruffly in answer to her question, "I ain't never heard of nobody named Marco." Then he hung up.

Cynthia tucked the folded page into her pocket and said, *"Bonne nuit,"* and *"Merci,"* to the concierge in her best Rosemary Hall French. She sneaked back into the dark room, stubbing her toe on the antique chest. She grimaced in pain, threw her raincoat over a chair, and limped to her bed.

· · ·

"Girls, I know she's difficult, but—" Mrs. Yates nodded as Cynthia came into the dining room.

A waiter pulled out her chair and she smiled bravely. *"Bonjour, bonjour,* everybody!" She knew what they thought. She'd been sticking with the story of mono, but now she knew they thought she'd had some sort of mental breakdown. Maybe I should tell them to just wait a minute. I'm on the way.

"We thought we'd spend the morning in the Louvre, and then have some sort of lunch in the Luxembourg Gardens . . ." Alison's mother was unbearably cheerful in the morning. Cynthia thought it was like trying to squint at the sun when you'd left your sunglasses at home. She drank the orange juice placed before her and tried to look happy, tried to be fascinated.

Alison and Harriet traded meaningful glances as Cynthia put her arm across her plate of scrambled eggs and a little yellow gob of it clung to her wristwatch.

They screamed with laughter in the elevator after breakfast as they left Cynthia behind with Mrs. Yates.

"She's out of it! Hopeless!"

"My God! She used to be such fun! What happened to her?"

"The mono infected her brain! That's what happened to her!"

The doors opened on the fourth floor and they ambled out, still giggling. "She'll never be able to go back to Smith," said Harriet as she fumbled with the heavy room key.

Harriet was right.

CHAPTER FOUR

Iris

Cutter Harrington smoked Marlboros and lazily exhaled smoke out of his nose. His eyelids were slightly hooded over dark gray eyes, his forehead smooth and wide under the black pompadour. Surprise would never cross this face. His sideburns were three inches long and his personal statement against the popularity of the Beatles. In the late sixties, Cutter was a testament to the celluloid memory of Marlon Brando's smoldering sexuality. At a desk, in the Carson's booth, or patrolling the halls of Morton between classes, he slouched with his broad shoulders low. When he walked, his narrow-hipped torso moved only slightly; he appeared to be sleepwalking a great deal of the time. A measured insouciance, a practiced nonchalance, governed his every gesture.

Ilsa was like a little doll beside him. A china doll, painted and hard and yet beautiful. They observed the ritual for steadies, arriving at school at eight, visiting their lockers hand in hand to retrieve the right textbooks, and strolling ever so slowly up and down the halls, talking to their friends until eight-twenty-five. Then Cutter would lean over Ilsa in the doorway of her history class, their mouths tantalizingly close but not touching, and she would reach up and stroke his dark sideburn and turn through the door, out of his reach for fifty minutes. He'd meet her at the middle staircase when the bell rang, and they would joke and flirt until they reached the gym, when he would be the one who left her at the door.

The attraction between them was palpable; it had a smell and a taste, it was fever. The noise his leather jacket made when he bent his arm to arrange his books was loud to Ilsa's ears. Her breath, when she tiptoed up to speak in his ear in the uproar of the hallway, was tickling and warm, and made his lips long for hers, those soft, pale lips only inches from his ear. They may have thought they were in love, and perhaps they were. But they were in heat, too.

On their second Saturday night at the movies together, Ilsa allowed him to reach around her small shoulders and touch her right breast in the pink angora sweater. It had been a week of great excitement in her life. The intoxication of being Cutter Harrington's girl, usurping Wanda, having everyone know about it, along with the nonstop attention of the only boy who had truly turned her on, was heady stuff. Ilsa decided that a week of foreplay was as long as she could drag it out. Besides, he knew her reputation; there was no point in playing innocent. But, thought Ilsa, as she watched Cary Grant on the screen, I like dragging it out. I like the suspense. And, strangely enough, Cutter seemed to like it, too. It was inevitable that they would, that they could, but Cutter was old enough to like the flirting, to play with the idea of conquest. He'd had years of easy, uncomplicated sex with Wanda. If I'm going to last with him, I'd better be a change from that, she thought.

Ilsa sighed as she felt his index finger softly stroke her nipple. She glanced at his profile in the shadowy theater. He was absentmindedly, with the point of his tongue, licking the corner of his mouth. She reached up and touched it with one finger, and he turned to her in surprise. Then he pulled her face to his, with his hand on the back of her neck, and kissed her hard. Her resistance was short-lived. Warm, very nearly gasping, they pulled apart a moment later and tried to watch Cary Grant drive a convertible down a country road. "Come on," he said as he stood up and gathered his jacket from the seat in front. "Let's get out of here."

On the back of his motorcycle, with her skirt hiked up to her panties, Ilsa wondered where they were going, where they would do it. Cutter's car had been sold, and losing her virginity on a Harley-Davidson seemed unreasonable, even to Ilsa. She pressed her face against his leather jacket and knew she was pressing her breasts against him with the same motion. They roared through, then past, the part of town she knew, and in a few minutes, with a few last growls from the engine, he stopped in front of a falling-down building. Its red neon sign pulsed ACANCY ACANCY. "Where are we? What is this?" She tried to sound confident, casual.

"It's a hotel a friend of mine owns. Wait here. Be right back." He took the steps two at a time and pushed open a glass door at the top. A ratty-looking leftover Christmas wreath flopped back into place when the door closed after him.

"Whatsamatter, Ilsa? Did you count on a suite facing Lake Michigan?" His voice was taunting.

"No." She was standing with her back to a window that had been covered with an old *Racing Form*. Yellowed swatches of Scotch tape held it into place. "No." She watched him pull the black V-necked sweater over his head, and then the white T-shirt. His chest was broad, smooth, nearly hairless; his arms were pale and very muscular. Black lines and irregular markings were visible on the inside of one forearm. "What's that?" She pointed.

Cutter laughed sheepishly. "Kid stuff. I tried to tattoo myself." He held out his left arm. "See that? Supposed to be a star. I cut it with a penknife and then burned it with matches to keep a scab from coming." He shrugged. "Didn't work that well. I'm a quick healer."

Ilsa hadn't moved. She stood with her arms at her sides, on the other side of the single bed. The sickly green cotton spread needed to be washed. The pillowcase was gray.

"Hey! We wanted this. We have ever since we started. Are you changing your mind or just losing your nerve?"

"I never lose my nerve." She smiled seductively. Yes. This is what I wanted, she thought. All this time. I'm here, Cutter's here. Only the place is wrong.

Barechested, with his faded jeans hanging perilously low on his thin hips, he stepped toward her. "You're sexy. You look like what sex would look like if it were in one package. I only know what your mouth is like." He put his hands on her face and stared down at her green eyes. "Are you gonna let me know the rest of you?"

Ilsa had undressed in front of boys before. She liked to. But it had always been in the back of a car, or sometimes in the front, banging an elbow on the steering wheel or bruising a kneecap on a gearshift. This was under a bright bar of white neon. Brighter than her doctor's office. Somehow the anticipation of being touched was always better than the actuality. The boys were rough, they were clumsy, and they bit her nipples too hard. She'd been the plaything of hungry adolescents. Cutter was waiting. He reached behind her waist and unfastened the skirt and slipped it down over her shoes and she stepped out of it, holding on to his bare shoulder. He rose and tossed it over the doorknob.

There was no chair, no table, no lamp, only the narrow bed and that glaring light on the cracked gray plaster ceiling. Should she tell him she'd never really done it? Never had anyone inside her? Never. Not once in all the hours of heavy breathing and kissing and touching. No. For once she wouldn't talk, wouldn't protest, wouldn't push away. And she'd forget about this room and just think of Cutter. As she had for years, alone in her own bed.

He gasped when her breasts were freed from the brassiere. "You're beautiful," he sighed, and touched each nipple gently with a forefinger. When he

had pulled away her panties, he led her to the bed and she lay back as though
she had done it all a hundred times and waited for him. He bent down, still
wearing his undershorts, and stroked her flat stomach with his hand and then
he was above her, atop her, face against hers, tongue inside her mouth, arms
around her shoulders. Ilsa felt she had been folded into heaven.

They lay on that bed with its protesting springs and paper-thin mattress for
hours. Cutter on top, then facing each other on their sides, petting and
exploring. His tongue was in her mouth, in her ear; Cutter kissed her shoulder,
her nipples, one after the other, back and forth. "So one won't be jealous,"
he explained. Ilsa petted the dark hair under his arms and then, impetuously,
put her face there. When he pulled her away, she sighed, "You smell like
Christmas cookies." He gave a burst of laughter and held her down and licked
under each of her arms as she squirmed and giggled.

The bed, the room, the cold bright neon didn't matter anymore when
Cutter began to touch her thighs. He is experienced, she thought. So this is
what Wanda got. This is what they taught each other. She stiffened when he
put his finger inside her and slowly moved it back and forth. She cried out
when he put two fingers in, and he pulled them away and stared into her
face. "Are you ready?" he asked.

Now or never. She nodded, not realizing her thighs were clenched closed
along with her teeth. Cutter kissed her belly and then stripped away his jockey
shorts. Ilsa stared at what looked huge and red and swollen and even angry.
Oh, God, she thought. It looks bigger than a Chicago cop's nightstick. Nightstick. Maybe that's why they call them . . . ohmygod. She cried out as he
pressed against her once, and then again. She thought she'd been split in
half, and then suddenly she was full of him, full of Cutter, and the stinging
and the pain seemed to be washed away. His face was above hers, and his
weight was on his elbows on either side of her head. She felt small, impaled,
but when she saw Cutter for the first time close his eyes in ecstasy, Ilsa was
transported to paradise.

·   ·   ·

"No, I don't think I have." Ilsa shook her white-blond mane and shrugged.
No, it was not like what she'd read an orgasm was supposed to be. She definitely
had not come. Gone. Left. Arrived. It just hadn't happened. Not like in the
book. She sat up, nearly naked, legs crossed Indian-style on the green bedspread. All she wore were white panties and a heavy silver ID bracelet with
several links caught up in a large safety pin to keep it from slipping off her
wrist. Her breasts were full and pink, and her face was flushed from the heat
of the room. The radiator hissed and spat steam from the corner. Cutter's
friend had given them a special weekly rate since they were there nearly every
night and on Saturday afternoons, too.

"So take off those things and let's . . ." Cutter said, grinning. He stood near the window, barechested, with his Levi's, as usual, slung as low as possible on his hips. Since October, Ilsa noticed, he had grown a little pattern of hair on his hard white stomach. The two of them had examined each other as closely as possible without the use of a magnifying glass. They knew each mole, each freckle, each ticklish spot, each point of highest sensitivity and yet . . .

"Turn to page thirty-two and tell me what you think of it," she instructed. Ilsa tossed him the dogeared paperback. It looked as if someone had dropped it in the bathtub. In fact, Brenda had.

Cutter read and then nodded. Then he read the paragraph again. "Sounds fantastic," he breathed. Then, in his terrible twangy fake Southern accent, he commanded, "Tek off dem panties, li'l gal!"

Ilsa giggled and then positioned herself. She lay back, legs apart, relaxed, waiting, as Cutter found the page again. She looked down and could see the top of his head and his big left hand holding the book between her legs. He was kneeling on the floor at the foot of the bed. "Do you see anything?" Oh, please find it, Cutter. Use your big beautiful eyes or your big thumb or just ask me to show you. Ilsa had found it for the first time the night before.

"No," she sighed. "No. Almost," she breathed. "Maybe just a little to the left."

Cutter was concentrating on being as gentle, as "featherlike" as the book said the hero was being. "My left or your left?"

Ilsa laughed.

"You're not supposed to laugh, Ilsa! Hey, this is serious!" Cutter began to laugh and the bed shook under them.

Five minutes later they had positioned themselves again. "Hey, why don't I just lick you there, and when I touch it with my tongue you just call out, 'Bull's eye!' and then we'll know, first of all, that you have this thing and, second of all, that it's findable."

"Jesus, Cutter! You are such a romantic!"

"I don't see what's romantic about this," he said, frowning. "This is science and biology . . ." He flipped the book across the room and it slid on the black linoleum floor, making a *sshhhh* noise. "Ready?" Cutter kissed the inside of one pink thigh and began. He was gentle and exploring for a few seconds. Then, when Ilsa almost rose off the bed and screamed, "Yes!" he used both hands to hold her thighs firmly apart, and his tongue moved slowly, methodically over the same place.

Twenty minutes later they lay in each other's arms, sated, dozing. Ilsa opened her eyes and moved herself even closer to him. She pulled herself nearer to study the way his lips curved, to think of what he had done to her. With that mouth. Oh, Cutter, I love you. He opened his eyes at that moment, as though she had said it aloud, and for a moment there was such tenderness on his face that Ilsa was afraid she had. Then he pulled her flat against him with one arm curved around her, and whispered teasingly and with unmistakable pride, "Hey, I found it, didn't I?"

. . .

From that afternoon of discovery onward, sex would be a drug for Ilsa Keller. She ached with wanting on Monday mornings when she awoke in her own bed without him. Hildemar noticed the way she was, but didn't know what to say, so said nothing. Her daughter was an enigma to her—a stranger coming and going at all hours, the subject of letters from this Mr. Lipscomb, the principal, the object of stares on the street and whistles as she crossed the parking lot below Hildemar's kitchen balcony. She'd watched her on the days she did appear after school. Ilsa was a woman, no doubt of that. She kept her room clean, she hung up her clothes, and her shoes were all in a row in the shoe bags, as she'd been taught as a little girl, but she obviously had a life her mother knew nothing of.

Hildemar could force her to eat a good breakfast, but she couldn't stop her from going out of the apartment half-naked, like some cheap movie star. She couldn't hold her head in the sink and wash that makeup off. She couldn't take scissors and cut that hair that was a foot high and stuck out like a kewpie doll's. And maybe what bothered Hildemar most of all was what she couldn't imagine doing anything about—that look of arrogant, female well-being. It shone in her eyes and actually seemed to make her mouth look beestung and full. Ilsa exuded a sense of confidence in her femininity that bordered on arrogance, and it made men of all ages look at her and wonder what she was like in bed.

Ilsa knew men looked at her, but Cutter was the one. Cutter knew how to find the place, how to please her. Cutter Harrington was her opiate, and she was his. There was no end to their appetite for one another. The grubby little room in the pawnshop district of Elliston didn't exist. After the first lovemaking, Ilsa had never noticed the neon light again—the room might as well have been lit by stars.

. . .

"Hey, look! There she is again!" said Ilsa. The unmistakable red head turned the corner and disappeared.

"She knows all about us, all about where we go," murmured Cutter as he pulled on a glove.

Ilsa's face was pink from the afternoon's lovemaking. She pulled on the knit cap and threw her leg over the back of the Harley. "Do you care?"

"Nah, I guess I don't." Cutter gunned the motor by turning the handgrips.

"I do!" Ilsa shouted above the noise. She resented it. Wanda Kowalski was a bitch, and Cutter had dropped her fair and square. So had lots of people, evidently. After the flushing episode, most of the teachers kept their eyes on her. The next week, Wanda was put on probation for smoking, and didn't come to school for most of October. Wanda Kowalski had lost all her swagger. Sarah Beck was nearly always with her; both looked a bit melancholy. Sarah usually seemed to be trying to convince her of something, whereas Wanda had developed a hopeless expression. She was an entirely different person since losing Cutter Harrington.

"She calls me, you know," Cutter leaned back and shouted when they stopped at the next traffic light.

Ilsa was furious. "Why? What does she want? I hope you hang up on her!" Her throat went dry. Yes. Cutter was hers now, but he had been with Wanda since seventh grade, and that was five long years. Five years of movies and kissing and hamburgers and trading secrets—Ilsa hated to think of all they knew about each other, of all they'd been through together. She'd been with Cutter for only four months.

"I don't have to hang up on her," he shouted back. "She just says my name and then *she* hangs up." The light changed to green and they roared off toward Ilsa's house, where they flagrantly kissed good-bye in the parking lot. Hildemar heard the motorcycle and stood on the balcony among her fluttering damp dishtowels, twisting her raw red hands in her apron. Her breath came in little puffs of anger.

"Cutter, promise me something," Ilsa said just before kissing him again. She put her warm little tongue in his mouth, the way he liked it, and then pulled back. "Promise me."

"I promise," he sighed, missing her mouth already.

"Okay." Ilsa was firm. "Don't talk to her. Just don't talk to her. Ever."

"Ilsa, have I? In all this time?" he questioned. He'd never heard Ilsa so dogmatic about anything.

"I hope not. I hope you haven't."

"I haven't!" he defended himself.

"Well, don't."

When she leaned up on tiptoe and kissed him lingeringly, her mother nearly screamed in rage from three stories above.

"Remember," Ilsa sighed as they broke apart. Her breath was warm and sweet on his face. "You promised."

.   .   .

"So you kids want a good car, a good first car, hunh?" The salesman in the brown suit with the too-short trousers scratched his head. "I think, let's see, let's jes' take a walk around the lot." Ilsa fell into step behind him, grinning, mimicking his long-legged saunter, the way he splayed his feet out in the brown-and-white shoes. Jerome Oakeshott, as his name tag spelled out, had just assumed they were getting married. He'd just assumed they wanted something economical.

Ilsa pointed and yelled, "That one!"

"Well, honey, you can't af—" Jerome began, but when he saw the dark look on Cutter's face, he stopped. "It's almost four thousand dollars is what I mean—"

"She said that one, and that's what she means," Cutter said.

Ilsa was leaning over backwards on the shining red hood. Her breasts were pointing impertinently skyward. Cutter knew what he wanted. "I want this one," Ilsa was saying as she patted the chrome. "Why don't we get this one?"

"You can't just buy a car on looks, now. We don't know what's under the hood, do we?" Cutter looked meaningfully at Jerome, who tried to decide whose side he was on. Did he want to sell the car, or did he want to side with the young feller who couldn't possibly afford it?

"It's a mighty fine car. Yessirree, your girl—uh, fiancée—has got the right instincts. This is one of our best little numbers. A Thunderbird convertible is sporty but perfect for a young couple with no children, and it's got all the extras." He opened the door and they leaned over his shoulder and noted the radio, the heater, the windshield wipers. "Two speeds, think of that," sighed Ilsa, making a face behind the salesman.

It was Jerome who suggested they "take a spin," and in minutes they were shrieking with laughter, racing down the highway toward Chicago. "We don't have to take it back, do we?" Ilsa wheedled.

Cutter steered with his left thumb and grinned. Ilsa's nearly white hair blew in the spring breeze. It was the first warm day of the year. "You're crazy! 'Course we hafta take it back!"

"But when he handed you the keys, he said, 'It's all yours,' and besides, what if we were foreign and we thought he meant it?"

Cutter shook his head. Ilsa got away with a lot, but that idea of playing foreign was . . . well, not cool.

"Well, why don't we go to Chicago in it? And have some fun? We could bring it back in a few hours. I mean, it's Saturday after all."

Cutter compromised, and they went ten miles toward Chicago and saw the skyline and turned around. Jerome was apoplectic when he saw them pull into the big lot under the plastic banners. "Where've you been?" he fairly shouted. Sweat was pouring down his face. "A spin doesn't mean California!"

Cutter got out of the car and stepped over to the thin, tall man. "Mr. Oakeshoot, I'm going to try to forget the way you have spoken in front of my wife-to-be. We *were* going to buy this car. We *were* very happy with you as a salesman, but I, for one, am now real disappointed in the way this has turned out."

As Jerome patted his damp forehead with the end of his garish yellow and brown tie, Cutter helped Ilsa out of the front seat as though she were a princess. "Come, sweetheart. I don't think we need to listen to this."

They walked away with spines straight, heads high, righteously insulted as

Jerome ran alongside them, sputtering, "If you want to name me a price, I'd be willin' to come down. Just as a favor to two kids startin' out . . ."

They rode the Harley to the hotel, where they tore off each other's clothes, laughing. "We should have never come back," Cutter sighed, as he remembered how pretty Ilsa had looked in the front seat of the red car.

Ilsa was giggling. "I've never seen anybody's head sweat like that before!" She began to kiss Cutter's shoulder blade. "And that tie he kept wiping it with!" she shrieked helplessly. "It looked like a poisonous snake!"

After their lovemaking, Cutter was awake. Ilsa, warm, silky, breathing deeply, lay in his arms, her cheek against his chest. He lifted a strand of her platinum hair to his lips and kissed it. Then he repeated in a whisper, "We should have never come back."

· · ·

Cutter kept his promise to Ilsa. Why is it so important to her? he wondered as he hung up the phone again and again the following week. Wanda's voice was like a spidery whisper that Wednesday night, the last time he heard it. He thought she said, "Please, please let me come," as Cutter, torn between his memories of Wanda and his loyalty to the fantasy he called Ilsa, hung up.

The next day it was all anyone could talk about. Mrs. Kowalski said Wanda had been very quiet at supper. She told her mother she was going to the Becks' house to do her homework, but Sarah called at ten o'clock and asked to speak to her. The two of them then found her in the storage room behind the Becks' store. She was hanging from a rafter by a man's necktie. It wasn't her father's, and the rumor around school was that it had belonged to Cutter Harrington. The note was all about him, too. That's what the rumors said.

· · ·

"She was crazy, Cutter! She had to be! Nobody does that if they're not crazy!"

Cutter and Ilsa went over it again and again for a week. He cried in the little lovemaking room, and she held him in her arms and repeated the mantra, "It wasn't your fault! Cutter, she was crazy! I'm telling you she was crazy!"

Cutter felt it was his fault, though, and the worst part of it for Ilsa was that she realized he thought it was her fault, too. That was the week her period didn't come.

· · ·

"You're fifteen! You can't have a baby!" Brenda had gone white with the news, and then had been so loud in her opinions that Gretchen had jumped up and slapped her hand over her mouth.

"My mother is downstairs!" Gretchen shouted almost as loudly.

Ilsa was silent, hands crossed over her still-flat stomach as though she were protecting herself from blows. "I want it. It's Cutter's and mine. It's half his, too."

"And he wants it? Sure! Sure! Come on, Ilsa, get smart!" shouted Brenda. Ilsa lit a Kent and dragged deeply, blowing smoke out of her nose, tilting her head way back. They all sat on the twin beds in Gretchen's pink room. Ilsa felt she'd grown up in this room, on these pink, frilly bedspreads.

"You know, of course, first of all, you're fifteen," Brenda began in her most irritating way.

"Don't be such a bitch when you're talking to her," said Gretchen. "You're being a pain in the ass."

"Right," nodded the very bleached blonde. "Yeah, and I'm also being the only one with any sense."

Ilsa took another drag on the cigarette. "Go on. Tell me how sensible you are." She sounded cool, detached, as if they were talking about someone else. Someone she didn't even know. Ilsa never cried. Never. Not since her father had died.

"You know he's not gonna graduate, don't you? You told me that he told you he's flunkin' everything except gym!"

"So?" Ilsa's face was a flawless mask.

"So that means he goes back to school a year. It means you drop out because you'll be as big as a house before May, and you won't have a chance at a diploma. Hell, you won't even graduate from the tenth grade!" She stuck a cigarette in her mouth and frowned as she flipped the lighter. The flame flared and she sucked at it until the cigarette glowed red. Gretchen and Ilsa were watching silently. "What about money? You think Cutter's pop is gonna support you, his son, and a baby on a Sears salary? I mean, Christ, his son may be the sexiest thing on God's green earth, but his father sells shoes."

Ilsa smiled. "He *is* the sexiest thing on—"

"Can't stop thinking about it, can you?" Gretchen shook her head. "Even now!"

"You have to get rid of it," Brenda said. "That's all there is to it."

"That's *not* all there is to it." Ilsa's voice sounded dead. "It's Cutter's and my decision."

Gretchen spoke gently. "What does he want to do?"

Ilsa didn't answer.

"Five to one she hasn't told him," snorted Brenda.

"I'll tell him tomorrow after school." Ilsa leaned back and stretched her arms over her head, luxuriating against the soft pink flowered headboard, a very pretty blond cat. The other girls looked at her. You'd have thought Ilsa Keller didn't have a worry in the world.

· · ·

Cutter had stopped all his pranks when he'd met Ilsa. She'd been game for anything, wanting to prove herself. It wasn't necessary; she already had a reputation as a daredevil. Cutter had pulled away from his gang, preferring to expend his energy in what the pair called "the Acancy Hotel." "I ache for you," they'd whisper to each other in the halls at school between classes, counting the hours until they could take off their clothes once more.

The occasional "duel" with a leader of a rival gang had stopped. The drunken brawls at the Shamrock and the petty burglaries at the newsstand were no longer so much fun.

Cutter had allowed his senior position in the gang to be taken by a stocky German called Wurst the Worst. He was big, ugly, and the first to use his fists. Cutter had stopped using his fists entirely. No one ever doubted his toughness; he'd proved it again and again. But he had drifted away from the high-school male bonding. His best friend was Ilsa.

"You're nuts, Ilsa. Entirely nuts." His voice was flat. Cutter rose on one elbow over her. Both were naked on the narrow bed.

"All we need is money. You know, Cutter, that's all there is, really. We go to school for the diploma so that someone will hire us for more money. And people live in houses and the more money they have the bigger the house, the nicer the furniture. And that is all because of money. And you can eat baked beans at the bus station or you can eat caviar looking out on the lake in Chicago and it just depends on how much money you have."

"I never heard you like this before," Cutter sighed, and lay back beside her. Both of them stared up at the neon light.

"So we need money to have a baby or to get rid of a baby, and we don't have it. And I thought it was at least a plan." Ilsa took a puff on her cigarette and then let her hand rest on her bare stomach. Spring. They'd spent practically the entire winter in this room. The radiator hissed. Cutter was silent. Ilsa spoke again. "After all, we almost did it once before."

. . .

Cutter was convinced at last—not convinced that it was a good idea, but that it was a way to get money. And he agreed with Ilsa. Money was the problem, money was the solution, and this was, as Ilsa put it, the only idea. So, in the eyes of Cutter Harrington, the adventure was begun by default.

The next night at nine o'clock he jump-started an old Ford, dark blue and unmemorable, and they were off. Ilsa wore a black wool beret over her bright hair, and Cutter wore a Chicago Cubs baseball cap. They both blinked behind dark glasses. "Dammit! I'm taking these things off! It's night, Ilsa! Nobody wears these at night!"

She sat under the rearview mirror, strangely exhilarated, pressed close to Cutter's arm. "Drive slow here. Be stupid to get pulled over before we're even outta Elliston." Her heart beat very fast, her lips were dry. She reached into the big canvas tote bag and touched the metal once more, just making sure.

Yeah, still there.

Ilsa and Cutter passed the junior high school and the high school and the turnoff to Ilsa's building. Neither spoke. They were never coming back. Ilsa turned on the radio—she had insisted they steal a car with a radio—and the Everly Brothers crooned "Dream, Dream, Dream." Our song, she thought. The first time she'd been in the car with Cutter and Wanda, that had been on the radio; and ever since then she could not hear it without thinking of being close to him. After tonight we'll always be together. Baby or no baby, Cutter and me. Cutter next to me in the morning. She put her hand on his blue-jeaned thigh, and he gave her a little half-smile in the dim light.

They left the town behind, the hospital where they'd both been born, their bedrooms full of teenage memorabilia, all the people they'd ever known in their lives, all four of the restaurants they'd eaten in, all the streets they'd ever seen. And, of course, the Acancy Hotel. Neither had ever been farther into the world than ten miles toward Chicago in the red Thunderbird that Saturday afternoon.

The highway stretched gray and straight before them, a smooth ribbon toward everything new. Ilsa stared at Cutter's profile: the straight, chiseled nose, the faintly hooded eyes, that corner of his mouth she lived to kiss. He knew she was watching him, and turned slightly toward her. "Hafta tell you something."

"What?" Ilsa sounded sultry. She knew that voice of his.

"There's nobody nobody nobody ever in bed like you."

She smiled and pressed her small, warm hand on his hard thigh just a little more. "I know."

Cutter grinned. He knew she knew. "Something else."

"Yeah?" She moved her thumb back and forth on the soft bleached fabric.

"You probably know it anyway. Nah. Nothing."

"Cut-ter! You tell me now! This minute! You know we don't have secrets!" Ilsa was sitting up very straight on her side of the front seat, regarding him with anxiety.

"Well, I've never said it before. Not to anybody." He sighed. She waited. "I love you. That's all I wanted to say." He faced the road, and the only movement Ilsa could see was that muscle flexing in his jaw. Sometimes he did it in his sleep.

She put her hand back on his thigh and nodded, staring out at the nighttime stretch of highway. "I love you, too." Her eyes were full of tears.

They were almost there; they had passed a sign that said CHICAGO 15 MILES when it happened. Literally out of the blue—or out of the black, as Ilsa would think later. The wailing horn, the screeching tires. There was no time to scream or pray or imagine pain. It was like being thrown from the top of a rollercoaster and passing all the bright lights of your life on the way toward meeting earth again.

· · ·

Bed. Clean sheets. Her fingers could feel the hem of the top sheet. A hotel. They'd done it. It was over. Ilsa smiled. Home free. No, not home. Yes. Home was wherever Cutter was. She was usually pressed against his warmth; they slept like spoons for twenty minutes at a time, sometimes for a whole hour together before going home for supper. But now, Ilsa thought drowsily, they could sleep entire nights together. She reached for him, but something stung her arm. It was hard to move. Where was Cutter? She opened her eyes.

"Mama!"

Hildemar Wirth Keller sat, wearing a dark blue hat impaled by a blood red hatpin, beside the white bed. Her best dress, which she usually wore only for church, was dark blue wool with a high neck. She wore it like a suit of armor, sitting straight as a soldier, one hundred seventy pounds of dignity. The Kleenex tucked in one of the long sleeves dangled like a paper flower over one of her red, swollen hands. She stood up, but didn't speak.

"Mama! Why are you here?" Ilsa realized colorless liquid was coming out of a bottle dangling above her and down a tube into her hand, which looked like the hand of a child. "How did you—"

"Ilsa, you were in an accident. A drunk driver." Hildemar made no move to touch her daughter. She watched the green eyes, whose depths she'd never understood, fill with tears.

"But where is he? Where is Cutter?" Ilsa began to whimper. It was a helpless keening sound, not quite human. "Where is Cutter?" She knew. She could usually smell him, feel him; she had lain beside him and willed her heartbeat to echo his. Now she smelled alcohol and something like Lysol. "Where is he?" she screamed at Hildemar.

A man with glasses and a white coat appeared and pushed her back against the pillows. "You're all right. You're going to be fine," he kept saying, as if that were what she wanted to hear.

"Let me see him," she wept. "Please let me see him." The IV had been yanked out, and she covered her mouth with both hands. "Just let me see him."

"I'm afraid you wouldn't want that," the doctor said quietly.

Ilsa screamed. "I do want that! I want to see him! I have to see him!"

"He died right away." He was stroking her hair on the pillow, the way Cutter used to. "He didn't suffer. He didn't know anything."

Then Hildemar spoke, and the three words she uttered would never be forgiven by her daughter. They were burned in her mind forever, with images so horrible she would awaken for years to come, screaming his name, seeing his handsome face, his sweet eyes, his smile, torn and crushed and bleeding.

The tone was cold, her mother's voice. "Massive head injuries."

. . .

Ilsa never went back to Elliston not to Cutter's funeral, not to pack the rest of her clothes. Her mother was given the toy gun, and the brightly colored ski masks, her mother saw the medical report concerning the miscarriage. Hildemar Keller stood at the foot of the hospital bed and told the small figure in the white robe that she was not to come home until she had changed. "Changed your ways," was what she said. "You have always been a bad girl."

When the door closed behind the stocky woman in the dark blue dress, Ilsa threw her water glass against the far wall and felt a curious delight in the noise and the flying shards. A nurse rushed in, gawked openmouthed at the girl whose face was as white as paper, and then padded out, calling for an orderly. Ilsa stared at the damp spot and said to no one, "Thanks for everything, Mama."

Four days later, Ilsa was kissed good-bye by two nurses and the doctor, who offered to buy her a bus ticket back home. She took the money and thanked him and walked down the steps of the hospital and through the little town, past a five-and-ten, past a bank, past a Texaco filling station, past the bus depot. She walked until she reached the Interstate, and then positioned herself on a patch of unmown grass near the cutoff that said EAST.

Traffic roared past. She'd meant to stand there bravely with her thumb out, but instead she sat on her suitcase and cried. She picked five of the bright yellow dandelions at her feet and, clutching them stickily in one hand, thought of Cutter. It must have happened within a few miles of here, she thought. Nearby. She stood up, wiped her face on her denim jacket, and then let go of the flowers. They fell in the knee-high grass and weeds and hung suspended upside down, stems askew, never touching ground. Ilsa stared at them, thinking of umbrellas, of parachutes, of falling, of floating in space. She remembered being thrown out of the car, away from Cutter. I wouldn't be here if Cutter hadn't died. I wouldn't be here if Papa hadn't died. Ilsa took a deep breath and decided she wouldn't think of it now. She fluffed up her hair and licked her lips, which tasted like salt, and stuck out her arm.

She was ready when the next truck growled to a halt with a great grinding of gears. The driver called down from the cab high above her, "Where to, little lady?"

Ilsa picked up the suitcase and answered, "Chicago."

. . .

At fourteen she became a woman with Cutter Harrington, at fifteen she became a widow of sorts and lost an unborn child, and the week after that she decided to become eighteen. No one asked her for a high-school diploma, no one asked her for a driver's license; they just looked her in the face and Ilsa, unblinkingly, lied. If she cried, she cried at night in the room she rented from the deaf woman on Lowther Avenue. When she wasn't crying, her green eyes looked as hard as glass.

The job in the diner didn't last long because the boss's wife didn't like having her around, so she walked across the street to the garage and talked the owner into letting her answer the phone and help the bookkeeper with some of the invoicing. The truckers killed time as they waited for repair work wandering in and out of the office or lolling on the puke-green vinyl chairs beside the coffee machine. They smoked and told jokes and guffawed and read dogeared racing magazines. They propositioned the pretty blonde for everything from coffee to trips in their rigs to bed. Ilsa smiled back as if her teeth hurt, thinking how ugly they all were, how beautiful Cutter had been.

Her initial delight in being handed a paycheck of one hundred dollars was soon dissipated with the news of taxes and health insurance. Ilsa felt the wealth swept out of her hands by the wind, and wondered if her future lay in tips and jobs like waitressing after all.

Two months later she left the garage for a job as a salesgirl in a lingerie shop a few blocks from where she lived. Ilsa felt miles from the Chicago she'd imagined, and finally, on a Sunday afternoon, instead of sunbathing in the backyard with her little transistor radio on the blanket beside her, she took the bus to the center of the city. She smiled at the great expanse of lake, bought a hot dog, walked in the park, and felt keen delight in the shining towers of steel looming above her. Lowther Avenue is like Elliston, she decided, a little, dumpy fringe area, away from the bright center of things. She bought a *Chicago Sun-Times* and sat on a park bench and looked at the "apartments available" section. She had done this for all of the Sundays in June, had come to watch the fireworks on the Fourth of July from this same bench, and thought of it as hers.

"Expensive," said a voice over her shoulder. She turned as a man with reddish hair sat down beside her. He wore jeans and a green plaid sport shirt and, unspeaking, crossed his legs and simply grinned at her.

Ilsa went back to the paper, trying to ignore him, refusing to look into his face. She was used to male attention and used to having to get away from it. It was a fact of life when you had platinum hair that fell to the shoulder, and a round figure atop long legs. Ilsa was wearing a red and white striped sundress she'd bought from Sears, and red sandals.

"You look like a candy cane," the voice said. "Did you just get here?"

Ilsa looked up at him then, fixing her green eyes on his face. She decided he was all right. "Been here two, three months."

"And you need a place to stay, right?"

She shook her head. "I have a place that's okay."

"You have a job?"

She nodded. He had a nice, uncomplicated look. Wrinkles around the eyes from too much sun were the only telltale mark of age. His body, the way he slouched, his hands, everything else about him, could have been twenty. His fingernails were short and clean. Ever since the garage, she had looked first at a man's hands.

"Ever do any modeling?"

"No. And I don't intend to." She tilted her head back knowingly and turned her lips down.

"I mean for an artist. A portrait painter."

"Are you a painter?"

"My name's Robert Tripper, and I am a painter." He put out his hand and Ilsa shook it. "Will you pose for me?" She stared at him, not answering. "For money? I'll pay you." When she still didn't answer, he kept talking. "I really *am* a painter. I had a show six months ago, and I'm working on enough canvases to have another." He stopped and smiled at her. "I like your face."

Ilsa laughed for the first time in what seemed like a long time. The woman who ran the lingerie shop had told her it was serious business and to smile often, but not to laugh outright. Ilsa hadn't felt like laughing since the reprimand. There wasn't much in her life to laugh about. She had called Gretchen once, just to hear her voice, and the tightness in her throat had almost strangled her in the attempt not to cry. After three minutes, she had gasped, "I have to go now. I have to pay for this." Ilsa had hung up the big black phone in the gloomy hallway with the red light beside it for the deaf Mrs. Tullis, and fumbled with trembling fingers for a cigarette. She wished fervently she hadn't called. I will never call again until I have good news, she vowed.

Robert Tripper's voice was friendly, without insinuation, without an invitation. And he isn't staring at my breasts, but at my face, Ilsa thought as she put the paper down in her lap. "Do you want to see my studio?" he was asking. "Hey, don't look like that! You really are too young to be such a cynic."

Ilsa followed him to a taxi, and then—thinking, What's the worst that can happen?—she got in. He pointed out landmarks as they rode: the Water Tower, the Art Institute, Marshall Field's. "But it's an apartment building!" she said with disappointment as they got out of the cab.

"Who says you can't paint at home?"

Ilsa made a face. A painter. A studio. Oh, why was she here, and probably miles from the bus back to Lowther Avenue? "I can't stay long," she said in the elevator, and he smiled again.

There were two doors on that floor and Robert stood in front of one: 17A. He turned two keys and pushed, and then stepped aside. After the gloomy twelve by fourteen feet of Ilsa's rented room, it seemed enormous. She nearly gasped at the expanse of shining dark wood floor, at the bright sunlight. "Go in," he urged.

A dozen canvases were propped against the walls at the opposite end of the room. They were oils of the palest pastel hues: pink, coral, lavender, rose. "Those landscapes were done last summer. Five are sold, and the others will be in the new show in October. What do you think?"

Ilsa turned back to him. "I don't know anything about art."

"You don't have to." He had a relaxed, nonchalant way that she found comfortable. "You could just tell me your impressions."

Ilsa had never met an artist before, never been to a museum or an art gallery. There had been a field trip once in eighth grade, but she'd skipped school with Gretchen to go to the movies. Now she wished she hadn't. She walked quickly across the room. So exciting. To be standing in Chicago in an artist's studio with his paintings, these amazing paintings before her. "I like the colors."

"Of course you do," he said. "Because they are your colors. Walk around that pillar and look in the mirror. Yes, with the sun in your face. Like that."

Ilsa stood before the full-length mirror and stared as if she'd never seen herself before. This man was looking at her so differently. What could he see that she had never seen? She saw a cloud of blond hair, curly with the humidity of the July day, pale skin blushing with sunburn, full lips faintly parted, and green eyes. Everyone commented on her eyes. They had since she was a little girl, sitting on her father's lap. Papa. The eyes clouded over.

"What is it?" he was asking.

Ilsa shook her head and turned away. "Nothing." Then she swallowed. "Suppose I was wondering what my father would say if he knew I was here."

"Will you tell him?" Robert asked.

"Never."

"How old are you?"

"Eighteen. April seventh." She had picked Cutter's birthday. He would have been eighteen that day. They had often lain in bed and talked of being twins, of the way they fit together, like two halves of an apple. Now she was his twin.

"Hey. Don't put me on." He shook his head.

Ilsa shrugged. "Believe what you want." His voice had pulled him away from admiring male to authority figure, and Ilsa naturally fell into her role of sulky, petulant rebel. "I have to go now." She started for the door.

"Will you pose for me?"

"Nekkid?"

He laughed. "Not necessarily."

She opened her basket purse and pulled out a package of Kents. Putting one in her mouth, she turned toward him. He frowned and fumbled for matches and, not finding any, said, "Hold on," and went through a door that must have led to a kitchen. He came back with a book of matches and lit her cigarette and watched her inhale. "Sit." He motioned toward the white sofa and matching armchairs that were grouped at the opposite end of the room.

When they were sitting across from each other, she took another drag on the cigarette and then said, "Does that mean yes or no?" He laughed. "You don't have to pose nude for me. You don't have to do anything. You can leave if you want. There's the door."

Ilsa didn't want to leave. The couch was new and pristine white. It was so unlike the cheap foam-rubber chair in her room. That horrible, lumpy mass was covered with a rough fabric and printed with enormous red cabbage roses. This great space was full of a light that seemed to belong particularly to a Sunday afternoon. Ilsa wasn't sure Chicago sunlight wasn't different from what shone down on Elliston or on Lowther Avenue. "Do you have a job?" Robert was asking. "What do you do?"

"I sell lingerie in a little store."

"Where are you from?"

"Doesn't matter where I'm from."

Robert stared at her intently. "Why doesn't it matter?" He seemed genuinely interested.

"Because I'm going to forget it. The only reason to remember where I'm from is so I don't make a mistake and go back there."

"That bad?" His voice was soft.

Ilsa sucked on the cigarette and shrugged as she blew smoke from her nose. She was proud of how well she smoked. Cutter used to tell her she had class when she pursed her lips like that.

"Pretty tough, aren't you?"

Ilsa shrugged again. "Tough enough to get along."

"What's your day off from this job?"

"Sunday."

"Only one day off?" he questioned. "I hope they pay you well."

"Not so great, but it's cash."

"I see." Robert stood and offered her a Coke.

"I've been drinking since I was twelve," she said archly.

"Want a beer, then?"

"Yes, please."

"Would you like a glass, or do you prefer to swig it out of the can?"

Ilsa turned her lips down, not understanding the question, but sensing he was mocking her somehow.

They drank out of cold mugs in silence. "Will you come back next Sunday?"

"I don't know."

He stood and fished for a card in his back pocket. "This is me. This is the address."

Ilsa stood. Robert was quite tall beside her. "Thanks for the beer."

He laughed then. "Here. Take it." He extended the little white card. "Twelve o'clock?"

Ilsa was already at the door. He walked toward her, extending the card, and she slowly put out her hand and took it. "No, let's make it eleven o'clock. One more hour of natural light." He was smiling at her as he opened the door. "Walk two blocks to the right and you'll see a bus stop. You can go anywhere from there. Want me to come down with you?" She shook her head. "Eleven o'clock? Next Sunday?"

She fixed him with cool green eyes. "I don't know."

· · ·

But she knew. She thought of it all week. Every day she thought of it. And she kicked the chair in her room and she dug the card out of her pocket as she ate the egg-salad sandwich that was the only thing Mrs. Tullis ever fixed for her lunch. The stale bread and soggy mess comes with that damned ugly chair, she thought on Wednesday. At the shop on Thursday, Mrs. Gordon's husband came in, and when his wife was in the back doing inventory, he patted her bottom. She ignored him, but felt as if she had been brushed by a snake. Then Mrs. Gordon popped out and called her "dear" in that sugary voice she used with customers. Ilsa always stared at her—a fat woman with black commas drawn over her eyes—and called her "douchebag" mentally for every "dear."

"Dear, would you get up on that ladder and find me all the pantyhose in extra long taupe? Oh, and with nude heels. And while you're up there, see if you can get two pairs of black sheer stockings for Mrs. Benjamin—that'll be size three—and one pair of the white stockings that young nurse likes. Size two. Thank you, dear."

Ilsa started up the ladder, with Mrs. Gordon's husband pretending to hold it for her as he looked up her skirt. Friday came and went, and then Saturday.

Ilsa told herself on Saturday night that her life wasn't too bad. Six workdays was a long week, yes, but she could get something better. Maybe the pharmacy down the street. And she could cover that chair with something. Maybe one of those Indian bedspreads. That would be cheap.

Ilsa opened the little closet and stared at her clothes. Nothing good. Nothing good enough for that apartment. She yanked hanger after hanger back and forth, and frowned at the sundresses. She stamped her foot, she was so angry at not having anything good enough. "Dammit!" she screamed, thankful that no one could hear her. "Dammit!" Then she flung herself facedown on the bed and thought, Maybe getting painted stark naked would be the best thing.

CHAPTER FIVE

Cynthia

Autumn 1967 — Beacon Hill

"I don't think it's possible. I don't think it'll make her happy, and I don't even think that—" Otis was saying.

"But she's the age! It's her year! If we don't, if she doesn't, what will people say?"

Otis turned away from the window. The Beacon Hill house looked out across Beacon Street to the bright green grass of the Common. The Kendall mansion had been designed by Charles Bulfinch and built in 1806; in true English fashion, there was an upstairs drawing room so that the family might "go down for dinner." They had eaten dinner in the oval-shaped dining room, and returned to the drawing room for coffee. They now sat behind closed doors, for Margaret Kendall loved closed doors.

Otis puffed on the cigar and asked himself, What haven't people said already? Aloud, he answered, "Who the hell cares what they say?"

"I care, and I know you do too," Margaret said stiffly.

"I care that my daughter sees a psychiatrist once a week and looks like someone who escaped from Auschwitz. I care that she"—his voice rose in anger—"that she can't get through dinner without tears in her eyes."

"And I think it's time she was pushed to snap out of it!" Margaret drained the china cup and rose from the blue brocade loveseat. "If she was with people her own age, people who were doing things, talking about things . . ." She changed the subject. "And as to her weight, we were shopping the other day and the saleswomen in Hunter's raved about how she looked in all the clothes. The tiniest waist, the most—"

"Oh, hell! I give up!" Otis signaled that the discussion was over.

"Does that mean I can begin getting things ready?" First, her name had to be put on the list, then there were the escorts to be invited for each girl's party. Then there were the dresses. So much had to be done in such a short time.

"Ask her! Why don't you ask Cynthia whether she wants to be involved in all this or not? She's the one who'll have to go through the blasted thing! She's the one!"

Cynthia had entered the room. "I don't want to go through it." This clear declaration was greeted by silence. She looked very beautiful at that moment, and both of her parents realized it. She was thin, but it lent her a mystical fragility, and with her blond hair flowing below her shoulders, she could have been an illustration of a mermaid or a fairy princess. Her face was smooth and pale, her cheekbones sharp, her eyes bright. They were deep green, and their sadness made her seem distant and untouchable. Her father thought, later that night, before he fell asleep, that his daughter was like some wild orchid of another country.

It was this Cynthia who consented to go to many of the parties of the "season," though she herself had not been one of the debutantes to "come out" the previous summer. The debut was a way of announcing the girls' availability, though not a way to gauge their suitability for marriage. Her mother delightedly bought her a new ball gown for every single dinner dance, and she was dressed and fussed over and bejeweled. Her very aloofness in the face of all the young white-tied men made her sought after. She was serene among the excited other girls, sophisticated, detached, a swan among lesser birds. Cynthia Lake Kendall, to her own astonishment, danced every dance, and not with Crosby Hyatt III, either. The phone rang nonstop every day from about ten in the morning onward. Cynthia, like everyone involved in the parties over Christmas vacation, slept until ten, then had a light lunch, shopped, telephoned, or otherwise prepared herself for the evening.

The curtains were drawn, her bedroom door was closed, and Cynthia lay on her bed from three to four in the afternoon, hoping to nap. She had not inherited her mother's talent for sleeping deeply for ten minutes and waking refreshed. "So good for the skin," Margaret often said.

Cynthia had only gotten a glimpse of him in the crowd the night before, but he was on her mind. Probably because I thought he was Marco, she decided. The same dark good looks, nearly olive skin, a strong nose. She had not yet seen him smile. Cynthia lay on her back and wondered who he was. Then she tried to imagine what she would do if she were face to face with Marco on the dance floor. Would they glide into each other's arms? Would her life change forever? But no, I'll never be face to face with him on the dance floor. He wouldn't be invited; he isn't suitable.

She had stopped crying over Marco Falconi, stopped planning to reach out to him, stopped daydreaming almost entirely. Not even her mother could have planned what had happened. Cynthia had been back from that perfectly awful trip with Harriet and Alison only two days when she'd gone to Cambridge to buy books to brush up on her French.

Summer was not quite over, and the streets and sidewalks were overrun with youths in shorts, T-shirts, and sandals or sneakers. It was a bright, hot August day, and the dazed freshmen were wandering around with maps of the Harvard campus clutched in sweaty hands. Cynthia had headed directly toward the Co-op from the subway stop. It was the biggest and best, she thought, for books. Standing in the Language section, she heard his laugh first. That laugh. Her heart beat in her ears and she felt weak. Then again, happy, carefree, Marco's laugh. Cynthia walked to the end of the row of bookshelves and saw him. His head was down, he was wearing a red jersey and white shorts. A girl with brown hair was pressed close to him, and he had his arm around her shoulders. They were bent over a book, laughing.

Cynthia stared at him for nearly a minute, and then, feeling almost frightened of how fast her heart was beating, fearful of fainting, she put down the French text and ran from the store. She ran to the subway and down the steps, and, with tears wet on her cheeks, stepped onto the train just as its doors closed. She sat down quickly, wishing she were in Paris, anywhere except there, so close to Marco and yet never farther away.

That night in bed, she tried to reconstruct the phone conversation one more time. She realized he must have thought the baby had died. Yes. No link between us anymore. And how could I tell him—him, of all people—that I had given it away? Marco, with five brothers and sisters, and who knew how many cousins. Marco, who was the one on the beach to bend down with the little kids and help them dribble wet sand and water into turrets and towers. Marco, who talked about having seven children and naming all the girls Cynthia. "We'll number them!" He would grin when she questioned the practicality of it. Marco. Marco, who hadn't seen her for a year. Marco, who hadn't answered even one desperate, pleading letter. Marco was happy with somebody else. Laughing. With his arm around her. As though I never happened.

That was the Cynthia who danced every dance, dressed in silk and taffeta all the colors of the rainbow, shod in satin slippers dyed to match. That was the Cynthia who drew the young men to her like moths to a flame.

· · ·

"May I cut in?"

Cynthia allowed herself to be transferred from one male to another and with a blink realized that she was dancing with the man who reminded her of Marco. Finally. And he was a man. Much older than everyone else. Mid-thirties? He had always been a head taller than the others in a crowd around the bar, or four tables away, or just leaving the dance floor on the arm of Patricia Marston.

"You're Cynthia Kendall?" he asked. The accent was not American. English was not his first language.

She nodded and glided into the way he waltzed. His steps were longer than the exiled Barry's, but Cynthia was tall, it was easy for her.

"*The* Cynthia Kendall?" he insisted.

She looked up at him. The emerald green satin left her shoulders bare. Her eyes took in the face, and she thought, Yes, how very like Marco. But don't think about that. Don't get distracted. "Unless there's another I don't know about, I must be the one."

He smiled. "You're even cooler and more self-contained than the rumors say you are. Does anything ruffle you?"

Cynthia didn't know whether she liked him or not. Why the teasing? "Should anything ruffle me? I'm waltzing in the ballroom of the Ritz Carleton. I've had a nice dinner and I'm among friends. One should hardly be ruffled under the circumstances."

"You're right, of course. How very Boston you are."

"And how very French you are."

He turned down his mouth in what Cynthia thought of as a totally Gallic expression and corrected her, "Swiss."

They waltzed together so well, moving as one, that a few of the older generation sitting out the dance actually began to follow them with their eyes as they disappeared and reappeared among the other dancers in the crowd.

"Look at him. Dances like an angel. Patricia must be seething," Patricia Marston's mother's best friend commented.

"She dances beautifully, too. Pity about the scandal. She seems a nice girl, though her mother . . ." said a woman in red silk who had never liked Margaret Kendall.

"They say she hardly speaks, been odd this past year. My daughter went to Rosemary Hall with her, and says that now she isn't the same person." Lilly Cates had leaned forward to put in her two cents.

"I've heard there might be a little, well, you know, mental instability there," added Mrs. Winston.

"She looks as cold as ice to me," Mrs. Cates observed, then she smiled. "But my sons don't think that's the case."

The other women turned to her. "Look," she said, nodding toward Cynthia, who was being cut in on as they watched. The Swiss was kissing her hand. He very nearly bowed from the waist as she smiled and then was swept into the arms of Crosby Hyatt III.

. . .

The next morning, at a little after ten, Cynthia came downstairs for a glass of grapefruit juice and a slice of cinnamon toast. She was always pale when she woke up, and today was no exception. Her blond hair, tied in a velvet ribbon low on her neck, was nearly white on the dark blue pullover; the blue jeans made her look pencil-thin. Her mother, who had been reading the paper in the living room, came down to join her at the dining room table. The winter sun shone brightly through the lead-paned windows on the Irish lace tablecloth, which was pristinely white; the pink orchids were the only splash of color in the dove gray oval room.

"His name is Jean-François Colbert, and he is from—"

"Oh, Mother, does it matter?"

"Yes. Maybe it does matter!" Margaret Kendall was irritated. "Maybe it matters that you pay attention to someone from a good family! For a change!"

"A cheap shot!" Cynthia's jaw clenched. Something in her relished the fights with her mother; she no longer avoided them by leaving a room or ignoring an innuendo. The rush of adrenaline amazed her, and she used it to sharpest advantage. There were no limits; nothing was sacred anymore. "I'm not like you, picking one good family and sleeping with all the men in it."

Margaret Kendall stood over her, white with anger. Her mouth was such a thin line it appeared to have been sewn closed. Crack! Her hand came across Cynthia's face. The juice glass flew out of the girl's grasp, and the liquid billowed in an arc across the Chinese carpet. Before Cynthia could cry out, Margaret Kendall had rung the little silver bell for someone to come from the kitchen to clean up the mess, and she herself was striding across the front hall.

The two women didn't speak for the rest of the day. They avoided passing each other in the corridors of the house, which was not difficult since the Beacon Hill place had six bedrooms in addition to the servants' quarters and a library and a sewing room and living rooms upstairs and downstairs and a pantry and kitchen that would have suited a small hotel. Cynthia dressed for the evening in her bedroom without her mother telling her she looked nice or advising her about pearls or where the diamond pin should be placed on the bodice. The doorbell rang, and the maid answered it and called up the stairs that her date had arrived.

The silence went on for three days, until her mother wordlessly put the newspaper in front of her one morning. It had been folded back to the society page, and there in the center was a photograph of Cynthia standing between Crosby and the Swiss. Both men were smiling at her, and Crosby appeared to be toasting her with champagne. Cynthia's expression was one of gentle amusement. Her oval face photographed well; she looked aristocratic and yet flirtatious. The camera had caught a spark; obviously, that spark was what had intrigued the men on either side of her.

Neither woman said a word to the other in comment, but that evening Margaret appeared in Cynthia's dressing room and asked what she was wearing. "This." Cynthia pulled at the hem of a lime green chiffon evening dress; the top was beaded with pearls and dark green sequins.

Her mother nodded approval. "Do you want to borrow my emerald earrings, or the pearls circled with diamonds?"

She'd never offered the emerald earrings before, though her daughter had often said they were her favorites. "Really, Mother! You'll let me wear the emeralds?"

Margaret stood behind her in the pink room, which housed a walk-in closet and a dressing table ringed by makeup lights. Both mother and daughter were reflected in the full-length mirror on the far wall. They stared at each other, and each thought the same thing: You made a terrible mistake the same night I did. And we were both caught in it.

"I'd love to wear the emerald earrings!" Cynthia was saying.

Margaret nodded. "They will be beautiful with that dress." What she thought but didn't say was, If this Swiss is the least bit interested, and he does appear to be, you might as well pull out all the stops.

. . .

Jean-François showed his interest in Cynthia, to the consternation of Patricia Marston, who had asked him to be her escort for every single dinner dance of the season. He danced with her, and then he cut in on Cynthia Kendall, and people watched and commented.

In his own patient, good-natured way, Crosby Hyatt was used to it; he knew he'd never had Cynthia's undivided attention, not at Edgartown, not now that he was at Harvard, not ever. Crosby was good looking, but he was a known entity—without allure, and certainly without mystery. Crosby was the perennial escort who picked her up and took her home, who helped her with her coat and fetched her punch, then years later wine and, these evenings, champagne.

The Swiss was an entirely different matter, Cynthia thought as they danced in silence for the third set. Her hand rested on one broad shoulder and her fingers could nearly touch the white piqué of his dress shirt. He had hardly spoken since that first dance, five evenings ago. The questions from him had elicited a basic profile of Cynthia Kendall. She had gone to Smith for a semester, which was not entirely true but sounded better than one month. She had no brothers or sisters, had grown up in one of the most historically important houses of Beacon Hill, spent her summers in Edgartown in a Martha's Vineyard landmark. There had been a family scandal a year or two before. Jean-François knew all the details about it that anyone else knew, for he'd telephoned an old Harvard classmate who had filled him in. Jean-François had shrugged. Every family had a scandal, otherwise they stagnated. Jean-François knew the history on both the maternal and paternal sides, and the wealth and the pedigree. He was totally satisfied. There was only one loose thread: the reason why Cynthia had spent months in the Bahamas last winter. Perhaps a sort of nervous breakdown, his friend had said. But he had stressed that he didn't know. It was just talk. She did look delicate, fine-boned, a lovely, high-strung thoroughbred.

"You're the only girl here who doesn't bore me to tears," Jean-François murmured as he gripped her waist almost imperceptibly tighter.

Cynthia laughed lightly. "And why is that? Because I never talk, and you amuse yourself with your own thoughts?"

He laughed with her. "Maybe. You've got the conceit right, anyway."

"And the arrogance too?"

"That too." He smiled, and they turned in time to the music. "I think you're the only debutante who's not trying to sell herself as a June bride."

"First of all, I didn't come out. I'm not a debutante."

"You might as well be." He swung her around in the two-step. "Everyone treats you as one."

Cynthia smiled. "Then I get all the benefits, I guess, without having to buy a white dress."

"And what are the benefits for Cynthia Kendall?"

Without a pause, she shot back, "Pleasing my mother."

He grinned, delighted. "Your mother is formidable, I take it?"

"*Très, très,*" she agreed.

When Richard Hardin cut in, they were animatedly discussing Françoise Sagan, and agreeing to disagree. "I want something from you, Cynthia," Jean-François said just as she placed her hand on Richard's shoulder. She looked surprised. "Lunch tomorrow. I'll pick you up at twelve o'clock." Before she could so much as nod, Richard had danced her out of earshot and out of sight.

. . .

"Marjorie Irskin was on the phone at half past eight about it!"

Cynthia poured milk on her cereal. The bananas were arranged perfectly in two concentric circles over the bed of Rice Krispies, and moved a little when the liquid hit them. She was tired and barely listening.

"Marjorie said he danced practically every dance with you except the first and the last! Patricia Marston's mother—"

"Oh, Mother! What does it matter? It's just a dance, and he's just another—"

"He's not just another *anything!*" Margaret Kendall was too excited to be annoyed. "And he's one of Europe's most eligible bachelors, with money and a good name—which, believe me, is rare. The two together, I mean." She sat down opposite her daughter and went on, "It's a bit awkward that Patricia met him in Europe and invited him here—invited him for everything, is what Marjorie said. And he isn't the least bit interested in her, evidently." Margaret sighed, without any sympathy whatsoever for the postmortem that was undoubtedly going on across town, in the Marston dining room. The girl might have completed her year at Smith, but she certainly wasn't as pretty as Cynthia. And the Marston name was practically nil before the last century.

"Why don't you invite him to lunch?" Margaret asked, and then, without waiting for an answer, continued excitedly, "Here! And we'll have Lexie do something special, something typically Boston, and it'll be something he'll never forget. And you'd be alone with him!" Margaret suddenly wondered if that would be an advantage or not. Cynthia didn't really sparkle with enthusiasm. Yes, she was beautiful, but the light had gone out of her eyes and her face in the last year. "Just the two of you, if you want," she continued. "He's a foreigner here, and . . ." Margaret went on to plan the menu as Cynthia played with the cereal.

"It's a bit tricky to call him, I guess," Margaret sighed. "How do you suppose we should contact him?" She didn't wait for an answer. "Of course, it would be ideal if you could bump into him on the street. Do you have any idea what he does all day? Where he goes? He can't be with Patricia all day. Goodness! A fate worse than death!"

"Patricia's not so bad. She's just . . . well, she talks too much, like her mother."

"Well," sighed Margaret Kendall as she smoothed nonexistent creases in the tablecloth with manicured fingers. "Do you have any ideas about finding him?"

Cynthia put her spoon down and looked at her mother for the first time since the monologue had begun. "Yes. He's picking me up at noon." She smiled. "For lunch."

. . .

"I know Cambridge. I went to Harvard."

"You went to Harvard?" Surprise was evident in her voice.

"Business School. There are still a few things you don't know about me. Can't learn everything on a dance floor."

"Did you go to school in Switzerland before that?"

He nodded as he scanned the menu. The restaurant was small, French, and one Cynthia had never been taken to.

The pale pink tablecloths and the brocade chairs made it formal, and she was glad she had worn her turquoise silk dress. "We'll have the house wine if it's very dry. Yes? All right, and then the paté? Cynthia, is that okay?"

She nodded. "Please go ahead and order for me. Anything but sweetbreads."

When that was taken care of, he turned his dark eyes to her. She sat very straight in the chair, hair billowing below her shoulders, cheeks bright pink from the walk in the snow, a choker of pearls on the outside of the stand-up mandarin collar. "You look like a fairy-tale princess."

To her consternation, Cynthia blushed deeply and then managed to say, "I'm just someone who lives in Beacon Hill that you don't mind dancing with."

He smiled. "Maybe more than that. You're past master at the Geneva understatement, though."

"Which is?" Cynthia put her napkin in her lap and tried to compose herself.

"I had a grandmother who had refined it to an art form. She'd say, 'That was fascinatingly boring,' 'That was horribly wonderful,' 'That was beautifully ugly.' "

" 'Beautifully ugly'?" Cynthia laughed.

"The Genevois are not like you and me," he smiled.

"But you're one!"

"Not when I'm in Boston, I'm not."

"What are you here?"

"I'm—believe it or not—a little freer, a little lighter. Maybe because less is expected of me or, correction, because nothing is expected of me."

Cynthia laughed. "How little you know!"

The wine was brought, and he inspected the label and nodded. Then he tasted it and nodded again. The Burgundy splashed into their glasses. "So tell me why you laughed."

She smiled. "You are an eligible male imported especially for the parties of the nineteen-sixty-seven season. Don't tell me you're that naïve."

He put down his wine goblet and shook his head. "Are you asking if I intend to marry Patricia?"

"You do cut through the formalities," she said dryly.

"Well, question asked or not, I will answer. She's a very attractive girl, but—" he shrugged. "She's one thing in Paris and another here."

"Oh, were you serious with her in Paris? Is that where you met her?"

"No, I wasn't, and yes, it was. I'm much more serious about being serious with you."

This time she didn't blush, but only stared at him with wide green eyes over the plates that had been put before them. She saw an older version of Marco, and the smile of someone who was teasing and sensual. His shirt was very white and his tie very blue, shoulders very broad. He seemed large, a very physical presence, across the tiny restaurant table. "Serious waltzing, now serious eating. I'm being held in suspense," she said sarcastically. What next? What could this Swiss possibly be alluding to?

"You read, don't you?"

She nodded. "A lot of Dickens, a lot of Greene, some Steinbeck—"

"Aldous Huxley?"

"*Crome Yellow,*" she assented.

They began to eat. Cynthia watched him covertly. She liked his accent, his darkness, the way he held his fork with the tines down. She hoped he couldn't sense her attraction for him for it felt blatant to her, obvious, even out of control. There hadn't been anyone since Marco. Crosby had kissed her a few times, but he would not dare to touch her breast, or even to *really* kiss her. Jean-François's hand on the table had long, thin fingers, shining pink nails, a gold signet ring with a coat of arms on his little finger. "How old are you?" she suddenly asked.

"Thirty-four in February." He swallowed some wine. "Do I seem like your great-uncle?"

"Ever been married?"

"No. It's something I haven't tried. Have you?"

"No." She looked down at her plate. I've tried other things, though, she felt like adding.

"Ever been to Geneva?"

"Once, for two days. I don't know much about it. The Protestant Rome. A lovely city on a lake. Seems quiet."

"You have an idea of it. Pretty fair." He sipped more wine and put the glass down. "Tell me. What are your plans?"

She smiled at him. He was very handsome, she decided yet again. "For the afternoon? For the weekend? For the rest of my life?"

"For the rest of your life," he answered without hesitation.

"No one ever talks to me this way." She liked the wine or the lightness she suddenly felt. Wine or Jean-François, did it matter? What mattered was— I'm not dead. I'm no longer numb. Shot full of novocaine to dull the boredom, to stop feeling anything at all. I am alive.

"How do they talk to you?"

"As if—" She stopped. No one talks to me except my mother, and she talks *at* me, as if I were faintly retarded, needing help to get dressed in the morning. Cynthia realized she talked to no one. She walked around with her arms crossed over her breasts as if to hold her thoughts inside. She looked up at him with such surprise, such wide green eyes, he wanted to reach out to her.

"Cynthia—"

"No. I'll tell you my plans. With great honesty—and you'll be appalled."

"No, I won't."

"There are no plans. Plans to get through the day, and then there are plans to get through the evening. What to wear, what time I'll be picked up, how many glasses of champagne I can drink without showing it. And when this is over and Christmas presents have been bought and opened and my thank-you notes written . . . then nothing. I have no plans to go back to college, to get a job. Nothing." She smiled sardonically. "Oh, that's not entirely true. I have an appointment for a haircut in two weeks."

Jean-François was astonished. This elegant creature was caught somehow under glass. What astounded him most of all was her admission of it. "What happened to you?" he demanded.

"I was hurt." Cynthia's eyes were full of tears. It seemed an act of great control, sheer will, that kept them from pouring down her cheeks.

He thought he loved her then, and he leaned across the table suddenly and pressed his mouth on hers as hard as he could manage, and he tasted the salt on her sweet tongue and heard her sharp intake of breath and he put his hands on the back of her neck and pressed her even harder against his face. Abruptly he let go of her and stood. The waiter materialized, and Jean-François jammed bills into his hand. The maître d' helped Cynthia into her coat and in minutes they were in a taxi. "What? Where—" she began.

"My hotel. My suite. My bed." Jean-François said it all so definitely that there were no more questions in her mind. He had decided and they were speeding through Cambridge, splashing great arcs of half-melted slush on either side of them outside the closed, steamed-up windows. The taxi was a warm cocoon, a submarine coursing through the gray December afternoon. He unbuttoned her coat and put his hands under the turquoise silk and up her thighs, which he pressed apart as he insistently forced his tongue between her lips. Suddenly she wondered if she liked it, if she could go through with it. My God, she thought. I feel as if I'm in an ambulance, being rushed to the hospital with a head wound.

. . . .

"You're lovely, you're, oh, so lovely," he whispered, looking into her face.

The room was warm and they were naked on the large double bed. Jean-François had thrown bedspread, blankets, everything on the floor and they lay on one sheet, bodies twisted together, heads on one pillow. Cynthia touched his cheek with her fingers and he pulled her mouth to his once more. She felt calmer, though not entirely satisfied. He had been quick and energetic, was all that went through her mind, and just as she had felt a throbbing deep inside her, it was over, with a near-scream from Jean-François.

"Are you all right?" he was asking.

She nodded.

He kissed her again slowly, sweetly, gently. "I had no idea. I'm sorry if I was too rough with you. Let me get a towel." He rose on one elbow and prepared to leave the bed. "I hope I didn't hurt you too much."

Cynthia was mystified. Yes, she had cried out when he came inside, but —then she looked down at her leg. My period! she thought with horror. Oh! Why now?

Gently he wiped the blood away and then pushed the towel between her legs. He seemed delighted, she realized. "I—why didn't you tell me?" he was nearly whispering.

She allowed herself to be pulled toward him once more as he lay down beside her and the kisses began again, delicate, warm, with such tenderness. Much better than the lovemaking, she decided.

The afternoon wore on with kissing and stroking and Jean-François touching her face with one finger as if to memorize the planes of her cheekbones, the line of her jaw. "I fly to New York tomorrow," he said quietly. "Then on to Geneva."

Cynthia said nothing. She liked the feeling of his skin on hers, his breathing, hearing his heart pound. She loved the muscles in his shoulders as he had arched himself in and out of her, the desperate holding back near the end, the crying out, the clutching her weakly afterwards. She wanted it again with him. She didn't want to think that this afternoon was all there was.

"So, my sweet girl with no plans, will you come to New York next Thursday and spend the weekend with me?" He waited. "My meetings will be over and we can go to the auction together on Thursday night."

"I don't even know what you do. What business you're in. What meetings you have," she said, drowsily turning on her back and staring up at the ceiling with a faint smile.

"I collect Egyptian artifacts, and Park Bernet sells them once in a while. I meet with dealers and collectors and we try to trick each other out of good pieces for the least money possible." He was silent, watching Cynthia's smile broaden. "Not a very proper thing to do, is it? I really should learn to say I'm in banking. Creates a much better impression than to lie here naked with an angel from Beacon Hill and tell her I'm like a little American boy who only thinks of his next baseball card."

Cynthia turned back to him and kissed him on the mouth gently. She knew she would go to New York, she knew she would sleep with him again; she loved what her skin felt like, what his lips felt like.

"So, my angel from Beacon Hill, you'll come?" he insisted in between kisses.

"I may be an angel," she said seriously. "But will you still meet me at La Guardia?"

· · ·

"Whatever you do, don't ever tell him," her mother was saying as she carefully folded the pink silk nightgown. In a state bordering on amazement, Cynthia had been watching her mother pack for her for the last ten minutes. "Just don't tell him. Stick to the mononucleosis story. Kate Grayson is your godmother after all, and she'd swear to that even if the Japanese were on hand to pull out her fingernails."

"On hand? Is that a pun?" Cynthia thought Kate Grayson perfectly capable of pulling out the fingernails of the Japanese herself. "As if any Japanese are desperate to know how I spent last winter."

Her mother ignored her daughter's contrariness and went on. "I don't think people really want to know the truth. Oh, they say they do, and your generation is running around 'letting it all hang out,' but honestly," she sighed as she tucked the black sequined evening bag in a corner of the Mark Cross suitcase. "They don't really want the truth."

Is this a dirty weekend? wondered Cynthia with a smile as she folded her cream crepe blouse carefully. And Mother just as happy as can be over it. Suppose the right last name makes a big difference. "Aren't the Swiss supposed to be insanely boring? And methodical and preoccupied with detail?"

Margaret Lake Kendall pursed her lips as she surveyed the other single bed. One pearl earring had been camouflaged on the pink flowered bedspread. She quickly picked it up and tucked it into the little white quilted satin jewelry bag. "I don't think I'd find Jean-François Colbert boring," she said, and looked across the room at her daughter. Yes, she is lovely. Cynthia's hair was nearly white in the sun that streamed in the window. She had perfect, ramrod-straight posture as she sat with her hands folded in the rose and white wing chair. But what does she talk to him about? Margaret was nervous when she thought of the weekend. Perhaps it was too soon for them to go away together. What she actually thought was that it was too long a time for her daughter to sustain the older man's interest. "What's he like?"

Cynthia blinked with surprise. What has come over Mother? This little woman-to-woman chitchat was totally out of character, without precedent. "Well, he's . . . you've seen his picture."

"Extremely handsome," said Margaret.

Suddenly Cynthia realized it was all a vicarious thing. My mother wishing she could do what I'm doing. Mother wishes she were going to New York. She wishes he had telephoned *her* twice this morning to talk from his room at the Carlyle. Aloud, she said, "What do you think of all this, Mother? Really think? I mean, you know I've packed my diaphragm and you know which nightgowns I'm taking and—"

"I think it's all very modern," said her mother, looking down at her hands. She sat as straight as her daughter on the edge of the twin bed, long legs in pale stockings, dark green suit with the jacket open, immaculately groomed as always. "It's fine. And of course it's all a prelude to—"

"To what?" Cynthia had no idea what she meant.

"Well, to marriage, of course. He wouldn't ask you to spend the weekend with him if it were just a—"

Cynthia fairly recoiled in shock. "Marriage? You think I'm going to marry him?" She was standing now. She felt bold. "Just because we're going to go to bed together, do you think that means—"

"Of course it does. He knows who you are. You're not some waitress at his hotel, you're not just anybody—"

"But, Mother!" she protested. "People make love because they want to! And *just* because they want to! It doesn't have anything to do with marriage!"

Margaret was calm. "Would it be so awful to decide this man is attractive and well educated and the right sort of person? And then to decide that marriage to him, living in a lovely place like Geneva, with a good name, having children with him . . . children who will be given everything . . . the right schools, the best of it all being the right name . . ." She took a breath and went on, "Would it be such a terrible thing to marry this man and to have all that?"

Cynthia suddenly saw Jean-François dressed as Santa Claus, bearing a big bag of all he could give her. She thought, Mother doesn't even know him! Doesn't even see him as a person! Or me, either, for that matter. I am to be sold to the highest bidder.

Margaret wasn't finished. "I know what you're thinking. But maybe it's time you thought differently. Sometimes you marry a man for what he can give you." Cynthia felt her throat constrict. "It's not wrong," her mother continued. "It's practical. Sexual attraction is a fleeting thing, but a house and a good name are for all the years you—"

"I can't believe you're saying this to me." The girl's voice was dull. She felt weighted down by her mother's words, as though she had fallen into the deep end of a swimming pool while wearing an overcoat. Her very arms and legs felt like lead. She wondered if this was why her mother had married her father. So she could live in this particular house in Beacon Hill. So her bank balance would always have lots of zeroes to the right of it.

Margaret Kendall stood and smoothed her skirt. She walked to the door without speaking, but her daughter thought, She isn't finished. No, she always has the last word. She won't leave yet. "And another thing, Cynthia. Think of the children you will have someday. Think of the father you're giving them. And think of what that particular father can give them."

Cynthia tightened her lips and didn't answer. She turned her face toward the window until she heard the bedroom door close behind her mother. "No, I won't," she said aloud. I won't think like that. She stood and walked across the room and stared at her face in the mirror. I won't be like that. Her green eyes shone with tears. And no matter what does or doesn't happen in New York, I'm going to remember what it was like to love Marco and to have him love me. We loved each other, even if . . . She couldn't finish the thought. We did love each other. And somewhere, she gasped near tears, there is a baby out there, that was made on the night we loved each other the most. She took a deep breath, suddenly not able to bear looking at herself, and turned to the window. I won't forget what it's like to be in love. She leaned with her elbows on the windowsill and stared out at the snow-filled Common. I promise I won't forget that. Her voice was a desperate, angry whisper. "And I won't end up like Mother."

CHAPTER SIX

Iris

1967—New York City

Ilsa stood in the empty room and then paced off the length with her small feet. Thirty of my feet, she thought, must be about eighteen real feet. And across was about twelve. Polished wood floor and white walls. A cell. "It's a cage," she said, looking out one of the two windows that opened onto an air shaft. "Scenic, it isn't," she frowned.

"Well, this is New Yawk!" said the realtor with a shrug. "You want Upper East Side Manhaddan, you gotta pay Upper East Side prices."

"How much is it? I told you I couldn't pay more than—"

"Two-fifty a month, and you aren't gonna find—"

"Two hundred and fifty dollars!" she shouted. "You must be kidding!"

"Look, you got a nice area, a doorman downstairs, an elevator building, for chrissakes."

"Two hundred and fifty dollars a month!" she repeated, ignoring him.

"And an address anybody in Queens would give their right arm for," he continued, unfazed.

Ilsa was standing over the little sink, the half-size refrigerator, and the two gas burners that made up the kitchen. It was less than one square yard. She was wondering if she could curtain it off, or maybe buy two old doors from a—

"Look, miss, if this is too much, I've got somethin' you might like down in the Village. It's a studio, but it has light and it's a little cheaper . . ."

"I'll take this," she said dully.

"But you're not gonna have the address, and I wouldn't want my sister down there in that neighbor—"

"I said I'll take it," she said again.

The realtor, Alfie Moskowitz, nearly jumped in surprise. "Okay, well, say, you're makin' a great choice. This is just great. Now we gotta go back to the office and sign some papers, and there's gonna be some little formalities like a deposit, and then it's all yours."

Ilsa sighed. Her head was down as she walked to the door. She felt frightened at how expensive it was, but it was the best she'd seen. And she would do anything to get out of the Barbizon for Women. She never wanted to see a female in curlers or underwear again as long as she lived. "Okay. Let's get it over with."

.   .   .

A week later she dragged in her Sears sleeping bag, her suitcase, which she opened on the floor and used as a bureau drawer, and a painting of herself. Robert Tripper had painted her nude for fifty-nine canvases, and she'd been featured in two of his exhibitions. When Ilsa had slept with him that first Sunday afternoon, it had been so disappointing she had wept afterwards in the big, beautiful bed in a corner of that sun-filled apartment she had thought was a piece of heaven.

The sex had never gotten better, but Ilsa was coldly philosophical about it. Perhaps, she decided, there is only one Cutter in every girl's life. If you're lucky. And after that, there are just "situations" with men who are not so bad or nice or who marry you.

Ilsa liked Robert best on the afternoons they walked through art galleries. He talked to her about technique and light, and would point out the way this artist used brushstrokes to create a feathered effect, or the way another artist depicted depth and shadow. The symbolism bored her, but she once told Robert, in a bout of enthusiasm, that the colors made her think of music. "What kind of music?" he insisted, staring at her as they stood in front of a Monet in the Art Institute.

Ilsa suddenly felt miserable, uneducated, a hick. All she could think of was Elvis or the Everly Brothers, and that wasn't the right music at all. Robert put his arm around her shoulders and said in a kind voice, "Never mind. What's important is that colors speak to you at all, and if they sing to you, why, so much the better."

That had been one of their nicest days, and after they left the museum they'd gone home and he had given her a brand-new sketchbook and five needle-sharp pencils. "Just draw what you see," he encouraged her. Ilsa had torn her first efforts into confetti but later she had let Robert look, had allowed him to help her.

Ilsa decided being with Robert might be the closest thing to love she would ever have, but one afternoon she came home unexpectedly and found the artist in bed with the old man who bought most of his paintings. Two naked, hairy bodies were locked in an embrace that sickened her. The scene changed everything.

They had parted on relatively good terms, just because Robert had not wanted her to leave. He felt Ilsa had learned a lot from him, and he had demanded only her affection. But the young girl had discovered new depths of manipulation, which he resented. They played power games constantly, and because sex was involved, Ilsa always won. He had begged her to stay; he had said that he would leave her alone except for weekends, he had vowed fidelity. Ilsa had decided she would move on. She took one thousand dollars he had hidden in the paintbox he used in the summer, and all the clothes he'd given her, and left a note. Robert would not be surprised; she knew he expected her to go and he expected her to steal.

· · ·

To Chicago by thumbing, to New York by bus. Coming up in the world, she thought. Ilsa spent her days getting dressed and going to employment agencies. She wore a simple black dress that Robert had picked out, and black slingback heels that made her legs appear even longer. A brassiere made her chest less conspicuous, and Robert, again Robert, had made her comb out the rat's-nest hairdo. She looked presentable, lied about her high-school diploma, lied about being able to type, lied about her age, and within a week she had a job as a receptionist for a small advertising agency.

Within three weeks one of the junior ad executives asked her out for a drink and then dinner; the next evening she went to his apartment for a nightcap. Playing hard-to-get, Ilsa waited until the fourth date to allow him to maneuver her into his bed. She was sympathetic about his boss, about what she termed his "going-up-the-ladder worries," and he was sure he was in love with her. This delighted her.

A few weeks passed. One evening after lovemaking, she bravely wiped away tears as she told him about her mother dying of cancer in Indianapolis. "All the money I can send," she sighed and then turned her pretty face away from him and into the pillow.

Instantly struck with sympathy for this blond darling who treated him like a god, he volunteered to help her if she needed it. Ilsa wasn't sure this was what she wanted to hear, and opened both green eyes very wide. "Oh, no, I couldn't ask," she sighed, muffling another sniffle. "I'll get through this. Somehow. I just wish . . ."

Behind her on the bed, Dennis stared at her creamy white shoulder and wondered if it would be bad form to start touching her again while she was crying. "What do you wish?" he asked, feeling himself aroused yet again. What was it about her that made him want to make love three times a night? "What do you wish?" he insisted.

"I wish I hadn't signed the lease for that apartment. I think I'll move out as soon as I can find something cheaper. Something down in the Village. I just shouldn't have committed myself to this." She sighed again, hopelessly. "It's too much of a burden."

"Oh, Ilsa!" Dennis sat up in bed. "You can't move! I mean, you're only three blocks from me, and it's so convenient. I mean, what I mean is, don't go to one of those dicey neighborhoods. New York isn't what it was five years ago. The muggings. The crime. Hell," he said, gaining momentum, "it's a garden of tigers."

She turned over, fixing her eyes on his face. He was looking at her amazing breasts. "You mean it wouldn't be safe?"

"That's . . ." He took a deep breath, feeling himself come alive once more. "That's exactly what I mean."

She squirmed closer. "But what should I do? Maybe I should get a roommate. I'll ask at the office . . ."

"A roommate! Ilsa! Are you nuts? You couldn't get a hamster in there!" And I could never go there on the spur of the moment, he added to himself.

"Well, I think a roommate would solve everything," she insisted. "Otherwise . . ." She sniffed again and buried her face in his shoulder, which meant her breasts were pressed against him.

Dennis did some quick figuring about his take-home pay and his own rent and decided if he could pay half of Ilsa's rent, that would save her for him. Exclusively. She would owe him, in a way. Not that she didn't want him as much as he wanted her. No. He wasn't that insecure. No, of course not. But it would make her very, very grateful, and any girl trying to live in New York and sending money back to Indiana . . . How brave she was, and how—she squirmed against him, and he felt her tears hot and wet on his neck—yes, how brave she was.

"Ilsa, darling, you know how I feel about you . . ." he began.

Yes, I can tell how you feel about me, smiled Ilsa. Hard as a rock is how you feel.

"I think you are trying so hard to make ends meet and I know what your salary is and how . . . well, why don't I pay half your rent for a while, just until you get a raise, just until you can . . ."

"Oh, Dennis!" she cooed. "Oh, I couldn't let you. Why, that's . . . that's out of the question. That just doesn't sound right to me. I mean, I know you are offering something so generous with no strings, but I don't think I could take money from you like that. I just . . ." She burrowed closer to him.

He bit his lip, nearly groaning. "Ilsa, it would be a favor to me. I worry about you, and I come to *your* apartment sometimes. You're usually here at my place, but I don't think I'm ready to live with anyone. You know how early I have to get up . . ."

Ilsa was horrified. She didn't want to live with a man again for a long time. They grew whiskers in the night. "No, I don't think we should live together . . ." Suddenly she was worried about the conversation's turn. Somehow they were getting away from the subject of money and rent. "Dennis, you wouldn't think that . . . if I did take—I mean borrow—this rent money, or you just gave me some every month . . . what upsets me is . . ."

He kissed one nipple and looked up at her. "What upsets you?"

"You wouldn't think that I was . . . oh, I can't say it!"

"Oh, darling! Say it! You can tell me!" He reached down between her legs, wishing this long talk would end.

"I wouldn't want you to think I was cheap." She sighed, too upset to continue.

"Oh, is that all! Of course I wouldn't think that, Ilsa! Oh, you are really something!" he laughed. He kissed her cheek and then her shoulder and then thought, Let's settle it once and for all. No moving. No roommates. "Ilsa, let me give you a check on the first of every month for half your rent. We won't even talk about it. Or let's make it cash. And if someday you want to pay—"

"Of course I want to pay you back." She batted her green eyes at him. "With interest," she emphasized as she sucked on his nipple.

"Ohhh," he gasped. "Okay, okay," he panted. "How much is your rent?"

Ilsa pulled her mouth away from his skin and said decisively, "Four hundred dollars a month."

.   .   .

The alarm jangled Ilsa into wakefulness, and she turned over irritably and threw the Kleenex box across the bare floor toward the sound. Eight months to the day after her arrival in the apartment on East Seventy-third Street, and she still slept "in the bag," as she called it. But it didn't matter to her. She thought of the place as temporary and bought not one chair, not one print for the walls, not one potholder. A single and never-used knife, fork, and spoon rattled in the kitchen drawer, along with a can opener for an emergency she had never had, and a corkscrew. Two wineglasses from the Pottery Barn and an unopened packet of pink paper plates sat on one shelf of the cupboard above the stove. The bathroom, in contrast, appeared to serve five vain women. The mirrored cabinet held all manner of creams and makeup. Sea sponges and loofahs and scented soaps crowded a plastic contraption that crossed the tub like a breakfast tray. Ilsa had twenty-two bottles of nail polish and twice as many lipsticks that she kept in a basket beside the toilet. She could apply makeup with a sponge, with one of several brushes, or with her fingers; she could brush her hair with seven different kinds of brushes, ranging from a tiny one to tuck into a purse to an enormous boar's bristle with a wooden back. There were five different brands of shampoo and three conditioners, not to mention the special once-a-week condiments.

The apartment was a place to recharge her batteries, to give herself a facial, to be alone for a few hours: it was for a night of sleeping alone. She changed her clothes there; it was her headquarters for deciding what went to the cleaners. The address mattered when people asked where she lived, and Dennis mattered because he took her to dinner and then to his bed four times a week. Of course, his money mattered too. She spent it on things he never knew he paid for. Seventy-five dollars' worth of eye shadow, culled from the street floor of Bloomingdale's on a rainy Saturday, for instance. Clothes that she always said she'd had "forever" or "since high school, do you mean you really like it?"

The job was where she spent her days, that was all. She put in time, she sat at the desk. She liked sitting in the royal blue and red reception area and seeing all the people who came and went, from messengers with clipboards to sign and packages to accept, right up to expensively dressed men who had appointments with the top brass. It was easy work for her, and if she'd been home she would have had to buy a television and knew she'd simply sit on the floor and watch soap operas all day. That had driven Robert totally crazy. He claimed to hear the theme song of "As the World Turns" in his sleep.

One day, Ilsa was wearing a short red wool dress that came to mid-thigh, a couple of black and red plastic bracelets from Woolworth's, and high-heeled red shoes. She had taken her phone off the hook and left her desk for coffee. When she came back a well-dressed man, waiting at the desk, said, "Wow! You must be new."

Ilsa smiled automatically and asked if he had an appointment.

"What about dinner tonight?"

That's how it always started. And it always ended with Ilsa moving on. To someone she thought more attractive. Usually the gravitation was toward a man with more money.

· · ·

Things do have a way of falling into place, Ilsa smiled into the mirror as she stroked pale sea green eye shadow on her lids. Dennis's money had been replaced within two weeks by a raise, which she knew Bill Van Horn had facilitated. And as for Bill, he was fun in bed and she liked the idea of being good to him after the misery he said his wife had put him through. Yes. Fun. She smiled. He needed to have fun. And me? she asked herself as she closed the tiny box. She dabbed perfume on her wrists and around her hairline and then her throat. Bill told her she wore too much perfume and had bought her something much lighter. Am I having fun? she wondered. Not fun like with Cutter. But then I loved Cutter. She stared into her eyes in the bathroom mirror and then told herself not to think. "Cutter is far away," she said aloud.

She turned off the bathroom light and walked into the other room. The tiny studio apartment had been transformed. Bill had said he would never feel quite the same about sleeping bags, but putting sentiment aside, he had insisted she buy a bed. He'd given her the money and let her do everything exactly as she wanted. There was a fold-out sofa bed of hot pink corduroy, a pink shag rug that Bill had said looked like cotton candy, and several gold lamps that Ilsa kept in their original plastic so that the white shades wouldn't get soiled. The Formica-topped coffee table looked so much like gray marble that Ilsa was still thrilled every time she thought of how cheap it had been. A big blue and white ceramic vase of cattails added just the right amount of interest by the front door. Ilsa was very proud of all she'd accomplished in such a short time.

The intercom squawked. "Miss Keller, a gentleman here to see you. Should I send him up?" Good old Hubert. Ilsa pushed the speaker button. "Yeah. I mean yes. Thanks." She had begun noticing certain things about herself. One of the secretaries at work had told her that ladies didn't chew gum, and after Ilsa's initial shock she had decided maybe the secretary was right. She never saw anybody really classy in New York chewing gum, only shoeshine boys and delivery boys and that girl who gave her manicures on Third Avenue. Ilsa dashed to the mirror for a last look, and then the doorbell sounded. She opened the door and pulled him in.

"Ilsa, baby! You look good enough to eat!" Bill laughed as he took off his raincoat.

"Oh, Billy! You wouldn't!" It appeared that he would. His teeth went after the straps of the black lace teddy, licking her bare shoulders in the process. Ilsa pretended to be upset for almost a minute, and then she simply stepped out of the wisp of satin altogether.

. . .

Ilsa was totally involved, as she always was when she was shopping. Her little white hands ruffled through the pile of lacy bikini underpants as quickly as a croupier's through a deck of cards. No. No. No. I have enough pink. I like the cream ones. Then she turned to the rack of hanging teddies. They were made of lace, with self-covered buttons from waist level to the low-cut bodice. There was only room for three of them. A veritable spiderweb on sale for only thirty-two dollars. Ilsa flipped one plastic hanger aside after another, and then stood back with pursed lips. Bill would like it. She flipped the hangers back again, and plucked a pale green teddy from among the others. "Do you have this in that cream color? In small?" She directed her questions at a gray-haired woman who stared quite openly at her bust and said, "I think you'd better try a medium. They run very tight."

"Okay. I think I might buy the black and the light blue, too, but the cream one is my favorite."

"Café au lait," the clerk corrected her as she disappeared into the stockroom.

Ilsa turned down her mouth in an expression of defiance and heard the chuckle that made her turn.

"I'm sorry. I couldn't help it," he began. A tall, bearish man in a gray overcoat was smiling. "Café au lait," he mimicked.

Ilsa noted the wide, sunburned face and the grin, and smiled back. She didn't say anything. Men came on to her immediately, at all times; she knew she needn't ever make an initial effort. She was completely aware that the way she looked was quite enough. Before she turned back to the rack of petticoats, she had taken in with appreciation his striped green and blue silk tie and the dark blue plaid scarf hanging around his neck. Ilsa had also taken in the fact that he was losing his hair, had a double chin, and could have a bit of a belly under that overcoat. Sunburn, she thought as she pulled at a petticoat trimmed in white lace, meant the Caribbean or skiing. But no, she could not imagine this burly man balanced on two skinny pieces of wood. More than likely he, like Bill, had been reclining on a bright towel laid across a chair with wheels in front of a resort hotel. A bright white hotel with a big blue swimming pool where pool boys dragged mattresses around and waiters walked quickly between rows of baking bodies, bearing rum drinks with imaginative names.

"I don't usually try to pick up beautiful young girls in Saks on my lunch hour," he began.

So why start now? went through Ilsa's head.

"But may I ask . . ." he almost stammered. Ilsa felt that he really wasn't practiced in seduction, and she softened a bit. A very little bit. "Are you an actress?"

"Not professionally," she shot back, without looking up from the latest petticoat.

He laughed and then she looked up at him and smiled very sweetly. The clerk returned and laid the teddies, pale blue, sea green, black, white, and, of course, café au lait, on the table beside the cash register. Ilsa's little hands tugged at this one and that one, checking the size labels, and when she confirmed that all were medium, she said grandly, "I'll take them all."

"Like a little girl buying candy," he said. Ilsa smiled as she fumbled in her voluminous pocketbook for her wallet. The analogy appealed to Ilsa, who bought five dollars' worth of chocolate often. She loved the sense of power she felt when she pointed a finger at the mocha, the chocolate-covered cherries, the ones with almonds, or the pralines. Yes, another six of those. Oh, and maybe four more of the ones with the cream centers, she'd say. It was a largesse she bestowed upon herself. Candy for Ilsa. Presents for a good girl.

"Would you have coffee with me?" he was asking at her elbow. The clerk sniffed with disapproval as she counted out the change. Ilsa had handed her two one-hundred-dollar bills.

Ilsa took the shopping bag and slowly turned. He smiled then, and the smile was full of longing and Ilsa saw the longing and read the need. She also noted again his silk tie and his apparent prosperity. She responded with one of her sweet, shy smiles, calculated to inflame. Men felt both protective and excited. They felt bigger, stronger; Ilsa's smile could make a man positive he could leap tall buildings in a single bound.

In minutes they were in a warm, crowded, noisy coffee shop on Sixth Avenue, sitting across from each other in a red leather booth just like the one she used to sit in with Cutter after home-ec class.

"Before we go any farther, my name is Harry Stoner."

"I'm Ilsa. Ilsa Keller."

"Ilsa," he repeated. "I produce plays. When I like the script, I put up the money, and then I get to have an opinion as to how it's spent." He stirred the sugar into the nearly black liquid.

Ilsa stared down into the heavy white china cup. She had just dropped five cubes of sugar in.

"Have you ever thought of acting?" he insisted suddenly.

"I do it all the time." She smiled up at him, giving him the total benefit of her great green eyes; all one thousand watts were turned upon him. "I don't have to think about it."

He laughed, but he felt the force of her gaze. His face felt warm, his hands cold. She was like a cat one minute, and a kitten the next. "I think you have possibilities."

She shrugged, and her breasts moved under the red sweater. He tried not to notice. Tried to keep his eyes on her face. "Do you have a job? Is this your lunch hour? Am I making you late?"

Ilsa sighed. "Oh, I guess I have a job. I'm thinking of looking for something else. It's just getting . . ." Her voice dropped and he leaned forward to hear. "Two sunny side up, one burger all the way, one man on a raft, tuna on rye, hold the mayo," chorused behind them. The din was deafening. Fine, thought Ilsa. Let him guess the situation I'm in. I don't know what it is yet. I haven't gotten that far. "It's just getting too complicated," she finished, deciding not to make it too easy for the man across from her. But she liked him. She liked the way he ordered the coffee, the way he had opened the door for her. Most of all, she liked his sincere smile and the way he smelled. She'd caught a whiff of his after-shave as he'd helped her off with her coat. A scent, a touch, could trigger in Ilsa oceans of emotion. "I'm supposed to . . . supposed to get married soon."

"Don't you want to get married? Do you love him?"

She shook her head mournfully and allowed her bright eyes to shine with tears. "I hate hurting him. I have to get out of it. I have to get away."

"Well, you must tell him. You have to be honest with him." How wonderful. Harry had heard of people catching other people on the rebound. A chance to comfort. A possibility to console. "Isn't there anyone you can talk to?"

The white-blond hair moved on her shoulders as she shook her head. "Nobody I can think of." She sighed and played with the spoon. "All our friends . . . you see . . . I wouldn't want to go behind his back, and all our friends were his friends first. It wouldn't be fair." A real Joan of Arc, she thought. I'll be up for sainthood soon.

"Your family? What about your mother?"

She hesitated. Would it be a sin to kill off Mama on a cold day in February in a downtown coffee shop? Ilsa had already given her cancer; death was the obvious next step. With a catch in her small voice, she stated, "She died last summer."

Harry Stoner flinched. Poor girl. He himself was very close to his mother. "Well, then, talk to me," he invited magnanimously. "I'm here and I'll listen. You need some advice."

Ilsa patted her nose delicately. She had practically trained it not to go red when she wept. She'd practiced in front of the bathroom mirror. Crying came in handy; summoning sudden tears was as essential as cab fare or a Tampax in the bottom of her purse.

When she didn't speak, he began gently. "Tell me about him. Are you sure you don't love him?" His own hopes soared. Father confessor, protector. She would fall into his arms to be comforted, and then she might fall into his bed. Suddenly he was reminded of all that lacy underwear and felt yet another strong twinge. "How long have you been engaged?"

"A year," she answered, wondering if too many details might not be a mistake. "I've known him for a year and been engaged for almost that long. It was sudden. He asked me right away. Maybe too sudden," she concluded.

"And when is the wedding?"

"I keep putting it off, making excuses. I know I'm not being fair to him, but I hate to hurt him." Good. But I do hope I don't sound too good to be true. An angel come to earth.

"Maybe you'd better not quit the job, then."

Ilsa's eyes filled with tears again, and her hand trembled when she dabbed at them. "Oh, it's a mess, isn't it? A job I hate and marrying the wrong man and the apartment that . . ." She wanted him to know she hated her apartment, too. And she did. She'd been reading *McCall's*, and nothing in their pictures featured bubble-gum-pink shag rugs. Ilsa sensed that she'd spent all of Bill's money on the wrong furnishings, and she felt a failure when she surveyed the little studio. It was like buying a dress and wearing it once and feeling like a lump and being told you had to wear it every day, forever.

"One thing at a time, honey," he said soothingly. "What does the apartment have to do with getting married to the wrong man?"

"Oh . . ." She rolled her eyes, wondering what to say. "It's just that it's not really . . . it's . . . well, it's going to be *our* apartment after the wedding and I'm fixing it up and now I can't bear to go home and be reminded of . . ."

"Oh, now I understand." And he did appear to understand. With amazement, Ilsa realized he understood what she hadn't yet made up. This nice man was filling in the gaps as quickly as she could toss them out with the occasional sniffle and blinking back of tears. "I think you're a special girl who's in way over her head. And I think you shouldn't lose this job, no matter how much you hate it. So let me walk you back." He dug in his pocket for change for a tip. Quarters and dimes jingled onto the blue Formica table.

Ilsa was helped with her black wool coat, and pulling on her red knit gloves, she felt a wave of disappointment. She'd liked him across the table from her at the coffee shop. He wasn't bad. She didn't know if she wanted to go to bed with him, but she was curious. He was too old, but she thought he might be smart, and he must have money to keep putting it in the theater like that. And his clothes looked expensive. And Bill was history. Maybe just one time. Just to see what an older man was like. Every man she'd ever had had been older, but this was *older*. They walked quickly; he took her arm to steer her between cars stopped at a traffic light.

"Right here." She imagined that she was smiling bravely. "This corner is fine." Her breath came in warm little white puffs in the cold. "Thanks for listening to me. I'm usually not so complaining and ridiculous." I can be lots of fun, she told herself.

"Don't say you're sorry for confiding in me. Then my feelings will really be hurt." Ilsa looked up at him in surprise. "Will you have dinner with me tonight? If I shouldn't call you at the apartment, will you give me your office number? Will you?" He was eager now.

Ilsa smiled slowly. "No. No phone numbers. Tell me where to meet you."

Harry Stoner looked up at the sky as if seeking to find a restaurant name above a skyscraper, and then blurted, "Sardi's. Do you know it?"

Ilsa smiled. "Sure." She'd heard the name, anyway, and there was always the phone book. Don't let him know you don't know anything.

Harry was happy. "Eight?" He grinned, and she thought he looked more attractive than when he was serious. "Ask for my table. Everybody knows me."

"But—"

"Remember. My name's Harry Stoner." He squeezed her arm. "Eight?" he cried again as she started to walk toward the revolving doors of the Pan Am Building. "You promise you won't stand me up?"

Ilsa shook her head, and he saw the platinum hair catch the weak, watery rays of winter sun and thought that her hair was more like light than sunlight itself. "I promise," she called back, and then was embraced by the spinning glass-and-metal partitions of the turning door.

I promise. Sardi's, she thought as she sat down at her desk. I'll wear that black dress that's so low-cut and so short Bill calls it a belt. She grinned impishly. And gallons of Chanel No. 5.

· · ·

When the lobsters arrived, Ilsa screamed in fright. "We're eating these giant cockroaches?" She recoiled as Harry Stoner shook with laughter and finally had to wipe tears from his eyes with the heavy damask napkin.

"I love you," he said before they'd ordered dessert.

Ilsa smiled and fairly preened with pleasure. She liked Harry, she liked the way everybody knew him, the way everybody came over to the table to say hello. And she liked being liked by somebody important. Ilsa Keller sat up very straight in the booth beneath the framed images of Katharine Hepburn, Spencer Tracy, Ethel Merman, Christopher Plummer, and who knew who else. Ilsa only recognized a few.

"I want to know everything about you," he insisted. "And you don't answer questions," he marveled. "Why don't you tell ol' Harry your life story?"

"Tell me yours first." Ilsa read the menu and then flashed her green eyes up at him. "Strawberries? Maybe I could have strawberries?" Bill always ordered for her, and she was unsure if her decision was appropriate.

Harry put his hand over hers. "Anything you want."

"With cream and sugar?" she added almost timidly.

That delighted Harry, who had gotten a glimpse of her little pink tongue and was reminded of a kitten once more. He instructed the waiter to bring lots of cream and sugar and lots of strawberries. The young man nodded and rushed away. "Now that the important things have been dealt with—the life story. But mine is longer than yours. Why don't we do yours tonight and mine tomorrow night? We'll start earlier tomorrow."

God, he's like a dog with a bone, Ilsa thought. Won't let up. Guess I have to tell him something. My mother's dead. As of this afternoon, she rehearsed . . .

"How old are you?" he was asking.

"You don't ask a lady that!" she smiled.

"You are hovering on the brink of turning twenty, is my guess. And that's really too soon to be coy about your age. Come on, Ilsa! Have you had any college?"

She twirled the stem of the wineglass in her fingers and didn't answer for a few seconds. "I didn't count on this. Just dinner. Just fun. Why do you have to know about me?"

"Hey, baby—"

"Don't call me 'baby.' Please." Bill always called her that, and she hated it.

"Sorry." He was instantly cowed. Ilsa noticed that his head was shiny. But he was a nice man and he smelled good and she liked his hands. She had decided she would go to bed with him when she caught a whiff of his after-shave for the second time. It had happened when he stood to greet her. Her perfume had mingled with the newness of his scent and she'd slid across the banquette, feeling the cool leather on her thighs, and simply decided she would let him have her.

She took a sip of the wine as he regarded her in silence. The little upturned nose, the full, pouty lips, the chin that was one degree away from being sharp. Her heart-shaped face in profile was lovely. "Are you running away from something?" he asked gently.

"Marriage to the wrong man," she said quickly.

Relief was evident in his voice. "Well, that's easy! You tell him no! No thank you! *Nyet! Nada!*" Harry didn't want Ilsa marrying anybody. To find her and then have her, shining and beautiful, slip from his grasp. He remembered when his childhood dentist in Queens had given him a tablespoon of mercury and he'd let it fall on the floor of the elevator and had cried and cried because the little silver balls couldn't be retrieved. They simply fell into smaller and smaller parts under his chubby, six-year-old fingers. "You have to tell him you won't!"

Ilsa turned her eyes to his. "How do you know when you're in love? Have you ever been in love? Really in love?" she insisted. Harry could talk about love for hours, she sensed it.

The strawberries came in a metal dish on a little stand with a white paper doily like a lace petticoat under the pedestal. Harry was animated. "A showgirl! In Vegas! Can you imagine anything so hackneyed? But I was only sixteen. Hell, my pop shouldn't've even taken me in that place. And I was sunk. I think I lost ten pounds every single time she walked on stage. Pop noticed." Harry burst out laughing, and people turned from the next table and smiled at him. "I guess waiters in the kitchen noticed! So he arranged for me to meet her after the show." He plucked a strawberry from Ilsa's dish. He chewed it and then swallowed, shaking his head. He'd changed his shirt, and the collar was very white against his tan. His dark eyes shone with delight at the memory. "Lot better ta lose your virginity that way than in the backseat a' some car parked in front of Frieda's house." He was relaxed, but animated, and the accent of his boyhood reappeared. Ilsa guessed it was Queens.

"Frieda? Who's Frieda?"

"Oh . . ." He looked back at Ilsa. "My wife. That is, my former wife." He stared at her face. "Well, no. She is my wife." He waited for Ilsa to speak. This would shock her. She is so young. She won't see me again. She'll be gone. One dinner. A few hours of her company. Gone. Like the mercury falling on the floor of the elevator.

"So. You're married." Her words fell like stones.

Harry nodded miserably. "I suppose it won't make any difference to you for me to tell you we don't get along. That's why you're here and she isn't."

"You fight? You mean you fight?"

Harry allowed himself a glimmer of hope. "Do we fight?" he cried rhetorically. Ilsa was staring at him, unblinking. "We fight," he finished dogmatically.

Ilsa made her decision. All over again. She wanted to know what it would be like to go to bed with this great bear of a man. His face was crossed with emotion after emotion. His eyes were little and brown and kind. Ilsa felt a great urge to curl up beside him. For warmth. She suddenly wanted to be held. Married? To someone named Frieda? Ilsa didn't care. She could compete with all the Friedas in the universe and still come out on top. She put her soft little hand on his big paw. "I'm so sorry for you," she said. Her eyes were soft with sympathy.

Harry tried not to gasp with surprise. He didn't dare look into that trusting face, but instead motioned for the waiter to bring the check. Her fingers were as light as rose petals on top of his hairy knuckles. He realized he might, after all, get to see Ilsa in one of the little lacy nothings she had bought this morning at Saks. Hope surged through Harry Stoner with all the warmth of the best claret.

CHAPTER SEVEN

Cynthia

1967 — New York City

"I knew a professor once who used to get impassioned over the idea of scientists, archaeologists, studying mummies."

"What do you mean? He loved the idea?" Cynthia looked at Jean-François's profile as he bent over the glass case. Inside, rows of scarabs, lined up like battalions of beetles, shone dully. They were every color from coal-black ebony to dozens of shades of blue faience to the whitest alabaster. Coming to the Metropolitan Museum on a Friday morning had meant they had the Egyptian Wing practically to themselves.

"No! Detested the idea. With religious fervor." He appeared to be examining the stones, one by one.

Cynthia shook her head. "I don't understand why. They have survived for thousands of years, been found, and we have the technology . . ."

Jean-François took a step to the left and continued peering down. "Professor Madison thought it was a sacrilege to disturb them in their eternal sleep. They'd been prepared to enter the underworld with a certain dignity, with ceremony, and there we were, a bunch of voyeurs in the twentieth century, undressing them, chipping away at bone samples, taking dental X rays."

"I never thought of it that way," she said, gazing toward the next room, which was lined with standing sarcophagi.

"I hadn't either, but we are disturbing them. And"—he looked up at her —"we don't have the right."

"Do you believe in life after death?" Cynthia's eyes were full of questions. Some shadow had fallen over his face, and she wanted to ask about it, wanted to know what Jean-François was thinking.

His mouth turned down, and he shrugged. "I don't believe in heaven or hell. We may have some sort of voyage to take, something to traverse like a river, maybe the way the Egyptians believed . . ."

"To prove our goodness?"

"Oh, my angel from Beacon Hill!" He laughed and put his arm around her and squeezed her shoulders. She smelled him, and felt the wool of his dark blue suit against her cheek. "I don't believe in goodness."

"You must!" she cried. "There is good and there is evil. They are twins, one dark, one light." His expression grew serious as she continued. "Don't you know about American cowboys and their white hats? Villains always wear black Stetsons."

He laughed. "Silly girl. Good and evil. Is this your New England upbringing?"

"Yes! No!" She grinned back at him as he folded her into his arms and looked down into her face. She blushed. "I don't know!" He kissed her forehead and leaned back, a cynical smile on his face. She continued, "But you aren't Catholic if you don't believe in evil."

"Of course I'm not Catholic. Geneva is full of old, old Protestant families who came there to escape those nasty Papists. Hundreds of years ago. But we had Jean Calvin to enlighten us about evil." He steered her toward the next room. His voice dropped and he pressed her close to him. "Tell you what, Cynthia. If you're very, very good to me until"—he looked down at his watch—"until half past twelve, I'll take you to a special place for lunch." Cynthia jabbed him with her elbow as an answer. He turned to deflect the blow, and continued with mockery in his voice. "And over trout amandine —it's always good there, and a good wine—we'll continue this talk of what's good and what's bad." He stopped walking and pulled her to face him, then kissed her very deeply on the lips. Cynthia looked up at him with slitted green eyes. She swallowed and caught her breath. "And then, after lunch, we'll go back to the Carlyle and do very evil things to each other."

Cynthia smiled coyly as she reached up to wipe a tiny spot of coral lipstick from his mouth, and he made as if to bite her. She answered him seriously. "No evil things in the afternoon," she raised her eyebrows, "unless lunch is *really* good."

He pulled her to him firmly, and she felt him, male and hard and exciting, through his wool suit and her winter coat. All she could think of was how happy she was to want someone again.

. . .

He didn't think he'd tell her. He'd make her wonder. He'd make her ask. He'd force her to ask questions, and then he'd only tell part of it. Jean-François dialed the number in Paris, glancing quickly at his watch and adding six hours. Nearly eleven o'clock. He knew she'd be preparing for bed, in a long silk dressing gown, dabbing on creams. Or reading a book in the salon, or propped up in bed, lace-trimmed pillows behind her. A glass of red wine would be beside her, wherever she was. It would be nearly full; he'd never seen her take more than a few sips. It was as though she wanted it there in case she needed it, not that she actually did. Cynthia was running the bathwater and couldn't possibly be out in less than fifteen minutes. He pulled the flowered quilt over his nakedness and then turned on his stomach, listening to the faraway ring.

" 'Allo?"

"Hello, yourself! How are you?"

The feminine voice was full of smiles. "Jean! Jean-François! Where are you, darling?"

"Still in New York. The Carlyle."

"Well, stay put. I think it's drizzling all over Europe. The skies are weeping in every corner of the Continent. No snow for skiers, no sun for the seasonably depressed." She sighed dramatically. "Are the meetings going well?"

"Hmmmm. Yes. I've cleared up several things with Chase. And they replaced the man I didn't like the last time I was here. This one is very laid-back American. California. But went to Harvard and he's a good friend of ol' Rheinhart's."

"Is *he* still in New York?"

"Says he can't come back to Geneva, and Zurich is out of the question. American wife, you know."

There was a little sputter of disapproval on the other end of the line.

Jean-François laughed. The reaction in Paris was predictable. "Maybe there's more to Susan than we know."

"Aah, yes. Sexual wiles. Physical attraction," said the woman's voice in a bored tone.

"Speaking of which"—he hesitated—"I have a lovely friend here in my suite. She's taking a bath right now."

Elizabeth reached over to the bedside table and turned the little enamel clock toward her. After lunch, before dinner. Why did he do this? Her friends weren't the recipients of confidences like these. If they were, they certainly didn't confess to it. Peculiar. Elizabeth wondered if she encouraged it. Jean-François went on. "I'm terribly attracted to her. She is the least boring of all the American girls I've met."

"Are you bringing her home with you?" She often feared he was going to tell her what the lovemaking was like. Maybe it came from not having a father.

Not having a brother. Elizabeth thought, Hell, I don't know from what it stems, and maybe I won't ever know. Why can't Jean-François distance himself when it comes to another woman? Did he consider her and the new one rivals? What message was he sending? Elizabeth sighed. Though not given to introspection, she often wondered what a good psychiatrist would say about Jean-François. What he would have said years ago. She told herself not to remember. With a trembling hand she reached for the glass of wine. It was as rich and crimson as blood. She took a deep breath and told herself not to think of it, then she put the goblet to her lips.

"I may. It occurred to me. She's been to Geneva once. What do you think? Could we stop off and see you in Paris first, or should we fly to Geneva and have you come there for the weekend?"

"Darling! Is this serious or what? And an American, too!"

"It might be. She speaks French. That's a plus."

Elizabeth understood a few things about Jean-François, and one thing was sure: whether or not the woman spoke French meant nothing as long as she made him happy in bed. She reached for her dark blue leather date book. "When will you descend upon me?"

"Don't have a reservation yet, and Cynthia might have to fly back to Boston for clothes, so not for at least three days."

"Cynthia. Hmmm. Nice, respectable English name." Elizabeth's concise English accent was suddenly pronounced.

There was silence on the line as Jean-François waited for a question, for another remark from Paris, but none was forthcoming. He couldn't seem to make her curious! Was it a game, to feign indifference? All these years and he still had no idea. Always off balance, still the little boy asking for attention. "I'll call as soon as we have plans. As soon as I know anything. I think we'll spend the weekend right here. The Carlyle. In case you need me." He knew she wouldn't telephone; she never did. Or very rarely. But wasn't it polite? Wasn't it normal to want her to know where he was?

"Fine, darling. I'm off tomorrow to Avignon. Just for a party tomorrow night, and then I'll drive back Sunday. The usual sort of thing. Should be fun."

"Have a good time," he said. He knew she would. She had invitations by the dozen, and people genuinely liked her, liked her chatty kind of fun.

"I always do, don't I?" Her voice was very nearly flirtatious. "And you, darling, try to enjoy yourself in New York!" She knew how much he loved the city. "Try very, very hard not to be bored." She laughed lightly, and he smiled.

"I'm not bored this trip. Not at all," he said suggestively as he heard the bathroom door open. *"Bon nuit, Maman."*

．　．　．

Their lovemaking began again when he saw her in the white towel. Cynthia was clutching it demurely to her as she tried to find a petticoat in a bureau drawer full of frilly white underthings. Jean-François stood behind her and touched the blond tendrils that had escaped the tortoiseshell combs, and then he found himself kissing her tiny ears and then her cheekbones. As Cynthia reached up to put her arms around his neck, the towel fell to the carpet; seconds after that the two of them were entwined again atop the twisted sheets of their previous coupling.

Afterwards, Jean-François dozed once more in a state of happy exhaustion, but Cynthia remained wakeful, her arm under his head, her pale hair spilling onto his chest. The hotel suite was utterly silent around the two figures on the large double bed. Jean-François's suit jacket had been hung over the back of the little desk chair, but all their other clothes were thrown and dropped around the blue and white chintz settee. Cynthia's shoes and his were at disparate angles where they'd been kicked off on the dark blue rug. The white ceiling was becoming gray in the pale winter afternoon light, which filtered weakly through the gauzy undercurtains. The din of Madison Avenue traffic rose from seven floors below—the Friday-afternoon confusion of honking horns and gleaming automobiles swimming up the wide thoroughfare among the schools of shining yellow taxis and the blue whales of belching buses.

Cynthia, however, could only hear the sound of Jean-François's breathing in the darkening room. She examined his face carefully, scrutinizing him as she had not dared to do before. His coloring reminded her of Marco: the dark skin that made her think of sun, of summer days, and the black-as-ink shining hair and straight black eyebrows. The mouth was different, though. Marco's lips had been fuller, almost femininely beautiful, but the Swiss had narrow lips, and in repose they could have been described as cruel. Cynthia had only seen him smiling or teasing or flirting. She could not imagine cruelty in him, though she did stare for a long time at the downward curve of his mouth. His shoulders were broad and straight. From skiing, she supposed, though he had told her he often rowed on the lake in a shell during the spring and summer. Jean-François's waist and hips were narrow and tapered down to long strong legs, as long as Cynthia's. Naked, lying in bed with feet in the air, they had compared them and decided Cynthia should be able to cross the Alps in record time. "Carrying me on your back," he'd laughed. She'd retorted, "On my back! Keep dreaming!" and he'd kissed her shoulder and said, "I love you on your back. You're best that way." Their playful wrestling had been a prelude to one more bout of lovemaking. Cynthia looked at him now, and felt a bit awed at his energy, his stamina in this hotel room. She hadn't realized a man could make love three or four times in twenty-four hours.

Carefully she began to move her pin-prickling fingers; her hand had begun to go to sleep beneath his head. He stirred and made a deep sighing noise, but did not awaken. Cynthia continued to stare at his closed eyes, and suddenly thought of her mother. All her talk of marriage. This man wants a very good time, she thought, and he's older and never been married and he's good-looking and I'm sure it's not difficult for him to find someone in any city, any country, who'll drink champagne with him and sleep with him.

Geneva is a world away, and so is his life. I'm just a good time and shouldn't dare think of falling in love with him, even though sometimes when he looks at me, when I look up at him and he's deep inside me . . . Cynthia felt her face go warm at the thought. Sometimes, then, I imagine that he loves me. I feel loved. She slowly pulled her numb hand away, and wondered if she should begin dressing for the theater. Before she woke him, she gently kissed one dark maroon nipple and felt a wave of melancholy at the idea of returning to her mother's house in Beacon Hill, to Crosby, or to someone else like him. But Cynthia was practical, and even as she pressed her cheek against his chest and inhaled the clean, warm scent of him, she told herself, Geneva is a world away.

· · ·

"Eight hours' flying time from Boston," he was saying. The bartender poured two glasses of champagne and placed them on the bar before them. They had five minutes to wait for their table at Lutece. The after-theater crowd kept opening and closing the door behind Cynthia, and she leaned forward on the high stool to make sure she'd heard him. Jean-François was smiling at her and asking, "Why not Tuesday?"

Beacon Hill

Barriers had fallen, veils were lifted, Cynthia thought, when we decided to take off our clothes, make love, go to New York. The Swiss was lighter, different from the silent, intense man she'd danced so many dances with in Boston. He's bright, and seems to think I am too, she thought with pleasure as she unzipped her suitcase on her bed at home. And when I ask questions, he thinks I am fresh and young and not unintelligent or silly, which I very well might be to someone that much older, someone that sophisticated.

"Cynthia!" The bedroom door opened and her mother stood there smiling. "When did you get back?"

"About ten minutes ago. I took a taxi in from Logan because I thought—"

"How was it? Did you have a good time? Did you go to the theater? What restaurants did he take you to? But what I really want to know is did he say anything about—"

Cynthia laughed. "Mother! I can't tell you everything at once! I did have a good time." She plopped down on the edge of the bed and put her hands in her lap. How she longed for a friend. A confidante. Anyone. But everyone she knew well was away at college. And she couldn't exactly phone her shrink and say, Oh, by the way, I don't think I'm still having a total breakdown, but may I make an appointment for ten minutes from now, because I have to tell someone about my weekend. Her mother would have to suffice. Dangerous as she felt it was to tell her mother too much about anything. "Actually . . ." She hesitated. "I had a terrific time."

The girl's face was alight with happiness. She flipped her hair back over her ears with quick gestures, and her mother noticed the emerald earrings. For daytime? She wondered, but decided not to remark on it. Cynthia seemed terribly pleased with herself.

"Tell me everything!" Margaret Kendall gushed uncharacteristically.

"No, I don't think I will." Cynthia stood up and began to transfer a folded black silk blouse to a pink quilted hanger. Three blouses were tossed onto the other single bed for the dry cleaners. Then she turned back to her mother, who sat speechless in the flowered pink wing chair by the window. "Mother, there aren't any secrets. It's just that . . ." She paused. "It was so special, I don't want to tell you everything."

Undeterred, the remark slipped out. *"That* special, was it?"

Cynthia felt as much as heard the unmistakable anger in the voice. Don't spoil things, she thought. Please don't. Don't let's fight. Just not tonight. Not when I haven't had a fight in all these days of being with a man, with wonderful Jean-François. Please let's not be like two cats in a too-small cage. Not now. "It was fun, Mother. He took me to Lutece, to '21,' to see the Supremes in concert at the Copacabana, which was hilarious because the place was full of people from New Jersey, and Jean-François thought they all looked like gangsters." She stopped and met her mother's eyes. Was it jealousy she saw in them?

"Mrs. Kendall!" called the maid from the hallway.

"I'm in Cynthia's room," she called back.

Agatha leaned in through the door. "Dinner is ready. Shall I put it on the table?"

"Let's wait for Mr. Kendall."

"Oh, he's here. He's in the library."

"Well, then, we'll be right down."

Without another word, the two women stood and walked down the hall, as distant as two people can be within the span of a corridor lined with family portraits, as foreign as two people who have no common language, as full of confused thoughts as only two people who have known each other for years can be.

. . .

After the dinner plates had been taken away, Cynthia looked from her father to her mother. Opposite ends of the long shining table, each precisely equidistant from the dried flowers in the centerpiece, each so far away from the other. Her mother seemed to be containing excitement, and kept pressing her to talk about the trip to New York. Her father, as always, appeared to be distracted. But there might have been embarrassment, too, as though it were "women's talk" and not for him to overhear. Or was it the idea of her spending a weekend with a man in a hotel room? A man she wasn't married to. Perhaps he remembered the last time he'd been in New York with her. Cynthia sipped from her water glass and felt her throat tighten when she thought of her father picking her up at the hospital. It's over, she said to herself. Over. And something new is happening to me. "I want to tell you both that Jean-François has"—her mother leaned forward expectantly—"has asked me to go to Geneva with him."

"Darling! How exciting!" Margaret Kendall had both manicured hands spread wide, framing her perfectly made-up face. She was almost girlish in her enthusiasm. Her voice was pitched higher than normal. "When? For how long? To meet his mother?"

"Margaret, just a minute. I'm not at all sure this is a good idea." Otis put down his spoon and pushed the silver dish of ice cream away.

"Not a good idea!"

"Well, to run across the ocean with this man neither of us has met. He's years older than Cynthia, and we don't know—"

"Don't know what? I'll tell you what I know!" Margaret Kendall had thrown her white linen napkin down on the table.

The gauntlet, thought her daughter. Why don't they just move out onto the Common and draw pistols? Then there'd only be gunfire instead of these voices. Her mother was in high gear now. "I know he is attracted to Cynthia—"

"Well, what man in his right mind wouldn't be?"

Cynthia smiled gratefully at her father. It was nice of him to say that. He had never paid any attention to her appearance until the last few months, when she was decked out in ball gown after ball gown, fussed over to within an inch of her life, and pushed by her mother to parade in front of him in the library before Crosby rang the doorbell. Poor Daddy, she had thought. He gets a quick glance at what he paid for.

"Yes! She is . . . well, yes." Margaret was sputtering. Cynthia felt her face go warm. "But he is from one of Europe's best families. One of the oldest Genevois families, very well connected." She took a deep breath as Cynthia wondered what all this had to do with the man with whom she'd spent most of the weekend naked. "A bachelor. A banker. Surely, Otis, you can understand—"

"All this would be marvelous if she were a few years older, but I think to push this as if—"

"As if this were the only man who'll ever be interested in me?" The words were out. Cynthia knotted her fingers in her lap and looked at her mother.

"Of course not! Don't be silly, dear." But her mother's voice held a note of doubt. Did she do it on purpose? Cynthia wondered. "But what if he did? Let's just imagine that all this is a prelude to marriage. What if he did ask her to marry him?" The question wasn't for Cynthia, but for her father.

"She's far too young even to imagine such a thing!" With these words, Otis Kendall flung his napkin down on the table. Cynthia thought it was her turn next. Otis pushed back the chair and stood. "Stop pushing her, Margaret. And I don't want her going anywhere with a young man who hasn't even had the courtesy to show his face in my house. As far as I'm concerned, he's a stranger, and I don't give a damn how 'well connected' he is in Europe!"

"Daddy! He wants to fly up from New York tomorrow to meet you."

"Oh!" was the simultaneous exclamation. Then Otis and Margaret were silent, standing expectantly at opposite ends of the gray dining room.

"Would it be all right for him to stay here? Or should I tell him that the Copley is nearby?"

"Of course he'll be our guest!" Otis was adamant. Expansive. "I would like very much to meet him." He smiled at Cynthia as though they were alone. "Especially if you're fond of him."

"Thanks, Daddy. You might like him." Once she was out of the room and into the hall, she raced up the stairs two at a time, surprised at her excitement. In less than a minute she heard his voice on the phone. "How's New York?" she purred into the receiver.

"Rotten," he said gruffly. "I have no one to be evil with in the afternoons."

• • •

"It's terrifying," she whispered into his neck. "I'm afraid to breathe."

"It's best this way," he whispered back as his hand curved around her breast.

They were lying in his single bed in the scarlet guest room at half past one in the morning, and Cynthia knew her mother was still awake and reading.

"So what do you think of them?" she asked as he kissed her cheek. The lovemaking had been quick, with Jean-François gasping into a down pillow to stifle the noise he invariably made. Cynthia couldn't decide what the cry was like. Something between triumph and pain. "Do you like them?"

He laughed softly. "Of course I like them. Your mother seems to think I'm fine, but your father is reserving judgment. I respect that."

Fine? Cynthia thought as she nuzzled closer to his warmth. Does he know, can he tell, that Mother would jump out the window for him?

"Your father is a very intelligent man." He kissed the top of her head. "And

I understand his not liking me too soon. After all, if you were my only daughter, I'd never leave you alone in the same room with me."

Cynthia smiled in the dark. "Oh, really?" she whispered as her fingers stroked his sideburn. "Don't you think I can handle you? Think you're too much for me? Is that it, Swiss banker?"

He pulled her on top of him once more, she felt him harden, and then as though she were a doll, she was lifted then lowered onto the shaft of him. Cynthia cried out, then put her hand over her mouth.

"You all right?" He stroked her flat, smooth belly as she gasped. She nodded and her blond hair caught what little light came in from the street.

"They'll hear us! I know they'll—"

He shook his head. "We're on another floor." He smiled up at her from the pillow. "And besides, they know what we're doing. Make no mistake about that."

"You think they suspect?" Cynthia's voice was full of astonishment.

"Of course they do! They *know*! Do you imagine that they think we spent the weekend in New York in separate hotel rooms?" His thumb was playing with her nipple, which was growing very hard, and a tight feeling ran through it and down between her legs, which were clasped around him, around his waist, around the very essence of him.

"Separate hotel rooms?" she repeated innocently. "You forget I'm from Boston. I told them we were in separate *hotels!*"

CHAPTER EIGHT

Iris

1967 — New York City

Harry Stoner had a wife. "I never touch her. Haven't for years. She doesn't like it." Harry had children. "I wish we were closer. Both girls are married, and they call at Christmas." He sighed with the appearance of genuine sorrow. "I feel alone so much of the time," he concluded one evening. He seemed to be a melancholy patriarch in a family of women who ignored him. Ilsa turned to him in the taxi and looked at his face with affection in the flickering lights of the oncoming traffic. He has quite a lot of face, she thought, what with losing his hair, his face went on forever. But it was a nice face, and Harry was a nice man.

She liked the apartment he had found her on Eightieth Street and Third Avenue, and she liked Harry. He paid all the rent for the spacious one-bedroom, and she worked three days a week at the corner drugstore for "walking-around money." My New York career is going backwards, she laughed to herself.

But the truth of the matter was quite different. Harry had the idea that Ilsa could be an actress. "You have presence, baby," he crooned. He couldn't break himself of the habit of calling her "baby," and at last she stopped letting it bother her. When he'd first asked if she could act, she had giggled, but the idea was very seductive to the Ilsa who loved looking at her face in the mirror, to the Ilsa who had adored taking off her clothes for Robert in Chicago, and for the Ilsa who feigned ecstasy when Harry mounted her.

She stood on the sidewalk under the awning as the doorman waited at the curb to close the door behind Harry. Harry struggled with the thick wad of bills he carried, counting and recounting and at last thrusting several singles into the cabbie's outstretched hand. Too much, thought Ilsa. But wasn't it better than being with someone stingy, someone like Dennis? Oh, anything, anyone was better than that. She'd eaten enough pizza with Dennis to turn into an Italian. And Harry only takes me to the best places. She smiled up at him as the elevator rose. He bent down and kissed her wide, pale forehead.

"Baby, what's on your mind?"

"What I'm going to do to you in five minutes."

"Five minutes!" he boomed, putting his hand under her coat and placing it firmly on her tight little bottom. "I have to wait five minutes?"

The doors whooshed open on the tenth floor and she squealed and ran down the hall crookedly on the new silver spike heels, as he pretended to chase her. Panting, they leaned against the big black door labeled 10J in brass letters. "Whew," Harry gasped. "I can think of nicer ways to have a heart attack."

"Oh, Harry, don't talk like that," she admonished him. "Not until—" He bent down and kissed her as the keys jingled in his hand.

"You little minx," he breathed, pulling away from the kiss. "You don't want me to die until I put you in one of my plays!"

"That's awful!" she shrieked. "You're just awful to me!" But, unbidden, the thought flashed through her mind like a bolt of lightning. Either a play or his will.

·   ·   ·

If there was a turning point in Ilsa Keller's ideas of what she wanted, what she feared, it might have come at that moment with Harry, as they caught their breath outside the apartment that wasn't in her name. They made love as they usually did, with Ilsa wishing he would lose about six pounds, all of it from his stomach. He held her in his arms afterwards, kissing her tenderly on each closed eye, whispering, "I love you, doll baby. Love you to pieces."

"I love you too," she whispered back, and often she thought she did. His arms felt so good around her, and he was warm. It was like snuggling up to a cuddly panda bear.

Harry snored. His wife hated it, Ilsa didn't even mind it. But tonight she curled around his wide back and pressed her face against his blue pajama top and wondered what would happen if he suddenly stopped snoring, then stopped breathing and never woke up. She turned on her back and, in the darkness, picked out the matching bedroom suite: the chest of drawers, the pair of bedside tables, the dressing table and the vanity and the little stool. All were in off-white with delicate silver antique-looking drawer pulls. The pale blue velvet Queen Anne chair sat solidly by the windows curtained in blue and white gingham. Both windows were closed behind the shiny blue shades, shutting out even the possibility of a pinprick of light, because they both preferred to sleep in a very dark room. Her eyes flickered toward the far wall, with its built-in television behind the sliding wooden panel and its little bar stocked with bottles and bottles of her favorite drink, Baby Cham. It was more luxury than Ilsa Keller had ever dreamed existed. Outside of a movie.

But what if he did die? she asked herself as she pulled the blue quilt up under her chin. Like Papa. Like Cutter. A sharp stinging sensation began in her nose, and Ilsa blinked rapidly in the darkness. Think, she told herself. The apartment has Harry's name on the lease and he pays the check every month and I couldn't even pay one month's rent anyway. My clothes are mine, and I could probably get away with taking the TV. But nothing else, she frowned. The rest would go to Harry's wife.

She made a face of disgust. Fifty pounds overweight, he said. She was pretty when I married her, he said. She used to be all right in bed, never wonderful, he said. Now she wore housedresses and red corduroy slippers all the time. Ilsa bet they went slap, slap, slap against her heels as she clumped around their apartment in Queens. And Mrs. Stoner would get all this! Ilsa suddenly felt it was wrong. When I make him laugh at dinner, when I do that thing with my mouth that he likes more than anything . . . Mrs. Stoner gets *my* dressing table! That Harry bought for *me* because I make him feel good!

Ilsa was too angry at the potential injustice to sleep. It was three-thirty when she tiptoed out of the bedroom and, wrapped in Harry's cashmere overcoat, watched *Some Like It Hot* on the television in the living room, which was even bigger than the bedroom one. At ten past seven, Harry found her asleep like a child in front of the morning news, and gently picked her up and carried her back to bed.

· · ·

When she woke at ten, she saw that he was gone. The coffee was cold and there were crumbs from the raisin bread all around the toaster. Ilsa carefully wiped the kitchen counter and rinsed the mug that was imprinted with the words, "It was good if the earth moved, fireworks exploded, cymbals crashed, and thunder cracked against the sky." Some actress had given it to Harry at a cast party. Ilsa opened the refrigerator, took out the Philadelphia cream cheese, an ice-cold can of root beer, and the strawberry jam. She stood on the kitchen stool to reach the Ritz crackers, then jumped to the linoleum floor barefooted, her coral chiffon nightgown billowing out like the most delicate of parachutes. Methodically, as she did every morning, she moved everything onto a tray and carried it to the living-room table in front of the television set. Settling back into the black leather cushions, she stared as though hypnotized as a man from Cincinnati won a pool table, a barbecue pit, and a golf cart with four-wheel drive. The cheering, screaming audience urged him to even greater heights of victory as he grinned and laughed and threw back his head in paroxysms of joy.

Ilsa snapped open the root beer and held the can to her lips. She loved the first burn of the day as it poured down her throat. She belched as loudly as she could and grinned, thinking of what Cutter would say, then began to spread the crackers with the jam and the cream cheese. Cutter. Papa. Harry. Suddenly she remembered being awake half the night with worry. Putting down the knife, she reached for the telephone, which sat on a pile of old *Glamour* magazines.

"Harry Stoner, please." She waited as the secretary put her through. "Mr. Stoner's office," came the second crisp voice. "Who's calling, please?"

"Ilsa Keller. Miss Keller."

"Oh! Right away, Miss Keller."

Ilsa licked jam off her thumb.

"Baby! Are you all right?"

"Of course I'm all right. Are *you* all right?" She crossed her bare legs and the coral chiffon fell in a cascade to the floor, exposing her white thighs.

"Well, you never call me here. I'm happy that you—"

"Harry, I want to tell you I've changed my mind about something. I've decided something."

His voice sank. He sounded weary, beaten, pessimistic. It was over. She was too good to last forever. "What? What is it? Tell me." And get it over with quickly. Like stabbing me with an ice pick. Or cutting off my favorite part. Harry bit his lip and stopped breathing.

"I want to take acting lessons. I want to do whatever you want me to do. What was it? Voice? Dancing? Dictation? All of that stuff. Whatever you think would be good."

Harry was amazed. With a grin on his face, he leaned back in the leather swivel chair. He'd talked his head off for weeks and gotten nowhere. "Baby, that's terrific!"

"And I want to start today."

He sat forward and reached for the bright green cylinder of lime Life Savers. Fumbling with the top one, he managed to persuade her that tomorrow would be soon enough; then he buzzed his secretary so that Ilsa could hear. "Pam, get Allie on the line and see if she can take a student tomorrow. A special student!" he added excitedly.

"But, Harry, you know I'll have to quit my job . . ." came the quiet voice, the wheedling little-girl voice he knew so well. That voice he loved so much. Harry liked to give her things, to protect her from what she didn't like, whether it was from overcooked steak or cheap underwear. Ilsa needed—deserved— his protection.

"Doesn't matter. You have a lot to do. These classes take time and energy. Don't worry about the—" He started to say "money," and realized Pam was standing in the doorway. "About a thing."

Ilsa was smiling, and Harry could feel the warmth of it over the line. "Harry, I love you."

He fairly purred. "Yeah, baby. I know. I'll, uh . . ." He hesitated when he realized Pam was still there. "I'll see you soon. Early."

Ilsa gave her throaty giggle and said, "I know what you mean. I know you're not alone. And I know exactly what you mean."

Harry felt his face go pink. She always knew when he was thinking about It. About them together. He hung up the phone and wiped his face with his handkerchief. Clearing his throat, he attempted to sound dignified. "Could you get that voice teacher on the phone for me? What's the name of the one that just took over for Hendrick? Marsha Allen! Yes, that's the one. And what about trying to set up beginner classes at the Olympia? You know. Start with ballet, probably."

Pam nodded. "I'll do it right away." She walked down the hall with a smile on her face. Right away. Because Harry Stoner had to get home to Miss Keller. Early.

. . .

And so it began. Ilsa went around to Hart's Pharmacy and told her boss she had to leave tomorrow to go to Europe with her uncle. It was actually easier to lie than to tell the truth. She did it without thinking. It was like talking about the weather.

Harry arrived at the apartment at five o'clock with an armload of white roses. One of the doormen was behind him, carrying another three dozen. The two men swept into the living room on a wave of the sweet scent as Ilsa squealed with delight. She threw her arms around Harry and he lifted her into the air with a grunt of effort. The green tissue paper was pulled aside as Ilsa gushed over how many there were.

"Oh, Harry," she said as they sat next to each other on the big black leather sofa. "This is going to be so much fun. Being an actress, I mean."

"You've got it, baby. What it takes. That sparkle. That presence." The bottle of Baby Cham just wasn't cooperating, and Harry fumbled with the cork. Ilsa held her stemmed glass out eagerly and waited. "But it's going to take work, you know." Harry nearly had it.

"Boom!" Ilsa giggled as the white bubbles frothed over the bottle neck and onto the coffee table and at last into their glasses. Harry hated Baby Cham, but to drink it with Ilsa was a small sacrifice.

"You're a great little girl," he grinned as he sipped at the overflow. Ilsa shook her white-blond hair out of her face and rolled her eyes. She dipped a finger into the pool of liquid on the glass table and licked it. Then she put her finger out for Harry to lick. He marveled at how adorable she was. Frieda would have rushed to the kitchen and run cold water over dishcloths, tut-tutting the "mess." When Harry took her whole delicate finger into his mouth, Ilsa stared at him intently, watching. Finally she drew it out slowly and outlined his lips with the damp pink fingertip.

Without a word they put down the glasses and walked into the bedroom. Silently they undressed, tossing everything onto the blue chair. Suddenly Ilsa giggled and, leaping naked onto the big double bed, asked, "Can this be the casting couch?"

Harry boomed with laughter as he held out his arms to her, watching her stand up and walk to the edge of the mattress, as pale as alabaster, with her champagne-colored hair wild around her face. He held her against him at face level, and then stepped away to stare at her. "I shouldn't have brought you white roses," Harry said solemnly. "You're not . . . not quite . . ." He was looking into Ilsa's wide-set green eyes, clear as a crystal lake, and glorying in the whiteness of her. "You know, you're more like . . . oh, I can't think of the flower." He stopped and hung his head while he thought. "You're like a white iris."

. . .

And so she became Iris Keller. The old name fell away from her like torn stockings, with that much ease, with just as little regret. She lay in bed that night listening to Harry snore, and thought of all the people who had called her Ilsa and realized, They're gone and I'm here. Gone. Beyond the New York skyline might as well have been beyond the curve of the earth. No one within walking distance, no one from her old life, or lives, for she began a new life with every man. No one to call her, no familiar voice on the other end of the wire to astonish or surprise her, for her name was not in the phone book. There was no way that anyone could even see her name in the lobby, since the directory said "H. Stoner, 10J." And now Ilsa had disappeared entirely.

She closed her eyes in the dark, and could hear her mother's voice calling her in for supper so long ago. She remembered her red coat with the wooden toggles and the deep pockets she stuffed with the rubber bands she found in front of the newsstand. She remembered her father's voice. Little Ilsa, he'd called her so often. And "princess." He'd called her his princess so many times as she sat curled on his lap. And "kitten." Papa had called her his little kitten. She turned and pressed herself closer to the warmth of Harry.

Without wanting to, she remembered the last man she'd been close to. The New York Hilton. Oh, I probably shouldn't have done it, she thought. But who's ever going to know? Harry hasn't caught me yet. And it keeps me with him, really. If I didn't have someone else once in a while, I might get snappy. Yesterday had been . . . well, she excused herself, he had been so sexy and they'd all had so much to drink. She'd been on the West Side yesterday, looking at shoes, just wandering, really, in and out of stores. Sometimes the Upper East Side was too orderly for Ilsa. The sky had started to spit rain just as she was crossing the street in front of the Hilton. Cars were driving up and driving away and the revolving doors were revolving and Ilsa thought, Shelter, and I'll buy myself a candy bar at the newsstand. As she crossed the lobby, a young man fell into step with her and asked her to a party. "Come on up to our suite and have a drink!" he urged with a friendly grin. He was wearing a pinstriped gray suit and had a nice haircut and an open sort of Midwestern way about him. Ilsa went with him to the seventeenth floor and entered a room full of men, all drinking, all loud. She was greeted by cheers as she stood in the doorway. Someone poured her a Scotch in a paper cup and she sat down on the bed to drink it. Everyone wanted to know her name and would she marry them. Ilsa remembered laughing and flirting; she also remembered thinking how young and cute most of the men were. A couple of women with beehive hairdos came in, and Ilsa wondered if they were secretaries. They were very relaxed about all the attention, and soon both women disappeared into the second bedroom. One man kept staring at Ilsa, and when she noticed him she stared back. He was by himself, standing by the window, holding a real glass, not a paper cup. He had black hair, black eyes, and very white teeth and looked more serious than anyone else. Ilsa thought he had to be Greek or Italian. As people began to leave for dinner, there was a place beside Ilsa on the bed. He walked over and sat down.

They didn't talk much. He stumbled over his name, changing "Marco" to "Mark," which made her laugh and tease, "Tell me when you've made up your mind." An arm reached between them every ten minutes to replenish the Scotch they were drinking. It seemed a natural progression for him to put his hand on her thigh. She was a little drunk and very turned on, so it wasn't difficult to let the dark-haired stranger take her by the hand and lead her down the hall to his room, to his bed. They licked and stroked and touched for what seemed like a long time. He was young and muscular and hard, and she gloried in his body; Ilsa could hear his heart beating, could feel the pulse of him under her experienced tongue. After he cried out, and at last pulled her by her hair away from him, he held her down, hands over her head, and concentrated on her lush, pouty pink lips, tasting himself as she tasted herself. Feeling as free as little forest animals, they played. It was past nine o'clock when wordlessly they began to dress, separating his socks from her stockings, her brassiere from his underwear. She pulled the brush through her tangled curls and only then thought of Harry. The movies. A perfect alibi every time.

Now she lay beside Harry and thought again, No. No one will ever know. I was Ilsa for the last time in bed with someone. The last time anyone said "Ilsa" with yearning.

"Iris," she whispered. Iris the actress. Yes, I'll do it, she thought. I'll even give up watching soap operas in the afternoon if they conflict with my classes, I'll take tap dancing until my legs fall off, and I'll get Harry to put me in the chorus of something. Won't matter if I'm in the last row, practically backstage. At first it won't matter. Iris tightened her lips. But later . . . later there'll be photographs of me, big ones, life-size. And IRIS written in capital letters. Pushing a strand of hair from her face, she touched her skin, imagining everyone knowing who she was, thinking she was beautiful. Everyone. All of New York at least. Yes. She pulled up the strap of the black nightgown. Capital letters. In red.

· · ·

As usual, Harry awoke before her. Yawning widely and silently, he rolled over to stare at her closed eyes, her faintly parted lips. After a moment he timidly touched the flushed cheek. He always gave a little prayer of thanks for her in the morning; he never ceased being amazed at her beauty. She was like a perfect peach. No, she was an iris. Iris.

She was his adored girl-woman, the baby girl who could reach orgasm, the lovely child who could make him scream with passion. Iris was also the sum of all her flaws. Harry let her be. She was spoiled and could be willful and bad-tempered. She had atrocious eating habits and was careless with money, spending it as if it were seashells and she needed only to take a walk on the beach later in the day to gather new coins of the realm.

But for all that, he was thrilled to follow her swaying little figure toward his table at Sardi's. He felt like Prince Philip, walking two paces behind his queen. His five-foot-tall queen with her high, round bottom atop slim, perfect legs, who would turn to him, invariably, with a smile as bright as the sun as she slid into the booth before him. The toughness of her, the fake worldly cynicism that he had found so ridiculous a façade, had evaporated the first evening with the arrival of the lobster. It was as if, by squealing in genuine horror, she had decided she could be vulnerable, she could stop the pretending. Why, even the way she held a cigarette was practiced.

Harry tried to be realistic about Ilsa. He thought she loved him, but would she love him if he didn't pay the rent for the apartment? Would she love him if he took her to McDonald's? Of course not. And Harry, with his expensive suits and his love of steaks and expensive wines, wouldn't expect her to. He touched a strand of the golden hair. Ilsa was wonderful to hold at night. He loved the silkiness of her breasts against him, the sweetness of her breath in his face as she squirmed against him for a good-night kiss. Her scent, her skin, made him hungry. He didn't think he could ever have enough of her, get close enough to her to want to move away. She wasn't like that about him, and he knew it. He dreaded the thought of her ever leaving him; it caused a pain in his stomach that was a mixture of fear and wanting and something akin to homesickness.

The possibility loomed all the time, since he couldn't marry her, and didn't every woman want marriage sooner or later? He couldn't divorce his wife. Frieda would take everything. And everything he had with Ilsa would go with her. Divorce reduces one's standard of living. Drastically.

For the last year his wife thought he had an office in Chicago. Well, he did and he didn't. He'd simply paid a friend's secretary an extra fifty dollars a month to say, if there ever was a telephone call for Harry, that she would ask Mr. Stoner to return the call. Meetings. By the dozen. And he always stayed with Bobby Katlin, who had an answering machine turned on twenty-four hours a day. Day and night. So no one in the household was ever awakened. It was so easy to be in Chicago, Harry thought as he put his arm over the curve of Ilsa's hip under the quilt. And so easy to be in this bed with this fair-haired satin doll.

She was young enough to be his daughter, but she was nothing like Liela or Myra. His own daughters had surprised him at puberty by becoming chubby, hairy strangers. They developed a shrillness, and they wanted the things their mother wanted: Princess phones in their own names; Ford Mustangs; short little mink jackets with big price tags.

A shame they weren't pretty. No one, except perhaps their mother, would call them that. But she would move heaven and earth to help them become less *un*pretty. He knew that the appointments Myra had had every Saturday afternoon were with a similarly hairy woman wielding a needle plugged into an electric socket. Harry had thought she should have tennis lessons, but Frieda had insisted on electrolysis, saying that Myra really shouldn't show herself in shorts until "the problem" was "taken care of." Liela had begun the appointments at age fourteen. Just one little patch at a time. Harry shuddered, imagining a furry daughter lying on a table under bright lights in the back room of the salon, until this shoulder and then that one were at least passable in a bare dress. He was freshly amazed whenever he considered it, for he himself was not overly hairy, and Frieda was not noticeably so. But they had bred gorillas.

Harry saw Ilsa, however, as a perfect doll, and now that he was to launch her, he saw himself as Professor Higgins with his very own Eliza Doolittle. The excitement filled him as Ilsa turned in her sleep. Feeling a different kind of excitement when her warm breast pressed against his arm, he gently pulled up her nightgown. He smiled as he saw her face soften, and knew she was only pretending not to be awake. With eyes still closed, she put her face against his shoulder and sighed. Frieda would never have put up with it. Never. She would have equated it with rape. Harry was kissing Ilsa's neck when he realized she was whispering something.

"Baby, what is it?"

"Don't forget, Harry. From now on. All the time. Don't forget to call me Iris."

CHAPTER NINE

Cynthia

January 1968 — Les Chênes, The Loire Valley

"So, you are Cynthia." The woman smiled behind large sunglasses. She extended a cool hand as Cynthia swung her shoulder-strap bag over one shoulder and smiled back. They shook hands lightly, and the young woman surveyed the tall, slim figure in black.

"How do you do, Madame Fortier?"

"I am delighted to meet you. Welcome to France, or"—she laughed—"to the suburbs."

"*Maman!*" Jean-François chided. "Behave yourself! I want Cynthia to like you."

Madame Fortier smiled warmly at her son, then turned to direct the chauffeur toward the pile of luggage sitting in the driveway. "Please, Paul, take it all into the front hall and let Dominique worry about it."

"Miss me?" Jean-François asked.

His mother laughed, with an easy, unselfconscious show of good nature. Looping her arm through her son's, she made a face. "Cried into my pillow every night, my dear."

Cynthia walked on the other side of him, feeling unsure of herself, her high heels sinking in the gravel. She was tired, and her skin felt dry and tight after the long flight; she wanted nothing more than a hot bath and a nap. But it was lunchtime and she was in front of an enormous chateau in yesterday's clothes, greatly desiring to make a good impression on the only member of Jean-François's family. More than I want the bath? she wondered as she followed the mother and son up the wide white marble steps. Twin fountains gurgled twenty meters away, surrounded by geometrically perfect flower beds and hedges. Though it was January, the grass was green.

The hallway could have been the reception area for a hotel. The rust and blue Persian rug seemed the size of a small lake, and yet only covered a portion of the shining marble floors. A chandelier twinkled above them, its thousands of prisms catching the winter sunlight.

"Now, Cynthia, let me show you to your room. I'm sure you'll want a bath and to change clothes." Cynthia nodded gratefully as Madame Fortier explained that lunch was not for another hour. "If you'd rather sleep, then please do. I'll have someone leave sandwiches outside your door, and we'll see you at six for drinks before dinner."

"I'd love to sleep! I think it's about six in the morning for me, and I'm beginning to fade."

Jean-François kissed her on the forehead. "Then let Maman take you upstairs. I'll see you in a few hours."

Cynthia followed the slim legs in sheer black stockings and expensive black suede pumps as they climbed the staircase. The hand on the balustrade was ringed with a single large, square diamond and a platinum wedding ring. It's as if she were still in mourning, Cynthia thought as she watched the figure in black open the door at the end of the hall. The room was large, papered in white and lavender flowered wallpaper, with a four-poster bed in the center. It was canopied in the same pattern as the wallpaper, with bouquets of violets and lavender ribbons on a white ground.

"Oh, it's lovely!" Cynthia sighed as she put her purse on an ornately carved satinwood bureau. The room was furnished in Louis the something, thought Cynthia. I'll have to ask Jean-François, just so I can tell Mother.

"It's my favorite guest room," said Madame Fortier. "I've been working for years on this part of the house. Sorting out the things that were put in storage when Jean-François's uncle died. Some of it is junk, some of it almost priceless, and a lot of it I simply shipped off to Paris to go on the auction block. Or to London. They fetched better prices in London." She shrugged. "I think I've spent years of my life talking to restorers."

"Well, it was worth it," Cynthia assented as she walked to the windows, which were closed against the cold. The tiny-paned windows stretched from waist level nearly up to the sixteen-foot ceiling. They looked out over the back gardens sculptured in green hedges; a fish pond covered with water lilies could be seen just past the cypresses.

"I'm English, and this garden is a mixture of French formality and the English confusion I so adore." Madame Fortier stood beside her, looking out.

"Look over there." She gestured towards a plot of wildflowers that grew in profusion around a marble statue of Pan.

Cynthia smiled. "I like the contrast. And I'm glad you're English. I've been practicing my French all the way across the Atlantic. A little nervously."

Madame Fortier looked pleased. She had removed the sunglasses, and her large, dark eyes were bright, rimmed with what appeared to be kohl. Her hair was twisted back and up off her long neck; the effect was dramatic. A pair of silver combs glinted in the black waves. Cynthia was reminded of Maria Callas.

Following a tap on the open door, a man with white hair and wearing a dark blue cotton jacket entered with Cynthia's luggage. "*Merci*, Dominique." He put the two suitcases down beside the wardrobe and left the room silently. "Is that all the luggage there is?" the older woman asked. "I was hoping I could keep you and Jean-François here for at least two weeks!"

Cynthia laughed. How relieved she was that she actually liked this woman. "Be careful! You don't know me yet, and two days might be enough!"

"I don't think so." Madame Fortier strode to the door and turned. "The bathroom is off to your left, and I think you'll find all you need. If you don't, just pull the bell cord by the bed. Someone will come." She stared at the tall figure with the flowing blond hair outlined in light from the window. A fairy-tale princess with green eyes. Jean-François was right. A maid came into the room, bearing a silver tray with sandwiches and a small teapot.

"Right over there, *s'il vous plaît*," Madame Fortier directed. When the maid had left, she cast another long look at Cynthia Lake Kendall from Beacon Hill. "Now sleep," she said. "And I'll send someone to knock on your door at five."

"Thank you."

Elizabeth Westerfield Colbert Fortier smiled again and said, "I think we're going to get along." Then she was gone.

· · ·

The moment Cynthia entered the *fumoir*, she felt something was wrong. The room was a small drawing room—more intimate, Madame Fortier had explained. It was dizzyingly crowded with antiques and paintings, but warm and softly lit. Cynthia sat on the edge of a small pink armchair and wondered why she felt ill at ease.

"Sherry? Champagne?" Jean-François offered. He knew the answer.

"Champagne, please."

"Always," said Madame Fortier as the same maid of the sandwiches put down a tray of three flutes. The maître d'hotel in a frock coat walked in behind her and began to twist the champagne cork.

"With the softest of sighs, not a 'pop,' " instructed Jean-François.

"Oh, darling! Leave Jules alone! I don't care if it makes enough noise to shatter all the mirrors in France, as long as we get to drink it afterwards!" put in his mother.

The maître d'hotel was expressionless as he turned the cork slowly in a white-gloved hand.

Cynthia glanced nervously at the tiny black hands of the delicate Sevres clock on the bureau behind Jean-François's shoulder and wondered if time had stopped. What if, owing to some planetary disturbance, the earth had simply stopped spinning, the universe had frozen in space? What if I will be trapped here forever in this uncomfortable chair between two people who seem only to notice each other? She told herself not to drink too quickly, to sit up straight, to look pleasant. How could she feel so foreign, such a misfit, here and now at six o'clock, when upstairs at noon she had felt so relaxed with this woman?

"Now, Maman! You know I have to go to Genève tomorrow, and I want Cynthia to come with me. Stop making all these plans as if we were planning to move in with you—"

"Darling! I only thought that it would be nice if you spent a bit of time here. After all, when else will I have the chance—"

"You'll have all the chances you want in Genève! Just come there and we can—"

"Oh! Must I?" she feigned horror. "Genève! Have you told Cyn—"

Neither ever finished a sentence, each so anxious to disagree with or dispute the other that they simply couldn't wait to leap in with their own ideas. It was an amazing sort of spoken shorthand, as if they were actors barking lines in a play. Cynthia used the time to study them. Jean-François was in profile, intense, dark, feigning irritation. His mother, with her black silk dress and lacy black stockings, was like a beautiful widowed queen, pearl earrings at her ears, several ropes of pearls around her neck. For all her words, she was not insistent upon getting her way, and Cynthia had the strange feeling that Jean-François was hoping he would have to give in to her. He seemed to want her to want him to stay. To insist. With more vehemence. And when at last she said, with a dismissive gesture of her left hand and a twinkle of the big, square-cut diamond, "Oh, do whatever you want," he seemed . . . what? Almost disappointed?

· · · ·

Dinner was better. There was conversation about Boston, about the deb parties, about how they'd met.

"So you danced her off her feet?"

"No. That wasn't the way it was. Cynthia kept following me around until it became embarrassing. Everyone was talk—"

"Jean-François! Stop it! She'll believe you! Everyone thinks American women are hopelessly aggressive," put in a horrified Cynthia.

"Well, they're right," he said as he reached for his wineglass. Immediately the maître d'hotel was beside him, filling it once more. "Absolutely correct."

"I think it's refreshing," his mother observed. "Women who know what they want. Women who have decided they want something all their own. Women who want to be something other than a keeper of the flame—"

"What are you trying to do? Ruin my chances with this angel from Beacon Hill? Sabotage all my dreams?" Jean-François seemed to be only half-joking.

Cynthia was silent. What *are* his dreams? she wondered. Does Madame Fortier accept my presence here as a *fait accompli*, the way my mother does? Why do I feel everyone else knows what's going on and I'm in the dark about it?

"I think I know your dreams," Madame Fortier said cryptically as she placed her knife and fork together at six o'clock on the plate.

Jean-François glanced at her with dark eyes bright with anger. "And you don't approve? Is that it, Maman?"

Cynthia put her napkin on the table and stood up. "Excuse me," she said, and walked, as quickly as she could without running, out of the dining room to the hallway and, with one confused turn of her head, took the stairs two at a time. In two minutes she was safe behind the heavy, ten-foot-tall door, in the room of floating violet bouquets. Safe? she wondered. Safe from what? From Jean-François, the man I'm supposed to be in love with? Safe from his mother, who seemed so normal this afternoon? Safe from this talk of marriage and dreams that I don't understand? Aren't I supposed to be downstairs, smiling at my fiancé-to-be and asking teasingly to be told of his dreams? Aren't his dreams supposed to be mine?

The green silk dress, the one Jean-François liked so much, felt uncomfortable. She longed for jeans, for a sweatshirt. She longed to go back to bed. It's not having any sleep, she decided in confusion. I'll apologize for leaving the table so suddenly. Cynthia stared out at the dark garden. Tiny chips of stars hung like diamonds over the faraway pear orchard.

There was a faint knock at the door, and she watched it open. Jean-François came in, closing it behind him. He held out his hands to her. "What happened to you? Are you not feeling well?" His voice was so full of concern, he had such a tender look in his eyes, that Cynthia found him irresistible. She was drawn to him, to his warmth, to his sureness. Nestled in his arms with her face against his cashmere jacket she felt everything was all right again. "Don't worry about Maman," he was saying. "We're always at each other. We're always . . . we've always been this way." He stared past Cynthia's blond hair as he stroked it, past the bed and out the window to the darkness of the garden. "Always," he repeated carefully. Then he amended it. "For almost as long as I can remember."

· · ·

They didn't go to Geneva after all, but stayed in the big house with Jean-François's mother. Day after day, Geneva was postponed. Cynthia could not decide who had got his way in the decision. Madame Fortier was very friendly to her, and the invitation "Please call me Elizabeth, dear," was soon forthcoming. They took walks in the garden together nearly every morning after breakfast, discussing what should be done before the warm weather. Cynthia helped unpack the new bulbs for spring, wearing borrowed garden gloves, a pair of old trousers nearly white from repeated washings, and some oxfords that Madame Fortier lent her.

Evidently the garden had been neglected for a long time. "Jean-François's Uncle Pierre, my first husband's brother, was quite elderly and lived here with a series of nurses 'round the clock for many years. He was nearly ninety when he died five years ago." She saw Cynthia's face and smiled. "I know you must be doing your arithmetic and feeling very confused. Let me say that he was about fifteen years older than my husband, and that my husband was twenty-four years older than I. I married Maurice Colbert when I was nineteen."

Madame Fortier paused, and Cynthia wondered if she would remark on the difference in her son's age and Cynthia's, but she didn't. How unlike my mother, flashed through her mind. Cynthia felt that her mother only saw life as it related to her daughter or to herself. No one else really existed. Everything was compared to herself and Cynthia. There were no other yardsticks, no other analogies. We do it this way and they do it that way, was the way her mind worked. Never, They do it that way because they think it's better. Margaret Kendall seemed incapable of even the faintest curiosity about why other people did things in whatever manner. "People like us" thought, did, wanted, even ate, in a "people like us" fashion.

She pulled herself back to the conversation. "Then this chateau has been in the family for a long time? I mean before your husband's generation?"

"Oh, yes. For several hundred years. You'll have to ask Jean-François for the details. The Colberts were Protestant at the time of the Reformation and most of them left France in the fifteen hundreds. Geneva had become a Protestant city and they were welcome there. There was no Switzerland at the time. No confederation."

She handed Cynthia gardening clippers. Cynthia began to trim the dead stalks of a palm in a big bucket. The greenhouse was crowded with trees waiting to be planted. "Don't make the same mistake I did and talk about Switzerland, about the Colbert family coming to Switzerland. They came to Geneva, and my, are they proud of it." She blew a strand of dark hair out of her eyes and then bent over a box of pine seedlings, checking the roots under the burlap-wrapped mounds of earth. "So they came to Geneva and settled and became private bankers. Jean-François carries on the tradition. But they are more Genevois than Swiss. Oh, don't ever forget that!"

Cynthia smiled. It was nice to be pulled into the older woman's confidence that way—as if the Englishwoman were taking her aside and saying, Watch out for the club.

"This chateau belonged to the Colbert branch who stayed in France, who stayed Catholic. Even though there was the fifteen-year age difference between my husband, Maurice, and Pierre, they were close. And I liked Pierre. So after my husband died of a heart attack, I continued to come to visit his brother from Paris. Just for dinner sometimes, driving back the next day. Rarely for an entire weekend." She nodded toward the row of palms for Cynthia to continue. "They'll go down at the edge of the driveway just when you make the turn. I think they should grow here. Should be warm enough. They have palm trees in Switzerland." She sighed as she pulled at the fronds of the smallest one. "Anyway, Pierre and I got along, and I guess I never realized how much he looked forward to my visits, or how much he liked me . . ." Her voice was a little sad. "So, when he died, he left me all this property." She threw up gloved hands in surprise. "I could hardly believe it. I thought it was a mistake!"

"So five years ago you moved here from Paris—" began Cynthia, thinking how sad it was that Madame Fortier had been widowed twice.

"Oh, no! I started renovating this place about five years ago. But I couldn't live here right away. It was impossibly gloomy and had gone to seed." She looked down at the dirty gardening gloves and the seed packet she held and laughed. "Pardon the pun."

"I think you've done an enormous amount in five years. I would have guessed those rooms had been that way for decades. There is that feel to them. The furniture belongs, the chandeliers are just right."

Elizabeth stood with hands on her hips and smiled slowly. "Thank you. Well said. That's just the way I wanted it to look."

"Now I'm mixed up. Do you ever live in Paris? Jean-François told me that—"

"I go there at least once a month for a few days. I have kept the apartment. You'll see it. Heavens! You two should go and stay there for the weekend. It's on the Ile Saint-Louis and it's a tiny pied-à-terre, but perfect for me or for a couple. Get him to take you this weekend!"

"He seems so happy here. I'll wait for him to suggest it."

Elizabeth didn't answer, but instead bent over a box of seed packets and quickly began to toss them into piles. It's true, thought Cynthia. Jean-François seems light and free here, even though he says banking makes him irritable and worried and he is involved with it all morning and then again late in the afternoon, when it's nine o'clock in the morning in New York and the Stock Exchange opens. Cynthia loved seeing him every day, every meal; she adored having him slip into bed beside her at night. His eyes were always bright, his face almost always smiling as if he knew a delightful secret. Cynthia realized she was in love with him. There was no doubt in her mind. New York had been a fling. Pushed into a fling by one's own mother! The invitation to Geneva had been a dare. She had also been very curious about this man who had paid so much attention to her, evening after evening in Boston. This foreigner. How did he live? What did he do? And most of all, how did he really feel about her? So the trip was also an exploratory junket. In Cynthia's mind the visit had begun with the question, "What do I have to lose and/or what would I be doing instead?" Now she was in love with Jean-François.

The difference in their ages attracted her. She liked the idea of Jean-François taking care of her. And because they were in a country other than her own, she felt still younger when some custom was explained. Thank God I took all those years of French, she said to herself a dozen times a day. But even understanding French, there was so much to absorb. She noticed the way Elizabeth held her fork in her left hand during the meal, with the tines pointed downward. Everything was stabbed, nothing was shoveled. And the knife nearly never left the right hand, and was used not just for cutting but as a guide. The second evening, at dinner, she wondered how on earth anyone half-sane could eat ice cream with a fork, but they had. At the top of each plate, both a spoon and a fork, facing different directions, were placed just for dessert. Cynthia had found it mystifying.

But day by day she felt more at ease with all the little nuances of the household. She began speaking French to Marie, feeling free to go into the library and read magazines without asking, feeling free to ask Jules, the old maître d'hotel, how long until dinner, feeling herself relaxed and less of a guest.

Lunch was always casual, and one sunny day it was warm enough for the three of them to have sandwiches on a table in the greenhouse. Jean-François had been on the phone to Zurich all morning, and he came out in perfectly pressed cord trousers and had to sit rather gingerly on a tarpaulin while his mother and Cynthia relaxed in old clothes and baggy sweaters.

"I really love looking at all those photographs of Jean-François in the living room," Cynthia said. "He looks so different in some of them." There was silence as Elizabeth poured herself another cup of tea. Jean-François reached for a second croissant, tore it open, and put in a slice of ham. "It's as if you were two people when you were a little boy," she went on. Elizabeth didn't respond. Jean-François put down the bread and reached for his glass of white wine. "The expression around the eyes is so different, especially in the one with the pet rabbit. You look so soft, so sweet!"

"Yes, well, I am soft and sweet once a year for the camera," he put in.

Elizabeth interjected, "I'm glad you like them. I grew up in a family where you never put personal photographs in the living room, only in your bedroom or on a dressing table. It's a change for me."

"Maman's second husband wanted them out on display."

"No, that's not exactly true." Elizabeth's face was suffused with sadness, and she toyed distractedly with the pearls she always wore. They were tucked under her dress or arranged over a sweater or cotton blouse collar and occasionally mixed in with another strand. Omnipresent. Today they were on top of a dark blue sweater.

"A present from him," was the surprising remark from Jean-François. Both women turned to look at him. His tone was sullen, petulant. Jealous? wondered Cynthia.

"Yes, these pearls were given to me on my birthday the day before he died."

Cynthia said nothing. Sometimes when she was with Elizabeth she felt the gulf between them was due to the fact that she was an American and the other woman English. Jean-François's mother was friendly but aloof; openly amused at things, but closed off about personal matters. She seemed to be open-armed and yet, figuratively, she averted her face.

Elizabeth cleared her throat and reached for her teacup.

"There was one photograph taken by the fountain that I loved. The one with you in the sailor suit." Cynthia continued, thinking she'd lighten the moment. "But was it here? The railing, the iron fence . . ."

Elizabeth dropped the cup, and tea splashed over the blue and white gingham tablecloth in a spreading stain. "Maman! Let me!" Jean-François stood quickly, pulling plates and napkins away while his mother clutched at her pearls as though they were a talisman.

Marie materialized and swiftly changed one cloth for another, and in two minutes the three were seated again. The interruption had not changed the dangerous quiet that Cynthia felt as plainly as the sudden chill when the sun moved behind a bank of clouds. What did I say? What could have upset her so? No. Upset *them*. Cynthia sipped from her wineglass and wondered, What secrets do they share?

·   ·   ·

Jean-François came to her that night as usual. Cynthia always felt him more than she saw him in the blackness or heard him in the silence as he crossed the room. He was warmth and hardness and strength as he slid under the duvet to press himself against her. "You are a cat," she whispered, and in response he purred into her neck between kisses.

"Tell me—" she began.

"Anything," he sighed as his head moved down toward her breasts.

"Why—how—I mean," Cynthia squirmed, and he pushed her back. "Please tell me how I upset—"

"Wasn't you," he said quickly. He knew exactly to what she was referring. Obviously the lunch scene had been on his mind too. But his voice betrayed irritation.

"But—"

He pulled away from her and propped himself up on one elbow. She could only see the plane of his cheekbones in the dim light. "Leave it alone, Cynthia. She's so . . . Maman is sensitive about some things."

"But photographs of you?"

He shrugged. "It's the past. She loved her second husband very much."

"And you didn't?"

"Why do you say that?" His voice was calm now.

"Otherwise you might call him something other than that. Maybe his name, or maybe even 'Father.' "

"We weren't close."

"What was he like?" she asked as Jean-François put his hand under the covers again.

He sighed in annoyance. "Now? You have to know now?"

Cynthia kissed his shoulder quickly. "Well, how else am I going to find out? I can't ask in front of your mother." She hesitated. "So, what was he like?"

Again, he shrugged. "All right, I guess."

"Honestly! Can't you tell me anything more than that?" She waited. "How did he die?"

The voice was calm, detached. "He had a stroke and he never regained consciousness."

"When? Was it just recently? Your mother still wears—"

"I was fifteen."

The subject was closed. The two figures in the big four-poster were still for what seemed to Cynthia a long time. Finally she felt his hand on her breast and his lips pressed against hers. She wondered if they were there to press away any more questions. But what other questions could there be? When he moved on top of her, she stopped wondering anything at all.

· · ·

In the morning Cynthia reached out one arm, wanting Jean-François's warmth. It was not only in bed that she was drawn to him, but when he entered a room, when he left a room, that she felt overcome with the idea that she was half of something wonderful. The other part was this foreign older man with the quick, athletic walk, with the darkness of a Latin, with the smile of someone delighted to see her. She liked the way he knew about wine, the way he was so particular about how the food was prepared. It showed sophistication, she thought, and was worlds distant from Crosby Hyatt's ordering a hamburger "well done" at the Edgartown Yacht Club.

After dinner, Jean-François often put a symphony on the stereo and told her about the composer. Cynthia knew about art and a bit about furniture— a very *little* bit, admittedly. Perhaps just because her mother was so keen on the subject of antiques, she had feigned disinterest. But she knew next to nothing about classical music, and was both impressed by Jean-François's knowledge and desirous of impressing him with her quickness and her memory of certain symphonies.

Cynthia watched him and admired him and, above all else, wanted to please him. When he put his hands around her twenty-three-inch waist and praised it, she pushed away her dessert that evening with apologies. He pressed his face into her hair and told her it smelled of the sun; so she noted the name of the shampoo she'd found in her bathroom and wrote it down in her diary. If he loved food, she would be a gourmet cook. If he loved tennis, she would be the best doubles partner this side of Wimbledon. Jean-François Colbert stepped into the role of the roommate she had never had, the best friend she hadn't had for years, and the lover she had longed for since Marco. He was her everything. And she would be everything for him.

On the eighth evening at Les Chênes, Cynthia and Jean-François walked away from his mother's manicured gardens, past the English confusion of flowers around Pan, away from the fountains, and toward the pear orchard. He held her hand so tightly she could feel the seams of his gloves pressing through her thin suede ones.

It was dusk, just before time for drinks in the *fumoir* and the dinner she had come to look forward to. After dessert they always moved into the living room and sipped cognac or Poire William as they played three-handed bridge in front of the fire. Talk was light. Elizabeth joked about the two of them as a couple. The tension of the first evenings was a faraway memory; Cynthia could not remember what had made her so uncomfortable, what had driven her upstairs and away from them.

Jean-François put his arm around her shoulders, draped in the coat his mother had insisted she borrow. It was green wool with a black velvet collar, and not as heavy as the charcoal gray coat she'd left Boston in. Boston, Cynthia daydreamed as she looked up at the pink sky. Did Boston still exist?

Each evening began in a blaze of color over the hills. The orange came after the pink, then the darkness descended on the corona of the blazing sun as it slipped behind the gray-green landscape. The air was scented with pine, with a cold cleanness, as they stood on the small rise, looking toward the orchard. Jean-François pressed her closer to him, and they turned to stare back at the house. The chateau was horseshoe-shaped, with a living room in the center extending all the way from front to rear. The windows blazed with light; only the third floor was dark, for the servants were downstairs preparing for the dinner hour. To Cynthia it looked like a small palace, a twinkling jewel on a dark green velvet cloth.

"Happy?" he asked, smiling down at her upturned face.

"Very. Amazingly happy."

"Why do you say that?"

Cynthia hesitated. "Because I guess I haven't been happy in such a long time. I'd forgotten what it felt like."

"Would you be happy with me?" Jean-François asked. "I mean, *could* you be happy with me? Not necessarily here, but—"

She reached up and gently put her gloved finger to his cheek, smiled, and waited. When he didn't continue, she nodded. "I think maybe I could."

"The chateau in Geneva is as large as this, and it needs work. The family stopped being interested about a generation ago. I want it to be proud and beautiful again. I want a garden like Maman's, and fountains that work, and perfectly kept tennis courts. I want a place for you, for us, for our family."

She would always remember that he didn't ask her. He *told* her.

"I want you as my wife. I want you to come to Geneva with me to be my wife."

Jean-François was holding her left hand, pulling away the black suede gloves. She saw the diamond, as bright as the first star of evening, and felt the cold metal pressed onto her finger. Cynthia looked up at the orange sky behind his face and thought, Yes, yes, yes. Pulling her into his arms, he kissed her slowly, tenderly. Cynthia thought, This is what I've always wanted. This is what my life has led to. This is the right thing. Finally.

·   ·   ·

"Fasten your seatbelts, please," chirped the stewardess, bending over her as Cynthia groggily fumbled with the buckle. She felt as if it had been weeks since she'd stood on the lawn at Les Chênes. Elizabeth had kissed her and pressed a bottle of wine into her canvas carry-on bag. "For your parents." Then Cynthia and Jean-François had gotten into his Porsche and raced over the country roads, bypassing the French capital and reaching the Paris airport in record time. Cynthia had not slept, but daydreamed all the way across the Atlantic.

·   ·   ·

Meanwhile, in France, in the Loire Valley, mother and son were linked by nightmares. Down the corridor in his room, fifty meters from where Elizabeth slept, Jean-François fell into a deep slumber, partially induced by the cognac and the long drive back from the airport, perhaps due also to the rather heavy dinner.

He was in a garden, running beside a lake. "Come on!" he shouted at the boy behind him. They were dressed alike, in blue sailor suits, white knee socks, and white shoes. It was a day in spring, and the sky above them was a blue dome. Yellow dandelions waved in the wind. "Come on! Hurry!" Jean-François called again, but the other boy couldn't keep up. He was thinner and slower, and his asthma was bothering him.

"If you'd just run faster!" Jean-François was fed up. He always had to wait for him, always had to slow down. It was boring. They were the same age, after all. But no, Jean-Paul was not strong. He was not well. That's what his mother always said. Jean-Paul was the one his mother hovered over, the one she embraced first when they came in after playing.

"Are you cold, my darling? Do you want me to send Louise inside for your sweater? Perhaps you should rest now."

Jean-François stood behind him, watching, listening. It made him angry. Maman never talked that way to him. She always said, "Oh, Jean-François! Must you be so rough! Don't leave him like that! Slow down! Be a nice boy!"

Jean-François's mouth opened in sleep and he began to breathe quickly in shallow pants. His white silk pajamas were soaked in perspiration. The moonlight coming through the open window on his face revealed an expression of terror.

"Let's go," he commanded in the dream. "Hurry up! I'm tired of waiting. Are you coming or not?"

The face below the ladder was pale. He didn't want to go up the workman's ladder. Maman had told them to stay away. The chimney sweep would be at lunch for at least another half hour. He sat under a tree at the back of the house, in his soot-covered clothes, taking bites from an enormous brioche with ham sticking out of it.

"You sissy! You coward!" shouted Jean-François from the top rung. He had already smudged his short trousers, and there was dirt on one white sock where it folded over just below the knee. Never mind, he thought. I can brush it off. Maman won't notice if I get inside the house first. "Oh!" he sneered in irritation. "You are such a baby!"

As Jean-Paul reached for the first rung of the ladder and drew up his leg with one spotless white shoe, Jean-François awakened. He was choking with the horror of it. His face was shiny with sweat, with tears. He whimpered, gulping air and crying. As he stumbled from the bed, his foot caught in the duvet and it slid onto the floor of the darkened room. Jean-François didn't notice. He swayed almost drunkenly toward the window and pulled it open. The biting chill of the air hit him like a wave, and he let his head fall back as he gulped the coldness of the night.

Jean-François stood with his fingertips on the windowsill for nearly twenty minutes. The light of the moon shone gray and sickly on his ashen face; perspiration became clammy on his body; his teeth chattered, and the tears dried on his cheeks. At last he turned and, surveying the room as though it were unfamiliar, found his way to the bathroom, where, letting his pajamas fall to the floor, he stepped under the shower.

Down the hall, Elizabeth turned on her back in restless sleep. Her nightmare always began the same way and always came in the hour preceding dawn. She dreamed she was walking through the garden, and Pierre was calling to her from his wheelchair. "Come and look at the roses," he was saying. She strolled toward him, feeling the soft spring breeze on her face, the gravel path crunching underfoot. Elizabeth was content, even happy, as she looked up at the blue sky, saw the path with the wildflowers, the Queen Anne's lace moving slightly in the fresh morning air. She wished she could persuade Pierre to tend the gardens, to call in gardeners, to order bulbs and seedlings. But these thoughts were short-lived, for she was drawing closer to the old man in the wheelchair and to his nurse—a figure in white, bright in the sunlight, with no face. Elizabeth, too, was dressed in white. When she reached Pierre and he extended a red rose to her, she smiled and then she heard the screams . . . screams like shrieks of an animal . . . no sound a human could make . . . screams of such shrillness, such terror, such pain. Elizabeth began to run toward the sound, desperate, horrified. The blue sky above whirling like a top gone mad. A spinning gyroscope whirring above the awful screaming. The screaming had become red and black and covered her face and hands and white dress like ink, like red and black silk scarves, like something alive.

Elizabeth sat bolt-upright in bed and fumbled for the switch of the bedside lamp. As it clicked on, the room, large, dark blue, the canopy above her, the four-poster bed around her, all blinked into focus. She wiped her eyes and glimpsed the mahogany wardrobe beside the door to the adjoining bathroom. The finials atop it made her gasp. Don't think. Don't think, she told herself as she saw the carved pinecones crowned with wooden spikes. Pulling the covers away, she got out of bed and went to the window.

Nearly dawn, she thought as she closed it against the cold humid air. Always the dream comes when Jean-François and I are here alone in this house with just the servants. As if it daren't show itself when another mortal is sleeping in this wing. And now Cynthia is gone. She must be back in Boston by now, being picked up at the airport, and the ghosts return. Elizabeth thought of Jean-Paul, of his innocent young face. Putting her head down, her black hair undone, dipping loose over her shoulders, halfway down the back of the blue flannel nightgown, she let her tears fall on the windowsill.

At breakfast, Jean-François was pale and quiet. "Do you miss her?" his mother asked.

He chewed his toast, far away, lost in thought, still troubled by his nightmare, and didn't answer.

CHAPTER TEN

Iris

1968 — New York City

"Well, I don't think it's necessary, and I don't much like being told something like that!" Iris had both hands on her curvy hips, and a sulk on her face. She was a cuddly figure in pale blue. The wool slacks fit her like a second skin, and there was the wrinkle of a V in front defining her sex. Harry tried to keep his eyes trained upward, at least up at her breasts in the fluffy angora sweater. Better still to focus on the annoyance in the green eyes.

"Baby," Harry began, and the sulk became a glare. "Iris, I mean. Iris. The camera adds five or ten pounds. Always. To everybody. Whether it's Katie Hepburn or Jane Fonda. So it's better to take that into consideration now, so when you're up for something no one will have to ask you to lose weight."

She was thinking. Not answering. Staring into space. The green eyes were glassy. Then she left the living room and closed the bedroom door.

Four hours later, amid the noise of Sardi's, she instructed the waiter, "A salad with vinegar."

Harry stared at her. He'd been sure she would put the idea of a diet out of her mind. That set to her little jaw, that determined gleam in her eye. He had expected her to demand a new dance teacher. "Make my sirloin rare, with french fries on the side. Double order. The usual." He turned to Iris, expecting her to add a steak to her order. A steak wouldn't hurt her. But she was silent, looking across the room as a woman was being helped into a white fur coat.

"You know, Harry, I've decided. I'm going to do everything you tell me to do. I'm lucky to have you tell me what to do and how to do it." She continued to stare at the mink. "And someday I'll be rich enough to have a coat like that."

Harry looked at the white mink again. Ten thousand bucks it had to be, at least. He put his hand in her lap and she wriggled like a little rabbit toward him. "Il—Iris, you're a good girl."

That night she made love to him, with her little pink tongue seeking out every fold of skin that immediately ceased being a fold, and then she placed herself atop him, "Pretending you're my pony," she cooed. Harry lay back and breathed with his mouth open, in great gasps, and sometimes he turned his head back and forth on the pillow as though crazed with the sweet sensation of her, and finally, when she at last let it happen, he screamed.

The next morning she had lost two pounds according to the bathroom scale, and that afternoon, after her singing lesson, a man delivered a big box. Iris tore away all the pink tissue paper and, with little squeals of happiness, buried her face in the white mink.

·   ·   ·

"Look at her, just look at her," urged Harry.

Richard Waterman was looking, all right. She was a knockout. Her high round breasts and deceptively long legs made his blood race, but her face shone with a radiance that reminded him of a Lolita-esque angel. She was a soft, cuddly little sister to Kim Novak, she was a Marilyn Monroe with a heart-shaped face that he found heart-stopping. The crystal-clear green eyes said, *Oh, I believe in you,* one moment, and the next they appeared to dare the onlooker to take her to bed. It was spring, and she was dressed in the uniform of youth. A red dress barely grazed her at mid-thigh, a black patent leather belt emphasized the curves above and below it, and little black slingback shoes made her all of five foot three. But, more important, they drew the eye to her delicate ankles and then inevitably up the length of her silky legs. They were amazingly long for such a petite girl.

"Wow! Wow and triple wow," Richard murmured. He was the new director, and nervous. *Aurora* had been through three writers and two directors and even had a theater booked for the previews in New Haven, but still had not been completely cast. He raked one slender hand through the few threads of hair on his head and sighed. "Harry, she's terrific, but . . ." he shook his head.

"I know, I know!" Harry was nodding. "Yeah, I know what you're thinking." He fumbled for a match in his vest pocket and lit the cigar he was holding. The two men sat in auditorium chairs ten yards from the stage, which was crowded with dancers in tights and sweatshirts. A group of ponytailed girls did warm-up exercises off to the left; Iris stood alone and quite still off to the right. She simply watched all the turmoil around her. Two men with a ladder asked her to move, and she stepped backwards carefully. Not a hair out of place, not a sign of nerves.

"Okay. The age-old question. Here goes." Richard stood up and shouted for silence. Fifty-six people froze as one; the primary colors of their exercise clothes were bright against the darkness of the wings. A ladder fell with a clanging noise, and a few titters swept the group. "We're all here today to see what you can do." Richard paced back and forth in front of the first row of seats, a rolled-up script in one hand. His other hand raked the top of his nearly bald head again and again. The quiet was respectful.

"Bertrand, get the dancers first. We'll start with the opening number." A shout was heard from the stage. "Oh, that's not the one you've practiced. Okay, do the high-kick one, then. The . . ." He looked down at the pages and thumbed through them quickly. "The one called *That's My Man.*"

The stage resounded with thudding feet; even with their ballet slippers the noise was loud. The piano tinkled out the most basic notes just enough to keep them in time. Bertrand sat on the other side of Harry and scrawled in a red spiral notebook. Richard leaned over every minute or so and hissed, "Boy in turquoise. Out," or "Girl with blond braid. Out."

To Iris it seemed to go on for hours, and still she stood. She tried not to look at Harry; she didn't want him to give her a thumbs-up sign or wink at her or make any of the others realize why she was here. They'd all been through one weeding-out after another, and she had simply walked in and joined the finalists. Iris thought it really wasn't very fair, but then she thought of the penciled black comma eyebrows of awful Mrs. Gordon, of the lingerie shop, of the deaf woman and the red light above the phone in the dark hallway, of doing things to Bill when she had been so tired . . .

"Keller! Miss Keller!" someone was shouting.

"Here!" she raised her hand like a girl in school, like the Ilsa in gym class. There was laughter around her.

"Okay. Know your lines? Let's go." Richard was being purposely tough on her. She was the little mistress of Harry Stoner, and he hated the favoritism, hated being put in a position of even seeing her, let alone knowing what she did to Harry at night in bed in order to be up on that stage now. "Step forward and project. Right back to the last row." He hoped he didn't sound too helpful, but something about her was so vulnerable. God, she looked about sixteen all of a sudden.

Iris hesitated for a split second and then curtsied as she and Harry had practiced. A French maid's curtsy. Her little red dress rode up to amazing heights and then slipped into place again at mid-thigh. "Oh, thank you so much, kind sir," she said loudly.

The theater was quiet. Harry leaned forward with his forearms in the brown suit on top of the chair in front of him. Richard turned to him. "She's fine, isn't she?" urged Harry.

Richard looked at this middle-aged bear of a man. Hell, he was the producer. Let him have it. Just this one thing. He nodded and then looked up at the small blonde on stage again. "Okay, Keller. Report to wardrobe."

They celebrated that night. Iris wore her mink to "21" and ate whatever she wanted for the first time in a month. She'd lost eleven pounds and had cheekbones, and her waist was the smallest it had been since she and Gretchen used to suck in for the tape measure back in the seventh grade. "I love you, baby doll," cooed Harry.

She resisted the urge to snap at him for calling her that. "This is a start, isn't it?" she insisted. "A good start, isn't it, Harry?"

"Hell, yes!" he gushed as he reached for the red wine. "It's not quite the lead, but . . ." He shrugged, smiling. "But you're going places, baby."

Yes. Iris was going places all right. Three weeks into rehearsal she went to bed with a musclebound dancer. Just to see what it would be like.

. . .

"Oh, Hárry, it's so boring." She was feathering a wand of mascara over her lashes for the dozenth time. She loved stage makeup, loved doing it herself. Iris was perched on the little dressing-table stool, staring with concentration into the mirror surrounded by makeup lights. "Really boring." She spent hours and hours in the drafty, unheated theater waiting for her cue, waiting to say that one line. She played gin with the well-endowed dancer and they made jokes about who would win what as a prize. He was quite something in his blue tights, and Iris was freshly amazed every afternoon at the sight of the tight little package between his legs. But really, it was dull, she decided. Nicky always lost. It was nice he wasn't gay like most of the other male hoofers, but his attraction for Iris was strictly from the waist down, and his value to the world had nothing to do with what was perched upon his neck.

Iris had much more fun with Harry. The emerald ring glittered on her finger as she slipped the mascara wand into its case. He is good to me, she thought as she looked at the two-carat stone for the hundredth time since he'd given it to her the night before. The radio beside her hairbrush was on, and Elvis Presley was crooning "Love Me Tender." "Boring," she sighed again.

"It's just like the army. Hurry up and wait." Harry paced behind her in their bedroom. Looking down at his watch, he inhaled sharply. "We have to leave this minute! Now, Il—I mean Iris—now!"

She grabbed her coat, a tote bag of red canvas that held more makeup, and a white bathrobe, and in minutes Iris and Harry were in a taxi. "Traffic jam," muttered the Puerto Rican at the wheel.

"Do you think this'll run forever?" she was asking. "That it'll be another *My Fair Lady* or *West Side Story?*"

"That'd be terrific. I'd get my money back and then some, but honestly, it doesn't have the music or the lyrics of a Lerner and Loewe show." He swung his arm around her in the backseat of the cab. "Don't worry. We'll open and you'll be fine. When it closes, you'll get another part. But it may run for . . . for who knows how long. A musical is an unknown quantity. Critics can say one thing and people will still buy tickets."

"You mean the critics might hate it and it won't matter?"

"Sure. It may not matter. Then again, last year, the critics loved *Night of Roses* and the public closed it. Just didn't go near the theater. It died on the vine with terrific reviews, all sorts of praise."

Iris was silent. Her face felt tight with all the pancake makeup. All I have to do is get into my costume, not fall down, and then say, "Oh, thank you so much, kind sir," and I'm home free. Broadway. A Broadway show. How could all this have happened to me? When Gretchen was probably worrying about her spring exams at someplace like Slippery Rock State College. And me! On Broadway! Iris snuggled closer to Harry and felt his warmth. Horns continued to honk in a cacophony of irritation, but the taxi, at last, began to move.

. . .

Half the cast and lots of husbands, wives, and lovers went to Sardi's after the show. The applause wasn't deafening, Richard Waterman said. But the audience was enthusiastic, Harry countered. Everyone hugged everyone else and gushed, "Great, just great!" There was an open bar set up in the private room, which contributed to the sense of bravado. Ice cubes tinkled amid the laughter and the loud voices, but the undercurrent of tension was as strong as the women's perfume.

The restaurant was still full of hangers-on when Ned, Waterman's teenage son, came in with the first of the early editions. A dozen people converged on him as he crossed the room. "Back! Back!" Harry pretended to wield a whip and took *The New York Times* from the young man. "Back, you animals!" He tossed the newspapers to Richard, who sat sipping a martini. He looked drained, but curiously tight with tension, like a father-to-be outside a hospital delivery room. "You do the honors!" called Harry. The composer and lyricist, Leslie Starke and Arnold Page, were both silent, nursing Scotch in a corner. Neither of them was gregarious. They communicated to the world on paper. Usually everyone forgot they were around.

The page was found and Richard hunched over, the *Times* open between his knees, and read. But not aloud.

"Hey! Let us in on this!" called the lead dancer, Natalie. "Come on! Don't kill us with suspense!" cried the set designer, who wore a yellow wool beret at all times, probably even in bed.

"It says, '*Aurora* has all the spirit of a funeral procession.' " Richard's voice was dead.

"What! What!" The voices were outraged. Natalie retreated to the window with tears in her eyes. "Who's the reviewer? Is it that damn Corkindale?" The room roared with angry voices.

"Shhhhh!" Harry bellowed. "Do you want to hear this or not?" The room fell silent. A knot of listeners stood in the doorway, another clustered around the bar, a half-dozen sat at tables, but almost everyone else stood, holding drinks, with long faces.

Richard cleared his throat as he opened the *Daily News*. Perhaps this one would be better. It was almost as important. " 'The dance numbers would have been original twenty years ago . . ." Bo Biddles, the choreographer, tightened a muscle in his jaw. Everyone in the room studiously avoided looking in his direction. Richard went on. "The lyrics lacked even a touch of origi- nality, but the songs were delivered with a certain charm and enthusiasm. Natalie Kane and Jess Barlow were appealing as the lovers, but must wither in embarrassment at the lines they were forced to deliv . . .' "

Richard tossed the paper up in the air, and the separate sheets of it sailed down on the heads of those crouched around him on the floor.

Harry went over to the bar and poured himself a tall glass of gin. One of the girl dancers picked up the newspaper and, with two of the male dancers, headed for the stairs. Iris touched Harry's elbow and he turned.

"Not great, huh?" she whispered.

Harry shook his head and poured still more gin into his glass. "I just lost a bundle on this. Don't imagine I'll ever see a cent of it again."

Iris immediately wondered if she'd lose her mink coat. Would he stop taking her to Sardi's? "But they won't close it right away, will they? I mean, there'll be other performances, won't there?" Iris was not only thinking of the financial loss; she was considering what a shame it was that just when she had conquered stage fright and gotten out her one line, she wouldn't have the chance to mince onstage in front of hundreds of people and do it again.

"We'll have to have a powwow about it. Have to decide whether to launch an ad campaign and risk losing more money. Tossing good money after bad." He smiled sardonically and sipped the clear liquid. "Or maybe we'll close it in a few days." He sighed at that thought.

"Harry . . ." She pressed herself under his arm. "Harry, tell me something honestly. I know the play wasn't great, but . . ." She turned her big green eyes, still in their stage makeup, toward his face. He was flushed from the heat of the room, perhaps from the alcohol too. "But was I good? Was I all right?" Her voice had a pleading quality to it.

Please tell me I'm good. Please tell me I'm a good girl, thought Richard

Waterman, who had overheard as he squeezed his way past them on the way to the telephone. He turned back in time to see Harry's face break into a broad smile. The older man put his hand on the blonde's shoulder and whispered, "Baby, you were wonderful. You were the best thing in the whole show."

.   .   .

On the Sunday following the Friday closing of *Aurora*, Iris lay on the living-room floor and read the comics section of the *Daily News*. She had also bought *The New York Times* because the Sunday magazine had an article on Broadway as the cover story. It was raining, Harry was in Queens with Frieda, and Iris felt a little lonely, a little depressed. She wished she had a friend to go to the movies with. There was only that other receptionist at the ad agency, but no, it had been too long. She wouldn't even remember me, Iris sighed. Iris had not had a girlfriend since Gretchen, no female she really trusted. Everyone knew about the man shortage in Manhattan. Phew, thought Iris. Why don't they call it Womanhattan? There were droves of females starving for romantic dinners, pining for escorts to cocktail parties, longing for love affairs. They spent every cent on their looks, lived in studios the size of shoeboxes, and fantasized about choosing silver patterns as a prelude to marriage to men who lived in one-bedroom apartments. Iris had spent all her New York time with men. Thinking of them, being with them—one man at a time, if you didn't count her afternoon interludes. Then, of course, at dinnertime she went home to Harry. It was still one man at a time. Basically.

Harry was her best friend—perhaps her only friend at this moment. In Queens with Frieda. Iris grimaced as she reached for the several pounds of newsprint.

The society section slid out onto the gray carpet. Instantly interested, Iris began to examine the photographs of the recently engaged and the married yesterday. The brides usually had long, straight hair, shining under a cloud of net, a string of pearls, and a smile that said, "Did it."

Iris read every word of the announcements on the first page, including the schools attended, the occupation of the fiancé, and sometimes of the fiancée, and whether or not they were descended from "strictly top-drawer" stock, as Harry put it. Most of them appeared to be. She turned to the inside page, curious, wanting to devour these strangers. "Cynthia Lake Kendall of Beacon Hill Weds Banker." Iris took a gulp of root beer out of the brown can and kept reading.

> Yesterday evening in a seven o'clock candlelight ceremony in St. Mark's Episcopal Cathedral, Boston, Cynthia Lake Kendall became the bride of Jean-François Colbert of Geneva, Switzerland.

The bride is the daughter of Mr. and Mrs. Otis Livingston Kendall III and the granddaughter of the late Mr. and Mrs. Preston Cabot Kendall of Beacon Hill. She is a graduate of Rosemary Hall, and attended Smith College. The elder Mr. Kendall was a founder of the commodities firm of Kendall, Wright and Caulfield; his son is chairman of the board of directors. On the bride's maternal side, the grandparents are Dr. Stoddard Lake, professor of European history at Harvard, and his late wife, Sophia Singleton Lake, also of Beacon Hill.

Mr. Colbert, a partner of Colbert & Cie., a Geneva private bank, is a graduate of Harvard University. The groom's great-grandfather, grandfather, and father were actively associated with Colbert & Cie. His mother, Elizabeth Westerfield Colbert Fortier, is the daughter of the late Dr. and Mrs. Richard Hayes Westerfield of London and Sussex, England. Dr. Westerfield was the director of obstetrics at the Royal Marlton Hospital in South Kensington.

After a reception and dinner dance for eight hundred guests at the Corinthian Club, Mr. and Mrs. Colbert left on their wedding trip to Gstaad. They will live in the Colbert family chateau, Les Colombiers, in Chambesy, Switzerland.

Iris inhaled through the straw. "Interesting," she murmured aloud. Marrying a Swiss person. Think of all that chocolate. And he's a banker. Think of all that money. Iris stared for one long minute at the pretty blonde. Long straight hair like all the others, curling faintly on her shoulders, gathered in pearl clips at her temples, so that the cap part of the veil could sit back from her wide, clear forehead. Cynthia Kendall Colbert gazed at the camera with light eyes, bright eyes, and her smile was Colgate-perfect. Iris thought of how the girl must feel, marrying a banker, going off to Switzerland with a foreigner, being taken care of forever.

"Being taken care of forever," she said aloud as she crossed her blue-jeaned legs; sock-footed, she leaned back against the leather sofa. Harry was good to Iris, but the musical was history, and professionally she was back at square one. "It's experience," Harry had consoled her. "It's something to put on a resumé," he said. And then he'd had to explain what a resumé was. But for Iris the excitement was over, had been over the moment of the last curtain call. Now it was lessons: tap, ballet, and the singing, where she simply croaked for forty-five minutes in front of a mirror and Mrs. Rowland shook her head and clucked.

Iris turned the pages and stared at one girl after another. They looked to be anywhere from twenty to twenty-five. Then she turned back to Cynthia

Lake Kendall Colbert, and wondered if she was marrying for love or for money. Would a Swiss be blond and Scandinavian-looking? Iris didn't know. Was a chateau like a palace or a castle? What did it mean to be a "private banker"? Iris folded the paper and tossed it aside.

Harry "bankrolls" plays. Harry has a wife. Harry won't marry me. I won't ever get my picture in *The New York Times* society section. Iris flounced into the kitchen, where she opened the refrigerator and reached for another root beer. Without sugar. She snapped open the top, and thought of those halcyon days of crackers with cream cheese and strawberry jam. Harry liked her rounder, but she liked herself this way, a whole size smaller in everything, even the painted-on blue jeans she considered her at-home uniform.

To celebrate the weight loss, Harry had given her his Saks credit card for the day, and she'd bought everything she could in the opening hours. She'd been there at a quarter to ten with seven other people, waiting for the big glass doors to be unlocked so that they could surge in past the counters, through the empty aisles, and be the first in every department. Charging like animals, charging, charging, charging, with the little plastic card.

But, Iris thought, I don't have money for the ladies' room tip at Sardi's. I don't have cab fare unless I ask for it in the morning, and then Harry gives me a brand-new ten dollar bill and a kiss on the forehead. She walked out of the kitchen and stood beside the modern square glass window overlooking Third Avenue. The rain pelted down in dirty-looking streaks. Harry with Frieda in Queens. The wife. Maybe someday the widow. Men always die first. And me in his—yes, Harry's—apartment with a mink coat. Me. No high-school diploma. No bank account. No fiancé. No chateau.

She turned down the corners of her mouth, remembering the image of Cynthia Lake Kendall from . . . what was the place? Oh, yes, Beacon Hill. Suddenly, Iris dipped low in a curtsy as she faced the expanse of gray buildings that stretched like mountains toward Central Park. In her best French accent she lisped, "Why, thank you very much, kind sir!"

CHAPTER ELEVEN

Cynthia

1968 — Beacon Hill

The Kendalls had gone all out for the wedding. Now, on Sunday at ten in the morning, Margaret showered and dressed then walked downstairs to see that all had been put in order. She had stayed at the Corinthian until the last guest departed at five past three, then Otis had paid the musicians, giving all fifteen of them very nice tips, as befitted his beneficent mood.

Yes, thought Margaret sourly, goodwill to all mankind and even womankind. Otis had tried to make love to her at dawn, coming into her bedroom and pulling the covers back and waking her. She had been surprised, then embarrassed, and had sent him away with a scolding for disturbing her. In his baggy white cotton pajamas with dark blue piping, he had, even to Margaret, seemed a rather sad polar bear maneuvering slowly through her bedroom, retreating in the gray light of dawn. Margaret sniffed. He hadn't pulled anything like that since long before his brother, Teddy, died. It might have been the summer Cynthia was away at camp in Vermont.

Cynthia must have been twelve that summer, and now she was married. At nineteen. The seven years were not what made Margaret smile. Cynthia married. Well married. It was what every mother dreamed about: a rich husband from a good family for her daughter. There was nothing else to wish for! Done, she sighed to herself as she moved the silver vase toward the center of the hall table.

"Mona!" she called, and the Irish maid appeared almost instantly. "These white roses haven't lasted, have they?" No answer was expected and none was forthcoming. "Maybe they should be thrown out if you can't put them in with the dining-room ones. No," she murmured as the maid took the vase and started to turn away. "On second thought, we are inundated with flowers. Just replace them."

"Yes, Mrs. Kendall."

The phone began to ring, and Mrs. Partridge answered in the pantry. She came into the hall seconds later. "Mrs. Kendall! Will you speak with Mrs. Grayson?"

"Oh, yes!" Margaret was pleased. She hurried toward the living room and the telephone on the drop-leaf desk. Picking up the extension, she heard Mrs. Partridge hang up. Good servants were hard to find. And once you found them, you had to find ways to keep them. Suddenly she worried about Cynthia living in a chateau and dealing with servants as the mistress of a household. "Kate!" she cried into the receiver.

"Well, it's over! You did it! And in grand style, I might add," came the dry response.

"Oh, finally," Margaret sighed.

"Finally? You'd think you'd just married off a fifty-year-old spinster who taught school and wore baggy gray cardigans and brown leather brogues!" Kate Grayson often told her childhood friend what a lovely daughter she had. Funny how Margaret seemed to assume the opposite. As if she simply didn't see Cynthia for what she was.

Margaret laughed. Mona heard it as she returned to the hall table with the vase of fresh flowers. First time I've heard that woman laugh in prob'ly a year, she thought. I'll have to tell the others in the kitchen. Then, cynically, it occurred to her, Maybe she's ill. A breakdown after all the excitement of the weddin'. She placed the silver container exactly over the little circle of maroon felt and turned it this way and that until the flowers were at just the right angle. Mrs. Kendall laughed again, and Mona winced.

"No, he's still sleeping. Let me close the door and we can really talk." Mona headed back to the kitchen as the double doors were closed firmly. She wondered what secrets those women had. Mrs. Partridge was counting silver coffee spoons and noting down totals in the dark blue spiral notebook that served as the household ledger.

"I heard her laugh," said Mona as she pushed open the swinging door.

Mrs. Partridge and Jake, the black man who came to do any heavy work, from furniture arranging to moving suitcases out of the attic, both laughed at the news.

"It's that Mrs. Grayson. She seems to cheer her up somehow." The house-keeper shook her head in wonder. "And to look at her you'd never think she had a sense of humor."

"I don't think she does. Don't think either one of them do," Mona stated firmly. She was holding her thumb under cold water in the sink. A thorn had nicked her. "They must be laughin' over Vietnam."

"To hear you talk, you'd think them two was real witches," Jake chuckled. Mrs. Partridge handed him a cup of coffee.

"Spell it with a *b* and you've got the right idea," chimed in Emily, who was called in to help with parties. She had been a mainstay at the dinner for the out-of-towners given on Friday night here in the house and she had been at the Corinthian Club with their staff until the waxing machines had been brought in to do the dance floor at four-thirty.

Mrs. Partridge smiled but didn't allow herself to join in the laughter of the others. Her broad bosom heaved as she sighed. She was the oldest of the staff, the longest with the family, and her personality placed her in the role of peacemaker among everyone "downstairs." She noted the number of salad forks at forty-eight, and tied the fourth bundle of velvet with the little ribbon. Then she began on the butter knives, lost count, and finally put the pencil down. The others chattered around her as she thought of Mrs. Grayson.

Mrs. Kate Grayson, who seemed always to have been divorced and somehow never married, had arrived just after lunch on Friday afternoon from the Bahamas. She was stylishly slim as always, in a chocolate brown silk suit; her face was very tan from the sun, and her dark hair had been tipped with blond streaks. Not from the sun, thought Mrs. Partridge, whose own hair was a sensible iron gray. The two friends could have been sisters as they walked with arms linked through the hallway to the living room, where, inevitably, the door was closed behind them. They had talked and laughed until past five o'clock, when Mrs. Partridge had had to knock and ask Mrs. Kendall if the bar should be set up in the hallway as usual, or perhaps at one end of the living room. Guests were to arrive in an hour for cocktails.

Mrs. Grayson had asked that someone call a taxi for her so that she could return to the Copley and change for dinner. She never stayed in the house, though Otis always invited her and teased her about being concerned over conditions being too spartan in the Kendall guest rooms.

The housekeeper had left the two women standing in the living room. Mrs. Grayson had been snapping her alligator pocketbook closed, and Mrs. Kendall had been saying something about how the party was going to be a success. I was distracted, Mrs. Partridge remembered. I was in a hurry. I was annoyed that I had to call the taxi from the pantry telephone when there was a phone on the desk within yards of the two women, who appeared to have nothing on their minds except gossip and getting dressed in time. Why can't I remember what was wrong? She picked up the pencil and absentmindedly began to chew the eraser. Jake was laughing about the waiter who had spilled red wine down the front of his trousers and had had to wear the only spare pair available—two sizes too small. "Yassir, he limped 'round ev'ry table all evenin' long!"

Mrs. Partridge was annoyed with herself. She hated the niggling little crumb of . . . what? It was like miscounting the forks and having to begin again, or finding that the linen in the laundry room had been folded and put away without being properly ironed. I went back to tell them that the taxi was there, and that was when I was struck with the idea that something was wrong.

"Mrs. P.! Mrs. P.! Are you among the living?" Mrs. Kendall stood over her where she sat at the kitchen table.

"Oh, yes! I'm sorry. I was . . ." she apologized.

"I just wanted to come down and tell you all that it went very well, and to thank you for working so hard." She gave a small smile as they all stared at her, and then she moved toward the stairs that led up to the upstairs pantry and to the dining room. Mrs. Kendall rarely thanked anyone for anything; you only heard about something if it was done wrong. The table with not enough places, the flowers in the wrong vase, the silver not polished, a chipped plate, a course taking too long to serve. Emily, Mona, Jake, Betty, and Mrs. Partridge composed a tableau with hands folded across apron fronts. Their mistress's footfalls were loud in the silence of the kitchen. It was Jake who called up to the figure in navy blue. "Miz Kendall, we was happy to do it. For Miss Cynthia!"

Mrs. Partridge raised her eyebrows, but the warning was too late. No one could see Mrs. Kendall's face, but the irritation in her voice was a giveaway. "Yes. Of course."

The door closed at the top of the stairs and they all burst into talk again. Except for Mrs. Partridge. She screwed up her plump, ruddy face as she picked up the pile of clanking butter knives and wondered one more time, What was so strange in that living room? Was it something I saw or something I heard? "Oh!" she said aloud in annoyance. Then she opened the ledger to the correct page and began to write carefully: *March 22, 1968, silver count. linen napkin count. china count.* Then, under the first column, in her bold handwriting, she subdivided *butter knives.* She shook her head one last time and thought, It'll come to me in the bathtub. It always does.

Gstaad

"What was that movie?" sighed Cynthia, curling under Jean-François's arm and putting her cheek against his chest. "That movie where someone asks the bride what she wants to see on her honeymoon, and she says—"

Her husband laughed. "Lots of wonderful ceilings!" Cynthia propped herself up on one elbow and kissed his smiling face. "Are you disappointed that it's just this one?"

She shook her head, and her long blond hair moved on her bare shoulders. The ceiling above them was that of the Chalet Edelweiss. Dark wood rafters crisscrossed the white plaster above their double bed with the colorfully painted headboard. The room was warm and romantic with pine furniture, a white duvet and heavy lace curtains; outside the elaborately cut-out shutters, the snow was banked up to the windowsill. "Like clouds," Cynthia had said. Her face was flushed, her lips swollen from kisses, her eyes half-slitted with sleep.

"My God! Are you ever beautiful!" said Jean-François. "You are the woman I always imagined I'd marry."

"What does that mean?" Cynthia tried to be more alert. She felt drowsy.

"It means that I knew I would marry someone beautiful. Someone charming, someone with perfect manners and good breeding. Someone worthy of being the mother of my children."

Cynthia didn't respond. She was reminded of her mother. But no, don't think of her now. Jean-François means all this as a compliment, not as a scheme, not as something contrived and premeditated. Still, she felt less warm, less drowsy.

He went on. "And I like the idea that you've never had to work, never had to be one of those career women with an apartment, worried about paying bills. I'm glad you haven't been exposed to all the shrillness of women's liberation."

Cynthia smiled. "No chance of that. It all seems very far away from me, from my life. I mean"—she snuggled up to him once more—"I feel a little strange in that I'm not in college, I'm not studying for a degree. But . . ." She paused. "I think that I would have graduated and gotten married anyway. I don't want to be someone's secretary!"

"Thank God for that!" He pulled her closer. "Just be my wife! Madame Colbert! Just be what I want you to be—"

Cynthia looked at the handsome face above her. He was serious. "What about what *I* want to be?" slipped out.

He laughed with delight. His elbows were on either side of her head and his face was inches away from hers. "Of course you can be whatever you want. But, darling, you're very young. Maybe being my wife will be quite enough."

He bent down and began to kiss her softly. First on the left side of her mouth and then on the right, and then tantalizingly near her lower lip, but not quite on it. Cynthia's heart pounded in her ears as she lay back on the big white square pillow and waited for him to finally, really, satisfy her with his kiss. In seconds she had altogether forgotten what they had been talking about.

Beacon Hill

"Look, I can't talk now. Otis will be down for breakfast any minute. Do you want to have lunch today? I just can't bear the thought of your leaving to-morrow, and I—"

"Good morning, Margaret," said the dark blue pinstripe-suited man before her. She never recognized him on Monday mornings, or perhaps it was the other way around. She never felt he was who he was on the weekends. Otis Livingston Kendall looked as if he had been born in a three-piece suit. A cesarean, of course. Or maybe a breech birth so that the solid, heavy-as-lead wingtip shoes could get out first.

"Oh, Otis," she said, cupping the mouthpiece. "I'll be right in." We may have separate bedrooms, she thought, and the servants know, of course, but we do have our meals together. That's only correct. "Kate? Yes. What about meeting me here at twelve, and we'll decide—" She was silent, listening. Kate could get annoyed over the smallest things. "Oh, all right. I'll come to you. The lobby at noon."

Margaret brushed the slight touch of perspiration from her upper lip and hung up the phone. Then she turned and walked—click, click, click went her black kid pumps—through the hall and then downstairs for breakfast with Otis. She seated herself at one end of the table and shook out the white linen napkin and then looked down, facing the half grapefruit on the Meissen china. Otis rattled the *Boston Globe* as he turned back the editorial page, and she looked up. He was entirely hidden behind the news of the day. Twenty-one years of mornings exactly like this, thought Margaret. Going on twenty-two. She sipped her black coffee and felt not only its heat, its caffeine, but con-solation. Only four and a half more hours until twelve o'clock. Until Kate.

CHAPTER TWELVE

Cynthia

1968—Les Colombiers-Chambesy

"Finally!" Cynthia exclaimed as the gray Bentley turned into the driveway of the chateau. She had seen photographs at Elizabeth's house but the reality, the enormity of the place, took her breath away. "You didn't tell me—I had no idea it was this big!"

"A pile of stones," said Jean-François, pulling her close to him in the backseat. "Dates from the late sixteen hundreds, but they considered it finished in 1723." He kissed her nose in a quick, affectionate peck, and then whispered, "Welcome to Les Colombiers. Nesting place of the doves. Or it used to be, at any rate."

Cynthia squeezed his hand and turned her green eyes up toward his face. "I'm so happy. Really happy."

The car reached the porte cochere and stopped on the gravel. Bags were taken out of the trunk by Christophe, who doubled as the chauffeur and butler, as two maids in black dresses and white aprons stood on the steps, watching. Jean-François introduced them to her in French as Silvie and Brigitte. "They will take care of everything in the house, outside of the kitchen, of course." He smiled as he put his arm around Cynthia, and told the maids, "This is the new mistress of Les Colombiers. Do anything she asks. I want her to stay here a long time." They all laughed and congratulated him, and each young, rosy-cheeked girl took Cynthia's hands and murmured, *"Tous nos voeux de bonheur!* Best wishes! All happiness!"

Jean-François then swept his new American bride off her feet and, to the applause of the maids and Christophe, carried her up the front steps and over the threshold of the Colbert chateau. "Put me down," she pleaded. "I've eaten nonstop for six days in Gstaad, and you can't simply—"

"Oh, yes I can!" he growled. "You don't weigh anything at all. Your overnight case weighs a ton by comparison." She laughed again, and he told her to be still or he'd drop her. "I want you always to remember this," he said seriously as he carried her through the enormous central hall, under the arched doorway, into the living room. The far wall had floor-to-ceiling pairs of French doors, small-paned, shining, that opened onto the lawn and the blue expanse of Lake Geneva and beyond, to the white peaks of the Alps in France.

"Is it real? It looks like a stage set!" Cynthia looked at nothing else as she was deposited on the Persian rug. The lake drew her. She thought of melted sapphires in the late afternoon sun.

"Now just across the water where you see those trees is Cologny, which is really the most expensive real estate in Geneva."

"But it's out in the country and so are we, so why do you say Geneva?"

"The canton of Geneva is what I mean." He explained that Switzerland was a confederation of twenty-two cantons that had banded together at different times since the thirteenth century. "Geneva was quite independent and among the last to join. It wasn't until 1815 that Switzerland became the country we think of today." He paused. "Our constitution is dated 1848."

"So the Genevois are very proud? Feel very different?" she asked, remembering her mother-in-law's comments.

"Oh, yes! We do! The cantons are all so different. When someone is very slow, very stupid, we say, 'He must have been born in Bern.' You never tell someone from Bern a joke on Thursday because they will laugh in church on Sunday." Cynthia shook her head, smiling. He was warming to the subject. "Geneva is . . . what can I say? All right. I'll tell you what Talleyrand said." Cynthia was staring out at the water, thinking she'd never seen a lake so beautiful. She was an ocean person, and yet she loved this lake. "Talleyrand said that there were five continents: Europe, Asia, America, Africa, and Geneva."

Cynthia smiled with delight. "Do you think I'll ever understand this place?"

Jean-François put his hand under her chin and lifted her face to his. "You probably won't."

"I might surprise you," she said flirtatiously.

"Understand Geneva?" He smiled slowly. "The place defies any explanation. But . . ." He stared into the almond-shaped green eyes. "What I want for you most is that you have a wonderful time trying." He put his arms around her then, and held her to him. Cynthia loved him achingly when he was protective of her, when he was teaching her things, when he ended any little discourse with an embrace. She hungered for his approval, to be the quick study, and thirsted for his touch that told her he was pleased.

"Excuse me, Monsieur," Brigitte said as she entered. "And Madame. The mail, there is so much, I worried that something might be important and couldn't wait until tomorrow." She held a stack of envelopes, many of them the size of invitations, in one hand.

"*Oui, merci.*" Jean-François broke away from Cynthia and took them from her. "Aah!" he sighed again and again as he turned them over to check the return addresses. "Perhaps I should take a look." He walked over to the drop-leaf cherrywood desk and began to slash quickly with a silver letter opener.

Cynthia turned in a slow circle surveying the room around her. Two marble fireplaces, each big enough to roast an ox in, were at opposite ends of the enormous room. To her far left was a seating arrangement of overstuffed chairs covered in brown flowered upholstery. Ugh, they're really hideous, she thought. An attempt had been made at making the room look cozy, but it had ended in dismal failure. Key word here is *dismal*, she thought. The furniture looked as though it should be put out in the garage to be picked up by the Salvation Army. The marble-topped coffee table was nice enough, but the yellowish alabaster vase on top of it was too large and very clumsy-looking. And empty, too, Cynthia noted with dismay. Is there a garden? I'll have to ask Jean-François if I can begin right away. Who would even want to sit in this room and read a book? Then she turned back to the glass façade and to the landscape leading down to the lake and out to the blue sky. Everything in this room should be focused on that view, she decided.

"Cynthia! Do you have any evening things you can get to? For tonight?" he was asking. He held a large square white card.

"Why, I don't know. I have all the stuff from Gstaad, of course—"

"Ask Brigitte if your things shipped from Boston have arrived. You'll need a long dress."

"For tonight?" Cynthia was tired. And disappointed. She had looked forward to their first evening together in this house. A relaxed dinner. Just the two of them.

He nodded. "The Genevois eat rather early. We're expected at the Bergeracs' in . . ." He checked his watch. "Exactly one hour and twenty minutes."

Six o'clock! In Europe! She remembered her ten-o'clock dinners in Paris and thought, This is crazy! But Cynthia also remembered Elizabeth's having talked about being a good sport. It might have been the credo she lived her life by, something to embroider on pillows late at night on quiet winter evenings in front of the fire. Her own mother wasn't at all keen on being a good sport. She liked something called "getting my own way." Well, thought the young girl. One woman has been happily married twice, and the other has successfully made one man miserable ever since I can remember. Cynthia smiled gamely and said, with perhaps a shade too much enthusiasm, "Great. I'll be ready."

Geneva

Well, no, thought Cynthia. I wasn't ready for this. She had her hand tucked through the dinner-jacketed arm of Jean-François as they were propelled by the crowd through a cobblestoned courtyard. The air was cold and damp, and she was glad to have the fur.

"This is the Vieille Ville, the Old Town of Geneva, the very heart of the place. Some of these buildings date from the fifteenth century." Cynthia wasn't looking at architecture, but at the women. They were nearly all older, all in long dresses. Cynthia's things from Boston had, unfortunately, not arrived and she had to make do with clothes she'd had in Gstaad: a raspberry velvet street-length skirt and a fuchsia silk blouse. She always wrapped an emerald silk cummerbund around her, showing off her tiny waist. It was one of her favorite outfits.

She tried to feel a bit more courageous, but the sound of all the French voices echoing up the winding stone stairway was daunting. The noise made Cynthia feel caught in a spiral of confusion. It's old, all right, she thought, noticing the lanterns embedded in the walls every few yards or so above their heads.

"Let me take this for you." Jean-François helped her off with the mink and handed it over to an elderly woman in a black cotton dress. Cynthia noticed it was the only fur coat in the little room beyond. Sensible black, gray, or tan wool coats hung in a row along the back wall.

One more landing, and they were at last inside a hallway with a receiving line. Two men in dinner jackets shook hands first and spoke in French. "*Enchanté, enchanté.*" A few steps farther into the room, two women were introduced and also shook hands. Jean-François was kissed by each, and they were very warm to Cynthia when they realized she was his new wife. Her French was halting, suddenly shy, and one of them smiled and said, "Don't worry about speaking French. We all speak English."

Jean-François had his arm around her waist, and led her into the high-ceilinged room, explaining, "This is one of the most elaborate houses in Geneva." Eighteen feet above them was a mural of angels, floating banners, and whipped-cream clouds. The room was so crowded with people it was impossible to see anything, not furniture, not a fireplace, not paintings. Only the Genevois. "I think it's dinner for fifty. That's usually the way the Bergeracs do it."

Cynthia was handed a sherry by a maid who maneuvered quickly through the knots of people with a tray. "Sip it," Jean-François advised. "You won't get another."

Couple after couple came over to kiss Jean-François and to be introduced to Cynthia. With dismay, she realized her double strand of pearls, the large diamond engagement ring, and the diamond lizard pin she always wore with this blouse were too much. She was overdone for this party. Perfect for New York, not even too much for Boston, but a Christmas tree in Geneva. The women were wearing very little jewelry; there was the occasional string of pearls, the small pearl-and-gold earrings. It was good and it was real, but it was subdued enough to make Cynthia feel flashy. In confusion she remembered that Jean-François had told her the guests would be from old banking families. She smiled at a woman in a long black wool dress wearing pearl earrings, and wondered if she'd misunderstood. A black *wool* evening dress? With tiny gold love-knot earrings and not one other ornament. The woman was regal, white-haired, and she held her chin very high. Her French was lovely, but she could have been a nun on her first night out of the convent. "She's the *grande dame* of the LeClerc family," was Jean-François's whispered explanation. As if that made any sense at all, thought Cynthia with frustration. She recognized the name LeClerc from something Jean-François had said in Gstaad, and associated it with wealth. I must have misunderstood, she thought yet again. Most of the other women were dressed very fashionably. Their dresses were classic, but in style, quietly elegant. Nothing that could have been labeled knockout, nothing to make a splash. She would learn later that these women usually had their own dressmakers who copied the styles from magazines.

A plate of hors d'oeuvres was offered to her, and as she began to shake her head and say, "Non, merci," Jean-François said something close to her ear.

She turned to him and said, "I couldn't hear you."

"I said you'd better take one. Just one, though." Cynthia looked at him as though he were completely crazy. "Just one." He motioned the maid back, and Cynthia obediently took a cracker with cheese on top. "That's right," he was saying. "You just get one chance around here. And only one hors d'oeuvre."

"Whatever are you talking about? I simply don't understand!" Cynthia had already swallowed the little tidbit.

"I mean that . . ." Jean-François looked to the right and then to the left as Cynthia waited. "I mean that they count them!"

•   •   •

In the car, on the way home, at a quarter past eleven, Cynthia demanded an explanation. "What is going on? There was no heat on in the house! I was absolutely frozen! And starving to death!"

Jean-François, at the wheel of the Bentley, began to laugh. "You have just met a Genevois banking family. Nothing to get excited about." He was smiling. "I should have warned you, but I always think it'll be better than it is."

"But—" stammered Cynthia. "Are they absolutely dirt poor? If they are, how can they live in that house, have servants—I mean, why have a dinner party and give everyone an ounce of roast beef and one glass of wine—"

"A very inferior wine, I might add," Jean-François put in.

Cynthia nodded. "Yes, it was not the greatest. But tell me—"

"I'll have to give you a book on Jean Calvin and Calvinism and a history of Geneva and the rise of Protestantism—"

She sighed. "Is Geneva—was that dinner party typical?"

He nodded. "Afraid so. It aptly illustrates how the Genevois feel about spending money, about being comfortable and well fed."

"But do they have money? You would think a banking family would have money," Cynthia insisted.

"Of course they have money! But that doesn't mean they spend it. It doesn't mean any one of those women has a mink coat. It doesn't mean they cannot afford one; it just means they won't wear their wealth."

"But, Jean-François! A mink coat is not just status with a price tag! It's for warmth. I grew up with the idea of never flaunting wealth. In Boston, women often use fur as lining only, but—"

"All right. I understand you." They were driving beside the lake now. Dark, shining water stretched off to the right of them under a half moon. Chambesy was nine kilometers from town. "But some people would see it as a symbol of wealth. Just because it's expensive and you obviously had enough money to buy it." He held up one finger, anticipating her interruption. "And furthermore, concerning warmth—the house *was* cold. I'm wearing more than you are, and I longed for the wine to be passed. At one point I wanted to rub my hands together and blow on them." Cynthia laughed. She'd put her hands in her lap under her napkin, pretending it was a muff. Jean-François kept on talking. "You and I were both chilled in that great big damp barn. They're human beings with the same body temperature as ours. They probably were cold, too. The point is—they don't live comfortably. I know it's difficult to catch on to. It has a lot to do with Calvinism. It also has to do with modesty."

They were pulling into the driveway now. Cynthia was surprised that her husband thought it was all so amusing, because she wasn't sure she did. Her mother had always said it was far worse to be overdressed than underdressed. Go for the conservative every time and you won't feel out of place. Heavens. And I'm from New England. Being low-key and understated is practically in my blood! Cynthia liked feeling well dressed and knew she looked well in clothes. She couldn't imagine giving up the satisfaction of wearing bright colors, her mink coat, the jewelry she loved. But everything must be in good taste, subtle. Mother is the same, she thought. It's something we share. Maybe the only thing, she thought with a frown. Cynthia worried as Jean-François drove the car into the garage. Was Geneva even more extreme in "modesty," as Jean-François called it? Will I fit here? Will I have friends? Will I have to serve hard-boiled eggs and tiny portions of sliced ham at my dinner parties as we all shiver in black, brown, or dark blue?

Jean-François opened the door for her. Taking her hand, he helped her out and teased, "Come on. It wasn't that bad. The Bergeracs are known for this kind of dinner party. Not all Genevois families are like that. You'll see. And the minute you understand this character Jean Calvin, you'll understand a lot about Geneva."

He slammed the car door behind her. What Cynthia suddenly understood—for the first time—was that she had taken on a lot more than a Swiss husband; she had taken on his life, his Geneva, his Switzerland, and all these Genevois. Whatever that meant, whatever they were! She looked up at the enormous dark silhouette of the chateau and thought, Life will be better when I can replace that horrible furniture.

Paris

Jean-François pulled the sheet away and yawned. He turned his head carefully to see if the woman was still sleeping. À *cinq à sept* was still best, he decided, as he cautiously moved toward the edge of the double bed. Suzanne's arms extended suddenly, and her long, manicured red nails playfully scratched his back. One hand closed quickly around his wrist.

Like a chain, went through his mind. "Ah, ah, ah," he smiled. "My plane is in fifty-five minutes."

"Come back," she pouted prettily. "Take a later plane. There are hundreds of planes to Geneva." A lock of auburn hair fell over her face. It was a lush countenance with pinchable cheeks and full lips. Her dark eyes were slitted with sleep.

"*Mon chère.*" He pulled away. "I must go now." He twisted from her grasp as she arranged the sheets over her large breasts and wondered whether to follow him into the shower for one last bit of persuading.

"You never stay long," she murmured. Suzanne made a face at the little crystal chandelier above her. This room was yellow and the other ceiling had been blue; again the traffic of the Paris evening rush hour could be heard faintly, like a river outside the window.

In minutes he had returned, pulling a tie into place, his hair damp with all the little comb marks showing. A quick scooping of coins from the glass-topped bureau was dropped jingling into his trouser pocket; the alligator wallet and the red Swiss passport with its white cross emblem were tucked into his suit jacket. He turned to her as she complained, "You never spend the night."

He sat on the edge of the bed, glancing at his watch. "I have to spend my nights somewhere else. You know that." He kissed her lightly first on one cheek then the other, though he could feel her anger as heat on her skin. That skin that had been warmed by his lovemaking only an hour ago. "I will telephone."

Jean-François stood up and wondered why women always believed him. Suzanne was an exception. He had actually called her for the second time. And the last. He smiled and winked and made a last little kissing noise. "*Au revoir.*" The door closed as she watched.

Then Suzanne rose up on her elbows and awkwardly threw her pillow toward it. It fell with a *poomph* noise on the carpet, at least a meter short of its target. With the same sort of *poomph* noise, the woman sank onto the bed again. "*Merde,*" she breathed to the empty room.

Les Colombiers

Cynthia fluffed up her hair with both hands, then sighed, took up the silver-backed hairbrush, and flipped the slight pageboy back into place. She smoothed her gray flannel suit with its pleated skirt and then grimaced in the mirror. "I look like a schoolgirl just released from a strict Catholic—"

"Oh, God! Don't say anything about the Catholics to her! She'll be clicking her false teeth for hours over that! I've made sure she knows you're Protestant, but your being American is bound to have upset her."

"Jean-François! I don't understand this!" Cynthia watched him pull his tie into place.

It was a bright Saturday a few weeks after their wedding in Boston, and Tante Helga was coming for lunch. "She's not really my aunt," he had explained. "She's my father's generation—a cousin. But she considers herself close to Papa and to Uncle Pierre. Both dead. But still close. Maybe she talks to them in prayer. Helga is an old German name. Means 'pious, religious, holy.' " He sighed. "Anyway, we must have her here. She has to inspect the new family member. She feels she has the right. She's sort of a matriarch of the Colberts."

"Why are you so nervous?" Cynthia insisted as he tore a button off his shirt sleeve and had to take off the tie and shirt and start to get dressed all over again.

When he answered, his French accent was more pronounced than usual.

"She's Swiss through and through," he murmured as he struggled with the buttons of shirt number two.

Cynthia looked in the mirror one last time, and then at her husband. "Swiss German," he stated gloomily.

.   .   .

Cynthia had been told not to speak unless spoken to. The woman was a large-boned figure in dark brown wool who hesitated suspiciously over every dish Brigitte presented to her. That long-sleeved, high-necked dress must be suffocatingly hot, Cynthia thought. She could at least take off her sweater. Is it spring all over Switzerland, she wondered, or just in Geneva?

Tante Helga, who used the title of her late husband, introduced herself to Cynthia as Frau Doktor Schweitzer. She was full of opinions. "Jean-François, this beef is far too expensive for a lunch such as this. You should tell your wife that boiled ham would have been quite—"

Cynthia said, "I thought meeting you was a special occasion." She smiled, and the woman nodded in her direction.

Helga Schweitzer was a widow in her early seventies. Stocky, wearing no-nonsense, sturdy brown leather shoes that tied, and a brown cardigan over her brown dress, she was a figure to be reckoned with. Her hair was a mixture of brown and gray and was knotted at the nape of her thick neck with two serious-looking tortoiseshell hairpins. Her face was round and high-colored. She looked, thought Cynthia, like a grown-up version of a Campbell's Soup child. Rosy-cheeked, robust, with intelligent blue eyes. She probably climbed an Alp before breakfast every day of her life. Her husband gone and her one son killed in an automobile accident, she was alone now in what Jean-François had described as "an enormous place filled with masterpieces of the art world."

Helga Schweitzer had inherited paintings from her grandfather and her father. They had both traveled extensively all over Europe, but mostly in France, which they had loved. They had had the chance to buy from certain artists before they became famous, and the good sense to do so. Her grandfather, for instance, had bought several things directly from Gauguin himself. Other paintings had been offered to him by an Austrian collector who had taken a bath in the crash of 1929 and didn't want his family to suffer. Indeed, he didn't even want them to know of his involvement on Wall Street. Now it all belonged to Tante Helga.

After lunch they walked into the *fumoir* and seated themselves. The older woman looked critically at the few changes Cynthia had made. "Didn't that bookcase hold some of the family silver?" she asked.

Jean-François cleared his throat and explained. "Cynthia thought—that is, we thought—that it should go in the dining room."

All three of them stared at the bookcase, which now held some handsome first editions rescued from obscurity in a packing box upstairs.

"Well," Helga proclaimed after what seemed like an entire minute of consideration. "I don't think the family would have moved the silver."

Implicit in that, thought Cynthia as she felt her cheeks go pink, is the idea that I'm certainly not "family."

The tisane, herb tea, was served and Cynthia, as instructed, sat in silence. She had never noticed how much Jean-François depended upon her for conversational openings. It amused her and pleased her, too, to watch him cast about for a subject.

At last they were able to walk Helga to the car, and to watch her settle herself laboriously behind the wheel of the old Mercedes. "Last forever, these German cars," she said as she put the key in the ignition. She looked very businesslike behind the wheel, Cynthia decided. She either passes everyone on the road or drives ten miles an hour and mutters under her breath as everyone passes her.

"Tante Helga, it was lovely to see you," Jean-François was saying. "I worry that you have such a long drive ahead of you. Perhaps the next time"—Cynthia gasped to herself—"the next time you should consider the train."

"I did consider the train, but when I studied the cost of gasoline, the train came out four francs more." She sniffed, and the sniff spoke volumes about what she thought of prices today, inflation, and the world economic structure.

Cynthia smiled and said she had been happy to meet her. Frau Doktor Schweitzer stared at her gray jacket as if she were about to ask about the quality. Would it be wearable in twenty years? Cynthia was unshaken and hospitable to the end. "Perhaps you should call us when you arrive?" she suggested. "So we won't worry."

"Oh!" said the elderly woman. "I wouldn't think of wasting money long distance that way! Someone else will call you if I don't arrive!"

With that, she floored the accelerator of the big black car and bolted down the driveway, leaving the young couple standing in her wake. Jean-François put his arm around Cynthia and shook his head. "Do you see what I mean?" he asked.

Cynthia burst into long-suppressed nervous laughter. "So that's Tante Helga! I feel as if I've been through a war and just barely survived to tell about it!" She stretched upward and kissed her husband on the cheek. "Why don't we go inside and get drunk?"

.   .   .

"It's simply that there are Swiss who love the outside, who love to travel, and there are Swiss who love their systems, the way they do things."

"But I live here now and I'm married to you and I'll speak French as well as anyone in a year or two. I'm sure I will," Cynthia said.

"Darling, it's not just speaking French. You are an American. You have a Swiss passport, but you are not Swiss and you never will be." He felt her stiffen beside him in the front seat. "This is what she has on her mind. And nothing will change her mind. I, on the other hand, think that it's better for the Genevois to marry outsiders, to bring foreigners into Geneva to live. Geneva is the way it is because of the American, French, and Belgian wives. I've always been most attracted to the women who are not of Geneva, and most particularly attracted to Americans who have traveled, spent time in Europe. Often they are very well educated and they are very interested in something, want to do something—and I don't count the Junior League!"

Cynthia was delighted. What an escape! If I lived in Boston, the Junior League is exactly what I'd be involved with. But Jean-François is attracted by women who are "very interested in something." What am I very interested in? I'll start with the chateau, she decided after a few minutes of silence in the car. I'll get it in perfect order and learn the history and next year we'll have a child.

It was a bright summer afternoon. They had driven along the lake to Lausanne, which was a leisurely hour from Geneva, then continued on to Bern, where they had eaten lunch. The Café du Commerce was known for its paella. Afterwards they had wandered through the Old Town, a place of fountains and flowers and streets lined with arcades. Jean-François told Cynthia that Duke Berchtold V of Zahringen had wanted to create a city on the site that was now Bern and told his huntsmen and his chief master of the hounds that he would name it after the first animal killed at the next hunt. That was in the year 1191, and the animal was a bear. So he named the town Bern and put a bear on its coat of arms. The city played a significant political role for centuries, and after Confederation it was chosen as the seat for the federal authority.

Now they were leaving Bern, and in a few minutes they would be at the Schweitzer family mansion in time for tea. Frau Doktor Schweitzer might have been the first Swiss German Cynthia met but luckily she had met others since. Jean-François had taken her to Zurich for three days on banking business and the young couple had been entertained at lunches and dinners by very hospitable, attractive Swiss Germans. Cynthia realized they were more likely to speak English than the Genevois, that St. Moritz was their place for skiing, and that, though sophisticated they were unstuffy and outgoing. They considered many Genevois to be insufferable snobs.

A banker's stunning ash-blonde wife from Interlaken was full of sympathy for Cynthia. "Ah! Geneva! The hypocrisy! Have you heard of the Genevois banker who was having an affair with his secretary but was so staunchly Protestant that he couldn't ask for a divorce until—" She took a swallow of wine. "Until the poor woman was pregnant with his seventh child!"

Cynthia laughed. "It can't be true! I've only been in Switzerland a few months but Geneva can't be—"

"Oh, my poor girl!" Claire-Lise continued. "Heinz is here in Zurich for now but the bank has moved him from here to Geneva, and to New York, and then back again. We have been all over, and—" She shook her head. "I am Swiss but not Genevois, of course. It was easier for me to go from Zurich to New York and make a life and be happy than for me to live in Geneva."

Cynthia brought herself back to the present.

Jean-François was still on the subject of Switzerland and the Swiss mentality towards the rest of the world. "Think of a Swiss as a patriarch at the head of a table. He eats at one table with himself as the head. Nothing is going to change that," he emphasized. "He is well aware that his land is poor. There is only water power and his own energy and ability to work hard. Nothing else here in Switzerland except what he makes of it. There are no minerals, no oil."

Cynthia sighed. She wondered if she would ever understand where she fit into all this. Yes, she could imagine a Swiss at the head of a dinner table being served first. The Swiss took care of their own. First. The city of Geneva even fed its pigeons bright yellow corn every morning at dawn. The public schools were excellent; some said the private schools were only for the foreigners or the very stupid children. And the laws were very strict about foreigners becoming Swiss citizens.

"But I'm married to you!" she burst out.

"Of course you are." Jean-François didn't know how to make her understand. "And I think it's beneficial for a Genevois to marry outside. These old families tend to be rather incestuous." He laughed. "A friend congratulating me on my marriage said he, too, had married a foreigner. His wife Ursula is from Bern!"

Cynthia thought of the Zurichois she'd met who had told her Geneva was impossibly introverted. "Why are you so different?" Her voice was flirtatious; she put her hand on his knee.

"Because Maman is English. Because I went to a school in France when I was a boy. Because I spent so many holidays away from Geneva." He smiled. "But the best reason I can give you for being the way I am is . . ." He grinned and she thought how attractive he was. "Because I am a very intelligent character."

Cynthia smiled and thought, Yes, he is. It was the reason he told her to go to Paris to buy clothes, to buy what she wanted at the market and "to hell with living as though we were using ration tickets in a war!"

"I love Switzerland," he said suddenly. "It's a country to be proud of. The tradition of hard work, honest labor, cleanliness—all of that is good. It's solid. It makes sense not to throw paper on the street. It makes sense to remain neutral in a world gone mad with war. Little wars everywhere." He sighed. "Neutrality is the key to the survival of Switzerland. When all of Europe was in turmoil, Switzerland was a little island trying to—"

"Why have I heard that the Swiss turned away Jews at the border and then watched the Nazis shoot them only yards away?"

"They weren't all turned away. There were large numbers of Jewish refugees in Switzerland. But some were not allowed in. Lots of non-Jews weren't allowed in, either." He sighed. "It was a very difficult political balancing act. A touchy issue for this country to know how many Jews we could accept and still not precipitate a German invasion. We always feared that Hitler would march in after them."

Cynthia stared at her husband's profile. They drove on in silence for a while. "Don't forget that what is now Switzerland has had a history of accepting refugees," he said at last. "Geneva was where the refugees fleeing the political clashes of the mid-eighteen hundreds came. They came from France and Russia and Germany. And of course, religious refugees, like the Colberts, came a few hundred years before and were welcomed." He stopped. "Garibaldi was here from Italy, and Lenin also came to Geneva."

"So I should just think of myself as another refugee?" Cynthia asked, lightening the moment.

Jean-François grinned. "*Oui!* And behave yourself with this old Swiss-German dowager, or I'll dump you at the nearest frontier!"

They'd had a big lunch, but Cynthia found herself wishing tea were over and they were deciding where to have dinner.

"I'll be very careful," she said primly. "I must be nervous. I'm absolutely starved."

"We're here," he announced as he swung the car into the driveway of the three-story house. "We won't stay long." He winked at her as he walked around to open her door. "Just long enough to be proper. Polite."

Cynthia sighed, and wondered if the bright green scarf over the white suit jacket was too much. She took Jean-François's arm as they stood on the front steps and rang the bell. There had been no question of their not coming, of declining the invitation. Well, Cynthia thought philosophically, even an appointment with the dentist doesn't last forever.

. . .

They discussed the weather, which was very good for this time of year. They all agreed on that. Then they discussed the traffic between Geneva and Lausanne. Cynthia looked around the living room. It must be sixty feet long, she decided. There was very little furniture in it; the little arrangement of chairs where they sat was strictly Grand Passage, a department store in Geneva. Utilitarian and cheap. The wooden coffee table could have been made by a carpenter in five minutes and then stained dark brown. But the architectural details of the house were good, and the high ceilings were in proportion to the huge room.

Covering the walls were *the* paintings. Gauguins, van Goghs, Picassos from his Blue Period, Seurats, Modiglianis, Cezannes, and several Matisses. The room was floor to ceiling with canvases. Millions of dollars worth of art in this one room alone, and, according to Jean-François, the entire house was like this.

Tante Helga broke in on her thoughts. "Cynthia, I see you are admiring my pictures."

"Oh, yes. They are beautiful. It's like being in a private museum."

"Would you like to wander around the hallways and look?"

"I would love to!" Cynthia stood and excused herself. The stairway was lined with paintings, every inch of the corridor's walls was covered. Cynthia was amazed at the work she recognized. Name after name popped into her head. She imagined Miss Crew, of her Rosemary Hall days, screaming in ecstasy. Cynthia was staring up at a Renoir when she sensed a presence behind her.

Tante Helga spoke. "Do you like that one in particular?"

"It's so lovely. The colors, that idea of sunlight on the girl's dress . . ." Cynthia sighed. "Yes, I do like it very much."

"You really like it?" asked the older woman again.

"Of course I like it! It's exquisite."

She turned and saw Frau Doktor Schweitzer smiling. "You know, Cynthia, I haven't given Jean-François and you a wedding present."

Cynthia could hardly believe her ears. She stood stock-still and waited.

"If you really like that Renoir, I will give it to you."

The girl said nothing. She could hear her heart beating in her ears.

Tante Helga had called for Rolf, her only servant in the huge house. Rolf was told something in German, and returned instantly, holding some sort of box.

Cynthia thought he would take tools from it and perhaps remove the canvas from the frame. But no, he had opened the wooden box, and Tante Helga was looking for something. Cynthia thought the box was filled with cards, file cards. She was confused.

"Aah!" came the cry from Tante Helga. "Here you are, my dear. Your wedding present."

Cynthia took the postcard and looked at it in amazement. It was a reproduction of the Renoir that hung above them.

CHAPTER THIRTEEN

Cynthia

Les Colombiers

Young Madame Colbert put away the fuchsia silk blouse and the diamond pin. When her clothes came from home, she hung the brightest in one wardrobe and anything neutral or pastel in another. Much of her trousseau from the best shops in Boston went into the first wardrobe. She held up the fur coat and stared at it—a present from her mother, who had said she was far too young for it at eighteen, but it had been recut from one of her own. "That's not extravagant!" Cynthia said aloud in the dressing room.

If anything was extravagant, it was the number of rooms in the chateau. And all of them needed replastering, repainting, wallpaper, and rugs and furniture. Jean-François had a pied-à-terre in town she had not yet seen. That was where he had lived until the wedding. Renovations at the chateau would begin now, working around the newly married couple. The biggest decision to be made was where to begin. The roof leaked in the west wing, and the wooden floors in several rooms on the top floor had buckled with the onslaught of the last hundred rainstorms.

Cynthia had found it hard to be enthusiastic when Jean-François gave her the tour. "Why don't we just live in part of it?" she suggested, but to her surprise he wanted all of it restored to its former glory. "But the heating bills alone—"

"Whose money is it?" he snapped.

Cynthia felt her face go pink. He'd never spoken to her that way before. She said, "Well, it's yours, but—"

"*Oui*. Mine," he said. His lips were pressed together tightly as he looked up at the water damage on the ceiling.

Cynthia followed his gaze and thought the dark, discolored spot hung over them both like a horrible gray cloud. Something felt heavy in her chest as she followed him silently down the stairs. Following, she said to herself. I simply do everything he tells me. Because he knows more, because he's older?

His voice cut into her thoughts. He was standing beside a fireplace in what had been an upstairs drawing room. "I want to make something very clear, now that the subject's come up." He leaned against the carved mantel, which desperately needed to be stripped, refinished, and polished, and slowly, methodically folded his arms over his chest. "The money. Household money, anything you spend. All you have to do is ask for it. I'll give it to you."

Doesn't sound so ominous, she thought. Why do I feel so tight inside? Cynthia looked down at the toes of her new blue suede pumps and thought, He'll never know how much these cost. Neither will my father. We don't do things this way. We. Meaning Mother and I. Meaning my family. Now I am part of a new one. Jean-François and I are a family.

"Just come to me and tell me how much it costs." His voice was firm.

Cynthia was reminded of her father explaining how her allowance would work. A quarter a week, he had said. Just come to me and ask. Just in case I forget.

"I'll keep the checkbooks in order. I'm used to it. It's easier. You won't have to worry about balancing accounts or checking figures." He smiled. "Don't look so gloomy. You know I'll probably spoil you rotten."

He unfolded his arms and held out a hand to her. She found herself unable to smile as he pulled her to him. His warm mouth was kissing her neck gently. Cynthia had her eyes open and was looking out the window behind him. A milestone had been passed. Something important had happened, and she had tacitly accepted it. No cry of protest, no argument. She reached up to kiss his lips and thought, He's older than I am, but I'll have to teach him my ways. Somehow.

· · ·

The idea was far too optimistic, because the subject was far more complicated than money. "It has something to do with being French," she was told when she had lunch with Comtesse Devereaux. "Just Veronique," the Comtesse had insisted immediately. Now she was saying, "A lot of Frenchmen are like that. Not every single one"—she held up a finger—"but lots of them. It makes them nervous when a wife has her own money."

Cynthia looked at the woman's carefully made-up face. She was undeniably good looking and had been the most attractive woman at the luncheon the previous Thursday. Summer had flown by with days of commandeering workmen at the house and evenings of long dinners with Jean-François and the occasional client he brought home. Now that autumn was here, Cynthia had begun at last to meet women her own age.

"I can talk about it, because I am absolutely seven hundred percent French. We're known for our stinginess." Cynthia laughed, and Veronique went on. "Like Scots and Jews. We are the last to pay for anything." She sipped her wine carefully, so as not to smudge her lipstick on the rim of the glass. Her auburn hair was caught in a low ponytail at the nape of her neck, and tied in a black velvet bow. The black cashmere sweater-dress was nipped in at the waist with a wide black and brown suede belt. Cynthia wished she'd worn something with a little more flair than her dark blue suit and white silk blouse.

"But what does it matter if I know what's in the checking account or not? Does he think I'm going to fight with him and run away to Rio?" The American was perplexed.

"Oh, what a good idea! To get out of this dump! And take our waiter with you," whispered Veronique with a sideways glance at the tall Spaniard to their left.

Cynthia was shocked. Veronique was married and had three children, though she was only twenty-five or twenty-six years old. "You don't like Geneva?" was all she could manage.

Veronique's wide face was horrified; her brown eyes flashed. "Like it? Am I supposed to like it here?"

"Well . . ."

"Louis dragged me from Paris. Because of his bank, of course. From Paris to Geneva! Do you know Paris?" she asked intently, leaning forward.

"Well enough, I guess."

"From Paris to Geneva is like . . ." She rolled her eyes. "It's like drinking your last glass of champagne and being told you will only drink milk for the rest of your life." Leaning back dramatically in the velvet chair, she announced to everyone in the Café de les Bergues dining room, "Skim milk!"

Cynthia laughed. "Oh, come on! It can't be that bad! Look at the lake! Think of—"

Veronique's voice dropped. "I *have* looked at the lake. I have looked and looked and looked at it. I can see it from every room in the house. I see it all the time, and I feel like putting stones in my coat pockets and walking right into it."

"You're not serious!" Cynthia loved the lake. From that first moment in Jean-François's arms. Of course, she'd glimpsed it from the car, but she wanted always to remember his showing it to her that first day in the chateau through the glass of the French doors.

"No. I'm not." Veronique was smiling suddenly. "I have only one thing to keep me amused in Geneva, and he keeps me from total insanity."

Their plates were taken away. "Louis?" Cynthia asked, and was met with a burst of laughter.

"Oh, my poor, sweet dear!" said Veronique in a tone of voice that Cynthia suddenly detested. It was condescending, full of innuendo. "He's . . . he's someone you probably know. This town is highly incestuous. I won't tell you, but you'll probably hear it."

"Is he married?" Cynthia's voice was cool. She wanted to erase the stigma of innocence in the eyes of this Frenchwoman, who seemed suddenly decades older.

"But of course! That's what makes it even more fun."

Cynthia had nothing to say. The bill came and she said, "Now, about money . . ." and Veronique laughed.

"I'll pay this time. It was my idea to meet, and you can do it next time." She tightened the black velvet bow and said, "Besides, I have to redeem myself in the light of all I said about the French being stingy."

"Seriously, Veronique. This situation with money and French husbands. If it's not about money, the amount of money, what a wife would do with it—" She took a deep breath. "Then what *is* it all about?"

Veronique looked at her with wide brown eyes and red lipsticked mouth, and said very distinctly, "It's about owning you. It's about power." She started to reach for her voluminous black suede bag, and stopped. "Worst of all, it's about control."

"Control?" Cynthia repeated.

Veronique nodded. "Many French husbands want a well-dressed, well-groomed little doll. And they want to control her." She put down the exact amount of Swiss francs. "And money is control." They both stood to leave the table, and as they were swished through glass revolving doors out onto the sidewalk, Cynthia tried again. "But Jean-François is not really French. He says he's Swiss."

Veronique laughed. "The worst of both worlds, I'm afraid!"

Cynthia thought of the Genevois she was meeting at dinner parties. She had so many questions to ask.

"Let me ask you one thing," Veronique began. "Did you tell him we were having lunch together?"

"Sure."

"And did he ask where?"

Cynthia nodded again. She had felt so strange this morning, as though she were asking permission.

"And did he then give you enough francs to pay for our lunch?"

Cynthia nodded miserably. She had hated it.

Veronique saw the agony in the younger woman's face, and put her hand on her arm. "Me too. Same thing. Probably synchronized. Eight minutes after eight. Now look." Her voice was softer. Cynthia was looking at her shoes. "You just got married, and you can deal with it."

Cynthia felt rage. "How can I deal with being treated like a child?"

"*Très, très facile*. Simple." She smiled brightly. "Just tell him you paid for our lunch. Then put the money away."

Cynthia smiled in spite of herself.

"And do it every chance you get!" Veronique kissed her on both cheeks and started to walk across the street. Then she half-ran back to where Cynthia still stood on the Quai du Mont Blanc, beside the lake. "I'll be late for my rendezvous with the dentist if I don't hurry, but listen! I will pay the bill in cash and later, maybe next week, tell Louis that it was ten francs more than it was!"

. . .

"I don't know if I really like her," Cynthia found herself confiding to Jean-François at dinner that evening. The dining room was nearly there, she thought, eyeing the chandelier that was to be hung the next morning. It was wrapped in bands of brown paper and lay on the floor in the candlelight like some mummified octopus.

"She's a very physically attractive person," Jean-François said.

Cynthia looked away from his face, hoping he couldn't see her expression. She felt uneasy with the description. Maybe I'm jealous, she thought. Or maybe I was silly enough to think that I'm the only "type" my husband would find attractive. "Oh, you think so?" she asked in what she hoped was a noncommittal tone.

Jean-François nodded. Cynthia waited for him to say that Veronique was too outspoken, too aggressive, but to her surprise he didn't. "She has spirit. She's—what would an American say? Gutsy!"

No one has ever called me that, Cynthia thought. Perhaps that was why she said what she said next. She knew as she said it that she was being mean. "She's having an affair." Was she violating a confidence? Veronique had been very decent to give her all the money advice. But Cynthia wanted desperately for Jean-François to take back his compliments, to reassess his estimate of Veronique.

"Oh, everyone knows that!" he laughed. "It's her way of coping with Louis. He can't be very much fun in bed."

Cynthia felt as young as she had at lunch. "Nobody at home talks about it like that. They just"—she shrugged—"don't."

"They have affairs in Boston, don't they?" he teased. "Don't proper Bostonians go to bed with each other?" His voice was full of fun, and made Cynthia smile.

"I guess they do. The population keeps growing." She wondered if he had ever heard about her mother. "You know about the Kendall family scandal, don't you?"

His dark eyes twinkled. "Oh, that weekend you ran away with a Swiss banker to New York? *That* Kendall family scandal?"

She laughed, remembering her mother packing for her. Then she became serious. "No, there's another one."

"The reason you were in the Bahamas all that time?"

Cynthia swallowed. No. Don't tell him. She could see her mother before her, waving red warning flags like someone in a jumpsuit on the track at the Indy 500. "I told you a million times, I had mono. What a colossal bore it was! Can't think of a nicer place to recuperate, though." Stop here, she told herself. Don't go on and on about it. It makes it too important. "The story about my mother."

He shook his head.

"I came in late one night from a party in Edgartown . . ." She so totally tuned out thoughts of Marco, of losing her virginity, that even she was surprised at what the human mind could manage. I am telling one story, and the other one has been wafted away like dandelion fuzz. "I heard Mother calling . . ."

Her voice broke when she came to the part about her mother's lover having died in bed. Cynthia took a gulp of wine. "I—I couldn't believe that he was so cold. And then to discover that it was Uncle Teddy!"

Jean-François was silent. Then he stood up and walked to her end of the long dining-room table and gently took her hand. She followed him into the living room, not speaking until he handed her a brandy. "I've never told anyone this story before," she said between quick sips of the warming alcohol.

"No one?"

She shook her head. "I think going to college for only a semester simply erased all potential friends from my life. There was really no one, after Rosemary Hall, that I could talk to." She thought of how close she and her prep-school roommate, Sophie, had been. But Sophie's excitement at being a UCLA freshman was a world away from the long days of someone who'd dropped out of Smith, from someone on an island in the Bahamas waiting for a baby to be born and forbidden to talk about it. Cynthia remembered the two terrible, awkward telephone calls she'd made from Nassau and her vow not to call Sophie again. "And so I guess I kept it all inside." She smiled ruefully over the rim of the brandy snifter. "In order to keep certain things from Mother."

"Aaah!" said Jean-François, pretending to stroke a nonexistent beard. "Vut vould Doktor Freud say about your muzzer?" He sat down beside her on the ugly couch.

"Don't ask me." Cynthia wondered so many things about her mother, but had never felt close enough to her to ask questions, and had never come close to any answers on her own. Most of them, she realized, were about sexuality.

"Funny thing," Jean-François said.

"What's funny?"

"Your mother. She's a very attractive person in the way she dresses and takes care of herself, but she's so orderly, so correct . . ."

"So dogmatic. So take-charge, is what you're trying to diplomatically step around!"

"*Oui.*" He sipped the brandy and tilted his head back. "And you say your father's brother was quite meek, that the only strong decision he'd ever made was to become a Catholic priest . . ."

Cynthia sat up very straight. "What are you getting at?"

"I'm just wondering if maybe your mother doesn't get her kicks from dominating men."

She didn't answer. Her father was certainly an unhappy man. Constantly criticized. Yes. *Dominated* was the word. Her mother had a laundry list of his shortcomings that she could recite at the first sign of a "discussion."

He went on. "What a person to pick to have an affair with! When you think of it—it makes no sense at all."

"Mother wouldn't sleep with anyone who didn't have a good family name," said Cynthia dryly.

Jean-François roared with laughter. "What about her daughter?" he laughed.

Cynthia swallowed and felt the warmth of the brandy in her throat. God. Does he know? Somehow, does he know? She began to cough, and he leaned over and patted her on the back until she got her breath again.

"Is all this talk of sex upsetting you?" he teased, taking the glass from her, then taking her hand and pulling her to her feet. "It's having an effect on me."

Cynthia looked up at his smiling face, and allowed him to kiss her. "It's good to talk this way," she said. "We haven't lately."

But for her husband the time for talk was over. He led her toward the stairs, holding her hand firmly. Like a little girl, not anxious to leave the lights and the talk for bed, Cynthia held back and wondered why her feet felt so heavy, why her body felt as if it no longer belonged to her.

.   .   .

Henry IV was assassinated in 1610, Cynthia wrote in the blue notebook on her lap. *Then came the rise to power of Cardinal Richelieu.* "Which, in short," she said aloud to the empty library, "was really and truly super bad news for the French Protestants." *Henry IV's Edict of Nantes was revoked by Louis XIV in 1685, causing the Huguenots to flee France in great numbers. They arrived in Geneva with marketable skills and a sense of diligence.* "Hmm," said Cynthia. "That's when the watchmaking and the textile industries began." *Bankers prospered while financing the extravagant excesses of Louis XIV.*

Brigitte entered the room with a silver teapot on a silver tray. "Madame? Would you like tea?"

When she had gone, Cynthia retrieved yet another book from the pile on the large leather couch. Geneva was the birthplace of Jean-Jacques Rousseau and the adopted city of Voltaire, she read. "In 1536, Jean Calvin, who had been trained in law, theology, and humanism, came to Geneva." He was to leave again, and then be persuaded to return. "In less than thirty years he had profoundly altered the character of the market town, making it a disciplined state. The government was formed by strict interpretation of the Bible. Calvin's Geneva was a bridge to the French-speaking communities. The fact that the two religions balanced each other was a deterrent against the entire Confederacy becoming involved in religious wars in Europe."

Cynthia turned the page and realized that this must have been the beginning of Swiss neutrality. She had already read of Swiss boys leaving the country to become mercenaries in wars fought elsewhere on the Continent, because there was poverty at home and no chance to change their lives. The Thirty Years War had been fought between France and the Habsburgs—with many Swiss mercenaries, who could attain a military rank and have a good career irrespective of their family or local status.

She opened the largest book to the bookmark. "In 1815 the five Great Powers, which were Britain, Austria, France, Prussia and Russia, issued a declaration on the subject of the integrity of Swiss territory. They recognized permanent neutrality."

The light was fading. Jean-François would be home soon. The last volume concerned Switzerland in the twentieth century: "Henri Dunant founded the International Red Cross after seeing the suffering of soldiers in the Italian War of Independence." The Red Cross building stood between Chambesy and Geneva, near the United Nations European headquarters. "After World War I, the Great Powers gathered at Versailles to sign a peace treaty. It was here that they decided to attempt to solve future disputes between governments through an organization that was to be called the League of Nations. It was the American president, Woodrow Wilson, who wanted Geneva as the site." Cynthia remembered Jean-François pointing out the building to her. "But when World War II broke out, the League collapsed. In 1945 the United Nations decided to have only 'victorious' countries as members, and neutral Switzerland was of course left out. New York became the world headquarters of the United Nations."

The door opened, but Cynthia didn't hear it. She screamed when she felt the arms around her and turned, her knees tucked under her on the couch, to face a laughing Jean-François. "You terrified me!"

He bent and kissed the back of her neck once more. "Your hair always smells like the sun. How can I stop myself?"

"Are you in the Swiss Army?" she demanded when he raised his head.

"Of course I am." He came around and sat beside her, putting one hand on her knee. "Several weeks a year, I will be away from my beautiful American wife—"

"This book says that after the Second World War, Switzerland has never had less than one hundred thousand men under arms at any time." She stared at him, nibbling a pencil, waiting for him to confirm this. Her eyes were very green above the green sweater. "The largest permanent army in Europe."

That smile, which everyone invariably described as "boyish," lit his face. "*Oui.* It is about five hundred thousand men. And we are literally under arms. I have a pistol and ammunition upstairs. A pistol because I'm an officer. The enlisted men have something much bigger and heavier. Rather like a machine gun." Cynthia's face showed amazement. "I know it's strange for an American to imagine every man between eighteen and fifty required to have a gun in his house, but we are responsible for our equipment. The bullets are in a case, and someone comes and inspects it to make sure the seal has not been broken. The gun has to be taken care of, kept clean and always in good condition. My uniform is in the upstairs closet." He smiled when he saw her expression. "It's defensive, of course. It's to deter attack. Some airmen were killed in the last war, but no one else. Accidents." He pulled her to him and put his face against her breasts. One of the books slid off the couch and onto the floor with a thud, but neither of them paid any attention at all.

Fifteen minutes later, as they struggled into their clothes, Cynthia asked slyly, "Is this what they mean by 'dressing for dinner'?"

· · ·

The screaming woke her, and probably woke the servants on the floor above, too. Jean-François was sitting up in bed, screaming himself awake, when Cynthia grabbed his shoulders and shook him into the conscious world, into their bedroom in the old chateau. "It's all right! It's all right!" she repeated as he rubbed his eyes and gasped for breath. Then he surveyed the shadowy room in the light of the bedside lamp, as though seeking monsters or ghosts.

Cynthia pulled all four of the pillows up against the headboard and reached around to rub his back. It was always the same. He would be covered in perspiration, nearly in tears, and panicked. She would stroke his back until he stopped shaking, and then they would lie down and press themselves together as closely as possible, like two teaspoons. After a while his breathing would quiet down, and she could turn off the lamp and hope that he would sleep soon after. And allow her to sleep.

Many times he reached for her in the aftermath of a nightmare, as though to affirm that he was still alive and not lost in some dark void. Cynthia wanted to give him warmth and caresses and comfort; she didn't understand why it had to be sex. The panting, the urgency, the inevitable cry at orgasm—it all seemed the opposite of what Cynthia wanted with him.

Now he turned to her and pulled at the hem of the silk nightgown. She thought, We made love only two hours ago, but she didn't push his hand away. She took a corner of the sheet and tenderly wiped the sweat from his

face as he began to stroke her thigh. "Darling, please . . ." she began, but
he was shushing her. "Please, tell me what you dream about. Tell me what
frightens you so much." One of his hands was between her legs now. "Maybe
it will help to talk a—"

"Cynthia!" His voice was insistent. "This will help. Not talk. Lie back. Lie
back," he insisted, until, reluctantly, she pulled the pillows away. She
never—not once—said no to him.

Les Colombiers

After the first six months of life in Geneva, Cynthia decided that the things
she had at first been attracted to in Jean-François were the very things that
were now wrong. His gentle, protective, let-me-take-care-of-you attitude suddenly became, "You don't know how to do anything, do you?"

"Where is the mail? Why don't I ever get to see it?" were the first words
out of his mouth one evening in the front hallway.

"Well, darling, I sorted it and took out what was for me, and put everything
else on your desk!" Cynthia stepped forward to put her arms around him. He
obviously had had something go terribly wrong today at the office.

Instead of putting down his briefcase and kissing her, he pushed past her,
saying, "I don't know why the simplest things can't be done my way! Why
do I want to walk all the way into my study to see what's in the mail?" His
face was an angry mask. "Does that make sense? Does it, Cynthia?"

She was too amazed to respond, but simply turned and went up the stairs
without a word.

"Can't you even answer a question!" he shouted at her retreating figure.

Dinner, an hour later, was silent. Course after course was served by the
new maid, who fairly rattled the dishes with nervousness. It was typical of
Cynthia to feel sorry for her.

As Jean-François dipped his spoon into the fruit compote, he said, "If you
could just manage things better, Cynthia."

She was almost paralyzed with surprise.

His voice was calm, reasonable, even sweet. "That's all I ask." It was the
voice of a martyr.

Cynthia decided to let the subject drop. She could not smile, but settled
for looking down at her wineglass and thinking, He must have had something
really unbearable to deal with at the bank. But he's home and this has blown
over. Maybe we'll have a cognac after dinner, and he'll relax and this will all
be nothing.

"Darling," he said suddenly, "you look absolutely ravishing in that shade
of pink. You must buy yourself lots of clothes in that color."

Cynthia looked at him. He couldn't say he was sorry in so many words. He was trying to apologize in his own way. She sipped from her wineglass and thought, Yes, darling. All is forgiven.

. . .

Cynthia Lake Kendall Colbert had learned at her mother's knee about running a house. She hadn't learned so much as *absorbed* the way to do things well. Margaret had managed the house in Beacon Hill and the house on the Vineyard as if they were small corporations.

Cynthia had always been a naturally organized person—an "A" student who always turned in her assignments on time, a girl who always had the right thing to wear in her closet.

Hence, when Jean-François found fault with little things, she boiled inside. Then she told herself that it was his house, that it was his money that ran it, that he had a right to have things done his way. She did everything he asked. The first time he mentioned it. "Don't let the maid put my dress shirts with the narrow pleats in with the wide-pleated ones." Fine. A little discussion about it, and Silvie was so quick. "I don't like orange juice in the small glasses." Fine. His place was set in the morning with a large one. "Don't allow the cook to butter the toast in the kitchen. I like to do it myself." A thousand details. But Cynthia said to herself, I love this man. This is the learning part of our marriage, this is the way he likes things. I can please him.

It was autumn in Geneva, and the air was fresh and the falling leaves were crisp underfoot. Earlier, Cynthia had been out with one of the gardeners, burning leaves, enjoying the smell, the sight of the orange flames as the sky darkened with the arrival of evening.

She had walked back toward the chateau, feeling refreshed and happy. She was lucky to have found Patrice. He loved the plants and was right on schedule with moving everything into the greenhouse before the really cold weather came. Cynthia rubbed her arms with her hands to get warm, and thought what a beautiful day it had been. The lake was a sheet of molten brass at the edge of the lawn, and the chateau's windows were little squares of gold in the fading afternoon light. The sun was setting behind the Jura.

She went in through the kitchen door to scrape the mud off her shoes, and then saw Jean-François in the front hallway. "You must come out and see the sun—" she began.

"Where have you been?" he shouted.

"Why, I—"

"I come home and you're not even here! Not only that, but no one is sure where you are! The mistress of the house, the chatelaine, has just wandered off! Disappeared!" His handsome face was dark with anger.

"Now you wait a minute!" she shouted back. "I was in the garden. I didn't just wander off!"

"Is that how you spend your days? Wandering in the garden?" he sneered. "Don't you have enough to do?"

She fell for it. "I have plenty to do, and some of it happens to do with the garden!"

"Well, I agree with you! You have plenty to do." His voice dropped into sarcasm.

"What is wrong? What is upsetting you?" she insisted. "I want it out in the open right now!"

"Oh, nothing," he said softly, but she could see the rage in his eyes. He looked down at her with his nose in the air, his head tilted back. He was holding a handful of letters.

"What has made you so angry?" she asked in a tight, controlled voice. Only yesterday he had been sharply critical of how long she spent in the bathtub. She had not allowed herself to be angry back.

He flung the letters over his head, and they fell in white rectangles all over the Persian rug. Then he shouted, "Pick them up! Pick them up and sort them! Or don't you have time to do the simplest things in this house! The most minor little things escape you because you have 'so much to do'!"

Cynthia turned away from him then to go up the stairs. "Don't you dare treat me like a servant!" she said in a cold voice as she started up the staircase. Her hand was damp with perspiration on the polished wood banister.

"Is it too much to ask that you put what I need to see on my desk in my study? Is that too much of a challenge for you?"

Cynthia went up to the room she called "hers," and closed and locked the door. She didn't feel like crying, she felt like throwing up. Who is this man? Whom did I marry? she asked herself as she looked out at the lake, which was fast disappearing from sight in the darkness. With tears in her eyes, she suddenly thought, It's not even the ocean out there. I'm so far from the ocean, and not even just on the other side of it from Boston. I'm smack dab in the middle of Europe, beside a little lake, in a chateau with a man I don't know.

Cynthia cried then, and as she was blowing her nose and wondering if she could survive dinner without tears, she suddenly thought of Crosby Hyatt III and began to laugh. I danced with Crosby practically every dance of my life until I met Jean-François. What a choice I had! Someone new and exciting and stimulating or Crosby—good, old, always-there Crosby. Marco flashed into her mind—his black hair blowing in the wind. Blue sky behind him. "Stop it!" she said aloud to no one. Then she walked to the bureau and reached for a hairbrush and lipstick. The mirror told her she looked fine. She slammed the drawer closed, checked her watch, and left her sanctuary. Cynthia walked, slowly, with head held high, down the stairs, through the main hall, and into the dining room.

CHAPTER FOURTEEN

Iris

1971 — Miami Beach

"So this is Miami!" enthused Iris. "Wow!" She was pressing her face against the little round window of the Delta jet. Royal blue water a thousand feet below looked solid, with waves and whitecaps unmoving as though the very Atlantic itself were an endless piece of canvas, an oil painting. Iris turned around. "I'm so glad you had this business trip!" Iris pushed her breasts against Harry's arm.

Two hours later they were curled up in the double bed of the newest hotel in Miami Beach. The Towers, it was called, and tower it did, over all the other hotels. Its lobby was a fantasy of white leather and burled wood; its hallways were covered, even the walls, with white shag. "Yikes!" Iris had screamed when they had stepped off the elevator. "I think it's alive!"

Harry had laughed, "Wait till midnight. Then this stuff undulates like undersea creatures." The white ceiling had inset spotlights that shone down every ten feet and reminded him of Jimmy Durante saying good night to Mrs. Calabash at the end of his television show.

Harry was sleeping deeply, as he always did after Iris took care of him. She watched his large stomach go up and down, up and down, for about ten minutes, and then slithered off the white quilted spread to what should have been the floor. She fell off the platform on which the bed stood like an altar, and with a stifled curse got up carefully, quietly. Then she showered, and putting on one of her new "backless, frontless, sideless little numbers" and her gold spike-heeled sandals with ankle straps, she eased herself out the door. This hall, she thought, shaking her head. It's as if it's been lined with Dennis the Menace's dog's fur. She stood beside the elevator and spritzed on about half an ounce of Joy. The doors opened, and she stepped in on a veritable cloud of perfume.

So sure was she of the admiration she evoked, she did not even glance at the three men who stared at her alabaster breasts, pressing upward and outward over the top of the parrot green jersey dress. Six eyes fairly popped with appreciation when they traveled down her long legs to the little feet in the high heels. Iris tossed her platinum hair disdainfully and turned her back to them, giving them an even more heart-stopping view. Her round bottom, obviously unencumbered by panties, looked firm and smooth under the skimpy dress.

The oldest of the three men was quite bald, maybe fifty-five, and a bit overweight. He pulled a handkerchief from the pocket of his yellow nylon polo shirt and wiped his shining pink pate.

The second one nodded and said, "Yeah, a heat spell in Miami's nothin' to fool around with."

The two stocky men wore madras sportcoats and black trousers and black city shoes. They could have been over-the-hill boxers gone to fat; they had the necks that athletes get ten years later, when the competition's over.

The third man, whom they called Cesare, was much younger; it was his twenty-fifth birthday, and there was to be a dinner for two hundred in the Towers ballroom that evening. Afterwards, he would celebrate again in his suite on the top floor with two hookers his father had paid for.

Cesare had a smooth olive complexion, an aquiline nose, and nearly black eyes, faintly hooded. He wore a gray sharkskin suit that shone one way in the artificial lights of the hotel and another way in the sunlight by the pool. The open-necked scarlet silk shirt showed a handful of chest hair and a single gold chain that looked heavy and expensive. It had been paid for by the gram in a shop in Beirut. He, unlike the others, was lithe and tight and sinewy. The others apparently worked for him.

In five minutes, Cesare had ordered a banana daiquiri for Iris, and after another she had decided yes, she would go to bed with him. The green dress rode up her creamy thighs as she perched on the barstool covered with fake zebra skin and smiled. "So, who ya down here with?" Cesare was asking. The accent was unadulterated Brooklynese.

"My father," she answered demurely as she fixed her lush pink lips around the pink and white candy-cane-striped straw.

"Like hell!" he laughed. "No father would let you dress like that!" He sucked in a breath as he glanced quickly at her round high breasts.

"Let me?" Iris echoed. "You think someone has to *let me* do what I want?" She took another sip of the drink.

He smiled slowly, lazily. Iris thought, with a catch in her throat as the cold, sweet drink went down, He looks like Cutter. He has hooded eyes and that mouth that takes just a few seconds less than forever to really get to be a smile.

Iris became the tough little cookie she had stopped being with Harry. "I always do what I want," she said in a low voice.

Cesare grinned and almost put his hand on her plump, little pink knee, but stopped himself.

Three daiquiris later, Iris was doing what she wanted, while Harry snored on on the twenty-seventh floor.

· · ·

They went at it like athletes. They sweated and with racing hearts went faster, then stopped on the brink of orgasm, then began again slowly, ever so slowly. Carefully gauging how much he could take, how much pleasure he could feel without exploding yet again, Cesare moved back and forth above Iris like a man holding his breath and counting to a hundred. He kept his mouth closed and breathed through his nose while Iris's mouth was open when she didn't have her lips pressed somewhere against him. She cried out often; he never did.

Before he fell asleep, he held her face in his hands and said urgently, "I love you! Do you understand me? I love you."

Iris shook her head. She hadn't believed any man who'd told her that between Cutter and Harry. No one had loved her the way Cutter had. Harry loved her the way he would love a daughter who pleased him, but Cutter . . . and Cesare . . . The intensity was the same, and there was also the matter of the hooded eyes. Her face was flushed from the exertion of lovemaking, her eyes bright green with excitement.

"No," she whispered, but even as she said the word, her mind whirled ahead, wondering what it would be like to be loved by someone like Cesare, by someone who made her remember Cutter and the way she had felt with him.

"But I do! I love you! I don't even know your name, and I love you." He sounded angry.

"You don't know me. I'm twenty-one years old and I'm from nowhere . . ."

"I'll be twenty-five tomorrow, and I don't care where you came from. You're here with me now."

Iris looked into the dark eyes, stared at the mouth that had done wonderful things to that place between her legs. "No."

"Damn you!" He stroked her white-gold hair, splayed over her shoulders. "I want to marry you." The voice was deep, serious.

Iris thought of all the times she'd wanted to marry Harry. For his money.

For the apartment. So that if he died, his wife wouldn't get her dressing table. She narrowed her eyes to little slits and said, "Why?"

He laughed then. "Are you that hard? Have you been around that much?"

She didn't answer, but with the quiet, intense curiosity of a child, she put her palm flat against his chest and wiggled her fingers in the hair. Just feeling it. He watched her and thought how uninhibited she was, how free, how happy to be naked. "I want to marry you," he said again as she curled up beside him and closed her eyes. "Think about it." That great need for sleep after being thoroughly satisfied was heavy upon him, like a drug. Iris said nothing, but nestled under his arm with her cheek against his chest. In seconds they were both fast asleep.

· · ·

At six o'clock, Iris opened the door of 2709 and called, "Harry! I'm back! Are you awake yet?"

Harry stepped through the open sliding glass door that led to their balcony, and smiled. He was wearing white double-knit trousers and white loafers and a blue and white sport shirt patterned with turquoise palm trees. They waved their fronds back and forth over his broad torso. "Where were you, baby? I've been missing you."

She flung her arms around him and kissed him, praying he didn't smell soap or notice that some of her hair had gotten wet in the shower.

"Where've you been, baby? Whatcha been doing?"

Iris gave him one of her sweet-as-sugar, little-girl smiles. "Just lookin' around."

· · ·

"Is this all right, Harry? Do you think it's too, too . . . ?" Iris had poured herself into a sequined white sheath that glittered and sparkled silver every time she so much as breathed. When she tottered from behind the closet door across the room to the balcony, she was a twinkling star of spangles and light.

"Wow! Do you shimmer and shine!" was the reaction from Harry as he pulled at his maroon cummerbund. Iris, still unsure, turned in front of the full-length mirror and studied her back view, lips pursed with concentration. "Did you ever see that movie with Marilyn Monroe, *Some Like It Hot?*" Harry asked.

"I think I did," she murmured, looking at her bottom covered with sequins, thinking of how Cesare had brought her to orgasm after orgasm. Then thinking not of her own bottom, but of his. A white, tight, firm, muscular . . .

"Well, she wore a dress like that. Thin, almost like a see-through net, with little tiny sparkly things that went crazy whenever she moved . . ."

Iris almost asked who. She had missed something.

Harry was saying, "This is really important to me tonight, Iris. Be super nice to this man. He has big, big, big money to spend and he wants to put a little bit in the theater. I want him to like me and you so much that he'll want to put a lot in. I want him to back *Turn Left at Paradise*. The whole show, think of it! And I want him to like me so much that I can direct. And you can probably have the part of Melissa just for the asking, just on account of the way you look."

"Wait a minute!" She turned with fire in her eyes.

"Oh, baby! I didn't mean it like that! You know I think you're a fine actress! It's just that the first thing people notice is how you look, and you look like Melissa should look." Harry talked with a desperate edge to his voice. He didn't want a fight with Iris, tonight of all nights. He needed her tonight.

Mollified, she went back to applying the third coat of gray mascara, then she dabbed on silver eye shadow. Iris preened for a few more minutes as Harry fussed with his bow tie. Then, satisfied at last, and remembering this afternoon's success, she spritzed herself up and down from bouffant hair to the tips of her toes with perfume.

"Thattagirl, baby! Oh, you are a knockout! And remember, just pour on the charm with this guy!" Harry swatted her on the rear and she yelped as they went out the door. "Remember how important he is to us, and remember how rich he is! Just gobble him up, baby!"

. . .

She did.

This isn't a bad assignment at all, she thought when she first saw him. Vito was short, just a few inches taller than she, but solid-looking, in his early fifties, sunburned, with a face that said, *Don't play with me*. He was rough-spoken and nouveau riche, which didn't faze Iris a bit—it was the *riche* part that was important. She decided he was handsome in a Kirk Douglas kind of way. His white dinner jacket was well tailored and looked brand new, as did the pale blue shirt, which made his skin seem even more bronzed. His cuff links were little horseshoes made of diamonds. Iris could hardly glance away from them.

"Where did you find this gorgeous gal?" he crowed to Harry for the third time.

Iris looked down at her plate and smiled. Her breasts were nearly leaping right out of her bodice, and she glanced down once in a while to make sure her nipples weren't exposed. Everything but that, she said to herself.

"She's an actress. Found her in the theater. I was thinking of having Iris play the part of—"

"More champagne!" Their host put up his hand, and three men in dark business suits seated nearby rose as one to make sure a waiter was given the message immediately.

"Gee," Iris observed, "you sure have a lot of assistants."

He roared with laughter at this, throwing his head back and showing perfect white teeth. They look sharp, thought Harry, wondering how he could get him a little less interested in Iris and a little more interested in Broadway. "A man in my position needs lots of . . . assistants," Vito replied. Ignoring Harry, he put his hand on Iris's and asked her to dance.

The ballroom of the Towers boasted a thirty-two-piece orchestra that was playing a Lawrence Welk-y version of "Yesterday" every third song. Every second song was "Strangers in the Night." Iris felt young and out of place when the man led her in between the round tables. Men were standing and practically bowing from the waist as they went by, and Vito nodded in recognition, this way and that. A little bit like a king, thought Iris. "Does everyone know you?" she asked as he put his arm around her waist on the dance floor.

"Well, ya see, it's my party." He pressed her against him very firmly, and she felt the three diamond studs in his dress shirt, cold against her bare breast. In spite of herself, in spite of that afternoon with Cesare, Iris was conscious of wetness between her legs. Was it the scent of him, or the muscles in his arms, or his voice? She didn't know, but something about him was arousing her. "The guest of honor ain't arrived yet. Said he had to take a nap. He'll be here any minute."

The music was slow, soulful. Iris allowed herself to be held very tightly and realized that Vito was aroused, too. She wondered if Harry would think this was going too far. The orchestra stopped for a few seconds at the end of that number, and Iris waited for him to release her, but he did not. Then came the strains of "Saying Something Stupid Like I Love You."

"I like you," he said, putting his face in her hair. "I really like you, Iris." She smiled and didn't answer. He went on. "Will you fly to the Bahamas with me tomorrow?"

She drew away from him then and demanded, "What about Harry?"

"What about Harry?" He shrugged. "He wants money for the show. I'll give it to him." He smiled slowly. "In exchange for you."

"I'm not a doll!" she retorted angrily. She tried to pull her hand out of his, tried to jerk away from his grasp around her waist. But he was very strong.

"I know you're not. There are plenty of dolls in this town, and you ain't one a' them." He pulled her back to him, and she again, unmistakably, felt him against the thin dress. "That's why I wanna get ta know ya better."

"I'm tired of dancing." Her voice was cold. "Let go."

He did. Elaborately shrugging broad shoulders in the white dinner jacket, he raised his thick black eyebrows. Iris hated herself for finding him very sexy, and turned to find her way between the tables. But she felt such power in the staring eyes behind her that she revolved back to him. His face was impassive, his mouth tight. "Don't walk away from me," he said sternly.

Iris was amused at his show of muscle; she was teasing. "Are you afraid people will think you're a bad dancer?"

"No. I ain't afraid a' nothin'."

Iris thought she'd gotten away from men who said "ain't," but Vito was different. Maybe the difference was that he said "ain't" and he didn't fix cars or work in a diner. He said "ain't," but he had money and he was giving a party in the ballroom of the Towers Hotel. So Vito was different; Vito was also the key to Harry's play. "Not even me?" she flirted, and then put out her arms again to dance.

When he pulled her to him a little bit roughly, she liked it. Harry treated her like fine china, and Cesare had treated her like a female animal. Cesare. Cesare. Vito's cold diamond studs made her stiffen, and when she did, the strong hand around her tiny waist pressed even more tightly. Iris felt his heart beating, sensed the quickened breathing. They danced in silence as closely as possible. He was conscious of the softness of her, the perfume, the hair like silk against his cheek, the white breasts like perfect little pillows against his chest.

"I got a plane tomorrow at ten. My plane. You comin' wid me or not?"

She shook her head, which was difficult to do, so close was she to him.

"I wanna make love to you."

She managed to tilt her face up toward his. Her breath was sweet in his face. "So do lots of men. So what?"

"I ain't lotsa men."

She actually felt a pulse in his erection, hard as a rock against her thigh, and said in a Mae West voice, "I guess you're not."

His laugh was deep. It was a wild kind of laugh; it seemed to release things he couldn't say.

"Ya happy ta be in Miami?"

She shrugged as though it were her one hundredth time, but she didn't fool him. Her green eyes were excited as they scanned the ballroom, taking in everything. She had sat up so straight at dinner and hesitated over when to begin eating the shrimp cocktail, looking back and forth at the others at the table before lifting her fork.

Assistants, thought Vito. That was kinda cute of her. Assistants and their bimbos of the moment. Cocktail waitresses picked up in the afternoons at places down the highway. The occasional stripper from a Miami topless joint. Sleaze. All of them. And this Iris. A natural blonde, at last. A little goddess. How the hell did Harry, this two-bit Harry, end up with her? That didn't matter now. "What about Vegas? Been to Vegas?" She shook her head. "What about L.A.? Rome?"

"I haven't been to L.A., but a friend at school came from Rome. She said the weather there was just terrible."

Vito looked puzzled. "Terrible?"

"You wouldn't believe the snowstorms, and it keeps snowing right up to Easter, practically." She put her head against his shoulder again.

"Rome?" he boomed incredulously.

She nodded. Positive.

They continued to dance. "I'd like to take you to Italy with me. That's my favorite place. That's where I live most of the time."

"Oh! I love Italian food!"

"Will ya come ta Italy wid me?" he insisted. "Will ya let me buy ya lots of new clothes for the trip?"

Iris was not answering. Would she lose Harry if she went on a little trip to Italy? He'd told her to be nice to Vito. Big money. The play.

"I'll talk to Harry about it for you," he said. "Don't worry about Harry. He'll understand. Every girl should go to Italy—the food, the art, the culture." The last word came out "cul-chuh."

They danced to two more numbers and then slowly, dreamily walked back to the table. Iris was thinking of Italy and of the dampness in her lace panties, and Vito was wondering if a trip to the Bahamas would quench his thirst for her. He didn't mind springing for a trip to Italy, and he could just send her back when he was tired of her, but the Bahamas were a lot closer. He could be in bed with her by noon tomorrow. "Hey, howya doin'?" people were asking as he went by. "Big party, Vito! Great *festa!*" called a man in a pink sportcoat.

Iris reached Harry, who patted her bare shoulder like a proud papa, and she smiled radiantly at him then excused herself to go to the ladies' room. As she was crossing the lobby, which seemed to be an acre of white carpeting, she saw Cesare coming toward her. "Why did you leave? Why didn't you wake me? How could you disappear like that?" Cesare took her arm roughly. His eyes were bright, as black as onyx. His white dinner jacket emphasized his broad shoulders, his narrow hips.

"Let go!" Christ! she thought. These men in Miami are like gorillas.

"Answer me!" he demanded. "And tell me your name! And your room number and . . ." There was desperation in him. "Why did you leave?"

Iris said coolly, "Places to go. People to see."

He grinned then. Perfect white teeth in a darkly sunburned face. "Marry me. Marry me. Marry me."

His hand was still on her arm, and Iris felt the heat of him, the animal strength coursing through him into his fingers, into the strong thumb. "To-morrow. Meet me here. Nine o'clock."

She looked confused. *Marry me. Marry me.* The words echoed in her mind. He was so young.

"I'm late. I have to go." He kissed her full on the lips. His mouth was hot, his tongue soft. Iris's knees buckled under the sweet assault. He broke away and took a deep breath, then wiped her pink lipstick off his mouth with the back of his hand. "Tomorrow," he commanded. "Nine o'clock."

He walked away from her in a great hurry, without looking back. Iris clutched her silver evening bag with perspiring fingers. God. What a kiss. "Nine o'clock," she said aloud. I'll meet him, but I can't spend the day with him. Probably wants me to go swimming, and I'll have to make up an excuse to him—or to Harry. Iris tottered on the high heels toward the ladies' room. She missed the step down as she passed the reception desk, and that was where her left heel broke off. "Damn," she muttered.

A young Cuban bellhop took her arm and helped her to the elevator, fetching her room key with a wide smile. That was why she missed the excitement and the applause in the ballroom. After twenty minutes, Harry excused himself and went to look for her.

"Baby!" he crowed when he opened the door of their room and saw her on the floor of the closet, looking for shoes that would go with the dress. "Baby! He's backing the play! Whatever you did to him on the dance floor, you did it good! He's backing *Turn Left at Paradise,* lock, stock, and costume!" He fell to his knees and kissed her neck. Iris laughed. She was happy for him.

Harry decided to return to the dinner, but Iris said she was tired. He understood completely. Iris could lose her mind over what earrings to wear, so a broken heel on a shoe, on one shoe of the only pair that would possibly be all right with the silver spangle dress . . . well, Harry had known Iris long enough to take it in his stride. "Order some champagne," he advised, "and put on your nightgown and curl up in bed. This thing shouldn't go on much later than midnight. I'll tell Vito you weren't feeling too well. The long trip, you know."

Harry was actually relieved not to have Iris at the table with them. She was creating a bit too much of a stir. Why, she was a sensation! The other women looked like beat-up beauticians at best, hookers at worst. Piled with makeup, top-heavy with beehive hairdos, their black eyelashes clotted with mascara. The one seated on his other side actually had wrinkled breasts. But Iris was like . . . like a flower, he decided as he stepped out of the elevator. And Vito saw her and approved of my taste, Harry thought. And he decided to give me the money because I am a man of taste! Harry squared his shoulders and walked into the ballroom, proud and happy.

· · ·

Iris brushed her teeth, thinking of his smile. She took a shower and soaping her hips, thought of Cesare's flat, iron-hard flanks. She dried herself, thinking of his hands on her body. She brushed her long blond hair, thinking of his hair, as black as a crow's wing—straight, fine hair. Then she thought, *Marry me, marry me,* and wondered what it would be like. Did he have money? He appeared to. They had made love in a suite on the top floor. That was nothing if not a New York accent, but where did he live?

Iris pulled on an ice blue peignoir and walked outside onto the balcony. She gazed out at the twinkling lights of Miami, awed at the view, at the expanse of sky over the ocean that was so unlike the skyscape of Manhattan. She smelled the salt of the sea and whispered, "Are you Cutter, come back to me?"

Harry had not returned at midnight, but Iris did not miss him. She wandered around the room, nightgown trailing behind her like the train of a wedding dress, thinking, wondering, fantasizing. At one o'clock she curled up in the big double bed and slept.

Her dreams were of Cesare, of his lovemaking, and of the floating words in space, *Marry me. Marry me.* She awoke to find Harry's arm heavy across her shoulder. Moving it away, she got out of bed and once more was drawn to the balcony. The cool night breeze ruffled her hair and seemed to caress her bare arms and shoulders. Iris stood very still for a long time and wondered, Do I dare imagine that I could love this beautiful stranger the way I loved Cutter?

.   .   .

"Hairdresser," she was explaining. "Only time they could fit me in."

"But, baby, at nine o'clock, when we'll prob'ly be by the pool all day?"

"I need a trim. I'm not going to let them do much." She was stuffing her little makeup kit into the pink leather bag. The pink linen coat dress with gold buttons across the double-breasted front was perfect, she decided. Perfect for what, she wasn't sure. Perfect for nine o'clock in the lobby with Cesare. She kissed Harry good-bye and said she'd call him if there was a big wait at the beauty parlor. "You can't ever tell how organized these people are. They get behind, you know." Then she dashed out of the room and down the fuzzy hallway.

Iris quickly repaired her lipstick with a little brush as she stared into the shiny chrome frame around the elevator door. By the time the door whooshed open, Iris was perfect. A dream of a blond, immaculately groomed, well dressed, pink with anticipation. If he has money, she decided as she watched the little lit numbers above the door go *ping-ping-ping* in downward sequence, I'll marry him. Harry will never marry me. I'll marry Cesare, but only if he has money.

She stepped out, heart beating quickly. Love doesn't last without it, she reminded herself.

He was where he said he would be. In white trousers and a white silk shirt and the gold chain. Iris thought he looked like a rock star, a movie star. Too beautiful to be anything but out of reach. A magazine cover. It's because I've gotten used to Harry, she told herself. And he's old.

Cesare kissed her on each cheek, which she thought was odd, and then slipped his arm around her waist, guiding her toward two overstuffed cream leather armchairs afloat on the fuzzy ocean of white carpet. "We don't have much time," was the first thing he said.

"Why not?" Iris looked at his watch, and it said two minutes after nine.

"Because I want to tell you everything. Before nine-thirty."

Iris stared at the dark face, the mouth set with determination. She nodded. "So. I'm here."

"I'll be quick. First of all . . ." He sat down with their knees touching; Iris's little feet were tight together in the white leather pumps. "First of all, I want you. I want you as the mother of my children. Second, I'm going to be very, very rich in a few years. When I'm thirty."

Iris nodded. Her hair was smoothly brushed and full and golden in the shaft of light coming down from a window high in the three-story lobby. Her mind was absorbing key words. *Children. Money.* "Very rich," he went on. "Because of my father." He stopped and took one of her soft hands in his and held it as if it were a rare treasure. "Because my father has lots of businesses and is careful about taxes."

"What business is he in?"

Cesare bit his lip. "Everything. He deals in cash, though, so it's a little hard to explain. He has interests in casinos in Nevada. He has hotels—he owns half of this one. He has apartment houses in New York. He has real estate in Texas . . ."

"Wow!" Iris gulped. "And so you help him in his businesses?"

Cesare nodded. "And when I'm thirty, I become a full half-partner. I'm the only son, and my mother died six years ago. So I know exactly what will be mine."

Iris was delighted. Imagine owning a hotel! Even only half of a hotel! Why, you could only sleep in so many rooms, even if you changed night after night, and room service was room service . . . Yes, half a hotel was fine.

"I have to be a sort of apprentice to my father until my thirtieth birthday, and then I'm home free. But now I have to do what he says, I have to please him."

"But that's not so long," Iris was saying. She loved looking at his face. It was the hooded eyes that she stared at the most. "What? Five years of pleasing your father?" Then the practical side of Iris asserted itself. "But where will you live in the meantime? How will you have money now?"

"I have money now. Money of my own. From little deals here and there. About fifty grand in the bank, and I get a suite in the hotel here whenever I'm in town. There are hotels in San Juan, in Mexico City, all over the Caribbean, too. You wouldn't mind living in a hotel for a while, would you?" He looked up at her with dark, questioning eyes.

She shook her head.

Cesare thought she looked like an angel then, when the light caught her hair and her big green eyes said, No, she wouldn't mind walking through hell for him. Barefooted. "Okay. I want you to meet my father. I want to ask him—no, I want to *tell* him—we're engaged to be married." He stood and she rose with him, still holding his hand. The little pink leather pocketbook was clutched under her arm.

"You're trembling," he said, putting his arm around her shoulder. "My father is a tough son of a bitch, but he means what he says. You can count on it. His word is law. We just have to hit him at the right moment." He looked at his watch.

"I didn't think it would be this way," Iris murmured. "I didn't think getting married would be—" She shivered again. The air conditioning was so strong in these public places.

Cesare bent down and kissed her. "You will marry me, then?"

Iris nodded, amazed at herself, amazed at the turn of events. No one had ever asked her to marry him. Not ever. Yet the idea of finding a husband had become a priority in her life. Iris had decided marriage was a step toward security.· A man to take care of her was Harry. That was one thing. But a man who legally had to provide for her was another. A man with money, whose money was hers by virtue of the wedding ring. Money was the biggest part of marriage in Iris's mind. How much there was, and how generous the husband was with it. She had wanted Harry to marry her, but she didn't think he would ever divorce Frieda. And if he did, Frieda, after bearing those daughters and keeping house for him all those years, would take everything. Then what would me and Harry have for us? was the question Iris had lain awake asking herself.

Cesare continued. "This part is business. It's my future. My father is my future. We try to get along, or rather *I* try to get along. It was easier when Mama was alive." He sighed. "I have to get along with him. That's why this is the first step toward getting married. He has to know."

They took the elevator to the top floor. "You mean he's here?" asked Iris. "In the penthouse?"

"Right next door to my suite." He raised his eyebrows. "Or you could say I'm right next door to *his* suite."

Cesare knocked, and the door was opened by a large man who looked beefy and familiar to Iris. "*Vieni qua, ragazzo,*" called a deep voice from another room.

His head was down, he was reading some sort of report when they entered the big yellow room he called his office. When he looked up and saw Iris, he immediately jumped to his feet. "Well, if it ain't Cinderella!" he boomed, taking her hand.

She was confused; Cesare was confused. Then Vito said, "You two know each other?"

One of the "assistants," who looked like a halfback in a red madras jacket, brought chairs in from an adjoining room. They were tucked under each arm like furniture for a dollhouse. Cesare motioned for Iris to sit, and she did, carefully pulling at the hem of her short dress. Vito was Cesare's father? It couldn't be! The man who'd asked her to go to the Bahamas with him—to Italy with him! But he was rich and he dabbled in lots of businesses—both Harry and Cesare had described him that way. Still . . .

Cesare was asking Iris, "You know my father?" She nodded. The young man cleared his throat and began, "Papa, I want ya to meet my wife-to-be. We wanna get married."

Vito, who had been leaning forward across his littered desktop to get a better view of Iris's bare legs, swallowed. Then his face was crossed with a look of horror. "No."

"What do you mean, no?" Cesare was shocked. If Iris had arrived yesterday, how had she met his father?

Vito stood up. "The meetin' is over. I got a plane to catch. Luigi's waitin' fer me."

"But, Papa! What's wrong? What is it? I'm twenty-five years old today, and that's old enough to get married."

Vito was pulling on his suit jacket. One of the old boxers was holding it for him behind the desk chair. It was gray sharkskin, just like the one his son had worn the day before. "I got nothin' more ta say. Why dontcha take Iris downstairs and buy her a drink and send her on back to where—"

Cesare was standing now, angry. "No! I want to marry her! She wants to marry me! We're gettin' married!"

Iris stared at the father's face and saw the son there. Yes, the nose was thicker, the eyes less bright, but it was the same face. Why hadn't she seen it last night? He was coming toward her, smiling. "Well, you can say you've seduced every member of the Luppese family. Father and son." He took her hand and bent down and kissed it. "Irresistible Iris."

"We are going to be married." Cesare's voice was calm now.

Vito turned to where his son stood. Iris thought Cesare looked smaller in the same room with his father, which was strange, because Cesare was taller. "If you marry her, you leave me." He waited for the words to sink in. His voice was soft, but the softness made it all the more ominous a threat. The room was utterly silent except for a gasp from the air conditioner. "You leave me and the business and Italy and all of it." He lifted his hand with index finger raised, and motioned for one of the "assistants" to come with him.

A refrigerator in dark blue madras opened the door for him, and Vito walked quickly from the room. Three more "assistants" followed. Iris and Cesare listened to the door of the suite open and close. She still sat demurely with legs crossed at the ankle, and he still stood beside his father's big wooden desk.

Cesare stared out the window at a cloudless blue sky as Iris wondered what time it was. He turned back to her, all grace and lean, young hardness beneath the white silk shirt, beneath the skintight trousers. His eyes were burning with anger. "Say you don't care," he demanded.

Iris gave a little start at the sound of his voice. She had been wondering what she would tell Harry about her hair.

Cesare's voice was hard. "Tell me you'll marry me anyway! Tell me the money doesn't matter!"

.   .   .

"*Ragazzo! Caro!*" Vito was on the line from the British Colonial Hotel in Nassau. "I saved you. Think about it. Thank me."

Cesare held the white phone to his ear and didn't answer. He stood wearing a large orange towel wrapped around his waist and nothing else. A cold shower after another session with Iris. She had left only four minutes before. Something about the hairdresser fitting her in at the last moment.

"She's a cute trick, all right," his father was saying. "But not to marry."

"She's gorgeous and smart and I love her. I fell in love with her the first time I saw her." Cesare hated the idea that his father knew Iris somehow. Had met her somehow. Iris told him they'd met at a party the night before. Cesare couldn't understand it.

"Yeah, yeah. So did I."

"Papa! What do you mean?"

"I mean she was at dinner last night wid a business friend of mine. If ya hadna been late, ya woulda seen her wid him."

The joke about her father. Cesare ran his fingers through his hair. So what? She certainly wasn't a virgin. A virgin couldn't do half the things she did in bed. "I don't care about that. I still want to marry her."

The voice was angry over the long-distance wire. "Ya *should* care about that! This is the mother of your children we're talkin' about! The mother of my grandchildren! Ya want a little tramp like that—"

"Don't call her names. She doesn't deserve—"

"Yeah, and you don't deserve a bimbo like that. Think of your mama, may she rest in peace." Cesare could see his father, off in the Bahamas, reflexively crossing himself. "She wouldna let a piece a fluff like that in the house!"

"Maybe you should wait and get to know her," began Cesare.

" 'Maybe you should wait and get to know her,' " echoed his father. "I know her already," he said ominously. "She's a type. You're young. You're a baby. You don' know these broads. A ballbreaker up there with the champions. So take her on a trip and screw her till your joint falls off, but don't marry her."

Cesare had his hand over his favorite piece of anatomy at that very moment, thinking that it might well fall off. His father hadn't paused to take a breath. "So, *caro*, take her to Puerto Rico for a few days. Screw her and get tired of her. My treat."

"I'm serious about her, Papa." Cesare listened to his father for another few minutes and then, luckily, another call interrupted them. "I've got Vegas on the second line," Vito said.

Cesare hung up at last. Then he gazed out at the ocean and imagined Iris in a bikini, imagined Iris undressed. He hoped she wouldn't get her glorious hair cut too short.

· · ·

Iris thought Miami was pretty tiring. She met Cesare every afternoon, telling Harry she had tennis lessons. Cesare typed up the bills on hotel stationery from the pro they named Raúl Gonzales. He picked and pecked, standing over the typewriter in all his naked glory, as Iris hurried in and out of the shower.

Yes, she could have been sweaty from tennis, "but I smell like sex," she had said after the first "tennis lesson." Cesare had agreed, then knocked her to the floor and begun licking her throat. Iris told Harry that Raúl had to be paid in cash, that he hated anyone watching, and that he exhausted her. Cesare teased her, saying he should get the money because her form was getting better and better "under me."

Iris told Cesare that she worked as Harry's personal assistant, but that she always made sure her private life was private. "There is no reason for my boss to know about you," she said primly. Cesare agreed. He was impressed with her discretion. And if she needed phony bills from a tennis pro to protect her valued privacy, why of course he would help her. It was a shame she always had to rush off the way she did, back to sending telexes and typing business reports. She was obviously very bright, and her boss was entirely dependent upon her to take care of his affairs. Papa was so wrong, Cesare thought as he kissed Iris good-bye that last day before she flew home to New York. Papa doesn't know the Iris I know. When he gets back from the Bahamas, I'll talk to him again.

But Don Luppese didn't fly back to Miami from the Bahamas. He flew directly to Kennedy and telephoned Iris.

· · ·

A week later, Iris was Mrs. Vittorio Luppese of Miami Beach, San Juan, Montego Bay, several other Caribbean capitals, Mexico City, Las Vegas, New York City, Rome . . . and Luppese, Italy.

CHAPTER FIFTEEN

Cynthia

1971 — Les Colombiers

Cynthia began the day at half past six. Pulling herself from bed, she ran the bath and sank gratefully up to her neck in the hot water. Low blood pressure, her mother had told her. Only aristocratic women have it. It makes you very slow in the morning, but something warm will help wake you. Cynthia often wondered if her mother had meant something like Jean-François. After three years of marriage, his sex drive still amazed her.

Cynthia dressed carefully and was downstairs at the table, her coffee set before her, at just about the time her husband was beginning to shave. They had separate bathrooms and dressing rooms, and it was easy to have complete privacy from the time she left their big bed. They never saw one another in the in-between stages of dress or undress or brushing their teeth. It seems "very European," she confided to Veronique, who said ominously, "Wait until you have separate bedrooms, and then you will really feel 'very European.'"

Cynthia hadn't answered her. She knew it was wrong of her to react to the possibility as a pleasant alternative to all this attention. I love him, really I do, she often thought. Why isn't the lovemaking better? Why is it over so quickly? Perhaps I'm not normal. I have had only one other experience, on a beach a long time ago, and he had so many women before getting married. Something must be wrong with me.

At seven-thirty, Jean-François pecked her on the cheek and took his place at the opposite end of the long table. A maid brought in the papers, which were fetched by the driver from town, and Cynthia poured his coffee. Croissants were kept warm in a large round basket surrounded by satellites of little dishes and pots containing jams and jellies and honey.

In twenty minutes he was gone, driven to Geneva over the lake road in ten minutes, so that he could stride through the nondescript door of a large, four-story stone building, just off the rue du Rhône, whose brass nameplate said simply, "C. & Cie."

Cynthia changed out of her suit and tore off her stockings and high heels and jewelry. She pulled on jeans, faded almost white, and a pullover in a bright primary color, and sneakers with holes in them. For Jean-François she "dressed," but for herself and for the house and for the workmen she still oversaw, after three years, she was comfortable. Jean-François had seen her in jeans the first summer of their marriage and given her hell. He had stood in the front hallway as she climbed the stairs and asked who she thought she was, dressing like that! Cynthia had blushed furiously, feeling almost naked under his critical glare, and answered that she was a housewife getting things done.

"You are Madame Colbert, with the French title of Comtesse, if we lived in France instead of Switzerland! How can you let the servants see you dressed this way?" She had been speechless. He had then commanded her to go upstairs and get dressed. She had "dressed" for three weeks, resenting every run in her stockings, every expensive silk blouse with a dust smudge on it, every chance of spotting her lovely clothes. Then she had compromised by spending the time in the morning and again in the late afternoon so that he could see her properly outfitted at breakfast and at dinner. What he doesn't know won't hurt him, she decided.

Cynthia, dressed in her "work clothes," *did* work. There were meals to plan a week in advance. Food was discussed with the cook from Normandy, and ordered in great quantities. Sometimes there were bank clients to entertain at dinner, over the weekend, for a week. Cynthia was used to it, always prepared, always very charming and hospitable.

The gardens relaxed her more than anything else in her life. She adored the rich smell of the earth, the sun on her bare skin, the idea of making something grow. The kitchen garden with its herbs and vegetables didn't interest her; the flowers did. Every third day she spent two and a half hours cutting blossoms and arranging bouquets for the house. The rooms were many and large, and the flowers had to be arranged in tall vases so as not to be lost in the vast proportions of the space.

Cynthia took lunch in the only room she felt was hers, her "office" or boudoir, her private sitting room. Located at one end of the first floor—what Americans would call the second floor—was her own living room with her private phone number, her favorite colors, and her favorite books from America. Watercolors of flowers and seascapes in simple gold frames reminded her of the Vineyard. She'd had the paneled walls painted pale sea green and the ceiling white, ignoring the wrath of Jean-François. Cynthia had stuck to her guns, saying, "I'm going to be the person in this room. Maybe I'll be here for another fifty years. After I'm gone, somebody else can worry about restoring the woodwork." This rare flash of willfulness annoyed her husband no end, far more than the actual painting.

A maid brought her tea and a sandwich, or a slice of cheese and a salad, which she nibbled as she sat at her desk. She carefully entered the household expenses into a notebook she kept in the bottom drawer of the antique desk. Math had been her favorite subject at Rosemary Hall, and she refused to accede to Jean-François's demands that she not "worry herself about money." It wasn't something to worry about, she told him; it was a normal thing to know how much was being spent. He seemed to humor her on the subject, which planted a seed of outrage in the practical side of her. Now she could not imagine not noting every centime in her own book, never seen by anyone else.

The telephone beside the bright green and pink and white flowered sofa was her link to Veronique, to Yves, to the friends she felt she didn't see often enough. Veronique was away in Paris for weeks at a time, and upon her return the two women would have a three-hour lunch and, as Cynthia said, "fill in the gaps." Increasingly, Cynthia's gaps were about her husband. He took the trips, he returned to the chateau with new clothes or paintings; Cynthia was the chatelaine. "We bump heads over nearly everything," she told her French friend. "If the gravy needs salt, it's my fault because the cook hasn't been properly instructed. If the front walk has a loose cobble, it's my fault because"—Veronique raised her eyebrows—"because the workmen haven't been told to fix it."

Cynthia's other best friend was Yves Rocard, who was gay in a Geneva where homosexuality did not exist. He was attractive in a polished way. His effeminate side could have been mistaken for an English education; there was nothing blatant, nothing high-pitched. "I'm just off key," he had laughed with Cynthia the only time they'd finally talked about it. She'd seen him on countless occasions at dinner parties—the extra man with someone's visiting cousin. He was always smiling, always telling a story. But he seemed what he was—the odd man, the extra. "I fill up the last chair," he had once said quite bitterly. "But in the best houses." No matter how nice the woman on his arm was, he was always alone—certainly not half of a couple, and not entirely accepted by the men who retired after dinner to smoke cigars and drink brandy. Cynthia adored him.

That first year in Geneva, the young American had plunged into every proffered social situation. She played tennis at Onex several times, and took golf lessons with a very witty Englishwoman. She volunteered for charity work and was at the Hotel des Bergues for the Protestant de Seminaire. She attended a meeting of the Dames de Morges, which had been formed by women of the oldest Genevois families; they grouped themselves by interest into discussions of art, literature, and other cultural topics. Cynthia found everyone much older and didn't go back a second time. She had lunches with women and knew how many children they had and where they lived, and Jean-François usually knew their husbands. She got along with the other wives well enough, but the person she invariably felt like calling for company was Veronique Devereaux. She was always lively and she seemed most understanding of Cynthia's situation with Jean-François. Cynthia was usually the first to leave after a tennis game without the iced tea and the chatter because something must be seen to at the chateau. Perhaps Jean-François would have left a message with the cook that he was bringing a curator home for dinner. The cook could handle that, but it would be the day Cynthia was between housekeepers, and so she would have to be the one to instruct a new young maid in how to manage hospital corners for the sheets on a bed in a guest bedroom. Or Jean-François would tell her at breakfast that he was coming home at four-thirty for drinks with six collectors from London who were on their way to see another collector in Zurich. Invariably it would be the afternoon she had planned to spend with an acquaintance, a potential friend, advising her about her garden. So the two women would try to meet later, but then the other woman's children had to be fetched at school, and the next day was no good because Cynthia was meeting with the contractor in town to go over a problem with the architect. Or Jean-François would have a new demand.

"Sabotage?" Veronique pouted. "Don't let him get away with it!"

"Oh, I don't think it's that. He seems happy that I know people, but it *is* a funny coincidence. Yesterday I was totally free."

"What did you do?" demanded Veronique, who thought Cynthia worked far too hard at everything. The American was a list-maker, a checker-offer of each thing to do.

"I met with the man who is going to redo the roof of the greenhouse, and we had a fascinating discussion about how big the pieces of plate glass should be. Then I went over the next week's menu with the cook, but it will certainly change since I never know from day to day what Jean-François will do. Then I drove to that nursery and picked out more seedlings to be planted down past the vineyards. And more rosebushes. Then I fought on the phone with the contractor who had nearly doubled the cost of the reflooring upstairs, then I went into town to see if I could pick out some other fabric for the dining room curtains since Paris is going to take six more weeks—"

Veronique gave a strangled scream. "Stop! Please. Cynthia! This was your 'free' day?"

"I know it," came the sigh.

Veronique included her in every lunch, in every charity activity. Other women liked Cynthia Colbert, but began to say, "You're busier than I am, so you call me when you have time." And the time slipped away.

. . .

"Because you listen," she was saying on the phone this spring day. "Most people don't."

" 'Most people' meaning adoring husbands?" Yves laughed.

"Exactly," she sighed, putting her feet up on the flowered sofa. It saddened Cynthia. She and Jean-François seemed to have their lives mapped out in some parallel way, and they only intersected at dinner a few times a week, or in bed. The latter less and less. Cynthia certainly didn't mind that. At the beginning the sex had been wonderful, or was it just the closeness she loved? Now what she thought so strange about it was the distance. When we are closest together, we are farthest apart. I can't see his face, there is no voice. There is only flesh, but flesh that seems to have forgotten *me*. I have never been so alone.

There was a period when Cynthia considered leaving Jean-François, asking for a divorce. She spoke to no one about it, not even Veronique. The evening she had planned to talk to him arrived, and she felt prepared. But almost as if he sensed a turning point, Jean-François came home and kissed her very gently, was quiet at dinner, and, after dinner, led her into the *fumoir*. There he sat beside her on the couch in front of the fire and, putting his head on her breast, nestled against her. He told her that there was a feud at the bank; two partners were behaving badly and forcing all the others to take sides. It was draining his energy to stay uninvolved. It was unheard of, such bad taste. Cynthia gave him her ideas and he listened, and with his head in her lap and his hands grasping hers, he whispered, "I need you. Don't ever forget I need you."

"He's a busy man. You know these bankers. It's all greed. Quiet greed. Not like Wall Street—never as gauche as all that—but there nonetheless."

Cynthia laughed and took a sip of tea. "Yves! You will never get over being in Switzerland! Being in Geneva!" She laughed again. "Most of all, you'll never get over being a banker."

"No. I won't." He had spent the last twenty years in Geneva, though he had been born in Paris and had gone to schools in England. He was involved in banking, but he made it clear that he thought what he did was boring. His fun was haunting auction houses all over Europe, dashing in and out of London to see dealers, sitting on the back row for the sales at Sotheby's and Christie's and filling his town house in the Vieille Ville with very good antiques. Because of this, Jean-François tolerated him at their table, at their parties.

Yves ran a hand through his sandy hair and blinked behind horn-rimmed glasses. "I'm off to Gstaad this weekend," he said into the telephone. "Do you want to come? It's two big dinner parties at the Palace. Just pack your dressiest duds."

Cynthia hesitated. "I guess anything would be better than the silly little house things I'm doing . . ."

"Thank you so much!" came the quick retort.

"Oh, Yves! We're good enough friends for you to know—"

"I know. I know. You just can't tell if it'll annoy him again. Well, I think you should come with me. Be with lots of people. And I have never understood why you haven't bought a chalet there. It's what you should have done the first year you were married."

"Jean-François always says he is away on business trips so much that it hardly makes it worthwhile to keep a chalet. But I think he likes coming back here and having it all in perfect order, with me waiting for him. I don't think he'd be happy walking in with his suitcase and having just the servants here and me off in Gstaad." She placed the empty teacup on the silver tray that sat on the marble coffee table. "I'll come! He'll be in London until Friday, and then it's Paris over the weekend. Yes!"

"*C'est bon!*" came the response over the line. And then he said what Cynthia was thinking. "Why shouldn't you have fun?"

They made plans to drive up on Friday afternoon, and Cynthia hung up the phone. She retied her sneakers, left her sanctuary, then almost skipped with happiness down the long hallway to the main staircase. Workmen on ladders were polishing the chandelier in the entrance hall. She addressed them in French. "When you finish, could you do the dining room one and the back hall, and then get the housekeeper to show you the other three upstairs?"

"*Oui, oui,* Madame Colbert," they chorused in very bad French accents.

Fabulous, she thought. These Swiss. And then she thought again. No. None of the workers are Swiss. They are Spanish or Portuguese, Italian or Yugoslavian. Thankful to have work. But always worried about their papers being in order. Worried about the families they weren't allowed to bring to Switzerland with them. Switzerland! With its zero unemployment!

Cynthia went to the kitchen and spoke to the newest maid about taking care of the household linen. She explained what to do about wine stains and how to assess which napkins should be replaced. A parade of maids in three years. The head housekeeper, who usually tended to such details, was away visiting her sick mother, and Brigitte had replaced her.

At last Cynthia retreated to the bathroom she loved, all mirrored and bright, and a long hot bath. Though it was only six o'clock, she decided she'd put on her nightgown, then she rang the kitchen, requesting that a tray be sent up to her bedroom. Just soup, nothing fancy. Why do I feel so tired? she asked herself as she slipped under the covers.

Before picking up *Le Figaro*, she surveyed the room. It's gloomy, she thought. The dark wood closed the space, and the long brown silk curtains, stretching twelve feet from the tops of the windows to the floor, shut out so much light. She longed to start over from scratch, but Jean-François wanted nothing done to his grandfather's room.

Cynthia thought of Yves and Gstaad. She loved the ski resort. Yves said it had nothing to do with Geneva and nothing to do with Switzerland. It was where the foreigners with money came together. He had explained to her that the influx of outsiders to Geneva had begun in the late fifties. Young entrepreneurs starting to build companies, Greek shipowners, the very wealthy Europeans who had so much money to spend and were flamboyant in a manner unimaginable to the Swiss, all came pouring into Gstaad. They sent their children to Le Rosey, the very expensive boys' school that moved its entire student body to Gstaad for the ski season; they kept their money in Geneva, shopped in Paris and London and Milan, and partied all over the Continent.

The old Iranian families seemed to prefer having houses in Geneva, and the wealthy Greeks bought houses in Lausanne, which was a quieter, smaller town, just fifty-nine kilometers away. Now everyone talked about the famous—and infamous—Bernie Cornfeld, who had moved his operations from Switzerland just over the border into France.

The phone rang on the bedside table, and she answered on the second ring. "Hi, darling. How's London?"

"Gloomy. Rain, rain, and, just for a little change—more rain."

Cynthia smiled. "Meetings going well?"

"Ummmm, okay," he acquiesced.

"I think I'm going to Gstaad with Yves for the weekend. If you're going to be in Pa—"

"With that fairy!"

Cynthia winced. While Americans were beginning to call homosexuals "gays," the Europeans still used epithets like "fairy" and "pansy." "*Oui*. With Yves." Her voice was quiet.

Jean-François was irritated. "I don't know why you have to do that."

She felt herself go warm with anger. "Because it's the last weekend of the season and I like Gstaad and I like Yves." Why did she have to explain going away for the weekend? His response would have been the same if Veronique had invited her.

"Go, then." The voice was deep, controlled. He didn't offer any wish that she have a good time; his attitude was more, "I can't stop you."

"Well, yes." Cynthia pushed her blond hair behind her ears nervously. "I think I will go, and I'll be back on Sunday night." She bit her lip and then said brightly, "I'll probably be home before you." Suddenly she realized she was talking to the dial tone; he'd hung up. "Damn him!" she said aloud, and slammed down the receiver.

The door opened at just that moment, and Silvie entered. She was known for her clumsiness, so Cynthia moved carefully away from the edge of the bed to allow her lots of room to put the tray down.

"Madame, are you feeling all right?" the young girl asked. She couldn't have been more than eighteen, pink-cheeked, plump with baby fat.

"Just a little tired. I don't understand it. I haven't done very much of anything today."

Silvie smiled and shook her head. "You work harder than anyone, Madame." She thought of her mistress in the rose garden before half past eight, and then later, down the hill toward the lake, showing two of the gardeners how she wanted the path to look. Before lunch, she'd gotten up on a ladder to explain to the Spanish workmen how to remove the wires of the tiniest pendants from the chandelier so that the prisms could be soaked in warm water and ammonia, and after lunch she'd gone out again to speak with the caretaker of L'Orangerie about getting the floors redone so that the place could be rented. "You never stop," she said.

"There's so much to do!" Cynthia sighed. "Just when one thing is taken care of—there's something else."

Silvie stood at the door and smiled sympathetically. "Will that soup be enough for you? Maybe I could bring some bread and butter?" Cynthia shook her head. "Just call me," the maid insisted.

"Non, merci. This is just fine."

Later, Cynthia slept without moving the tray from the bed, and woke at dawn with one edge of it digging into her heel. Groggily, she placed it on the floor and then, curling up on her side, slept again.

At eleven o'clock the phone rang, and Veronique asked if she could come by for lunch. Amazed at the time, Cynthia said, "Sure, love to see you. Give me twenty minutes!"

She pushed down the button and then dialed the line for the kitchen. "Brigitte! I have one guest for lunch. Just salad and cold chicken, if there's any left. Something very simple. It's Comtesse Devereaux, and you know how she is always on a diet. Oui. Oui. Merci beaucoup."

Cynthia leapt from the bed and ran into Jean-François's bathroom to run the shower. Friday noon! she thought, and in a few hours Yves will be here and I'm not packed. She waited for the water to warm up before stepping under the spray, then suddenly thought of her shampoo in the other bathroom. Opening her husband's medicine cabinet, she reached for his. She had started to swing the mirrored door closed, when she noticed something and opened it wide. On the top glass shelf, beside little wafers of hotel soaps, there were several condoms in black, shiny foil packages. "He never uses those," she said aloud.

On the contrary, Jean-François wanted her to become pregnant. Both of them were disappointed that she had not yet conceived. The box, with the printing in French, was on the bottom shelf. "Contains twelve," she read. There were two inside, and on the shelf were four. Six gone.

The hot water was running full force, and steam was obscuring Cynthia's reflection in the mirror. She pulled her white silk nightgown over her head and then carefully closed the cabinet. Her face was wet with tears when she stepped into the shower.

. . .

Veronique was already downstairs, reading *Paris Match*, when Cynthia walked into the grand salon. She stood and they kissed one another on each cheek. "*Ça va?*" queried Veronique.

Cynthia smiled. "I'm off to Gstaad this afternoon, so things couldn't be better."

"Good girl!"

"Well, why not? Jean-François will be in Paris, and . . ." Her voice dropped as she sat on one of the dark green brocade wing chairs. At last the room was finished, and everyone who'd seen the "before" version praised what she had done. Even Cynthia's mother, on a visit from Boston, had been impressed with this daughter who had shown no interest in what she herself had been doing in fits and starts for years in the Beacon Hill house.

"You should go. And why don't you look around while you're there?"

Cynthia knew exactly what she meant. "Oh, Veronique! I'm not like you! I can't! Remember how American you always say I am."

"Suit yourself," sighed her friend. "But you can have everything. That's my motto, my credo." She hugged herself in the gray sweater. Ropes of silver beads hung around her neck. Louis thought they were a present from him, but Thierry had given them to her. Veronique had asked Louis if she could buy them, and he'd given her the money, which she pocketed. Now she was free to wear the necklace as often as she pleased. And please both men. And get three hundred fifty francs out of the deal. "You *can* have everything," she repeated.

Cynthia laughed. "Anything to get you through this vale of tears, yes? Please needlework it somewhere and send it to me for Christmas."

"I'm serious. Look at you. You're *superbe*, and anyone who sees you thinks so. You dress like a Parisian—which, as we know, is the highest compliment I can give." They both smiled, and Cynthia looked down at the tan cashmere trousers with the narrow brown alligator belt and the white silk shirt with pearl buttons. She wore low-heeled brown alligator shoes with small gold buckles across the instep. "And you look like a mixture of Tuesday Weld and Catherine Deneuve. Sort of European quiet, well-bred sexuality and all-American—"

"Stop! I can't take any more! I'm going to be so conceited I won't be able to have lunch with you!" Cynthia had her hands up as if to ward off blows. "How can you—"

"I tell you these things for your own good!" Veronique insisted. "I'm your best friend. But you should believe me. You need masculine appreciation. It's vital for the sanity. Physical appreciation, too."

Cynthia shook her head. "I get physically appreciated. As you put it." Why was Veronique pushing this so hard today? It wasn't the first time she'd brought up the subject, but why today so outspoken? More outspoken than usual. She told herself not to think about what she'd seen in the bathroom cabinet.

Veronique responded quickly. "After two years of marriage, husbands don't count."

"What!" the American gasped, though she'd heard it before.

"I think you should have an affair."

Silvie had entered the room. "*Excusez-moi*, Madame. The lunch is ready whenever you would like to come."

"*Merci.*" Cynthia's face was a mask. The minute the maid turned her back, she raised her eyebrows and hissed, "Do you think she heard you?"

"Doesn't matter." Veronique shrugged, getting up from the chair. "I'm sure she agrees with me."

· · ·

Yves's sleek black Jaguar hugged the hairpin curves as they sped toward Gstaad. Snow-crowned Alps, looking as though they'd been sprinkled with sugar, were bright in the sunlight; the sky was postcard blue. Yves concentrated on the winding road without speaking, and Cynthia was silent with her own thoughts, hands clenched tightly in tan suede gloves.

I saw them, she said to herself. In their little, black, shiny envelopes. She marveled at whatever instinct or talent it was that allowed her to forget temporarily, to put aside pain. Perhaps inherited from Mother, she decided. The ability to do what had to be done, calmly and efficiently, no matter how your stomach felt, or whether your eyes were blinking back tears. Mother could probably go to a wedding reception five minutes after major surgery. And no one would suspect a thing. Or have a heart attack during intermission at the opera and file right back in with the others for the last act. Heart. My heart hurts, Cynthia decided. She felt that same tiredness of the day before sweep over her, and she leaned back in the red leather seat, closing her eyes against the glare.

The lunch with Veronique had been typical. She always gave a running commentary on the latest between her and Thierry, how much she loved him and how she was "handling" Louis. The logistics of an affair were formidable, Cynthia thought. Just the geography of it was a challenge in a town as small as Geneva, where people were always bumping into friends and constantly seeing acquaintances across the dining rooms of the few good hotel restaurants. Forgetting about emotions.

The car swerved and Cynthia moved toward Yves, who braked and shifted into a lower gear. Affairs. So Jean-François, who sleeps next to me as many nights as he's in Geneva—or does he?—is having an affair. The things are here and not in his blue kit bag that he throws into his suitcase, which means he sleeps with someone here in Geneva, she realized with shock.

Yves broke into her thoughts. "You are far away!"

"I'm already in my ski boots." She tried to smile.

Yves laughed. "Oh, my dear!" he mimicked a glamorous non-skier from Paris they both knew well. "Gstaad is not for skiing." He lifted his left hand from the wheel as though its fingers twinkled with jewels. "Gstaad is *après-ski.*"

They laughed companionably together, and he began to tease, "They say that the only downhilling some people do is from the lobby of the Palace down to the Gringo to dance the night away."

"Yves, you are my favorite man!"

He sighed and rolled his eyes. "My God! That doesn't say much about your life! I'll have to do something about that!"

"Don't you start with me!" she warned. How much can I take without bursting into tears? Without telling all? But neither Yves or Veronique would be shocked. They'd only be shocked that *she* was. Suddenly Cynthia felt quite alone, quite foreign. No one else would take her revelations seriously. Her voice was soft as she began, "Why do you and Veronique think you know so much about my marriage?"

Yves pushed his sunglasses farther up his nose. "Because we do."

"Do you know things I don't know?"

He turned to look at her face and then answered very carefully, "I don't know what you know, do I?"

Cynthia blinked back tears. "So I am the fool, right?"

"No. You just don't see the picture. You are so young—"

"I'm not! Veronique is not so much older than I am, and she—"

"She was born a cynic, and you have been brought up wrapped in cotton wool," he ended.

There was silence in the car as it whirred along like a toy, with the massive mountains to the right. They were riding a mouse darting back and forth over the personal landscape of sleeping giants. "I don't think my life has been that protected."

"I think it has." His voice was kind. "Cynthia . . ." He stopped and then put his hand on her knee for just a moment, then placed it on the wheel again. "Veronique and I grew up in Europe—here and there all over—and what she does is normal. What she thinks about it is commonplace. Husbands and wives just—what is that English expression?—they 'make do.' We don't expect to love the person we marry forever. Or even in the beginning."

Cynthia was unprepared for the tears that coursed down her face. She pulled off her gloves and swiped at her cheeks with quick, hard, outward motions.

"Do you love him? No! Don't answer that!" Yves was shaking his head. "Because don't you see that it doesn't matter?"

"Doesn't love matter?" she demanded with a sniffle. "Doesn't trusting someone matter?"

He nodded with a frown. "I can't explain it to you. I wish I could. My parents had separate bedrooms, always. But they must have made love once, or I wouldn't be here."

"Maybe your father isn't your father," Cynthia said gloomily. "I mean, if your mother—"

"No." Yves shook his head, and the glasses glittered in the bright sunlight. "That's part of the arrangement. No snags with the will, no inheritance problems."

"Sometimes I think that the children of a Frenchman are more important than the wife." She tightened her lips and willed herself to stop crying. "I know that Jean-François is Swiss, but even after—what is it?—two hundred fifty or sixty years, he seems to be very French to me."

"He is very French. Let's face it—holidays there, cousins there, summer house there, mother there, early education there, all make him French. He can't help it." He stopped.

"And having a mistress is very French and he can't help it. Is that it?" she demanded.

He nodded, refusing to glance away from the road, knowing she was suffering. "I don't want to be harsh with you. Oh, Cynthia!"

"But why! Why, when I'm always there! Why, when I'm a good wife!" Her voice was shrill.

"Because . . ." Yves didn't know how to tell her the things that had been obvious to him since he was a small boy. Obvious in families. Obvious when fathers and husbands left their dinner tables, were gone all evening, and quietly closed the front door behind them at midnight. Obvious when they arrived for August vacations a week late, and left their wives and children a week early. Cynthia blew her nose and apologized. She hated herself for all this drama, particularly when Yves didn't consider it the least bit dramatic. "Because . . ." Yves tried again. He saw the slender spires of the Palace Hotel on a peak in the distance. An enormous red flag with the white cross of Switzerland fluttered in the breeze. Yves sighed and finished his thought. "Because he's French."

Palace Hotel, Gstaad

"I hate having a dog in the house, watchdog or not. I mean, it's all right in Ankara, where we have the garden, but in Istanbul . . ." The woman in

chocolate brown silk blew twin streams of smoke from her nostrils in irritation, then stubbed out the cigarette. "My husband insisted, but I finally told
him—"

Her Turkish industrialist husband leaned forward and interjected with a
broad white smile, "She told me, 'Either the dog goes or I go!' "

She put her hand on his arm, and smiled with girlish delight. Her dark
eyes were bright. "I won't miss the dog."

Another voice was going on. "When we go to Paris, we always stay with
my mother-in-law, who insists we dine with her every single night, and that
means sitting down for five hours of—"

"It's not that I mind going to Milano for clothes, but as a city I so prefer
Rome. Rome is Italy, and Milano is—"

Yves said softly to Cynthia, "You look very pale. Do you feel all right?"

"I think I'll get a little bit of fresh air." She nodded and rose from the table.

They were attending a dinner party for forty at the Palace. The hotel, the
most chic in the ski resort, sat atop a mountain like an illustration for a fairy
tale. The dark wood-paneled dining room was crowded, and several people
were smoking between courses. Noise seemed to rise in crescendoes of voices
and laughter, and then drop off again. This was Yves's Gstaad—the Gstaad
of only six weeks a year: two weeks at Christmas and New Year's, and the
four weeks of February. Then "everyone" moved on. The Caribbean, Hawaii,
a warmer place, another party. Cynthia found it fun for a weekend or two,
light and frivolous after Geneva. She enjoyed Yves's brand of humor, and
though he always made her feel a part of things, she considered herself an
innocent bystander.

Now Cynthia felt the voices around her as if they were touching her skin.
She walked very carefully, squeezing on tiptoe between the chairs of the black-
tied men and the women in their brightly colored evening dresses, and then
hurried out to the hall and to the ladies' room. Fifteen minutes later she was
back at the table, with fresh pink lipstick and a pleasant expression. Luckily
she'd saved the rose chiffon sheath from any damage. I'm absolutely never
sick, she thought as she raised the wine to her lips and sipped carefully. The
London banker on her left was speaking to her. "And what does an American
think of President Nixon? And the trip to China! Imagine having it all start
with a game of Ping-Pong!"

Cynthia nodded, then began to speak. She'd read an editorial only yesterday
in *Le Figaro*. Her stomach felt strange, but she smiled and went on. The
thought flashed through her mind as another wave of nausea hit her: I am
certainly my mother's daughter.

·   ·   ·

Saturday was "bright and shining," Yves chortled at breakfast. "I don't miss
that damn fog of Geneva one bit!" He excitedly buttered one piece of toast

after another. Cynthia marveled at how he appeared to live on carbohydrates and never gained an ounce.

"I don't miss it either." She suddenly thought of the condoms in the bathroom, and her spirits sank. Don't think. *Do not* think, she told herself. Not until Sunday on the way home. You owe it to Yves because he invited you. What would Elizabeth say? Be a good sport.

"What the hell are you meditating about? You seem mesmerized by the decision of whether to have honey or marmalade."

Cynthia smiled. "About being a good sport."

"Am I that awful to have breakfast with? Wait till I get you out on the slopes! That'll be the true measure of a good sport. Those ninety-degree-angle *pistes*, no lunch, no rest, forty-seven degrees below zero, and the wind will be howling . . ." He was waving a piece of toast in the air effusively. The honey poured off in a golden stream and clotted in the middle of his new red sweater.

They both stared at the sticky glob and began to laugh. Yves put down the bread and sopped his napkin in the water glass. "Oh, to be a good sport," he sighed.

"Let's go up to the Eagles Club for lunch," Cynthia suggested. "Let's really do this right. If I'm going to be a good sport, let me be one in the best places."

The skiing had been exhilarating, they agreed over the buffet four hours later. The Eagles Club was "hyper-exclusive, which is why they let me be a founding father," Yves joked.

"I'm surprised they let you in," laughed Cynthia. "Your table manners leave something to be desired."

"Don't taunt a man wielding a fork," he threatened.

She followed him through the dark wood dining room with its big wide windows overlooking massive peaks in the distance. "It always looks like a stage set. I remember painting sets at school for things like *South Pacific* and thinking it all looked ridiculous, and then seeing it on opening night—"

He stopped her. "We never did *South Pacific*. We did *The Importance of Being Earnest*, where we all fought over who got to be in drag."

Cynthia laughed as they found two places at a table on the porch. Pushing her tray into place, a woman reached up to kiss her on both cheeks. "Cynthia! Haven't seen you anywhere for simply ages!"

"I've been undercover." She smiled. She sat down and regarded the woman, who had dyed red hair, an obvious facelift, a diamond ring with a stone the size of a marble, pear-shaped diamond earrings, and a brand-new and never-to-be-christened hot pink ski suit.

"But you should come out more! I'm having a dinner next Thursday, and I insist you come!" The bright red lips smiled widely.

Even the teeth are false, Yves thought. "Oh, Christine! You'll never get her to go anywhere. She's taken a vow. She communes with nature, she reads, she meditates. No dinner parties for this girl!"

Cynthia tried to think of a remark to make light of it all, but what Yves was saying was so close to the truth that she found it difficult. "I'll see if Jean-François is free, and if he is, we'd love to come."

"If he isn't, bring Yves!" The Austrian baroness was insistent.

Moments later she had finished her wine, and her party rose to go, leaving Cynthia and Yves to themselves. Yves moved beside Cynthia to lean against the wall and face the sun. "Whew!" she breathed. "What do you do with someone like that? And Jean-François wouldn't be caught dead at one of her parties! I'll have to make some elaborate excuse if she calls me. Like having someone tell her I'm dead."

Yves speared an artichoke heart and laughed. "You don't have to go that far. Don't you realize you have a reputation for not going anywhere? People don't expect you to accept their invitations. And you're so far up in the stratosphere socially that they don't even get their feelings hurt."

"What do you mean?" Cynthia put down her glass of white wine.

"I mean that people notice your absence and think that their party isn't good enough for you."

"Oh, that's ridiculous!" But she wondered if it wasn't true. The Colbert name was pretty illustrious. And the old Genevois families simply didn't pay much attention to the foreigners who, like the Baroness, were apt to spend money ostentatiously, flouting the principles of Calvinism. With a frown, she remembered how many skimpy portions of meat, served in chilly dining rooms, she had endured in the past few years.

Cynthia was perpetually amazed at the bounty of engraved invitations that came in the mail. The phone rang constantly with this hostess and that one asking for Monsieur and Madame Colbert's presence at dinners four weeks in advance. Jean-François's frequent traveling was a good excuse. He rarely wanted to go out, and Cynthia had stopped being excited at the prospect of yet another dressed-up evening. When she did accept, it was more and more often with Yves at her side.

"The Baron killed himself, you know." Yves was speaking.

"He did? When?" Cynthia wished she had been kinder to poor Christine, with that awful hair. But if the truth be known, she was less fond of the Baron than of the Baroness.

"Two months ago. Drinking a bit. Sort of fell off the balcony of the chalet into a snowbank."

"You mean it happened here? In Gstaad?" Cynthia was astonished.

Yves nodded and reached for another piece of bread. "You see? You really are a hermit."

"Did he break his neck?" She was horrified.

"No. There was a big soirée going on, and nobody missed him and he froze to death."

My God, thought Cynthia. And the Baron always thought of himself as the life of the party.

"*Ciao, bello!*" It was Luciano from Rome. Big, handsome, irresistible, and newly divorced from his Argentinian wife.

Yves rose to kiss him on each cheek. They clapped each other on the shoulders playfully. "*Ça va?*" Cynthia stood and was kissed and complimented on the little sprinkling of freckles across her nose.

Suddenly she felt her knees give way, and realized she had fallen to a sitting position again on the hard wooden bench. No one had noticed, but she felt all strength drain from her limbs. Excusing herself, she found her way through the exuberant din of the dining room and down the stairs to the ladies' bathroom. Best bathroom view in Switzerland, she thought as she passed the lockers and the mirrors and the windows overlooking snowy, jagged peaks against the deep blue sky. Holding her arms across her stomach, Cynthia was grateful to be alone.

Five minutes later, after rinsing her mouth and splashing cool water on her face, she made her way upstairs again, to be embraced by Luciano and offered more wine by Yves, who stood up to let her have a place on the bench beside him.

"You and Cynthia are coming to La Cave tonight," Luciano was insisting. "Last night was great. Hedy was singing song after song. Roger Moore was there, and Bob Wagner, and then, at about one, Polanski showed up . . ."

Cynthia leaned back. Closing her eyes against the brightness of the perfect spring day, she was glad there was a Gstaad, glad there was an Yves to bring her here, glad to be in Switzerland. Animated voices filled the clear, fresh air. She squinted at the row of tables and saw the glass carafes of wine on each, half-full, bright in the sun with their contents like liquid rubies or topaz. But something deep inside was hurting. She told herself not to think until just before facing Jean-François on Sunday. Just *be*, she told herself, listening to the chatter around her. If my heart is breaking, why is my stomach upset?

Geneva

"So you're going to have a baby!" Veronique exclaimed, leaning forward toward her wineglass on the glass table. The two women were in her apartment in town, which was glass and steel and shining chrome. One wall was mirrored, and reflected the lake and the sky before them. They often had lunch together here at the Devereaux apartment, when Cynthia had errands to run in Geneva. The sun had burned the fog away at noon, and the modern furnishings, spartan and shining, made the brightness of the interior dazzling. Double doors were open onto a small balcony, and before them stretched an expanse of water and skyscape.

"Wait! Wait!" Cynthia held up her right hand. On the third finger glittered a square-cut emerald set in platinum.

"Wait yourself! Where did that rock come from?" Veronique's brown eyes were wide. "He gave you that for getting pregnant!" It wasn't a question, it was a euphoric statement of fact. "Well, then, my dear girl, please produce a child immediately, so I can see what you get for actually coming through on the deal!"

Cynthia smiled and reached for her wineglass. "All I want to tell you is . . ." She sighed and went on, "Jean-François wants a child very much. He is finally talking about it." She didn't know whether to say anything to Veronique about the condoms she'd discovered in his bathroom. No, I will not. She had debated whether to accuse her husband or to ignore the whole thing, which was probably what Veronique and Yves would advise, or to remove the little, black, shiny packets so that he would know she knew. Cynthia decided she would keep count of them, and if one was ever missing from the cache, she would confront him. He had become so solicitous in the past two weeks, so interested in her, so tender toward her. She had felt ill Sunday evening as she unpacked and Jean-François had been concerned enough to call Dr. Marceau.

"Maybe it's the best thing. The best thing for your marriage. I know that Louis and I have changed so much since our oldest was born." She hesitated. "Let's say that the marriage has . . . evolved."

Cynthia tried not to smile. Jean-François didn't think that Veronique and Louis had a marriage. "They have dinner together once in a while," was the way he'd put it.

"So get pregnant and be happy," was her friend's final advice. "You won't believe how men act once they've . . . what do the Americans say?" She laughed her deep throaty laugh. "Once they've knocked you up! They go around as puffed up as roosters, and suddenly the mother-to-be takes on the qualities of the Virgin Mary, and before you know it, you have a husband nibbling from your hand. On his knees." She laughed again. "And loving it. And loving you. And loving what he's done to you! Oh, the male ego. Pride. Masculinity. Virility." She sipped wine with a big smile on her face.

"Oh, Veronique! You can be so mean! Jean-François is like an angel these days. He looks young and vulnerable to me. The way he did before we were married. Something in him that I loved has resurfaced . . ." It was true. She had fallen in love with him all over again.

"Cynthia! You have really bought the whole package, haven't you! But then again"—she turned her mouth down cynically—"the package is just reflection, isn't it?"

"What do you mean?"

"I mean that if someone looks at you as if he loves you, then you think 'I am lovable' and you love yourself and then you love the person who makes you love yourself, who makes you feel wonderful."

Cynthia let out a sigh of exasperation.

"Admit it!" Veronique demanded. "That's how love works!"

"Love and work aren't even words that go together, Veronique!"

"Do you believe that people 'work' at their marriages?"

"Oh, I hate that!" cried Cynthia. "It's the newest thing to talk about. I guess this decade in America will be known as the days of everyone 'working' at their marriages!" Veronique laughed at the vehemence of the reaction as she continued, "I imagine men and women wearing wedding rings through their noses, being led on chains, with pickaxes on their shoulders, to the salt mines!"

Veronique was grinning with great self-satisfaction as she leaned back in the Eames chair of cream suede. Her white silk blouse was festooned with amber beads, her vivid coral nails matched her carefully lipsticked mouth. "I don't feel that I'm working at my marriage. Louis knows what it takes to make me content, and I know what he needs and we allow it." She shrugged. "And we have the children in common."

"Sounds so simple," said Cynthia, looking at the expanse of mirror showing the two friends placed on a reflection of water behind them. We look like something created by Dali. Made up. A fantasy from the mind of an eccentric. A painting titled *Two Wives of Geneva Discussing Marriage*.

"You'll see," Veronique said sagely as she emptied the bottle into their glasses. The white wine looked like sunlight. "Please hurry up with this baby! I adore being a godmother, and besides, I can hardly wait to see the new jewelry!"

CHAPTER SIXTEEN

Iris

1973 — San Juan, Puerto Rico

Iris thought marriage was great fun. Vito was so generous; anything she wanted, anything at all, was hers. She only had to point at it and smile, or squeeze his arm and look up at him. It was bought, wrapped, and delivered to the Luppese suite that same afternoon. The first months of their marriage were lived in the penthouse of the Luppese Palace Hotel in San Juan. Iris spent her time trying on new clothes and then giggling as Vito took them off her. The newlyweds often went to Montego Bay or to a hotel in Martinique or Santo Domingo, but returned to San Juan after a week or two.

Iris loved living in the San Juan suite. One would imagine that she'd been born in a first-class hotel. She'd always hated doing dishes, and thought anything vaguely related to a kitchen awfully boring. Room service was such an obvious alternative. Why should she have to make a bed when people could march in and do it for her? Vacuuming? Cleaning a bathroom? It wasn't Iris's style. Her energy was better expended in getting to and from various appointments, though lately she'd had the hairdresser and the manicurist come to her. And there was shopping. Serious shopping.

In a boutique she liked, Iris could spend several thousand dollars in a matter of an hour. If a silk blouse pleased her, she was liable to buy one in every color. If a pair of trousers were a little snug, she often bought them and the next size up, too. And in every color. Vito adored going with her to pick out lingerie, and usually sneaked into the dressing room to okay the little lace teddy or the brassiere with the push-up wire cups. He'd been horrified when she confided that her mother used to make all her underwear by hand. "Something to do with hygiene," Iris had said, shrugging as if it were nothing. But when she thought of all the awful little cotton bloomers banded in gray elastic, she clenched her teeth. And then, of course, to make up for the bad memory, she picked out an ounce of lace that cost sixty-five dollars.

"You know, Vito, you're a big part of why this marriage is so great," she cooed up at him.

He laughed with his head thrown back. "Oh, baby bride! Ya take the cake! Ya made me the happiest guy on the planet!"

Then they'd go to bed for a while. Vito worshiped her body. They had that in common. Iris's short career as an actress had given her an excuse to stare into the mirror for hours. She resumed this habit of self-examination, but now the retinue of retainers who joined her in this preoccupation was enlarged.

A major admirer was Hatfield, the big (six-foot-three and built like a pro halfback) black hairdresser in San Juan, who was king of the salon at the hotel. He told her endlessly how wonderful her fine platinum tresses were. And Dotty the manicurist, who said she had the softest hands and feet of anyone she'd ever worked on. "I mean, honey, if I didn't know better," she'd say with her Doublemint gum in midair between swacks, "I'd say Mr. Luppese had hired somebody ta jes' cart you 'round like a queen so those little velvet feet of yours never had to suffer the shock a' hittin' ground!" Juan had given her the first massage at the Luppese Palace, but Vito hadn't liked the way he'd smiled at Iris afterwards, so now José did it. Like Hatfield, he was so gay, as Vito said, that "he prob'ly wore purple tutus around the house." The "assistants" in their madras jackets snickered behind their big, hairy hands whenever José arrived for his appointment. Gay José simply raised his penciled eyebrows and pursed his lips, then sniffed disdainfully through his tiny nose.

Between all this maintenance and getting ready for the evenings with Vito and trying to get enough beauty sleep in the mornings, Iris's days flew.

Her husband used one bedroom of the penthouse suite as his office. So it was easy to have lunch together in the suite and often a "little nap" afterwards. Iris liked to do it before Hatfield came to do her hair. She found that if she put Vito off for even one afternoon, he was liable to drag her away from the dinner table in front of guests. Then her hair was really a sight when she reappeared for dessert.

Iris Luppese was happy without reservation for perhaps the first time in her life. She had no financial worries, and she was secure in her position as Mrs. Luppese. The role was an easy one, and she fairly glowed when the hotel staff made a fuss over her. Furthermore, she could easily accomplish what was expected of her, which was simply to be beautiful, sexy, and available for Vito.

Iris loved sex. There was nothing she didn't love about it, from the first unzipping of a man's fly, all the way to the stickiness on her thighs afterwards. She loved the heaviness of the male animal, the sense of being filled with him, the taste of him, the smells, the moans of pleasure, the deep sleep of the satisfied. She was an acrobat in bed, especially for a woman who couldn't do a sit-up if someone held a gun to her temple. She was a giver, as unselfish as a saint. Iris, who wouldn't voluntarily open a door if a man was within fifty feet to do it for her, was tireless in her ministrations over the male organ. But perhaps what men loved about Iris was what came to flower with Cutter and again with Vito. She was funny, she was irreverent, she was playful.

"Oh, my God in heaven!" she squealed as Vito flipped her over like a little doll and mounted her from behind.

"Mary! Mary! Mother of Jesus!" he groaned in ecstasy as he clutched her tight little white bottom, which made him think of the marble statue fountain in the big piazza of Luppese. "Mary! Mary!"

"My name is Iris, you lunkhead!" she called back to him, which made him tremble with laughter.

"Don't do that, Iris!" he begged while his eyes watered with hilarity. "I'm losing it! I'm losing it!"

She wriggled away and turned onto her back, grinning, and then looked up at him as he loomed over her on all fours. "We'll get it back, Vito! Don't you worry!" He dipped down, bending his arms in a sort of push-up to kiss her. Then she scrambled behind him on the big double bed and reached under his big, muscular buttocks and between his thighs and began to stroke him gently.

Vito was vocal about this. He cried out, he swore, he praised her. Then, helpless with desire, he shouted, "Iris! Come in front of me! I can't see you! I want to see you!"

Iris smiled and continued stroking. "Use your rearview mirror!"

. . .

Vito and Iris were compatible. "This happy marriage routine—it's all expectations," Iris said to Hatfield. "I give him what he wants. I think I even give him more than he thought he could have." She shrugged as Hatfield wielded a big brush, back-combing her hair into a bouffant that would just go through doorways. "And he likes having a little doll."

Hatfield was surprised at how bright Iris was. "Hmmm," was all he said, but he was taking it in. Then he couldn't resist. "I never saw his first wife, but I heard about her. She was no doll."

"Oh! Tell me what you know!" Iris put both manicured hands on the arms of the chair and rose right up off the seat. Dotty had applied acrylic Dragon Lady nails and lacquered them a deep orchid purple, which was perfect for the lavender chiffon dress she planned to wear at dinner. "Hatfield, you have to tell me! I don't know anything, and of course I should know, so that I don't make mistakes."

"You ain't makin' no mistakes." Hatfield grinned with a row of ivories that made Iris want to reach for sunglasses. The reflection in her dressing room mirror was dazzling. His gold silk shirt was open to the waist, and his broad chest was hairless and as smooth and rich-looking as the darkest chocolate. White trousers hugged his hips so tightly that Iris wondered if he could sit down. But then he didn't sit down, with his job. Hatfield stood all day in his white patent leather Guccis—little tassels, no socks. He toyed with a side curl, artfully suggesting that it was natural. Then he whooshed about three ounces of hair spray on that one tendril. Iris held her breath, closed her eyes, and waited. "She was jes' one of them Italian mamas, you know?"

Iris winced. Mama. *She* was Cesare's mama. He had sent a telegram saying simply, "Congratulations. Cesare." And both Iris and Vito had stared at it and then at each other. Neither said a word, but they had one thought: it had to be sarcastic. Didn't he have the right to hate them both?

Hatfield was going on. "You know, like on the spaghetti ads. Real fat. Arms like seal flippers. No lap, just rolls. A face like the Pillsbury Doughboy's and gray hair back in a bun. And a big housedress with little print flowers on it."

"How do you know all this?"

"I saw her photograph. Mr. Luppese had it on his desk for about four years after she died. I came up to do—"

Iris was suddenly very alert. "To do whose hair?" she demanded.

"Some . . . somebody he had stayin' here for a while, but she di'n't last . . ."

Iris's green eyes flashed. Well, of course a man like Vito had to have women. And his wife did die six years ago and maybe she wasn't all that great in the sack before she croaked. No, forget it, Iris told herself. "So the first Mrs. Luppese was a real frump?" Iris stared at herself in the mirror. Hatfield was concentrating on a backwave.

"Don't call my mother anything, you two-timin', lyin', cheatin', piece a' garbage."

Hatfield turned with the brush in his hand, his wrist arched, and Iris jerked her head around just in time to see Cesare, a vision in white, strike out with his fist. Orange stars exploded in front of her, she heard Hatfield's high-pitched scream, and then there was only darkness.

"Oh, baby bride," Vito was whispering. "Wake up, darling!"

Iris opened her big green eyes and focused on his darkly suntanned face. It was full of concern, and judging from the red nose, he was full of liquor. She took his thumb in her hand and held on to it.

He smoothed her forehead with his other hand and smiled. "Oh, you're all right. I thought you were gonna sleep till tomorrow. How do ya feel?"

She tried to talk, but couldn't. Her jaw was wired shut. Her eyes showed panic as Vito tried to explain. "Just for three weeks, that's all. You have to drink out of a straw, but I've already told the kitchen that anything you want you get ground up, pulverized, liquefied. Anything!"

Iris put up her hand in horror. " 'E broke my jaw," she muttered through clenched teeth.

"I know!" Vito's voice boomed. "And there's a warrant out for his arrest! I want him caught and brought back to me so he can apologize!"

Apologize to me or to you! wondered Iris. Oh, shit! What does my face look like? She motioned for Chiquita, who hovered nearby in her pink maid's uniform, to hand her the mirror on the bureau. "Agh!" was Iris's anguished reaction when she saw the green, blue, and black bruises circling the ugly metal.

Vito was stroking her hair on the pillow. "Iris, baby. I'll get him for this. I'll get him for hurting you. You are my precious dollbaby," he crooned.

Iris dropped the mirror on the yellow flowered spread and wondered who would get her for what she did to Cesare. For hurting Cesare. She remembered the urgency of his proposal ("Marry me. Marry me.") and his fevered love-making. She remembered Harry, too, weeping on his knees, in their apartment as she told him good-bye. A broken jaw isn't enough, she thought. If this is all there is, then I got off cheap.

CHAPTER SEVENTEEN

Cynthia

1973 — Les Colombiers

A bright orange fire sputtered and hissed in the fireplace at one end of the master bedroom. Cynthia made a mental note to ask the gardener to be more careful about keeping the wood dry in the shed, and glanced uneasily at Jean-François, hoping he wouldn't notice. She continued to brush her hair as she walked toward him, big belly preceding her in the cream satin quilted bathrobe. Jean-François was sitting at the desk with a pen in his hand, studying typed pages with the bank's letterhead. He scratched little notes in the margins, and then sighed and bit his lip.

"Darling," she said, putting her hands on his shoulders, "will you come to bed now?"

He turned slowly in the chair to look up at her. "I don't know. I don't know if I will or not."

Cynthia didn't answer, but her hands kneaded the muscles in the back of his neck, her thumbs worked at loosening the tightness in his broad shoulders.

"If that's an invitation, then the answer is yes. But if you're just in need of being 'cuddled,' as you say, then why don't you buy yourself a stuffed animal?"

Cynthia dropped her hands and walked quickly away.

"It's always like this, isn't it?" he taunted. "You want to be pregnant, so I take care of that. You have Michel. *Brava.*" He had turned completely around in the chair, and had the chair back under his chin, his legs on either side of it, knees wide apart. "I do my bit for you."

"You can't say that—" Cynthia was folding back the duvet and unbuttoning the robe. They had had an early dinner, it was a cold February night, and all she wanted was to be warm in the big four-poster bed. Warm, with Jean-François close to her. But that was not to be. Not in his present mood.

"Oh, can't I?" His voice was mocking. "So now you're pregnant again and not so very interested—"

"We made love last night!" Pulling the robe away, she thought she looked as if she had a basketball under the nightgown. Maybe I should simply be pleased he wants me. She could hear Veronique telling her that.

"I hardly remember it. So memorable was it." Jean-François was standing now, coming toward the bed. Cynthia hated him when he was like this. His lips curled in a nasty way, his eyes bright with anger, his face dark, as if the blood had rushed to his head. "What the hell do you do?"

Her voice was cool and detached as she slipped her bare feet under the ironed, clean sheets. "What do you mean?"

"I mean—what's your modus operandi? How do you do it?"

Cynthia reached toward the little clock on the bedside table and turned it to face her. Her hand trembled, and she hated herself for that. She looked at her fingers as if they had betrayed her, and prayed he hadn't seen.

His voice was rising. He was standing over her, still dressed in his business suit. "What I'm asking is, what do you lie back and think of? Surely it's not England. Is it Switzerland? No." He smiled sarcastically. "I know!" He snapped his fingers close to her face, leaning down. Cynthia willed herself not to blink. "I know! You lie back and think of Beacon Hill!"

"No." Her voice was nearly inaudible. She fluffed up the pillow behind her, but she couldn't close her eyes.

Cynthia didn't look at her husband. He could go on that way for hours. About sex. About the way she "mismanaged the household," about Michel still crawling, about anything. She knew he wasn't finished.

"How do you think it is for me? Do you think I like having sex with a corpse?"

Cynthia swallowed thickly, her face flushed. She put her hands outside the covers and smoothed the mound that was the new baby. Don't listen, she thought to herself. Little one, don't hear this. Aloud, she said, "Why do you say 'having sex' instead of 'making love'? I always hope we are making love."

"Oh!" Jean-François threw his head back. "*Pardonnez-moi!* Yes! Let's be delicate about it, shall we? Sex is dirty for Cynthia, but making love is okay." He was staring at the fire and nodding as if he finally understood. "Maybe that's the problem between us. I want you to spread your legs wide and let go and have sex with me like a bitch in heat, and you want Cary Grant to kiss you for three hours with background music, and then he might possibly be allowed to slowly slip out of his dinner jacket—"

"Stop it!" Cynthia reached for the bedside lamp. "I'm tired."

"I'm tired, too!" There was a threat in his voice, but Cynthia couldn't fathom the meaning. Tired of me? Tired of talking?

The room was dark except for the desk lamp and the glow of the fire, which was orange and yellow and flickering. The hissing of the damp wood was loud in the room; the sweep of the alarm clock's second hand was the only other sound. Jean-François's profile was strong and handsome, but the downturned mouth was sullen, petulant. He stood like a statue beside the bed for another two or three minutes, and only when he moved away and left the room did Cynthia's rigid muscles relax, and she allowed herself to close her eyes. The door slammed behind him and she heard him descending the stairs, calling for Christophe to bring the car around. Cynthia sat up with both hands clenched in fists.

Year five of happy marriage, she thought cynically. The only thing that's really changed since year three is that he no longer makes any secret of sleeping with other women. No, that isn't true, she admitted. Being pregnant with Michel was bliss. Everything Veronique told me was true in spades. Jean-François was in love with the idea of a baby in the house, in love with me, and in love with himself for being so clever as to make it all possible. She thought of the presents; the little things he had held behind his back teasingly had pleased her most. There had been fancy perfumed soaps from Roger Gallet in their bright plastic cases, and once he had brought a dozen velvet ribbons each a meter long for her hair. Jean-François had seemed softer then, a man who adored his wife. Marriage had taken a new shape, as if, for the first time, they were together, waiting for a baby they both wanted, anticipating even greater happiness.

Cynthia lay back, the blond hair she still kept very long splayed on the white pillowcase, and folded her hands across her swollen belly. How surprised she'd been to have undergone a cesarean, and to awaken flat and empty, to be told it was "all over." She remembered groggily trying to focus on the face of Elizabeth. And tiny Michel! They had picked a name that was easy in many languages for the little boy. She had cried and cried when he was put into her arms. No one could really understand why. She had been thinking of her firstborn somewhere . . . somewhere far away. The baby she had never even held. I never saw your face, I don't know your name. Oh, stop! she told herself. He or she is happy, almost six years old. And this new baby will mean two babies to keep, to have and to hold, to love and protect—they are to help me forget. Please, little new one, she smoothed her round belly, be a happy child. She thought of the great happiness Michel had given her—just by existing, just by his bright eyes lighting on her when she entered a room, just by having tiny fingernails. She bit her lip and stared up at the ceiling, thinking she had to get up and turn off the desk lamp. Maybe things will change with Jean-François. Maybe it's his age, the bank, something . . . something besides me. Let us find what we used to have, she prayed, when Michel was a dream, safe inside of me, growing like a flower underground, waiting for spring to make an appearance. Oh, Jean-François, why can't I bring out the good things in you again? I hope . . . Then she told herself not to finish the thought. But too late, she said to herself. You can't not finish thoughts. They speed ahead and there they are. She frowned and then thought it again: I hope I can stop hating him.

. . .

Stephanie Elizabeth was born on a rainy afternoon in May at the Hôpital Cantonal Universitaire Genève. Mother and baby are fine, Jean-François was told when he arrived at Les Colombiers from the airport.

"Paris. On business." Cynthia's voice was calm as she told Elizabeth. "He's on his way."

Elizabeth looked angry for a moment, and then said in a brisk, well-let's-get-on-with-it manner, "The most important thing is you! How do you feel?"

Cynthia nodded, but her great green eyes were filled with tears.

Her mother-in-law yanked a Kleenex from the box on the little metal bed-side table and handed it to her. "Don't worry. Often happens. I felt like crying my eyes out for days after . . ." A look of sadness crossed her face. "Afterwards."

"Talk to me," said Cynthia. "Please talk to me about something other than babies and . . ." Her voice faded. "Just . . . just tell me how India was."

Elizabeth reached for her hand and took it. It was rough from gardening, like her own. "Oh! How I wish I could help!" she sighed. "But what can I do? Is there anything you can think of? Anything you want to talk about?"

Cynthia seemed to take on strength from Elizabeth's concern, or perhaps it was pride that made her blink away the tears and feign complete control. "I'm fine. Everything is just fine, Elizabeth. I talked to my parents when you went out for coffee. They're so excited to have a granddaughter. Now tell me—is the Taj Mahal all it's cracked up to be?"

"It's better!" Elizabeth's face was younger than her years; her hair was still jet black and had been blunt-cut to shoulder length. Sunburned, with those dark eyes like Jean-François's, she looked to Cynthia like a gypsy suddenly dressed in elegant clothes. "My friends and I realized that we could be there on a night of the full moon, so we postponed Burma—talk about getting visas!—and hired a car and raced along from Delhi to Agra after this spec-tacular dinner. The food was so hot that—"

"I'm jealous! Why can't I do things like that?"

"Because, my dear, you're busy having babies. When Stephanie Elizabeth is two, you can come with me!" She thought, That would show my son what's what!

Cynthia smiled broadly. "You're amazing. You're what I want to be like." She nearly blushed with the implied intimacy. She and Elizabeth shared the way common to both old and New England of not saying things close to the heart. But they understood each other just because they had been taught not to express too much in words.

"You breastfeed my little granddaughter, and then we'll talk. I don't see why Jean-François should keep you chained to that drafty old chateau—"

"Hello, Mother dear," the voice oozed sarcasm. Jean-François stood in the doorway of the white room. They didn't know how long he'd been listening. His gray pinstriped suit, one of three he'd had made for him in London, was beautifully tailored; his dark blue tie was perfectly knotted over the white oxford-cloth shirt. He appeared to have just showered and dressed. "Fomenting revolution, are you?"

"Darling! You have a daughter! Come here and give your wife a kiss!" Elizabeth ignored his snarled remark.

His face was set in the scowl his wife was beginning to know so well. He didn't speak for a moment. Both women were astonished when he said, "How can you invite Cynthia and not me?"

His voice sounded like a little boy's asking why his friend could stay up later; why his friend got a bicycle for Christmas; was he loved as much as another?

Elizabeth managed to laugh. "Oh, silly dear! You can come too, if you behave yourself! Now come over here." It was a command. "And show Cynthia how much you appreciate all she's been through today!"

He entered the room then, and kissed his mother on the forehead and then sat on the bed carefully and bent down to kiss Cynthia's lips. "The baby— she's all right?" he asked her, and she nodded.

"I arrived here at about seven-thirty, just before—"

Jean-François turned to his mother. "How did you know to—"

"Cynthia called me at four, when the pains started, and I thought, false alarm or not, I wanted to be here!" She smiled. "So a mad drive to Paris and then the early flight . . ."

Jean-François wasn't listening. He was holding Cynthia's hand very tightly, with downcast eyes. "Did you call my hotel?" he asked quietly. She nodded. He wouldn't look at her.

Elizabeth pressed her lips together and stood up. The little white metal chair made a *scrawk* noise on the linoleum when the legs scraped the floor. "Would you like me to stay for a few days or shall I go back home?" She smoothed the skirt of the black linen dress with a flash of a hammered gold bracelet, a wink of the large square-cut diamond.

"Please stay on!" Cynthia said. "I'd love to have you there when they let me out of here. And Michel will be ecstatic. Really!"

Elizabeth smiled. "Well, we've all heard a thousand mother-in-law jokes, so . . ."

"No. Stay, Maman! Do stay," urged her son.

"All right! Now, what can I do for the new mother? Shopping? Anything from home you want me to pick up? Face cream? Chocolates? Trashy novels?" She put out her arms. "I'm here to serve you! So take advantage of it!"

Cynthia smiled. "Chocolates! And the worst romantic novel you can dig up. English or French, I don't care, just as long as the heroine wears a hoop skirt and is a virgin . . ."

Elizabeth waved from the doorway. "And the hero has to wear riding boots all the time! And skintight trousers!" She disappeared.

Jean-François still held Cynthia's hand. She saw his face suffused with guilt, eyes downcast as if fascinated by the hem of the sheet. He was contrite, like a badly behaved little boy.

But he is wonderful to look at, and he is my husband. We do have a son and now a daughter together. Cynthia put her other hand over his.

"Jean-François, do you love me?" He had never told her. She had complained to Veronique, who said European men seldom say it. It's the Americans who say it all the time. They wear out the phrase. Forget it. Of course he loves you. Forget about his saying it, though.

He looked up at her, into the clear, shining green eyes that were like transparent forest pools.

"Tell me if you love me."

"Of course I love you," he replied.

"Tell me."

His dark eyes dropped to their hands again. Then he spoke. "I love you," he said in a dead voice.

Cynthia was silent, waiting.

His voice was strong this time. But absolutely flat. *"Je t'aime. Je t'aime. Je t'aime!"* He frowned and then looked right into her face. "There! Are you satisfied now?"

Zurich Airport

"That blonde." Jean-François nodded toward the tall, slender stewardess behind the check-in counter of Swissair.

Alain Didier laughed. "You never stop, do you? I can't think of anything but my bed—and alone! After that meeting today, you can't possibly have the strength!"

Jean-François shrugged. "Some men like a game of squash after a hard day, but I like a good fuck."

Alain shook his head. He was the same age as Jean-François and had been married a few years longer, but he couldn't imagine behaving the way his colleague did. It was always some woman. Get her to bed and then get her out again and catch his plane, make his appointment, usually leaping from a cab, running up the steps, dashing down a hallway to the boardroom.

Alain now watched him stride over, his broad shoulders in the well-cut suit ramrod straight. The face of the young woman was smiling, then her expression gave way to pretty confusion. Jean-François moved aside as more passengers arrived at the desk to hand her boarding cards. But she was glancing surreptitiously at him, a faint pinkness suffusing her face and neck in the open white cotton blouse. Alain watched his friend step forward again and make what appeared to be a joking remark. The girl looked down at her desk and then up into his face for a few seconds, judging him. Then she broke into a smile and nodded. As Alain watched, she took Jean-François's boarding-pass stub and matched it with one in her own pile. He took it from her hand with a slow smile, which seemed to perplex her, but she was smiling back at him all the time.

Alain opened the *Neue Zurcher Zeitung* and shook it out to the editorial page. Christ, I hate to watch, he thought, remembering Cynthia, the dazzling American wife. He wondered how often they went to bed together. She did have a veneer of cool aristocracy, but his own wife, Charlotte, had told him she was a warm person. Charlotte said you had to take the time to get past her shyness, and perhaps it was shyness about her French. Whatever it was, thought Alain, she was smashing. When he had met her the first time, she was wearing a red silk dress with bouffant sleeves that bared her white shoulders. The party was in Paris around Christmastime, and she said she had dared to wear emeralds that were so big as to be taboo in Geneva. They had shared a few jokes about the "Protestant Rome" and tipped their champagne glasses "to Jean Calvin."

The memory troubled him. Cynthia was very nice, very young. He tried to focus on the editorial about the latest French election.

"Hey, I'm not flying to Geneva with you." The voice was over his shoulder.

"Are you nuts? It's the next-to-last flight. You're not going to take that awful eleven P.M. one, are you? That's the worst—"

Jean-François shook his head. "No. I'll come tomorrow. Early." He grinned. "I've got a date. Right here in Zurich." He turned to look at her once more and she smiled, knowing that he was talking about her to his friend. "Pretty cute, isn't she? From Interlaken. Her French is a travesty, but who cares?"

Les Colombiers

Cynthia did not examine her marriage, she simply got on with it. It was life, it was children, it was routine. She loved her children and she was happy in her garden and everything flourished under her capable hands. She was often reminded of her mother's advice. How many times had she told Cynthia to think of what Jean-François could give their unborn children, to think of the life he could bestow upon her as a wife and chatelaine. It sounded like Veronique. Like Yves. How very practical it all was. A house. Servants. Children. Security. The whole nine yards. Because she had fallen in love with Jean-François, Cynthia simply wanted him, but was nonetheless not unpleased with what he possessed, or his position in life. Cynthia sighed. Still, what about being happy to see your husband walk in the front door at the end of the day? Where did that fit in? Or where had it gone?

Michel was a sturdy little boy with chunky legs and dimples in his pink knees that showed between knee socks and short trousers. Black-haired, with dark eyes, he was a clone of his father. Elizabeth doted on him, and Cynthia's mother thought he was an angel and sent packages from Boston nearly every month. He outgrew the clothes while they were in the mail, Cynthia told Veronique.

Stephanie was a small-boned, delicate, golden-haired little girl, with her father's big dark eyes and her mother's features. She wanted to attempt anything Michel could do, and experienced deep frustration at finding herself not tall enough, not strong enough. She was so self-critical, she cried when she felt she had failed. Cynthia called her "my little perfectionist" and consoled her when she was angry at not being able to zip her snowsuit without help. She seemed to thrive with other children, couldn't wait for first grade, and came home grinning with pride, waving her perfect scores on this spelling test or that arithmetic homework. A less-than-perfect grade would make her frown. Cynthia would say, "But you did so well." Cynthia assumed it was competition with her older brother, but eventually she realized it was simply Stephanie's character to care deeply about pleasing, about achievement.

Both children were fluent in French and English, and when Michel was four, Jean-François hired a German nanny. The French nurse who had tended both children since birth was very young and had a fiancé in Lyon she longed to return to, so there were no hard feelings and the transition was easily accomplished. At the age of six, the little boy was trilingual, and Stephanie, four at the time, was also nearly fluent in German.

Cynthia kept them home until they were six, then Michel was sent to the public school at Chambesy, and later Stephanie followed. When they were ten, both children transferred to the prestigious and private Geneva International School.

Their mother liked taking them to school. They chattered in the backseat like birds about their friends, their teachers, their projects. And they fought, too. Usually Stephanie started the "touched you last" games. The chauffeur fetched them for lunch or the nanny of the moment. If Cynthia didn't get a glimpse of them before they were shepherded back at two o'clock, she always tried to sit with them when they had their supper. Sometimes it was difficult to arrange, but she felt guilty when she couldn't be there.

They were bright, lively children, and Cynthia made sure they had friends for ice-skating, invited groups to swim in the pool; she supervised memorable birthday parties, and hired the *de rigueur* piano teacher. They both learned to sail off the dock at the lawn's edge. Invitations for playing after school or lunch on Saturday were more formal than anything Cynthia could remember from her own New England childhood. It meant telephoning the mother of little Pascal and asking if it would be all right for him to spend the day with Michel, then there were the logistics of picking up and depositing home again. It was all mapped out in advance, very carefully.

Each December twelfth, Cynthia took them, bundled up, looking like fat dwarves, to see the reenactment of the Escalade. The affair was a parade that commemorated the night in 1602 when the Genevois fended off the Savoyards at the city's gates. Cynthia bought Michel and Stephanie each a chocolate in the shape of a cauldron to symbolize the pot of hot soup a housewife had poured over the wall onto the invaders. The handmade costumes of the procession were carefully passed from one generation to the next for this particular holiday, which was the most important Genevois celebration. Some of the participants rode on horseback, some in wooden farm wagons; others led cattle and came with their dogs. They were bearded and bonneted and carried muskets and pitchforks. Michel and Stephanie always loved it.

One year, Mimi and Antoine Bonnell invited the Colberts to celebrate with their extended Genevois family. Antoine had known Jean-François all his life. December the twelfth meant a dinner with all forty-five relatives—brothers and sisters and in-laws and children. There was pheasant as a main course; the table was laden with food, and extended from the dining room into the salon. All twenty-three of the children cheered loudly when servants arrived carrying the giant chocolate cauldron. Nicholas, at fifteen the oldest of the children, brought out the family's ceremonial sword, and—*swak!*—with one powerful stroke broke the pot open. Out poured marzipan and chocolate candies, symbolizing what the housewife had poured down on the French. Cynthia had such a wonderful time in that crowd of people at the Bonnells' chateau that she wondered fleetingly if she should talk to Jean-François about having more children.

Jean-François is an only child, and so am I. How sad it is for my two to have not one cousin, if it means this much fun on a holiday.

Stephanie appeared to be more gregarious away from home, at school with the little girls her own age. Michel was slightly introverted and preferred to play alone in the garden with imaginary playmates, or to sit for hours with a box of crayons and paper. He would come solemnly into Cynthia's room after school and wait for her to finish a phone call, standing patiently, his big, dark eyes fixed on her adoringly.

One afternoon he said, "Maman! Bernard and I are going to build a house in the faraway garden!"

Cynthia smiled and held out her arms to him then pulled him onto her lap, muddy shoes and all, to be cuddled. "A big house? Big enough to live in?" she asked, and he pulled away and looked up at her.

"Big enough for me to make my drawings. Big enough for you and me and Bernard." He set his mouth with determination. "No one else allowed." Then he amended. "Except both grandmeres!"

"What will you build it of? Wood?"

He was anxious to begin the project, and wriggled off her lap. Halfway across the room, he turned. "Wood? No, Maman! It's going to be made out of gold!"

The clatter of his feet across the marble floor and echoing down the staircase made her smile. She knew how he held onto the banister with one hand and with the other held onto the invisible Bernard, helping his "friend" down the stairs.

Cynthia's early married years revolved around availability for Jean-François, looking her best for him and being with him at receptions and dinner parties. There was a perpetual parade of houseguests, but she quickly developed a system whereby she gave them a car and told them what was of interest in town or in nearby France, and they were not allowed to imagine seeing her again until drinks before dinner. By the late afternoon she was dressed and happy to be entertained by their adventures. Often the guest was a curator from a museum, anxious to discuss his collection with Jean-François. All Cynthia really did was make sure they were comfortable and well fed and had a desk or a large table to lay things out on. Photographs or artifacts or catalogues. Less often they were clients who had become friends, which was typical in the world of private banking. They spent one night and half a day, conferring with Jean-François all morning, or he would leave the bank early and they would talk before, during, and after dinner. The following morning there would be an early drive to the airport. Sometimes special guests stayed over the weekend.

The house was filled with flowers, the food was always beautifully prepared, and Cynthia was comfortable with all kinds of people—from the most flamboyant collector to the most introverted, professorial researcher.

Often, entire days were spent with the account book or on the telephone, for there was so much repair work to be done on the house. The second-floor rooms where she and Jean-François and the children lived were finally papered and painted, but there were new mantelpieces to be carved for two of the rooms, and tiles to be picked for four of the bathrooms. Besides all that, there was the Colbert social life. When Jean-François was away Cynthia had her own invitations.

The wives of Geneva often met for lunches at one house or another. Six or eight of them arrived at noon, in their elegantly tailored suits or silk afternoon dresses, and were served by maids in the family dining room. Sometimes in the late spring or summer, a table was set out on the porch, with a linen tablecloth and silver, though there was never an attempt at informality. They still wore white gloves, Cynthia wrote to her mother. Both guests and servants, she added in the margin. Her mother approved of the custom.

The evening dinner parties were black-tie, often in a tent outside the big houses. The women wore evening dresses bought on their latest shopping trip to Paris, and an orchestra provided dance music under the gaily striped marquee. Two hundred guests was a normal crowd, with dozens of staff wending their way through the guests with trays of champagne held aloft. "But the party givers are the foreigners," Veronique pointed out. "They are not the Genevois. The Genevois don't believe in this kind of show. They'll come and they'll be well-mannered, but they'll leave early!"

"You mean they'll drink the best champagne, but they won't approve?" asked Cynthia.

"Oh, yes, exactly! They'll choke it down!"

Golf was played in Onex, and there was talk of building a golf club in Cologny, directly across the lake. Jean-François told Cynthia that he could remember his grandfather telling him that when he was a boy at the turn of the century he would ride horseback all over the area, and it was owned by only four families. Many of the houses across the water from Les Colombiers were occupied only a month or six weeks every year; they were the summer houses of the wealthy Genevois. Tennis was very popular, and there was a great deal of sailing on the lake.

Cynthia found her time at the chateau spent in constantly having things perfect for Jean-François's arrival. The children seemed to sense his imminent appearance from the airport and, like rabbits, ran to their rooms. Stephanie wasn't nearly as intimidated as Michel by his temper, and though their papa often brought little presents, they waited until after dinner, which they took in the kitchen, to come and kiss him *bon soir*.

Sometimes Cynthia felt more like another child than a wife. I am well-behaved, I am obedient, she thought one morning after Jean-François had been particularly irritable at breakfast over some imagined sin. Perhaps he'd noticed that a hedge in the back needed pruning. Or perhaps it was a silver tray that needed polishing. It was all the same—a rebuke, and then Cynthia saying, "I'll take care of it." But just when those prickly, unhappy thoughts settled on her, her husband would arrive home in a delightful mood with tickets to Wimbledon given to him by a client, asking, "Can you be ready day after tomorrow? I have a suite at the Dorchester!" Or he would kiss her in the front hall and make her guess which hand held the jewelry box behind his back. He goes too far, thought Cynthia, and then he's sorry. He's like a little boy who has a tantrum and then comes home with something he's made at school. Often she thought of him as a spoiled, bad-tempered child, though he was older than she by fifteen years, and treated her as a child so much of the time. Cynthia never felt that she was his equal, that she could say things. Ask, yes. Apologize, always. But not express too many opinions. And never was she allowed to say what she wanted or didn't want in bed. Jean-François and his ego had already mapped the four-poster as his territory. She was his, his wife, his property, once she pulled the sheets back.

. . .

"At the end of the day I don't ever feel that I can say 'I did this' or 'I made this,' " she complained to Veronique. "It's all maintenance. It's all taking care of things and, of course, taking care of people." She sighed. "Why do I feel like that when I get into bed at night?"

"You're supposed to feel Jean-François when you get into bed!"

"Oh, stop it! I do! But there must be something—"

"Look. Don't get all American on me! There are no jobs for anyone here in this little town. We both do our good deeds with the Foyer Handicap." The charity was run by the socially prominent women of Geneva. Veronique frowned. "If we were in Paris, it would be a different story. You could work for a fashion house or a publisher or an art gallery. There would be any number of ladylike occupations for the wife of a rich man, but here . . ." She threw up her manicured hands. "Nothing!"

"Thank God I have the garden," Cynthia murmured. "At least I can see progress . . ."

"You mean you don't clap your hands with joy when Michel outgrows his Sunday shoes? What kind of a mother are you?"

Cynthia wondered if she dared say it, even to her closest friend. "Do you ever . . . do you sometimes—"

"Out with it. Odds are I probably do," urged Veronique.

"Do you ever wonder why no one told you how boring it all is?" Cynthia took a deep breath, and the oatmeal wool dress swelled tight across her small breasts. The gold chains she wore twinkled in the light. She expected Veronique to laugh at her, but her friend didn't say a word for a moment.

"It's Geneva. The sky is too low." Her voice was serious.

"No, Veronique. Really. I think sometimes that it's not worth it." The words slipped out.

The hand was on her arm like a vise. "Don't you *dare* say something like that! Don't you dare even *imagine* that!"

"What do you mean?"

"I mean that lots of women absolutely crack here—can't take it—the sky *is* too low. And there are all those positive ions trapped by the Alps in the middle of Europe, concentrated right here in Geneva."

"Positive ions?" Cynthia echoed, puzzled.

"Yes!" Veronique nodded vehemently. "And we're supposed to thrive on the negative ones. Leave it to Geneva to be a hotbed of the wrong kind of ions!"

The moment for serious confidences was over. She managed to smile. "So we're stuck with the positives that make us feel negative?"

"Exactly." Veronique nodded with a straight face. "And it's ruined this town!"

Geneva

"He's had his face lifted so many times he can barely get that hors d'oeuvre in. Look at him now. That sliver of smoked salmon . . . he's dying for it! But no, no! For a man who can't smile, a Schneiderman buffet is an impos—"

Cynthia shook her head at Yves to silence his second-by-second progress report. She leaned forward and allowed herself to be kissed by Madame Longet. "*Bon soir.* So nice to see you again." Three kisses. Back and forth and back again. The Geneva way.

"Are you here for a while?" the older woman asked.

"*Oui.* I must spend the next few days at the apartment in town, packing up things for Jean-François. Egyptian things for New York. They're going into a sale, and should have gone off two weeks ago." He'd asked the house-keeper to take care of it, but she hadn't, so then he'd blamed Cynthia for hiring an "incompetent," though it was the only botch-up in Madame Poirot's five years at Les Colombiers. "Then the children are arriving in three days with their *grand-mère* from France, which is wonderful."

She thought of the workers who were still in that second-floor bathroom, hanging wallpaper. She had to get them out before Elizabeth arrived. And the just-cleaned curtains must be rehung in the guest room she was so fond of. Cynthia sighed. The very idea of all the supervising bored her.

"Ah, my dear!" Madame Longet threw up her hands and, as if reading her mind, empathized, "I know what you are going through. I was thinking the other day of all the time we give to our houses. Seasons changing and people arriving. A week to close one house and a week to open another, and then in May another week to leave Geneva and another week to open the summer place. It's a month missing from every year."

Cynthia smiled, thinking, You left out the chalet in Verbier. Beginning in mid-December, that must be in order for the skiing season. And the damned roof still needs work. I must drive up on Monday and call the contractor to meet me.

Yves was touching her arm to get her attention. He whispered in her ear, "There's one of the best golfers ever. Geneva Golf Club. Did you know he left his wife because she was so cruel to him? Sometimes when he came home she wouldn't speak, and—"

"Yves!" She tried to quiet him though she never would have been at this party without him at her side. He was her comic relief. "How is the golf?" she said smoothly as Georges bent to kiss her hand.

"I'm playing my age," he said. Old Geneva, he was a man in his early seventies with hair going gray. He had courtly, Old World manners that made Cynthia think of Maurice Chevalier. A wide white scar ran across the top of his right hand, and he wore a very large gold signet ring on his little finger. "And every year," he laughed, "it's getting easier!"

Yves spoke. "We must play sometime. Do you always play with the Syndicate?"

"Oh, no! They give me a complex!" Georges smiled again.

The Syndicate was a group of the club's top golfers, numbering approximately fifty, who played together, pooling francs and vying for the purse. Many of them played five and six days a week and were much better than the weekend golfers. It was their names that were called on the awards night to stand up and be applauded and to walk forward for their little silver coaster engraved with the date.

"The Syndicate always sounds too serious," remarked Cynthia. "I think of the Mafia and Wall Street and—"

Yves burst in. "And you're right! The Syndicate is very serious and is definitely up—or would it be down?—on that level."

"You're just jealous," came Mimi Bonnell's voice. Georges nodded and turned to greet a golfing friend. Mimi was the very pretty Frenchwoman married to Antoine Bonnell of the enormous Genevois family who gave the Escalade parties. Antoine was a banker approaching eighty, and Mimi was in her late forties, with lots of energy. To Cynthia she seemed perpetually packing for Paris or unpacking her new clothes bought in Paris.

"*Oui.*" Yves nodded vehemently, smiling. "Totally green. As green as the green." Mimi kissed Cynthia, and then Yves.

"Tell me, how was Paris?" Cynthia asked the tall brunette in the dark blue velvet suit.

"The same," Mimi sighed. "The showings were so-so. I bought nearly nothing."

"I hear that Ann-Marie was there with you-know-who . . ."

"Oh, Yves! Shame on you!" Mimi chided. "Do you think I would know anything about that, or that I'd breathe a word to you if I did?"

Yves slipped his arm around her. He was quite a good-looking man, thought Cynthia. Too bad he was becoming known as Geneva's most notorious gay, but then again it didn't appear to hurt his feelings, did it? He was lively and full of fun, the perfect escort for anything, be it a Genevois dinner party or a dogfight.

Mimi was talking. "May I be the first to tell you that there is more than one hotel in Paris? And I didn't see them in mine."

Yves bubbled with laughter as a waiter in a white jacket poured more champagne into his glass. "I knew I could get a confirmation from you that Roger is, in fact, concubining in the City of Light."

Mimi and Cynthia shook their heads and rolled their eyes. Mimi asked, "Jean-François? Is he here?"

"No," answered Cynthia. "Paris!"

They all laughed. Yes, I can laugh, too, Cynthia thought. She sipped from the champagne tulip and thought of the ridiculous little packages in the medicine cabinet. So long ago. And I broke my promise to myself. She sipped again, conscious of the laughter and conversation around her as mere background for her thoughts. I counted them and I watched and I recounted, and when they were gone I never said a word. Paris, she thought again. Maybe it wasn't ever anyone in Geneva. He always has so much to do in Paris.

CHAPTER EIGHTEEN

Iris

1973 — The Caribbean

Señora Luppese's first years of marriage were heaven. From the wedding at City Hall in downtown Manhattan right through the months of living in the penthouse suite at the Luppese Palace in San Juan, in Mexico City, in Santo Domingo, in Montego Bay. Iris's life was idyllic.

The country didn't make much difference to her; she never handled money or worried about the weather. The suites were basically the same. Room service was always there with whatever she wanted, whether it was a cheeseburger or caviar, a Tab or a martini. Vito had laughed so hard when she asked for Baby Cham that she'd never done it again. She missed Hatfield, but she had Minnie, Juan, Rita, and Samuel, or others who performed the same services. Shopping was more limited on some islands than on others, but Vito took her to Miami with him about once a month, where she hit the stores with a vengeance. "Hurricane force," joked Don Vito. There were more credit cards than she knew what to do with, and her husband was as benevolent as a Santa Claus.

Vito told her she could stop World War Three if she could get the Russians in bed with her. She smiled like the coquette she was and asked, "All of them at once?" Iris batted her big, green, heavily made-up eyes, and purred, "Oh, Vito, you're such a joker."

Then, one day at lunch over a Caesar salad in Trinidad, he broke the news to her. "Iris, honey, I've decided to go back home."

You've decided! she almost screamed. What about what *I* decide? And where the hell *is* home, anyway? But she smiled sweetly and waited for him to elaborate. Iris was in a good mood, having received seven evening dresses she'd ordered from Saks Fifth Avenue in the morning mail. She thought she might keep at least six of them.

"You're gonna love it, and everyone's gonna love you, too," he was insisting. "The house is homey and comfortable and—well, I grew up there. I came to New York to make my fortune, and I did." He nodded proudly. He clutched a beer in one hand. "Now it's time to go back home and drink the local wine and hear that music and just . . ." Words failed him in moments of great emotion. "Just be there."

"Is there a hotel?" was Iris's first question.

He boomed with laughter, and when he had finished, he reached forward across the glass dining room table and grabbed her hand. "No, honey, there's a house! We'll live in a real house like real people! A big house, right in Luppese!"

"No hotel?" she said plaintively. What she meant was no room service.

Vito laughed again. "You'll be the queen of the town. Because you're my wife. You're the bride of Don Vito Luppese. People gotta—everybody's gotta treat ya with respect."

Iris was quiet for a moment, and then she smiled. It might not ever happen. He might change his mind. He might get an urgent phone call from Vegas or New York. Then again, being the wife of the man whose ancestors had named the town Luppese, after themselves, might not be so terrible. Iris left her chair at the table, and rushed to throw her arms around his neck. "Do you promise I'll like it?" she asked in her cutest little-girl voice.

Vito beamed and kissed the insides of her silky white elbows. "I promise, baby bride. And remember—" He raised his thick black eyebrows. "Queen of the town!"

.   .   .

Iris got so excited going over the Atlantic that she and Vito did everything but make love right there in first class. The blankets hid a multitude of sins, but not everything. A stewardess walked by quickly when she saw Iris's blond head moving back and forth over Mr. Luppese's lap. What had really given it away was the look on Mr. Luppese's face as, with eyes rolled back in his head, he bit down on the rolled-up in-flight magazine.

Luppese, Italy

In Rome, they went directly to a suite at the Hassler. It had been redone for a prince of the church, Vito told Iris as she gawked at its deep red splendor. She hadn't known the Catholics had royalty. The little balcony overlooked the crowds on the Spanish Steps and, below that, the Via Condotti and the best shopping in the Italian capital.

The next morning, Iris was standing outside Gucci's with her face pressed to the glass when it opened. At eleven o'clock she met Vito for coffee and tiny chicken sandwiches at Caffe Greco, and then dragged him down the street to Bulgari's. Vito himself never used "plastic," and it was quite a sight watching him peel off all those hundred-thousand-lira bills to pay for the diamond necklace.

The necklace was the first thing Iris had seen in the window, and the first thing she had tried on. It was of tiny square diamonds with a seahorse pendant made of diamonds and an emerald eye. She threw her arms around Vito in the shop, and the elegantly dressed man behind the counter lowered his eyes and thought, American.

"You are a darling to go shopping with," Iris gushed. She was looking forward to meeting the women of Luppese in her new clothes—couldn't wait to have a dinner party and wear the necklace with her deep green satin evening gown.

Iris bought ten pairs of suede gloves in a shop near the Spanish Steps; the colors ranged from basic black to a very peculiar orange sherbet color. She didn't care how much anything cost, and neither did Vito.

Two days later, with three "assistants" following in another Fiat and one "assistant" driving them, Iris and Vito left Rome and proceeded southward. Iris was horrified at the driving habits of the Romans and then of the Italians in general. At one point, she clutched her husband's arm in terror and another time simply put her head in his lap, which could have led to personal problems in the backseat of the little car, had Iris been in a better mood.

They passed Naples—well, not really. They spent four hours lost in it, having made a wrong turn. The sticky heat caused perspiration to soak their clothes, and shortened their tempers. "Goddammit, Giorgio! We've lost them again! You've gotta slow down and keep a lookout."

"Vito, if I don't have somethin' to eat soon . . ." whined Iris. He ignored her. A few minutes later she told him she had a migraine.

"Whaddya mean, a migraine?" he roared. "You ain't never had one a' them before!"

Iris wiped the dew from her upper lip with the index finger of her strawberry pink glove and said delicately, "I just never told you."

The traffic noise was deafening, and the two cars of the Luppese entourage were continually losing sight of each other. "It's either a parking lot," Vito complained, "or a damn racetrack." They were stopped near the railroad station in a sea of honking taxis in several acres of baking asphalt populated by belching buses and trucks and little *cinquecentos*. Vito reminded Giorgio in a tight, angry voice that they had already circled the train station twice. A big, plump, shiny green fly the size of a bumblebee buzzed in the window nearest Iris, and she shuddered with distaste. "Jesus, a goddam B-52," Vito swore. Iris then attempted to shoo it out, but Vito's face got in the way of Iris's pink glove and she gave him a solid whack on the nose. It upset him.

But not half as much as it upset Iris to be spoken to that way. She called him a shit and he called her a whore, and they both retreated to their separate corners of the little Fiat. They had never addressed each other any less affectionately than "baby bride," "honey," "sweetie pie," or "precious."

Giorgio drove on through the madness that was Napoli with a furtive glance in the rearview mirror every few minutes. Silence in the backseat. An ominous stillness in the car as the snarled traffic outside squawked and backfired and growled like so many zoo animals in a too-small cage.

Things got better once they were out of the Calcutta of Europe. "The Amalfi coast," Giorgio said expansively as they drove along the curving highway on cliffs above a sparkling Mediterranean. The two in the backseat were still silent. Iris was wondering if any of the dry cleaners in Luppese would ever be able to get the perspiration stains out of her shocking pink linen dress. Vito was beginning to wonder if Iris would want to make love to him that night after the long drive. Neither one felt very confident about either situation.

Finally Vito said, "Pretty, huh?" gesturing at the scenery.

Iris nodded. "Yeah."

Two hours later, after leaving the main highway and after passing several fruit stands manned by little boys in ragged clothes, they began the approach to Luppese. "City of my ancestors," Vito said, smiling, and Iris took his hand and moved toward him.

She smiled back. "I can't help but be excited." That was just before Giorgio hit a pothole on the dusty yellow road and both Vito and Iris cracked their heads on the roof. They cried out in pain and anger.

The car stopped in the center of the village, where it was surrounded by boys and girls no older than five or six years old, barefooted, with big, dark eyes, cheering their arrival. Iris was horrified. She rubbed her head and thought how poor everyone was. It was like a Sophia Loren movie, she decided. To the right, a bakery and a shoemaker seemed to be the only stores on the street. People sat out in front of them on little wooden chairs, talking, playing chess, knitting.

"The piazza," Vito beamed, nodding to the left. He was happy to see his favorite nude statue, and hardly noticed that the little fountain wasn't working and that there were discarded Coke bottles and papers in the scrubby brown grass around it. A little girl of about three, with no underpants and a torn pink dress, sat nonchalantly on the edge of the curb, legs apart, elbows on knees.

"My God," Iris whispered.

Vito had reached up and clapped Giorgio on his shoulder. His madras jacket was clammy with sweat. "*Bella! Bellissima!* Great to be back, huh?"

Giorgio nodded and then nearly wrecked the car, dodging both another pothole and a black cat. "Almost home," he said, as he wrenched the steering wheel back and forth in his chubby pink hands. The street broadened a bit and seemed smoother as they left the town behind. Iris was confused. The car proceeded toward a house about fifty meters down another dusty yellow road. "The house you grew up in?" popped out of Iris's mouth.

"Well, I say that, but the truth is we tore that house down and built this." He beamed. The car stopped in the dirt driveway and they all got out.

The one-story yellow ranch house appeared to be made of concrete. Stucco, Iris would learn. Turquoise and orange molded plastic chairs stood out front, looking a little disconsolate in the unmown grass. They appeared to have been abandoned after the last social gathering in better times. A painted statue of a black boy in a red coat held his hand out for the reins of a horse. "Life-size! Ain't he great, Iris? Had him shipped over special from Brooklyn. This guy I know . . ."

Iris wasn't listening. I'm supposed to live in this dump? I'm supposed to sit in a chair like that? Orange and turquoise! What'd they do, rob a Howard Johnson's? I'm supposed to go shopping in a town with two stores? I'm—

Vito took her by the arm. "Now we're *really* home, baby bride." He swung her up in his arms and boomed, "Open the door, Lorenzo! I'm carryin' my bride over the threshold!" Then what he said chilled Iris to her very bone marrow. "No more hotels, no more fancy towns! Home, sweet home!"

The interior wasn't any better. Iris was reminded of her first studio apartment and her attempts at decorating. At least no one here had ordered hot pink shag carpeting, but the effect was very much the same. All the lamps had bases of gold naked women, and the big white shades were still carefully covered in cellophane. The vinyl-covered, pastel blue sofa had buttons the size of fifty-cent pieces, covered in a gold metallic material. All the edges of anything that could be fringed were, and when the five small electric fans oscillated back and forth, the entire living room seemed to undulate in a friendly manner. The bedroom was dark and small; its wallpaper printed with giant orange sunflowers. When Iris woke in the morning or fell asleep by the light of the lamp in the hallway, each flower looked like a head. The head of someone she had known, had left behind. Iris swore the wallpaper gave her nightmares. Vito expansively told her she could change it anytime she wanted to go back to Naples and order a new pattern. Iris had snapped in response, "Back to Naples? I'd rather have my appendix out, with no anesthetic."

Iris was sure that Vito couldn't last without good restaurants and room service and a Cadillac on call night and day, but she was wrong. Signora Perrini, a native Luppese woman who weighed about two hundred pounds and had a very pronounced mustache, did all the cooking, and Vito raved about it. No more little shrimp salads for Iris. It was pasta and rice and great loaves of bread washed down with a raw, coarse red wine that always gave her a headache.

As for the car . . . why, Vito never went a step farther than the grubby little piazza. It was three minutes' walk, but still close enough to the house to hear the incessant screaming of the children playing tag or soccer with a nearly airless rubber ball that thudded instead of bounced.

"What do you mean, there's no dry cleaner?" Iris had shrieked on the second day.

"What do you mean, I can't get my hair done because there's no one to do it?" she shrieked on the third day.

And so on. No manicures. No pedicures. Vito tried to give her a massage, but she cried out that he was bruising her and he left the house, slamming the door, and she didn't see him again until late that evening.

And the evenings! Vito didn't seem to miss the casino in San Juan or the floor shows of the big hotels. Vito left his wife to go out with his boyhood friends who played games together.

"Games!" Iris had shouted at him in amazement. Cards at Mario's house because his wife had died and there was no woman to bother them, was the way Vito put it. And something that looked like bowling in a dirt pit on the other side of the piazza. Iris was not encouraged to stay and watch. Or Vito and his "assistants" would park themselves at a certain table outside the only trattoria and drink pitcher after pitcher of the red wine and talk and laugh. Then Vito would come home smelling of alcohol and cigarette smoke, and clumsily maul her in bed. Iris became a zombie, and barely paid attention to what he did to her.

"You can't!" she cried out the first time she saw him. "You can't wear a sleeveless undershirt like that! Not without anything on top!" Iris was sincerely horrified. Don Vito resembled a woman seven months' pregnant, and his bare, flabby arms and paunch were not a pretty sight.

"I'll wear anything I wanna wear!" he shouted back as he slicked back his hair with a tonic he had bought from the local barber. The liquid had a sickly sweet smell Iris hated. "It's hot here, and it's August. In case you hadn't noticed."

"I *have* noticed," she responded with disgust. "It's like living in hell." Iris got up every morning and took a cool bath and applied her full makeup, then put on one of her dresses, complete with jewelry and perfume. Everyone in town had strong feelings about Don Vito's wife. The men were agog, but knew that she made their *capo* miserable. The children stared at her and followed her through the streets when she left the house, which was rarely. The women hated her.

She was hardly the queen of Luppese. She was lonely beyond anything she'd ever imagined.

Only the "assistants" had ever seen Iris be sweet to Vito, had ever known the two to bill and coo. The squalid village of Luppese, in the throes of the blistering flush of August, had baked all the affection out of them. The blue sky over the little town was like a dome of heat. Not a leaf moved on a tree, the grass was as yellow and dry as straw, and the palm trees in a circle around the piazza seemed to be stretching themselves away from the scorched earth, toward cooler air at a higher altitude.

Nothing pleased Iris, and she no longer pleased Vito. He often left their bed in the middle of the night to make telephone calls to the States. She would reach out and feel the empty mattress, and wondering if he would pull her into his arms upon his return. But he rarely did, and Iris usually fell asleep before he came back anyway. The room was suffocatingly hot; the ceiling fan seemed to revolve too slowly to make a difference, as if it, too, were enervated by the heat.

Against this background of sweat, red wine, sleeveless undershirts, and bickering, Iris discovered she was pregnant. "A son!" crowed Vito to everyone in the piazza. He never mentioned Cesare, who seemed to have vanished without a trace. He had eluded the three men Vito paid to find him in the Caribbean, and the man in New York had had no luck, either. His bank account had been emptied the day after he broke Iris's jaw, so he had money.

Iris wanted a little girl, an ally; she couldn't bear the idea of raising another Vittorio Luppese who would stand in the dusty street with his friends discussing the Juvenitus soccer score.

That same evening, after her big announcement, Iris was sitting with the enormous, mustached cook, watching a John Wayne movie dubbed into Italian. *"Ci vediamo! Arrivederci!"* he drawled as he sauntered away from two men in black Stetsons and toward his horse. Iris sat with bare legs on the white plastic coffee table, waiting for one of the electric fans to turn its breeze upon her. Signora Perrini absentmindedly fanned herself with a handkerchief, her large, hairy hand lazily waving it in the direction of her shining pink face.

A divorce was what she wanted, Iris decided. The pregnancy was the last straw. She didn't want a child. Had never wanted one. The idea of going through nine months of losing her figure, literally getting uglier every day, and then! Then you had to endure something so awful no two women on earth could agree on how horrible it really was. Forget it. It was like a ship in a bottle. Iris understood how it got in there, but it seemed absolutely ridiculous to try to get it out. But Vito was excited enough for twelve mothers-to-be. And besides, she thought, a child would always need to be taken care of. Always need a nice place to live, and clothes. Vito would not deny this child anything, ever. Especially since he felt he had lost his son. Suddenly

Iris thought of Cesare. She rubbed her jaw and wondered where he was. In the spring, she thought, Cesare would have a little half sister or half brother.

With a child, Iris realized, she would get more money from Vito. Every month or every year, or just one fat number that she could invest. Iris knew her husband had money, but she kicked herself for never having bothered to find out how much. The nocturnal phone calls were usually in Italian, and though loud, they were confusing. Iris wasn't the least bit interested in listening to her husband have a long-distance argument in a foreign language. She sensed that things hadn't been going well for him since their move to Italy. But then he drank and seemed placid, with the same fatalistic attitude of "what will be, will be" that the other men of the village seemed to possess. Vito had lost all the sharpness, the keen edge of competitiveness that had drawn her to him. He had exchanged his beautiful tailored silk shirts and sharkskin suits for undershirts and sandals and baggy trousers. He had gained weight, become soft.

Iris thought of Cesare again. His tight body, his flat stomach, his shoulders. She had wanted the father *and* the son. They smelled the same, she remembered. And Vito had the same slow, easy smile that turned her on. And the strong hands. The same skin. Vito had been brighter, rougher than his son. He had earned it all the hard way, and the son would get it on a silver platter as some faraway birthday present. Until Luppese, Iris had never regretted her decision to marry Vito. The lovemaking was good. The shopping was great. The clothes, the room service, the Cadillac: she liked it all. But that was all gone.

I'll just have to ask for the divorce, she told herself. He's never said no to me before, and he's as miserable as I am. What future is there in this godforsaken little dump? The girls became women with breasts and periods at eight or nine, were married at fourteen, became pregnant on their wedding night if not before, then settled into a plump, early middle age by the time they were twenty-five.

Their husbands worked as laborers for the most part, had rough hands with perpetually dirty fingernails, and expected nothing more from a woman than good cooking and sexual availability. Children were treasured and adored, but grew up quickly, inheriting the hardships of their parents' lives.

No. I will leave here, have the baby in New York, and then I can live wherever I want. Vito can fly in to visit me and it. That's settled.

"*Signora? Signora?*" Signora Perrini was asking. "*Un po di gelato?*" She held a mixing bowl of chocolate ice cream in front of her, and dipped into it with a stainless steel serving spoon.

"*No, grazie.*" Iris shook her head in revulsion. She looked down at her stomach, straining at the buttons of her pale blue dress, and was reminded of the seven pounds she'd gained. I'll lose my figure entirely if I don't watch out, she thought.

Once again, she tried to be involved in the gunfight on the main street of a Hollywood backlot, but it was difficult. Vito Luppese. Don Vito. He'd explained that the title was a show of respect. He wasn't a huge godfather sort—"Just medium," he'd responded when she asked. They'd been having dinner at the Luppese Palace in Vegas. Iris had swung her little bare foot up under the long tablecloth and put it squarely in his lap. She smiled like a kitten and said, "I don't think you're medium," as Vito gasped. Now she sighed and wished they could turn on all seven fans at once. But the house wasn't wired correctly, and it was two living-room fans maximum with the television. Seven fans was blackout time.

John Wayne certainly swaggered, she thought. Oh, Vito, how wonderful I used to think you were. How wonderful you used to be. She remembered his shining suits, the diamond ring he used to wear on his pinky finger, the perfect haircuts and shaves he used to get when Miguel came up to the suite in San Juan in the morning. Now he did it himself with a dangerous-looking straight razor in the little bathroom. That whole half of the house, but especially that bathroom, smelled perpetually of mildew. *Muffa.* Yes, I would come to Italy and live in the shit heel of the boot and know the word for mildew, Iris thought. Other people lived in Rome and spent their lives shopping and learning how to say things like "What other colors do you have?" and "Charge it, please," and I learn the word for mildew.

I can't stay here, she said to herself again, as she watched Signora Perrini dip into the bowl of *gelato* with the oversized spoon. There were large circles of dampness under the woman's plump arms in the cheap cotton dress. Iris went back to staring at the television.

I can't be his wife anymore. I'll go away and have the child and start a new life. Iris felt quite cheered at the prospect of leaving Luppese. Who knew what might happen? Maybe this would jolt Vito out of this hole! Maybe he still loves me enough to come with me. It all went wrong when he decided to come here. Why can't we go back to the Caribbean or to New York or to any Luppese Palace and start over? Why can't we have fun, make jokes, make love? I want to go shopping again, she sighed.

The movie ended and then the ten o'clock news was over, and the next movie, *Return of Frankenstein*, began. When it ended, Vito still wasn't home. Signora Perrini had left, waddling out the kitchen door in her pink housedress and her green rubber thongs. Iris fell asleep with her arms crossed under her head at the kitchen table.

When she opened her eyes, Signora Perrini was standing over her, holding a cup of coffee. "Where is he?" Iris asked angrily. The cook raised her eyebrows and nodded toward the hallway.

Ignoring the coffee, Iris stormed out of the kitchen, down the shadowy hall, and into the bedroom. Vito was facedown in his sleeveless undershirt and jockey underwear, snoring. Iris couldn't control herself another minute. She screamed. Vito jerked upright in fear, and Signora Perrini raced to the doorway.

"You pig!" Iris shouted. "You fat, filthy pig! You don't come home! You drink all night, playing cards with your friends, and you expect me to live my life in this dump! It's supposed to be October, and it's still two hundred degrees in here!"

"Iris!" he began. The powerful man she had been intimidated by on the dance floor that first night was gone. He was soft, and she knew it and he knew it. "Iris!" he shouted, but nothing would stop her now.

"I'm not staying here a minute longer! I'm going back to civilization, and then I'm going to—" She looked up and saw the faces of the village children outside the open window. "Get out of here!" she shrieked, and they scampered away, giggling, like little animals.

"Iris! Wait a min—"

"No! *You* wait a minute! I can't live here. I hate every minute of what you've done to my life!"

Vito had leaped from the tangled gray sheets and was holding her by the arms. She could smell that awful stuff he drank on his breath. *Grappa.* She tried to wrench away. "You're not going anywhere until we talk," he said.

Iris was too angry to talk. She was too tired to think. All she could do was react to the fury she felt inside. A rage that had started the first time she'd been told there was no dry cleaners. A rage that was fueled every time she saw that large brown cockroach that lived behind the toilet. "I'm leaving you! Leaving this!" She wrenched herself free. "And I'm going to get a divorce!"

She stormed from the room and out to the garage where they kept their suitcases. Vito stumbled down the hall to the bathroom and began to shave. He had to get dressed and had to stop her. "I love you," he said softly to the bathroom mirror, as if in rehearsal. He noted with disgust his protruding belly, his pudgy arms. Maybe the boys are right when they say they wanna replace me. I shouldna come back here. I've let myself fall apart. And the organization, too.

"Lorenzo! Giorgio!" Iris was shouting. "Help me with this stuff!"

Both men came running from the side of the house. They were bleary-eyed from being with Don Vito all night, celebrating the impending birth of his child. They were potbellied like him, these boyhood friends who'd been with him everywhere. In Luppese they had shed the madras jackets and wore their shoulder holsters over T-shirts. Iris thought it was ridiculous. She understood having guns and bodyguards in an American city, because Vito had lots of money and he was important. He hadn't told her much about his business, but some of it might not be on the up-and-up, she had once confided to Hatfield. "I think he's sort of an underground businessman."

"Help me get this ladder up there to the loft." Iris was a sight. She still had not washed her face or combed her hair after her hours of sleep at the kitchen table. The blue dress was wrinkled, and she was wearing no shoes. "Just hold it for me. I'll go up." The garage had once been an old barn, and the upper part still had hay in it along with filing cabinets and a wardrobe with the first Signora Luppese's things in it.

"I got it. I got it," Lorenzo insisted, gripping the old ladder. Iris climbed it quickly and saw what she wanted. The hay under her bare feet made her wish she were wearing shoes.

Iris would later recall that she'd heard something that made her think those ratty little kids were back. That they were around in front of the house near the bedroom window where she and Vito had been fighting. But she couldn't have heard anything. The garage was in the back, yards and yards away. Her hand was on the handle of the big Gucci suitcase when the noise tore through the quiet of the October morning.

Those brats, thought Iris. What are they doing! Then she heard Lorenzo and Giorgio shout. Both began running back toward the house, their feet thudding on the dirt lane. The horrible noise came again, and Iris knew what it was. She fell down the rungs of the ladder, screaming, "Vi-to! Vi-to!" in short, staccato shrieks as she ran toward the house.

. . .

Iris would never forget the metallic smell of blood in the early-morning heat of that day. It was somehow worse than what she saw, what everyone tried to keep her from seeing. Giorgio and Lorenzo had drawn their guns, but stood over the body of Don Vito Luppese as helpless as children. The automatic pistols were like toys in their big, meaty hands, shiny black in the light, like licorice. Tears coursed down their cheeks and they sobbed with their arms around each other; sweaty, unshaven, overweight, grown men weeping.

A pink and blue flowered sheet had been yanked off the clothesline by Signora Perrini and now covered Vito, who lay just beside the front steps. The shotguns had mowed him down when he answered the door. His bare white feet with pink bunions, long overdue for a Luppese Palace pedicure, stuck out like a bird's feet. They seemed to have nothing to do with the bulk under the blood-soaked sheet.

The crowd began whispering, then murmuring. Like people waiting to buy a ticket for the movies, thought Iris, as she turned away from the body. She sobbed silently, feeling all the eyes of the town upon her. Signora Perrini was the only one to come forward to comfort her. The big woman towered over Iris, who was the only blonde for a hundred miles, the only woman who shaved under her arms for two hundred. Iris allowed herself to be led away from the house, down the dusty road to the Perrinis'. With every step she took in her bare feet, she thought of how everything was gone. I'm fat, I smell, I haven't bathed since yesterday, and Vito is gone. Iris was crying uncontrollably by the time she reached the Perrini kitchen. Why did Vito have to see me for the last time looking like this? She reached up and tried to push her fingers through her tangled hair. Screaming like that? Screaming about a divorce? Suddenly it occurred to her that that was what all the subdued voices were about. They would mourn their native son forever, but Iris was the foreign witch who'd made their Don Vito's last months a misery.

. . .

"Signora Luppese! Signora!" The voices at the door made her jump with surprise. Hardly anyone ever addressed her, save Lorenzo, Giorgio, or the cook. "Can we ask you a few questions?" The two men were American. They wore polo shirts, dusty blue jeans, and loafers. One carried a small tape recorder, and the other held a steno pad. When they tried to open the screen door, Giorgio leaped out of nowhere and shouted at them to go away. "We've come all the way from Rome!" one called plaintively over his shoulder as he ran down the garden path.

"Who were they?" Iris asked when Giorgio had come back into the kitchen, red-faced and perspiring from the effort of moving so quickly in the heat.

"Reporters. Newspaper clowns," was the growled answer. "The Italian ones Lorenzo took care of."

Iris didn't ask what that meant. There were too many other things on her mind. She would never see Vito again.

"She cried all day," the good-hearted Signora Perrini reported to anyone who would listen. "Cried until she couldn't see. Wouldn't eat. Wouldn't change her dress. Cried all day."

But no one came to the Perrinis to tell Iris they were sorry, and no one came to bring food. All the flowers were at the Luppese house, where Don Vito had been washed and laid out in the low-ceilinged living room. He was between the cyclops of the television and the shiny blue vinyl-covered sofa, lying like a beached whale on the dining-room table, his best black suit cut open in back so that he could be stuffed into it. Electric fans whirred around him, turning their propeller heads this way and that, this way and that, all seven of them turned up high. The refrigerator had been unplugged to prevent a power failure. One strand of his black hair moved up from his powdered forehead eerily, and then lay down again. Up and down, every ten seconds.

Iris began sobbing again when she saw him. She remembered the Vito she had adored, the man who had danced with her that first night of the party, the man who had made love to her at least twice a day for so many months, making her laugh, making her love him. Tears poured down her face when she looked at his hands and saw how waxen they looked.

The funeral was the next morning; it was necessary to have it so soon "*in questo tempo,*" in this weather, Signora Perrini had explained. The town was still and every single citizen, even babies, wore their best clothes to Mass in the little church beside the piazza, and then walked silently to the graveyard beyond it.

Vito's widow, in her best black crepe dress and a black veil Signora Perrini had lent her, walked between Giorgio and Lorenzo, head down, slowly. At the graveside she watched as the coffin was lowered into the ground and men and women cried unashamedly. The priest had told Iris she could throw the first handful of dirt in the grave when he finished the prayers.

The Latin liturgy mixed with Italian prayers seemed to go on forever. The singsong quality and the priest's robes brought back her childhood Sundays, so long ago and so far away, sitting beside her beloved Papa. The pew was cool under her bare thighs, her long legs dangling in white knee socks, not quite reaching the kneeling cushion.

The sun beat down on the little band of fifty-three mourners, baking them in their black finery. Iris could feel rivulets of perspiration between her breasts. The chanting of the priest stopped and he looked up at her from his prayer book. She bent down, scooped up a handful of earth in her black-gloved hand, and then let it fall into the ugly hole, onto the shining wooden box that held her husband. It sounded like sand falling on the hood of a car. She wondered if Vito knew what was happening, somewhere, if he could see her now. If he could forgive her.

A second shower of dirt fell onto the coffin. Iris looked up and, across the yawning chasm of the grave, saw a slim figure in a white suit. Cesare had returned to Luppese to bury his father.

When Iris looked up again, after the last prayer, he was gone. Like a vision, Cesare had materialized and vanished. He must have pushed his way through the crowd, which closed behind him like water. Her heart was pounding in her ears. She wanted to talk to him; she *needed* to talk to him. Lorenzo took her arm when she began to look around in confusion. There was no sound of a car leaving, no way to see over the heads of the mourners. Oh, don't disappear again, she begged silently. Please. Not yet.

No one approached the widow Luppese in the moment of silence that followed. She turned away from the grave, with Lorenzo and Giorgio still on either side of her, and walked slowly back toward the empty piazza. She was a tiny figure in black, dwarfed by the two big, gentle men in black suits with pants too short for them, ankles showing in white nylon socks. The death of their friend and *capo* had shattered them. Unlike the townspeople, they blamed themselves, not Iris.

Like big puppies, they followed her into the silent house and sat at the kitchen table, watching her move around the room. She fixed coffee for them, and scrambled eggs that weren't bad. She was reminded of the days before Vito, the days of Harry and cinnamon toast and Philadelphia cream cheese and cold root beer.

"I'm leaving," she announced as she buttered a piece of bread.

"Where ya goin'?" Giorgio asked in his Brooklyn accent.

"I don't know. But I won't stay here." Her green eyes darted around the kitchen. Children's faces peered in the open windows; Iris threw the dishtowel in their direction and shouted. It fell short and lay on the tile floor, but they ran away in a flutter of bare feet and whispers. At least they aren't giggling, thought Iris. She knew what everyone was saying, that it was her fault, all her fault. If she hadn't been about to leave him, screaming about a divorce, if she hadn't had to have help with her suitcases, Lorenzo and Giorgio would have been where they should have been. Doing what they should have been doing. Taking care of Don Vito.

"May I come in?" It was Luigi Rizzo, short and balding, perspiring in his black suit. He was the closest to what Vito could call a business partner in Luppese, and Iris knew that he was a notary who often went to Naples on errands.

"*Si, certo,*" said Iris. She offered him a chair at the kitchen table and poured him a cup of coffee. The two giants shifted themselves and their plates to make room for him.

"I want you to know how sorry I am." He bowed and kissed her hand before seating himself. Iris nodded, touched by his courtliness. "Many of the men want to tell you that, but . . ." He shrugged before picking up his cup. "The women. The women don't want their men to come to you." He rolled his black eyes and then smoothed his mustache.

"*Grazie,*" said Iris.

"You must know about the will. It's very simple, really. A child and a wife are left the same. You and Cesare will split all the money and property equally." He paused. "And if it's true that you are pregnant, then the will leaves you each a third." When Iris didn't respond, he thought she had not understood. "That child will get one-third, as will you and Cesare."

Iris tried not to look delighted. It was so easy. And the child growing in her belly meant she would have two-thirds of everything Vito had. She nodded, keeping her lips closed. Then she lifted her coffee cup in front of her face and listened as he explained the necessity of meeting with lawyers in Naples.

In twenty minutes it was over. She thanked Signor Rizzo and told him that she would like to leave the next morning. Lorenzo and Giorgio could drive her. Yes, they knew the address. Yes, she would stay in a hotel called the Vesuvio. Yes, she would see him the following morning at nine o'clock in the *avvocato*'s office.

That done, Iris began to pack. She wondered what she should wear, and decided it had to be black. She wondered about income taxes, and then told herself that Vito's lawyer certainly knew about that. Didn't Cesare tell her that he paid no taxes? Cesare! Will I face him across a desk, or will he let Luigi represent him? Oh, God, Iris suffered as she surveyed all her dresses in the old wardrobe. Please, God, she prayed. Please let me still fit into that divine black linen suit.

Naples

Once she left Luppese, Iris missed her husband desperately. The meeting in Naples had not produced Cesare, but only five men who treated her with deference and great civility. But it was Signor Zaccheroni who made a long statement on behalf of Cesare and then, taking off his glasses, asked the others to agree. They did. Iris was then told that the money and property could not be divided until she produced the second child of Vito Luppese. Only then would the estate be probated.

"But that's seven months away!" she cried.

They nodded sagely. She saw in Zaccheroni's eyes the slightest hint of veiled mockery. Perhaps he did not believe she was pregnant! It was certainly in his client's best interest that she not be.

Iris had no choice but to say, "*Certo,*" and agree to bring the child back to Naples after the birth. "As soon as I can travel," she amended.

Thank God I have money, thought Iris as the men droned on about getting papers in order. Papers from New York. Papers from San Juan. Iris had seen Vito hiding the money the first week she'd been in the house. Hundred-dollar bills were folded tightly and stuffed into what resembled a very large plastic sandwich bag, tucked under a loose piece of linoleum in the hall closet, where he kept his good suits. She'd counted the bills one night and discovered that the total was over seventy thousand dollars. I'll be all right for seven months on that, she thought.

The meeting was over, and the men dipped their faces low over her extended hand in farewell, not quite kissing it, just brushing her knuckles. Iris thanked them all and returned by taxi to the Hotel Vesuvio for her bags. She saluted the volcano from her corner room and thought how beautiful the blue bay spread before her was. "But no," she said aloud to the sky. "Not Italy."

In six hours she was at Rome's Fiumicino Airport, and in one more she was settling herself in the first-class section of the Alitalia jet. An hour later, the young man beside her bought her a drink. She sipped the vodka, thinking, It's been so long since I've felt this way, so long since I've been among people in real clothes, in real shoes. She missed Vito suddenly, and wished he were beside her. Wished they were on their way to a Luppese Palace together. The man laughed at something he was saying, and she smiled back, trying to pay attention.

"Where do you live?" he asked as dinner was placed on the little drop-leaf trays before them.

Iris gave him one of her looks that said, I'm so lucky to be me, and answered, "Paris. I've decided to live in Paris."

CHAPTER NINETEEN

Iris

Iris did very well with money of her own. It was the first time in her life she'd had more than a few hundred dollars to spend as she pleased, and no one to report back to on how she'd spent it. First, she rented an apartment. Her clothes and jewelry said it all to the realtor. She told him the truth about herself, which wasn't nearly as fascinating as the diamond rings or the spectacular seahorse necklace with the sparkling emerald eye. She simply said that she had arrived the day before and was staying at the Ritz, that she would have a bank account in a few days, and that she wasn't sure about papers, but would find out from the American Embassy.

Iris thought the address was very good, and that was important. The apartment was small but it had a second bedroom for the baby. Delightedly, she set about furnishing it. All the times in New York she'd gotten it wrong, and now, after the luxurious hotel suites and several thousand magazine photographs, she knew what she wanted.

The owner told her she could do anything she wanted as long as the apartment was white when she left, and so Iris brought in the painters he recommended, and told them the whole place was to be the color of her eyes. Unfortunately—or fortunately—the three of them all mixed their paints separately, and every room was a slightly different color green. "Oh, well, it's not the least bit monotonous. The living room is the color of my eyes in the morning, and the kitchen is the color of my eyes when I'm wearing green, and the bedroom is my nighttime eye color." The second bedroom was left white. Iris had rather daring plans for it.

The painters gave her the names of shops for furniture, and she took taxis from one to another and back again. In one morning she had ordered the sofas, two of them to face each other, and two club chairs, all to be upholstered in a glazed chintz of dark green and emerald green leaves. The coffee table was glass, with silver-colored bamboo legs, and the carpet over the shining parquet floor had a large geometric design in exactly the color of the living-room walls and white and lettuce green. Three weeks later it was delivered and all in place. Iris loved it.

She called a language school and, after two group lessons, arranged for someone to come to the apartment to teach her French. It made her happy and reminded her of the good times with Vito. Room-service French, she said to herself. Surprisingly, for she had never been anything but a mediocre student, she made great strides, and the teacher, a woman in her early thirties with buckteeth, often nodded her approval.

Iris kept putting off what she wanted to do most. Finally she walked into an artists' supply store three blocks away that she had passed every day for weeks. She stood in front of the counter and in adequate French told the young man what she needed. He added a can of turpentine, rags, a few things she had forgotten. But Iris knew what she wanted from the days in Chicago with Robert. She paid in cash and left the shop, feeling panicked.

After white wine and onion soup in a little bistro, she walked home hoping she hadn't missed the delivery truck. Five minutes later the doorbell rang and she told the man to put everything in the second bedroom. She didn't have the nerve to call it the studio.

Two weeks passed—six French lessons, a doctor's appointment, a haircut, and two manicures—and still she couldn't bring herself to approach the room or the still-wrapped packages.

One afternoon when she particularly missed Vito, she filled the apartment with pink roses. She put them in a white pitcher, in a glass wine carafe, in a silver vase Vito had bought her in Rome. The apartment was fresh and bright and, as Iris thought, "a clean green in feeling." The jungle-print slip-covers were brought alive by the pink flowers around the big, airy room. Restlessly she paced the apartment and finally went out to buy magazines. Fashion magazines. Something to look at, not think about.

The newsstand was crowded with people quickly tossing centimes at the old vendor as they rushed to the Metro. Iris stood off to one side, out of the way, and fumbled in her bag for her wallet. She would buy *Vogue*, both the French edition and the American, too, if it was there. Iris moved back to keep from being pushed by a man with an umbrella as he hurriedly reached for *Le Figaro*. Her leg bumped the pile of bound magazines on the sidewalk—they were old ones, unsold and out of date. Iris looked down to keep from falling, and saw herself weeping at the kitchen table in Luppese. Vito's smiling face was the top right-hand photograph. The caption was in French, but the meaning was clear. "Death of a Mafia Capo." Fumbling with the twine, Iris managed to break two nails before she asked the old man to help her. There was a lull in customers, and he bent over the magazines in his canvas apron, gesturing and talking.

"*Oui, oui,*" she insisted. "I do want to buy this," she kept saying as he shook his head. Finally, with a quick turn of his penknife, he cut the cord, and Iris grabbed the wrinkled top issue and then the second copy and the third. The man took her money and shrugged.

She fairly ran down the crowded sidewalks to her building, clutching the magazines to her chest. She pushed her way past an elderly couple, racing up the front steps and through the lobby, nodding at the concierge. Minutes later, Iris was barefoot, sitting on the edge of the jungle couch, leaning over the open magazines spread on the coffee table. Vito's face grinned at her. The old Vito of Caribbean days, the Vito of the evenings at the casinos, the Vito of the shopping trips, at the racetrack. Then she turned the page and saw the bloodstained sheet, that ridiculous pink and blue flowered sheet, draped over his body beside the front door. How shabby the house looked, she thought. I wasn't imagining it. And the crowd. Someone in the crowd must have had a camera. Unless . . . unless whoever killed him had told the press first. Iris leaned over the glass coffee table, head between her hands, staring, mesmerized by the images.

She examined each photograph as if she were looking for clues as to what had happened to her, to her marriage, to her love for this man dead of gunshot wounds. Standing up, she went to the bookshelf and took down the French-English dictionary. Translating from the French, then scrawling each English word in the margin, she at last, after two hours, could read the article.

LIVE BY THE GUN AND DIE BY THE GUN

DEATH OF A MAFIA CHIEFTAIN THIRTY YEARS TO THE DAY AFTER FATHER'S ASSASSINATION

Vittorio Luppese was born in the village his family owned. Their fiefdom, called Luppese, is a dusty little town of about sixty people, deep in the hinterlands of Calabria. Luppese, with its unpaved main street and its single trattoria, represents only one facet of the violent and powerful empire of the Luppese family.

"Violent and powerful!" Iris echoed in amazement. She continued to read.

The young Vittorio emigrated to the United States when he was nineteen, leaving behind an older brother, an uncle, and an elderly father, all three of whom were known as "men of respect" in their native Calabria. During Luppese's years in America, all of his male relatives would meet sudden, savage deaths at the hands of their enemies. Through his father's connections, Vittorio was introduced to the Pallotti family, which ruled the numbers rackets and prostitution in Brooklyn and Queens. Vittorio was an errand boy for several years, a bodyguard, an enforcer, and then a fearless hit man specializing in killings that no one else would attempt. He was picked up by the New York police on several occasions, most notably for the murder of the president of the Longshoreman's Union, but no involvement was ever proved.

Iris read the paragraph again. Vito killing people? She shook her head, but she shivered right down to her bare feet. Then she flipped through the magazine. It was a trashy movie magazine with articles on Princess Grace and Yves Montand having an affair; there was a big headline announcing that *Flash!* had obtained a photograph of Catherine Deneuve topless on a yacht. "It's just gossip and dirt," said Iris softly, but she turned back to the Luppese article with trembling hands.

The infamous gang war of 1959 between the Pallotti and Salvatore families resulted in Luppese's true worth being appreciated. He was positioned as the trusted *consigliere,* or counselor, for the victorious Salvatore family. Within three years, fired with ambition but tempered with a cool head and a cold ruthlessness, Luppese had removed both Salvatore brothers and their cousin and heir, Cosimo Salvatore. At that point Luppese began acquiring hotels in the Caribbean and purchasing casinos in Las Vegas. With money, with power, he no longer had to answer to anyone. He ran the Salvatore family like a benevolent monarch, meting out rewards and justice. But with his personal fortune growing beyond his wildest dreams, he made the mistake of pulling away from the men who had put him on the throne.

Some say his "defection," his getting soft, began after the death of his beloved wife, Maria. She was his childhood sweetheart from the Old World of his ancestors, a woman who baked bread, wore black all her life, and kept house in Luppese's giant haunt in Queens behind electric fences, armed guards, and German shepherds. See photo, page 47.

Iris turned the page and saw a grainy, black-and-white oval photograph of someone who looked as if she had lived in the nineteenth century. The hair was twisted back from a heavy, round face with kind eyes. The black dress was pinned with a cameo brooch at the V of the neckline. Under the picture was the caption, Maria Colombo Luppese, wife of Vittorio and mother of Cesare. The son has not been seen since his father's remarriage, to an American named Iris Keller.

Iris jumped. They must have somehow gotten access to my passport, she thought. I must get another one. The marriage license had "Keller" on it. Another passport is what I need. I must get rid of the name Luppese. She returned to the article and skimmed it. It listed more hotels than she had known about, property in Florida and in Texas, a diamond-smuggling operation out of Amsterdam, twelve casinos, several construction companies, and what the article called "dummy" corporations that listed Vittorio Luppese as the president. The list of his assets seemed endless. Some sounded like bars and nightclubs; there were vending-machine companies in New Jersey and Ohio, and several company names that were described as loanshark operations in the United States. In Naples, it said, thirteen clans controlled eleven different quarters of the city. Tobacco- and drug-smuggling alone provided for about half a million dependents. Luppese was named as the godfather for the region, extending from Pozzuoli to the north to Poggio Marina in the south. The main article continued to describe Vittorio, known for the last five years of his life as "Don Vito," as a callous but brilliant leader of thugs. His power, it said, extended to three continents and brought in millions of dollars per month to the criminal organization he ran. Arrested for assault, armed robbery, arson, and four times for first-degree murder, he had never spent a single day in prison. The last paragraph then repeated what a violent, cruel man he had been and insinuated that to be gunned down among his own in a little town in Calabria, just as his father had been, was to be expected. The last sentence about his murder said, "No witnesses, no suspects. The assassination of Don Vito Luppese goes unsolved just as his death goes unmourned."

Iris stared at the photograph of Vito in a white dinner jacket, drinking champagne, grinning at the camera as a younger man. She saw him sitting with dark glasses, smoking a cigar, in a chaise beside a swimming pool in Palm Springs. Yes! There in the background were Giorgio and Lorenzo. Iris traced the familiar faces with one pink, polished nail and then began to cry.

She cried until the page was sopping wet, and then she walked into the kitchen and folded it up as though it held crumbs or had been stained by food, and crushed it into the garbage. Iris took the other two copies down the hall into the bedroom and placed them in the bureau drawer that held her scarves. They lay flat under dozens of colored silk and chiffon squares. She held her arms over her bulging stomach and told herself to think. Think about the baby, the baby's name. Think about what she would inherit and what could be taken away. By whom? By the U.S. government? By people who had hated Vito? By the people who had killed him?

She poured herself a glass of red wine and sat in the semidarkness of the living room, lit by only the one reading lamp. I'll just do what I have to do. I'll have the baby, of course. And go to Naples and see what happens there. Maybe I'll take a French lawyer with me. Maybe between now and then I'll find someone I can trust. And if I don't—she made a little moué of "So what?"—then I'm on my own. She sipped from the wineglass and said aloud, "On my own." Before Paris she had nearly always been with a man, but she had had to learn to sleep alone, had consciously thought of it every time she prepared for bed. Iris comforted herself that the situation was temporary. Pregnancy and celibacy.

Late that night she awoke and, in her nightgown, walked down the hall to the kitchen. She drank Perrier and stared out the window at the lights of the city. The trees along the Seine were bare. She thought of the view from the Miami hotel that night after making love to Cesare, and wondered where he was. She wondered if he hated her, and the baby to be, for taking part of his inheritance. Maybe he doesn't hate me, she hoped. I'll be in Naples in seven or eight months, and maybe Cesare will be there, across the table from me in that office with all the lawyers. Maybe . . . She remembered his hooded eyes. Then she thought of Vito making love to her. They'd laughed so much in bed. Iris put down the glass and walked down the hall to her bedroom. But sleep eluded her and she got up again and went to stare at the easel, the canvases, the wrapped packages of brushes and tubes of paint.

Church bells were tolling nine o'clock before she next thought of the time. It was morning and the canvas before her was finished. "I did this all wrong," she said aloud. "I should have had northern light and never begun in the semidarkness and . . ." Then she broke into a smile. It wasn't bad. The pink roses appeared to fall in space in front of a night cityscape. Iris had watched Robert twist his brush a certain way to make something appear rounded, and she found she could do it. She also knew about leaving what she thought of as "holes" or blank spots on the canvas for what would later look like lights.

Iris spent her entire pregnancy learning French and painting. Her kind Dr. Dumas warned her about varicose veins, so she had a carpenter build a sort of platform atop the kitchen stool and she sat cross-legged on it, leaning forward. It was hell for her back, but she thought it was worth it. She painted canvas after canvas, and then painted over many of them, but there were twenty she considered good. Flowers made her feel happy, so she had a standing order with the florist on the corner. Tiger lilies, roses—any color but red—pansies, violets, were all delivered two times a week. Iris would put all one color in the living room or mix all the flowers in one big white ceramic vase on the coffee table, then paint her favorite bouquet.

One day a week she painted not a stroke, but went to the hairdresser and had a shampoo, and Lisette blew her dry and Danielle gave her a pedicure and a manicure. After lunch in the Ritz dining room with white wine and a chocolate dessert, she went shopping. But not for clothes. She wandered in and out of bookstores, looking at art books for ideas. Sometimes she bought hundreds of dollars' worth of books at a time, and had to take a taxi home.

Iris started with Picasso and went backwards through the Impressionists to the Renaissance. She loved Alma-Tadema and Matisse and the Belgian artist Delvaux. At first she didn't read the text, but just ran one perfectly polished nail over the colored plates, whispering, "Wonder if I could do that. Wonder how he got that color."

By May, Iris had discovered the art galleries of Paris. She went to the Louvre three times, and then decided she would comb the Boulevard St.-Germain to see contemporary paintings. She wandered up and down the rue de St.-Pères, the rue Bonaparte, the rue Jacob, and the rue Seine, in and out of the galleries. On one of these Wednesdays, as she stood before a large abstract canvas, belly sticking out, hair fluffed like a golden bell, wearing new pink leather shoes and a blouson cotton dress, a voice asked her in French, "What do you think?"

"I would have done it differently, but I like it anyway," she answered in her American accented French.

She turned and saw an elderly man with white hair, smoking a pipe. He wore a very wrinkled beige linen suit, for the day was warm, and a green silk tie. The conversation led to coffee at a nearby café, and to Iris's shy confession. "I paint. I mean I try to paint. It's something I have to do every day. This is my day off. I can hardly wait until tomorrow morning." She looked at her perfect pink polished fingernails, and told herself to remember to wear gloves, as Danielle had advised.

Monsieur Le Sage ordered more coffee and smiled. "When may I see your work?"

Iris gasped. "No. You can't see it. I mean—no one has ever—"

"But it's my business," he said gently. He was very amused at this young pregnant woman, hardly more than a girl, obviously alone in Paris, painting in secret. "I would be a terrible art dealer if I didn't insist upon seeing your work."

"You own that gallery?" she asked with wide green eyes.

He nodded and took a sip from the new cup of coffee.

"But you didn't even lock the door."

"Oh, I have an assistant in back. I come and go all the time."

"Why—I mean how did you get your gallery?"

"You really are a funny one," he laughed. "And I'm not flirting with you, because you must be one-quarter of my age."

"Please," Iris insisted. "I don't know anything about art or artists or galleries. Tell me how you got your gallery."

Etienne Le Sage told Iris about his father, who had owned the gallery first, and about his own desire to be an artist. "But I wasn't good enough," he finished, and began to light his pipe again. Iris's heart sank. Perhaps *she* wasn't good enough. And just when she had decided to show him her work! Now she could not, because he would have to be polite and not hurt her feelings, or else he would have to say, "You aren't good enough." He lit the pipe and finished the sentence. "But I was wise enough to realize it, and lucky enough to have a father who taught me everything I know about the business side of the art world."

They spent two hours in the café, with Iris asking questions and Le Sage answering them. At last, as it was getting dark outside, he called for the check and said, "Now we take a taxi to your studio."

Iris blushed. "I don't have a real studio. I mean I—I just call it that in my head, to pretend that—"

He helped her out of the taxi in front of her building, and then followed her into the lobby. The concierge, perpetually knitting, nodded curtly as the pair got into the elevator and closed the little glass doors. Iris's throat felt dry. "I hope I'm not going to embarrass you," she said.

Le Sage laughed. "Why would you imagine that?"

"What if they're so bad you don't know what to say?"

"Don't worry, Iris," he said solemnly. "I have much experience in these matters." He would not normally have addressed a woman, any woman, by her first name on such short acquaintance, but she had shrugged when he asked for her surname. She had repeated "Iris" until at last he called her "Madame Iris" and then she corrected him. "Just Iris."

She twisted the key in the door and stepped into the living room. "This is it." She smiled. "Would you like a—" She started to offer him a cup of coffee, and then shrugged in embarrassment. There was something so refined about him that Iris, particularly on her own territory, felt herself wanting. She was suddenly aware of how pointed the toes of her spike heels were. She suddenly wondered if she was wearing too much perfume. This man was a gentleman. His clothes, his manners all say class, she thought.

"*Non, merci.* But I can't be kept in suspense another minute." Etienne Le Sage was standing in the center of the room, tall, aristocratic in bearing, obviously pleased with the living room. The white woodwork was fresh against the green walls; the fabric of wild leaves was charming. And the silver vase of tiger lilies was bright and naïve and totally uncontrived. No matter how she painted, he thought, she had somehow developed a good eye. He had noticed the perfect nails, the lovely hair, and had not imagined for a moment that she lived in squalor in one room, but this apartment overlooking the Seine was still quite a surprise.

"Okay." Iris's voice was soft. "But remember . . ." She turned as he followed her down the hall. "I just started."

It was dark enough to turn on the ceiling lights; Iris walked quickly in to her workroom and began to switch on the standing lamps in the corners. Etienne Le Sage stood in the doorway and stared as Iris turned to face him on the other side of the room. She stood with her hands clasped over her round-as-a-watermelon belly, face solemn.

"Tell me about them," he said softly.

"There's not much to tell. I like flowers. I like to paint at night when I wake up. I actually try to wake up so that I can paint in the dark."

"The colors are extraordinary," he said as he bent down to examine a canvas lying on the floor. He propped it against the wall, and then stepped back for a better look. Iris was holding her breath. So far, he had said something nice. Now came the criticism and the "you're not good enough" part. But he was so kind. Monsieur Le Sage would probably say "I'm sorry" first.

"How many do you have?"

What a strange question, Iris thought. "Well, they're all here. They've never left this room. Just what you see."

"Ten, eleven, five more behind the stool, and one, two, three, then four there, and . . . four behind me. Does that make twenty-seven?"

Iris counted, then nodded. "Right."

Etienne Le Sage was visibly excited. "Iris, I want to give you a show. I want to put them all in my gallery and see what happens." He was smiling, full of delight.

"You what? You what?" Iris kept repeating. "You want to do what? You mean you *like* them? You mean you think they're not—I mean you think they're good?"

Once he had convinced her of his intentions, they had a glass of wine to toast her success. He took her telephone number and walked to the door. "Remember, don't let anyone else see them."

She nodded. She felt light and breathless. Closing the door behind him, she walked slowly to the studio and stood on the threshold, looking at all the canvases propped against the walls of the little white room. "I did this," she whispered. "By myself." Then she remembered the things that Monsieur Le Sage had said: "Extraordinary." "Amazingly original." "So few lines evoking so much." She reveled in the prickles of pleasure she felt in recalling his voice, his words. She said it aloud. "Iris, I really like these paintings."

The little figure in the pink dress began to cry. No one had ever complimented her on anything she'd done. Not ever in her life. Not even "What a great cup of coffee." Iris cried and cried. The only compliments she'd ever gotten were in bed.

CHAPTER TWENTY

Iris

Men were attracted to Iris. They always had been and always would be. The most impervious male would stare into her green eyes and wonder . . . or catch a glimpse of the deep cleft between her white breasts and find it hard to look away. "You smell like a woman," one of her French lovers waxed poetic, lying on his back in her bed. "It's female musk. It's something so primitive . . ." he found he could not go on speaking as he realized that Iris had her lips pressed around his favorite possession.

The men arrived in tandem with the first show. During her pregnancy she had painted and read. The afternoon encounter with Etienne Le Sage had changed her life. The idea of Iris as an artist astonished her; made her stare in the mirror hours longer per week than usual, wondering Am I fooling everyone? She wondered when Etienne would find out what she was really like, and she told him this. He didn't laugh, but took her hand across the desk of the gallery and kissed it as if she were a queen. "That's what I think of you. That's what the *real* you deserves. It's not every young woman who could come to Paris and learn French and have a baby in a strange country and, on top of it all, develop herself as a painter alone in her apartment."

Iris said nothing. She had never even told him her last name until they discussed what the invitations to the opening would read. He nodded when she said she spoke a little Italian, but he didn't ask any questions. Etienne could be sensitive and intuitive almost to the point of being psychic about his protégée. He had suggested that she be known simply as Iris.

Her first show was well received by the crowds that packed the gallery, but the critics were "critical," said Iris. All the canvases were sold, though the two newspaper reviews had described them as "nothing more than pretty pastels" and "rather romantic canvases that make one want to see her work in a few years, when it reaches a more developed stage."

The men arrived that evening of the opening. They held her hand just a little bit longer than necessary after kissing it, then they looked up into those impossibly green eyes and stared just a little bit longer than a woman would have. They sent flowers to the gallery, for she would tell no one where she lived. They sent boxes of chocolates in silver and gold foil; they sent art books and letters of praise and adoration, but most of all they extended invitations —to this party and that dinner and this play and that opera.

Iris went to them all. She loved drinking champagne at the bar at Fouquet's before dinner, under the pictures of Marilyn Monroe and Edith Piaf, and she adored Sunday lunch at L'Interalliée. The eighteenth-century mansion had once been the Russian embassy, and then belonged to the Rothschild family before it became a club. It was opulent, each room high-ceilinged, gilded, and more splendid than the last. Iris wore her very best daytime clothes, and one Sunday, with a French count she didn't much care for, was introduced to both the Aga Khan and the President of France. She put a little star in her datebook that evening before taking off her eye makeup for bed.

By dint of singleminded discipline, Iris had gotten her figure back within a month of her son's birth. It was diet and exercise and a thrice-weekly massage. No one except the nurse she hired, the concierge, and Etienne knew of the child's existence. No escort ever picked her up at her apartment or took her home at the end of the evening. She swore she loved taxis, and laughed about a secret life. She made love in hotel suites, and her lovers imagined a jealous husband. She said she simply had to go home, and she was so young that sometimes they fantasized she was going to be late for a family breakfast. She never told anyone, not even Etienne Le Sage, that she'd been married.

The baby was as dark and good looking as his father and half brother, and she named him Stefano Luppese, in honor of Etienne. He was two years old when Iris had her second show at Galerie Le Sage. At four o'clock on the May afternoon of the show's opening, she was hurrying to get across town at five.

"No! No!" she cried in irritation as little Stefano raked tiny fingernails over her stockings from her knees to her ankles. "Don't do that!" Iris sat at her dressing table, trying to dab on eye shadow. The boy hit her elbow, and her finger went into her eye. The sharp pain made her cry out, and as she put her hand up to her face, Stefano dropped her compact and the mirror broke to pieces and the powder spilled like pink dust on the rug. His crying was too much. She grabbed him by the arm and walloped him as hard as she could. "Look what you've done!" she screamed at him, which only made him sob more loudly.

Iris jumped up from the little stool and threw him down on the bed. She sat over the chubby little boy with the red tear-stained face, holding his arms over his head, and said slowly and distinctly, "Sometimes I hate you."

Stefano was immediately silent. His breath came in little gasps. Suddenly horrified, Iris was ashamed of herself. "Darling, I do love you," she began to cry, pulling him into her arms, his little wet face sticking to her lacy slip. "I do love you. I do love you so much." She stopped and thought of her ruined eye makeup, of how she'd have to start over. "I just . . ." she sighed and sniffed and realized her nose was running. "I just don't think I'm a good mother. I don't seem to like being a mother, but I do love *you*." She put her cheek against his silky little black curls and rocked him back and forth. Both of them sniffled for a few minutes, and then she released him and walked quickly into the bathroom to wash her face.

As she stared into the mirror, she said to herself, What is it? The fourth time this week that we've had that scene? It's always when that damned nurse is fifteen minutes late! I guess my threshold is only so much and then I break. She shook her head in sadness, and began to feel tears come again. The most important male person in my life, and I can't deal with him. I don't want to deal with him. I never wanted to be his mother or anybody's. She watched her eyes fill with tears again and saw them race down her cheeks. She splashed cool water on her face and whispered, "I don't know how to be any different."

. . .

Iris stood beside Etienne Le Sage—she in her new St.-Laurent black dress, black lace stockings, and the seahorse necklace, and he in his black dinner jacket with the purple cummerbund—greeting everyone. People called her paintings "fresh" and "vibrant," and they bought them. One little red circle after another was affixed to the frames. Etienne was a generous host, and treated the gallery openings as he would his own party. The champagne was Dom Perignon and not in short supply. The hors d'oeuvres were puff pastry and paté from the best caterer in Paris. The gallery resounded with laughter and the voices of people having a good time.

Iris spoke fluent French in a lilting, flirtatious way, and was surrounded, as usual, by men of all ages who, tonight, were openly admiring the low-cut dress and the little Vidal Sassoon haircut. It was the newest thing in London to have the side part and the geometric **W** on the nape of the neck. Iris's Parisian hairdresser, Carita, on the rue du Faubourg St.-Honoré, had copied it from an English newspaper photograph with great success. Viewed from the left side, Iris resembled a beautiful young boy, and from the right she looked like a twenties vamp as the shining blond wing fell straight to the line of her chin, sometimes covering one eye.

"*Non, non, non,*" she was protesting sweetly. "I can't just leave Paris and go to the Sahara with you!"

Jacques insisted that he was serious. "But the colors! It's too magnificent to describe . . ."

"Don't you dare lure my Iris away from me!" Etienne interrupted as he turned to join the conversation. His white hair was mussed as usual, but his dinner jacket was perfectly pressed, and the tie, though it had seen better days, was straight. Iris had bought him the cummerbund, which he loved.

"But it's a professional venture!" Jacques exclaimed. "This is not a romantic interlude I have planned!"

Three other men booed him and laughed. Maurice then invited her to the Pacific to study the color of the water, and Alphonse asked her to go to the Arctic to see the colors of the glaciers.

"But I'm serious!" Jacques defended himself. "The sunsets of the Sahara—"

"Sorry, *mon cher,*" cooed Iris. "You must go, though, and I will miss you." She winked at him. "Bring me the photographs to look at."

Etienne took her elbow and smilingly led her away. "If I weren't old enough to be your grandfather, I'd be raging with jealousy." Iris laughed and he went on, pushing her through the crowd, which was slow going, since everyone wanted to speak to either her or him or to congratulate both of them. "Have you ever met a prince?" he asked her when they'd reached the back of the room.

Iris raised her eyebrows in horror. "Oh, no! I don't want to! I mean, not now! I'm not . . . I'm not ready!"

"Of course you are," he insisted, pushing her forward. Iris tried to turn back, but it was too late. She was hissing, "Do I bow?" when she was face to face with her first prince.

"*Enchanté,*" he murmured as he bent his lips to her hand. Prince Ivan was as dark as Iris was fair. He had black eyes that burned like coals, and high cheekbones and a full pink mouth under a David Niven moustache.

"*Oui,*" whispered Iris, staring into his face. At that moment he put his hand up to smooth his shining black hair back, and Iris did the same thing with her own blond sidesweep. The three of them laughed. He asked if she wanted champagne, and in minutes Iris was at ease, answering questions about her work, and Etienne had slipped away with a little smile on his face.

The Prince, who was from some Slavic country Iris had never heard of, was a romantic figure in luxurious exile. There were lots of minor monarchs in Europe, but what made Prince Ivan different was his money—lots and lots of it. It meant his name appeared in the society columns and his photograph was taken at this charity ball or that polo game. Iris became the woman in the picture with him.

. . .

Yeah, yeah, yeah, thought Iris. Across a crowded room. That's how these things always start. Prince Ivan was tied up in London and wouldn't be back until Sunday. Iris had been very cranky when he told her that he would miss this party, but now that she was dressed and here, it didn't make any difference. There were plenty of men to give her attention. She did not look again at the man six or seven yards away, but felt a flush of warmth as the dark eyes assessed her body from platinum hair right down to the high-heeled, black suede pumps. Juan Carlos put his hand on her bare arm and she turned toward him with a little smile. "I demand undivided attention," he said in his heavily accented French.

"And you get it," she responded. "When I'm in the mood."

He laughed with very white teeth and then leaned down as if to kiss her bare shoulder. Iris moved away coyly, leaving him smiling. Nice to know I speak better French than a little count from Barcelona, she thought. Some pretender to some throne, she decided as she was handed another glass of champagne. How could you keep a straight face with everyone knowing you were only "pretending"?

"Madame Iris," said the voice to her left. "I'd like to present Principessa Claudia di Saturnia." Iris nodded and smiled. The older woman was wearing a silver-colored silk suit that matched her short gray hair. Iris took it all in, made polite conversation, then offered sincere-sounding regrets and moved away. All within forty-five seconds. Women never interested her.

"Madame Iris, I would like you to meet . . ." It happened again and again as she navigated the room, until at last she was near enough for him to approach her. "I know who you are," stated the man with the dark eyes. "I'm Jean-François Colbert."

"What? No title?" she laughed up at him. "I don't know if I can waste my time with you!" Her green eyes beheld him mockingly.

Jean-François wanted to give her a hard slap on her bottom, which was plainly visible in the black and emerald green silk dress which seemed to have been pinned in place and then sewn on the living woman. "Well, then, don't." His face had flushed dark with anger.

As he turned away to push through the crowd, her voice was full of fun. "Have some champagne with me. It'll cool you off."

He was unused to such behavior, but faced her once more. A tray of flutes materialized, and they both replaced their empty glasses. "So this is Iris," he said sardonically.

She nodded with raised eyebrows. "*C'est moi.*"

"Someone told me you were American. You really must have worked to divest yourself of the accent."

She shrugged, her bare shoulders moving almost imperceptibly in the low-necked dress. Jean-François thought her skin was the color of cream. Rich, rich cream. But it was her cat's eyes that held his attention. Mischievous, taunting. And taking me in. Jean-François couldn't remember a woman looking at him with such boldness. He decided she was both willful and spoiled, and it made him want her.

Iris didn't answer him. She had never forgotten a conversation with Etienne when she'd first come to Paris. "Iris," he'd said, "your French is lovely, but your English . . . well, may I say that if I were you, I would forget the English or else go to a school in London and learn to speak the way . . . the way you look as if you should speak." Darling, kind, dear Etienne! It was all about class. And she didn't have it as an American speaking a mixture of Midwestern twang and the Brooklynese she'd picked up in New York. She rarely spoke English anymore at all. She knew Etienne was right. It gave her away.

The crowded room buzzed with conversation. Jean-François could see the faintest pink shading between her breasts. He leaned down and said softly in one little seashell ear, "I want to make love to you. Let's leave."

Her laugh was like tiny silver bells. Her green eyes closed as her wet, pink lips curved into an O of hilarity. She laughed until she had to wipe the tears from her cheeks. When she stopped to catch her breath, he was gone.

Sir Geoffrey was beside her. "Iris, darling, whatever is so funny?"

She smiled at him and said, "The French. The French!" and he joined her in the laughter.

. . .

They were waiting for her when she waltzed in on that September afternoon, hair in layers blowing around her face, the white linen dress showing off the faintest golden tan from sunbathing on Prince Ivan's yacht.

Iris heard her before she saw her, and the voice from so long ago, so many lives ago, was like an electric shock. "Ilsa! Ilsa! It's really you!"

Etienne, at his desk in the middle of the room, an island among the paintings, opened his mouth to speak, but was too late. Iris looked up and saw the man and woman at the back of the gallery coming toward her. At first she didn't recognize the woman. The heaviness was gone, both in her body and in her manner. And she was wearing a rather stylish red suit and red leather pumps, and most astonishing of all, she was smiling.

"Mama!" cried Iris, not moving. A thousand questions bombarded her mind. What was she doing here? How did she find me? Who is this man? How can she look like this?

Hildemar Wirth Keller—now Mrs. Melvyn Leonard—took her daughter's hands in hers and beamed. "You look wonderful! You look so beautiful! So beautiful!" Her eyes shone with tears.

Iris had nothing to say; she was too overcome with the change in her mother. That tight woman of few words who had rarely shown her any affection in all her growing up years. That woman who had left her in a hospital room, telling her she was a bad girl.

The balding, round man in the light blue sportcoat took over. "I'm Melvyn. Your mama and I have been happily married for two years, and I been lookin' forward to meetin' ya every day of those two years!" He smiled ingenuously, tried to shake her hand, which was held by Hildemar, and then, in embarrassment, simply patted her on the shoulder. Iris said dully, "Melvyn."

Etienne had stepped forward. "I think this calls for a celebration of sorts, and so I propose that we go around the corner to a little café for lunch."

Iris had still said nothing except "Mama" and "Melvyn." Wordlessly she allowed the couple to precede her out the door, and then, rolling her eyes at Etienne, took his arm. "Help me," she mouthed silently. They walked in two pairs to the bistro Iris and Etienne knew so well, and then, with loud *bonjours* from the owner, were seated at their regular table in the corner.

"I saw your photograph in the window and told Melvyn that it just had to be you! That was yesterday afternoon, and I couldn't sleep and couldn't think of anything else." Hildemar looked younger—was it possible?—than she had the last time Iris saw her. She was a size-twelve dress now, and at least fifty pounds thinner, and her hair was no longer in the tight bun. It had been cut and permanented. She was wearing mascara and red lipstick and even little, square, red enamel earrings! All Iris could do was stare.

Melvyn began to talk. "I didn't think it could be you! The name was different and here you are, all the way over here in Paris, France!" Iris experienced a sinking feeling. All these years of shedding where she'd come from, the girl she'd been, and now she was faced with someone who knew her as Ilsa Keller.

Etienne suggested they order boeuf à la ficelle and a bottle of red wine. "A fillet of beef is wrapped with string and then plunged into boiling water. Three minutes per pound," he explained. "They serve it with a variety of vegetables, a pot of mustard, and coarse sea salt." Everyone was enthusiastic about it and the waiter took the order. "But first, some shrimp!" Etienne insisted. "And three glasses of vin blanc."

Melvyn was talking. "I don't blame ya for not knowing your mama! When I met her she was real different!" His smile and his Midwestern accent were both so totally friendly and unaffected that, as Etienne said later, no one could not like that man.

"I've changed a lot, Ilsa." Mama's voice was soft. That may have been an apology of sorts, Iris was to think later.

If Etienne was surprised at it all, he showed nothing on his craggy, lined face but polite interest.

Hildemar went on, "I met Melvyn and wanted to be happy. Just suddenly thought it might be fun to be happy."

Iris spoke. "I never heard you ever use the word 'fun' or 'happy.' " Her voice was dry, dead, tired.

"I guess I didn't until Melvyn came along." Her mother's voice was sad.

Bowls of cold shrimp arrived, and they all began to separate shells from the bright coral flesh, and conversation came to a halt.

"How long will you be in Paris?" Etienne asked.

"We leave in two weeks. Then we go to London and then home. We came last year and went to Rome and Capri, but this year we decided to do something different." Melvyn smiled that rather sweet, homely smile of his and went on. "Hildy and I don't like to go to twelve countries in nine days."

Iris thought, How amazing. Hildy. My mother in Europe, after all her sad stories about the war. My mother married to someone who says "we" with affection. My mother looking happy and even a little bit pretty! Iris realized her mother couldn't be over fifty. That wasn't very old. But she had always seemed angry, dried up, and matronly when Iris was a little girl.

Etienne was a great help with conversation. What had they seen in Paris, where were they staying, were they interested in art galleries, did they like the food? Iris felt frozen by the whole encounter. Surprised, not sure she wanted to see her mother again, not happy, only confused. And amazed. The woman before her was a stranger.

At the end of lunch, Iris had made the decision to take them home with her. Etienne put his arm around her shoulder as they all stood on the sidewalk outside the café. He squeezed her as if to impart courage, and smiled like a co-conspirator. "Do it," he whispered. "They're nice people."

Iris would ask him later, time after time, if he had known what she was going to do. "But I didn't know I was going to do it!" she would insist. "How could you have known?"

Hildemar cried when she saw her grandson and he leaped into her arms with a squeal of joy as if he'd known her all his short life. It seemed more of a reunion than a first meeting. Iris had tears in her eyes when she said good-bye to them that night after a dinner of omelettes and wine.

She cried all day, two weeks later, as she packed her son's clothes in two big Gucci suitcases, and she cried so much when she kissed Stefano for that last time that she thought her heart was splintering inside her chest.

"I love you, Stefano," she said to the little boy clinging to his grandmother's pink blouse with one chubby fist. Iris could not remember ever having kissed him as he was being held by someone else. The thought made her tears fall even faster. "I love you," she said again and, with one soft hand, patted his flushed cheeks and made him smile back at her.

"Ilsa—I mean Iris . . ." Melvyn began. He was really trying to get used to her name. "We'll write you and tell you about him, about how strong he's growing." Melvyn's eyes were red and watering. He was an emotional man who did magic acts at children's birthday parties in his spare time. He built things in what he called his "hobby room," and he loved baseball and eating Hildy's potato salad at the church suppers they went to on Wednesday evenings after choir practice. "And I'll take good care of him. We both will." Hildy was his first wife. He told Iris that he had been waiting for the right woman to come along. He could not have children because of a bout with mumps during the Korean War. Now his eyes were overflowing with tears as he pressed Iris's hand and breathed, "I've always wanted a little boy."

At last Iris had helped them into the taxi for the airport. She knew that in three hours they would be checking into the Clayton Hotel in London, and that a week later Stefano Luppese would be starting a new life as an American living in Cleveland, Ohio, the adopted son of a banker and his wife. Stephen Leonard.

Iris watched the little yellow taxi until it disappeared at the right turn onto the boulevard, and then, weeping, she ran into her building and up all five flights of stairs and into her apartment. She poured herself a glass of wine with trembling hands and then sat down heavily on the jungle-print couch in the living room. Something sharp dug into her thigh, and she leaned to the side to see what it was. One of Stefano's plastic racing cars. Bright green, with a decal of the number "3" on its side. Stefano would be three years old without her this next year. Iris put the little automobile on the glass coffee table and tried to stop crying. Finally she took a deep breath, and said aloud to the empty apartment, "I know I did the right thing."

CHAPTER TWENTY-ONE

Cynthia

Margaret never thought to mention it to Cynthia. Why upset her? Why bring back bad memories? She certainly never saved any of the clippings. Her eyes picked out the black-and-white image once in a while, and with tight lips, she would turn the page. A name from some faraway past, from a summer she'd rather forget, a summer she'd rather not have happened.

The first mention of him Margaret Kendall saw was a little filler, probably two inches square, noting that Marco Falconi, or Mark Falconi as he was now called, the first-term Rhode Island state representative, had married Cornelia Postell, the only daughter of Max Postell, the publishing tycoon, of Chicago. "Should be a help in any future campaign," Margaret said under her breath. "All he has to do is toss his hat in the ring." She saw no reason to mention it that evening at dinner to Otis, who was silent as usual, except for noting the attributes of the summer squash.

It must have been two years later that she saw the photograph of him "with the former Cornelia Postell." Not very pretty, Margaret decided. Rather large-boned, with a somewhat strong jawline. Falconi was in Providence announcing his candidacy for the United States House of Representatives. As a Republican! Margaret was amazed. In a Democratic state like Rhode Island, with all those second- and third-generation immigrants and all those Catholics! Why, he doesn't have a chance, she said to herself, and didn't let Mark

Falconi cross her mind again until she saw in the *Boston Globe* that his name was listed as a freshman congressman on the way to Washington.

Margaret turned the page, and then another and another, looking for the "Dear Abby" column. No, she decided. I won't bother sending this to Cynthia in Geneva.

Les Colombiers

One evening, Jean-François arrived from Paris, coming from airport to dinner table and—it was obvious—from bed to Les Colombiers. Cynthia smelled the perfume on his suit jacket when he kissed her at the front door, and then saw the scratch marks, three parallel red lines on his cheek, disappearing into his shirt collar. She exploded in pain and anger, for perhaps only the third time in their marriage.

Cynthia seethed during dinner, but, ever her mother's daughter, she waited to go into the *fumoir* and have it out with him, away from the ears of the servants.

"If you were a woman, you'd be called a whore!" she said stiffly as he closed the door behind him. "A slut, a tramp, someone with no morals!" He made no response, but she saw the muscle in his jaw move as he walked toward the humidor.

"I mean it, Jean-François! I'm sick of it! You wave it in my face! I'm sick of pretending it isn't happening!"

He laughed a mocking laugh as he lit the Montecristo, turning it slowly. "So don't pretend. Know that it's happening. I don't deny anything."

"But why!" she shouted. "Why do I feel that it's happening all the time? Every time you are away! Who is she? Do you want to marry her?"

This amused him greatly. "*Mon dieu!* Of course not!"

"Who is she? Who is the woman?" Cynthia's voice was low. She felt herself trembling with rage, but with fear, too. I don't want to know, she told herself. Don't tell me. Just tell me it isn't happening.

"Who is she?" he asked in surprise. "It isn't one woman, it's lots of women."

Cynthia felt tears in her throat. "But why? I never say no to you! Never! Not when I've been pregnant, not ever!"

"I need it." His voice was detached. To Cynthia he sounded as if he were ordering something from a menu.

She opened her mouth to say something, but instead walked over to him and with her nails started for his face. "I'll add to what's already there!" she cried out.

Jean-François dropped the cigar and, rising from the chair, grasped her wrists. Cynthia was so angry she felt imbued with enough strength to pull herself away. Tears streamed down her cheeks. "Oh, I like this! A little spirit from my Beacon Hill Puritan!" he taunted her. Suddenly he pulled her toward him and tried to kiss her. "No!" she screamed, and wrenched away. "You make me sick!"

The air between them seemed charged with electricity. Jean-François suddenly wanted to make love to her. On the floor. Anywhere. Cynthia wanted to hurt him. Physically hurt him. "You disgust me," she said coolly. Her face was pink, tear-stained.

Rejected, suddenly swept with anger, his face darkened. "Don't be so American, Cynthia. American women all labor under the misconception that they own their husbands. You don't own me, and I'll do as I please." He added, "Any woman, anytime."

A palpable silence filled the room. "Any woman but me." The moment the words were out, she regretted them.

"*Ça va.* Okay." He picked up the cigar, straightened his suit jacket, and left the room. As he had done the other times, he packed a bag and drove away in the Bentley.

Cynthia went to bed without him, woke up without him, did all the things she usually did. Veronique came for lunch, and again gave her the standard lecture. "It's normal, darling! Normal. *Tant pis!* Just forget about it. Go on with life. He's the father of your children, your husband." Cynthia stared at her across her boudoir. It was winter, and there was a fire in the fireplace. They both wore dark blue slacks and high-heeled shoes and bright sweaters. "And you don't own him. But the other side is he doesn't own you either. You owe it to yourself to find someone to make you happy." Cynthia bit her lip. "One man cannot be expected to be everything."

Babette entered with the tisane and the teacups on a silver tray, put the tray on the glass coffee table, and exited quickly. Veronique said too much in front of servants, Cynthia always thought, but her friend disagreed. "They listen at doors anyway. Let them get the story accurately!" Now she was saying, "Look. My mother is a countess and my father is a count. I was told a thousand times to marry a gentleman, an aristocrat. Marry an aristocrat. From the time I was fourteen!" She shook her auburn hair. It was in a shoulder-length pageboy this year, and touched the yellow sweater. "Marry an aristocrat! So I did. I thought I'd live happily ever after because I did what Maman told me to do!" She sipped the tea. "And what do I get? An aristocrat who is not terribly clever at business things and has managed to lose a lot of my inheritance. An aristocrat who is allergic to thirty different foods, which makes planning the simplest meal a royal pain. An aristocrat who has had bad breath for seven years from smoking those Gauloises cigarettes." Veronique turned down the corners of her mouth and lifted the teacup in a mock toast. "But—" she said sarcastically. "All's well because, after all, Louis *is* an aristocrat."

Cynthia was silent. Veronique did her best to talk her into having dinner with a colleague of Louis's. "He's hunting," she said. "And he's divine. If I weren't involved . . ."

At last she had gone and Cynthia was alone, looking out the window at the early winter darkness. I don't think I love him anymore, was what kept going through her mind. It worried her more than the fact that he had stormed out, more than what had been spoken between them. Cynthia knew Jean-François would come back; she knew where he was. Antoine Bonnell had seen him at the Beau Rivage. He liked the bar there better than the one at the Richemond. So Jean-François had moved into the apartment between the two hotels. How convenient. He could walk to work; the last time he had left it had been summer and the boats were running and so he had taken the boat to the bank in the morning.

The first time, he had stayed away two days, the second time four, and this time on the fifth afternoon Jean-François returned. Shouting for her in the hallway to come down and greet him as if he had returned from some triumphant journey, he arrived bearing, as he always had before, flowers, and a jewelry box from Van Cleef and Arpels.

Cynthia called Veronique the day after and when she heard the cheerful "Allo!" she simply said, "He's back."

Without missing a beat, Veronique demanded, "What did you get this time?"

Cynthia stared down at her wrist. The bracelet was three diamonds wide, dozens and dozens of the stones set in platinum. "A bracelet," she answered quietly.

"Oh, do cheer up!" Veronique would never change. "If life is all that bad with him, you still have the bracelet. Think of the resale value!"

. . .

As if somehow sensing things at Les Colombiers were once more "locked into position," Elizabeth arrived the next day after lunch. "Oh, Cynthia! I'm so happy to see you!" she exulted and Cynthia felt, as always, that her mother-in-law really meant it. The two women kissed in the salon and then broke apart.

"Now, how long can you stay?" Cynthia smiled. "I hope this is a real visit and . . ." She stopped, realizing that a tall, very handsome man was staring at her from behind Elizabeth.

He stepped forward. "So you are the ravishing Cynthia," he said. "I am Tony Forbes-Todd, Elizabeth's aide-de-camp." Cynthia extended her hand and he shook it.

"Aide-de-camp, my eye!" laughed Elizabeth. "Cynthia, this man is a scamp, a renegade, a—"

In minutes they were all laughing, seated facing the lake, toasting each other with champagne that Elizabeth had brought with her in a silver ice bucket shaped like a top hat.

"I feel alive again," Cynthia sighed as she put her glass down on the coffee table.

The others stared at her, suddenly silent.

She smiled. "Must sound awfully strange, I guess!" She wished she hadn't let herself say it, but Elizabeth took her hand and squeezed it as if she understood. Tony suddenly began to talk about Geneva. "I hear it's the most multilayered, most bizarre little place on earth."

"What makes you describe it that way?" Cynthia asked.

"Well, I was in Geneva last night for a dinner party, and was amazed at how rather *tight* things are, and yet—"

"What do you mean, Tony? Didn't they give you enough to eat?" Elizabeth teased.

"Oh, it wasn't the food. It was the furnishings of the house. Grand house. Spectacular architecture, but shining parquet floors that would have been marble in Italy or in France. A few small Oriental rugs, a painting of a Madonna and Child that you knew was worth a fortune, but such a . . . how can I describe it?" He hesitated. "Such a sense of coldness."

"Simplicity as religion," spoke Elizabeth.

Tony laughed. "I can hardly believe Bernie Cornfeld chose Geneva for his IOS! He must have turned this place on its ear!" He poured more champagne in their glasses.

"He did," Cynthia put in. "You can see his chateau just down the lake."

Elizabeth said, "People talked about his private jets, his Rolls-Royces, his castle in the Haute Savoie, complete with moat, his apartments in London, Paris, and New York—"

"They were also talking about all the 'nice' girls in Geneva who 'worked' for him!" smiled Cynthia.

Tony laughed. "And everyone running for the French border when the Swiss discovered almost nobody had work permits!" He began again. "It's just such a contradiction. Geneva. All this 'goodness' in this funny town. I remember a banker I met a few years ago. Little character. Innocuous. Unimaginative. The story is that in the 1960s there was a great parade of Genevois men who used to drive to a bordello in France." His voice dropped, and his blue eyes were bright. "Shocking!"

They all laughed. Cynthia thought she had rarely seen such an attractive man. Tony was the young banker from London with whom Elizabeth traveled. She'd been hearing his name for years, but had never dreamed he'd be so good looking. Elizabeth had told her that his wife had left him for his best friend; a few months later Tony had impetuously asked Elizabeth to join him on a trip to the Far East. He must be Jean-François's age, Cynthia decided.

"The madam had someone come out every evening and cover the license plates with little towels. Dishtowels, hand towels. And . . ." Tony was thoroughly enjoying himself, and gave in to laughter. "This Genevois banker, a pillar of the community, drove all over Geneva for a whole day with a pink and white dishtowel over his license plate." The three of them thought this hilarious.

"Wish you could run away with us," said Elizabeth to Cynthia. "Why don't you think about coming to Mombasa in the autumn? We're going to hire a guide to take us everywhere. Animals. Game reserves. I want to see all the things that I worry might disappear in the next decade."

Cynthia was not without a pang of envy. To be so free! Jean-François would never consider it. He would list all the things she had to take care of right here in Chambesy. He would make her feel she should not have brought it up. And he would not go with them, either. Elizabeth chattered on, with Tony putting in his dry comments. They were so compatible, Cynthia thought, wondering suddenly if they were having an affair. "She runs circles around me, you know. I have to take a handful of vitamins with every meal just to maintain a steady pace," he was saying. "And then there's the glucose to keep my blood sugar up . . ."

As the sky over the lake darkened and the lake itself turned from blue to gray to black, they realized the afternoon had flown. "Wish we could stay, darling, but we both have the seven-o'clock flight to Paris." Elizabeth was standing by the fireplace, pulling on black kid gloves.

"You've never told me what you came to Geneva for," said Cynthia. How she wished they would stay—for dinner at least. Perhaps, though, it was just as well they didn't, she thought, for she had caught herself staring at Tony just a few seconds too long. And he had stared right back. With eyes intensely blue, alert, intelligent. He had classically handsome features and a really dazzling smile. "What *are* you doing here?" she laughed.

"Tony had business here yesterday with a bank, and I . . . I . . ." Elizabeth fluttered her hands. "I was in Paris this morning and just decided to come and see you!"

Cynthia was pleased and amused. She picked up the phone and requested that the car be brought around. When she replaced the receiver, she was smiling. "You know, of course, that you are not normal?"

Elizabeth embraced her, and then Tony kissed her once on each cheek. "Neither one of us?" he twinkled. Cynthia felt terribly attracted to him then. "Neither one of you," she answered a bit flirtatiously.

"Thank God for that!" Elizabeth said as she heard the car on the gravel drive. In less than a minute the two travelers were outside in the car. Elizabeth's waving hand showed at the back window, then Tony's, but in seconds the Bentley had reached the end of the driveway and was gone from sight.

. . .

Cynthia sat at her desk all morning and wrote on her blue stationery. The fountain pen scratched quickly across page after page. She turned each finished one over, and put it under the silver seashell weight. Once she stopped and traced the ridges of the silver scallop lovingly. A wedding present. How appropriate.

Sometimes she stared into space, trying to remember Jean-François's exact words, then she would nod and frown and put her head down and begin to write again.

Cynthia wrote late at night when she couldn't sleep, and sometimes a part of her was thrilled with the idea that Jean-François might come downstairs and see what she was doing. The possibility also terrified her. She planned again and again what she would say, how she would wave the pages in his face. She would confront him rather than simply contend with his temper.

Usually within a day, the pages would be rolled into a tight scroll and tied with white string—always the same, this little ritual—and then buried in the garden.

And as Cynthia patted the dirt around the pale blue pages from Tiffany's and lovingly made sure no roots were disturbed in the process, she very nearly smiled. I don't know why, she thought, but it makes me feel better.

CHAPTER TWENTY-TWO

Iris

Paris

Dear Iris,

I'm fine. Hope you are fine.

I play Little League baseball every Saturday but so far every one has rained! School is okay. I got A in spelling and C in arithmetic and all the rest B's. History is my favorite subject and science is second.

Mom and Pops are taking me to the Ringling Brothers with four friends for my birthday next Sunday. They are Freddie, Lester, Mike, and Billy. We are all in the same class and all play baseball, too. Almost forgot to tell you. Mom is baking a big cake with strawberries all over the top just for me!

Hope Paris is nice. Mom says invite you to visit.

With love, Stevie

Iris put the letter in the pocket of the white satin dressing gown and wiped her eyes. She had read it three times since its arrival in yesterday's post. Slowly, deep in thought, she walked away from the window. Mama never did anything like that for me when I was a little girl, she thought. Never. Iris took a deep breath and reached for the silver bell on the mantel.

"Madame?" Anna, the newest maid, stood in the arched doorway of the bedroom. She was just eighteen, as petite as Iris, with gold-colored hair.

Iris sipped the black coffee. "*Oui*. I have to buy a birthday present. For a little boy. He must be . . . hmmm . . . ten. Maybe a baseball glove. Maybe a . . . oh, I don't know," her voice drifted off. "Yes, a baseball glove. Could you do it for me this morning? Forget everything else, and we'll get it off by courier to Ohio."

"*Oui, madame*. I'll get my coat."

"I think there's that store for athletes . . ."

"*Oui, madame*. I know the one."

The bedroom was a large square with five tall windows that made it very bright at this hour. It was nearly noon. The furniture was Louis Quinze; Iris had pieces made by Cressent, Foliot, and Delanois. Sconces of the same period hung above the carved mantel and were placed in pairs here and there above a bureau or a seating arrangement. Iris sat on a green, white, and coral striped loveseat whose fabric was made entirely of embroidered satin ribbons. The walls were covered with apple green silk and hung with small pen-and-ink drawings by Rembrandt, presents from an admirer. Each was framed in a narrow band of gold. The bed seemed colossal and was; larger than king-size, all of its sheets of satin had to be specially made. The green brocade canopy above it fell from a gesso-covered carved crown five feet in diameter. The baldachin itself was crowned with ostrich plumes of parrot green, and bird of paradise feathers. A silver candelabra bearing fourteen candles stood on Iris's side of the bed. In the nearest drawer was a silver box of loose powder, a sable brush, and a mirror, so that Iris could look nearly perfect in the morning without leaving the bed and risking waking her companion. She had arranged everything in her bedroom to convey a sense of opulence and romance.

"*Merde*," she said aloud as she stalked to the bathroom. Anna still hadn't learned to run her bath immediately after she brought the coffee. Of course, it was an unusual day. Iris usually slept until one o'clock or two, then bathed, dressed, and took the poodle for a walk. She would return to the apartment for a light lunch and begin to prepare for her evening with a visit from Maurice, who did her hair. Twice a week, Fleurette arrived to do her nails. More often than not, after a dinner party an admirer would bring her home and stay the night. In that case, Iris looped her white lace bed jacket on the ornate gold handle of her bedroom door. It was a signal to Anna that a breakfast of shirred eggs, croissants, and grapefruit juice was to be presented on twin silver trays at eight o'clock. That gave the man of the moment time to shower and shave and go to his office if need be. Most men Iris slept with had to be nowhere at such an ungodly hour. They telephoned their stockbrokers or banks much later in the day, if they did anything at all in the way of commerce. Usually, Iris looked forward to the breakfast as a way of regaining strength, and after the trays had been cleared, there was often more athletics. Men seemed to like sex in the morning, she had discovered early on. They seemed to have more drive then.

Today is a day to paint, she sighed as she sank down in the bubbles. She had five hours before her manicure, and Etienne was waiting for the final canvas. The show would be in just three weeks; the invitations had already been mailed.

Iris had become a celebrity in the years since she had first looked through the window of the Le Sage Galerie. Her name, simply Iris, was constantly in the social columns, and often on the lips of people who saw her shopping or on the street. There were those who sniffed at her talent and called her a magnificent example of what good marketing could accomplish, but there were also those who loved everything she painted. Men continued to fawn over her; women loathed her, but were usually too intelligent to say this aloud.

Iris would have said, if asked, that her life was full. She closed her eyes and luxuriated in the heat of the water, in the scent of the oil.

There were no money problems, even without what she secretly called "the Naples dough." The Naples meeting all those years ago had been unforgettable, with little Stefano intermittently dozing and smiling and gurgling, all to the delight of the lawyers. My! How those Italians loved babies! Iris had immediately handed him to Zaccheroni, who, as Cesare's representative, had seemed not to be nearly so argumentative as he had been ten months before. Indeed, no one could have called him the antagonist as he beamed down at the little rosy-cheeked face and cooed, "*Caro bambino! Bellissimo! Bravo ragazzo!*" Iris watched with faint amusement from the opposite side of the wide table, hoping Stefano wouldn't ruin everything by peeing on the *avvocato's* immaculate gray suit.

She herself had spent hours preparing for the reunion. Black was best. I am a widow with a child, and besides, it's my best color. Dressing carefully at the Hotel Vesuvio, in her room looking out toward the volcano, Iris had been excited at the thought of facing Cesare. As she sprayed on the White Shoulders perfume and blotted her pink lipstick, then adjusted the little black veil of her adorable Parisian hat, she had imagined lunch with him, laughing with him, making love with him. But when she entered the conference room, with Stefano in her arms, she was disappointed to see he was not there.

Perhaps it's better, she consoled herself, as the lawyers babbled on. After all, we are dividing money, and that isn't always pleasant. Especially when I've managed to cut his inheritance by thousands and thousands of dollars. She soon learned it wasn't thousands and thousands. Vito's shares in the fourteen hotels alone were worth several million dollars, even with the quick buyouts that had been scheduled. Luigi Rizzo explained that he had not thought she would be interested in managing, directing, or worrying about a hotel, so he had recommended the sales go through. Evidently, Cesare had not been interested in the hotel business either, so the money was now there to divide—and there were the nightclubs and finance companies, the restaurants, bars, vending-machine and trucking firms, and the construction companies.

The inheritance and income taxes were staggering, but Zaccheroni and Rizzo had worked out a plan between them that seemed very intelligent. Iris was impressed when she was shown how much tax money she would save. Rizzo had arranged for a Swiss bank account to take care of the European revenue, and the American assets were to be juggled between her and Cesare for three years, preventing a big bite from the Internal Revenue Service.

At first Iris was on her guard, for she had told herself on the plane a thousand times, Just take all the money and get out of this. She didn't want anything left unfinished; she was suspicious that something might go wrong the minute she left Italy. Her instinct was to walk away with her share and not ever look back. But she listened to the outline of the situation, and she trusted Rizzo. So she signed the papers, and sure enough, in three years it had all come to pass just as he said it would. When Rizzo took ten percent, she didn't begrudge him a lira or a dime of it.

Iris had become a woman of means with the blast of a shotgun. Suddenly she possessed a Swiss bank account and a nine-room apartment in one of the most elegant neighborhoods of Paris.

After the Naples meeting, alone in the suite at the Hotel Vesuvio, she had said aloud, "There's nothing I can't have. Nothing I can't buy. Nothing beyond my reach."

She told no one of her trip to Naples, not even Etienne Le Sage. Upon her return, she reported her passport missing, and with a little help from the American Ambassador, whom she'd met through Prince Ivan, she was issued a new one. No one blinked at the birthdate, and though there was a fuss over her refusal to use a last name, Prince Ivan made a telephone call. The Ambassador became annoyed at the delay, and finally, Etienne Le Sage stepped in as a Parisian to vouch for her, and at last it was official. Iris. Six years younger. Prince Ivan thought it amusing and fey, Etienne thought it was silly but didn't say a word, and the Ambassador never knew about it at all.

Iris pulled the plug from the bath with one elegant little pink foot and stood up to dry off. Her body was pale, shining with the oil, and plump. No chocolates today, she chastised herself as she looked down at her little round belly. "Well," she said aloud, wrapping herself in the fluffy fuchsia bath sheet, "none in the studio anyway."

Anna had still not returned, and the apartment was quiet without the shrill barking of ZiZou. The phone began to ring as Iris applied cream around her eyes at her dressing table, and she looked at it in irritation. No one I know calls me at this hour, she thought. It must be a tradesman, or perhaps it's for

Anna. It continued to ring as Iris patted her cheeks with moisturizer. Turning toward it on the little green brocade covered stool, she made a face. "Damn damn damn," she muttered, strode across the room to her bedside table, and angrily picked up the receiver.

Iris said *"Oui?"* three times, rolled her green eyes toward the ceiling, and listened. Her impatience disappeared, she smiled coyly and said, "Jean-François Colbert? *Oui.* I think I do remember you."

. . .

Iris told Monsieur Colbert that she was engaged all week except for tomorrow evening. Would he care to come for dinner? The invitation surprised him, for usually he did the inviting and the squiring and the choosing of the rendezvous, and suddenly it was out of his hands. He hung up, feeling a tickle of anticipation.

Jean-François usually spent no more than three days and two nights in Paris, but this week he had scheduled a meeting with an Egyptian curator from the museum in Berlin, who wasn't to arrive until tomorrow. He had three amulets that needed to be assessed for a possible auction in New York at Sotheby's the following spring. And this evening was the dinner with the painter, so of course he would plan on its being—well, at least a very late one. He could not possibly go back to Genève before the day after tomorrow. Cynthia won't perish without me, he thought. She's handled it all these years.

Jean-François's banking business usually occupied no longer than an afternoon and the following morning or a single-day meeting, interrupted by lunch. He often went to a client's house for reasons of confidentiality. As a young man in the bank, he had been told by one of the partners never to allow the client to see a piece of paper with his name on it or even a figure, particularly in France. They feared that the police would spot a Swiss banker meeting with a Frenchman, and the tax authorities would swoop down in an instant. "But how do I tell them what is in their account?" insisted the young Jean-François. "If I'm meeting with six people in two days, how will I remember all the numbers?"

The older man, one of his father's best friends, had laughed. "You write the balance on a tiny piece of paper, and as you're going up the stairs you look at it. Very simple. Then you are welcomed and seated, and in a few minutes you tell the client the amount. He will be amazed and delighted. We encourage them to think we have everything in our heads and *only* in our heads."

Geneva was so close, an hour by plane, that it wasn't reasonable to stay over, though Jean-François often preferred it because of his evening arrangements. There were always women to call, women to see and to sleep with.

At fifty-two, he was still a magnetically attractive man. His carriage was ramrod-straight, his face was always either windburned or sunburned a dark tan and he moved quickly, easily, like the athlete he was. His suits were made by Lanvin on the rue du Faubourg St.-Honoré, at least three new winter ones and the same number of summer ones every year. His shoes came from a *bottelier* his father had used and his grandfather, too, on a side street far from any fashionable Parisian neighborhood, but his shirtmaker came to him. Or rather to Geneva. He was an Indian who arrived from Hong Kong three times a year and stayed in the Beau Rivage for three days and met with his customers. Jean-François's measurements were on file and hadn't changed in years, so all he did was pick out the fabric and decide if a collar should be wider or narrower according to the fashion. The shirts arrived from Hong Kong six weeks later. When he took off these clothes, usually flinging them over the chair of a strange woman's apartment, his body was muscular and lean. He loved his body. He loved what it could do.

That explained a lot about Jean-François. The pursuit of the female was a game, but sex was a sport, a good form of exercise that could be performed with a minimum of fuss. It was easier than finding a squash partner, a lot less trouble than reserving a tennis court.

He had a history of one-night stands. Oh, sometimes he called the woman again, if she was exceptionally beautiful, but the thrill was gone. It was more exciting to admire her in the restaurant, to drink in the way she walked or held her head. The challenge of the hunt evaporated once he knew she could be had. Jean-François never thought of making love; it was "having" a woman or "bedding" her or "jumping on her bones," which was an Americanism he liked to use, or it was "screwing" or "fucking." It meant dominance and control and getting his way and self-satisfaction. For he could look down at the woman's smiling face either as she lay in tangled sheets or just before the obligatory farewell kiss and know that he wouldn't bother with her again. She was used, discarded, without interest for him now.

But Iris had laughed at him, and he hadn't liked it one bit. Her laughter rang in his ears long after he'd stormed out of the drinks party. He'd been annoyed at himself for thinking of her during the long conversation with the curator. His mind had wandered, but then, the room had been too warm; he'd had too much wine at lunch. Now he would see her again. He thought of her alabaster breasts exposed, no, flaunting themselves was more the case, in the black dress. He would put his face against them. He would lick the nipples until she cried out for him to stop. Oh, Iris, he thought. Tonight I'll pay you back for that first meeting. Tonight. He smiled at himself in the bathroom mirror as he carefully scraped the razor over his suntanned face. Tonight, he thought again as he rinsed the blade under the running water.

· · ·

Everything was ready. Iris called Anna and told her to light the dining-room candles just before she announced dinner. She didn't want any fussing around as they were seating themselves. "And Anna! I think the white roses on the hall table are too much. Try them on the little square table in front of the window down the hall. *Oui*. Toward my bedroom."

And the bedroom was certainly ready. Each lamp had been treated with a few drops of Iris's favorite perfume, which was Chanel No. 5 this year, and then turned on for a few hours to allow the scent to pervade the room. The lace-trimmed, sea green satin sheets gleamed where they had been turned back against the moss green velvet spread. The four square pillows were propped up invitingly against the carved headboard. Anna always came in during dinner and switched on just one ormolu lamp so that there was no more than enough of a glow to undress by. A little silver book of matches with a white iris outlined on the front was beside the candelabra. Iris always let the man light them; with a gesture she could actually convince most of her suitors that it was their idea.

Iris sat at her dressing table, lightly dusting her face with a last touch of powder. Her hair, worn longer these days, had been twisted up atop the crown of her head, giving her the silhouette of a Gibson girl. Little curly wisps fell around her ears and on the nape of her neck. Critically, she surveyed herself, and then sighed. Past thirty, went through her mind. But, she smiled, Jean-François Colbert must be past forty for all his swagger and narrow-hipped splendor. She spritzed a last bit of perfume in her curls and walked into the living room to await him. He was due to arrive in a few minutes and she liked being calm, appearing nonchalant when the doorbell rang. Iris smiled. This was going to be fun.

· · ·

"It's difficult to believe you are American," Jean-François said, and instantly regretted it, thinking, Now she will say, Hard to believe that you are Swiss, and I will have to explain things, defend my country.

But Iris didn't react as predicted. "*Oui*, isn't it?" she replied in perfectly accented French.

"Did you paint in America?"

"No," she said. "I modeled for a painter when I was very young. It was fun to be on that side of the canvas and to lie very still and daydream the hours away. And be paid!"

He laughed. Had she ever been concerned about money? The Dom Perignon slipped down his throat in a cool rush as he surveyed the surroundings. The salon had the original paneling of Louis XV, and the furniture was all original, too, covered in royal blue brocade silk velour. Jean-François had written her very good address in pencil on a pad at the Ritz, and stared at it after hanging up the phone. She must be kept, he decided, for he could think of few unmarried women who could afford to live on the Rive Gauche of the Arrondissement Setième in a *hôtel particulier* of the late seventeenth century.

A *hôtel particulier* was originally a private house for one family, but in modern times had been divided into apartments. Apartments as big as a house. The massive wrought-iron exterior gate was on rue de Varenne. After passing through it, one crossed the courtyard toward the building itself, which was situated between courtyard and garden. High windows set in the six-meter-tall ceilings overlooked the fountain and the borders of violets in front or the plum trees and white roses in the back. Iris occupied the first floor, which was considered the prize location in a *hôtel particulier*.

"Tell me why you come to Paris," she asked him.

"I play with money. Mostly other people's, but some of it is mine."

"There are other reasons, too," she said cryptically. "You were with Monsieur Jaccard, weren't you, that time I met you?"

"I'm surprised you remember." His voice was tight. He had hoped she wouldn't refer to their previous meeting. His eyes tried to avoid her face, those big green cat's eyes, but then they only dropped to the amazing breasts, which seemed scarcely contained in the cream-colored silk. The neckline was scooped, and the dark pink of a nipple was merely a centimeter from exposure.

"Jaccard deals in Egyptian artifacts, doesn't he?"

"*Oui.* That's why I see him. I collect them, and he advises. Sometimes we swap pieces. Sometimes we argue over authenticity. And sometimes we band together at auctions to make sure we don't ever bid against each other for the same thing."

"A cult of death . . ." Iris's gaze went upward toward the high ceiling. "Do you think of it that way?"

He nodded. "Sometimes. But mostly I think of it as life. All that activity, all that artistic ability—craftsmanship in a land of heat and desert and the Mother Nile—that anxiety about the protection and nurturing of what will pass . . . pass into, not oblivion, but to another life." Jean-François obviously relished such a question, but even with his enthusiasm, a part of him could step away and think, Shrewd woman, to get me to talk this way.

"Where are the pharaohs now?" She sipped champagne and gazed directly at his face.

"Pardon?" He was confused.

"Where are they now? Where do you think they are?"

Jean-François blinked. "Why, they . . ." He smiled. "They are in another Egypt."

"An Egypt without overpopulation problems, without Mubarak, without an Israel." Iris laughed. Her smile was open, flirtatious, fun. Small, beautifully shaped fingers held the champagne tulip to her lips. Each nail was painted blood red.

"I didn't think a painter would know much about Egypt," he said seriously.

"I didn't think a Swiss banker would know very much about . . ." She hesitated just long enough to let him know she meant to mock him, that she had almost said "anything." But then, with a radiant smile, she finished the sentence with "Egypt."

"You don't think much of bankers, do you?" he asked.

"Scum of the earth," she twinkled.

He wanted to kiss that laughing mouth then. Those full, very red lips that seemed to become more lush with every sip of the Dom Perignon. Iris was a flirt and a tease. She played. She was baiting him. He knew her type and, oh, he looked forward to bedding her. *Perhaps we will skip dessert, or we might, judging from the look in her eyes, have it in her bed.*

"Madame." Her maid, standing under the archway that led into what Jean-François presumed was the dining room, said, *"Est servie."*

. . .

Jean-François found Iris curiously guarded about her life before Paris, and said so. "Most Americans tell you more than you want to know."

Her long gaze from the opposite side of the dining room table told him that she didn't fall into the category of "most Americans." The candlelight lit the planes of her face in an extraordinary way. The chandelier helped. If he'd looked up, he might have noticed that the bulbs were all pale pink, and that that had a great deal to do with the glow of her complexion. On the table between them sat a silver basket of gardenias. Several of the flowers seemed to hold drops of dew, but upon a closer look one realized they were strategically placed pearls.

"I am positive life does not begin when you're born, but only when you want it to. Only when you're ready."

Jean-François's dark eyes were black in the light of the white tapers. "And when were you ready?"

Iris wondered why she was talking this way. *I forgot to drink milk before his arrival, that's why. The champagne has taken its toll.* She thought of the Acancy Hotel, of Cutter, of running away—in a flash, a piece of a dream. But something crossed her face and Jean-François saw it and was intrigued.

"I think I was about fifteen," she said.

"What?"

"Monsieur Colbert, would you care for more pheasant?" Iris cut him off and nodded toward Anna, who held the silver serving dish at his left.

. . .

It was like that all evening, he thought later. *Iris played me like a trout,* he said to himself angrily as he walked home along the Seine. Dinner had been yet another playful preamble to bed, to sex. *She was a damnably attractive female,* he thought again and again as she dipped toward him again and again.

Offering him the pepper with one pale, bare arm extended and breasts near enough to touch. Then leaning forward to touch one petal of a gardenia gently and to watch it turn black with a peculiar fascination. They both stared at the dangerous-looking, lacquered red nail on the delicate flower, and then gazed up at each other like co-conspirators. The same thought passed through both of their minds at that instant of eye contact: You can be cruel.

After the raspberry sherbet and the little curls of wafers had been eaten, Iris suggested they move to the *fumoir*. It was a smaller, beautifully appointed room all in yellow and gold brocades, with canary yellow watered silk covering the walls, and a Venetian chandelier with amber pendants above them. "You look like a gardenia in a garden of sun," Jean-François said as they stood in the doorway. He reached to touch her pale hair, and she smiled, then moved away and took a chair at the opposite end of the room. He moved a chair next to hers, lifting it carefully so as not to wrinkle the Persian rug. Iris realized she could smell him, a musk that made her lean toward him yet again with the cognac.

Jean-François clapped his hand over her wrist and, with the other hand, took the glass away and placed it on the table. Then he pulled her toward him and kissed her very, very gently. She neither participated in the kiss nor rejected it, and when it was over, without the slightest flush to her face, or the most infinitesimal shortness of breath, she asked, "Who are you?" It was the same tone one would use to ask "When are you returning to Geneva?" or "Did you like the wine?" Polite, not quite disinterested, but demanding an answer.

He breathed through his nose with his lips a hard line. The bitch. The hard-as-nails, cold-as-ice, smoldering, lush, perfumed, half-naked bitch. "I am Genevois but I come from an old Protestant family in France. My pedigree is as long as one of your alabaster arms. I might do well," he said cynically, "to ask you that same question."

She was amused again. "Oh, Jean-François!" She had a way of purring his name. "I'm Iris. Half of Paris knows who I am." She smiled coyly and sipped the cognac. "The half that counts."

"Why won't you speak English with me? With anyone? Not even with your English friends?" He remembered that evening so well. Maneuvering around the room to be close to her. Listening.

"Because we are in France. What's wrong? You don't believe I'm an American, after all?"

Jean-François let it pass. It was strange, though.

"Are we fighting about something?" she teased. "Do you doubt me, my veracity? Should someone like Jaccard be called to attest to my authenticity?" She pinched the top of one bare arm with her fingers, and the red marks her fingers left on the white skin made something stir in Jean-François. "I think

I'm alive. I think it's Paris, therefore I am." She and Etienne always joked that way. It was second nature to her after the years of lunches and dinners with her mentor. Her French was a patter of sophisticated plays on words. All picked up from Etienne and the people he surrounded her with.

Jean-François looked at her lips again; he was impatient. She was being the coquette and taunting him. He hated her, and hated himself for wanting her so much. "Let's go to bed."

Iris didn't laugh this time, but raised her bright eyes to his and said, "You don't know me very well." With dignity she stood and left the room.

Jean-François half expected her to reappear in a negligee or even naked, but five minutes later he was still alone. He sipped the cognac, nearly disbelieving what had happened, when he sensed a presence near him. It was Anna. "Monsieur Colbert? Madame says she must sleep now, for she has many important things to do tomorrow. She asked me to see you to the door."

The young maid feared he would crush the little glass to splinters in his hand. His eyes were as black as onyx with anger as he stood. "Show me, then," he said with clenched teeth.

Now, beside the river, looking at his watch, he saw that it was midnight. "You don't know me very well!" he mimicked her. Then, scowling, he repeated, "You don't know me very well." He took a few steps and stopped, his hands in the pockets of his dark blue suit. "Don't know you very well!" he roared. "Oh, Iris! You little whore, you vixen! You witch, you bitch!" His face was dark with fury. He was nearly shouting under the benign gaze of the full moon. "I'm going to know you inside and out!"

· · ·

Iris was at her dressing table, pulling the mother-of-pearl pins from her hair. The nightgown she wore was strapless, of ivory silk; she had planned to wear it for Jean-François. Behind her, a lamp had been lit, the bedroom was full of scent, the bed turned down just so, all as it should have been, for the encounter with him.

She patted cream around her eyes and smiled at herself in the mirror. Maybe next time, she thought. She pulled a Kleenex from the little, lace-covered box. What fun!

Iris finished her ablutions and slid into bed. She ached for male attention, but it would be worth it, she comforted herself, not daring to even smooth the silk across her belly. It all felt too good. The champagne, the sherbet, the kiss, the cognac. Iris felt her senses singing. Jean-François was too good to be true. And, she smiled as she reached for the bedside lamp, I'm going to have to be bad enough to deserve him.

Les Colombiers

Jean-François knew that, as a Swiss banker, he couldn't go to Paris once a week and shouldn't go more than five or six times a year. But as a collector of Egyptian artifacts he did not arouse suspicion among the French tax authorities. It worked very well. Still, Colbert & Cie. was a very real responsibility—he couldn't dash away every time he felt the urge for a walk on the Champs-Elysées. And now, at his desk in his study at Les Colombiers, he was seized with frustration. Iris would have to wait until the next sale at Christie's, when he could stop over in Paris on his way home from London. Eighteen days away.

The paper was fresh, ecru-colored, from Pineider in Rome. An affectation of his mother's: she'd ordered boxes of it for the Les Colombiers stationery. He stared at the clean expanse for a moment and began in his strong hand to write. Black fountain pen slashes covered the page. *Dear I,* he read to himself. *Dear Me, Myself, Dear You are like me. Why do I want you so keenly?* He crushed the sheet, then unfolded it and tore it to pieces. That kind of woman would love to have something in writing. Think of next year, next month, tomorrow. I won't feel the same, so don't write it. "That kind of woman," he said aloud, staring at nothing, seeing nothing. Yes, that's why I want you so keenly.

· · ·

"Highly unoriginal, perhaps," read the card. "But maybe I can please you after all." The white irises arrived by the dozen, laid carefully in the long, white boxes of the best florist in Paris. La Chaume, old and established, on the rue Royale, was opposite Maxim's, which was convenient, for a chasseur was often sent out by a diner and told to return with flowers to match his love of the evening's eyes.

"But why doesn't he call me?" cried Iris in frustration, waving the first and only card in front of Anna. "Why doesn't he show himself? Won't he ever invite me to dinner again?" She wondered if she'd gone too far, and made Anna carefully describe his facial expression at least three times, his exact words that last time she'd seen him. "And then he turned in the doorway," she said. "And with this terrible scowl—I swear his face was a thundercloud—said, 'Tell your mistress to sleep well.' " The young maid never tired of telling it, and added more facial expressions and more of a growl in her voice every time.

In seventeen days, Iris received twelve dozen irises. All in white boxes tied with wide silver ribbons. They banked the fireplaces in her bedroom and in the living room, they stood in tall silver vases on the Louis XIV commode in the hallway, they were put in blue-and-white pottery jars from Portugal and arranged in Iris's bathroom. Everywhere she looked, there were white irises. All from the silent Jean-François Colbert. Iris gnashed her teeth when a visitor asked about the flowers, said they were from "an admirer," and tried to look pleased. She only succeeded in looking petulant and thwarted.

On the afternoon of the eighteenth day he telephoned and asked to speak with Madame Iris. Anna ran down the hallway from the kitchen and whispered, "*C'est lui! C'est lui!*" practically jumping up and down with excitement. Iris nonchalantly picked up the extension and purred, "*Allo.*"

"It's Jean-François Colbert. I wonder if you would like to have dinner with me tonight."

Iris had plans, but nothing a case of the flu wouldn't fix, and she sensed that she was being given a last chance. Take it, she told herself. Go. Don't play with him anymore. Aloud she said, "That would be lovely," in a musical but totally insincere voice.

"I will come for you at eight."

The line was dead. Iris stared at the phone for a second with raised eyebrows, and then put down the receiver. "Anna!" she shrieked. "It *was* him! And he's taking me to dinner! Tonight!" Anna materialized instantly, for she had been standing just on the other side of the archway, listening. "God knows where he's taking me, and God knows what I should wear!" Iris rolled her eyes and stood up. "And God knows what will happen!"

·   ·   ·

With a sense of exhilaration and anticipation the two met in the spring twilight of the courtyard at number 11 rue de Varenne. Iris had decided not to invite Jean-François upstairs for a drink, fearing it would stir uncomfortable memories. She fairly floated past the fountain in a black silk dress printed with— what else?—white irises. The bright green of the leaves was exactly the color of the emeralds at her ears and around her white throat. Jean-François took her small hand in his and lifted it nearly to his lips. He didn't look into her eyes, but she noticed how dark his suntanned face was, how firm his grasp. Tucking her arm in his, she allowed herself to be led to the waiting taxi and in minutes they had crossed the bridge and were at a small restaurant on the Ile Saint-Louis. Iris was led by a dinner-jacketed maître d' to a table in a corner and seated. She approved of the pink linen tablecloth, the pink roses, and the single silver candlestick with the pink candle. Pink and candlelight were so flattering. A familiar green bottle sat in a silver ice bucket beside the chair of Jean-François.

"*Très, très belle,*" she murmured in appreciation as the Dom Perignon bubbled in their glasses.

"*Oui.* You are." His voice was serious, his eyes were black in the candlelight.

They had foie gras, they had oysters. They talked of politics, of Mitterrand, of Giscard d'Estaing. Iris had done her homework. She'd spent all afternoon reading the latest issues of *L'Express* and *Time* as Fleurette painted her toenails and waxed her legs.

"Tell me about the 'Mitterrand effect' on your banking," said Iris.

"Oh, he hasn't driven as much money to us as one might think. I talked to someone at Banque Privée—"

"Is that the Rothschild bank?"

Jean-François nodded, impressed. "He said he thought eighty percent of their funds were from France, but I think it's more like fifty percent." He smiled. "The rest is what I call 'frightened capital.' "

Iris laughed. "From little dictators and little kings and big Arabs . . ."

"I don't care how tall they are," Jean-François said in mock seriousness, "but I do think they should be able to carry their own bags of money. I mean, how does it look for our porter to have to leave his desk and rush out to help someone lift a—"

"You mean that they arrive with bags of money?"

"Of course they do! And we get it downstairs and throw it in the walk-in vault."

"Must be fun to see it," mused Iris. "Must be fun to touch it. I just stare at numbers on a page and subtract things or figure what the interest will be—" Jean-François wondered how she could be so damned wealthy. No. Wealthy wasn't the word. *Rich*. Iris was rich. "Must be so much fun to actually have it in your hands."

Jean-François looked at her pretty little fingers with the pink, polished nails and thought of being in her hands. "*Oui*," he said absently, then sipped his champagne and swallowed.

"Is it true that there are special French police who do nothing but photograph French citizens going in and out of Geneva banks?"

He nodded. "But a few years ago the Swiss caught two of the agents and slapped them with a charge of—I forget—maybe it was espionage. They were escorted to the border very quickly. It's expensive for the French to bother with all that." He paused. "The French have been bringing money to Geneva since before the Revolution. The aristocrats came running to Switzerland not only to save their heads from the guillotine."

"Oh! The French! Hiding money, not paying taxes, why, it's a national sport!" Iris smiled.

So's lovemaking, thought her dinner companion. "But we don't take just anybody's money, no matter what you read."

"What do you mean? Wouldn't you take mine?" she said archly.

"Depends upon how you acquired it." Jean-François was handed the wine list, and quickly flipped through the pages of calligraphy.

"So, if I were Eva Perón and arrived at your bank, you might have qualms about helping me out of the taxi with my suitcases?"

He nodded and told the wine steward to bring them the Chateau Petrus.

"We turned away Tshombe's money. He arrived from the Congo in 1953 with quite a lot of it. Trujillo of Santo Domingo approached us. Pictet et Cie. turned him down, too."

"Are you trying to convince me that Swiss bankers have scruples?"

The subject was a prickly one for Jean-François, and he wasn't the least bit amused. He was proud of his bank, proud of being a Swiss and of being a private banker. "You know, Iris, Switzerland is a rather complicated country. It never had a country gentry, and the men who controlled the cities were businessmen. The upper class was composed of Swiss merchants or bankers. They were the aristocracy. They were entrepreneurs in their own right, and dealt with factories and railroads. They created the biggest insurance industry in the world. Never call them simply financiers. They built the country."

Iris had sense enough to drop her bantering tone. "There's so much I don't know," she said quietly, staring at his face. Yes. And so much I want to find out, she thought. Not particularly about banking.

Jean-François looked at her shining green eyes and heard his voice explaining about the Secrecy Act, the Banking Code passed in 1934. He was reminded of those first few years with Cynthia. No. Maybe it was only the first year when she asked so many questions, was so interested. She read every book about Switzerland she could find. And she absorbed information like a sponge. What happened? he was asking himself. "There was a Gestapo agent named Georg Hannes Thomae who came to Switzerland asking questions. In 1933, Hitler ordered every German citizen to declare any foreign holdings. The Nazis were suspicious, to put it mildly, of the close German-Swiss ties. Anyone who didn't come forward and was found to have a Swiss bank account would be executed. Thomae went to Zurich and settled himself. To make a long story short, he used bribery to obtain information about Germans with accounts, but that didn't always work, so he had another scheme, which was to approach a bank and say that he was depositing money in the name of so-and-so. Now if so-and-so had an account there, it was up to the judgment of the clerk to take the money or not. A bank would never have given information in the face of a direct demand, but communications had broken down, and they weren't prepared for the tricks of the Gestapo. In those days the story of how hard it was to bring the money over the border, and the idea of a personal favor for Herr so-and-so, was very believable. Unfortunately for the Germans whose accounts were exposed. At least a dozen accounts were discovered that way. Sometimes the person was of high enough rank to get off with a fine, but if the depositor was a Jew, the least that could happen to him was placement in a concentration camp." Jean-François shook his head. "Because of Thomae, many people were tortured and killed."

"*Mon Dieu*," breathed Iris. She wondered if it was bad form to take a bite of the duckling while discussing this.

"So the bankers were in a terrible situation. Sometimes customers they knew would arrive to close their accounts with a stranger by their side. Or wires would arrive, properly coded, asking for the money. If they sent the money, it was a declaration of guilt, but if they didn't, they could be holding money back from the owner. This sometimes resulted in the torture in Germany of the depositor."

"I'm beginning to understand some things," Iris sighed.

"The Banking Code of 1934 was a landmark in Swiss history. It gave the banker a code to adhere to. Morally and legally. It was written in stone. It also declared to foreign governments, to the world, that foreign deposits would be safeguarded. The Swiss depositors were also happy about this because of their own distrust of Bern!"

"Is it true that all the money left by Jews who died in the war was kept by Switzerland?"

"No." Jean-François shook his head. "There was a law that unclaimed money stayed in the bank, but after World War II it was decided that the money in accounts untouched for twenty years would go to the Confederation and then be turned over to the Red Cross. Most of it was. I have to be totally honest and say probably not every Swiss franc, but most of it was."

Iris thought how Swiss it was to be so careful with the exact phrasing. She was also thinking how attractive he was. But a little dull, perhaps. Men usually pay more attention to me, she thought. "Good for Switzerland. I guess my zillions are in the right country."

"Zillions?" He winked. "Seriously, how did you begin painting? How did you come to Paris? Where were you born?"

It is a testament to the savvy of Iris that not only did Jean-François not receive an answer to any of his questions, but that he became involved with his own life story. "No brothers or sisters," he was saying. Iris thought she noticed a flicker of his eyelid, and wondered why he would be ill at ease making such a statement.

The sexual tension was there, but they began to enjoy each other's company, too, and the adversarial roles were dropped as the wineglasses were lifted. Iris was laughing. "I met someone who told me his grandfather was arrested for dancing the tango in his navy uniform!"

"In Germany under the Kaiser!" erupted Jean-François, who was delighted. "I have a confession to make." He leaned forward toward the lemon sherbet. "I've never danced the tango!"

"Well, my dear," Iris drawled dramatically, "you haven't lived. And you certainly haven't sinned!" With any other man she would have found it quite natural to place her hand on his at this point, but with this Swiss she hesitated.

"I think I probably have sinned." He smiled very slowly, and Iris thought, My God, I feel as if he's touching me. *There.*

"I bet I've done worse things than you," she teased, opening her lips for the silver spoon of glacé. "Probably much worse."

"Perhaps much better," he laughed. He considered leaning across the candlelit table and kissing her then, but he did not. She looked, with her lips a little shiny from the sherbet, as if she were as sweet as candy. Her pale arms were plump and made him want to touch them. Her hair, as fine as spun gold, fell in tendrils upon her neck. The effect was of great innocence, as though she could have stepped from a painting, draped only in a few yards of fabric, with cupids escorting her through a sylvan landscape.

"Have you stolen?" she asked with great insouciance.

His dark eyes narrowed with concentration. "Sometimes women have given me things that belonged to their husbands."

Iris loved this. "*Oui. Exactement!*"

"Don't think I'd call it stealing, though," he continued seriously. "Would plundering give me any status in your eyes?"

"*Mais oui!*" Iris began to point out the cheeses she wanted from the cart in front of them. The waiter was filling a plate with slice after slice. "I love this. I love all this," she whispered.

"All what?"

"All this food! Isn't it beautiful? Doesn't it taste like heaven? Don't you adore eating?" She gushed like a child.

Jean-François grinned and stared at her in profile as she instructed the waiter: "And that one. *Un petit peu.*" Totally uninhibited. He had imagined her loving the taste on her tongue, the coldness of the champagne, the color and richness of the Chateau Petrus. Don't say a word about appetites, he warned himself. Just think it.

"What about murder? Have you done murder?"

His throat went dry. "I was far away," he coughed. "Murder? Did you say murder?"

"*Oui.*" She shrugged. "Don't act so guilty. I will wonder about you."

Jean-François took a sip of the wine and swallowed. "You do have some curiosity, then?"

Iris fixed him with her great big green eyes and gave him one of her half-smiles, calculated to incite.

· · ·

The Ritz was closer, and neither of them cared what bed they used. They walked quickly past the grand *escalier d'honneur* and the Aubusson tapestries near the impressive staircase. Singlemindedly, neither glanced to the left at the bar, which Hemingway had called a paradise. Once they were in Jean-François's suite, there was little sentiment involved in undressing. They yanked impatiently at their clothes as if in a childish race to see who could go skinny-dipping first. Jean-François tore off his shirt without undoing his cuff links, and fumbled helplessly to undo them from the opposite side of the cuffs. Iris's zipper was stuck until she could pull it up again, and she cursed as she pinched the flesh.

At last they stood facing each other at the foot of the big double bed, both entirely naked. Iris was as white as a marble statue, rounded and lush. Her breasts were large, but firm and erect. Jean-François, dark and muscular and tall, was two feet in front of her, simply staring. He reached for her nipples of dark rose with both hands, and when Iris moved closer he spoke a sharp command. "No! Wait."

Iris opened, then closed her mouth. Let him have his way. He still feels angry with me. Later I will have my way. She swallowed, and her lips went dry as he twisted her nipple between thumb and forefinger. The tight hard knot at the tip of each breast was pulsating, matching the pulse between her legs. She felt the erect nipples cold in the air. Still he played with her, and still did not move closer. Iris felt her knees weaken and still he kept on. She leaned her head back and stared up at him with lips parted, breathing through her dry mouth. He did not look at her face, but only concentrated on her breasts. Iris stared at the ropes of muscles across his shoulders and down his arms. She watched them move under the olive skin and tried to think of them as separate from the hands and fingers that now cruelly played with her. At last he hurt her, and she cried out and struck him with her flattened palm across his face.

"Bitch!" he shouted, but at the same instant scooped her into his arms and threw her on the bed, where he pressed her knees apart and began to lick her thighs.

"You bastard!" Iris yelled back at him as she writhed to push his face away. But he was strong, and she couldn't. She grabbed a handful of his black hair and yanked, causing him to shout at her and grab her hands. Then he flipped her over on her stomach and struck her on her round, white bottom nearly as hard as he could. Twice. And twice Iris emitted high-pitched shrieks of pain.

Jean-François commanded her roughly to shut up, which made her all the more furious and all the more determined to scream. After another few minutes of struggling, with Iris trying in vain to get out of the tangle of sheets and with Jean-François at last grasping both of her wrists in one hand, he was on top of her once more. She looked up at him, face flushed, green eyes fairly blazing with fury. He held her wrists above her head and stared at her. Then he laughed. She did not. His white teeth suddenly looked cruel to her, but his mouth—she still wanted his mouth.

"You'll be a good girl now, won't you, Iris? If I let go of your hands?"

She nodded and he released her and she slapped him as hard as she could across the face. But she didn't get off the bed soon enough, and in seconds she was beneath him again in the same position, breathing hard. "Good girl?" He raised his eyebrows.

"I'm not a good girl. I thought we established that a long time ago." Her voice was low, controlled, but she was still angry. "You don't hurt me and get away with it," she said, staring up at him defiantly.

"You don't hurt *me* and get away with it, either." He hadn't meant to say that. But I won't see her again, he thought, so what does it matter?

Iris was silent. Their breathing slowed to normal, but they still stared at each other in the silence. He let go of her wrists and then reached down and spread her thighs. She offered no resistance, but was surprised when he knelt and suddenly entered her. "*Mon Dieu!*" she cried as he forced himself deep inside. Iris curled up toward his shoulders, toward his face, like an animal seeking protection, but when he whispered hoarsely, "Am I hurting you?" she shook her head. Wide-eyed, she clung to him as he rocked back and forth and she saw closed eyes and black lashes and his mouth a straight line and the muscles of his jaw clenching and unclenching as he entered her and pulled away, entered her and pulled away. In minutes it was over and he lay sweating, exhausted, spent, in her arms.

Iris was tired and cranky and dissatisfied. He didn't bother! she thought to herself in amazement. Selfish bastard. He was already asleep. Iris pulled herself out from under him, wincing at the sensation of his falling out of her. Damn it. Damn it to hell. She looked up at the ceiling, totally awake. I've had better nights at a suite in the Ritz. Hell, she thought, as she tenderly touched her sore bottom, I've had better *afternoons* here.

• • •

Anna was beside herself when she woke up the next morning and saw her mistress's door closed. She began to wrack her brain, wondering if she had perhaps closed it herself. Was Madame really back from dinner with this Monsieur Colbert? Really back and sleeping in her own bed? There was no wisp of lace on the door, so no breakfast was expected—unless, of course, things had been so passionate, so wild . . . Anna flushed with excitement. So . . . so whatever that Madame had not had time or had entirely forgotten the signal. She bent down and squinted through the keyhole, but could see only a mound under the white satin quilt. Whether it was two bodies or one, she could not be sure, and with a sigh of frustration she stood up and tiptoed down the hall to the kitchen to make herself a cup of tea.

By the time the bell rang, summoning her to the bedroom, Anna had stood outside the door two more times in a state of high curiosity. Now she raced down the hall and, throwing open the door, wanted to cry, "What happened?" but didn't. Iris stretched and yawned, then asked for tea, croissants, blueberry jam. Seeing Anna's face, she said, "I know you're dying to know what happened." She shook her head, still feeling a handprint of heat on her left buttock. Iris sighed and looked a bit forlorn. "I don't know what happened. When I figure it out, you'll be the first to know."

Anna stood there a few seconds longer. "*Oui, Madame,*" she said tentatively, and left the room to fetch the breakfast tray.

Iris opened the little cabinet beside her bed and extracted a hairbrush and a pair of ivory combs. As she twisted her hair into a knot, she thought of Jean-François. *Mon Dieu!* He did not satisfy me! But her eyes narrowed as she thought of his arrogance, his toughness, his bullying, his damn pride. She smiled faintly. The next time I do what I want, and *he* will do what I want. She thought of his body, of his face above her, and of his fierceness. "*Mon Dieu!*" she whispered. Jean-François Colbert, you *do* excite me.

· · ·

He stretched out his arm and reached for her. Then he turned over and stared in amazement at the rumpled sheets. He bolted out of bed and walked quickly to the bathroom. The door was open. Naked, he stalked heavy-footed to the living room of the suite. The curtains were open, the door to the hallway closed; her black silk evening bag was not on the table. Indeed, there was no sign of her anywhere. His own clothes lay where he'd dropped them. Jean-François rubbed his eyes and blinked. She had actually left his bed, dressed, and gone! "*Merde!*" he swore as he reentered the bedroom. He sat on the edge of the bed and reached angrily for the phone. Then he banged down the receiver and said, "*Merde!*" once more.

He ordered breakfast, called Swissair, and showered. Staring at himself in the mirror, he yanked his tie into place and laughed. Jean-François still couldn't quite believe it.

· · ·

That was how it started, with appetites and confusion and lovemaking that Iris later described as "gladiatorial." Jean-François flew back to Geneva that morning, thinking only of her. Iris walked in the Bois de Boulogne, thinking only of him. She painted all afternoon while Jean-François sat in his dark blue office and stared out the window at passing clouds.

Geneva

"I wonder if you're free for dinner tonight."

"*Un moment,*" answered Iris. "Anna! Please bring me my book!" He heard the pages being turned and thought what a bitch she was. "*Oui.* As a matter of fact, I will be free. After . . . after a little drinks party. After eight?"

"*D'accord.*" Without a good-bye, he hung up the phone and then summoned his secretary. "Swissair, Jacqueline. Get me on a flight that arrives in Paris no later than six." She stared at him. He had meetings tomorrow morning. Back to back, one right after the other, until lunch. "I know. I know." He nodded. "I'll be here in time."

In two minutes she reappeared. "Flight two-oh-seven, leaving at four-thirty-five. Can you make that?"

He was already standing, slamming his desk drawer closed, tucking his bright red passport into his jacket pocket. "Have to make it." He winked at her as she stepped aside to let him pass, and in seconds he was gone.

The pretty redhead returned to her desk and sat down slowly. She hoped no one else called for him today. She hoped none of the other bankers asked for him. She could cover to a certain extent, but . . . She spread her hands and shrugged. Monsieur Colbert. Had he lost his mind? Why, he had just returned from Paris before lunch!

Paris

Dinner was not to be. Anna opened the door and showed Jean-François into the salon, where Iris waited. She wore a cream satin dress that was slightly off the shoulder, with fitted long sleeves. Ropes of pearls lay on her bosom and hung to her waist. One square-cut diamond was at each ear. Her hair was brushed back into ivory combs and cascaded onto her bare shoulders.

Jean-François could think only of vanilla ice cream. He wore the same gray suit of the evening before, but someone at the Ritz had pressed it. His pale blue shirt made him appear more olive-complexioned than he had looked seventeen hours before, when Iris had given him a last look by the light of the bedside lamp. His black hair, still damp from the shower, shone like patent leather. Iris visualized the bathroom at the Ritz. She now knew what his shaving kit looked like, that he had his shirts made in Hong Kong, that his shoes and suits were made in Paris. Iris definitely approved of the tall, handsome man before her.

"Champagne?" was all she said. "I'm one glass ahead of you." She sat down on the little Louis Quinze side chair as he positioned himself near her on the loveseat. Iris leaned forward to fill the tulip flute, and he stared openly at what he thought were the most exquisite breasts he'd ever seen. She knew what he was looking at, and had calculated exactly what he'd see. Brightly, she began, "I met a man this evening who insisted upon speaking English."

Jean-François felt rage rush through him. He hated it. The jealousy. This was the first time Iris had made him feel it. "What was his nationality?"

"He was from Paris, but he was exceedingly proud of his English."

"Which you never seem to speak." The little dart at her was because of his jealousy. You pinch me, I pinch you. Pinpricks. Little arrows.

She smiled. "Anyway, he spoke wonderful English and we talked and at last I asked him where he'd learned and he said, 'Why, right in France!' And when I thought a certain school, he said, 'Oh, no! I read all the plays of Oscar Wilde the summer I was seventeen!' "

Jean-François managed to smile. He loathed the man. Wished him . . . dead? How childish. He swallowed some champagne. "And what do you read?"

"Etienne—Etienne Le Sage—is always after me to read this or that best-seller, but I confess . . ." Her shoulders, as pale and rich looking as cream, went up in a shrug. "I just don't. I try to know who's president of the Republic . . ."

It was false modesty and they both knew it. She had proved herself quite well informed the evening before.

"I think you are more a visual person than anything else. The colors of your canvases . . . you never told me how you began to paint, or even when."

"I started to paint in the middle of the night. In Paris. When I was very sad about something."

He stared at her and waited for her to continue. She was silent. "And did the sadness go away with the painting?"

Iris shook her head, remembering the tacky little magazine and seeing the photograph of herself at the kitchen table in Calabria. "No. I guess some sad things are like old suitcases in the back of a closet."

"I don't understand."

"Well, you know they're there, and once you had a use for them, but now . . . now they are back there in a dark corner, and they take up space in your life, but you can't seem to get rid of them, either." She smiled quickly to bring levity back again, but Jean-François noticed how forced it was. She told herself not to drink any more. Not to think of Vito dead on the front steps.

Jean-François didn't speak.

Abruptly, Iris stood and reached for a silver bell on the table between them. Anna arrived on the third jangle, for she had been lurking in her favorite haunt, the archway leading to the dining room. "Throw this bottle away," Iris instructed, "and bring another."

He didn't ask for an explanation, but understood. A bad bottle. Bad spirits let loose. He couldn't stop himself from a last question. "Why did you say you had a use for them? Is there a use for sadness?"

"Sometimes sadness can change you. Can make things happen to you."

"Once I was so sad, I didn't grow for a year." His own voice shocked him. "I was eleven."

Iris poured their glasses full from the new bottle, and wondered what could have made such a strong person so desolate. What could have touched such a selfish person so deeply. Suddenly she wanted him. Naked. In her arms. In her bed. Iris wanted his vulnerability. But she wouldn't hurt him, not tonight. Not as she had planned. She looked into those black eyes and offered, "Let me do nice things to you. Very gentle things."

He nodded curtly. Jean-François was unused to the female of the species offering anything other than her body, beautifully wrapped, to be sure, and well tended, obviously.

They drank in silence, occupied with their own thoughts. The clock chimed nine as Anna, unsummoned this time, entered with a silver plate of paté and little toasted triangles of thin bread. Iris refilled the glasses and they ate a bit for energy—for strength.

Iris took his hand then, and together they stood and walked through the semidark apartment, down the hall where the vases of white roses stood on the table with the letter opener and the unopened mail. Past the latest declaration of love from Carlo. Past the watercolors of Capri that Prince Ivan had had framed for her after a cruise. The bedroom was waiting for them, a warmly lit, scented haven. "You've never really kissed me," Iris whispered as she looked up at him.

He put his hands on either side of her head and bent down. He tasted of cold champagne at first, but his tongue was warm and soft in her mouth. She realized she was holding on to the lapels of his jacket for balance when he pulled away and began to lift the pearls over her head. Then he undid the tiny buttons on her dress from the neckline to the waist in back, and pulled the yards of satin over her head. Iris held her arms up like an obedient little girl. She wore a cream lace camisole and a garter belt. Jean-François knelt on the carpet to kiss the soft flesh between the stockings and her panties, and nearly moaned when he inhaled her scent. He pressed her backwards onto the bed and pressed his face against her thighs as she reached to undo his tie. "No," she whispered when she feared he would make love to her fully clothed. "Please let me undress you."

Jean-François stopped then, and she rose upon her elbows and then stood and tugged the tie away, and then the shirt. Her little fingers pulled at his belt and then the clasp above the zipper. Her hands brushed his hard, erect maleness and then he took down his trousers and stepped from his shoes and socks.

"You are almost terrifying," she whispered with a little smile.

He laughed as he took her hand and they turned toward the bed again. They lay on top of the satin sheet, staring at each other, admiring the lines of flesh and pinkness and the hardness and the softness that was male and female. Iris bent to him and put him in her mouth quickly. She moved her tongue round and round the shaft, and then her lips back and forth over the line of circumcision. She always pitied the poor adult male this cruelty he had endured as a baby, and she was as tender to that little seam as if it had happened in her presence only yesterday.

Jean-François could not be still for her, and pulled her away and tried to hold her down and come inside. Iris kept whispering, "No, no. Not yet. You must wait." And with her little velvet hands she stroked him until he thought he would burst with wanting to be in the hot, silky wetness of her.

At last she could not hold him away any longer, and he was inside her, moving back and forth, and no matter how she implored him to wait, to go slowly, he could not. Or would not? And he came with a cry of something that sounded like pain and then lay in her arms and slept.

Iris stared up at the green canopy and counted the peacock feathers clustered at each corner. Then she counted the egret feathers and then she reached to turn off the lamp. In the darkness his face was before her, flushed with passion, eyes slitted, lips faintly parted. Iris touched his muscular back and listened to his breathing in the silence of her bedroom. Selfish bastard, she thought again. Two nights in a row, and he doesn't care. Two nights in a row, and I will probably want him again anyway. She felt cranky and wide awake and confused.

When she awakened in the morning he was not beside her; his clothes were gone, and the bedroom was without any sign of his ever having been there. Iris rubbed her eyes and wondered if she had dreamed him.

CHAPTER TWENTY-THREE

Cynthia

January 1988 — Vieille Ville

"What is it, Cynthia?" Yves's voice was soft. When she didn't answer, he went on. "Sit down. Let me get you something. Wine? Something stronger?"

She shook her head. Her blond hair hung just to the shoulder of the tan linen dress. A large topaz sparkled at each ear. Her shoes were tan kid, slingback. As usual, Cynthia looked like a magazine cover. Always *comme il faut*, Mimi described her. Just so. The little wrinkles around her eyes were the only sign that she was past thirty.

Yves pulled the cork on a bottle of Chateau Lafitte and splashed two glasses quite full, then extended one to his guest, who sat up very straight on his big, dark green leather chesterfield. The sun streamed through the high living-room windows of his house in the Old Town, and all the brass nailheads around the arms of the sofa shone in the light. The dark wood of the antiques gleamed richly. Everything was polished, lovingly cared for by old Pierrette, who limped through the rooms every morning with a dust cloth, silver polish, brass polish, and furniture wax all in a basket she hung on her wrist.

"It's Jean-François again, isn't it?" Yves asked as he took his place on the other side of the coffee table.

Cynthia sipped the wine and then tried to smile. "Isn't it possible to stop by and drink wine with an old friend?"

"Not with me, it isn't! You owe me things," he said, trying to sound sinister but failing.

"Oh, Yves!" For a second he thought she might cry, but she didn't. She didn't continue, either.

"Look, dear Cynthia. Do you want advice? Do you want someone to talk to? Or do you want a sounding board? I can be anything," he insisted. "A shrink?"

She put the wineglass on the table and then spread her hands helplessly. "I don't know what to do."

"Well, first start at the beginning and tell me what you're talking about."

"The beginning?" Her laugh was brittle, self-mocking. "It all started right at the beginning. The beginning of everything, the beginning of our marriage, the beginning of our life together."

Yves looked down into the red wine and frowned. Cynthia had come to him before, close to tears, full of pain. It happened about once every two or three years. He never helped. He tried, and she went away smiling bravely. Tough, beautiful Cynthia. Being beaten to death. Slowly.

"I think it's serious this time, Yves." She sighed and picked up the wineglass. "Veronique has seen him in Paris with her. Mimi saw them together in that restaurant he loves. He's away more than ever. And when he's in Geneva, he's more bad-humored than ever—"

"Why the hell do you let him get away with it?" Yves burst out.

"With the women?"

"No! With the shit he gives you! 'Do this' and 'Do that' and 'This isn't good enough'!"

She laughed. "You've been listening to Veronique. She thinks—"

"I don't have to listen to Veronique. I can see Jean-François with my own eyes," he interrupted.

"But he's always been that way. I don't care anymore. It's always something." She looked down at her beautifully manicured hands, the result of a New Year's resolution to have manicures like all the other women she knew. "Something is wrong, and if it isn't—if everything is perfect—he invents something. It's an excuse to shout, to ruin a dinner, to not make love." Cynthia stopped and stared up at the Venetian mirror over the Louis Quinze bureau. "I'm used to it. I really don't think I care."

Yves wondered if anything would dynamite Cynthia out of her stupor. Would the years go on this way? She was the wife Yves would have wanted —if he'd ever wanted a wife. Bright and kind. Intelligent. A reader. Glamorous, with an aristocratic subtlety. Perfectly groomed at all hours of the day or night. A good mother. A good organizer. A charming hostess. The perfect chatelaine.

Cynthia went on, "It's the women I still care about. I don't know why, but I feel that he belongs to me."

"Nobody belongs to anybody," Yves said cynically. He stood up and walked to the window. With hands in his pockets jingling his change, he remembered Alphonse telling him good-bye. After two years. Just like that. Nobody belongs to anybody.

"I don't know what's right anymore." Cynthia sipped her wine. "No. That's not true. I know what's right, but let's say my ideas about fidelity have been battered to pieces in Geneva."

"You're American, darling. When are you going to understand one thing? Veronique and I keep telling you. It's just one thing you have to absorb."

"What is it?" She turned her big green eyes upon him.

"Marriage has nothing to do with your sex life."

"Oh. I know that." Her voice was hollow. She was thinking, Marriage means I don't *have* a sex life. Everyone else does. Not me. That part of me has died. I still miss it, so maybe it hasn't died. It's just . . . wounded. "But here everyone accepts the unacceptable. It's unacceptable to me, anyway. Everyone tolerates the pain."

"It's simple prostitution in many cases. Love? No. It's money. One marries to consolidate one's position. Land or business."

Cynthia thought of her father's money, her father's bank. She wondered if that had helped Jean-François fall in love with her. Yves went on, "When some penniless East European princess marries a German who made all his money in Australia from stones popping out of the ground, or from oil in Venezuela . . . when the money was made five years ago and no one has ever heard of him but his bankers." He laughed. "Or the concierge at the Richemond!"

Cynthia said softly, "I guess it means something."

"And it doesn't look like undying love to me!"

Cynthia didn't speak. Wordlessly she held out her glass to be refilled. He poured more wine into both of their goblets and sat down again. They were both thinking the same thing. "It's not your imagination," he said quietly.

"I know it isn't." She waited for him to tell her.

"She's a blonde, an artist. She's American. Funny thing is—she's a short, slightly plump version of you."

"Should I be pleased?" Cynthia said huffily. At last, she thought, he's being straight with me.

"No. I mean she has hair the color of yours and eyes every bit as green. The same complexion."

Marco flashed into Cynthia's mind, unbidden. Same colors. Do we repeat ourselves? Are we drawn again and again to the same type?

"She might have been from Madame Claude's. Ten years ago she could have been. She's . . ."

"Mimi was up against one of her girls, wasn't she? Didn't Antoine fall in love with a Madame Claude girl?"

"Yes. And Mimi knows that she very nearly lost him."

"Did they ever marry their clients?" asked Cynthia in shock.

"It happened. Madame Claude, as you know, taught them everything to please a man. And one of the things she said was, 'If you marry, marry very well and make it a good marriage.'"

"Sounds like every mother."

"I have to hand it to her. Picking these beautiful girls and preparing them to spend the evening at Paris's best dinner parties with Europe's most prominent, most important—"

"Richest. Don't forget richest."

"Yes. Richest men," Yves assented.

"I heard that sometimes they would go on trips for two or three weeks . . ."

"*Oui*. And behave impeccably. The whole point was for someone like Giscard d'Estaing to have a 'companion' who could be of a very good family and who would amuse him totally. No one should have been able to guess they were from Madame Claude."

"But Mimi was talking, and she said that they were *so* beautiful that they stood out."

"They were spectacular sometimes, but . . ." Yves realized he was saying too much. Cynthia had successfully deflected the conversation away from herself. Now all he was doing was making her suffer with the descriptions of how clever and attractive her competition was. Idiot! He began again. "Look, Cynthia. This woman Jean-François is seeing in Paris—she was not from Madame Claude. It doesn't matter. Madame Claude was closed down for tax reasons under Pompidou. She never went to jail because she knew too many secrets. They let her off with a fine." He sighed. "But none of this matters. This woman—what matters is what you think about it."

"I hate it." Her voice was flat. "And I hate him, too."

Yves was surprised. "Don't you love him anymore?"

She shook her head. "But I have two children I love and—"*and worry about*, she thought to herself. Especially Stephanie. A photograph of the honor students from the Academy had arrived yesterday. Stephanie was in the back row, smiling. Cynthia thought she looked terribly thin, somehow not right, not herself.

"And a lovely house and servants and a good material life. *Un train de vie*," Yves said.

"Is that so bad? No one in Geneva ever seems to give those things up in the name of love. No one ever leaves a rich man. I've been watching." She smiled faintly. "Unless it's for a *richer* man."

"Ha!" came the delighted laugh. "You're catching on!"

"What do I do, Yves?" she persisted. "What do I do?"

"Have an affair, for Christ's sake!" He wanted to shout, *Find someone and fuck your weekends away*, but he couldn't with Cynthia. She didn't use words like that.

She shook her head, and her hair was platinum in the sunlight. "Then I think I'll get a divorce. I've never considered divorce because it's always in my mind that Jean-François is the father of my children. That will never change. But perhaps *I* am changing." Her voice was strong. "I'm not like you and Veronique."

"Well, let's just say neither one of you are like me. But then again, we have one thing in common—we're all looking for the right man!"

She laughed brightly, then became serious again. "I mean that if I wanted to make love to someone, if I found someone like that, then I'd want to be with him. All the time. Wake up with him. Make plans with him. And I think if I felt that way about him, then to even have dinner with Jean-François would be absurd. I would be repelled at the idea of sleeping next to one man when I wanted to be making love to another!"

Yves put his face in his hands. "Oh, Cynthia! Haven't you been listening? Veronique and I have been giving you lessons in how to be cynical—how to be Genevois, how to survive in a loveless marriage—for all these years!" He sank dramatically to his knees and feigned weeping on the little French commode.

Cynthia laughed in spite of herself. She had resolved nothing by coming here. Everything was still a mess. But the wine had made her feel a bit better, and Yves—just seeing him was comforting. But she and he were poles apart in their ideas on love; she couldn't embrace the attitude he proposed.

Yves returned to his chair, then leaned forward and, bright-eyed and smiling, shook his head in defeat. "Cynthia. You know what your problem is?"

She shook her head, and the amber earrings flashed in the light.

"You're just too romantic for little old jaded Geneva!"

Verbier

Cynthia would always remember that weekend in Verbier as the last, though actually it was not. It was, however, the last time before things began to come apart. Before Easter, before the beginning of the end.

Jean-François had driven up on Friday night with Jacques Dubois and Pamela, a banking colleague and his young English wife. He was in high spirits, affectionate with Cynthia, making toasts at dinner, effusively offering everyone brandy. He and Jacques had gone upstairs to the room Jean-François thought of as his study.

When the two women had washed the dishes, for there was no help at Verbier, they moved into the living room of the chalet. "This is my favorite place," Cynthia sighed as she sat down beside the fire in the dark brown leather chair. Most of the other furniture was old pine antiques. It was a large room, all wood-paneled, decorated with American Indian rugs as wall hangings. Cynthia liked their bright primary colors, especially in the daytime, when one saw only white snow and blue sky to the north beyond the curlicued, carved wooden porch railings. The original chalet was built mostly of old pine, which was too expensive to use nowadays; the Colberts had bought the place and the next-door lot, then added on a second story and another wing. Pamela arranged herself cross-legged on the white fur rug, with her cognac in front of her.

"You love it more than Edgartown?" she asked.

"No. I confess I don't. I always look forward to every other summer there. But I think it might be a tie. Who could not love this?" She waved her arm lazily behind her at the wall of glass. It was dark and impossible to see outside, but Pamela understood her to mean the evergreens laden with snow, the jagged peaks against a black sky.

"How do you do it?" the younger woman suddenly asked.

"Do what?" Cynthia asked, gazing into the orange flames.

"Have a happy marriage to a Genevois."

If Cynthia had known her better, she might have laughed. But she was instantly sympathetic instead. "It's not easy, I know."

"Nothing is easy about it!" Pamela burst out. The pretty brunette in the white sweater then lowered her voice. "Geneva isn't easy. Jacques's family isn't easy. Sometimes I just feel like getting on a plane to London and saying, '*Au revoir* and screw you,' to all of them!"

Cynthia took a sip of the cognac. "I had a simpler time than you're having. My mother-in-law is English, and she is Jean-François's only family. No one else was around to express dismay that I wasn't from good Genevois stock." She hesitated, and then decided to be totally frank. Pamela was bright, with a mind of her own, and had been married only a year. She was twenty-six and could take it. "But what we have to understand is that we are second-class."

This statement was followed by a cry of dismay. "What! What are you talking about?"

Cynthia nodded. "Second-class citizens, and we always will be. Always." She put up a finger. "I will always be an American, and that's not as good as being Genevois. Now, my children are Genevois. That's fine. But me?" She shook her head, and her hair shone nearly white in the firelight. "Never. I am second-class."

Pamela was silent for a moment, and then fairly exploded. "Do you know what a woman said to me at a family gathering? I could hardly breathe, I was so angry! It was one of Jacques's aunt's friends. She and I were talking last summer out on the lawn, and she took me aside and asked me if I was from a good family!"

Cynthia burst into laughter. "That's because the first thing they say here is always, in French, 'She is a what?' A Devereaux, a Pictet, whatever. I know of an American woman who, upon marrying into a very old Genevois family, was forced to sign a marriage contract stipulating that all property would forever remain separate. It was as if they didn't trust her. And when her husband dies, their child inherits three-quarters of his fortune and she gets one-quarter."

Pamela groaned. "And how do I handle all these . . ." She sighed. "These things I'm supposed to do in order to be a proper lady."

"What are you talking about?"

"The keys to the big, gloomy cathedral. Les Clefs de St.-Pierre? Whatever. Raising money for renovations by making jelly. The charity work just bores me silly. The idea of it makes me cringe!"

"Then don't do it." Cynthia was definite. "But you'll meet people that way. Other women. Other foreign wives. And you'll somehow sift through the ones who love to do needlework for bazaars and the ones like you who'd rather be . . . I don't know . . . playing tennis?"

Pamela smiled. "Close. Golf."

"So join the golf club. Cologny is heaven."

"We're already members, thank God. Since the waiting list is six years!"

"Well, aren't you lucky?" said Cynthia. "So spend every minute there! And the rest of the time, do what you have to do to keep your marriage intact. Simple. Simple advice from a longtime married crone."

Something in Cynthia's voice made Pamela reach for the Remy-Martin to refill their glasses. She had had no one to talk to in Geneva for months. No talk like this. Her long-distance bills to her best friend in London were so big that she was using grocery money and making all her calls from the post office phones. "What was Geneva like? What were you like when you came here?"

"Geneva was *so* different. Fewer cars. Still signs of how the country had suffered during the war. They say that right after World War II there were only five taxis in all of Geneva, and almost no one could afford to take one unless there was a funeral! It was a town of bicycles. I came in the sixties, when there was no Christie's or Sotheby's, no Habsburg, Feldman. Now there are so many art galleries and nonstop openings." She sighed. Too many invitations. "There used to be so few restaurants that everyone had dinner parties at home. There were very few shops, but we all had fun going to Paris or having our dressmakers make our little afternoon dresses. We flew to London for sweaters and good wool winter clothes. I felt my clothes were too bright when I arrived from the States, and that I was always wearing too much jewelry, but you can see the Genevois women are now *très, très* chic. I think they're more chic than the Parisians. But Geneva was a small town."

Cynthia took a sip of the liqueur. "So Geneva was different and so was I. I was nineteen and my husband was my whole life." Cynthia shook her head. "I wasn't secure enough about myself." She suddenly wondered if she was now. "I just wanted it to be fine." She realized Pamela was watching her intently. "I wanted to have a marriage, and that was my life. There was no idea of getting out of it, of leaving Geneva. That never entered my mind as a possibility. I never thought of going back to Boston." Well, only once. Because Mother was there and a whole life I didn't want. Not even when Jean-François was horrible did I ever imagine starting over as Cynthia Kendall of Beacon Hill, with my mother pushing me toward . . . toward another marriage. That would have been my fate if I'd gone home. No college diploma, and big fights over whether I should go back and get it. I can hear Mother being worried about my social life as a twenty-something-year-old freshman! "Oh . . ." Cynthia sighed aloud. "The things you're taught to think are important. And one day you wonder if they are or not."

"Did you do all this charity work?"

"I did the first year, and then I sort of dropped out. It seemed that the things I had to do—renovating the chateau, starting the garden, social things for Jean-François, expanded to fit the hours in the day. So I never felt I had a free minute. And then I had the children, and though I had plenty of help, it was a whole new set of . . . of situations. School. Measles. Piano lessons." She took another swallow of the cognac. "Jean-François has always been a demanding man. I guess the time . . ." She stopped and gazed into the flames. "The time just slips away."

"What would you change if you could?"

Cynthia was suddenly alert. "Are you writing my memoirs?" she smiled.

"Sorry. It's just that I wonder where I am, what I'm doing here. It's nice to talk to someone like you."

Cynthia put her hand out and touched Pamela's shoulder. "If you love Jacques, then talk to him. And if he's not sympathetic, then find a good friend. Come and talk to me! And if you keep on loving him, then stay. But make sure he's a part of your life, of what you're going through."

Pamela's brown eyes were shining. "You sound so wise, I feel like taking notes. And after seeing you and how you've managed . . ." she marveled.

Cynthia thought, if you only knew. I stopped loving that handsome, affectionate man you met at dinner years ago.

The conversation became more general. Cynthia felt like a liar, an impostor, an actress playing the role of cherished wife. But Jean-François was the actor. Such was his charm that he had that power to make people think he was really there. Really existed behind the fresh, quick, boyish smile. But he was always somewhere else—enduring a nightmare he would never describe, or off on a "business trip," which meant never in his room at the Ritz. Jean-François, the master of illusion. But when he put his arms around Cynthia in front of guests, they adored him. They were sometimes jealous of her, but they invariably loved being witness to something they imagined was typically a private show of affection between two happy people.

"Bed!" Cynthia yawned. "Breakfast is anything within reason, which means anything you can find in the kitchen. And it's anytime you want it. I usually get up early and spend time with my notebook and . . ." It had slipped out. "And then I'm down here in the dining room at about eight. I'm going out with Maurice, my ski instructor, tomorrow at nine. You're welcome to come with us, unless you want to go off on your own or with Jacques and Jean-François."

Pamela put her hand up to cover her yawn. "Oh! I'll make all decisions tomorrow!" She smiled. "Thanks for . . . for being open with me. I . . ." She couldn't finish. Cynthia put her arm around her shoulder, and suddenly wondered why she wasn't more that way with her own daughter. It was somehow easier with her son, but physical affection was so hard within her family. The Kendalls and now the Colberts. Sins of the mothers. Cynthia joked, "Remember! We're second-class citizens, but that doesn't mean we have to suffer. So, starting tomorrow, do what you want to do! It'll make you happier and Jacques, too."

Pamela nodded. "Right. No more squeezing myself into a mold."

"And tomorrow my best friend, Veronique, will be here, with or without her French banker husband, and Mimi and Antoine, who is another French banker, and . . . you can just be an anthropologist." Cynthia nodded. "Yes. We'll have lunch on the terrace at Vieux Verbier, and I'll keep your wineglass filled."

They kissed good night in the European way, and Pamela went upstairs wondering why she sensed an undertow of unhappiness in Cynthia Colbert. After all, she thought, she has everything. A husband you'd stare at on the street and a chateau that is really magnificent inside and out from what I've heard, and two perfect children, good friends, and she herself is bright and beautiful. What else could she possibly dream of having?

Cynthia turned out all the lights in the downstairs, and checked the front door, which was a new habit. Switzerland was changing, everyone said. Too many foreigners. As she passed the closed door of Jean-François's study, she heard the two men still deep in conversation.

She reconsidered Pamela's question as she prepared for bed. What would I change? Cynthia undressed and slipped into a nightgown, and then arranged the duvet and turned out the bedside lamp. The outside shutters were drawn back, and she could see the black sky with its stars as bright as diamonds. What would I change? she wondered as she shivered at the open window. Just one thing, she decided. I would marry a man who loved me. And I would love him back.

· · ·

There was a crowd around the table in the sun when Maurice, Pamela, and Cynthia arrived for lunch. The Vieux Verbier had good, simple food and a faithful clientele that spilled out onto the large wooden deck. It was located just a few minutes' walk from the center of the village and only a few meters from the cable cars silently going past above the tables of the brightly dressed skiers at lunch. Cynthia, rosy-cheeked, in a lime green anorak and a white *combinaison de ski*, introduced everyone. They, too, were tanned, and smiling behind sunglasses. "Pamela, why don't you sit between me and Louis. He'll fill you in on Verbier. It's Pamela's first time here."

Fendant, the local white wine, was ordered and then Antoine insisted upon having a bottle of Dole Blanche, too, which was a little pink in color. "Where's Jean-François?" Mimi asked.

"He and Jacques left at nine this morning from Savoleyres for helicopter skiing," said Cynthia. "They're at the Glacier du Trient."

Plates arrived almost immediately with bacon, ham, the *viande sechée*, small sausages and pickles and little onions the size of marbles. Black bread came in baskets.

"Verbier was nothing until the 1950s," Louis was saying. He was a man of sixty with snow-white hair and a dignified manner. Veronique had told Cynthia that when she was young she had actually been attracted to what she now called his "stodginess." He seemed a kind man and a good father, if a somewhat dull husband and companion. Veronique had her own ways of coping—coping was called Thierry and Roget and André and Jean-Luc and now Gérard.

"I've been coming here since 1957. Our chalet is one of the oldest ones. Like the Colberts', it was built in the 1920s," Louis said, sipping wine.

"I really love the Colbert chalet," Pamela was saying. "How long have they been coming here?"

Louis said, "You must get Cynthia to tell you the story of how she and Jean-François happened to buy Le Grand Combin."

Everyone at the table had heard the story, but it was fun to hear Cynthia tell it in her understated way. "Well, a Genevois banker who shall remain nameless—"

"Only because we all know his name!" Veronique added, grinning.

Cynthia went on, "He had the terrible misfortune to fall in love with an American, and he went so far as to marry her." She shook her head in sympathy. "This banker liked to come home for lunch, which he did every day. He actually had the temerity to expect his American wife to have a nice lunch for him and to sit there and eat it with him. Now," Cynthia said solemnly, "we all know how impossible American women are. How spoiled and lazy." Everyone laughed. "This American wife hated these lunches, had things to do on her own, and rebelled. She finally exclaimed, 'I married you for love, not for lunch,' and they divorced and their chalet was sold for a song." Pamela laughed along with everyone, and Antoine and Mimi applauded. Wineglasses were refilled.

Maurice began to describe last year's trip to the Himalayas. "Unbelievable skiing. Untouched."

"But getting there!" signed Veronique, who had gone with Gérard unbeknownst to Louis, who had been led to believe she'd been with a group. "You arrive in Delhi at one in the morning—"

"I don't think that's so bad," put in Cynthia, who would have loved to have gone. "One in the morning. You just pretend you've gone out to a party."

Antoine, Mimi's husband, was eager to go. "But I'm taking my own wine."

Louis was worried about getting sick. "I would take two hundred Swiss francs worth of medicaments. I'd buy morphine in England and—"

"Medicine! I'd go a step further. I want to take my own blood!" exclaimed Antoine.

Cynthia and Pamela both began to laugh. They were imagining the group, all now dressed in hot pinks and tomato reds, turquoise and yellow parkas, in the bright white sun of Verbier arriving in the middle of the night at the Delhi airport. All carrying ski equipment and bottles of wine and plasma.

As the plates were cleared, Cynthia put her hand on Pamela's arm and said quietly, "You know my phone number at Chambesy, don't you?"

Pamela nodded. She seemed so much more relaxed than she had upon arrival the evening before.

"You can call me anytime."

"But you're so busy—" Pamela began.

"Yes, I am. But I think I have to stop being 'busy' and make time for really important things. I thought for a long time after I went up to bed last night."

Pamela smiled. "So did I." She surveyed the group of laughing people and the white peaks against a cobalt blue sky. "I think I'm going to be all right."

Les Colombiers

"I can't talk now! Louis is home for lunch! I'll call you later!" Veronique banged down the phone.

Cynthia hung up and sighed. She kicked off her green leather flats and stretched out on the sofa in her "office," her boudoir. Gérard had somehow found out about Veronique's trip to the Seychelles with Louis. "Louis is my husband!" Veronique had shouted at him. "I have a right to go anywhere with him!" "And I have the right to be jealous and to ask you not to go!" Gérard had shouted back. Oh, thought Cynthia. It was so difficult to keep it straight.

The phone rang, and Veronique's voice began as if there had been no interruption at all. "Louis is in the garden, talking with the gardener about geraniums. So now," she continued breathlessly, "the worst has happened."

"Louis found out about Gérard?" Cynthia ventured.

"No! No! He knows about him already," Veronique fairly snorted with irritation. "I told you what happened yesterday with the letter, didn't I?"

Cynthia couldn't remember a thing about a letter, but said, "Oh, yes. Yes! Now tell me the worst."

Veronique was talking quickly. "Gérard says that if I don't go to the Seychelles with Louis, he will take me to the Maldives with him! But I don't know how to get out of going to the Seychelles without developing some deadly disease, and then Louis is so sweet he'd probably want to stay and nurse me back to radiant good health. I mean, Cynthia! How can I possibly *not* go?"

"Not go to the Seychelles with Louis, or not go to the Maldives with Gérard?" Cynthia was wondering what it would be like to pack for a trip with someone you wanted to be with. Wondering what it would be like to be excited.

"Well, yes," said Veronique slowly. "I think I'm a little confused. I mean, well, yes. How can I not do—or do—both?"

"You sound a little unsure of things. Now you just have to concentrate," Cynthia urged. "I mean, the Maldives and the Seychelles are both good for getting a tan, but really, with all these warnings about skin cancer . . ."

"Cynthia! Are you putting me on?"

"And the food will probably be about the same, and there's good wine everywhere nowadays. I'm sure neither Louis nor Gérard would put you in a second-class hotel, so that's equal. Strictly first-class. Ah! Now you'd better check—before you decide where you're going—whether the plane tickets are first-class. And if Louis is economizing, then go with Gér—"

"Cynthia!" Veronique screamed, and then her voice dropped to a frantic whisper. "I have to hang up! He's back!" She banged down the receiver.

Cynthia rubbed her ear and replaced the phone. Veronique! Always on a diet, always getting a facial, always getting her legs waxed, always in a state of trauma over a love affair. She swung her feet down and put on her shoes. Louis seemed like such a nice man. Even with the bad breath. It would be easy to be married to him, she decided, staring out the window at the cherry blossoms. I'm going to tell Veronique to go to the Seychelles.

Connecticut

"Stephanie! Are you on a diet again?" Lisa practically shouted so the whole table could hear.

The tall blonde nodded. "I want to wear the tightest jeans in school." She counted five carrot slices.

"Size two?" Lisa insisted.

Stephanie didn't answer, and the conversation bobbed off in other directions. There were three hundred girls in the Walliston Academy dining room, six at this particular table, and every girl had her big orange tray propped beside her chair. The table itself was round and covered with glasses of milk and orangeade and iced tea, heavy white plates with what the girls called "mystery meat" and its attendant gravy and mashed potatoes. String beans and carrots were served separately, in the same little dishes that the fruit cocktail or ice cream came in. Rolls were on every plate, soggy on the underside from sitting in the gravy.

Stephanie felt ill when she smelled the food. It was disgusting. She looked down at her blue-jeaned thigh and thought, I won't eat tonight or tomorrow, and by the day after tomorrow I will have lost two pounds. And my legs will be thinner.

The laughter around her was louder. Kathy was on her third chocolate pudding, and they were applauding. "Well, being on a diet," she was saying as she plunged the spoon into the gooey mass, "doesn't always mean giving up chocolate!"

Stephanie's mouth watered. No, she told herself. You ate the carrots. You ate five slices. Now stop. She looked down at her thighs again and imagined them the size of sequoia trees. At last the scraping of the chairs on the stone floor signalled the end of another dinner. Stephanie fell into step with her roommate, Kim, and joined the chatter about the European history exam. "If anyone should get an 'A,' it's you!" Lorraine insisted. "I mean, you live there!"

Stephanie shrugged. It was almost Easter vacation, and she dreaded going back to Geneva. "I don't think I live there," she said quietly. "I just exist."

The girls, who knew all about the Colbert family, were quiet for a moment as they approached the front steps of Browning Hall. Then Lisa asked, "Stephie! Would you mind 'existing' with me for three hours while I try to figure out what the devil the Habsburgs had to do with the unification of Western Europe?"

Geneva

Cynthia found herself less and less interested in the parties of Geneva, and seldom showed herself. But Yves often telephoned the day before and was insistent and beguiling about it all. "Oh, come with me! Get out of that house! Jean-François is away, so what will you be doing? A light supper alone and a terrible French movie on television. You can do better, Cynthia! Let me take you!"

As she resisted, she wondered what to wear. Yves could talk her into most things.

This is certainly old Geneva, she thought as she surveyed the room. Nearly everyone was a familiar face to her, and a familiar name given to a street or a quai or an art gallery acquisition. The men prospered as bankers or *avocats* or businessmen; the women were active in raising money for the restoration of St. Pierre's Cathedral, and once or twice a year might stand in a display room at the Richemond or the Beau Rivage for the Christie's or Sotheby's jewelry sale. But basically they were wives and mothers. They were never photographed for magazines or written up in the society pages or interviewed for any reason. They wore elegant dresses, usually classic in style, and good jewelry. Nothing flashy, of course.

Yves leaned comfortably with one elbow on the wooden mantelpiece, looking quite handsome. Cynthia smiled. Yves had his moments, for all his fear of getting older and his vanity about the wrinkles he called "shopping bags" under his eyes. Guests talked in groups, and floated from the upstairs drawing room to the little library beyond. It was one of the chateaux facing the lake; its turrets and the sweep of emerald lawn made it easily recognized from a passing sailboat.

"I went to a reception last week, yet another art gallery opening, and met the strangest Lebanese girl," Yves began.

"Why was she strange?" asked Cynthia.

"She was convinced that the hors d'oeuvres served at most of these parties are lowering everybody's sex drive."

Cynthia almost choked on the triangle of toast and paté as she thought, Well, Jean-François is certainly not affected. He never shows his face at these affairs. He has his own "affairs."

"She explained everything about Geneva to me in terms of microwaved hors d'oeuvres."

Cynthia managed to swallow and then laughed. "Oh, Yves! I've been struggling to understand the Protestant Rome since my first dinner party here. And now you tell me—" A silver tray bearing dozens of appetizers was thrust between them. Cynthia took a stuffed mushroom cap and continued, "Now you say that the key to Geneva has been in front of me—"

Yves interrupted her. "Literally under your nose, darling, all this time."

CHAPTER TWENTY-FOUR

Cynthia

Connecticut

Stephanie Colbert's roommate was the only one to see her changing from blue jeans and layers of sweaters into her nightgown. Her legs had gotten so thin she had asked for permission to wear sweatpants in phys-ed, saying she'd lost her shorts. No one except Kim saw Stephanie's spine, which was a rope of easily countable knots, or her shoulders, which reminded Kim of the newborn baby bird she'd found dead in her backyard years ago. No one except Kim saw the swollen stomach under the sharply outlined ribcage. "You look like somebody from Africa," she burst out in March.

"I just want to lose a few more pounds," said Stephanie.

"But—but can't you see what you look like?" Kim insisted. "I mean, last fall, yes, you were a little bit heavy, but Stephie! You've gone too far! You have to stop this! You have to eat!"

"I do eat!" Stephanie defended herself. "I'm eating very healthy things. Just things that are good for me. Carrots—"

"You ate four carrots at lunch again today! I saw your plate! Stephie, you have to start eating again! Like a normal person—"

"I don't know who's normal," the girl sighed. "Most of the world eats too much."

"But, Stephie, it's not chic. It's . . . it's . . . you're getting ugly." She said the word reluctantly from across the room, glasses low on her nose, book and papers in front of her on the desk.

"Am I?" Stephanie stood up from where she was sitting on the edge of her bed. She had been tying her tennis shoes like a robot in slow motion.. Every movement tired her. She turned to the mirror between their two chests of drawers, and stared at the old person in the glass. Her face was drawn and tired. Her skin was stretched tight across her sharply etched cheekbones. But perhaps most unattractive of all was the color of her complexion—a sickly gray. Her blond hair was no longer shiny, but her dark eyes were unnaturally bright. Stephanie turned to the side and examined her narrow waist and straight silhouette. Yes, I have lost weight, she admitted to herself. Just five more pounds, and then I can relax and eat again and not worry if I gain one or two pounds back. She pulled at the loose skin on one of her forearms and said, "Ugh."

Kim shook her head and tried to concentrate on her Latin assignment. She wondered if she should go to the school nurse, but then thought, Stephie would never forgive me; I'd be tattling. She'll snap out of it. Besides, in three weeks we go home for Easter, and her mother and father will talk some sense into her. She'll have to eat in Geneva.

. . .

Two days later, Stephanie Elizabeth Colbert fainted on the front steps of the science lab building. Miss Dexter, the librarian, was the one to rush to the telephone as the girls gathered around the limp form like so many chirping, panicked chickens among a fallen comrade. A stretcher arrived, carried by two janitors, since Walliston Academy had only a day nurse and a night nurse and Dr. Bowden, who lived in town. The men were astonished at how light she was. By this time, Stephanie was alert and embarrassed, trying to sit up and worried about missing a class. They carried her to the infirmary anyway, with Kim and Miss Dexter walking on either side of the entourage. Kim was secretly relieved it had happened this way, for she'd been fighting with herself over what to do, knowing that she *should* do something and feeling responsible. Now Stephanie was in the hands of adults.

Nurse Gainor asked them all to leave, and then helped Stephanie behind a white curtain and asked her to undress. When several minutes had passed and the girl did not reappear, she pulled the partition aside and saw Stephanie sitting on the metal chair with her head between her knees, fumbling pathetically at her shoelace. Her hands trembled and her thin fingers could not grasp the cord.

The nurse was unprepared for what she was to see. Slowly undressing her newest charge, she bit her lip, trying not to gasp at the emaciated body. Nurse Gainor thought of famines and concentration camps—places and situations that had nothing to do with an elegant prep school in the Connecticut countryside. Nothing to do with a little rich girl whose address on the chart was a chateau in Switzerland.

She helped Stephanie into a white cotton garment that tied in back like a hospital robe, and then supported her across the cold linoleum floor down the hall to a bed. Her teeth were chattering, so she was put under blankets and told to rest. Before the nurse turned away, wondering what lab tests Dr. Bowden would want, Stephanie was fast asleep.

Geneva

"Madame Colbert! Telephone!" It was the new maid calling as the intercom buzzed. She couldn't seem to comprehend that the household had twenty-three extensions and that she didn't have to depend upon voice power.

Cynthia had just finished a lunch of endive salad and homemade bread with slices of Gruyère and Appenzell, her favorite cheeses, and was at her desk, going through the mail. She took a deep breath, preparing to shout back at Danielle in the hall, but then merely sighed and picked up the phone. "*Oui. Allo.*" Then she switched immediately into English, realizing it was long-distance. The line was very bad. She wished the caller would hang up and start over. Cynthia pressed the receiver to her ear tightly, after pulling off one jade and silver earring.

"Yes! Yes! This is Madame—Mrs. Colbert," she said loudly, distinctly.

The noise quieted and she could hear.

"Mrs. Colbert," the woman said Col-burt in an American accent. "This is Mrs. Harvey calling from Walliston Academy."

Cynthia felt a terrible lightness sweep over her like a cold wind. Stephanie, she thought. Oh, please, not an automobile accident. Oh, please let her be all right. Stephanie! "Yes, Mrs. Harvey," she answered coolly.

"I have some bad news. It's about your daughter."

"Yes." No. No. No. Cynthia's fingers tightened around the telephone line. If I can count to four before she tells me, then it'll be all right. One, two, three, four . . .

"She's in the hospital in Stamford. She's very ill, and we think—"

"What happened to her?" Cynthia was suddenly indignant. What was this woman going on about?

"She's lost a great deal of weight, and simply needs to gain it back and to have bed rest."

Cynthia felt total confusion. She thought of diseases of her grandparents' era. Diphtheria. Did people still have tuberculosis? Cholera. No. That was in the Third World. Tetanus. Stepping on nails barefoot in summer. "What are you talking about?" she erupted in a rare show of impatience. "What has happened? What is wrong with my daughter?"

"She collapsed yesterday at school, and Dr. Bowden, our school physician—" Cynthia remembered her mother saying she disliked people who said "physician" when "doctor" would do. "Dr. Bowden thought she should be hospitalized immediately to prevent further dehydration, so she was taken to Stamford General Hospital. She's getting the best treatment, but I thought you should know."

Should know. Should know. *Of course* I should know. "But I still don't understand what happened to her!" Frustration and anger came over the wire all the way from Geneva to the headmistress's office in the white colonial building in Connecticut.

Mrs. Harvey hadn't wanted to use the medical term. She'd felt she had to telephone this morning, but had hoped she could wait for the doctor in Stamford to make his call to break the news. Dr. Bowden was sure, and Dr. Letterer said he thought it looked "open and shut," so she supposed she had to tell this Mrs. Colbert something. Too bad she was one of the few mothers she had never met. Mrs. Harvey took a deep breath. "Dr. Letterer wanted to wait and speak to you later today—"

"Please," said Cynthia. One hand held the receiver and the other curled around the mouthpiece as if she were capable of wringing the words from it.

"It appears that your daughter is suffering from anorexia nervosa."

Cynthia frowned. She'd never heard of such a thing. Anxious? Nervous? "What is it? What did you say? I don't know that I understand. Mrs. Harvey?"

"Yes, I'm still on the line."

"What is that? What did you say? What is it in English?"

Mrs. Harvey sighed and looked down at the sheet from the admissions office. There was a photograph of a smiling blonde in a bright red turtleneck sweater. The address was Chateau Les Colombiers—"Of the doves," she translated. And the phone number of course. "Mrs. Colbert, in plain English, I'm afraid it means that Stephanie has been starving herself."

. . .

Cynthia was told by some supervisor—some nurse, she supposed—that she couldn't speak with Stephanie, that she was sleeping. It alarmed her. It was ten in the morning there. Then she called her mother, who offered to drive to Stamford and pick up her granddaughter so they could decide what should be done.

"Cynthia, we just can't leave her in the hospital! She should be here at Beacon Hill where she can be taken care of properly. I can't believe from what you tell me that she's ill enough to be in *any* hospital, but if—" Then it should be Boston Memorial, where the Kendalls had given so much money, had so much influence, she insisted. Cynthia hated her mother's take-charge voice all of a sudden. It said a thousand things and above all it said, *You don't know what to do, and she's your daughter.*

"All right, Mother. Let me know if I should fly over. I really appreciate your driving to pick her up." Cynthia felt she was talking through clenched teeth. Being grateful with a hand at her throat. "Then we can have Dr. Sutton's opinion and . . ." The arranging continued, and still Cynthia hadn't spoken a word to Stephanie. What is happening? she wondered as she hung up the telephone at last.

Jean-François was not in his suite at the Ritz. She hadn't expected him to be, but just once, she thought, couldn't he be reachable? She left a message for him to call her immediately and then thought, with a great sense of exhaustion, What's the point? He can't do a thing from Paris. It doesn't matter, she realized. I can tell him tonight if he calls, or tomorrow if he doesn't. With a sigh, she sank onto the green and pink flowered sofa and stared into the fireplace, which was banked with ferns in bright fuchsia pottery jars. He'll be irritated that I bothered him at all. She was reminded of the time Michel broke his leg in Verbier. She had thought his father would want to know, and finally reached him at seven-thirty the next morning in Paris, but instead of being concerned, he'd been annoyed. The corners of Cynthia's mouth turned down and she absentmindedly fingered the diamond on her finger. She understood now. Jean-François had been annoyed because of something in Paris. He wouldn't have been in his hotel room at all if things had been going as planned. That was the year she'd found the notes from someone named Yvonne in his coat pocket. Cynthia took a deep breath. Poor girl. Probably only a girl. She seemed obsessed. She'd written of love and wanting and missing. Things that Jean-François couldn't understand.

Suddenly, Cynthia felt very tired and near tears. She felt helpless, and all she wished for was to see Stephanie, to stroke her face, to know that she was all right. Her eyes watered. Anorexia nervosa. Starvation. Why would Stephanie want to starve herself? There must be a mistake. The American doctors are wrong, she thought. Cynthia did not allow her tears to fall, but suddenly, decisively stood up and walked to the telephone.

"*Oui*," she said to the concierge at the Ritz. "Madame Colbert calling from Geneva. It's not important that Monsieur Colbert call me back. Don't bother to give him the message. That's right. Cancel the message. *Merci.*" Slowly, like someone in a dream, she replaced the receiver. Why do I feel, she wondered, that that was a positive thing to do?

·   ·   ·

Mothers and daughters, went through her mind. All three generations of us on the telephone. "She's very weak, Cynthia, but she wants to talk to you."

Cynthia could imagine Stephanie in the red guest room with the four-poster bed, speaking into the extension. The red guest room that her father and I spent the night in so long ago. Before you, before marriage, before—

"Mother!"

"Darling! How do you feel? I've been so worried."

"All right. I guess." The voice was faint, even distracted.

Cynthia pulled at the garland of pearls around her neck. "What do you want to do? Have me come there or you come home early for Easter or what?"

"Cynthia!" It was Margaret Kendall's voice. "I don't think you understand how ill she is."

"Mother! I'm trying to under—" Cynthia was angry and her voice was tight and showed it.

"Mother, I want to come home." Stephanie's voice was tired.

"Well, then, darling, have your grandmother make the reservation. Swissair is best. And just come. Call me and let me know what—"

"Cynthia!" The voice was sharp. How often have I heard my name spoken like an oath, thought her daughter. "You don't seem to know how . . . how weak she is." Margaret Kendall wished that Stephanie weren't still on the line. "Stephanie, dear, why don't you let me talk to your mother. You try to sleep some more before lunch."

"But I don't want—"

Cynthia listened helplessly to the conversation in Boston and frowned. Granddaughter and grandmother get along no better than Mother and I, she thought. Then she heard the click of the extension being hung up. "Are you still there?" her mother asked.

"Of course."

"Cynthia." This time the voice was low, full of concern. "She can't get on an airplane by herself. She'll need a nurse to travel with her, a wheelchair."

"What?" Cynthia felt a sense of shock. "She can't walk?"

"Barely. With me and Mrs. Partridge's daughter Janice—I've had her come to help out these last two days—with both of us holding her between us to go back and forth to the bathroom."

Cynthia was biting a thumbnail. She suddenly felt very frightened. "Mother?" Her voice sounded young and pleading suddenly. "Could you bring her here? Would you?" She felt tears in her eyes. "Can you?"

Margaret Kendall's voice was firm, full of authority, but her daughter was grateful for the way it sounded. For once. "Certainly, dear. I'll take care of everything."

.   .   .

Two days later, Stephanie was in her own room at Les Colombiers. She had been examined by Dr. Marceau, and everyone in the household knew exactly what anorexia nervosa was. But not what it meant.

"Mother, I don't think Dr. Marceau nor I, nor anyone, can force her to eat. Something is obviously more deeply wrong when she simply refuses. It's not just spooning vitamins down her throat."

Margaret Kendall nodded and stared out at the lake. The two women sat in the enormous living room in their nearly identical Chanel suits. "The morning before I went to pick her up, I told your father I thought it was all too dramatic and that that Mrs. Harvey should be shot. I thought Stephanie had just gone too far on a fad diet—the way so many teenage girls do—and fainted. Nothing to it, I said to your father. No reason for a hospital, and no reason whatsoever to alarm Cynthia in Geneva!" She sipped the tea, thinking how nice her daughter's life was. Servants who lived in. This really beautiful house. And Jean-François was still, after all these years, a very attractive man. She continued. "But"—she almost shuddered—"when I saw her . . ." She put down the teacup. Cynthia said nothing. She stared out at the blue water and thought of Stephanie's big eyes in the gaunt face. "When I saw her and got her settled in Beacon Hill, I called Dr. Heatherington."

An image of that tall, gray-haired, bespectacled man in his darkish brown leather office flashed through Cynthia's head. She hadn't thought of those Thursdays and Tuesdays for years. She wondered if he still had the artificial flowers on that table by the curtained window. Daffodils that always needed dusting. Was he even still alive?

"Well, Dr. Heatherington no longer practices, but a young man named Haggerty has taken over, and we talked for maybe twenty minutes on the phone. After I told him who I was."

God. And who are you, Mother? Mrs. Otis Kendall. Mother of a desperately unhappy daughter treated by a colleague in nineteen-sixty-something before being saved by love affair with desperately good-looking Swiss leading to desperately unhappy marriage . . . no, don't think it, Cynthia chastised herself.

"Are you even listening?" Margaret was irritated. "He said that anorexics definitely need—"

"Anorexics! Mother, do you think she is? It sounds so . . ."

"Serious. It is." When Margaret Kendall's lipstick wore off, one noticed how much older she suddenly was. Most of it was on the lip of the Sevres cup. "Anyway, he said that he definitely thought she should have some help. One of his colleagues is here—well, not right in Geneva, but in Switzerland—and he thinks very highly of him. American. Advised me to get in touch."

Cynthia nodded. She'd sat on Stephanie's bed for hours, just stroking her forehead and holding the bones of the emaciated hands. And part of her wanted to scream, "Why did you do this to yourself? You beautiful, lucky girl, with everything good in life waiting for you. Why? Why?" But she had said nothing. "Why is this American psychiatrist here? Why in Switzerland? And where?"

"His name is Charles Galveston. He's on a sabbatical of sorts, working on a paper. I think he's in Lausanne."

"That's wonderful. It's only sixty kilometers away." Cynthia felt encouraged. Help was on the way. It could all be taken care of, if it was organized properly. If you sat down and figured out how to handle it. A good doctor. Lausanne. "I hope . . ." she sighed as she stood up and pushed back her long, blond hair with the brown velvet band. "I hope he's good, and I hope Stephanie likes him."

· · ·

Stephanie didn't speak for the first hour the doctor sat beside her bed. Cynthia had placed a *fauteuil* there, upholstered in sharp, parrot green watered silk, but then decided it wasn't restful enough and had a maid help her carry another armchair in, one that was covered in dark blue leather. Stolen from the library.

"You think a change of chairs will help?" Margaret asked. Cynthia shrugged. The two women were having coffee in the living room. And though neither would say it, they both wanted to be nearby when Dr. Galveston came loping down the front stairs.

It was the afternoon of the second session, and he reported that Stephanie hadn't spoken that hour either. They asked him to join them.

"Coffee? Sugar?" asked Cynthia.

He was big, tall, athletic-looking, Margaret noted, staring at him. Probably over six feet one, with light blond hair, and dark eyes set in an intelligent face. He had what Margaret called "a good straight nose" and fine features. She worried that he wasn't old enough, experienced enough, but then again, wasn't it a sign that one was getting old when policemen and doctors started looking terribly young?

Dr. Galveston nodded when the sugar was dropped in the cup. "Is it true what I heard about the Swiss?" Both women looked at him, waiting. "That when they mention sugar, they ask, 'One lump or none?' "

Cynthia laughed. "But that doesn't apply in this household."

"And you're among Americans right now, so you can relax," Margaret said in her most charming way. "Now, will you have five teaspoons or six?"

The young doctor grinned, and his smile was very bright. "Better hold it down to two." He crossed his long legs.

After two sips of the coffee, he suddenly became serious. "I wish I could tell you something you don't know, but until she wants to talk, she simply won't let me in on her secrets. It's anorexia, all right. She exhibits certain patterns of behavior that correspond with those of other sufferers from the disease."

"Disease." Cynthia's voice was soft. Jean-François wouldn't accept that word. He had come back from Paris the day before, seen Stephanie, and refused to believe there was anything wrong that ice cream and lots of carbohydrates wouldn't cure. She was glad he'd be in London for a while. Even Mother had been amazed at his behavior, which, anyone would say, was offhand at best. *Callous* was more descriptive.

"What patterns?" Margaret was insisting.

"Well, she keeps a notebook under her pillow. I don't have X-ray vision, but I'll bet it's a list of all she eats."

"I've seen her writing in it," Cynthia remarked. "But she puts it away when she sees me come into the room."

"What happens next?" Margaret was asking. "What should we do? Do you think Dr. Marceau has the right idea?" Margaret felt no compunction about asking an American doctor what he thought of a Swiss one.

Dr. Galveston sighed. "He's a general practitioner, and certainly knows about protein and vitamins and what a person should eat. But . . ." his voice drifted off. He put down his coffee cup. "It's going to take some doing to get her to *want* to eat again. That's where I come in. I have to discover what made her want to stop."

"But she didn't want to do it! She doesn't want to look this way! She doesn't want to be in bed over Easter vacation instead of skiing in Verbier!" Cynthia felt anger. The doctor was on the wrong track. She'd had such hopes, but he didn't know what he was doing after all. This man didn't understand anything.

He turned his brown eyes on the excited woman before him. She was quite beautiful, with all that blond hair, and dressed in a simple sweater and pink wool skirt, which suited her. Lovely enough to be rather intimidating. "Madame Colbert," he said slowly, "she doesn't *know* what she looks like anymore. Skiing in Verbier is the last thing on her mind. And with all due respect to you, she did it on purpose. Right now it's *control*. The only thing in her life she feels she can control is what she does or does not put in her mouth and swallow. But it's anger, too."

The mother and the grandmother stared at him. The room seemed to breathe with the silence. Outside the window, the lake was as still in the afternoon sun as a splash of blue paint on a canvas. His voice was low, but the words sliced the quiet like knives. "I'm afraid Stephanie is in the first stage of killing herself."

CHAPTER TWENTY-FIVE

Cynthia

Les Colombiers

The atmosphere at Les Colombiers was changed. Stephanie's illness had a great deal to do with it, of course. The arrival of Michel home for Easter from Exeter added to the change, as did the presence of Margaret Kendall, who found the routine of the household much to her liking. She made no reservations back to Boston, though Cynthia expected her to announce that she had done so any minute. Dr. Galveston had moved his suitcases, books, and papers, in various sausage-shaped duffels, from his hotel in Lausanne to an upstairs bedroom. Jean-François was in Paris more than ever, and for more days at a time, which meant that Yves and Veronique found more reasons to drop in for tea or a glass of wine before dinner. Cynthia often asked them to stay; Yves never declined, though he would have made excuses had Jean-François been home, and Veronique would always accept the invitation unless Louis was waiting for her.

Cynthia felt heartened by the sense of camaraderie around her, and she realized one afternoon, as she poured tea for the six of them, that a certain loneliness had been a great part of her life in Geneva.

Margaret was asking Michel about his grades. So grandmotherly, thought Cynthia with a half-smile as she passed the cup to Dr. Galveston. Michel was on the Dean's List. "You're bound to get in anywhere next fall," Margaret was saying. "What colleges have you applied to? Harvard must be one of them. Like your father."

Michel was now just seventeen, six foot one, and a strikingly handsome young man. A clone of Jean-François, but only in looks. His dark eyes would cloud over at the mention of banking, at the mention of tennis with his father, at the idea of a ski weekend with him. They didn't seem able to occupy the same room for more than a few minutes without a disagreement about something. It could be an editorial in that day's newspaper, or it could be tension over whether Michel would be playing golf that weekend at the club in Cologny. He reached for the cream before answering. Yves was telling Veronique not to get her hair cut, and Dr. Galveston was staring at the newly acquired Renoir over the fireplace.

They occupied two sofas and two wing chairs; Michel was on a footstool, knees almost touching his chin, near the marble coffee table. "I'm not applying anywhere." His voice was even.

"What did you say, Michel?" Cynthia thought she'd misheard.

"Mother," he sighed, as though preparing for a confrontation, "I don't want to go to college."

"Darling!" It was his grandmother, who thought the only people who didn't go to college were those who manned cash registers in supermarkets or spent their days lying under automobiles, wearing grease-stained overalls.

"I mean I don't want to go, and so I'm not going." Michel, who realized all conversation had stopped, blushed a deep rose.

"Well, what do you propose to do instead?" Cynthia tried to keep a noncommittal voice. All hell would break loose when Jean-François heard about this.

"I want to paint." Michel delivered this bombshell and then placidly sipped his tea. His moment of embarrassment was over. It wasn't a matter of not doing the expected and announcing it. That part was over. Now he could tell them all what he intended to do. Bang. Decided. *Fait accompli.*

"I've seen some of your paintings," Yves put in. "The ones in the library hallway. And they're damned good."

Margaret shot him a look that could have killed. "But, darling, one just doesn't say 'I'm going to be an artist' one day and then . . . then . . ."

"Oh, I want to study. I want to work at it. Maybe New York. Maybe share a loft in SoHo with a friend of mine who's flunking out of school. Maybe live in Paris on my own for a few years."

Veronique was glad it wasn't her child talking that way. My God. Poor Cynthia will be between the two men in her life when this—how do the Americans say it?—hits the *ventilateur*. The fan. Hits the fan. Dr. Galveston was silent, listening.

"Why can't I do it, Mother? Why should we all be programmed like robots just because our fathers or our mothers want us to do what they did, be what they are?"

The psychiatrist said gently, "No one's fighting you, Michel."

The boy laughed. "It's good to have a family shrink on the premises! We're going to need you when Père hears this!"

They all laughed. Veronique said, "I think I'll book a flight to Rio so I don't have to hear anything and be disturbed in town. I mean, Les Colombiers is only nine kilometers from Geneva . . ."

Cynthia sipped her tea and then said brightly, "Get two seats in the non-smoking. I'm coming, too." There was general laughter again. Funny, she thought. If I'd been alone hearing this, I would have had an entirely different reaction. I would have been planning rationally how to "handle" it, how to tell Jean-François in the most careful way. And I would have been afraid of his thunderous reaction. But these people are on my side! Against the "difficult" man I married. And Michel is growing up. Maybe he doesn't need me as negotiator and peacemaker. She listened to him carefully outlining a plan of action, and was proud of her son. Maybe he doesn't *want* me to help him, either! Cynthia had a little smile of satisfaction on her lips as she lifted the cup again.

"Being a banker has never appealed to me. Never," he was saying decisively.

"I understand your point of view perfectly," Yves said, and they laughed. He went on very seriously. "But you know, you don't have to be just a banker. You can be a banker part of the time or for a few years and then take the money . . . and run." He smiled wistfully and they all waited. "I wish I'd done that." It was a rare moment for Yves to speak so seriously about himself, to be so introspective. "I wish I'd gotten out. Wish I'd taken my shares and set up an antiques business . . ." He looked down at his teacup in the ensuing silence.

It was the youngest one of them who said the wisest thing, Galveston was to remember later. Michel's voice was clear. "It's not too late. It's never too late, Yves."

Yves toasted his godson almost imperceptibly with his teacup. Cynthia realized that the two of them would be allies. They'd always liked each other, but something important had transpired this afternoon. She knew Yves would help Michel any way he could in the battle against Jean-François.

· · ·

"Mother, do you know what I almost said?" Michel was standing beside the bureau in her bedroom as she arranged the ropes of pearls around the neckline of the black and white silk dress. She was frowning at herself in the mirror. "The other day when Yves and Veronique were here?"

"No, darling. What?" Cynthia was distracted. Jean-François should be at the airport now. It was eleven minutes' drive away, and the Bentley had been sent to fetch him already.

"I almost said, 'It's not too late unless you're dead.' "

Cynthia's head snapped up to look at him behind her in the mirror. "Now stop it! Right now. I don't know what to say to you. Except that your sister is very ill. We simply have to—"

"Let her do anything she wants!" His face was pale. "Let her starve herself just because she's on strike against the world!"

Cynthia quickly applied the coral lipstick and blotted her lips and then applied it again. I'm nervous, she thought. I'm sorry Mother is in town at the concert, but glad Charlie Galveston is here. Jean-François has always felt he can say anything in front of the servants. I know he doesn't like Charlie, thinks the whole business of psychiatry is "American," but at least—

Michel was going on. "Why is she—"

Cynthia realized her son was near tears. She stood up and turned to put her arms around him.

He gave her a hard squeeze, which nearly took her breath away, and then they drew apart. "Mother," he said in a desperate whisper as she stared up at him. Up at him! "I don't want Stephie to die!"

"We're not going to let her die! You're not and I'm not and Charlie's not!" She knew she hadn't included Jean-François. Cynthia felt hollow inside, and frightened. She hadn't wanted to say it. Dying. The possibility had been buried the way she buried notes in the garden. Unspoken. Unseen.

Michel blew his nose and Cynthia thought, Maybe I've done something right. I have a son who is capable of feeling, can let himself cry.

"Madame Colbert! Monsieur Colbert is arriving!" It was Danielle knocking on the door.

"*Oui! Oui! Merci!*" She put one cool hand on Michel's cheek and he tried to smile. Then Cynthia gave herself a last look in the mirror and pulled at the pearls for the twelfth time.

"Cynthia!" He was "arriving" all right. Other people came and went. Jean-François made the act of arrival an ongoing important verb. "Are you even home?" His tone, even while shouting from downstairs, betrayed irritation.

Michel looked at her and said, "You look beautiful." She nodded and made a face.

"Cynthia!" Her husband's voice came from the bottom of the staircase.

She took a deep breath and said, "Well, here we go." They left the bedroom together and started down the hall.

· · ·

"What was all the shouting about?" Stephanie asked. She had gained three pounds since being brought home, but that had made very little difference in her appearance. A skeleton with a yellowish tinge to her complexion, she sat propped almost upright with pillows around her. Blond hair was below her shoulders. Her mother brushed it every day until the girl begged her to stop, saying she had to lie down again.

Charlie Galveston sat gingerly on the edge of the bed. "Your father's upset."

She gave a weak impersonation of a shrug. "Oh, that's not new. He's *always* upset."

The psychiatrist wondered if he was approaching her all wrong. Maybe the informality of the situation—the use of his first name, living in the same house and seeing her several times a day, just stopping in the doorway to say hello—was getting him nowhere. Perhaps he should have kept his distance, kept his title, and remained a bit of an antagonist.

"Nothing new?" It was one of the first things she'd volunteered, other than a general unhappiness with life. "What do you mean?"

"I mean he's a bastard and Mother puts up with it. Mother is just so . . . so . . ." Her lips were a thin line, almost a sneer.

Charlie's tone was casual. "So *what?*"

"So *perfect!*" She spat the word. Charlie didn't interrupt. He was on a roll. "Look at her! Look at my grandmother! Being a shrink, you must have looked at them!"

"What am I supposed to see?"

"Ha! I don't have to tell you." She stopped and folded her arms across the front of the pink nightgown. Little roses were embroidered in a row across the bodice, delicately smocking it. Suddenly Stephanie wanted to talk. "Look at the way she looks! She looks perfect. Her hair is perfect, her face is perfect, her lipstick, her nail polish, her clothes never wrinkle. When she had the flu last Christmas, with a fever of a hundred and one, she still looked good enough for the cover of *Vogue.*"

"Do you think she tries to look perfect?" he asked, not looking up at her. Charlie concentrated on a corner of the white summer quilt trimmed in eyelet. Patterns, he was thinking. Loops and holes and stitches and patterns.

"She . . ." The question seemed to confuse her, but she had too much to say to stop talking. "Mother has always *been* perfect. Period. A perfect life." She laughed without humor. "Until she met Père, that is."

"Then what happened?"

"Now she *pretends* it's perfect. She's so good at that. Nothing bad ever happens. There is never a bad bottle of wine. There's never an argument, only a 'discussion.' That's what tonight was—a discussion. You'd better catch on to the codes if you want to survive in this house."

"You'll have to help me, then. I'm not sure I understand anything around here."

"The first thing to do is to watch Mother. She runs the place without even trying. It's called living in a perfect world. And the garden!" She rolled her eyes. "Have you seen it? The minute there is a change of one degree in the weather, she's out there getting rid of some plant and putting in another one, a better one, a more perfect one." Stephanie's face and voice, even her shoulders, curved in anger. "So this house is Mother's perfect, perverted little world."

"Perverted?"

"Because . . . because . . ." she stammered. "I don't know why I said that. Really."

"Do you think your father has anything to do with how your mother runs the household?"

"Oh, it's all for him! Anything to please him. No. To placate him. To postpone his anger. Pardon me! To avoid a discussion! She jumps through hoops like a trained poodle."

"Do you think she tries to be perfect for him?"

"Yes!" Then she realized what she'd said, and it was too hard, too soon to give up all the anger she felt for her mother. She took it back. "I mean no! She *has* to be perfect for herself, too. She holds herself together with Scotch tape." She frowned, her gaunt face showing fury. "The kind of Scotch tape that doesn't leave a mark. Mother would make sure of that. Seamless. The invisible kind." There was silence in the pink bedroom, and then, almost inaudibly, she said, "And I'm a mess. I feel it whenever she comes near me."

"Explain. Please."

"I mean . . ." Stephanie sighed. "She never really touches me the way she touches Michel. When Mother touches me, it's always to adjust something. It's because my hair is in my face or my collar is turned up. It's to let me know I don't look right. I wish . . . I wish she'd just hug me the way she does Michel."

The two of them sat together for a few more minutes, but it seemed that the emotion had drained the girl of energy to continue. Charlie turned off the bedside lamp and then gave her hand a pat. "Shall I leave the door open?" he asked from the hallway. The light shone on the lower half of Stephanie, barely a curve under the white quilt. She nodded with eyes closed. "Sweet dreams," he wished her, and walked quickly down the hall to his own room and to his notebook.

Les Colombiers

"Stephanie, her illness, her arrival at Les Colombiers," Charlie Galveston wrote in his notebook, "has triggered events in concentric circles that radiate from her bed as if she has become the vortex of the Colbert clan." He stopped and nibbled at his ballpoint pen. Disgusting habit. He looked at the toothmarks, a guide to time spent in contemplation, and thought of Cynthia's reaction. The cheap plastic made a satisfying *clack* as it landed in the wastebasket.

"Cynthia Colbert seems to be the key to her daughter's illness. Her mother is all Stephanie talks about. Stephanie resents what she calls her mother's perfection, her own feelings of not being loved enough, her idea that her mother cannot really love. Stephanie feels her mother is only surface, an automaton getting through the days with a minimum of fuss."

Charlie stopped and leaned back in the leather chair. The ceiling above him was a deep terra-cotta color, with carved white moldings. Cynthia had suggested he take over this room at the end of the second floor, where he could have complete privacy and all his books and papers in one place. A desk had materialized one morning, a massive, flat-topped, wonderful old desk, carried in by three men. She was a thoughtful person, a kind person, who loved her daughter.

Yesterday he'd stood in the doorway and seen Cynthia sitting beside the bed. She was asking about school, asking about roommates. And Stephanie was answering in monosyllabic grunts. When she noticed the psychiatrist, Cynthia had stood and smiled as though everything were just fine, and greeted him and left the room. Had it been a trick of the sunlight streaming in the tall windows, or had he seen the glint of tears in her eyes?

Don't fall in love with her, he warned himself. Christ. Don't do that. Love? Where does that fit into this household? Michel loves his sister, but has no conception of her pain. He wants to live more than anyone else, is thirsty to paint. Cannot understand why anyone would allow herself to be in bed when the world was waiting. Cynthia loves her children. Period. Cynthia's mother loves Cynthia, but is jealous of her life. She even seemed upon arrival to approve tacitly of the long absences of Jean-François, though her manner toward him changed upon her return from her junket to Paris. He was extremely charming to her in the face of her coldness. Arctic temperatures, that first dinner back. Stephanie's grandmother, Margaret Kendall, seems to prefer Michel. Stephanie knows it. What Stephanie feels toward her father is a question mark.

Charlie stood up and stretched. Almost ten o'clock, and he'd been at his desk since half past seven. The trees were green outside the window, and birds were making a frightful racket. He'd never seen such big crows in his life. They were nightmarishly big. Refugee extras from Hitchcock's *The Birds*. Stephanie, my dear! he thought. I think I will go up and ask you what you think of your father. Me, Charlie Galveston, house detective. No, he corrected himself, chateau detective. He smiled and rolled down the sleeves of his blue plaid flannel shirt, and buttoned the cuffs. Chateau detective. I like that. And I'm here to discover why all the Colberts, except Michel, seem to suffer so.

• • •

"I used to love him. I guess I still love him." Stephanie paused and looked down at her hands, folded in the lap of the blue nightgown. "I think I was about five or six, just starting school, when something happened that changed things. He was shouting at Mother on the stairs, and I remember thinking that he would never shout at me like that. I remember thinking she had done something to deserve it. I didn't think in those words, of course, but the idea was that."

Charlie nodded from the wing chair at the foot of the bed. Jealousy of the same-sex parent. Very normal at that age. "But he came storming down the stairs and knocked me out of the way and I began to cry. I fell on my knees just on the side of the first step where it's all wood and no carpet. And I was crying and he yelled at me and then he turned around and picked me up and set me on my feet like . . ." Her voice faltered. "As if I were a lamp that had fallen, as if I were an object. And he shouted something else at Mother and ran from the house. Then he was driven away."

"What do you mean 'driven away'?"

"Well, he was. Our driver took him somewhere and he didn't come back for what seemed like a long time."

Charlie stared at her. Yes. The Colberts had Roget as their chauffeur, but there always seemed to be someone coming or going on the gravel driveway lined with cypresses. "Driven away. You said your father was driven away."

She smiled. "Freudian slip?"

"I don't know. What do you think about it?"

"Yes. I thought Mother had driven him away. But now I don't. I think that . . . I don't know. Sometimes I think I *am* an object like the one he suddenly set upright and into position again."

"Your father placed you where he wanted you on the rug?"

"He's been placing me all my life, and maybe it's caught up with me."

"Do you think he does the same with Michel?"

She nodded. "More. Michel is the oldest, and the only son. I know it's horrible for him lots of the time with Père. And now look at what's happening."

"What?"

"The fight about being a painter. Père is like a rock, isn't he? I can hear things going on when I sit on the top stair. There's some kind of channel of sound waves . . ."

Charlie made a note to be careful of what he discussed with Cynthia in the big salon. "Your brother is fighting hard." And I want you to fight, too, he thought.

"I know, and . . ." Her eyes suddenly filled with tears. "I'm proud of him." She reached for the Kleenex on the night table and blew her nose. "He isn't only fighting Père, but Colbert & Cie. and our grandfather and great-grand-father and all the Colberts all the way back to France, four hundred and forty years ago." She smiled, and even though her nose was red and her face too thin, Charlie thought, *She looks like her mother. Undeniably pretty.* "It's hard fighting dead people. Hard to fight what people expect of you," she said.

"You're awfully wise for fifteen," Charlie said gently. "Why don't you tell Michel how you feel about all this?"

"Oh . . ." She was embarrassed. "He's my big brother," she said, shrugging. "He knows anyway."

Charlie shook his head. "He would like to hear it from you. And he's not having an easy time of it." She looked tired, and he stood to leave. "Would you like to talk to him? If I send him up after lunch?" She smiled when Charlie squeezed her hand. "Michel would be happy to have you as an ally."

Stephanie nodded. "Okay." Her eyes were filled with tears again. Her emotions were on the surface at all times. *Frail. Fragile.* But her voice was strong. "Send him up, Charlie, and I'll tell him that I'll beat up anybody who looks at him cross-eyed!" She weakly made two fists. Charlie winked at her and waved from the doorway.

．．．

That evening, when the psychiatrist went to say good night, Stephanie didn't mention Michel or his visit, but suddenly said she'd been thinking all day of something. "Tell me what," Charlie urged. The room was lit only by the one pink porcelain ginger-jar lamp on her bedside table. One window was open to the cool spring night. It was a teenage girl's room of pink rose wallpaper and flowered chintz.

"I think that nobody drives Père away."

"And?"

"And I think he *likes* to be away. And I think he leaves because he has to. Because he wants to. And I wonder if he's happy wherever else he is."

"You don't think he's happy here at Les Colombiers?"

She laughed. "Are any of us happy here?"

"What makes you unhappy here?"

"I have no friends here because they're all from school, all in the States, so that makes it hard even to go to the movies."

"I hear that you played a lot of tennis last summer. You couldn't have played alone."

"Oh, that. Yes. I did make a few friends at the club." She seemed to switch gears. "But that isn't it. Not really. Les Colombiers gives me a feeling of isolation."

"Why don't you ask your mother if you can stay in town once in a while with Michel? He does it, doesn't he?" *Watch out. Don't compare her to her brother, who everybody likes, when she feels second best.*

She nodded. "I could."

Charlie found himself irritated with her. He remembered his own teenage years of working at Paxton's Drugstore from the minute school was over until the day before it began again. Delivery boy. On that bicycle that had three flat tires one summer. A record for Carter, Iowa. He pulled himself back to Stephanie. Progress. She no longer talks about dying the way other people speak of returning a book to the library.

"Charlie, do you think my father loves my mother?"

He was caught totally unawares. "I don't know. I just . . . don't know." He had wondered what kept them together. Was it this house? Money? Security? Cynthia could leave anytime. Anytime she realized she could.

"I don't think they love each other, and it terrifies me."

"You shouldn't worry about marriage and love just because you don't see what you want in your parents' lives." She didn't answer. "You know, Stephanie, the first marriage we ever see, the one we know the most about, is our parents'. That's the one that we absorb first and the one that most likely imprints us with what we expect from our own marriages."

"Are you married?" she asked suddenly. He shook his head and she continued, "Divorced?" He nodded. "Why don't you get married again?"

As he stood up to terminate the conversation, he thought, Because there aren't many women like your mother.

"Why not, Charlie?" she insisted. She was a pest of a fifteen-year-old at that moment. Wise one minute and a bratty little kid the next. "Why don't you?"

He tweaked her nose and growled as ferociously as he could manage, "Because no one will have me! Now go to sleep, you little monster!"

She actually giggled as he closed the bedroom door behind him.

·   ·   ·

"Will this forever be known as the Summer of Fish Sticks?" Cynthia groaned as she passed Charlie in the downstairs hall.

"Don't despair," he smiled.

"I can't even stand the smell of them anymore." She rolled her eyes. "Oh, by the way, she's drinking milk now instead of water! I put it on the tray three days ago and didn't say a word, but . . ." She looked triumphant. "The glass is empty when the tray comes down to the kitchen again!" Cynthia started up the stairs.

Charlie didn't want to depress her, but he knew how devious anorexics could be about hiding food. They usually insisted upon eating alone and, like Stephanie, often at a precise hour. Potted plants mysteriously died. Birds gathered on rooftops outside windows. Clogged toilets. Laundered pieces of toast in pajama pockets. Patients could be diabolically clever when it was important to be. But perhaps, he thought, as he walked down the hall to his "office," perhaps she saw no need to hide food. Perhaps his theory of not forcing her to eat was working. She could have been put into a hospital and fed through a tube up her nose when he'd arrived. He shuddered. But those patients, in his experience, became even more rebellious and began to treat everyone around them as the enemy. Their mothers and fathers put them in the hospital and allowed them to be subjected to the humiliation of nude photographs, of daily weighings, of constant supervision. They usually prided themselves on fooling the doctors and nurses who had, in effect, become their jailers. It was hard to break through this sense of imprisonment and isolation and discover how to help them emotionally.

Yes, thought Charlie, as he sat down at his desk and opened his notebook, I understand that a doctor has to save their lives first. But if the problem all started with feelings, then shouldn't we reach out to their anxieties, their fears first? He knew he would have to tackle Dr. Marceau tomorrow after his weekly examination of Stephanie. "I hope I'm not imagining," he wrote on the clean page, "that she is improving. I hope I'm not too close to see the reality."

There was a tap on the door, and one of the maids peeked her head in. Complete with little white cotton mob cap. "Like something out of a movie," Charlie had written in his diary that first week here.

"Sorry to disturb you, *Professeur*, but Madame Colbert wanted me to tell you lunch is ready."

"*Merci.* I'll be right there." He stood up and was rereading his last sentence when she spoke again. "In the garden, *Professeur*."

He nodded, knowing that the table would be set with white linen and silver and Baccarat wineglasses. Cynthia's pink roses were in full bloom in the little area surrounded by sculptured hedges that left the table in a manicured green clearing free from the wind, bathed in sun. He read his last sentence again, and then shook his head. Reality!

Geneva

Alain Didier stood in the doorway of Jean-François's office, not knowing whether to go in or not. His colleague was on the phone, nodding. "*Oui, oui! D'accord!*" he said, and looked up and motioned Alain to come and sit down.

The call was terminated with a euphoric "*Merci beaucoup!*" and Jean-François replaced the receiver with a big grin on his face. "Christ! Alain! This calls for a celebration! We need a drink!" he insisted as he rose and buttoned his gray suit jacket.

The Hotel Métropole bar was a few minutes walk through the cool spring dusk. Daylight savings time was in effect, and though his father had kept his watch on "God's time" until the last minute of his life, Jean-François loved the long hours of sun.

When they'd each ordered Scotch, Alain asked what they were drinking to.

Jean-François took a sip, savoring it, and then, with eyes towards the ceiling, swallowed. "To good health." Alain didn't respond. "Christ! How often do we drink to good health, and we don't even think about what it means to get sick and to die!"

"You're a lot of fun today," Alain said cynically. He squinted blue eyes behind wire-rimmed glasses. "Do you want to tell me what you're talking about? Or should I just enjoy my drink?"

"I mean that I had myself tested for SIDA—AIDS, the plague of the eighties—whatever you want to call it . . ." He paused. "And I'm fine!" He grinned with delight. "Clean bill of health." He shook his head. "I read yesterday that Switzerland has the highest number of AIDS cases per million people in Europe! Of course I think that's just because we keep the most accurate figures!" He smiled. "And because they come here for treatment. But I'm not a case, thank God!"

Alain didn't say anything. He stared down at his Scotch glass. Something about Jean-François repulsed him at that moment. He thought of that pretty stewardess in the Zurich airport, of Laurent's secretary, of Roger's young assistant, of his own secretary's kid sister. That was only the beginning of the list. Jean-François slept with anything that moved. Nothing stopped him from finding ripe, usually young bodies to leap upon. "What about Cynthia?" The question burst from him unbidden.

Jean-François put down his Scotch glass and shrugged with a happy smile. "What about her? If I don't have it, she doesn't have it either."

Alain stared at him for a long moment. "Am I to believe that one of the great cocksmen of all time is about to change his ways?"

Jean-François smiled that smile that women loved, and shook his head. "Wouldn't bet a franc on it." He took another swallow of Scotch. "If you use a condom—"

"Do you keep score?"

Jean-François looked down at his hand curved around the glass and didn't answer for a moment. Alain worried that he'd had a long day and was drinking too quickly. Maybe it was anger. Damn. Why did I ask that? I'm goading him into a fight. And nothing will ever change. Nothing I say will make any difference to him. Why should I care? I've known him since we were in university, and he's always been like this. Alain broke the silence. "Hey, just jok—"

But Jean-François said, "So far this year, which is four months old, I guess it's been about twenty to twenty-five. *Oui*." He stared into space, thinking, computing. Alain was speechless as his friend continued. "That's about right. Twenty different girls, but there is one that I screw every chance I get. In

Paris. And she's not a girl. She is a woman. Capital letters. So this is not a typical year for me. I guess I've been with her about twenty different times since Christmas."

He turned and saw the expression on Alain's face and, misreading it, laughed and said, "What can I do? I guess I just love women!"

Alain looked down again, willing himself not to respond. But the thought occurred to him: No. You hate women.

CHAPTER TWENTY-SIX

Iris

Spring 1988 — Paris

"It always amuses me," Iris was saying. Her voice came from under the straw hat with the straight little brim. She was immaculate, delicious, Jean-François thought, in the pink linen short-sleeved dress. The hat was festooned with pink roses; only Iris could have worn it with such aplomb. "I always wonder what—"

Jean-François followed her gaze and then glanced back at her. Two older women, well dressed, perfectly suited and pearled, were sitting three tables away, having an afternoon coffee. The pollution hung heavy in the air, the traffic noises were almost unbearable, but the sky was blue and the outdoor café was still a good place to be on such a day in Paris. "What are you talking about?"

"Lesbians!" she said. "What . . . why . . . what do they get out of it?"

"But how can you tell?" Jean-François prided himself on understanding women. He'd paid to watch lesbians make love more than once, and thought it a sensuous sight, but he could never pick any but the most masculine out of a crowd.

"Look carefully," said Iris softly. "Do you see their fingers touching on the tablecloth? And under the table? The shin turned awkwardly just so it can touch the other knee?"

"*Mon Dieu!*" he laughed. "You're right. It's the most subtle . . ." His smile died as one of the older women turned in her chair to recross her legs and faced him.

She smiled faintly with recognition, and then said something to her friend, who also turned. Then she stood and made her way between the tables toward Jean-François and Iris.

"Oh!" gasped Iris. "She couldn't have heard us, could she!"

Jean-François stood and embraced Margaret. He did not so much as glance at Iris, though his mother-in-law stared down at her with great interest. The pink silk roses, all handmade at no little expense, seemed to wilt under the force of her gaze. Jean-François was saying smoothly, "It's so nice to see you here. Cynthia told me you were coming to shop. Are you enjoying Paris?"

Margaret Kendall looked him straight in the eye and, tight-lipped with disapproval, said, "Yes. Are *you* enjoying Paris?"

Jean-François met her steely gaze volt for volt, and said definitively, "I'm not in Paris."

She turned without another word and returned to the other woman, to her now-cold coffee, to her chair in the sun.

· · ·

That evening, ten minutes after Margaret had asked the concierge to reserve a table for two on the first floor of Fouquet's, the phone rang in her suite at the George V. "Could you get that?" she called from the bathroom. "I bet they're full tonight! Tell him to try that other one you were reading about, the one two streets over—"

"Hello? Oh, just a—why, is this Cynthia?"

"Is it—? Why—how are you?" Cynthia tried not to act overly surprised. She sank down on the flowered sofa in her boudoir and listened. "So you're buying out the town! Now that's why I'm calling. I know Mother's filled you in on . . . on Stephanie and what's happening," she sighed. "I thought if she was anywhere near Hermes perhaps she could pick up a scarf for her, something bright. Just . . ." She bit her lip. "I don't know, just even to tie around her neck over a nightgown! I feel I want to do anything and everything, and it's . . . it's . . ." Cynthia wasn't one to complain, so she stopped herself short of saying, *It's so hard.*

"Of course we will buy a scarf! That's easy. Are you sure there isn't anything else?"

So matter-of-fact, as always. Weren't those two like peas in a pod? "Well, tell Mother to have a good time, and if you want to come back to Les Colombiers with her, I would love to have you! Really! We have guest rooms by the dozen!"

"Thank you, Cynthia, it's a lovely invitation, but I'm flying to New York day after tomorrow."

"The next time, then. Well, so glad to talk to you. Have fun. 'Bye."

Cynthia put the receiver down slowly, and then, staring into space, said aloud to no one, "How odd. How really odd that Mother never mentioned meeting Kate Grayson in Paris!"

. . .

Jean-François was angry. Kick-the-furniture furious. In a rage, as a matter of fact. He lay awake for hours with clenched fists. The next morning he snapped at the maid who arrived to do the room while he was shaving. An hour later he snapped at the Ritz's concierge about a detail on his bill, which was not a wise move, for the man had more power than most generals. Then he cursed his taxi driver and accused him of taking the long way to the airport. He arrived in Geneva with clenched teeth, ready to take a bite out of anything that crossed his path.

"Goddammit, Cynthia!" He shouted in the library, though she wasn't even downstairs. "Goddamn you!" Jean-François slammed the desk drawer closed and then began to pull one auction catalog after another from the *étagère*. Christie's and Sotheby's were separated, each house arranged chronologically, starting from the window.

Charlie Galveston opened the door and then said, "Oh, excuse me!" when he saw Jean-François. "I'll come back."

"No, no! Come on in!" Jean-François urged him. "Just come in. I'm looking for a certain sale that should be in a certain catalogue that should be in a certain place, but *no!*" His voice rose. "No, that's too simple. Cynthia has let things go again. She can't handle a household this size. She can handle a garden. But she can't take on anything more."

Charlie didn't answer. He had left a book on adolescent depression on the brown leather chesterfield, and now bent to retrieve it.

Jean-François had chosen to focus on him as another male, a co-sufferer. "Ever notice, Charlie, how women can manage what they want to do, but there's never time to do the things they don't care about? Not like men. We earn money. We have competition. They can take baths and read novels and eat chocolates all day if they want! It must be a lovely life! Idyllic," he sniffed.

Charlie started to leave the library, and then turned before reaching the door. "Stephanie has been asking for you."

"Oh, yes!" The voice was a sneer. "That's what you're here for, isn't it? To pull my daughter out of the doldrums. To get her to eat." He held several of the glossy catalogs in his arms. "Tell me, what happens next?"

"Do you want to talk about Stephanie?" Charlie felt his control ebbing away.

"Not really. No."

The psychiatrist was astonished. "Did something happen . . . something go wrong? In Paris?"

"You bet!" snapped Jean-François. "But now I'm in Geneva where things go wrong."

Charlie didn't know whether to stay or leave. "Do you want to talk?" he offered. "Or shall I see you at dinner?"

"A shrink won't help," Jean-François said unpleasantly. "But a competent wife could. Have you seen her today?"

"I think she's up with Stephanie." As he started toward the door, the voice said quietly, "Tell her to get down here. Now."

. . .

"Dinner was tough going. Do you want a drink?" Charlie and Cynthia were alone in the *fumoir* with after-dinner coffee. Jean-François had said he had to "straighten out the mess" in the library, Michel was back at Exeter for the spring term, and Margaret was still in Paris until tomorrow. Cynthia finished her coffee and stood up. She strode quickly to the silver tray on the bureau that held the bottles of Scotch, vodka, gin, liqueurs.

"Sure. I'll join you. A cognac would be very nice." Of everyone in the household, Charlie felt the most relaxed with Cynthia. She was straightforward in the New England way he admired, with a sense of humor that showed itself only occasionally. Cynthia cared deeply about what was right and wrong; perhaps she judged herself too harshly. He watched her go through the day at Les Colombiers, well-meaning, kind to every servant, keeping her thoughts to herself. So he was taken aback when she handed him the glass and then said, "I know you wonder why I stay." She sat down carefully in the flowered cotton print dress and crossed her long legs. Her pearls shone in the light, her hair was pale and shining, and her waist, circled by the blue leather belt, was very small. Charlie was reminded of Grace Kelly in the old Hitchcock films.

He nodded and took a sip of the cognac.

"It's easier than it used to be." She stared at the Utrillo behind him. "Because I don't love him anymore. You stop being hurt. You stop feeling anything, and then . . ." She smiled tightly. "Then you are really free. To do what you want."

"What do you mean, 'do what you want'?"

"Well, I don't try to please him so much. I can't anyway. I guess that's all I mean." She stopped. "I just do the best I can. The dinners are good. The house is in order. It won't be perfect, but I can't do much better. He'll shout about it anyway. Like the missing Christie's catalog."

Charlie wanted her to keep talking.

"I've always been bored by this." Her glance took in the large room; the corners were in darkness, away from the glow of the two lamps near them. The *fumoir* was a terra-cotta-colored cube about seven meters on a side; the ceiling was seven meters above the Oriental rug of deep greens and tan. The furniture was less ornate than that in the salon.

Charlie appreciated the rich comfort of the modern, down-filled sofa. He absentmindedly stroked the fringe of the coral Thai silk cushion beside him. "Bored by what?" he asked.

"Taking care of a house. This house. Planning meals. Making sure the cook doesn't quit because she's had a fight with the gardener over something inane like bruised strawberries." Cynthia spoke matter-of-factly, so he was surprised when she said, almost in a whisper, "I hate it. I hate it here."

"Do you ever consider divorce?"

"Every day!" she laughed. "But . . . is this the time? With Stephanie upstairs?"

"May I tell you something about her?"

"Please do." Her voice was gentle, pleading. "She will hardly speak to me. I know she's angry. But I don't know what it's about. What I've done."

There it is again, he thought, but decided it wasn't the time to talk to her about it. "Stephanie is full of ambivalence about you. You are one of the biggest things in her life. She sees herself in you, wants to be like you, and"—he paused and then decided he'd better get it over with—"is jealous of you, and you're correct. She's angry with you, too."

"Give it to me straight. Why is she jealous?" Cynthia uncrossed her legs and planted her feet in the slingback blue leather pumps solidly together, as if to keep her balance. She leaned forward with her hands in her lap.

"Because you are beautiful and she doesn't feel beautiful. She said she's been overweight—no, in her words, 'fat and disgusting'—all her life." He swallowed a bit of the cognac. "Everything is self-image, you know. I'm writing a paper on it. Who you think you are, self-fulfilling prophecies. Don't get me started." He waved one hand. "We'll be here all night."

"Why is she angry with me?" Cynthia's voice was almost tender.

"She says your life was perfect before you married her father, and now you *pretend* it's perfect and you go on and on with it. As she says, 'like a saint, like a martyr.' "

Cynthia blushed. "I didn't think she really thought that much about my marriage. She's away at school. I know she and her father were close. Maybe up till the age of five. He was close to both of them. He seemed to be a happy father. Really until . . ."

"Until they started having opinions, their own personalities," Charlie ventured.

"Exactly right." She nodded, and her hair was a flash in the light. "I remember Michel not wanting to play golf. He wanted to learn to ride. Jean-François hates horses, so it was out of the question. The same kind of thing with Stephanie. Where to go to school. She won out, though. She fought to go to the States."

"Did you take her side in it?"

"Yes. But I suppose she felt I didn't do or say enough. She was strong about it. I admired her at the time."

"Stephanie has told me she hates the way you try to please him."

"What else should I do? Should I just tell him to go to hell? Tell him there's no dinner and he can make a sandwich? Tell him I've given his books away and turned his library over to the maid for her ironing?" She began to laugh. "You must be a good doctor, Charlie! You're getting me to tell you the things I'd like to do!"

"You said you hated it here. Do you consider leaving?"

Cynthia nodded. "But I won't leave until the time is right." She pushed her hair back from her forehead and looked Charlie directly in the face. "Do you know that sometimes I think I have already left. I'm not really here. I *have* gone."

"What do you mean?"

"It's just that my life is all duties. I don't have anything with Jean-François. I can think back, all the landmarks—no! All the milestones," she laughed. "Or are they millstones? in a marriage . . ."

Charlie smiled quickly, continuing to stare at her.

"All the biggest events in a marriage. For instance, having a child. He was in Paris when Michel was born. Not in his hotel room at three in the morning. Same with Stephanie's birth. No one could find him." She said nothing more. With Cynthia, it was all understatement; she would let Charlie imagine her in labor, wanting her husband and knowing he was in bed with another woman as she gave birth to his child. "And now, with Stephanie's illness, he's not involved. It's sort of *my* marriage, in a way. He doesn't have a thing to do with it."

"He must have, in the beginning. Was it very different then?"

Cynthia leaned back in the chair and gazed at a far corner of the room. "It's such a hard question. I remember being so young. I even *felt* young. But especially with Jean-François. And then coming here. His house. His country. His Geneva. I wasn't always terribly happy, even in the beginning. I remember so few times that we really were free together. Skiing." She smiled. "Weekends in Paris. Maybe just two of them. I do remember one time feeling that he was 'with' me. That he understood. There was such a closeness that night."

"Tell me," said Charlie.

"Every Christmas before Michel was born—that must have been three or four times—we would go to the midnight service at Cathedral St.-Pierre in the Vieille Ville on Christmas Eve. It's the oldest church here. I think part of it was built in the twelfth century, the rest later on. Anyway, I remember the first time we went together."

Charlie listened to her every word, and realized she had told no one this story before. The phrasing was such that it was an old memory, unearthed on this spring evening. Oh, Cynthia! he thought. All the sides of you are intriguing. He felt himself there with her as the nineteen-year-old bride on Christmas Eve. A damp, gray cold had hugged the city day after day that December. She and Jean-François walked, after parking the car, up the cobblestoned hill overlooking the lake, toward the old cathedral with its tolling bells. Cynthia had her hand tucked in her husband's arm, trying not to shiver, trying not to be annoyed that he had advised her not to wear her mink. Once inside, she understood, for the congregation was a study in brown and black. No little girl wore a red ribbon, no woman wore sparkling earrings. The impression was of total bleakness. There was not one flower, not one candle, not one sprig of holly or color. On this, the most joyful of all Christian holy days! Six men in black, with white, starched collars extending like miniature breastplates over the fronts of their robes, marched in as an unseen choir sang. They were, to a man, unsmiling, gray-bearded, and dour. During the sermon in French, which was filled with admonishments, Cynthia was reminded of the Pilgrim fathers and the Salem witch trials. Electric lights blazed above them in round wooden candelabra. At last, after the Communion, when the service was nearly over, one of the rectors walked behind the altar and began to light white candles on a Christmas tree. Cynthia swallowed thickly, suddenly feeling near tears as they sang "O Little Town of Bethlehem" in French.

"It was all so familiar and so unfamiliar," she said. "My first Christmas with my new husband in my new country." She looked near tears at the memory. "We left the cathedral and walked through the dark, cobblestoned streets and then up the hill overlooking the lake. I felt so close to him then. Jean-François put his arms around me . . ." She smiled faintly and looked away from Charlie. "And he said, 'Don't worry, Cynthia. You'll make it.' "

Charlie didn't speak. He wanted her to go on.

"Sounds like such a little thing when I say it aloud, I guess. But it made a big difference to me. I lived and relived that, again and again. It was like putting on a favorite warm sweater when I felt cold. I felt close to him then."

"What happened? What changed?"

"Other women happened." She shrugged. "I *stopped* happening. I became caretaker of the marriage, I guess." She frowned. "His whole life became away from here, away from me, away from all of us."

But he needs you, is what Charlie didn't say. Should he tell her what he'd seen? Was living in the household—becoming a part of it, even—a dangerous thing?

"Do you realize that your husband blames you for everything?" Charlie thought, She's receptive and much less defensive than I ever imagined. She's open. I can dare to talk about it.

"Oh, I realize it." She smiled sardonically. "Even the weather is my fault."

"I have to tell you that you are bound to each other in this."

"What do you mean?"

"I mean that you have become your husband's accomplice. You agree with him, you go along with it."

The phone was ringing and she stood uncertainly, as if she didn't know whether to answer it or not. "Go along with what?" she asked as she moved toward the end table behind them.

"You agree with the idea that everything is your fault."

As she reached for the phone, it stopped ringing as if someone else in the household had picked up.

Charlie thought it a good time to say good night. He stood and walked toward her, then put the glass on the silver tray. His voice was kind. "It's a very, very difficult thing to absorb. Make me wrong. I would like that." He smiled and she smiled back. "But think about it. Don't be locked in as his accomplice. Stop letting him make you believe that everything out of order, out of sync, is because you made a mistake. He needs to control you for this. He needs to make you believe that it's all your fault!"

"And he does control me?" Her voice was soft. She was thinking that she would have to go upstairs soon, and she wondered if he would pull up her nightgown and . . . and . . . was it making love?

"Only you know that. Good night, Cynthia."

She watched him close the door behind him, and then she reached to turn off the lamp, thinking of all that had been said. And Stephanie. Does she think that her father controls me? Does she think I'm weak and pathetic because I try to "please" him?

Cynthia left the room behind her in darkness and closed the door slowly. The thought came to her in the hallway: If this had been a bad time with Jean-François instead of a talk with Charlie, I would close the door just this same way, and in my thoughts, too. I would close my mind and not think of the unpleasantness in the air of the *fumoir*, and I would go upstairs and let my husband have me. The next thought chilled her. I would blame myself for getting him upset, and think that letting him make love to me would calm him down. I would owe him one. Her hand clutched the silky wood of the banister as she mounted the first step. He's always made me think that.

· · ·

Jean-François wanted to continue to be angry with her, but he couldn't sustain it when he heard her voice on the telephone. He couldn't even be angry with her for calling him. At home! *Mon Dieu!* At this hour! "Yes. I want you all the time. And I don't want some fat little prince from some sandbox lifting his robes and climbing on top of you whenever you think I'm not around!"

Iris fairly purred in Paris. Her laugh was light. She adored the idea that she could make Jean-François so upset. What power! What fun! "Well, I don't know. I really don't know," she said sweetly. "I love Paris. Why don't you just come here?"

"What about the bank?" His voice was loud. Silly woman! Did she think he could just waltz away from Colbert & Cie.? My grandfather, my great-grandfather, my great-great-grandfather made it what it is, and I can't just . . . !

"Well, of course! The bank!" She held one palm over the receiver and tried to stop smiling. What a little boy he was! It was all so easy. "I'm happy you miss me, darling. We'll just continue as we have been. It's been, what? Two years? Surprised you're not bored. So let's just relax . . ."

"No. I know what you're saying, and I don't like it."

Innocence oozed over the wire. "What are you talking about? You're here every week!"

"You mean let's go on with your doing as *you* please—"

Knowing it would infuriate him and push him closer to what she wanted, she said, "I've always done what I pleased."

"All right." His voice was firm. She was not going to keep going to bed with everyone she enjoyed at dinner. He would put a stop to it if he had to buy a chastity belt from Boucheron. Jean-François sighed. "All right. You come to Geneva. Live here."

"But . . ." Iris thought it was clever to resist. Never let him think it was anything but his idea. "I don't know if I want to live in Geneva. It's little and drab and gray, and besides, what do you mean, 'live here'? With you and your little wife?"

Jean-François thought quickly. Of course she wouldn't want to leave Paris for Geneva, but she had hinted about getting married, and if he left her in Paris, someone, some asshole count, was very likely to marry her. No. Iris had to come to Geneva. Just for a while. Just until he grew tired of her. "Of course not here at Les Colombiers! I want you nearby, but that is extreme!"

"I can't imagine there's any place pretty enough in Geneva to make me leave my apartment!"

"Yes, there is, Iris! I will find you the *plus belle pied-à-terre* in Switzerland, let alone in Geneva! I know the perfect place!"

Iris hoped one couldn't hear a smile over the telephone. She said, with a trace of petulance in her voice, "Where will I live?"

"You shall have the most beautiful suite in the Beau Rivage!" He jotted down *B.R.* on his pad. Call them and find out exactly how many francs I'm in for. But do I have a choice? he worried.

Iris didn't sound ecstatic, or even convinced that it was a good idea. "Are you sure I'll like it?"

"I'm sure. I'll get you rooms overlooking the lake. You'll be in heaven. Now, sweet dreams. And tomorrow—"

Like a little cat about to lick cream from its paws, she asked, "Tomorrow?"

"Tomorrow you get Anna to pack your things!"

"Oh, Jean-François!" Suddenly Iris was nervous. "She has to come too!"

"Anna?" He thought he might lose his temper. *Mon Dieu!* Iris could be so spoiled. A lady's maid! It was like the nineteenth century! "*Oui! Oui!*" he sighed.

"And ZiZou!"

Jean-François grimaced. That yapping, furry rat didn't like him. Perhaps it was jealousy. Nothing like a lesbian poodle in your life. He sighed. "*Oui.* And ZiZou too!"

Paris

"Anna! Anna!" Iris called in excitement. "Guess what?"

The maid stood at the foot of the big bed, smiling. When Iris was happy, the world was one big chocolate soufflé.

"We're moving to the Beau Rivage! Monsieur Colbert and I have talked and . . ." She shrugged her pretty, bare shoulders in the black nightgown and fairly cooed with delight. "It's all set! Now, tomorrow I must call the concierge and tell him to forget everything! He's bright, so he most likely has, but still . . . *Oui*, I had better call." She put one palm against her cheek.

"*Incroyable!* The Beau Rivage!"

"No, it's *not* incredible," Iris corrected her. "It's just a little planning, and . . . and men can be led." She smiled impishly. "Like little ponies."

The two women laughed together. Anna was the nearest thing to a female friend Iris had, for she posed no competition. Iris didn't confide everything to her young maid from Brittany, but she told her more than she told anyone else, and the rest, of course, Anna gleaned by virtue of sheer proximity. Etienne, her oldest and closest friend, for instance, knew only a fraction of what went on in the apartment on rue de Varenne. When others were present, Iris behaved like an empress to the little maid, but alone, she was different. Anna still got hell if she forgot something, but she was clever enough to understand that this American didn't know how to treat a servant, didn't understand the class system. Perhaps if I were a Negro, Anna thought, things would be very different. Her mistress was complicated, arrogant, and could be a sulker, but Anna was fond of her, and the perks were magnificent. The food was always the finest quality, and Madame never checked a bill or questioned a price or even asked, "Where did all that caviar go?" The apartment was kept toasty warm all winter, and she was given Madame's cast-off clothes and allowed to wear them on her day off or when not in uniform.

"Oh, Madame!" Anna's eyes were bright. "Do you think we'll have the suite they showed us last week?"

Iris giggled as she thought of their little day trip to "case" Geneva. She'd seen the bank, the chateau, and then investigated both the Richemond and the Beau Rivage. "Why not? Why shouldn't that be the one? Monsieur Colbert knows how spoiled I am, and he said a view of the lake!"

"Do you want me to telephone tomorrow, or shall I wake you so that you can call before Monsieur Colbert?"

Iris groaned. It was past midnight now, and she loathed the early hours of the day unless there was someone to play with in bed. "I'd better be the one to speak to the concierge. I'll thank him profusely, and when we arrive, I will tip him outrageously." Iris had learned a bit about hotel living with Don Vito, and one thing was sure: a concierge could be invaluable. It was always nice to have an ally at the front desk. Iris's green eyes narrowed. "And perhaps I should hint that when Monsieur Colbert calls—well, that suite we liked so much, perhaps that will be the only one available. *Oui!*"

Anna nodded, and then, in a whirl of coral chiffon, a cast-off from her mistress, called "*Bon nuit!*" and left the room.

Iris felt great happiness as she lay in the dark of her enormous bedroom. Genève. Jean-François. Everything was moving in the right direction, and Jean-François thought that it was all his idea. She turned on her side and thought of his lovemaking. I've had better, she admitted. He can be a selfish bastard. Well, never mind. He can be taught. Even after a few years, it's not too late to demand more. And things must be really rotten with the wifelette if he wants me so close to him. If he would risk having me in such a small town as Genève! If I'm very clever, she smiled—and I am!—then living in the Beau Rivage could prove to be the last step before living at Les Colombiers as Madame Jean-François Colbert. *Oui.* She closed her eyes and pulled the satin sheet up under her chin. If I'm very clever . . .

· · ·

"Madame . . ." Anna began haltingly. Well, she had to tell her. The breakfast of tea and croissants was arranged carefully on the lap tray as Iris moved the pillows behind her into a more comfortable position. She'd had her conversation with the Beau Rivage, slept for three more hours, and felt refreshed. As good a time as any, thought her maid. "Madame, there's been another note."

Iris rolled her eyes as she lifted a croissant to her lips. "Probably some jealous wife." The notes made her more angry than afraid. "Did you throw it away?"

"Not yet. Do you want to see it?"

"Not particularly, unless it's more fascinating than the last." Iris stirred her fifth teaspoon of sugar into the steaming tea.

"Maybe you should read it." Anna pulled a square white envelope from her apron pocket. It was good-quality stationery, but the note inside was written by hand on the cheapest sort of foolscap. A schoolboy's notebook page, five holes on the side.

Iris unfolded the page. Always folded twice, always with the message in the center of the lined page. Blue ballpoint pen. Printed. Letters exactly the same size, all capitals, slanted neither to the right nor the left. YOU HAVE ENE-MIES. "Oh, honestly!" Iris exploded. "So I have enemies! That's not headline news. Everybody knows I have enemies. Well, half of Paris anyway." She sounded a little proud of it, Anna mused, still standing beside the bed. "Why, every person in the world with any spirit has enemies! Don't you have enemies, Anna?"

"Hmmm. My cousin and I don't get along, but—" Reluctantly, she shrugged. "*Non*, I guess I don't."

"Well," Iris said sulkily, "I think you're an exception. And anyway . . ." She stared at the page once more before refolding it. "I just don't get it. This is number three. Is it a warning? 'You have enemies.' Is it telling me that someone other than the person who wrote this is . . ." She couldn't finish the sentence. And in English. *Mon Dieu*, she was glad it wasn't in Italian. Don Vito. She shuddered when she thought of what his enemies had done to him.

"I don't think it's a warning. I think it's from the person who is your enemy, because the other two said . . . what was it?"

"They're in my top left-hand drawer. Yes, that desk."

The maid fetched the other identical envelopes, and Iris quickly pressed them open and flat on the white satin quilt. "*D'accord*. Number one: 'WATCH YOUR STEP.' Number two: 'WE KNOW ALL ABOUT YOU.' " Iris shook her head, and her blond tendrils moved on the shoulders of the lime green bed jacket. "Well, I'm not worried. This is ridiculous. I bet it's somebody's wife I slept with." Iris and Anna began to laugh. "The . . . the husband of somebody's wife . . ." They laughed merrily as the pages were refolded and put away. When she could control herself, Iris lifted her teacup in a mock toast. "To enemies! They make life ever so much more exciting than friends!"

·   ·   ·

Anna had taken care of the breakfast dishes and tidied the big bedroom and arranged the flowers that had been delivered. The flowers always came on Fridays and Tuesdays. A standing order. Now she stood in front of her bedroom mirror, quite the nicest maid's room she'd ever seen, and primped before going out to pick up smoked salmon and that very thinly sliced whole-wheat bread and a few odds and ends. Nearly everything was delivered to the apartment, but Anna liked having a walk in the fresh air, liked an excuse to look in the shop windows. She pinched her cheeks the way she'd seen Madame do, and brushed her hair over her head to make it fuller, the way Madame did. Ready to face the world, she thought, which was just what Madame often said. Anna pulled the fitted navy coat from the closet and buttoned it, for it was a windy, cool spring day. She turned to admire herself and thought for the thousandth time what wonderful luck to have these marvelous clothes!

An hour later she put the key in the lock with trembling hands and realized with horror that her nose was running. Could your eyes water and your nose run from fear? she wondered. Anna dropped the big key, and then the wicker basket she used for shopping slipped from her grasp, and as she bent to pick them up, she realized she was sobbing.

"*Qu'est-ce que c'est?*" Iris was demanding in the open doorway. "I heard all this noise and . . . Anna!" When the girl looked up, Iris saw the white face and the frightened eyes. "What's happened?"

One cognac later, the story was out. "I was standing on the other side of Boulevard St.-Germain, just a block away, waiting for the light to change . . ." She wiped yet another tear from one blue eye. "There were maybe five or six people around me, but I was nearest the curb. I was in the front of the crowd. Nearest the street. And a voice said, 'You could be pushed into the street and you could die.'" Anna's eyes filled with tears yet again. "It was a foreigner, not a perfect French accent."

Iris leaned forward, listening intently. She wore a long, emerald green silk kimono and sat on a stool, her elbows on her knees, her deep sleeves touching the Oriental rug. "A man or a woman?"

"*C'est un homme.* With a deep voice."

"And you didn't see him?" Iris sighed. "You didn't see how tall, how old, how . . . anything . . . he was?"

"He evidently pushed through the crowd and . . ." Anna shook her head, then took another swallow of the Courvoisier. "The thing is, there was all this traffic. The light had just turned green when he said it." She shivered.

Iris stood and walked to the window. I *do* have an enemy. Someone nearby, someone who may be watching the front gate. She stepped away from the window. "Anna," she said, turning, "I think you should do your hair differently and stop wearing my clothes."

"*Oui, Madame.*" The girl was still trembling.

"And now we must think of other things. Etienne is coming for a drink tonight with two other dealers and . . . you didn't lose the smoked salmon, did you?"

Anna gave a big hiccup and shook her head, which made them both laugh. "And there's packing." Iris started to leave the room. "Don't worry, Anna! We're on our way to Geneva! Switzerland is one of the—no, probably *the* most civilized country in the world. I expect it can be awfully dull at times, but won't that be a relief!" She smiled. "Forget about this morning. It's in the past. These things don't happen in Geneva!"

Les Colombiers

When Jean-François awakened in the morning, he found himself alone in the big double bed. He'd been glad that Cynthia was asleep when he came upstairs, and he had felt free to lie awake for a long while, thinking of Iris and of the plan to ensconce her in the Beau Rivage. Risky. Anyone would agree. With the rue Aldemar Fabri apartment next door. Just how often did Cynthia use it? he wondered. He knew she sometimes left things there on her way into town for errands—the chair to be re-covered, the Venetian prints to be framed. Michel had stayed there with two friends from Exeter after a late concert; Margaret had stayed in town once or twice. So risky, having Iris next door. Well, then, I shall never tell her I have the apartment. She shall only know of Les Colombiers and nothing else. I can keep clothes at the apartment and call her from there, and she won't be able to call me back or go there if she is unaware the place even exists. Just a precaution. He sighed then smiled. Iris nearby. His heart beat more quickly as he felt suddenly, physically, totally awake. His hand grabbed Cynthia's pillow. Too bad she wasn't lying beside him. But Iris stirred him. Sugared innocence in the thinnest layer over tough, what-do-I-care sulkiness. She was as hard and brittle and sweet as candy. Jean-François nearly groaned aloud when he embraced the pillow. Then he suddenly kicked the duvet away from his nakedness and walked energetically toward his bathroom and a cold shower.

An hour later the Bentley had deposited him near Place Bel Air, on the other side of the River Rhone. The four-story building of pale pink gave no hint of what transpired inside save for the presence of curlicued wrought-iron bars on the windows. The brass plaque beside the entrance said simply, "C. & Cie." Everyone who should know, would know that that stood for Colbert. A Colbert, at least one, had walked through this doorway nearly every day of every year since 1795.

The glass partitions slid open and Jean-François nodded at the porter, who sat at a desk a few meters away across the expanse of white marble. *"Bonjour, bonjour."* Jean-François mounted the stairs two at a time, then paced to the end of the hall and entered the conference room. It was a corner salon with tall, tiny-paned windows, the same dark brown and black octagon-patterned carpeting that covered all the bank's floor area, and chocolate brown walls. The central piece of furniture in the room was a large, shining, oval oak table. Around it were fifteen armchairs, upholstered in fawn-colored suede. The decorator, who headed his own chic firm in the Vieille Ville, had cajoled the partners into accepting a modern lighting fixture that reminded Jean-François of icy stalactites aimed dangerously down at those now present.

"*Bonjour, bonjour,*" went all around the table. There were a dozen men greeting him, the last to arrive, but it was still only 8:27. These twice-weekly gatherings were to hear from one or another of the portfolio managers, of whom there were thirty, or from any of the partners, of whom there were seven. It was to talk about Wall Street, to discuss what Zurich was doing, how the yen was reacting to the latest bribery charges leveled at Prime Minister Takeshita. Someone would invariably ask everyone to look at the latest issue of *Neue Zurcher Zeitung* and to note the article on the mark. The Zurich paper was regarded as the best German-language newspaper in the world and one of the two top political observers in the world. Swiss economic analysts watched every American election, considered every word of every Mitterrand speech, and knew the power, temperament, and leanings of every Thatcher cabinet minister.

In forty-five minutes they were all standing, ready to go to their desks and their computers and their telephones. Three of them were planning to lunch at Le Bearn, which was a short walk away on Quai de la Poste, elegant and expensive. The wine list impressed the most sophisticated client, for the 1970 Chateau Lafitte was priced at seven hundred Swiss francs or over four hundred dollars. No Swiss would *ever* be extravagant enough to order it. The bankers from Colbert & Cie. took clients to the restaurant, but never wives or mistresses.

Jean-François made a joke to Alain as they gathered their papers and several of the others laughed. "So I said to Kashoggi, unless you tell me where Imelda buys her shoes . . ."

Jean-François entered his office with a sigh of happiness. It was his haven. I should spend more time here, he thought. The walls were covered in dark blue fabric woven very subtly with a fan pattern. Jean-François often leaned back in his chair and thought it looked like idealized waves of Lake Geneva, and it soothed him. The motif went well with the two portraits of Korean entrepreneurs who stared at him from the far wall, looking proud and prosperous in their ceremonial kimonos. Two small Oriental rugs lay atop the solid blue carpeting; full-length, peach-colored curtains hung at each corner window. The other walls were hung with modern canvases; one painting was of a bigger-than-life-sized face, and instead of eyes there was only endless sky behind the pupils.

He told himself not to think of Iris, not now. He told himself not to think of the constant shouting at Michel right up until he'd flown back to school. He told himself not to think of Stephanie, not now. He told himself not to wonder why he avoided the green eyes of Cynthia. She was angry that he wasn't going to fly over for Michel's graduation from Exeter. Cynthia was going to do it all in the span of three days, and jet lag be damned. She didn't want to spend too much time away from Stephanie. He'd given the bank as an excuse, but the truth was Iris. If he was to be away from this office, it would be because of Iris. So don't think of it now. Not now. The phone rang as he flipped on the computer, and the voice on the line said, "*Buon giorno.* It's La Tosca. Do you have any news?"

Jean-François greeted him effusively in Italian. He could visualize the prince in a grubby phone booth at that terrible train station in Milano. He turned in his chair and tapped a few keys on the Toshiba and carefully, very carefully, began to tell him what he'd done with the last deposit.

CHAPTER TWENTY-SEVEN

Iris

The Beau Rivage

ZiZou was racing back and forth from room to room, wagging her tail and barking. It was a high-pitched bark that annoyed most men. Three porters, all tall, good-looking Portuguese, deposited suitcases in one of the bedrooms and, trying not to stare at Iris, retreated to the salon, where they opened the curtains and made sure everything was in place.

"*Oui, oui.*" Iris nodded in approval as she counted. Twenty-three Louis Vuitton cases, four hatboxes, and ZiZou's carrier and basket. She nodded at Anna, who began to dole out Swiss francs to the young men.

When they had gone, Anna exclaimed, "*Magnifique!*" The suite was actually two adjoining suites consisting of two large bedrooms, two salons, and two bathrooms. The one of white marble was for Iris. Her bedroom, on the lake side, faced the Quai du Mont Blanc and the *jet d'eau*. A high-ceilinged room like all the others, it was paneled, with a large wardrobe and prints on the walls. One salon was cream-colored, with white woodwork and blue carpeting; the other was pale peach with coral curtains to the floor, and a ceiling mural complete with cupids and drawn bows. There were marble fireplaces in each of the sitting rooms and a sense of light and space. The second bedroom, for Anna, faced the Brunswick Park in front of the hotel.

Jean-François arrived while they were unpacking. He ordered champagne, and after they had toasted "Genève," he and Iris walked from room to room in approval. "So you know all about Empress Sissy?" he said when he sat down again. They were on a loveseat in the coral sitting room.

"I know nothing at all about her." Iris sometimes felt so tired of pretending to be well educated and worldly; it could be exhausting. Her usual response would have been a smile and, "Of course I know a bit about her, but I want *you* to tell me everything!" But today she had no patience for the game.

"She was the young Empress of Austria, and was staying at the Beau Rivage for the second time when she was—"

"Wait! How old *is* this hotel?" Iris looked up at the twinkling chandelier and the high ceiling. The tall window was open to the green leaves of the park outside.

"It was built in 1865 by the Mayer family, who still run it. I thought, you little, demanding, spoiled minx, that you'd get excellent service. If Prince Rainier likes it, and Gina Lollobrigida is happy here, and Catherine Deneuve and Peter Ustinov . . ." Jean-François laughed at the look on Iris's face. "So far, how do you find the staff?"

Iris breathed, "Wonderful," but she was thinking, Wonderfully attractive, and where did that Mayer family find all these tall Portuguese? Must be better diets than their fathers had. My God, they were handsome. Right off a movie set. "Simply wonderful," she repeated. "But tell me more about the Empress."

"She was young and beautiful and very well loved and . . . assassinated, unfortunately when she was getting on a ferry just after she left the hotel." Iris thought of Vito; MAFIA ASSASSINATION, one headline had read. "They brought her back here, to this suite, and she died a few minutes later. She was stabbed."

"Here?" Iris looked around nervously as Jean-François nodded. "But the rooms have, of course, been redone, with all the original furniture sent to Vienna. Don't look like that, Iris! It was a long time ago—1898." He laughed and pulled her to him. It was a warm day, and Iris smelled sweet from her bath; she was as soft as a little girl to Jean-François. But the little-girl idea ended there. "Why don't we christen your bed?" he whispered, and she stood up; the lavender negligee was nearly transparent against the bright light coming in the window.

She called to Anna, who was hanging things in the wardrobe in the second bedroom. "Anna! If anyone calls, tell them I'm . . . I'm . . ." She smiled radiantly at Jean-François who was unknotting his tie. "I'm involved!"

· · ·

Iris had resisted showing up at the Christie's pre-sale cocktail party, though it was practically next door at the Richemond and Anna had heard that eight hundred invitations had been sent. Nearly mad with frustration, Iris paced the coral sitting room, halfway watching French television. "The Scarecrow and Mrs. King," then "The Bold and the Beautiful," then "Santa Barbara," and, with the last of the Dom Perignon, "La Roue de Fortune." "My God!" she cried out as the winner of the word game was shown what he could pick as prizes. "How can anyone know what to choose from that garbage! Nothing so bad as the taste of the French middle class!"

Anna stayed out of her way, thinking that she'd rather be in a cage with a wild animal. Iris knew that Jean-François would have been invited to the auction, and that he would have Cynthia at his side. A few meters away! How Iris longed to see Madame Jean-François Colbert of Les Colombiers!

Jean-François had told her nothing except that she was blond and American, and these two facts had been divulged only after extended questioning. He never complained about her, nor did he praise her. She was his wife. Nothing else. Iris did not imagine she would be anything but beautiful. Her heart pounded at the thought of being in the same room with Jean-François and having him acknowledge her in surprise with a flicker of recognition and then be forced to avoid her with his wife at his elbow.

The evening seemed endless, punctuated only by room service. Iris usually ordered one hundred grams of *entrecôte*, finely cut, and string beans, also finely cut, for ZiZou, which arrived on the white linen-draped cart along with dinner for Iris and Anna. The waiter placed the three silver dishes for the little poodle on the floor of the first salon, near the window. He was a new waiter, Iris realized. French and good looking. He quickly arranged the chairs and glasses, opened the wine, and poured a bit for Iris to taste. She nodded her approval, and he filled her goblet. When he started to leave, she called him back. "You forgot the water for ZiZou!" Iris pointed to one empty silver dish. The white poodle turned her head away from the steak, and looked at him with big brown eyes full of reproach. He apologized, and then, trying not to seem unduly interested in Iris's wisp of a peignoir, asked nervously, "With or without gas?"

"Evian," answered Iris. "ZiZou prefers Evian."

．　．　．

Sunday morning, Iris was awake early, drifting around the suite from room to room, holding a goblet of orange juice. She wandered through the French doors to the balcony just above the big awning over the entrance of the Beau Rivage, and looked out at the water and then out to the front of the hotel. People were alighting from cars and taxis. "Dressed to kill," she hissed under her breath, "and all going to the Sotheby's brunch downstairs." She fairly growled into her orange juice, and then, reentering the suite, shouted, "*Merde!*"

"What about this?" Anna asked, holding a white silk sheath with long sleeves for Iris's inspection.

"I'm not going," said Iris. "I'll only get into trouble. I know it would make Jean-François furious if I did go." The minute that thought was out in the open, she had made her decision. Anna watched her pull off the turquoise caftan, and suddenly her mistress shouted, "*Oui!* Run the bath, and then come back and help me with this jewelry! And do you think I should wear silver shoes, or is it too too much since it's only high noon?"

. . .

The diminutive blonde had filled in the deep V neckline with pearls, and wore her favorite pearl-and-diamond earrings, which Vito had bought from Harry Winston's in New York. She hadn't yet visited the shop in Geneva, but she would. Iris intended to walk up and down the rue de Rhone some afternoon; Adler was tops on her list, and then Van Cleef & Arpels, and Boucheron and Cartier and Bulgari. There was no such thing as too much jewelry.

Iris was noticed in the crowd, for so many people knew each other, saw each other two and three times a week at such gatherings in the spring and in the fall, but no one had ever seen Iris before. Yves saw her and wondered why she was alone. Her face was soft, open, receptive, her skin luminous. She was strikingly beautiful and stood out, even with three hundred others milling from room to room, leaning over glass cases of jewelry.

"Amazing," noted Cynthia, concentrating on not spilling her champagne. She was forced to hold it at eye level like everyone else in the crowd. "The old and new Geneva. There must be millions of francs' worth of jewels here, and twenty years ago all I noticed was restraint. Modesty. And now . . ."

"Oh, it's the foreigners!" quipped Yves. "Cynthia! You have to be more *au courant*. You have to blame the foreigners!" He turned to the left, also holding aloft his champagne. "Ahh!" he was saying. "Look! There's my favorite couple." His voice dripped sarcasm. Cynthia followed his gaze to a man and woman in their late forties, suntanned from a cruise, off by themselves, scanning the crowd with darting eyes. "That German Count and Countess Aren't We Wonderful! So stuck up you can't even invite them to dinner!"

Cynthia shook her head. "You're awful, Yves! But tell me the name of that older woman in the red silk suit over there. She looks so familiar."

A tanned blonde in her early fifties, with the big hair popular twenty years ago, pale lips, and eyes rimmed in dark liner, stood across from them. "She used to look like a lioness, and now she just looks like an old fox," Yves said under his breath. "That's Princess Lewandowski. She used to sleep with everybody, but mostly princes, and one of them finally married her and then keeled over dead, practically on the honeymoon. What luck!"

Cynthia laughed. She agreed that the princess looked like a fox. "Was the prince really ancient? Was she the one people were talking about when they said, 'Too bad she can't put him in the bank and sleep with the money'?"

"That's the one, all right," Yves said, grinning. He took two more flutes of champagne off the tray before them, then he and Cynthia made their way toward the long buffet table of scrambled eggs, cheeses, and smoked salmon.

"Where's Yvette?" Cynthia asked after Albert had kissed her the required three times. "Oh!" was the response. "Yvette is not allowed to look at jewels!"

"Cynthia!" so many people greeted her. She rarely went out these days, and when she did, she felt besieged by people who wanted to say hello.

Mimi Bonnell came over and kissed her and then Yves. "Are you losing weight?" she asked him as she tried to step back and get a good look at him. It was not possible, for there were so many people. "You *are*, Yves!"

"Not so, my dear," he answered as he took a bite of a croissant. "I'm just not wearing my credit cards."

They laughed and then decided to try to make their way back to the first salon. "Cannot see anything," Mimi was saying to Antoine. "Madame Bonnell, Madame Colbert," the gray-haired man said, trying in vain to bend down in a sort of halfway gesture toward kissing their hands. They greeted him and moved on in the crush of people to the stairs. "He's a banker friend of Antoine's," Mimi was saying. "Old Genevois. Antoine told me—" She stopped on the step above Cynthia to wait for people going up to pass.

Perfumed, glittering, gleamingly well-tended women and handsome men, thought Cynthia. I feel good. Her green and white silk shantung dress, her emerald earrings, the large diamond ring on her left hand. Nothing was too much. Nothing overdone. Geneva has changed, she thought. It's all so much more lively than I remember. There was a blond woman who lived in Monte Carlo sometimes, London other times, wrote poetry, and was in Geneva to see her banker. The tall, well-built man who would be King of Italy was with his wife and son. Cynthia recognized a very married banker between his wife and his mistress. Yves had told her the mistress had a code name. Wanda.

The sale would begin in five days; people from all over Europe and the Middle East, some Japanese, and some Americans would come to bid on the jewels. There was an air of anticipation, though few of the guests tonight would be bidders. The Swiss franc was as strong as ever but it was more than that. Whether it was due to the multitude of foreigners or Swiss or that other species, the Genevois, Cynthia felt surrounded by prosperity, by personal wealth.

They were in the lobby again, and Mimi was about to finish her story. "He told Antoine that his grandfather was so stingy he always used to give the same thing to each of his grandchildren for Christmas." A man stepped in between them to greet Cynthia and to ask about Jean-François. "He's at home with the catalog of this sale!" she laughed. "Mimi! I'm sorry! This is a madhouse. Please tell me what the grandfather gave to each child! Quickly! Before someone else interrupts us!"

Mimi, intrepid in the sea of chattering champagne drinkers, had not lost her train of thought. She leaned forward and said distinctly, "One half of an apple!"

Geneva

"You know Mimi's gone," Yves said. They were having lunch at Le Dorian, a French restaurant in the Vieille Ville. Twelve o'clock was early, but soon the bright dining room of windows looking over the square would be crowded, every table taken, every inch of every velvet banquette occupied.

"Paris?" Cynthia asked, wondering why Yves would even mention such a commonplace event.

"No. Left Geneva. Probably for good." Yves sipped the Monseigneur Badoux. "Nice. 'Seventy-nine. Very nice. Does anyone care if we have red instead of white? I like this. Wonder if I should order a case."

"Oh, I don't know." Cynthia shrugged. "What do you mean, she's 'left Geneva'? We just saw her at the Sotheby's brunch. What happened? Where is she?"

"She cracked," said Veronique. "I felt it coming. She was with me one afternoon. We bumped into each other at Fendi's, and then had a lunch at the Entrecôte and . . . well, we talked until six. She was going on and on about not belonging anywhere. That her children had no home, were strangers in Switzerland. That we were all strangers in a strange land. She said, 'At least you speak your native language, but I'm Slavic—' "

"She's French, isn't she?" Cynthia interrupted.

"Yugoslavian," Yves said.

"She said her children weren't at home anywhere. The schools in England, the holidays here and in France, the invitations to parties of their friends in Spain and Italy. Antoine's family is old, old Genevois. Always had money. They were well off back in the thirteenth century. His first wife was Greek, and he has the son. Mimi's first husband was Egyptian, and she has one daughter, and then the children between them, who have godparents of every nationality. Hungarian, English, German." Veronique paused. "She had tears in her eyes, as though she had suddenly lost her bearings."

"She's right about the children not knowing where they belong." Cynthia spoke quietly as she picked up her wineglass. "I often think that."

"Well, look at us. Not one of us was born here. Louis is here because of his bank. I'm here because of *my* bank. Cynthia, you've married someone born here, but your children spend, what, two months a year in Geneva?" Yves was warming to the subject. "But if you go way back, all the oldest families, these old banking families, have names like Turrettini. Pictet is French, Lombard is probably Lombardy . . ."

Cynthia had heard all this before. She wanted Veronique to get back to Mimi. " 'It's a town of strangers,' Mimi kept repeating. The diplomats come and go, and unless they are wildly attractive, which is rare, they stay clumped in their own crowd and aren't invited to our houses. Then there are the old Genevois who are opening up . . ."

"Since the early sixties," said Yves. "Since foreigners started businesses here. Then the old banking families *had* to invite them. If one did, then the others had to compete with him and couldn't exclude the new blood. Couldn't afford to. It meant money."

"But what really happened to Mimi?" Cynthia insisted.

"Veronique thinks it has something to do with the last lover, but I think it's more than that. I mean, she's had so many affairs in . . . what's it been, fifteen years? What's one more breakup?"

"She's very conscious of getting older, Yves. We all know that." Cynthia knew that Mimi had had her eyes "done" at a clinic, but she wouldn't tell. She could see the difference. Everyone had suddenly begun to say that Mimi looked so "rested" last spring. "She takes great care of herself, though." Cynthia could see the bright-eyed brunette in her mind's eye, chirping about Paris, about the latest fashions, about what she'd bought. Always beautifully groomed, every hair in place, her lipstick a dark, deep, Paloma Picasso red.

Yves sighed. "Well, so maybe it's a combination of events. But suddenly she began ordering things . . ."

"What do you mean?" Cynthia imagined waiters in restaurants taking Mimi's orders.

"Ferraris. Lamborghinis. A few weeks ago, three Ferraris were delivered to the Richemond. For her husband," Veronique explained.

"What are you talking about?" Cynthia leaned forward, chin on her hands, then she moved back again as their waiter arranged the plates of *poulet rôti*.

"So the Richemond sent them away. Returned to Ferrari. But you can imagine the commotion. Let alone the traffic jam! Then, the next Thursday, evidently five Ferraris and five Lamborghinis were delivered to the Richemond. They had all these drivers standing outside the open doors, waiting for Monsieur Bonnell to arrive and sign the forms. The Richemond doorman sent them away."

Cynthia imagined the regal Pierre in his white gloves and his maroon uniform and the matching billed hat with gold braid, "sending them away." Imperiously. "But why did she do it? And why to the Richemond?"

Yves shrugged elaborately in the red cashmere sweater. It was a "day off" for him, and he was enjoying his long lunch, his sport clothes. "She suddenly just . . . snapped." He sighed. "So anyway, Antoine arranged for her to go to France and 'rest.' He seemed to want to make a joke of it when I saw him yesterday. Said it just showed how good his credit was—the idea that so many automobiles could be put on his account with no questions asked!"

"What a stupid man! How cold!" Cynthia put down her fork. "Maybe *he* has a lot to do with how Mimi feels."

"And maybe Mimi is right," Yves continued. "Look. Look at this place." It was the most popular watering hole for the private bankers. Le Dorian was located near the University, near the Grand Theatre in the old quarter. But the diners were not all Genevois. There were Arabs at the next table, and two very well-dressed men speaking Spanish just behind Cynthia. Across the narrow aisle sat a tall, thin man with very blond hair, reading the *Wall Street Journal*, and next to him on the banquette a Japanese sat stabbing at capers, then carefully arranging them on each slice of smoked salmon.

"The world," Veronique said, smiling.

Cynthia said, "I like it here. I remember WASP-y Beacon Hill and homogenized Anglo-Saxon summers on Martha's Vineyard." She suddenly thought of Marco and wondered if either of her friends saw any change in her expression.

"You amaze me!" Yves cried with delight. He put his hand over hers and squeezed it.

Veronique pushed a strand of auburn hair back. Her new ruby-and-pearl earrings caught the light at the same time she lifted her glass of red wine. "I think Mimi's right. We're all strangers here."

Yves looked at her and grinned. "Let's drink to strangers!"

Veronique corrected him, "To lovers and strangers."

Cynthia lifted her glass and thought, I go along with all of it, and still I am a stranger in the way I think, even with these two. But she laughed and mimicked them, comfortable because they understood her. "To lovers and strangers."

Geneva

Never mind, Iris thought. I don't have to worry about my reputation here in Genève. Paris counts, but this is small-town stuff. She looked around the nearly empty three rooms and saw perhaps twenty people walking slowly from one painting to another, holding champagne glasses. They were well dressed, respectful. Jean-François had persuaded Etienne that the opening would be a good idea, which was why, on this summer night, she was dressed in a lavender and white flowered silk dress and her favorite "small" diamond necklace. Her dyed-to-match *peau de soie* shoes made her at least five foot three, and though they were killing her feet, the added height was a comfort.

Of course he isn't here, she thought in annoyance. The bank. The family.

Unbelievable, really! "*Bon soir*, Madame Fontaine! *Mais oui!* Of course I remember meeting you in Paris. How nice of you to come tonight." Etienne was smiling at her from across the room, and she excused herself to go to him. What a wonderful friend he'd been all these years. From the very beginning in Paris. When she was young and pregnant and knew nothing. She kissed him on both cheeks and then leaned back. "Don't you look divine!" she cooed. "The purple cummerbund is very *you*. It's uplifting to see you making a fashion statement," she teased him.

"I'm relieved one of us is beautiful. Let's leave it at that," Etienne laughed. His dinner jacket looked as if he'd spent the night on a train sleeping in it, and his white hair was mussed. His priority wasn't to look bandbox perfect. Getting dressed always seemed to interrupt telephone calls or work at his desk. He'd been a little boy with shirttails flapping out over his short pants, and socks that scrunched down in rings around his ankles. "Come with me, Iris, to meet some of these patrons of the arts." His tone was the slightest bit sarcastic.

There were a few Arabs, a few couples speaking German, an Italian count and his countess, a smattering of diplomats, and a group of a half-dozen joking in French near the table bearing the hors d'oeuvres. A tall, black-haired woman in white linen approached them purposefully. "*Bon soir!* I am so happy to meet you. A friend of mine has a book of your watercolors, and I would like to know when you began to paint and how and what you're doing in Geneva and will you be staying long and—"

Iris and Etienne stopped talking and Iris introduced her mentor, and he took the woman's hand and bowed slightly. She is, thought Iris, very elegant, and though in her late sixties, is still beautiful, straightforward, entirely confident. Iris didn't mind that Etienne obviously took to her.

"My grandson is keen on becoming an artist. Now, I don't know enough about what you do to know what being an artist really means, and perhaps he doesn't either. All I know is"—the woman took a sip of her champagne —"I think the boy deserves a chance to try. He's seventeen and scheduled for a slot in his father's private bank."

"Has he had any studies? Any—" Etienne began.

"Oh! I don't even know! Perhaps an art course at prep school. An American school. You know, they let them try all sorts of things under this heading of 'liberal arts.' But anyway, the family is totally torn apart over this. The bickering at the dinner table alone sounds rather like the ominous first shots of a world war." She continued, oblivious of their laughter. "I'm his grandmother, and I want to risk the wrath of everybody by giving the boy a chance, and I don't know . . ." She hesitated. "Would you ever—do you ever, Madame Iris . . ." She took a deep breath. "Do you ever take on a pupil?"

"Never. I really don't think that I could—"

"Now, Iris," Etienne said, "don't react too quickly. The boy is seventeen and eager, and you are here in Genève for the summer. Perhaps you will have time on your hands, and it might be . . ."

Iris couldn't believe her ears. Etienne, who always wanted more and more of her canvases, was actually suggesting she take time away from her own painting to devote to a schoolboy!

"Just one or two times a week," the woman was saying. "I think it might turn the tide one way or the other for him. And for his father, my headstrong son. What he needs is to be shown that the boy has talent. Or the boy needs to know that he does *not*. Do you understand?" she implored them. "His life is at a crossroads and this summer could make a difference for him. If he doesn't have the chance, he will be funneled into Harvard and caught up in the schedule of what he 'should' do, and in the blink of an eye he'll be in business school and behind a desk and perhaps twenty years from now he'll wonder if he could have spent his life better in a studio, painting."

"When you put it that way," Iris responded, "I cannot say no to you!"

"Shall I have him telephone you tomorrow?" Elizabeth felt a surge of triumph. An artist with a Paris reputation, right here in Geneva! She'd read a tiny, one-inch-square blurb about the showing in the arts section of the *Journal de Genève*, and counted on there not being a big crowd. She'd also counted on no one asking to see her invitation. And she'd been right. The doors of the Vieille Ville gallery were open to the little cobblestoned square and the bubbling fountain outside.

"You might as well just have him come to me. We can decide on a schedule together. I am living in the Beau Rivage, and will expect him . . ." She hesitated. "In the afternoon. Four o'clock?"

"Four o'clock. He'll be there."

Etienne took her hand again as they said good-bye, and then cast a sideways look at Iris, who seemed a bit subdued by the entire encounter.

"What do you think?" Iris asked.

"I think you'll be glad you did something nice for the boy. I don't think you'll be sorry about taking him on."

"Hmmmph," Iris snorted, in one of her little-girl piqued moods suddenly. "You, dearest Etienne, who run my life, are now even arranging for my good deeds!"

Etienne, who understood Iris better than anyone, smiled. "Is it so bad to commit an unselfish act once every ten years? Does it hurt so much?"

"I saw the way you looked at her," Iris said archly. "Let's not discuss good deeds and going to heaven. Please."

Etienne allowed his glass to be refilled by a Spanish waiter and then smiled broadly. "Oh, Iris! You are a bad girl! Couldn't you see this for what it is?"

Iris turned her green eyes upon him and shrugged. "All right. I'll try it your way. Art lessons for a young boy. Totally innocent."

The Beau Rivage

When Anna answered the door and led the young man into the coral sitting room, Iris rose from the chaise rather dramatically. She wore a long scarlet satin robe and came forward extending her small, white hand festooned with rubies.

Michel took the hand and bent slightly toward the glittering rings. *"Bon soir*, Madame Iris. I am Michel—"

"Michel! One of my favorite names! Anna, why don't you bring us some refreshment?" She motioned for him to sit across from her. "Would you care for wine or champagne? I only drink champagne in the afternoons."

"Oh, champagne would be fine. *Merci.*" He nodded, wanting to please her, longing for a Heineken. My God, her breasts are enormous, and the top of that red thing is so . . . so tight. Michel swallowed and then folded his hands in his lap. Then he decided that wasn't the place for them after all. He couldn't take his eyes from her face, for when he did, they dropped to the shiny red expanse of cloth covering . . . he shouldn't imagine. Not now. Michel thought she was the most beautiful woman he'd ever seen. She was kittenish with him, joking about the champagne, and sultry when she talked about the heat in Paris and how Geneva might suit her for the summer. She was a vamp when she leaned forward to refill his glass, and maternal when she told him to wear old clothes he didn't care about ruining when working in the studio.

She went to her bookshelves and pulled down volume after volume of art books and brought them to the little table where the champagne glasses sat. Then she sat next to him on the little coral brocade loveseat and he could smell her perfume, the powder she had used after her bath.

"I've just arrived, as your *grand-mère* might have told you. By the way, what is her name? Neither Etienne Le Sage, he owns the gallery that shows my work, and he is . . . well, everything to me . . . uhmmm, what was I saying?" Iris had suddenly noticed Michel's lap.

"*Grand-mère* is Madame Fortier. She lives in Paris a lot of the time now."

"Fortier? And her husband, your grandfather's name?" Iris wanted to assess her importance early on. The boy wouldn't repeat this.

"Her husband was Alexandre Fortier, but he died about . . . I don't know . . . I never knew him. He was with a law firm in Paris . . . but—"

"That was my next question. Well! I didn't know your *grand-mère* in Paris, but I'm glad we met in Geneva!" Satisfied that she was dealing with a family of influence, she opened the book of Dubuffet on her lap and began to ask him questions about what he liked, who his favorite artists were, his favorite periods.

Two hours later, Michel Colbert was striding through the Beau Rivage lobby, past the fountain circled with pink flowers, past the dark blue blazers of the porters, and out the revolving door. He noticed nothing. It was all a blur. Michel was overwhelmed, a little high on champagne, very happy, and totally in love.

Les Colombiers

"Stephanie, darling," Cynthia breathed, sitting on her bed. "Do you want soup for lunch? For a change? Cream of asparagus, bouillon, or chicken and rice?"

The girl shook her head. She looked better than she had a month ago, and was able to spend some of the day sitting in the chair by the window, but she was uninterested in anything but M&Ms and fish sticks.

"Okay. Fish sticks it is!" Cynthia tried to sound enthusiastic, as she left the room and started toward the stairs. Both Dr. Marceau and Charlie had instructed her to allow Stephanie anything she wanted. The diet could be diversified in the future, but now they just wanted her to eat.

Lately, Charlie seemed pleased after his sessions with Stephanie, though he would not communicate their content to Cynthia. Stephanie appeared to like him and often asked for him in the morning, which was the time he spent working on his paper in his room.

Cynthia was sure it had been a good idea to add him to the household. He no longer made her think the word *psychiatrist* when she saw him. Charles Galveston had seemed almost invisible for the first part of his stay. He volunteered so little about his life, was quiet, appeared for meals, disappeared after them. Now she noticed the laugh lines around his brown eyes, and his bright white smile, and knew that he could hold his own on the tennis courts with Michel. Sometimes he actually beat him! The two would come in laughing together.

"Oh!" she gasped as the object of her thoughts appeared at the bottom of the stairs.

"Didn't mean to scare you!" Charlie apologized. "I think I'll sit with Stephanie until her lunch tray comes." He respected the girl's demand that no one watch her eat, and suspected that she stripped naked and weighed herself afterwards. Cynthia's scale was not in her bedroom, but in the bathroom down the hall, so that Stephanie had to take the trouble to walk there. "I don't want you staring at it all day long!" Cynthia had protested when she had asked it be moved to her room.

"It's a fish-stick day," Cynthia grimaced. "How do you think she is?"

"Do you have three minutes?"

"Absolutely. But let me speak to the cook first."

Cynthia was back in an instant, and they sat down across from each other at the dining-room table. It wasn't yet set for lunch, and seemed the perfect place for a conference. "Okay. How is she coming along?"

Charlie nodded. "She's talking. That's the best thing. She can't seem to stop telling me . . . telling me how the only thing in her life she can control is the food."

"She actually says that? That's just what you said that first day!"

"She has not said it in words, but she *knows* it, which is the most important thing. The highest hurdle is realizing it, and she does. But what I wanted to ask you is, what if she told you she wanted to live at home next year, to go to school in Geneva?"

"Oh, Charlie! Anything she wants is fine! I'd love to have her at home. Jean-François is the one who is so keen about boarding schools. We'd have to fight him about her actually living at home." She hesitated. "But we would. *I* would."

"It's good to hear all this. I think it would make a difference to her. She feels, along with all the other confusion, somehow responsible for your 'perfection.' She calls it 'good behavior.' "

"But why?"

"I don't know yet. She also continues to think of you as perfect and herself as someone falling short of you. You are the yardstick she measures herself by."

"What if I were to talk to her about . . . about her father? About what I feel?"

"Not now, maybe later." What Charlie didn't say was that he didn't think Cynthia was ready for that.

"What if . . . what if she were to discover . . ." Cynthia's voice died. No. Never. Too dangerous. In a jagged thought, like a clip from a movie, she saw herself, big-bellied and barefoot, standing on Kate Grayson's terrace overlooking the turquoise sea. Me, she thought, a few years older than Stephanie.

"I'll go on up now," Charlie said. Whatever she'd almost said had deeply troubled her, but Cynthia with secrets? Jean-François was the one with secrets.

"See you at one, then. It'll just be you, Michel, and me. I think we'll try to have it on the porch, so bring a sweater," she smiled and then returned to the kitchen. How peculiar, she thought. I miss my mother. Gone twenty-four hours, and I'm beginning to think she was good company! Then she thought of Stephanie upstairs, weighing less than one hundred pounds at five foot seven. But she's gaining weight and she's talking. And me! What do I have to do with it all? And my mother with who I am? She looked down at the Sevres china dishes piled with shining black caviar and said aloud, "Mothers and daughters."

· · ·

Cynthia sat at her desk in her boudoir. It was midafternoon, and the house seemed to sleep peacefully around her. Jean-François was away, and she felt free. She was barefoot and wearing white Levi's and a red T-shirt. Red plastic combs held her hair back from her temples. Cynthia adored spending a few francs on things like combs and ribbons and bright bandannas, which she kept in one drawer completely separate from her "good" things. A straw bracelet she'd paid two Swiss francs for, roughly a dollar and a quarter, was on her wrist. She stared out the window at the green leaves and thought, No matter what happens to any of us, the summer holds such a sweetness. The swans were on the edge of the lawn with their four tiny little ones. Swans mate for life, she thought, and felt a twinge of melancholy. Cynthia put her head down and nibbled at the end of the fountain pen. The black ink soon slashed across the page, then another page and another. She twisted her long hair up into a knot, tucking the combs in to hold it.

The ringing of the phone startled her, and she turned in her chair and gave it a malevolent look before rising. "My line," she said aloud, and picked up the receiver. "*Allo?*"

"Cynthia! You won't believe me when I tell you what's happened!"

"Veronique! I probably won't, but tell me anyway."

"Oh, you never change, do you?" Veronique did not understand that Cynthia's blasé attitude had been formed that first day at lunch all those years ago, when she'd felt like such a ninny facing Veronique's sophistication. "I will tell you! I . . . I think I have to."

Such reticence isn't like the Veronique I know, Cynthia thought, and realized her throat was very dry. "Veronique?" Her voice was anxious.

"*Mon dieu!* I couldn't wait to call you. I have my legs propped up and I tried to run to the telephone and now I—"

"For heaven's sake, what *is* it?"

"I'm your friend, remember?"

"Yes," Cynthia responded with a bit of hesitation.

"Well, I . . . I saw her! I saw her again!"

Cynthia's voice was sharp. She knew exactly who Veronique was talking about. "Who? Who did you see?" Her heart was pounding in her throat now. Don't tell me. Don't let it be true.

"That same woman. The blond one from Paris. She's staying at the Beau Rivage." Silence on the line. "The one with Jean-François! The one from Paris!"

"I know. I know." Cynthia's voice was only a whisper. "I guess I'm not surprised."

"I saw her on my way to Sotheby's. I was just past the Brunswick Memorial and about to cross the street, and for a minute I thought . . . the hair . . . I thought it was you! But she's small—tiny, actually—and she was making her way up the steps toward the revolving door, and all I could think was what is she wearing, and I want a good look at her face, and I was hurrying and I got hit by a car!"

"What! What?" shouted Cynthia. "Are you all right? Veronique!" Cynthia was standing now, ready to go to her friend. "Are you in the hospital? Shall I come?"

"I'm at home. I'm in bed. My legs are all swollen. I have no ankles. I was knocked down but I'm all right."

"My God, Veronique! You're sure you shouldn't go to a hospital? Please let me—"

"No. I'm happy here. I'm drinking cognac."

"You are amazing!" Cynthia wiped a fine film of perspiration from her upper lip. Darling Veronique. Crazy Veronique. My best friend for years.

"Cynthia?" the voice came over the line.

"*Oui?*" Cynthia thought, I should go to her. I'll tell Simone to serve dinner without me.

Veronique's voice was full of life. "Don't you want to know what she was wearing?"

The Beau Rivage

The poodle leaped onto the bed, and Iris cuddled it. "No, Etienne! It's just ZiZou! I'm not being unfaithful to Jean-François—yet."

His laughter came from Paris. "I miss you! Now tell me how you are. What do you think of Geneva now that you've been there awhile?"

"Well, it's more filled with flowers every day. Manicured little parks here and there. Pots of flowers along the sidewalks, in front of shops, in window boxes. It's sparkling clean. Really lovely. I thought I'd be awfully homesick for Paris, but I'm not! And this hotel is splendid. You know I've stayed in lots of . . ." She hesitated, then decided it would give nothing away. "I've stayed in lots of American hotels. The really modern ones. Sort of plastic and new, with those paper loops across the toilet seats, and ice machines that go 'clunk' in every hallway, and . . ." So long ago, she thought. "It's just that the Beau Rivage is so *elegantissimo.*" She fell into Italian. "It's so Old World charming and so . . ." Iris finally said, "Refined." ZiZou yelped in irritation. She was hungry, and Anna had forgotten to call room service. Iris patted her head as the brown eyes looked up imploringly.

"How is ZiZou? Does Anna walk her on the quay?"

"Oh, no! I've arranged for Portuguese porters to take care of that. At seven o'clock Luis comes, and at noon there is Manuel and at four o'clock there is

Joao. Anna likes the night duty because I think she meets someone." Iris cooed to ZiZou. "I pay them ten Swiss francs for twenty minutes, and they all seem to like her. They're very kind."

"That's an expensive piss," Etienne snorted. "And what about Anna? Is she happy there?"

"I think she loves Genève. After all, we have room service, so there is no kitchen to take care of, and the dry cleaner is around the corner for all my clothes. Someone comes in to vacuum every day, and to change the sheets. I brought my own, of course, but we may sometimes, in a pinch, use the hotel ones. I think living in a hotel is by far the only sensible way to survive in this world of constant maintenance."

"You sound like a very jaded Eloise at the Plaza!" laughed Etienne.

"Eloise who?"

"I'll send you the book. Now, my last two questions. What about the studio?"

"Jean-François is seeing about a little place on the lake between here and where he lives, which is a place called Chambesy. It's about eight or nine kilometers out of town. It was to be a gardener's shed, but it sounds perfect for me. Lots of light, a view of the water, and all the work on the house next door has stopped for some reason. I can probably move my things there in a few days."

"But if the studio is out of Genève, how will you get there?"

"By taxi. And lots of them are driven by women! Buses, too, according to Anna! Though I haven't been near a bus in . . . well, in decades." Her voice dropped. "But I must say, it's fortunate that I'm very rich, because there are three kinds of taxis here. Expensive, *mon Dieu*, and you must be kidding!"

Etienne laughed. "And the student? Tell me."

Iris gently stroked ZiZou's little white head and thought of Michel with a smile. "In a word—adorable! Young and eager to learn everything he can! Oh, I think he's so sweet, so—"

"Now, Iris! Slow down!" His voice was warning her, though Etienne doubted she would pay any attention. When she wanted a man, even a very young man, he couldn't stop her. If only that *grand-mère* had known!

"Oh, you are so silly. Do you honestly think that—"

"I won't let you finish! When you use words like 'honestly' after we discussed 'innocent motives'!" He was laughing as he bid her *au revoir*.

Iris giggled softly, pulling the white satin negligee over her breasts as she hung up the phone. "Oh, Etienne is so silly, isn't he, ZiZou?" The dog looked up at her mistress adoringly. "I mean, really!" Iris smiled like a little cat thinking of cream. "Michel is not so young!"

Les Colombiers

"Yves Rocard? Did you say Yves Rocard?" Tony asked. Anthony Forbes-Todd held his drink at waist level and looked totally at home in the grand salon of the chateau. He stood silhouetted in the window with the lake behind him, and all Cynthia could see was that he was a tall man with very dark hair. It had been two years since she last met Elizabeth's friend and occasional traveling companion.

Elizabeth glanced at Cynthia. "That's Yves's last name, isn't it darling?"

"Yes. Do you know him?" Cynthia stood beside the mantel, arranging flowers in a Chinese porcelain vase. Her back was to them all as she tucked ferns in with the white roses.

"Why, I went to school with him! In England. He went to Eton, didn't he?"

"I think so." Cynthia couldn't put her finger on it, but Tony Forbes-Todd made her slightly ill at ease. Maybe she wasn't used to the English. But no, Elizabeth was English and she was always delighted to be with her.

"Stop fussing, Cynthia, and join us! The sun is over the yardarm and it's time to drink!" Elizabeth poured her daughter-in-law a glass of champagne and extended it to her.

"Leave her alone, Maman," Jean-François said. "It's the only thing that gives her pleasure." All three of them looked at him. "Fussing," he said definitely.

"Thank you so much," Cynthia said, taking her glass. No one knew if she was speaking to her husband or to Elizabeth, and there was a long silence. "Tell me," she began, "all about the latest escapade."

Tony put up his hand. "But no, wait! Before we get onto Kashmir, I want to hear about Yves. Is he a friend of yours?"

Jean-François laughed. A bit unpleasantly, both his mother and his wife thought.

"He's a very close friend of mine," Cynthia said. "A very loyal, wonderful man."

"Emphasize the word 'man' when you talk about Yves." Jean-François was becoming more aggressive, and both women looked at him sharply.

"What are you talking about?" Tony asked equably. No one answered him. "He wasn't gay at school. Not at seventeen, which was the last time I saw him. And I'd like to see him again. Could we—"

"Yes," Cynthia interrupted. "We'll have him to lunch tomorrow, unless you'd rather he invited us all around to his house. All I have to do is telephone him." She suddenly thought she liked Tony Forbes-Todd. He was all right after all. Jean-François had been firmly but gently put in his place!

Tony was staring at her over the edge of his glass. She felt suddenly that her dress was too short, but that was the fashion, or that it was too fitted in the bust, but her dressmaker had assured her the "big" look was going out. The color was always good—pistachio green—and the style classic, a linen coat dress trimmed in white at the collar and the short sleeves. She'd been in Geneva with errands all day, and had come home to find surprise houseguests off a plane from New Delhi.

"How's the family business, darling? Should I switch to an inferior champagne?" Elizabeth looked just the same, thought Cynthia. That strong face, with a few more wrinkles around the eyes, but one knew they were laugh lines. The clear red lipstick was still her trademark, along with the black and white clothes and the heavy jewelry. She was forever elegant, with a great sense of her own style.

"Don't you dare!" Tony put in when Jean-François didn't respond. "I don't drink inferior champagne. You'll lose me as a friend."

"They come and go, don't they?" Elizabeth laughed. "You'd think after sixteen years he'd have an ounce of sentiment . . ."

"I don't, you know. It's all for show. I saved her life only yesterday, but she's conveniently forgotten."

"Are you going to drag out that old 'rampaging bull elephant' story?" Elizabeth laughed.

"No. I was thinking more on the lines of the 'wounded she-lion' story."

Their pleasure was contagious, and Cynthia found herself laughing with them. Jean-François nursed his Scotch and seemed to be thinking of other things. Cynthia had noticed it the last time he and his mother were together. Was he angry with her? He was the same Jean-François she had seen with his mother all those years ago in France, before the wedding. The son who wanted her attention. Who wanted to be begged to stay longer, who wanted to be dissuaded from going to Geneva. And now she sat in her own living room and saw the mother-and-son sparks again. Twenty years later. Nothing had changed except that Elizabeth had become someone with more fun in her life than a garden and a pied-à-terre in Paris.

"What? What did you say?" Cynthia asked.

"I said that you and Jean-François should dash away with us the next time." Tony seated himself directly across from Cynthia.

"Count me out. Responsibilities, you know. Someone has to hold the Colbert family together."

"I'm not really a Colbert, darling. Don't count on my having a highly developed sense of responsibility," Elizabeth said.

"As highly developed as a lily of the field perhaps." Tony grinned at Cynthia, who smiled back.

"I can't imagine Elizabeth spinning or toiling," she put in.

They all were laughing as Charlie came down the stairs from his before-dinner visit with Stephanie. He held out his hand to Elizabeth and then Tony. "Charlie Galveston. I'm happy to meet you."

Cynthia thought of Charlie as a sweet, unsophisticated American, but when he took his place beside Tony on the white brocade sofa, she suddenly saw him as a rather good-looking man. Tony was handsome, but Charlie was as tall, as broad-shouldered, as slim-hipped. Tony's face was etched-on-a-coin perfect, while Charlie had the rather ordinary good features of a grown-up Kellogg's Cornflakes boy. He was tan from writing at the table in the garden, and his hair had turned quite light from the sun. Cynthia suddenly wondered why she'd never noticed any of these things before. The third male presence was, of course, Jean-François, lounging opposite her in the wing chair, his knees wide apart in the tan summer suit. His darkness still attracted her, but he never satisfied her longing for tenderness. She looked at his hands curved round the glass, and thought of them touching her. It was a purely intellectual exercise, for she felt nothing anymore.

Simone stood behind Cynthia and announced dinner in a low voice.

"No, no," Charlie was laughing. "I don't give family rates."

Elizabeth said, "Oh, but you should. Jean-François was never very normal." The group was standing, preparing to walk to the dining room. Jean-François's face was dark with rage. "You would know, Maman, wouldn't you? You were always there! Always watching, weren't you?" He tossed down the last swallow of Scotch and went on. "But *not* watching me! Never *me!*" He put the glass down on the coffee table, said, "Excuse me," in a cold voice, and left the room.

They all turned as one to watch the tall figure disappear, then they heard his feet on the stairs. Cynthia said, "I think everyone should go in now. Elizabeth, perhaps you could place my guests and . . . and I'll be right down." She cast a nervous look over her shoulder. "You start without me." She tried to smile.

Flowers and vegetables from the garden, a lamb that had been studded with garlic cloves and cooked to perfection, and the best wine made for an appealing meal. The three of them gamely made conversation, but the party had been spoiled, and the forks seemed to make too much noise on the china.

Charlie was lifting his wineglass in a toast to his first summer in Switzerland when they heard Jean-François shout, "I hate you! You're just like her!" and then a door slammed.

Elizabeth blushed, but said cheerfully, "That's the thing about living in a chateau. The doors are so big that when you slam them . . ." Her voice cracked.

Tony put his hand over hers on the Burano lace tablecloth. "There's so much more door per slam."

Cynthia did not reappear for some minutes. When she did, she looked frightened and small coming quickly into the dining room. And terribly young, thought Charlie. Like a girl late for dinner. Vulnerable.

She spread the napkin in her lap hurriedly, and instructed Simone to bring her a piece of the lamb and a salad. Then she looked around at the faces in the candlelight and smiled. "Those doors! Sometimes there is a sudden gust of—"

Elizabeth interrupted. "Don't be brave with us, Cynthia! We're your friends!" She nodded at Charlie, who was filling her glass from a decanter. "Drink some wine and let Tony and me tell you all about ruby smuggling in Burma."

Chambesy

"Like it?" Iris stood in the open doorway and gestured widely at the one big room.

"Like it? It's fantastic!" Michel marveled.

The studio was thirty by thirty feet, with a concrete floor now covered by one of Iris's Oriental rugs. The white plaster walls were festooned with newspaper clippings thumbtacked here and there, sketches for paintings not yet started, and postcards and snapshots that Iris liked. A photograph of the familiar *jet d'eau* seen through a rainbow was at eye level and made Michel smile. At one end of the room, easels and a table of planks laid on saw horses were set up; at the opposite end, a mattress lay on the floor, covered incongruously with four of Iris's fringed shawls. Each of the shawls had a story: there was the black and red one from Spain, embroidered with red roses; the silver and white one from Portugal; the heavy lace one that Etienne had given her from the Art Nouveau shop in Paris; a pale green silk from India. Each was from a male friend. At the head of the bed were pillows, all Thai silk, piled in shiny pastels of orange sherbet and ice blue and parrot green and lemon yellow. An ice bucket sat on a table in the center of the room, with two glasses.

"Champagne?" Not waiting for an answer, Iris filled the glasses from the bottle she'd opened just before his arrival. Michel took it and sipped. "It's hot today. Amazing for Geneva to have such a long streak of good weather."

"Mmmm." Iris realized he was nervous. Maybe because they were really alone now, and not in the hotel, talking, with Anna in the next room. "Best for last. Let me show you the best part of this place." She walked to what appeared to be a garage door, and grasped a handle and pulled it upward. A door swung up and in, and then slid above them, flat against the ceiling. The lake was twenty feet away, sparkling in the sun, like a length of shimmering blue silk. "Pretty nice, isn't it? I still can't get over the dimensions. An architectural aberration." She turned back to him and noticed that he was staring directly at her breasts in the white piqué dress. Michel blushed.

"Okay," she said. "I want to know where you think we should begin. Since this is the first time we've actually been able to paint, and so far I haven't seen anything but your sketches. So what first? What do you think?"

"I want to tell you something, Madame Iris," he began.

"Just Iris." They spoke to each other in French. God. I'm not too old to know what you're thinking.

He cleared his throat. "Iris. Okay, Iris. I like the way we only talk about things that matter. What art I like, what I think about Jasper Johns or the last Van Gogh sold at auction, what I want. Most people . . ." He sipped from the glass, liking the tickling cool feeling in his mouth. "Most people ask me if I have brothers and sisters and where I go to school and where I have applied to college, and you . . . well, you don't, and I like it." Christ. I must be drinking this stuff too fast, he thought, and blushed again. Her eyes are as green as Mother's. Don't think of Mother now!

"I know you have things on your mind," she said cryptically. "It's good to meet someone and feel you can connect without the details or the statistics."

The heat was there. Iris felt it, and so did Michel. They both took another sip of the champagne and Iris quickly reached for the bottle and refilled the glasses. They drank in silence, standing in the center of the room. The ducks were honking outside, and a cool breeze was blowing in off the lake through the open door. Michel stared at the ice bucket as if memorizing the lines. He could feel the tightness of his jeans becoming almost unbearable. He didn't dare look at Iris.

Iris was amazed at how much he suddenly reminded her of Jean-François. That darkness. But Michel was sweeter and, of course, younger. It was something about the dark eyes that made her think of her Swiss lover. Same type, she thought. And I'm definitely attracted to it.

Okay. Can't stop myself. No one will know. He's not a baby. Can't stop myself. "Michel," she said softly, as she put down her glass. "Could you undo my dress for me?" She turned around without meeting his eyes, and then heard him place his glass on the table and felt his fingers brushing against her skin. "That's better," she whispered, and turned back to face him. "Let me." She reached for his top shirt button, and at that moment the sundress fell to her waist and her full, firm, pale breasts were free. Michel gasped and bent down to kiss her mouth. Too hard, Iris thought, wincing. I shall have to teach him things. His hands on her bare shoulders were too rough.

Moments later they were on the mattress in a tangle of fringed shawls, both naked, Michel's head between her silky white thighs. Iris was teaching him things.

CHAPTER TWENTY-EIGHT

Les Colombiers

Perhaps it was the influence of Charlie, of his direct questions, that made me ask, thought Cynthia. She immediately said, "Elizabeth! I'm sorry! Don't answer me! You don't have to!"

On the afternoon following Jean-François's explosion, the two women were alone in the gazebo, having tea. Michel and Charlie were playing tennis, and Tony had driven into town with Yves. It had been an amusing lunch, with the two old classmates joking about the eccentricities of their tutors and playing "wonder what happened to . . ." about their mutual friends. There was that bully who became a Methodist missionary in Malawi, and that con man who tried to trick the Egyptian zillionaire out of buying Harrod's.

"Sometimes I feel I have never known your son. The nightmares are the closest thing to finding out what's inside him." Cynthia stared off into the distance. The grounds were green, lush, after all the rain of April and May. "And he won't explain them. And I . . . we . . . I hold him afterwards and wonder about his secrets." She stirred the tea and then put the spoon down as if laying down or putting aside all reticence. "I hold everything in. Good manners. You know my mother. You know me. But Jean-François has never let me really touch him, and sometimes . . . ." Her voice was soft. "Sometimes I think it's too late."

Elizabeth sensed desperation. "It's time we talked. The idea of this conversation has haunted me for years. Ever since I first laid eyes on you."

Cynthia stared at her. What was she talking about?

"You know about Jean-François's brother, don't you?"

"No," Cynthia breathed. "He's never mentioned having a brother!"

"He hasn't told you anything, then? No wonder." Elizabeth poured herself more tea. "He had an identical twin brother."

"Where is he? Who is he? Did they fight? Why—"

"He's dead, Cynthia," Elizabeth's voice was calm. "An accident when the boys were ten." Neither spoke for a moment. "I can hardly believe he didn't tell you."

"Is that why—I seem to remember a strange lunch we had, when I was talking about family photographs and you were so upset you spilled the tea all over the table. Do you remember?"

Elizabeth nodded. "Yes. The pictures were of Jean-François and Jean-Paul. It just happened that you never saw a photograph of the two of them together."

Cynthia remembered thinking how gentle Jean-François had looked. The mouth was ever so slightly softer in expression. It must have been his twin. "The nightmares? Then they have something to do with the accident?"

Elizabeth nodded. "I . . . Cynthia . . . we'll talk again. I'm sorry. I find it difficult." She was wiping tears from her eyes with a fresh white handkerchief that had appeared from a pocket of the white linen dress. "So sorry," she murmured.

Cynthia stood up and moved toward her. She put her arm around her shoulders and waited for the older woman to speak again. But Elizabeth abruptly stood and whispered, "I'm sorry. Please excuse me." She walked hurriedly back to the house.

· · ·

Tony was full of charm at dinner that evening, but Charlie seemed more reserved than usual. Michel was in good spirits, and even challenged his father to a tennis game on the weekend. "Pretty daring of you," quipped Jean-François. Cynthia looked at him with new eyes. What else has he kept from me?

"So I told Elizabeth to stay put while I went to buy water for us. The next thing I knew, she was on a camel and waving merrily at me about half a kilometer away!"

"Lizzie!" groaned Michel, who adored his grand-mère. "You can't desert someone as helpless as Tony in Algeria!"

"Quite right, dear boy! I won't last! I'm not as self-sufficient as I should be."

"What happened?" Jean-François insisted, appearing to be genuinely interested. Cynthia wondered why the change in him and then thought, I won't ever know. He won't ever tell me what he thinks.

"Yes, what happened?" Michel put in.

"I had to get on this asinine beast and catch up with her! The wretched animal tried to bite me, tried to toss me off into the sand, and then swung his head around and tried spitting something very like tobacco juice all over my feet!"

"I had no idea this man would so antagonize the sweet little dromedary," Elizabeth murmured, looking down at her filet of sole. They all laughed, and Simone entered with another bottle of white wine.

Jean-François suddenly directed a question toward Charlie. "What if we sent a piece of this very good fish up to Stephanie?"

"I don't think she'd be interested. Though," Charlie hastened to add, "it is very good, I agree." He realized that the girl's father had not the slightest comprehension of what his daughter was suffering from. It was only the third or fourth time he'd mentioned her to Charlie.

"Do you think she's making progress?" was the next direct question.

"I spoke with Dr. Marceau on the telephone this afternoon, and . . . well, I think it would be a good idea for you and Cynthia and me to talk after dinner." Charlie was worried. The results of Stephanie's physical examination had been a disappointment.

Elizabeth turned to Tony. "And how was it, seeing Yves again?"

Tony laughed. "He looks so much the same after all these years! I could hardly believe it. You know, when you're that young—excuse me, Michel, this is someone ancient talking!" Michel grinned. "You think you'll never have gray hair, never have a wrinkle, and it's all so gradual that you don't see yourself anymore . . ." Charlie thought of Stephanie upstairs. She didn't know what she looked like. "And so, when a contemporary looms into view, you're usually shocked. But not so with Yves." He sipped his wine and smiled. "Incidentally, he thinks the world of you, Cynthia."

She was pleased. "Well, he's pretty wonderful, so I'm highly complimented." She didn't say that he had invited her for lunch as soon as she had a spare moment. She wondered if it concerned Tony.

Strawberries from the garden were brought in, and a silver pitcher of cream. Talk over coffee, over cognac, in the *fumoir* afterwards, was of banking, which Tony was involved in, and of what would happen to Switzerland in 1992. The country's having refused to join the European Community would change nothing, according to Jean-François. "Look at us geographically," he emphasized. "And historically . . ."

Charlie waited for a sign that they should talk privately, but none came. Not for the first time, the psychiatrist wondered about Jean-François. He glanced at Elizabeth and thought, She must know. Then he looked at Cynthia, bright-eyed, listening, interested. Charlie thought, She doesn't know. He has never let her know him. The words of the evening before came back to him. "I hate you! You're just like her!" Was it jealousy? The feeling he owned his mother, owned his wife? "You never watched *me*!" Was that what he had said? Who was Elizabeth watching, then? Charlie took a sip of the cognac and started to reach for the large brown leather humidor. "Cynthia, may I?" She smiled and nodded. "Please do. Help yourself. There are clippers in there somewhere."

"No, no. I mean, shall I go outside to smoke it?"

She laughed. "No, Charlie! I'm a strange woman—I adore the smell of a good cigar!" Tony smiled at her, and took the humidor from Charlie.

"I'm a strange woman, too," Elizabeth said. "You know Davidoff is still alive. I saw the cigar czar himself taking a walk downtown the other day. That Russian must be about eighty."

Tony chimed in. "Davidoff? Wonderful! Great country, Switzerland!" He grinned at Cynthia and Elizabeth as he struck the match and turned the Cuban cigar slowly. Then he looked at Charlie, who appeared to be blissfully happy. "Yes, Charlie. Lucky us. Good cigars and . . ." he winked. "Strange women."

· · ·

"I think I run to get away from everyone. I think it's to leave it all behind." Cynthia lay on her side, propped on one elbow. Her legs were outstretched, and she held a green leaf to her lips as she spoke.

Charlie had come upon her on one of his long "thinking" walks, and she'd waved, circled part of the vineyard, and come back to him. He'd never seen her in shorts before. She looked great—long legs, golden tan, hair in a pony-tail, face flushed with the heat.

Now they sat under an oak tree and gazed off into the distance at the vines. Row upon row on the hillside, soaking in the summer sun after all the spring rains that would culminate in their autumn harvest.

Charlie ran his finger across the wire spirals of his notebook and said nothing. It was so new to see her this way. The imperfect Cynthia, actually perspiring, without lipstick, with white-blonde hair mussed prettily in the dark green ribbon. Perhaps she was really "away," and a different person from the one who organized Les Colombiers so capably.

"And what do *you* leave behind?" she asked, surprising him.

"What do you mean?" He sat up on one elbow in the khaki trousers and Topsiders. His blue plaid shirt was open at the neck showing how tanned he'd become playing tennis.

"In the States. Home. All those phone calls every afternoon." Cynthia smiled at him. "Sorry. But I'm curious."

"The phone calls are business. I'm a psychiatrist, but I'm also—well, let's just say I wasn't always one. I graduated from Harvard and then went into my uncle's business, which I hated. It was insurance. He died and left it all to me. Feeling guilty as hell about it, I sold the company." He laughed. "I went crazy at that company. I was so young to have it dropped into my lap, and my uncle's heart attack was so sudden that he had not designated a successor." Charlie smiled at her. "Just imagine me—this twenty-three-year-old as head of an insurance company in Hartford, Connecticut. I'd stroll in every day with an empty briefcase. No! No, I take it back. I usually had a Hershey bar in the bottom and a Sidney Sheldon or Irwin Shaw paperback."

Cynthia shook her head in amazement. "But didn't you work at all?"

"Not really. I had a wonderful office, though."

"Well, what happened?"

"I was going through a stage of wondering what I wanted, and all I knew was that I didn't want to bet on people getting sick, having accidents, and dying. I saw it as a giant crap game, with people giving me money to guarantee the worst."

"Never would have thought of it that way!" Cynthia stared at him. Insurance was a great part of her bookkeeping. Against theft, against loss during shipping, against water damage, against fire. All of Jean-François's Egyptian artifacts were behind bulletproof glass in the bowels of the chateau. "So what did you do? How did you get out of it?"

"I realized I was very interested in why people behaved the way they did. My secretary's husband was taking antidepressants, which was quite a new thing in those days, and I found myself asking her all sorts of questions about the situation. I became her confidant, I guess, and soon found myself going to the library and reading all I could about enzymes, hormones, the pituitary gland, and all sorts of body chemicals. Then I began reading about stress and optimism and the effect of a positive outlook on the immune system."

"But that's only now being researched!"

Charlie smiled. "How did you know that?"

"Because I read about it only a few days ago. They are coaching cancer patients in dealing with pessimism, and it seems that they are producing more active T-cells."

"And do you know what T-cells are?" Charlie tried not to show his incredulity.

"Of course I do!" She sat up and swung her legs under her. "They fight infection. I believe that T-cells are what people with the AIDS virus aren't producing enough of."

"Hmmmm . . ." Charlie looked down at his notebook. "So you read these articles, do you?"

"When I can."

They didn't speak for a moment, and then Cynthia said, "Tell me what happened next. In Hartford."

"Well, it took me almost two years to realize I had to do something else.

Finally, I enrolled in night school. All premed courses, and then I began to think psychiatry was the only thing I wanted. So I sold the insurance company and used some of the money for all the years of study. Most of it went into a real-estate firm in Boston. Maybe you've heard of it. I kept the old name. Harcum and Rowlands?"

"That's it? Why, everybody knows it! It's the top one." Cynthia laughed. "I can't believe you're involved in that! How really . . ." she hesitated. "Fascinating."

"I like it. Actually, I love it. But another part of me wants to be in a place like this, writing. Working at my research papers." He paused. "I have to have my escapes from Boston."

"What about your patients? You can't just desert them."

"Oh, I deal with very few nowadays, and your call came at the best time for me. I wanted to stay on in Switzerland."

Cynthia suddenly realized that Charlie, in his perpetual khaki trousers and plaid shirts, was a man of means. She had never thought of him as a businessman, as a practical planner. He had always appeared good-humored, listening, sometimes half in a conversation and half off by himself. As though he were watching a play. "There are two very different sides to you," she said, not looking at him but stroking the delicate veins of an oak leaf.

He laughed. "I hope there are more than two! That's what makes being a shrink so much fun!"

She laughed with him. Then, seeing his watch, she said, "I have to go back." She stood up and brushed the grass from her shorts. Her long legs were perfect, her stomach was flat, the green T-shirt clung to her small breasts.

"I'll walk with you." Charlie tucked the pen in his breast pocket and grabbed the notebook. "There's another reason why I came to Les Colombiers."

"Stephanie. You mean Stephanie, don't you?"

"Yes. Before I knew her as a person, she was a case. The number of anorexics in the States is growing every year. Mostly teenage girls, overachievers in school, overly anxious to please their parents—to earn their love."

"Do you think she doesn't think I love her?"

He nodded. "But I don't think that's your fault." He sighed. "I'm not supposed to use words like that, but—"

Cynthia finished for him. "But you knew I would be thinking the word 'fault,' and it was the only way to get through to me."

"Very clever," he said. "I think a doctor can study and read and think and observe, but there comes a time when he has to decide what to do on his own. Which brings me—"

"To what you want to say to Stephanie." Cynthia sighed. She dreaded this. They'd had the conversation before.

"Right. Dr. Marceau thinks I'm being too easy on her. And I must say she is still in lousy shape physically, and summer is here. I am disappointed."

"In her?"

"No. Perhaps in my reading of her. In the way I've handled the case." They were walking in lockstep through a freshly mown green field. "And I use the word 'case' on purpose. Not to be cold, but to remind myself that though I love her as a young girl, she *is* a case. I am responsible for what happens to her."

Cynthia's voice was soft. "You love Stephanie?" How open he is, she thought. How free to be able to say something like that.

He nodded. "She's going to be a wonderful woman someday, but now she's confused, that's all." He added, "And she is very lovable. She doesn't think so, though."

The house was before them. Simone was waving her white apron up and down. Cynthia sighed and said, "It's probably the telephone for me. Or the wine wasn't delivered or there's a problem with the water." Just when Elizabeth and Tony have gone and the curator from London is due any minute. Something else. She shook her head and both of them walked more quickly. "Don't you see why I want to run away?"

The Beau Rivage

The notes began to come to Iris's suite at the hotel. Maddeningly slipped under the door. "I don't think I'll tell Monsieur Colbert about this," Iris confided to Anna. "What can he do, anyway?" Except assume I have had a checkered career, she nodded silently. Which I have.

Iris, following her habit of staying in bed on Mondays, sipped her Dom Perignon and orange juice with a drop of Cointreau. "Mimosas, I adore," she cooed as she drank from the icy stemmed goblet. The maid was straightening the lace-edged pillow cases behind her mistress. ZiZou was snoring on a pink velvet cushion near Iris's ankles; the telephone was within reach, along with several issues of *Vogue*, both the French and American editions. Iris thumbed through *Elle*, but she was distracted. She reached for the latest missive on the bedside table and opened the envelope. YOU'LL BE SORRY. Iris blinked. I've practically never been sorry, she said to herself. I can't remember the feeling. Etienne had told her years ago she was one of those people who were not sorry for having done something, but only for having got caught at it. She had nodded vehemently.

Iris called room service and requested they serve her dinner at seven o'clock, so that she could have a long night of beauty sleep. She had no way of knowing that the room-service waiters flipped francs for the privilege of entering her suite. Her shapely charms were usually well displayed in a negligee "no thicker than a spider's web," in the words of one of the young Spaniards. After deciding upon tortellini with salmon and filet mignon, very rare, and asparagus with Hollandaise sauce, she felt drowsy. She fought against sleep as she read about the latest "in" French spa but dessert was to be chocolate mousse with fresh strawberries and cream, and she really couldn't imagine existing on a lettuce leaf and designer water, no matter how much it cost per day.

Iris slept and Iris dreamed. She was in a ballroom, dressed in a long white dress, a simple string of pearls around her neck. The walls were lined with hundreds of men, but not one of them came forward to take her arm, and though the scene made her imagine dancing, there was no music. Just silence and all those men with faces she could almost recognize. She thought she saw Harry, then there was Cutter, or was it? Iris began to feel panicked, alone in the center of the tremendous room, under a sparkling chandelier. She was confused, and wanted someone to come to her. She found she couldn't move away from where she stood. It was as if she were paralyzed, unable to shorten the distance between her aloneness and the men with shadowy faces. Then someone in the crowd said, "You'll be sorry."

Iris woke with a little cry, and ZiZou yelped and jumped off the bed as the doorbell of the suite rang. It was time for the porter to take the poodle to the park. Exactly four o'clock. Iris sighed and reached for the Baccarat goblet, then leaned back upon the pillows, trying to understand the dream. *You'll be sorry. You'll be sorry. You'll be sorry.* The phrase disturbed her. She picked up the note where it lay on the sheet, and tore it into little pieces, lengthwise and then crosswise, and then she put them all back into the envelope.

Cologny

Veronique carefully folded her napkin beside the cheese plate and swallowed the last of her white wine. When she heard the Mercedes start she rushed from the table and down the hallway and out the kitchen door. A sick cook, a night off for the maid, an empty kitchen and a simple dinner. It all meant no one was there to see her. Veronique watched Louis's car turn left at the end of the driveway. Ha! To town to pick up some papers! She ran across the gravel and in seconds was in her little black Jaguar following her husband on the road. The road towards France.

· · ·

The next evening, Cynthia and Veronique met for dinner at La Perle du Lac. Situated in a lovely park right on the lake, it was one of the most elegant restaurants in Geneva. "Your family can live without you for one meal,"

Veronique had insisted. Now she sat down in her red and white silk dress and grinned. Her hair was cut these days in a little cap of curls, and somehow the light, fluffy style made her seem even more animated than usual.

"So you kept our rendezvous," she said. "I have to talk to you, Cynthia, and I didn't want to risk anyone else hearing. I mean household servants especially. Louis is on a business trip. Or so he says." Veronique raised her eyebrows. A waiter materialized and they discussed wine and then decided to have a bottle of Moët et Chandon.

Cynthia looked around. Nearly every table was full. They were outdoors on a terrace with the water, a streak of black just a few meters away. Veronique lived on the other side of the lake, but Les Colombiers was just down the road. "Okay. I'm ready. What have you done now? Or is it Gérard who's done something?" Cynthia shook out the big damask napkin.

"It's not me! It's not Gérard!" Veronique leaned forward and hissed. "It's Louis! He's having an affair!"

Cynthia resisted the impulse to say, *It's about time.* Veronique had been unfaithful to Louis for as long as she could remember. Yes, the first lunch. Veronique said it was self-preservation—that her marriage would have ended years ago if she'd had to depend upon her husband for excitement. Cynthia kept her voice even as she asked, "How do you know?"

"I followed him. Too many times in the last month after dinner he's had some reason to go back into town. Back to Genève. *Oui, absolutamente!* I didn't believe a word of it. So I—how do you say it in those gangster movies?—put my tail on him."

Cynthia's first reaction was amazement. Stodgy, quiet, dull banker Louis! Her second thought was, Please, don't let Veronique speak English tonight, because I will laugh at everything she says. A few days ago she had told Cynthia she had bought a "snailskin belt," and she talked about "not having belief in my hears." "Speak French," Cynthia insisted now.

"So where does he go? To France. To a little house with a big dog out front. The dog barked his head off, and I thought Louis and this woman might come out to see what was wrong, so I turned around and drove home." She gulped the champagne placed before her. "So now I know everything." She leaned back in the chair as if she wanted to fan herself from exhaustion.

"What do you mean, you know everything?"

"I know when he sees her, if they stay at home or go to a bistro for dinner or drinks. I know."

Cynthia ordered lake perch, and Veronique said, *"Moi aussi,"* and the waiter suggested mixed salads and disappeared.

"How do you know if he goes to see her or not? How?" Cynthia insisted. "Are you racing around in the Jag behind him every time he leaves the house?"

"Simple mathematics." Veronique smiled proudly. "I know it's fifteen kilometers to her house, and every evening when he comes home from work and walks in the garden and every morning while he's in the shower, I dash out to the garage and check the kilometer thing."

Cynthia began to laugh. Veronique didn't so much care who the Frenchwoman was, or that her husband was betraying her. But the idea of one-upmanship, that he hadn't fooled her, was enough to make her content. "So, *cherie*, fifteen kilometers means her house, drinks and bed. Thirty is a round trip, of course. Thirty-five kilometers means a romantic dinner at the Auberge Gaston down the road. They have liver with onions as a specialty, so that's what Louis orders every time." She shrugged nonchalantly. "His favorite. It's eleven kilometers to town, so I know if he sees her on the way home from the bank." Taking another sip of champagne, she philosophized, "You can't depend on men, Cynthia. That we know." Cynthia was still laughing. "But mathematics! Whether it's the value of a jewel or the number of kilometers to Louis's mistress in France, *that's* dependable."

Les Colombiers

"He's not here yet?" Charlie leaned forward in the big wing chair in the *fumoir*. It was just past six in the evening.

Cynthia sat on the sofa across from him, looking worried. The pink linen dress showed her narrow hips and small waist; a pink quartz necklace sparkled around her neck. "He's not coming."

A typical example of the absent, mysterious father figure, said Charlie to himself. No wonder Stephanie rarely talked about him. It was all "my mother this" and "my mother that." "Well, I'm sorry you have to decide this alone. Dr. Marceau and I have talked, and it's his opinion that medically she is abusing herself to such a degree . . ." He sighed and crossed his legs. "It's just that we cannot allow it to go on much longer."

"What are you proposing? Force-feeding her?" Cynthia's throat felt tight. She realized she was frightened. Had been terribly frightened since the phone call, all those months ago.

"She still has no period. She is low in electrolytes, which has an effect on the regularity of her heartbeat. That alone is dangerous. Her vision is blurred. Cramps in her legs at night, which she wouldn't tell me about, are the result of not enough potassium. Her gums bleed because she hasn't enough vitamin C . . ." Cynthia's face was full of such anguish that he could not go on.

"What do we do?" Cynthia's voice was only a whisper.

"Dr. Marceau wants her to go to a hospital to be put on a strict refeeding program, which involves rewards for gaining weight. She will have no privacy, no chance to hide food, and under this constant supervision she will gain weight."

"What aren't you saying, Charlie?"

He leaned back in the chair. "I'm saying that that regime is fine for her body, but it is the most terrifying program imaginable for her emotionally. What she fears most is losing control." He stood up and walked to the carved oak mantel and leaned one elbow on it. His eyes were troubled, a golden brown in the suntanned face. "Cynthia, it's a terrible decision for you to make on your own."

"Jean-François is always very busy. He doesn't consider this his affair."

"Not his affair!" Charlie almost shouted. "That his daughter is . . ." He nearly said *dying*, but stopped himself. She wouldn't die because there were too many people who wouldn't let her. Alone she would die. Never realizing, never thinking it was possible.

"The house and the children, you know." Cynthia looked down at her hands folded in her lap.

"Okay." Charlie stood up and pushed his hands into the pockets of his white trousers. "I'll be very straightforward with you. When I arrived here, she was hostile to me, then she played along for a while, but the idea was, 'I'll pretend to pay attention, pretend to talk to you, and not let it affect me. This is my secret. My secret is what I eat. You can't touch that. Nothing else in my life is controllable, just what I put into my mouth.' Hostility is normal."

"She seems anything but hostile to you now. I feel the hostility directed at me."

"Before we talk about where you fit in, she has had to accept me as a listener. First, just a listener with no judgmental ideas, no criticism. None of this, 'But you are ruining your health, you are such a pretty girl,' stuff. I've tried to comprehend how she sees her world. I wanted her to tell me how she feels. For a while she had nothing to say."

"Why not?"

"Because, as is often the case with anorexics, they don't really have a sense of who they are. She had really never considered how she felt. Stephanie said she thought she'd always been told how to feel."

Cynthia sat up very straight in the chair. Her jaw muscle tightened. He went on. "It's the idea that she sees herself reflected in the eyes of everyone around her, but there is a blank when she looks in the mirror. She is your daughter and she is an honor student and she is class vice-president and she won the tennis championship at the club last year." He raised his hands in a restraining gesture. "I know it's hard to comprehend, but she feels mystified as to who she really is inside. She sees all the things I've said as how other people see her. She says she is afraid that if she lets up for one minute, it will all be swept away."

"Why?" Cynthia asked, leaning forward.

"She's running as fast as she can to *be* all these things for other people, and if she relaxes the real Stephanie will come forward. And that Stephanie will be exposed as unpopular and ugly and stupid." He grimaced. "And fat." He was silent for a moment. "The dieting in the States now is ridiculous. They've done surveys of kids in the third grade and found that almost half of them, especially the girls, thought they were too fat. And many of them had already been on diets! At age eight!" His voice was disgusted. "All the advertising we are bombarded with! Every successful career woman is thin. Every good mother holding a box of detergent on television is thin. And fat people are greedy and lazy." He shook his head and continued, "Anorexia only exists in the industrialized countries, where we have plenty to eat and prize thinness. The disease doesn't exist in the Third World." He put an elbow up on the mantel again. "I could talk about it all day. Mysticism. Denial of the body. Spiritual superiority. What is also interesting is that in these teenage girls, all secondary sexual characteristics disappear. No curves, no breasts, no menses. I don't have the idea with Stephanie that she wants to deny her femaleness. But many girls do. It frightens them, and when they stop eating, these adolescent changes go away. They don't progress into womanhood."

"What about boys? Men and anorexia?"

"Very rare until recently." Charlie was silent. He hated telling her about the treatment Dr. Marceau recommended, but how could he not? And yet, by telling her, he knew he would turn her against it and she would give him one more chance to reach Stephanie. His way. "Cynthia, Dr. Marceau isn't here, so you can't ask him anything." I'll try to be fair, he told himself. "Do you have any questions about the hospital program?"

"You didn't tell me if they would force-feed her?"

"In a life-threatening situation, yes. A tube through the nose to the stomach, and drips to stop dehydration."

Cynthia shuddered. "But what did you say about rewards for gaining weight?"

"Its rewards . . . well, if you do *not* go along with the program you are deprived of . . . certain privileges."

"Like what? Do you mean she would be kept longer in the hospital if she didn't gain weight?"

"Television would be denied her if she refused to eat, or she might be deprived of visiting privileges, or not allowed to make or receive telephone calls."

Cynthia was silent.

Charlie didn't say anything. He knew of cases in England in which girls were not allowed out of bed until they had gained ten pounds. Books were taken away, pencil and paper for writing letters were not allowed, and sometimes pillows were confiscated and the patient was not allowed to sit up. All as a punishment for not eating, for not gaining weight. "That is the plan Dr. Marceau wants for Stephanie. Once she is in the hospital, it is difficult for you or me to have any say about her treatment."

"Please, Charlie! What do you think would be best for her? Would it be good for me to be removed from all this? To let her be treated as a patient, as a very sick person who doesn't know what's best for herself anymore?"

"This behavior-modification idea came into vogue in the 1970s, but it's still widely used. I'm opposed to it."

Cynthia tried to smile. "Thank you. So am I."

"It's putting a fragile personality, whose only sense of control lies in maintaining this low weight, into a situation of punishment. It usually results in depression, even suicide attempts, as their only control is taken away. I can't sanction it." He stopped. "But what I want to do, with your okay, is to have Dr. Marceau explain to her all the things that are happening to her body. She knows it now, and I know it's just one thing she worries about, but I think she should hear it from him. I don't think it'll make a difference, by the way. I want him also to tell her about the hospital regime."

"I find that idea absolutely terrifying."

"Well, maybe she will too. If we could get her to eat a little more while I continue grappling with this psyche of hers . . ."

Cynthia had tears in her eyes. "I keep wondering if it's something I did as a mother. Did I make an issue of her eating her spinach? Did I talk about—"

"Stop it, Cynthia!" His voice was kind but firm. "Don't accept blame so easily! Please!" She closed her mouth and leaned back in the chair. He's right, she thought. I've gotten in the habit of letting Jean-François blame me for everything that goes wrong. Charlie went on, "I do think Stephanie constantly compares herself to you. She sees you as perfection, and yet there is this ambivalence about your life. I can't say any more without compromising her, and maybe making you feel awkward when you're with her."

"All right. What can I do now? That's my question."

"Just be there for her. Try to make her understand you love her. Love without reservation." Charlie stared out the window at the dusk. The green leaves were thick, and smelled fresh through the open windows. No screens, he thought. Clean. The swans were just visible in the fading light. Proud, serene, gliding on the smooth as glass water. Switzerland. Some purity here, somehow. "I don't know why, Cynthia, but I think—I *feel* more than think —that Stephanie is on the verge of a breakthrough." He spoke softly, as if to himself. "Something is going to happen."

CHAPTER TWENTY-NINE

The Beau Rivage

"Christ!" Jean-François was saying. "It's all going to hell in a basket!" He waved the glass of Scotch at Iris from where he sat on the coral loveseat. She listened as he went on. Wound up. Tired. Tense. Sometimes they had dinner in Le Chat Botté downstairs, or a drink in the bar, but Jean-François preferred staying in the suite. Jean-François saw her three or four times a week. Iris smoothed the lime green silk dress over her knees, and then recrossed her legs. She sipped the champagne and watched his face. "It's this Elisabeth Kopp affair. I think the whole thing will blow up in everybody's face within a month. It appears her fool husband has been laundering money."

The name was familiar to Iris. Kopp was the first woman member of a Swiss government, in a country where women couldn't vote in federal elections until 1971. An attractive brunette, she was known to be extremely bright, efficient, worthy of her position.

"It's her husband, really. He's the one. We all knew about him. I mean, we bankers. I think it was a setup. But she warned him that there was to be an investigation of his firm."

"Wouldn't that be the most natural thing in the world to do? To tell her husband!" Iris insisted.

"No. Not if you're Justice Minister. Not if you're going to be President of Switzerland next year."

Iris winced. "I didn't realize she was that high up."

Jean-François nodded. Thank God Iris reads the papers, he thought. Cynthia used to be so good about it, but since the beginning of the summer, she is distracted and can't seem to concentrate on anything. "Vice-president now, and a damned good one." He shook his head. "And all this money-laundering scandal linked to someone that well known is such bad publicity for bankers—for all of Switzerland, really."

"You amaze me sometimes," Iris said softly.

"Why?" Jean-François realized his tone was softer, too. Iris is good with me, he thought.

"You are so patriotic toward this country, toward what it stands for. It's a beautiful thing to see." She went on. "From my great distance, I look at the United States with a jaundiced eye, and read about how Reagan's cronies have left the White House with millions, and that the situation with the homeless is worse than ever, and I don't feel the least bit responsible. Even if I lived there, I wouldn't feel it had anything to do with me. I guess that's the difference. You seem to feel a personal responsibility for what goes on in Switzerland."

Jean-François nodded. "Maybe I do. We're a proud country and there are just six million of us. I care very deeply about what the rest of the world thinks of Switzerland."

Hoping to distract him from the Kopp affair, she said, "Why don't you take off that tie? And why don't we take a nap before dinner? Would you like that? A back rub? Maybe I could pet you a little bit."

Jean-François smiled and jerked the tie away from his throat, then pulled at the buttons of his shirt.

In moments they were standing in Iris's big bedroom, and he was tearing the few clothes she wore away from her. She only wore a dress and lacy panties, which were transparent, and wet with her sweetness. Jean-François put her down on the bed on her back, and when he was naked, he thirstily began to suck at the most lovely nipples he'd ever seen. Iris had insisted he always wait a few minutes before entering her, and he told himself he would try. The intensity was always pounding in his head, his body. The urgency of having a woman made him hurry. But tonight he bent down, and when she opened her thighs and whispered, "Please," he gently spread her pink lips and methodically, back and forth, licked the juices from her. In a few minutes, when she could no longer stop herself, Iris screamed and raked his back with her nails. Jean-François continued until she was sobbing and had buried her face in a pillow to stifle her shouts. "Please come inside me! Please!" she insisted, and he rose and entered her easily with one sure thrust of his lean, tanned body.

"I love you," she cried as she held on to his shoulders and, with closed eyes, fell into his rhythm. "I love you."

Jean-François could think of nothing. For him it was all feeling. It was a taste in his mouth like honey, it was a stroking of his loins with a warm sweetness he could never remember afterwards. He could not cry out *I love you* any more than he could have stopped what was happening to him, starting at his toes. Jean-François closed his eyes and groaned in ecstasy. No words, no thoughts, no pictures flashed behind his lids. He cried out like an animal at the end, and then sank, exhausted, beside her on the bed. Iris smoothed a lock of his black hair away from his perspiring forehead and kissed his eyes and hoped he would forget what she'd said.

Les Colombiers

Cynthia stood in the open living-room doorway and wondered how to interrupt Charlie and Elizabeth, who were deep in a discussion. She started out to the terrace and then heard Charlie say, "If an early relationship was complicated, sometimes a person cannot express love in a sexual way. He may only be able to have sex with someone he doesn't love."

"So that is a big cause of infidelity?" Elizabeth was asking.

"*Can* be a cause of it," the psychiatrist agreed carefully. "But there are men who constantly seek conquests, new experiences in bed, to prove themselves lovable. Or, at middle age, to prove that they are still attractive, virile, strong. The wife, whatever is between them, has little to do with it."

"May I listen?" Cynthia asked shyly.

"Of course, darling!" Elizabeth seemed glad to see her, and Charlie immediately pulled a wicker chair up to the glass table holding their glasses of lemonade. He hardly looked at Cynthia, but continued, "There is something new, according to a sex therapist called Dagmar O'Connor. She sees a 'choir-boy/stud complex' growing prevalent among women."

Cynthia was all ears, fascinated, not speaking. She had never talked about sex with a man in her life. Only Jean-François's way of talking about it, which was to belittle her and call her cold. Having sex—for she no longer thought of it as making love—was a joyless exercise with someone who bullied her. And here in the sunlight, at eleven o'clock in the morning, this conversation was taking place! It was as easy as discussing a tennis match. She found herself staring at Charlie's mouth and wondering, Would he be as free with a woman in bed as he is with the two of us, talking about it?

"It's the flip side of the madonna/whore complex. A woman is attracted by men she sees on the street, but she cannot be physically aroused by the man she loves at home, the father of her children."

"Interesting," Elizabeth said. "Of course it seems reasonable. I've just never heard of it."

Charlie didn't know whether to attempt to direct the conversation or not. There were so many things he wished he could let Cynthia know. She was like a starving child in ways. The thought shocked him when he connected it to Stephanie upstairs. But she was starving too. To be touched. Emotionally and physically.

"Infidelity," he mused aloud. "There are all kinds of reasons. Some men are terrified to have only one woman in their lives. One is the counterweight to the other. There is a terror of attachment. And so much power is involved. Not only power over another person, but a sense of being able to fill some emptiness inside themselves. Some men only feel whole, complete, when they are literally in the throes of sexual intercourse." He stopped. Cynthia was staring at his hands so intensely that he thought he could feel heat from her. "It's a starvation. They long to be satisfied with something that's been missing since childhood. So . . ." He stopped. My God, he thought, I'm sitting here with the mother and the wife of a man with the most full-blown sexual problems I've ever seen. He smiled. "Okay, class! Any questions?"

Both Elizabeth and Cynthia laughed. "You make it sound like an addiction to alcohol, to drugs," Cynthia said.

"It is just that. A craving to be satisfied, but the satisfaction is short-lived. The man has to move on. New woman, new conquest. There is a recklessness about it. And a thirst for what the man sees as an almost whorish kind of woman whom he can have and leave. His wife is on a pedestal, the virgin, the mother of his children. He needs other women constantly, but they only nourish him temporarily. This kind of man cannot form a lasting attachment."

"But infidelity implies that they are married. Isn't that a lasting attachment?" insisted Cynthia.

His voice was very gentle. "There are all kinds of attachments, aren't there? Some are emotional and some are . . ." Oh, how he hated to hurt her!

She was staring, green-eyed, trusting, at his face. "And some have to do with property and children. Isn't that right?"

Neither Elizabeth nor Charlie said anything. Why can't I think of words? Charlie castigated himself. Just at that moment, Simone appeared in the doorway to announce lunch.

They stood and walked in silence into the house. Elizabeth was wondering if anything could have changed her son as a little boy. If anything she could have done would have prevented his becoming the selfish, cold man he now was. A lot of what he is is my fault, she thought as she took her place at the dining-room table and shook out the white damask napkin.

Cynthia was thinking of attachments. I am just what Veronique and Yves tell me I am: the chatelaine of Les Colombiers. I am what Stephanie thinks I am: trying to be a perfect person, fulfilling my duties all the days of every season, unfolding into years. Days and nights of duties. She suddenly looked again at Charlie's mouth. Jean-François had stopped kissing her years ago.

"Mother!" It was Michel at the opposite end of the table. "You're blushing! All I did was ask for the mustard!"

. . .

Even though the Genevois said, "It only lasts five minutes, so make the best of it," Cynthia felt the summer dragging by. She tried to swim every morning, and sensed that her day was not complete when she didn't manage to get into the icy water of the pool. With every passing week, it and the lake would both be warmer. Michel was already windsurfing without a wetsuit at the edge of the lawn. "Summer really doesn't begin until the Bol d'Or," she had told Charlie earlier. To her surprise, he'd said he'd sailed in the race the year before, adding cryptically, "I'm not totally new to Geneva." The Bol d'Or, Europe's biggest sailing race on a lake, usually took place in mid-June. Starting at nine on a Saturday morning, the boats all sailed up the lake and back, covering a course of one hundred sixty kilometers. "A catamaran can do it in about nine hours, but we straggled back to the Société Nautique after twenty-four!"

"But the Société Nautique—" she began.

"Oldest yacht club in Switzerland," he interjected.

She wanted to know how he even *knew* that, but decided not to ask. And how did he race, and with whom? And how does he know so much about Geneva? He'd been the one to tell her about the bomb shelters. It seemed that every newly built house had to have one. "It's been the law for about twenty years," he laughed at her surprise.

"There isn't one at Les Colombiers."

"That's because this is an old house. So we'll all have to huddle underground in the shelter at Chambesy with the other villagers."

Sometimes Cynthia felt she'd known Charlie all her life, but then she told herself it was because he was American, because he knew Boston, because he wore Topsiders. Then she denied that, for Michel and all his friends, whether Swiss, American, French, or Italian, had sort of an international uniform based on blue jeans, polo shirts, and Topsiders. Charlie was a hundred percent American, but his French was quite good, he seemed to know as much about the European Community as any dinner guest they'd ever had, and he was totally relaxed in the household. It occurred to Cynthia that she would miss him when all this was over.

Over. The summer seemed leaden. The days drooped past. Michel was away several afternoons a week with no explanation; Stephanie, upstairs in her room, seemed to be making little headway, and Jean-François, though in Geneva most of the time, was often at business dinners that went on till after midnight. Charlie was always good company, however, and Cynthia found she liked it when she discovered him in a corner of the living room, reading, or sitting under a tree with his notebook on his lap. He would put his work aside with a smile and make time to talk to her.

Still, Cynthia looked forward to the return of Tony Forbes-Todd, and mentally planned dinner parties around him, with Yves and Veronique and Louis. Elizabeth and Tony had developed the habit of arriving unannounced, which was fun for everyone. She and Jean-François seemed to be the only ones who didn't enjoy each other unreservedly. But he was so moody, so mercurial, that Cynthia actually preferred it when he suddenly announced at six, after a day at the bank, that he was "going out." And if he didn't care about having people around, that was fine, too. Charlie got on with everyone and was easygoing and genial—in short, the perfect host. But there was a mystery about Tony. She fantasized about him. She told herself it was childish, but she remembered the way he looked at her . . .

Cynthia had never instigated many gatherings at the chateau, for the salon was so grand, so enormous, that even in the winter with both fireplaces burning, it was difficult to make people feel comfortable. But in summer, with the doors open to the lake, using the terrace as the dining room, the setting was dreamlike. There was no hunting allowed in the canton de Vaud, and Cynthia often saw blue herons in the morning, hawks circling lazily in the sky, and, of course, geese and ducks and the perpetual swans, serene, white as snow, gliding on the water. Michel counted twenty-four one night at dinner.

. . .

The Saturday of the Bol d'Or arrived, hot and clear and bright, and Cynthia impetuously called Veronique and Louis and Pamela and Jacques to come for a picnic. Pamela, whom she had seen at a few drinks parties, seemed to be adjusting to Geneva surprisingly well. It was the fiftieth anniversary of the race and there were six hundred fifty boats entered. The cook prepared several kinds of salads, and Simone laid out a buffet of patés and cheeses and melon with prosciutto on the terrace. The lake was white with sails; then within a few minutes ablaze with bright spinnakers. An Englishman they only knew as Patrick floated above it all in one of his hot-air balloons. Charlie passed Michel the binoculars. "See that white eight-meter?" he asked, and Michel nodded. "That used to belong to Switzerland's last general, General Guisan from Lausanne—"

"Last?" asked Pamela. "What do you mean last?"

"We only have a general in wartime," answered Jean-François. "Appointed by the Federal Assembly."

"The boat was called *Le Tigre* and it was sold to someone who—" Suddenly a blast from a trumpet coming over the water interrupted Charlie. "The boat is now known as *Le Tigre à Poil*, or the *Naked Tiger*, because the owner likes to sail naked and demands that everyone on board go naked. He also plays the trumpet." There was another series of notes.

"Give me those binoculars!" cried Veronique.

They all laughed at her, refilled their wineglasses with the chilled Aigle from Sierre in the Valais, and bantered away the rest of the afternoon. Strawberries from the garden were served in a cut-glass bowl, and the guests helped themselves with cries of delight, for the berries were as sweet as honey. Jean-François smiled at Cynthia several times for no reason, and she, ever hopeful of connecting emotionally with him, moved her chair next to his and put her hand on his bare, suntanned forearm. So she was surprised when she heard him say a few moments later, "I have to go into town."

Veronique and Cynthia tried not to look at each other, and were silent as the men stood and bid their host *au revoir* and *merci*. Both women found themselves staring down at Veronique's still-bruised shins.

The moment Jean-François had left the terrace, Charlie moved into his chair and said almost under his breath, "It isn't over yet."

Cynthia heard him and leaned forward, looking mystified. Charlie merely winked at her, and then carefully dropped two strawberries into her wineglass.

· · ·

"Oh, yes! Of course I'm glad you feel free enough to call and ask! I think we can find a bed for you tomorrow night." Cynthia was smiling into the phone. She felt a strange sort of giddiness suddenly, and hoped it didn't show. "Well, it's because you're a friend of Elizabeth's, and she *is* my mother-in-law," she teased. Don't say his name, she told herself. You might say it with too much affection in your voice. Don't say it. She listened to him and then said cordially, "Okay. So we'll expect you for dinner. No. Elizabeth won't be here. She dashed back to Paris day before yesterday." Cynthia listened. "Yes, yes. Sounds wonderful."

She hung up and sank back into the pink flowered sofa cushions with a great sigh, arms raised over her head. I shouldn't dream about him, but I do. I shouldn't think about being kissed by him, but I do. I suppose it's normal for married women to have these fantasies when real life is so . . . so wrong. She smiled. He was so terribly attractive. When Veronique had met him that first time, she had screamed at her for an entire lunch to have an affair with him. "Why not!" she had insisted. Cynthia stood and jammed her hands into the pockets of her white slacks. "Because I'm married!" she said aloud. Then she walked to her desk and thought of his rather lovely name. Anthony Forbes-Todd.

"Pardon, Madame Colbert." Simone stood in the doorway. "I must—"

"*Oui.* Is it about dinner?" Cynthia thought, This is what it all comes down to. Discussing whether to have baked potatoes or rice. My life is full of details that no one cares about. Least of all, me.

"The peaches, Madame, they are not ripe. Shall I make a soufflé for dessert? Perhaps lemon?"

"*D'accord.* That would be fine, Simone." Cynthia followed Simone out of the room and then proceeded down the hall to visit her daughter before dinner. And Stephanie's dinner? More fish sticks, a small glass of milk, and a package of M&Ms. Not much had changed since June. She was still postponing the shock tactic of threatening her with the hospital. It sounded much too cruel, but perhaps Charlie was right that it was the only way to reach her.

"Stephanie, how are you?" she greeted her daughter brightly as she carefully sat down on the edge of the bed. The wan face smiled halfheartedly, but Stephanie didn't answer. Cynthia glanced around the pink bedroom, thinking, I'll never get used to the paleness, the sharp little cheekbones, and the collar bones that seem to be laid on top of her skin. But her voice remained cheerful, as though she were greeting someone returning from a picnic. "Darling, did you have a nice day?"

Vieille Ville

"What do you think of Tony Forbes-Todd?" Yves was leaning back in the wicker chair, his arms over his head. His terrace was small but sunny and brightly bedecked with terra-cotta pots of orange geraniums. They'd had a light lunch, and Pierrette had cleared the dishes away.

"I hardly know him," said Cynthia carefully. "But I like him. He handles Jean-François so well that my husband doesn't even realize he's being handled!"

"He's smooth, all right." Yves closed his eyes and tilted his face back to catch the sun. "Must say, he thinks you're really special. So chic, he said. So beautiful, he said. So elegant, he said."

"I'm blushing!" Cynthia lifted the glass of iced tea from the glass table.

"He talked a lot about Elizabeth and Jean-François."

Cynthia didn't respond. So this was the reason for the lunch. Yves couldn't keep secrets. He adored gossip. The fresher the better. *Chaud* off the press, Veronique called it.

"Aren't you going to get the least bit curious?" came the lazy voice.

"Mmmmm. I am. I guess." Cynthia took a sip from the glass and the ice cubes rattled. "Yves, did he mention that Jean-François had a twin?"

"Christ!" Yves sat up suddenly, wide-eyed, and stared at her. "So you know! I swore I didn't think you knew!"

"Elizabeth told me when she was here."

"Just then?"

"Mmmmm." Cynthia didn't look at him, but had her eyes closed behind her dark glasses and knew he was staring at her.

"And the accident. And all the messy feelings behind it."

"Okay, Yves. You can start talking now." Cynthia gave him her I-surrender voice.

"She didn't tell you about the accident?"

"All I know is that his identical twin died. Nothing else. Oh, yes, they were ten years old."

"Cynthia, do you want a glass of wine?"

"No. I love this iced tea. What—" Cynthia opened her eyes.

"Are you ready to hear something a little bit—a little bit strong?"

She took off her sunglasses and squinted at him, then nodded.

"First, I'd better tell you about the accident. It happened one spring in France. Nobody here in Switzerland knows the details. All the family vacations were at the house in the Loire Valley. Colbert had already died. So the family was really the old uncle and Elizabeth and her twin sons. Jean-François's brother—"

"Jean-Paul." Cynthia had a chilled feeling. The sun was warm, but goosebumps covered her bare arms. She resisted rubbing them away.

"Jean-Paul was smaller than Jean-François, and he always had health problems. He seemed to be the one to catch colds, he had the measles for days longer than Jean-François, he—"

"How do you know all this?" Cynthia sensed she was about to hear something she didn't want to hear. She wanted to punch holes in the story as soon as possible.

"Elizabeth talks very freely to Tony. I mean, my God, they've logged a million miles together. I trust Tony."

"Do you think Elizabeth would want me to know?"

"Cynthia! Your scruples drive me mad sometimes! This concerns your husband. Don't you want to know!?"

"*Oui.* Go on." She was staring intently at Yves's face.

"Jean-François was always after his twin to run faster, daring him to do things. He was a bully with him. And Elizabeth told Tony she always worried about Jean-Paul."

"I understand. Please." Cynthia thought of the photograph of the little boy with the sweet-looking face.

"It was in the morning, and there were workmen doing something to the roof of the main house. Les Chênes, of course. They left ladders and went off for a break. I don't know, lunch, maybe. And the two boys went up on the roof, and one of the gardeners later said he saw Jean-François waving at Jean-Paul, daring him to walk from one chimney to the other. Elizabeth kept telling Tony that she couldn't be sure, no one could ever be sure, but it seems that the two boys were holding hands and then struggling . . ."

"Maybe Jean-Paul was falling and Jean-François was trying—"

"Nobody knows."

Cynthia was sorry to have heard the story, and angry at Yves for telling her. "So the twin fell off the roof and died. Is that it?" Her voice was sharp, matter-of-fact. She crossed her legs quickly and wiped her perspiring palms on her skirt.

"No." He shook his head. "He slid down the angled roof and tried to grab the edge but missed and somehow . . ." he stopped.

"Go on." Her voice was without emotion.

"He was so small and fell so quickly that he didn't drop straight to the ground, but landed on the spiked iron fence that went around that side of the house."

Cynthia felt icy perspiration bead on her face and between her breasts. She forced herself to ask, "You mean he was impaled on one of the metal spikes?"

"Yes." Yves couldn't look at her.

"But there's no reason ever to think that—" Her voice was childish and lost-sounding.

"Cynthia," Yves said gently. "Jean-François was horribly jealous of his twin."

She got up then, hearing Jean-François's screams in the night, seeing a little boy in a sailor suit bleeding on a metal railing, and stumbled toward the nearest geraniums. Carefully pulling aside the blossoms that in her tear-filled eyes seemed suddenly blood red, she fell to her knees on the stone terrace and vomited.

· · ·

"There's always been the idea that it wasn't an accident." Yves's voice still rang in her ears. So that was why Elizabeth was always a shade different, less relaxed, when Jean-François was around. But what if it *was* an accident, and all these years he's been punished for it! By his mother! By her every glance! But that makes sense, too, that jealousy idea, thought Cynthia in confusion as she sped along the road to Chambesy in the red Ferrari. By the time she turned into the driveway, she had decided. She pulled the little car up beside Charlie's green MG with the familiar Massachusetts license plate, and for the first time she wondered vaguely how he'd managed to get it over to Switzerland. Cynthia turned off the ignition and pushed her hair back in its blue velvet band. So many things I don't know. She got out of the car and slammed the door. She clenched her teeth with resolve and started across the gravel, feeling angry, confused, but determined. *I have to talk to Jean-François.*

· · ·

The Bentley was in the garage. She'd seen it. He was here. Home early. Tapping three times on the study door, standing on one foot, then the other, she at last opened the door and went in. His head was down and he seemed lost in thought. "Jean-François," she began, but he interrupted her. "Do you think we will have houseguests forever?" he asked in annoyance.

"Well, Tony is one of your mother's best friends!"

He stood up and put the pen down. "He's an idiot who follows her around! I object to him!"

"I don't think he'll be here for more than a few days. But let's not talk about this. I want to tell you something—ask you something. Jean-François!"

His head was down and he was staring at a color photograph of a granite cat sculpture. Suddenly he said, "I'm going out. I won't be here for dinner."

"But—Jean-François! Didn't you hear me? Please, could we talk? It's important!" she implored him as she watched him swing on his suit jacket and slam the desk drawer closed.

"If it's about Stephanie, you handle it and tell me tomor—" He was nearly at the door.

"It's not! It's about you! It's about me! It's important!" Cynthia went to him. He had one hand on the brass door handle. She put her hand on his arm and begged him to listen. "Please! I'm asking you to talk to me!"

His face was above hers. Suntanned, eyes as black as jet. Once she had loved him more than anyone. More than anything in her life. Now he stood before her, far away. As handsome as the Jean-François she'd danced with so long ago in Boston, but unreachable. "We don't touch each other anymore, do we?" she said quietly.

"No." He opened the door and she watched him go down the hall and listened to his footfalls on the marble, and she thought, I don't know you. I never did.

· · ·

I never did. I never did. I never did. Cynthia realized it was half past five when she swung the Ferrari out of the driveway. She needed to drive. To drive fast.

As she passed the Chambesy post office, she saw the scarlet flag with the white cross hung over the front door. An accident. Not an accident. Her vision was blurred by tears. Poor Elizabeth. All this time. Cynthia took a swipe at her nose, which was pin-prickly with the threat of a full-scale crying jag. She wiped her wet cheeks with the back of her hand and then switched into high gear. The little car lurched forward, racing beside the lake. Cynthia saw what she called a killer fridge snap a photo of her license plate and thought, Damn it, another one. The machines, which resembled refrigerators, stood beside the road and, with great flashes of light, nailed speeders. Within days the owner of the car had a ticket in the mail with specifics as to the speed of the car, the date, and the minute and the location of the violation. There was no arguing about it. Swiss efficiency.

Jean-François. Your twin brother. Impaled. She cringed. An accident. Her heart pounded. Don't think. Not now, she told herself, and glanced anxiously in the rearview mirror at her face. No one could tell anything. I am my mother's daughter, she thought grimly. Cynthia made a quick right turn and pulled into a parking place opposite the Beau Rivage, which was next door to number six. She stared at nothing. Why am I here? Hoping to see him with that awful woman he sleeps with?

Suddenly, Cynthia found herself reversing the Ferrari and driving back to Les Colombiers, walking upstairs as if in a trance, stripping her clothes away, and sinking into the bath. She closed her eyes, and the past came flooding back to her. Marco. Edgartown. Living in the Bahamas under "house arrest" with Kate Grayson. Marco. Never getting his letters! And he never got one of mine! Vanished from my life. The hospital in New York. Not being allowed to hold the baby. Taken away. It wasn't given away. *Taken* from me. Marco. Cynthia could see him in the bookstore, laughing with that girl. She relived getting on the subway, wanting to die of unhappiness.

She did not hear the phone, only the voice. "Madame Colbert cannot come to the phone at the moment. May I—" Cynthia could hear Babette in her bedroom, speaking her careful French for someone on the telephone. She rose in the soapy water and tried to hear.

A soft knock came at the half-closed door. "Madame Colbert? *Excusez-moi . . .*"

"*Oui*, Babette. Who was it?"

"It was a Monsieur Forbes—Forbes Toad," she mispronounced the name. "He says he cannot come until a few hours. The plane is late from London."

"Oh! I forgot all about him anyway! *Merci!*"

The door closed and Cynthia stood up in the bathtub and looked at her gleaming, slim body reflected in the mirrored bathroom walls. Three children? One is inches from starvation upstairs, Michel is with friends, and one . . . ? She stepped from the tub and grabbed a big towel. Her eyes were filled with tears when she looked in the mirror to put on eye makeup. She stared at herself for a long time without moving.

· · ·

Jean-François was silent at dinner. He said nothing about her demands to speak with him, and neither did she. Cynthia didn't trust herself to say a word. The fish stuck in her throat.

They ate like two strangers in a restaurant. The new maid almost tiptoed in and out of the dining room with the serving dishes. It had been a long time since they had eaten without the presence of Charlie or Michel, who were in town watching a tennis match with Yves. After the cheese was taken away, Jean-François stood and said he had to go back to Geneva. Cynthia knew why, and she was glad to see him go.

Cynthia couldn't sit still, but wandered through the house aimlessly. Stephanie was asleep with the light on, and she walked in to turn it off, but stood for a few moments over her sleeping child. She stared down in anguish at the sharp, pinched little face. Please, she prayed. We have to save her. She turned off the bedside lamp and made her way toward the doorway outlined in light from the hall. Light at the end of the tunnel, always darkest before dawn, she thought. Slowly she descended the stairs and paced the salon, then felt herself drawn to the darkness of the garden.

"Cynthia! Are you there?" The voice on the path was Tony's.

She'd forgotten about him. How many times had she forgotten about him during this interminably long day? Before she could answer, he came up to her, and Cynthia found herself encircled in his arms. He pressed her to him and said soothingly, "It's all right, Cynthia, it's all right." The scent of roses was heavy in the air.

"But it's not all right," she whispered, hoping her face wasn't tear-stained, wondering what he meant. "Nothing is all right." She looked up at him, but could only see the dark outline of his shoulders and his head. She wanted to see him. So many hours of this summer had been spent fantasizing about his face against hers, his mouth kissing hers. "Tony," she said. Desperately wanting him to kiss her, she would remember the hunger she felt on the garden path in the darkness of the August night. She would remember her desire, but she would also never forget that he turned his face away.

. . .

Cynthia was vague, nervous, high-strung at lunch the next day. A dozen red roses arrived, and she thanked Tony profusely even as she thought, I loathe red roses. Any color but red. And didn't they connote passion? Don't be stupid, she told herself. They are a house present from a houseguest. Forget it. You were upset and you threw yourself at him and you're a fool. Stop it.

"Cynthia!" It was Charlie, asking her something. "Are you all right?"

She nodded. "Fine. Perfectly fine."

Tony laughed and said, "Then maybe you could pass the pepper, please!"

"Oh, oh, absolutely." Everything is too much. The story about Jean-François. Don't think. She bit her lip and tried to pay attention. "A friend of mine here in Geneva was very close to Cristina Onassis when she lived here. During her pregnancy. And Cristina was put through hell." Charlie poured more wine for everyone and then for himself. "A doctor in New York City called her every day of her pregnancy and told her to get an abortion!"

"Why?" Michel erupted.

"Because she had evidently taken a sleeping pill during the first month, before she'd known she was pregnant, and this doctor would tell her every day that her child would be born deformed."

"But was it true?" Michel insisted.

"No! Her doctor here in Geneva told her there was no danger, and to relax and be happy. But some people didn't want her to have an heir. The baby would have changed everything."

Charlie was staring at Cynthia, and when she noticed it, she smiled automatically and nodded. She heard Tony repeat, "The child would change everything."

The word upset her. She remembered being with Yves on his terrace. *An accident*. A child. A baby. Cynthia suddenly pushed her chair back. Excusing herself, she walked quickly from the room. The boudoir was home port. She kicked off her white sandals and then sank heavily onto the pink flowered sofa. Don't cry. Don't start. Until this summer, I never cried! Not since that other summer, she realized with a little jolt of surprise. Coming full circle. She sat up very straight and pushed a cushion behind her. Just decide what to do. It was when she pushed the second pillow into place that she felt the sharp corner of it—a chocolate bar. How funny! Here! Cailler. Her favorite. The gold and brown and white wrapper was torn open quickly. With the first little square on her tongue, the sweetness made everything better. I'm alive, she thought. And I have a brain and I can decide what to do. She ate another square, and then another. Strength. To get me through this.

. . .

"No, that's fine. You know the way I approach these things," Charlie said on the phone to someone, in French. "I don't want to be involved." He sighed and switched the receiver from one ear to the other. "Fine. Use your own judgment." He listened for a moment and then said, "No, I can't be reached. I want everything taken care of according to the list you were given. And if it's not covered on that page, then do what you think is best. As if it belonged to you. I'm sure Madame Bardot told you. *Oui. Oui.*" He nodded. "That's the whole point. I do not want to be involved. Now that we understand each other . . . *oui. Merci. Au revoir.*" Charlie hung up the phone and thought, And if she doesn't catch on to that, then I get rid of her, interview others, get someone else.

"Charlie!" Cynthia exclaimed, materializing before him in the salon. He felt a rush of guilt, and he must have blushed, for she looked at him with her head tilted to one side and smiled. "Michel says he's not hiding chocolate all over the house. And Stephanie is not doing it!" Her voice was light. She was pleased, adored the idea of someone having such fun with her, because she thought, They're for me! Someone is teasing me. It's like coming upon Easter eggs as a little girl. "What do you think?"

"What do I think?" he repeated. "I am in favor of chocolate."

She looked into his face long and hard, and then smiled quizzically and left the room. Confused.

I shouldn't lie to Cynthia, Charlie thought. But it isn't a lie, he decided. I've simply left out things. What was that prayer? Sins of omission. Yes. That was it. A sin of omission. He closed his address book and thought, But now it doesn't matter. I'll tell her if it matters. He rolled up the sleeve of his blue striped shirt. Absolutely.

CHAPTER THIRTY

August 1988 — Les Colombiers

The large brown manila envelope arrived from Kate Grayson the day after she received a letter from her mother telling her that Kate had died. Cynthia held the package in her hands, staring at the handwriting that she'd seen every birthday, every Christmas of her life. The return address was always the same size as the address. The wide *s* that was almost like a figure eight, the sprawling capital *K* and *G* that dwarfed the rest of the letters. She sighed, took the envelope to her desk, and picked up the brass letter opener that Elizabeth had brought back from Tunisia.

Cynthia had written to Kate two months earlier, when she'd found out about the cancer. She evidently hadn't wanted anyone to know, but Cynthia was glad that her mother had broken the promise and let her in on the secret. Paris had been Kate's last trip.

Cynthia had taken three afternoons, off and on, to compose, very carefully, a letter that conveyed affection for her godmother, but didn't show that she knew of any illness. It was a very difficult letter to write, and the moment she had handed it to the woman at the counter of the little post office at Chambesy, she had felt a weight off her shoulders.

Now she stared at the return address and wondered what would happen to Tower-on-the-Hill in the Bahamas. In 1983, *Architectural Digest* had done a four-page spread on Kate's property. Kate had had to be talked into it, for she was frightened of burglars. Margaret had written Cynthia: "I told her for twenty minutes on the phone, long distance, that I couldn't imagine burglars reading *Architectural Digest*. They read things like *Police Gazette* or the Sears, Roebuck catalogs." Cynthia had laughed so hard at the story, and even Jean-François had seen the humor in it. Dear Mother! It was typical of her—the "people like us" mentality.

She slid the brass knife under the flap and tore it open neatly. Inside were letters! Dozens of unopened letters. Cynthia pulled them out with a cry of shock. They were addressed in her careful teenage handwriting, in her blue ink, to Marco Falconi, at the University of Vermont! Tears filled her eyes as she held the bundle wrapped in brown grocery twine, and turned it over in her hands in disbelief. Then she realized there was another bundle in the big manila envelope, and when she touched the paper, before she pulled it out into the light, she knew. Tears streamed down her face.

"Why am I crying? Why now?" she said aloud. There they were. All the letters she had longed for, ached for. All the letters Marco had written to her while she was pregnant, while she had been tortured by the idea he no longer cared what happened to her. Bound in the same brown twine. American stamps. Red and blue air-mail envelopes. Dozens of them. Tissue-paper thin. Typed. Cynthia's tears fell on the top one, and with a burst of rage she banged her fist down on the desk shelf. The hinges gave way and the drop front fell onto her knees and then slid to the floor with a crash. Amazed at her own strength, thinking sourly, An antique desk, hope, faith in someone, let it all break to bits! She ran from the room clutching the envelope and the letters in trembling hands.

Simone heard the noise from Michel's bedroom, where she was changing the sheets, and hurried down the hall. As she entered Cynthia's boudoir, she anxiously scanned the room looking for something broken. Simone stared at the pieces of wood on the floor, then she folded them in a sheet of the newspaper that was stacked beside the firewood on the hearth. Madame Colbert was outside; Simone saw her blond head bowed. She was holding something to her breast, walking slowly beside the lake.

Cynthia was gasping for breath, trying to stop crying. She wished she knew which she felt more, anger or sadness. There was rage in her like a fire, and yet such a sense of betrayal mixed with the sad memory of all those months of wanting any sign from Marco, any sign that he still thought of her. She thought of the child growing inside her, week after week, and of all the times she'd excused herself from dinner to go to her room and write him. To tell him how she felt, how her body was changing, how much she missed him. All those letters! She'd always walked to the village to mail them early in the morning, before the eight o'clock pickup, and licked the stamps herself. She actually remembered kissing the envelopes before handing them to the old postmaster.

Kate must have made a deal with him. Cynthia began to sob. She cried like she'd never cried before, and the lake before her became a blue-gray blur and still she couldn't stop. There was one last thing in the envelope. She pulled out the one sheet of stationery, dove gray, with the dark blue monogram KHG, for Katharine Harcourt Grayson. Cynthia read the three sentences: "I know you will never be able to forgive me. I knew it was wrong. I did it for your mother. Love, Kate."

Vieille Ville

"I'm going to try! Why not try?" Tony was saying. He sat with long legs stretched out in white linen trousers. He was barefoot on Yves's terrace. They were both drinking vodka with tonic.

"You can't do it! You've tried before, remember? Remember what happened? Your wife left you. It won't work." Yves was trying to control his anger. He would not let this happen to Cynthia.

"That was years ago. I didn't understand certain things, and I think I do now. What a woman wants—"

"Right! Let's start right there!" Yves was pacing back and forth in a pair of khaki shorts and a polo shirt the color of his geraniums. "She wants a husband, not an escort, not what she's had up till now!"

"She's had nothing, unless you count up all the material things. She's got diamonds and designer clothes and she lives in a chateau . . ."

"In effect, she sleeps alone." Yves thought of all the times he and Veronique had tried to push her into an affair. They had agreed a hundred times that she lived an unnatural life. "Without affection, let's say." Tony was determined to win this argument.

"Yes. Definitely. But what can you give her that she doesn't have?" It was a cruel question, and Yves felt the atmosphere change between him and his friend. He started to backtrack. "I didn't mean it. I know that you think you love her. I'm sorry, Tony." Yves bent down and pulled at a little weed in one of the terra-cotta pots. Not wanting to stop the conversation to go to the garbage bin, he hesitated, then put the weed in his pants pocket.

"I *do* love her, and I know that the other night in the garden she wanted me. I don't know what held me back. I don't know what stopped me. Maybe I'm a better person than you think I am, but I didn't take advantage of that beautiful woman in the moonlight." He took another sip of the cold alcohol and stared down at the slice of lime. "I could ask her to go on a trip with me, with me and Elizabeth."

"Now I've heard everything." Yves shook his head and gazed at the sky as if addressing a higher being. "Superb idea my friend has. He proposes that a woman run away with him along with her own mother-in-law." He took a swallow of the vodka and turned to Tony, who still sprawled in the wicker chair. "That's great. Neil Simon? Or Woody Allen? It has possibilities."

"Forget the sarcasm. I can't take it. I do love her. I have since the first time I met her. And you know what? I don't think Elizabeth would mind one little bit if Cynthia left her son for me."

"He's easy to hate, isn't he? I'm inclined to agree with you in a way, but is . . . is there something more than that gruesome story about the twin?" Yves didn't tell him that he'd told Cynthia. He never knew where loyalty to one person stopped and loyalty to another one began. His friends were his family. He was genuinely concerned about all of them, and if things that shouldn't be told or should be known overlapped, well, then, he had a hard time with the information. But when in doubt, he usually told. He adored the mystery, then revealing it, and finally the amazement crossing the face of his companion. It was power to know secrets and benevolence to tell them.

"I'll need more vodka for this," said Tony, extending his glass. Yves took it and disappeared into the coolness of the living room for the bottle and more ice. Tony ran his hand through his hair. I can imagine it very easily. She is perfect for me. So lovely, so calm, so precise. And some women don't care about the physical side of things. Or not nearly as much as we read they do. Christ! If you believed *The Hite Report* or anything else these days, you would assume the world was filled with bitches in heat! Panting to be satisfied. No. Cynthia isn't like that. And I could shower her with everything else. She's fabulous in clothes. She loves her house, and it's wonderfully done, but she could have a town house in London and one in the country. There's that place in Surrey up for sale. Cynthia would be very happy in London, the kids would be off at school, and I have my own time. I think she'd love to travel. I've seen her face when Elizabeth and I have told our tales at Les Colombiers.

"Well, spill it," Yves ordered as he handed him the glass and took a chair opposite him in the shade.

"I don't know. Elizabeth isn't sure, but—" He frowned and Yves stared at his face and thought, not for the first time, what an astoundingly handsome man he was. "When Jean-François was very little, maybe only five, maybe four, his father died. Elizabeth tells me he became maniacally jealous of his twin, and more and more attached to her. He would literally fight with his fists to sit next to her in the car, and she would arrange to be in the middle, with one on either side when it was possible, and he still wasn't satisfied. Jean-François wanted his mother to himself. According to Elizabeth, he began to resent the very existence of his twin." He reached for the glass and swallowed. "We all know what happened."

"Christ!" was Yves's only comment.

"When Jean-François was about twelve, Elizabeth married Alexandre Fortier."

Yves felt the short hairs on the back of his neck stand up. He listened intently to every word.

"Jean-François tried to talk his mother out of it, and even on her wedding day he came to her and told her it was a terrible mistake. She thought it was something he would get used to, because evidently Fortier had two grown sons and liked Jean-François. But things became worse. Jean-François refused to be sent away to school, so he was in the house all the time. He hated for his mother to so much as laugh with her husband, and he was constantly inventing ways to keep him away from his mother. If they planned a trip together, Jean-François would invariably come down with some 'sickness' the day of the journey, forcing Elizabeth to stay behind or to cancel the whole event."

"What a little shit," Yves breathed.

"But it was when he was about fourteen that it happened."

"*What* happened?" Yves had never liked Jean-François, and this confirmed everything he'd suspected. A spoiled brat. A pompous man who was used to having his way with women. Starting with his mother.

"He was in the pear orchard with his stepfather, helping him trim dead branches for firewood. Elizabeth looked as white as a ghost when she told me this, because usually Jean-François never left her side. Especially if Fortier was going out, since he liked having her to himself."

"Didn't she realize that was twisted, wrong?" Yves interrupted.

"I don't know. I think she had the idea it would pass. He would get older and grow up." Tony thought of Elizabeth as a stable, commonsense sort of woman. Like Cynthia.

"So what happened?" Yves insisted.

"Fortier fell from a tree and never regained consciousness."

"Christ! I thought he died from a stroke. That's what Cynthia thinks, too." Yves stood up and drained the vodka in his glass. "Is it possible?" he demanded.

"That might explain a few things. Like why Elizabeth isn't herself around him."

"Years ago," Yves put in, "Cynthia told me how formal and proper and 'different' Elizabeth was that first time at Les Chênes in France. She was very nice, but not full of stories, not at all the fey person she is now."

"She told me she finds it difficult to be with him, and hates herself for being this way, hates herself for the things she cannot get out of her mind. I told her that sometimes I thought she and her son 'flirted,' and the minute I'd said it I was sorry. But"—Tony raised his eyebrows—"she nodded. She told me she sometimes listened to her voice and couldn't believe it was hers. Elizabeth says she sometimes pretends he isn't her son, just so she can force herself to be nearly normal when she meets him. She said the worst is meeting him after an absence."

"God! It's so awful!" Yves groaned. "But what would you do? Turn in your own son on the suspicion that he is capable of such a thing?"

Tony hesitated. "But she says she'll never know. It's the terrible jealousy that makes her suffer so much with the idea—the idea that he could 'get rid of' anyone who took her attention." He closed his eyes. "I think the death of the little boy, her son, is something she'll never get over. He was . . . he was just adored by her."

Yves spoke. "You know, of course, the bastard is still reaching out for his mother's love. Jean-François sleeps with anyone and everyone he sees. And now he has installed his little mistress in the Beau Rivage. Their best suite, overlooking the lake. With her French maid, no less!"

"Really?" Tony wasn't unhappy about the information. It might make it even easier for him to persuade Cynthia to leave her husband. She was so close to it.

"I think Jean-François is just going through life loving and leaving women. Cynthia is the chatelaine and the mother of his children, but the others . . . why, three years ago there was a suicide in Paris, and I heard that Jean-François had been involved with her. Though it's hard to imagine. He's the king of the one-night stand. This painter in the Beau Rivage must be a piece of work to have kept him interested this long."

"Sounds like he uses women. Then he punishes them." Tony had disliked him in an instant. Especially because he felt such a strong attraction towards Cynthia. "Will you help me?" he found himself asking.

"Help you? With Cynthia?" Yves was watering a geranium with the hose.

"Yes."

"No. I've told you how I feel. I love Cynthia. It isn't fair to her. I don't want her to be hurt."

Tony took a deep breath and then said, "I love her, too."

"You hardly know her. You've hardly had a conversation with her. It's entirely unrealistic." Yves's face was hard.

"Everything about love is unrealistic," Tony said.

"Well, again I will say it. I don't want her to be hurt."

"Neither do I!" Tony insisted.

"Then stay away from her. You and I know what you are. We've known since Eton. Tony, listen to me as an old friend." His voice was gentle, barely audible above the gurgle of the water splashing on the stones of the terrace. "Leave Cynthia alone."

Les Colombiers

"You had no right! Mother, how could you do such a thing? How could you pull Kate into it? Didn't you know—couldn't you imagine—how I suffered, not hearing from him? Not a word, not ever—" Cynthia fairly yelled into the bedroom phone. The door was closed, Stephanie was asleep, but she didn't trust herself to speak normally. She was angry beyond the point of tears, angry to the point of screaming.

It was nine o'clock in the morning in Boston, and Margaret Kendall sounded crisp and courteous, like an executive secretary protecting her employer from a nuisance call. "It seemed the proper thing to do. You were seventeen years old. I don't think it's anything we have to discuss."

"I think it's high time we discussed it!" Cynthia held a Kleenex in her clenched fist. "All these years, twenty years, and we've never mentioned that summer in Edgartown again. What happened to you, to Uncle Teddy, to me. Convenient, isn't it? If we don't talk about it, it'll go away. We'll pretend it never happened, and someday we'll forget it entirely. Is that the reasoning?"

"Cynthia, you're hysterical. Calm down!" Margaret's voice was firm.

"You know what, Mother? This is a turning point for me. Getting that letter from Kate made me realize how my life hasn't been my own. I see how other people have pushed and pulled me into what they wanted—"

"I don't know what you're talking about. You're not making any sense. You're overtired. You must not be feeling well."

"I suddenly feel very well, and I'm going to do something I should have done years ago. I'm going to find my child. I want to know him—or her— if he wants to know me. But I will give him the chance. I will find him and write. He or she is old enough to—"

There was silence on the line from Beacon Hill. Margaret moistened her lips and then dabbed with a white handkerchief at the tiny beads of perspiration on her upper lip.

"Mother! Are you there?"

"Yes," Margaret answered. Her voice sounded dull, tired.

"I know that you and Dr. Halliday arranged the adoption. I know he was there all the time, I talked to him after they—" Cynthia's voice cracked. "After they took the baby away."

Margaret Kendall said nothing.

"I know that you must know where he is. The parents. The address . . ." Cynthia held the receiver with both hands. "Mother?"

"Perhaps the . . . the child won't want to see you."

"Maybe not. But at last I am doing something. Giving him a chance to know me, to know I . . ." Her voice was little above a whisper. "I cared."

Neither woman spoke for a moment, and then Margaret said, in a voice full of resignation, "All right. If you must. Call him. Dr. Halliday is about eighty and retired. He lives in his summer house on Cape Cod. I think it's in Annisquam."

"I will. I am. Now." Cynthia scribbled "Dr. H" on the pad and drew a diamond around it.

"You were only seventeen," Margaret repeated. Her voice was hollow. "I did what I thought was right for you. Remember that. Whatever I did was for your own good."

Cynthia took a deep breath, still angry. "Good-bye, Mother." She hung up and dialed the international operator and explained in French what she wanted. She replaced the receiver and stared at the phone. Three minutes later it rang, and she was given Dr. John G. Halliday's number.

Cynthia sat on her bed and stared out the bedroom window at the green trees against a postcard-blue sky. August. Heat. She heard ducks quacking. She tried to think of what she would say. Oh, no, please don't tell me I have no right to know. Please trust me to do the right thing. I won't hurt my child. Haven't I hurt him enough? Isn't giving someone away, being given away by your own mother, enough hurt for fifty lifetimes? A baby. Helpless. Little. I never held you.

Cynthia had to go into the bathroom and blow her nose three times before she could dial the number. Her rage at her mother had wafted away like smoke, now that the idea of what she was about to do had taken hold. She dialed the number. Dr. Halliday was home. His wife said she would call him in from the garden. He remembered her. How was she? How had she found him? Cynthia told him she had just spoken to her mother and that she felt, after all these years, that she must find her child. That the child was old enough to decide whether or not he wanted to see her.

There was silence from the old doctor. Cynthia swallowed. She could hear him breathing, so clear was the connection. "Margaret didn't tell you?" was his question.

"Tell me what?" Cynthia thought the room moved crazily, as though she were dizzy or drunk. The sunlight coming in through the windows looked gray suddenly, not yellow.

"The parents took him home from the hospital. Home to St. Louis. He . . . the boy . . ." he hesitated. "I'm sorry, Cynthia, the little boy died of pneumonia when he was three."

Washington D. C.

The little office was packed with men in summer suits. The air-conditioner was doing its best, but fighting Washington's sweltering heat was a losing battle. All three chairs were occupied and men stood behind them and leaned on the arms and others stood in the open doorway, all hanging on the words and trying to read the face of the man behind the desk. He was young for what was happening to him, and very handsome, which could be an asset or a drawback. No one could tell about women voters these days, Tom Newton thought. A too-handsome candidate could come off as a lightweight, a pretty face with no substance. But, he decided, listening to the senator's intelligent answers, that was unlikely.

"I think all this is a bit premature," the senator was saying modestly with a twinkle in his eyes. The reporters were laughing.

"Premature!" hooted someone from the *Washington Post*. "I hear your wife has already bought her outfit for the inauguration!"

"I haven't seen it yet," he bantered. "Or the bill either!"

"Hey, come on, you guys! We've got work to do! Enough!" Bill Brady was hustling them out. "You've had twenty minutes, which is plenty! Hit the road!"

The room emptied and the senator stood up and stretched. His suit was a light tan: the pale blue shirt beneath it set off his olive complexion. "Glad that's over," he sighed. "What's next?" He sank into the swivel chair.

"Glad you asked," Newton said. "Listen to this." He held a brown folder. "This ominous-looking file is your bio. I want to make sure it's all in here. Or what shouldn't be isn't. Get me?"

"No. I don't." The senator sat down and leaned forward, elbows and arms on the desk.

"Don't look so worried! I'm sure you're as clean as a cub scout. It's just that the F.B.I. is going to be looking at every move you've ever made. There'll be the tax audits, the value of everything you own, every piece of jewelry your wife owns, the boat, the summer house, mostly assessment stuff. You know, the net worth stuff they always publish. And you'd better get Ferguson in here for legal advice and to set up a blind trust. No conflict-of-interest calls." Newton stopped. He was staring down at the open file. He turned a few typewritten pages. "You never cheated at Harvard, did you? Think of Teddy Kennedy."

"I've never been in a car accident either," the senator said dryly.

Newton grinned, then looked down again. "Marijuana. Remember Ginsberg." The senator shook his head. Newton turned another few pages. "Married for seventeen years. Looks good."

There was silence in the room. Brady sat in one of the chairs to the left of the desk with his blond head down. He was trying to decide if an impromptu press conference just before the convention would look staged. He crossed out one line after another on the page.

"Kids? No drug problems?"

"I'd know." The senator was known to be a family man, often cited as a good father.

"Okay. Just remember Geraldine Ferraro. Son at college. Drug dealing. And her husband. Anything we should know about your wife or her family?"

The senator almost made a remark about his own family and the Mafia, but he didn't. Most other people had stopped that. "No. Nothing that I can think of. Her family has had money for generations. They haven't exactly had to scramble for anything or bend the rules."

Newton nodded. Brady put his papers in his briefcase and looked at his watch.

"Okay, the last. There isn't any bimbo who's going to tell some reporter in Podunk, Iowa, that she fucked the vice-president, is there? I mean, that you had a hot and heavy weekend together in the past or that you like to do it wearing socks on your ears?"

Brady laughed. "Come on, Newton! This guy's Mr. Clean . . . " He waved an arm toward the senator.

The senator shook his head. "Not unless I was too drunk to notice it wasn't my wife."

They all laughed and Newton got up and put on his suit jacket. "Well, that does it. Have a good weekend. You're a shoo-in! All that convention stuff is just for the masochistic television viewers. A mere formality."

· · ·

The senator arrived in Houston for the Republican Convention the day before it officially started and checked into a hotel suite with five television sets. Newton and Brady were with him all the time. Neal and the two kids arrived the day before the nominations for president were made.

The speechmaking and the carefully orchestrated "impromptu" demonstrations seemed endless. Newton was right. Carson Birch, former secretary of the navy and governor of California, was named on the first ballot to be the Republican candidate for president of the United States in the 1988 election. And, as everyone knew he would, he announced the senator from Rhode Island as his running mate. "A great ticket" was the consensus. It had it all: an elder statesman and a young-thinking go-getter. The geography couldn't be better and the broad appeal was obvious to all. A blue-blooded Californian with cabinet experience, a governor of the most populous state coupled with an Easterner with Washington experience, an excellent record in Congress, and a liberal background that made him outspoken on human rights and the protection of the environment. "And no one can overlook the ethnic thing," gushed one delegate draped in red, white, and blue banners and wearing a white straw boater. "I mean really! Think of how many Americans are gonna love voting for a second-generation American named Mark Falconi!"

· · ·

The dreams began that night. He hadn't thought of her in years. He didn't think he had. Is it the unconscious or the subconscious I'm dealing with, he asked himself as he yanked his tie in place a few mornings later. One time. I guess it was a one-night stand. New York. Why should she haunt me when

Cynthia Kendall was really the only one? Cynthia. Geneva. Married at nineteen. He remembered the shock of seeing her picture in the paper and calling the house. Cynthia on her honeymoon. Gone. The housekeeper had told him. His thoughts returned to . . . what was her name? No name but a face like an angel's and Cynthia's green eyes. That's what had pulled him to her across the hotel room with all the drinking, loud voices, and confusion. No. Forget it. Then he told himself what he'd heard as a little boy: *If you dream of someone, they dream of you.* Was that true? Could she possibly remember me? So long ago.

He walked out of the bedroom and into the front hall of the Washington house. It felt empty. Neal and the kids were at her parents'. But outside the place was surrounded by Secret Service agents. Not very subtle, he thought as he glanced out the window at the contingent with walkie-talkies, all with identical haircuts and tan summer suits. Someone had left the new *Time* magazine on the hall table and he saw that he was on the cover, arms raised in victory with Birch. Grinning as the crowds yelled and the band played. God, it was as good as an orgasm. Mark thought of her again. So many years ago. I was a baby. Cheap. Common. Like someone who'd sell tickets at the movies. But a goddess in bed with eyes as green as Cynthia's. He picked up the mail and the *Newsweek* that was under it. My face again. A nearly identical photograph, just off to the side a little instead of dead-on. Euphoric with the excitement of the moment. He winced as the thought came to him. She could find me if she wanted to.

CHAPTER THIRTY-ONE

Les Colombiers

Sweat was pouring down Cynthia's face but she kept running, wondering if she was blinded by tears or perspiration. Just one more time along the last line of vines and then I'll go back.

Why does it have to be this way? she kept asking herself. Marco! Marco Falconi. She could see his forty-one-year-old face smiling at her on the hall table from the cover of *Time* magazine. She had felt like fainting.

Senator Mark Falconi was the Republican Party's candidate for Vice President. That man I loved, no, that boy I loved. A stranger now. Far away, with bodyguards and a wife who looks well-bred, and rather ordinary-looking children. And I keep coming back to Jean-François and his twin and . . . Cynthia stumbled, regained her footing, and then, rather wearily, slowed down and stopped in the field. Her left ankle was all right, she decided as she wiggled it in a circle. Suddenly, Cynthia had the distinct feeling of another presence, and when she turned, there was Charlie. He was sitting against an oak tree, reading from a spiral notebook; the sleeves of his green and white striped shirt were rolled up to the elbow. Papers were spread out on the ground all the way down to his crossed feet in their sneakers. Fifty feet away, but he looked up and saw her. "Cynthia!" he called out.

No, she thought. She shook her head and waved and continued walking toward the house. No. Not now.

"What is it? What's happened?" He had fallen into step beside her, and she thought, How tall he is, how big he seems.

She shook her head, not trusting herself to speak. With one hand she reached up and yanked the blue ribbon and the rubber band from her hair, hoping that it would make it more difficult for him to see her expression. "Stop!" he insisted, and when she didn't, he grabbed her shoulder and swung her around to face him.

Cynthia's face was pink, and her eyes sparkled with tears. Her shoulder-length blond hair hid nothing. She bit her lip and shook her head. "I can't tell you." She put her hands up to cover her face as he took her by the elbow and led her back to the tree. "Sit," he commanded.

Cynthia held her breath for a moment, with her head down. She sat cross-legged in her white shorts, like an Indian, elbows on knees and face in hands. I can stop. I know I can. I don't have to cry in front of Charlie. I really thought I never cried, and for the last few days it seems it's all I do.

"I can wait all afternoon," he said gently.

"Oh, Charlie! This isn't anything to do with you! It's all me! It's Jean-François and me, and it's something that happened a long time ago that I try to never think about. And it's too many secrets. Awful secrets. Things people do and want to forget . . ." she gasped for a breath.

"Can you try to look at one part at a time?" he asked.

Cynthia wiped her eyes on her navy blue T-shirt. She didn't answer for a moment, and then she said, "What if you have to do something, take care of something that you thought was in the past, was over, and you don't know if you have the strength because you realize you never take the first step."

Charlie waited for her to explain. The Cynthia of the last few days was at the breaking point.

"I let it all happen around me. I always do. As if it were an act of nature, and then I decide whether to put up an umbrella or to go indoors. Things seem to happen *to* me, and I feel suddenly weak, defenseless, and I hate myself for not being able to act." She stopped and looked up at the sky. "And I cannot *not* do something. It's as if all these years—here, in my marriage, at Les Colombiers—I've willed all the confusion out of my life by this awful maintenance of meals and schedules." Her voice wavered. "I suddenly know too much, see too much, and . . . and . . ."

She took a deep breath, holding back tears.

"Is it too late?" Charlie had no idea what she was talking about. Could she mean her postponed talk with Stephanie?

"I don't know." She was silent for a moment. "Funny. Stephanie thinks I'm a hollow little doll, just getting through the days, pleasing Jean-François, and I'm beginning to think she's right." Her eyes filled with tears again. "And me, the 'perfect' one she thinks I am, has made a 'mistake' that is twenty years old and is suddenly in front of me . . . to shake my life. To shake my perfection." She looked up at Charlie, and there was such pleading in her face. "To give me a chance."

"Then take the chance. I think you're suddenly sure of what you have to do." He smiled that bright smile of his, and his eyes were all-seeing. Cynthia nodded, and tears slipped down her cheeks yet again in two wet trails. They stood up together and she said, "Yes, I know what I have to do." With a wave of her hand, she left him standing under the oak tree, watching her walk back towards Les Colombiers.

· · ·

She quickly showered and decided she would wear her new white suit. Yes. Cynthia felt tan and healthy as she stepped into the skirt bare-legged and pulled the pristine white linen up around her waist. The women of Geneva, even in their designer clothes, went without stockings from late spring to mid-September. She splashed on perfume and brushed her hair, all the while staring intently at herself in the mirror. Cynthia had made up her mind: I will send a telegram from the main post office in town. A letter will take too long. I've waited too long as it is.

The Last Afternoon

Michel was playing tennis at the Dietrichs' house. The tennis courts were down the faintly sloping green velvet lawn, near the lake. "We made this even with about forty-nine earth-moving machines, which woke me up every morning for a week last summer," Jochen laughed.

The boys were well matched, and it was always a close game. "Hey, unfair, that duck quacked just as I was serving!" laughed Michel.

"*Oui!* And that goose honked just as I hit it back. It would have been a much stronger shot without that interference in my concentration."

They joked in German and French as they played. Michel allowed himself to daydream of Iris for too many minutes, too many serves. The view of the lake here reminded him of the view from her studio—the view from the mattress, to be more specific. He didn't think she went out there on Thursdays. She was at the Beau Rivage this afternoon. He tucked in his white shirt, and when his hand brushed his bare skin, he was reminded of her hand. Then he thought of her tongue. Jochen's serve shot past him before he could even lift his racket.

"Okay, Colbert, want to play again?"

Michel walked to the net, shaking his head. He bent down for his windbreaker and his racquet cover. "No, another time. My mind isn't on it. And I have to stop in town before I go home."

"A beer? A shower?"

Michel smiled. "*Oui*. Both of the above. We'll drink to your season at Wimbledon."

Jochen slapped him on the back, and they fell into step together. One boy was thinking of an ice-cold beer and the other was thinking of a soft, perfumed Iris.

Les Colombiers

It was nearly four o'clock, and the house was quiet. So quiet that the insect noises from the garden could be heard along with the occasional buzz of a faraway motorboat towing a skier on the lake. Charlie was still outside, sitting under the tree, making notes on the prevalence of bulimia among anorexic teenage girls, but his mind was on Cynthia. Stephanie was upstairs, dressed in shorts and a T-shirt, for she had felt better the last few days, had actually eaten more than double her usual intake. She told Charlie she felt that a cloud was passing over her, that something was about to happen. Jean-François was at Colbert & Cie., and Michel had left a note on the dining-room table saying that he would be back before seven. His mother had questioned him once about his afternoons, but he had merely smiled and said, "It's better that you don't know." She took this to mean that it was something he didn't want his father to know, and that she would be compromised. Cynthia had asked nothing more and had told her son to "have a good time, whatever it is." He had grinned and kissed her and dashed out to the garage to race away in the Fiat. Now, whenever he left Les Colombiers in the afternoon and didn't specify tennis, she assumed it was his mysterious errand.

Cynthia was brushing her just-shampooed hair over her head when Simone walked into the bedroom. "Madame," she said. "*Le téléphone. Un américain.*" Simone watched Madame Colbert's face go pale.

"I'll . . . I'll be right down." Privacy. Away from Stephanie, down the hall. She turned and watched Simone leave as she swept her hair into place with nervous little strokes. It could be anyone, she told herself. Her hand holding the brush trembled; her wrist felt weak, as if she'd been playing too much tennis. Cynthia rose from the stool and walked decisively out of the room, down the hall, and down the stairs. It occurred to her it was one of the most important journeys she'd ever made. In one minute she had taken forty steps to speak to someone who had resurfaced from another life.

She sat on the loveseat with the blue lake spread before her on this Thursday afternoon in August, and clutched the receiver with pounding heart. It was twenty years away from Martha's Vineyard, from a time when things could have been different. As she heard his voice, Cynthia saw today's *Le Figaro* on the coffee table. Marco's face was smiling at the camera. A grainy black and white photograph of someone from a lost dream.

. . .

Cynthia hung up the phone. A curious calm suffused her.

"Mother!" It was Stephanie.

"You're downstairs!" exclaimed Cynthia. It was the first time since her arrival from school, all those months ago.

"Oh, Mother!" Stephanie was crying, and with remarkable strength she crossed the big salon and folded herself into Cynthia's arms. She was looking better, though the shorts and the cotton blouse flapped on her thin frame.

"Darling! Oh, darling one!" How good it felt to hold her daughter.

Stephanie pulled away and stared at her mother. "I listened on the stairs. Mother, I heard almost everything—what you said about having a baby. You really got pregnant when you were seventeen? When you were in Edgartown?"

Cynthia nodded. There were no more secrets. "It's true. It was a terrible time for me. Maybe all these things . . . these twists and turns when we have no idea what's ahead, what might happen . . ."

Stephanie said, "You're different. You're not the person I always thought you were."

Cynthia held her close and kissed the top of the blond head. "I love you, little one. I can't always say what I feel, and I'm sorry about that. But will you know from now on that I love you?"

Stephanie nodded and said, "I love you, too, Mother. It's been easier to hate you for the last year, and I don't know why. But Charlie has helped me figure some things out, and I know that I don't hate you."

"I never really thought you did. I want you to get strong and eat and live and be gloriously happy and fight for what you want." She stopped. "And to have what you want. Whatever it is."

"How funny," said her daughter, almost in a whisper.

"What's funny about that?"

Stephanie looked up at her mother's bright eyes and smiled. "That's exactly what I wish for you."

The Beau Rivage

Iris was nervous. And I never am, she told herself. Self-assurance had come with Paris, with age, with money. She smiled into her little dressing-table mirror and inspected both sides of her face in the triptych glass. I have everything, she thought. Really I do. I'm famous enough. Successful enough. And

I've been rich enough ever since that meeting in Naples so many years ago. All I want is a husband. A husband I want, she amended. Anyone can get married, she often told Etienne. If I wanted to simply *be* married, then I would be married!

She dabbed on the faintest silver eye shadow and lowered her lids demurely to check them with the hand-held mirror. Her lips were a full pink, the color of camellias, and she had doused herself with Shalimar, which was Jean-François's favorite. She thought of him now: He'll be cranky after a day at the bank. That's normal. He'll be hot—it's seventy-five degrees outside—and I'll undress him.

Her mind returned to that delicious lovemaking of a few weeks ago. Jean-François usually didn't take so much time with her. And he hadn't since. But that had been exquisite. And Michel. The boy was so sweetly unselfish in comparison. He had all that energy, which meant it could go on and on and even again on and on. Iris licked her lips and sighed. Okay. Forget the boy! Think of Jean-François. No threats. No ultimatums. Nothing in bad taste. Nothing out of "Dynasty."

Just a reasonable, "We are good friends," and "We are well matched," and "This is what I want from you." *Oui*, nodded Iris to her reflection. He is a practical man, he hates fucking his wife, and . . . she sprayed perfume between her breasts and closed her eyes with the delicious coolness of it . . . and he loves fucking me.

. . .

When he parked the Fiat, he remembered it was Anna's day off. Doesn't matter, he thought. Maybe that's a good thing. He walked through the lobby, past the little fountain, without stopping at the reception desk, and started to go up the stairs. But instead he stepped into a waiting elevator.

Inspecting himself in the mirror, he saw a sunburned face and black hair shiny and wet from the shower. In the elevator's display case, he admired the diamonds and thought, If you were trapped in a Beau Rivage lift, there would be lots to look at, to think about. The ruby rings reminded him of Iris. Everything reminded Michel of Iris.

The elevator stopped, and he pushed open the gold-colored door. At Iris's suite, Michel lifted his hand to ring the doorbell, and then dropped it and tried the handle. It turned. Room service, he smiled to himself. Won't she be surprised to see me!

. . .

But Iris didn't see him. She never knew that Michel had tiptoed into the salon and heard the voices. He could see both of them clearly through the partially open bedroom door.

His naked father was shouting. "You think . . . you *dare* to entertain the dream—that you could be my wife? What makes you think I want a wife? *Any* wife at all?"

Iris was naked too, wearing only her biggest diamond earrings, which hung in pendants almost to her silky white shoulders. Her blond hair was tousled, and she sat on her knees on the bed among the tangled white satin sheets. Her face was flushed and her breasts were pink, the way they became after lovemaking.

"You don't know what it's like to have a wife. To come home to someone who wants you. Who wants you in every way." Her voice was determined.

Jean-François was mocking, sneering. "And you as my wife? You can't even live in a suite at the Beau Rivage without a maid! You can scarcely take care of yourself, let alone a chateau with servants and meals to plan and houseguests who might stay for two weeks at a time and . . ."

Michel suddenly felt that he might vomit. He wiped his perspiring forehead with one hand and blotted it on his jeans. Then he tiptoed to the hall of the suite and carefully opened and closed the door. By the time he'd reached his car, he was panting; his chest was heaving, and he was gasping like a swimmer who'd spent too long underwater. Michel managed to open the door and get in. Slick with sweat, his hands couldn't hold the key. He dropped it on the rubber mat and fumbled for it with fingers gone numb. On the third try he succeeded in putting it into the ignition.

Les Colombiers

Stephanie had gone upstairs again, and Cynthia thought, I need a drink or a walk. It's almost too bad I've been running today, for I feel such energy, such a charge of adrenaline. She took another cool shower, hoping it would calm her, and dressed. She was experiencing a keen excitement, an exhilarating tension that was new to her. I must think. I must plan. I must pack. But what loomed largest in her mind, like a big, bright yellow balloon, was the thought, I must find Charlie.

He found her instead. She was in the rose garden, a tall figure in a white dress, surrounded by white roses. She was staring out at the lake with her hand up, palm flattened against the glare of the setting sun. Her hair was platinum in the last rays of the afternoon.

"Cynthia!"

When she turned, he thought how different, how changed she was. Her face was radiant; she looked like one of her roses after a spring rain. "I did it," she said. "I finally did something good and right, without being swept along on a wave of circumstance."

Charlie stepped close enough to touch her then, and she impetuously walked into his open arms. His hardness, her softness met through the thin cotton of their clothes. "Charlie," she said, "I'm leaving Jean-François. I'm leaving here."

"Mmmm," was all he said, kissing her forehead.

"Don't you have anything to say?" She looked up at him, thinking, He's kissing my face and it's all right.

"I know. I know you're leaving him. I've known it for weeks." Charlie kissed her forehead. "You knew it, too! You've known it before today!" He pulled her closer, and Cynthia looked up at the brown eyes, the wide smile, at the Charlie she suddenly felt as muscles and skin and maleness. She did not resist when he put his finger under her chin and gently tilted her face up toward his. The kiss went on for hours or days or for all the rest of the summer. It went on and on, with a sweetness that exaggerated the scent of the roses and the blue of the lake behind their closed lids.

Cynthia held onto his shirt collar as though it were a lifeline in a stormy sea, or the only thing between a cliffside and the earth a thousand meters below her dangling feet. She felt her skin wanting him, and her tongue softly touching his, and she longed for this man with a hunger she could not remember ever knowing before.

From the third floor of Les Colombiers, Stephanie watched from her bedroom window and silently applauded.

CHAPTER THIRTY-TWO

Cynthia climbed into Charlie's MG, and in minutes they were driving into Geneva and then across the Pont du Mont Blanc to the other side of the lake. "Where are we going?"

"To my house. I want to make love to you."

That frightened Cynthia. It reminded her of being in the taxi with Jean-François all those years ago. Of plowing through the slush-filled streets of Boston toward his hotel, his bed. "No." She shook her head, thinking, Oh, Charlie don't ruin it. Don't disappoint me. "What are you keeping from me? I can't stand another secret!"

He looked at her as he pulled into the driveway of a house half-hidden by trees. Behind it gleamed Lake Geneva, a wide swath of blue, turning silver in the dusk. "Come here." He pulled her across the front seat into his arms. "I'll tell you everything you want to know. This is my house. I apologize for not telling you about it, but it wasn't livable when I got the call from you about Stephanie. I really didn't have a place to stay. And then when I could have moved here, when the last carpenter left, I was amazed at all I was absorbing about your family. It was an invaluable experience to be able to understand Stephanie's ideas of who she is." He waited for her to speak, and when she didn't, he asked, "Do you forgive me?"

She nodded. "But . . . but will you live here? Do you live in Boston? Do you . . ."

"I have no wife. I have no children. I have houses in one, two, three—actually four countries, if you count Nantucket as another country. All run by housekeepers who only know I might arrive without a toothbrush in the middle of the night and stay for two days or two months." He spread his hands. "That's all there is to know about me. The perks of being in real estate. I can live anywhere with my books and my typewriter. Fieldwork is where I choose it to be. Boston is three months of the year at the clinic. I feel very free."

"No more secrets?" she asked.

Charlie shook his head. He was staring at her pretty mouth. "And you?"

"May I . . ."

"Come on. A glass of wine. In my living room."

It was glass-walled and all lake before them. The house itself was peach-colored stucco, modern in its lines, like an adobe house in New Mexico. Every room had glass doors that opened onto a terrace, both ground floor and first floor, and every terrace was like an altar dedicated to the gods and goddesses of Lake Geneva.

Prints hung on the walls, but there was very little furniture, just a few pieces of glass and chrome on polished wooden floors. It was clean and shining, with a sense of space that made Cynthia imagine she could dance from one room to the next. Barefoot.

"I can tell you everything because I'm no longer ashamed or angry. I feel somehow that what I did this afternoon cleared so much darkness away. A heaviness is gone from me." She took the white wine and watched him settle down across from her in a big wicker chair. "I got pregnant when I was seventeen, and my parents sent me to the Bahamas to be hidden away. The baby was born in New York, and . . ." Her eyes filled with tears. "And I gave it away. A little boy. And he died." Cynthia took a swallow of the wine. Charlie was listening, watching her face. She took another sip. "I only respond when I have to. I react to what's put in front of me."

"But today you didn't."

"No, I didn't." Her voice held such joy. "Today I talked to the baby's father. Yes!" she marveled. "He was that. And he was someone I loved very much. And now . . ." Her eyes were staring out at the lake. "We talked about so many things. We touched each other after all these years. And now he is simply someone who was terribly important for a slice of time, a piece of my life. At last I seem to be moving forward. To be free of all ghosts." Cynthia was silent for a moment. "I won't stay in my marriage any longer. I won't be Jean-François's accomplice. I realized the next day, after our talk in the *fumoir*, that you were right. It's been like that for years. I am a pleaser. Stephanie called me a martyr, but I think that's not quite it. I was a pleaser, a smoother of rough edges, and when there was a splinter and Jean-François was annoyed, I was in the wrong. It was always my fault that he wasn't happy." She sighed and looked out at the lake, past Charlie. "I wonder if I ever knew the man I married. I feel as if I haven't seen him for years. And yet we had breakfast together this morning." She frowned. "No. Not together. We were two people in the same room. I suddenly don't hate him anymore. Do you know what it's like to have someone make love to you while you're hating him?"

"No. I hope I never know." Charlie stood up and put his wineglass on the table in front of her. "Come with me, Cynthia. Come upstairs with me. I want to make love to you because I love you."

She took his hand and allowed him to lead her through the house and up the stairs to a white bedroom overlooking water and sky.

Charlie unfastened her sandals and then her dress, and when she stood before him in white silk panties, he said, "You undress me," and with fumbling fingers she undid the first button of his shirt. Then, when she realized there was no turning back, her hands became purposeful. She drew the shirt away from him. How often she had seen him pull himself out of the pool, these strong tan shoulders flexing with the effort. Cynthia almost shyly traced the fine white line of the scar on his collarbone, the one he'd gotten ice-skating on the Charles River, as she'd heard him tell Michel.

When he was naked before her, he reached out and, with one quick motion, pulled her panties to the floor, and she stepped out of them. Then Charlie clasped her hand and led her to the big white bed, and they lay down together in each other's arms.

She stared into his brown eyes, and he into her green ones, until they could not keep their smiling faces apart. He kissed her closed lids and then bent down and kissed her nipples, then circled each one with the tip of his tongue. Cynthia swallowed and did not move, did not speak. "Are you praying?" he asked her, and she reached down for him. "Please come back. Up here."

He pulled himself to face her on the pillows again, and could see that she was frightened. With one big hand he stroked the line of her neck, the curve of her shoulder, very gently, as though he could lull her to sleep, and when she was relaxed enough to close her eyes, Charlie put his hand on her belly and moved it back and forth. She made no gesture to stop him, but opened her eyes and stared at his face and was still staring when he reached between her thighs and began to touch a place that Jean-François had always neglected. Cynthia dug her fingers into his shoulders and bit her lip and breathed through her nose as if in pain, but her eyes remained locked with his. Charlie leaned over and kissed her cheek, but never stopped the slow, methodical movement of just one finger, and her clear green eyes would not leave his face. "Let me give you pleasure," he whispered, and Cynthia thought, Give? Give *me* pleasure? Take. Take me. Take what you want.

When she cried out and arched her back, he put his mouth on hers and entered her as she trembled and clawed his chest. There were no words between them, no thoughts; there was no Geneva, no lake, no house, no room, no bed. Just happiness like a drug coursing through their bodies.

The Beau Rivage

Iris took the heavy door in both hands and, when Jean-François was at the stairs, slammed it as hard as she could. The noise reverberated through the atrium, down to the lobby, where it sounded like a gunshot. The concierge, in his immaculate white jacket, flinched and looked up, worried. Iris, however, found that the loudness gave her some satisfaction; then, still naked except for the diamond earrings, she went back and stared at the rumpled bed.

Finished. *The last time I make love to Jean-François Colbert.* She sat down on the edge of the bed and suddenly felt bone-tired. "I'm not going to cry," she said aloud. "I'm going to take a bubble bath and then get good and drunk."

Anna's day off, wouldn't you know it, she thought as she bent over to run the tub. Even ZiZou was gone. Anna had taken the dog at Iris's request. That little self-pitying thought triggered the tears, but by the time the bath was ready, she was all right again. She dried off, as always, admiring her pink, lush body, and then, as was her habit, carefully applying creams from her toes up to her neck. She changed her mind about getting dressed, and opened the wardrobe with her dozens of negligees. She put on the black one from Christian Dior, then took it off, then put on the peach-colored one with the lace top, and discarded it. She pulled the pink one over her head, stared at herself in the mirror, and pulled the silk over her head again. It went with the others in a pile. Anna was invaluable at times like this, for Iris never put anything away, never hung anything up. *White. Virginal white is what I want.* She slipped on the newest white negligee, tied the little satin ribbons across her breast, and stared with satisfaction in the mirror. *Oh, Jean-François! Look what you're missing and weep!* Then Iris suddenly felt her eyes sting, and with a bold sense of purpose she sat down at the dressing table and made up her eyes and powdered her breasts and rouged her cheeks. She stared into the mirror. *Only two hours ago, I was getting ready for him, now he's gone for good.* Through the open balcony doors she heard the horn of the big white boat that cruised the lake like a *grande dame.* "Heart and soul," sang Iris, for it was unmistakably the first three notes of the horn. "I begged to be adored. Lost control and tumbled overboard . . . madly . . . that little night we kissed . . ."

Iris thought of his sneers. Jean-François had insinuated she was from nowhere—no, he had *said* it. That she wasn't good enough to be his wife.

Her green eyes flashed with anger as she opened a side drawer in the little chest and began to scramble through curlers, clips, ribbons, and rubber bands until her hand felt what she wanted—a small rectangular packet. A reminder of the past of Ilsa Keller, of the high-school days with Gretchen and Brenda, of being tough with Cutter as they strolled the halls before the first bell.

Iris opened her jewel box and put on three diamond rings and a pair of diamond earrings, then a matching necklace of square-cut stones. She smiled. Diamonds never fail to make me feel better. Whew, get out the sunglasses! Then her little manicured fingers tore open the package. Iris thought, I haven't done this for years. She tore off one piece of silver foil after the other, and stuffed the gum into her mouth. Then she smacked to her heart's content in front of the mirror, staring at herself in the diamond necklace and the white lace and the white satin ribbons. Smack. Smack, smack, smack, went the whole pack of spearmint gum.

Les Colombiers

Michel had washed his face, and now sat with Stephanie out on the terrace. She told him the story of their mother's phone call and their discussion of what it meant. Michel said nothing. "And then I saw Charlie out in the garden, and they were kissing!"

Michel held a beer in one hand. He stared down at it. "You know Père's been having affairs all along, don't you?"

Stephanie nodded. There was color in her face from the heat, and she looked rather pretty, but still too thin.

Her brother nodded again, in misery, thinking of the scene at the Beau Rivage. "Where's Mother now?"

Before Stephanie could answer, there came a "Yoo-hoo" from behind them. "Honestly, don't you think someone could have picked me up at the airport?" Elizabeth was standing in the doorway in one of her white dresses with lots of noisy silver bracelets, hair pulled back severely, with oversized dark glasses covering most of her face. Cynthia had said Elizabeth always looked like a celebrity traveling incognito. "Did you all forget me?" she asked.

"Lizzie!" Michel stood and walked over to embrace her. "We didn't know you were coming!"

"Darling," she cooed. "I didn't know I was either! And Stephanie! Why, you're out of bed! I called Dr. Marceau yesterday, and he told me you were much better . . ."

"You talked to him?" Stephanie's voice betrayed her dislike of the general practitioner. She would never forget the meeting between Dr. Marceau and

Charlie and herself, and what he had wanted to do to her. Charlie had been on her side.

"Yes, I did!" Elizabeth unpinned her straw hat with the black and white striped ribbon and put it on the table, then allowed Michel to seat her between him and his sister. "I think it's time I acted a little less like a grandmother and a little more like Auntie Mame." They waited. "Simone is opening the champagne, and then I'll . . ."

Simone appeared with a silver tray and glasses. Babette followed with the green bottle and an ice bucket.

"Now," said Elizabeth, when they all lifted their glasses, "I know that Stephanie isn't going back to school until after Christmas, and that you said you weren't going to college." She winked at Michel. The art lessons would always be their secret. Her grandson got up and came to her chair and put his arms around her. "Thanks for everything," he said softly.

"What's that all about?" came Stephanie's voice.

"Something that's over, but was wonderful while it lasted," said Michel as Elizabeth turned to look up at his face.

"Well, as I was saying"—she lifted her glass again—"I have tickets for a ship that sails the Greek Islands. We board on Wednesday if you feel up to it." She tipped her glass toward the two others, and she and Michel drank.

"I want to go!" Michel said. I want to go far away and forget Iris and the Beau Rivage and all I heard a few hours ago.

Stephanie did not answer.

Elizabeth said, "And I want to have fun! And dance all those crazy Greek dances and break dishes and drink ouzo and buy lots of junky jewelry and sing!"

"Sing?" the young ones chorused.

"But of course! I am going to sing my way through Lesbos and Skiathos and Mykonos . . ."

Her grandchildren laughed and Elizabeth toasted, "To singing!" Then she asked suddenly, "Where's your mother?" There had been no sign of dinner preparations when she'd given Simone the champagne.

"She went away with Charlie," said Stephanie. She knew how it sounded, and she thought, Yes, she did. I've never seen a kiss like that. Except in the movies.

"Well," was Elizabeth's response. "Well," she repeated, absorbing the information. Michel refilled their glasses. "Would anyone like to join me for dinner? Let's go to the Lion d'Or and pull out all the stops."

Michel nodded. "I would. Let me go up and put on a tie."

Stephanie was hesitant. "Do you think they would have fish sticks?"

"I think a restaurant with all those stars has anything you can imagine, darling."

Stephanie smiled tremulously, thinking, Everything is changing, or I'm changing. For the better. Mother isn't the same. I'm not the same, she said to herself for the fiftieth time that afternoon. And this is the first time out of the house in months, first time in a dress, first food outside of the bedroom. She felt a little leap of excitement inside and wondered, Am I hungry? Hungry for all kinds of things outside this house? "I'll be down in five minutes," she said.

Elizabeth told everyone in the kitchen to take the night off, and Babette and Simone immediately decided they'd catch the train to town, to go to the movies. Elizabeth, Michel, and Stephanie took the Fiat and were laughing together as they pulled out of the driveway. As they drove beside the lake on the Quai du Mont Blanc, they passed Jean-François, who had been drinking in the Richemond bar after leaving Iris. He didn't see them, and neither his mother nor his children noticed him.

. . .

Les Colombiers. Cynthia. Stability. Jean-François passed the Red Cross head-quarters up on the hill to the left, and shifted into fourth gear. No matter what has ever happened in Paris or London or New York or Geneva, Cynthia has always been at home, waiting for me, looking beautiful at the other end of the dining-room table. My serene blond wife with her perfect taste in clothes and jewelry. Nothing gauche, not ever. Elegant. Lovely in her simple un-derstatement. And an aristocrat. She could be a princess. Ha! He frowned. Iris! Iris thinking she could ever be my wife! That she could ever take Cynthia's place! Completely *fou*! Madness!

Jean-François decided he had made a narrow escape. Now I'm rid of her. She can go back to Paris with that silly French maid and that little bitch of hers that growls and shows its teeth whenever I walk in the door. Bitches! Aren't they all!

. . .

"Are you awake?" Cynthia whispered. In answer, Charlie's hand moved to her face, pressed against his chest, and with one finger he touched her cheek.

The doors of the terrace off the bedroom were open, and the lights across the lake were visible. Cynthia could see stars against the black sky. She smiled and he whispered, "What?"

"It's a perfect night for what I used to do, but now I don't have to do it anymore." Her voice was light and happy.

"What are you talking about?"

Cynthia kissed him and then wriggled into her position under his arm again. "I used to write down things about Jean-François. Things he'd said that were particularly terrible. Like . . . he used to tell me that being in bed with me was like making love to a corpse."

Charlie pulled her up into his arms, and they faced each other on the pillows. "Pretty lively corpse," he remarked.

Cynthia smiled slowly and kissed his shoulder. Charlie. His skin, the way he tastes, the way he smells, his muscles against me. It's more than wonderful. There is no word for him, or for the way he makes me feel. It's all so natural. So easy. Wonderful. Full of wonder.

"So you wrote all this down and then went up to bed with him?"

"Oh, no. I'd wait until he was asleep and get out of bed and go down to the desk in the salon and write. Then, when I'd finished, I'd go out in the garden and bury the pages."

Charlie was silent, and then he said, "I saw you one night from my window, just after I'd arrived. I thought it was the most bizarre thing to see a beautiful woman in the moonlight wearing the most transparent, sexiest . . ."

Cynthia laughed. "It is a little strange, I guess." She sighed, remembering how sad the notes had been, how alone she had felt in the dark house writing that way. "I suddenly realized I didn't have to bury the pages anymore. I still write. I still put away what I write, but I don't literally have to bury it . . ." Her voice trailed off.

She kissed his cheek. "I may have to keep you around, Charlie. I probably need a good psychiatrist."

He nodded and said in a soft voice, just before beginning to kiss her again, "I'm going to hate being around you."

The Beau Rivage

Iris heard something in the salon and called out, "Room service! I'm in the bedroom!" There was no answer. She was still seated at the dressing table, enjoying the sight of herself chewing gum. But the noise wasn't in the salon and it wasn't room service. Iris screamed when she felt the cold metal on her neck.

A voice said, "I've hated you all these years, and now I'm gonna kill you so that I don't have to waste any more energy hating you."

Iris was terrified. She couldn't turn to see in the mirror, but was at an awkward angle, facing the door to the salon. "Who are you?" she said, and realized with a shock that she was answering this man in English. He had spoken in English. And his voice . . . she knew the voice. "Let me see you," she breathed. Iris could feel the vein in her neck moving in fear. My pulse is probably a thousand, she thought.

"You don't have to see me to remember me, do you? Think hard, Iris. Have there really been that many men you've fucked? Fucked over? Fucked and thrown away?"

The voice! The accent! Iris desperately tried to remember.

She heard the click of the safety being released, except she didn't know what it was, just that the gun pressed even harder against her throat. It occurred to her that she was about to be murdered while chewing a whole pack of spearmint gum. Maybe as a last reflex she could spit it out as the gun fired. Or maybe as a last request he would let her toss it through the open window. But to die with it in my mouth! How embarrassing! After all I've been through.

The voice said, "Oh, you can guess if you really think about it. You've fucked lotsa men, but you can't have married all their fathers."

"Cesare!" she shrieked, and turned on the stool to face him. He stepped back in surprise. She wasn't supposed to do that. The gun was aimed at her heart, but also, he realized, blinking, at those luscious breasts that seemed to be bulging out of the top of that lace bodice with the ridiculous little ribbons tied in silly little bows. Cesare thought the entire get-up looked very insubstantial, as though it might tear or break under the weight of all that flesh. He could see her pink nipples under a pattern of white lace. His mouth was dry.

"Cesare! Where have you been all these years!" Iris was standing with her arms out.

He was confused. She should be terrified by now. As Cesare debated what action to take, a French-accented voice sang out, "Room service!" and a trolley with a white tablecloth was wheeled into the bedroom. There was champagne in a frosted silver bucket, and a large plate of smoked salmon, sliced just the way Iris liked it—so thin you could read the *Journal de Genève* through it. The waiter tried to get a good look at Iris so that he could report downstairs, and only just barely managed to open the champagne and pour it into two of Iris's Baccarat glasses she kept on the bureau. Luckily he had an extra fork, but he'd thought the order was for one. He never gave Cesare a second glance.

By the time he had gone, Cesare had put the gun down and was holding a glass. "What the hell are you doing here?" he asked, though he knew about Jean-François. He'd seen him coming and going. He hadn't missed his last departure, or the door slamming, either.

Iris looked at the handsome, olive-skinned face and, with a leap of her heart, those hooded eyes. She took her gum out demurely and put it in the dish where she kept safety pins, behind her on the dressing table. Cesare's eyes were on her face. He hadn't seen her close up for years. Now he simply stared at the wide-set green eyes, the full pink lips, the ivory-pale skin. Her hair was pinned up loosely in back and curling on her neck, and when his eyes moved downward, there were those amazing breasts, straining to free themselves of the inconsequential covering.

Iris knew what he was looking at. Her voice was soft, little-girlish. "Cesare, I've missed you."

"Christ, Iris! Don't pull that stuff on me! Ya go to bed with me, then ya dump me for my father—for his money, I guess—then ya manage to get pregnant so that my inheritance is sliced away by millions of dollars, then ya—"

"You know what a Swiss banker friend of mine says?"

"No." His voice was sullen, but he did take a swallow of the champagne. Leave it to Iris. Dom Perignon. He approved.

She smiled coyly. "I don't agree with him, but he says, 'God rules in heaven and money on earth. Even the devil dances for gold.' "

Cesare was staring at her mouth. Goddamn! What nerve! She can actually say it! Somehow it made it better for her to say she'd married his father for his bank account. How he had suffered, thinking of them in bed together. So it had been money. Nothing more. Maybe not much more. Yeah, well, Iris was Iris.

She read his mind. "I have a lot of money, but you must have a lot of money, too." Her eyes took in his tight trousers in the tan fabric, and then her eyes flickered upward, inspecting his suit jacket that fit so well. His shoes looked handmade. Good body, as always, she thought. "I don't need any more money," she said. "I want other things now."

Cesare refused to take the bait. "Christ! Ya think ya got enough diamonds? They're makin' a glare and hurtin' my eyes!"

Iris was staring at his mouth. It looked a little cruel, which had always turned her on. Miami. A million years ago. "I don't need any more diamonds. I need other things."

They sat down then, she on the loveseat and he in a little Louis Quinze chair beside her. The negligee fell open and he got a good look at one long, silky leg as she poured the rest of the champagne into their glasses. The bed was rumpled behind them.

"Do you still want to kill me?" Her little pointed pink tongue licked the corner of her mouth.

He shook his head. "Nah. I won't get anything out of it, and you're right. We both got enough money." Cesare stared openly at her breasts now. "Tell me, Iris, what were all these hints about wanting 'other things'?"

"I want to make love."

Cesare's heart began to pound, though he would think later that nothing about Iris should ever surprise him. He saw the gun, cold, metallic, evil, on the little marble table beside his champagne glass. Then he looked at Iris. She was warm, perfumed, and he could smell her musk. She looked soft and willing and full of wanting. He had never tired of remembering those afternoons in Miami. The memories had tortured him. He'd never married because of Iris. She was ever-present, all too vivid in his mind, and always got in the way of the other woman. And yes, the woman of the moment was always the "other" woman. Iris was Iris.

Again, she read his mind. "Remember the tennis lessons?"

Cesare burst out laughing, and then stood up and said roughly, "C'mere!" He pulled her out of her chair and began kissing her. When he could breathe again, he said, "Oh, Iris, you were always such a bad girl!"

Collonge-Bellerive

Cynthia and Charlie awoke for the second time at about midnight, and snuggled together under the white sheet. The night air from the lake cooled their skin and felt clean.

"Cynthia," he began. "You know you can go back to him."

She was shocked. "Tired of me already?" What was he saying?

"No! But he would take you back, and maybe things would change."

"Things *have* changed. I want to be with you." There was silence. She took his big hand in hers. "Listen, Charlie. I used to think all the time, every year, that things would change. That somehow I could have the man I married back again. That it could be fun again. That I would be happy to see him when I heard him come home from the bank. That he would take me in his arms and . . ." She stopped and then began to speak in a matter-of-fact voice. "Now, you must know about illusions. Self-delusions. Secrets." She smiled. "Did you know that a lot of the Swiss Alps are riddled with tunnels and roads and giant caves? Military secret. They are full of soldiers and supplies, even hospitals and fighter planes. So you drive to a beautiful place like Gstaad along a highway where the median posts are removable so that the road can be a runway for planes in wartime, and all these glorious mountains are nearly hollow against a sky too blue to be real, and you . . . you never know . . ." Her voice died.

Charlie squeezed her hand. "Cynthia, I love you. I think I've loved you for a long time. I held myself back. I hid the chocolate because I didn't trust myself to speak. It wasn't the right time." He reached up and stroked her hair. "Let's talk. Let's try to be realistic." He sighed. "I don't have Colbert money. I have what I think of as lots of money, but it may not be lots of money to you. I can do anything I want. I have money for plane tickets, for fun, but I don't have the kind of money you're used to." He hesitated. "I don't have money to buy you diamonds."

"Oh, Charlie! I have plenty of diamonds." She rose on her elbows and stared at his face in the starlight reflected from the water. Then she kissed his cheek tenderly. "I think I want what I've never had. Things I've never had until this summer—until tonight." She smiled flirtatiously. "Things like chocolate."

Clarissa McNair graduated from Briarcliff College in New York majoring in American history. In Toronto, she was a researcher for *Connections,* the six hour, award-winning CBC-TV documentary on organized crime. In Rome, she was a news writer, broadcaster and producer of political documentaries for Vatican Radio and was also the weekend news anchor for WROM-TV. While writing GARDEN OF TIGERS, she was in charge of international publicity for a film company. Having had adventures from Afghanistan to Zanzibar, she is now a private detective specializing in criminal cases.

CPSIA information can be obtained at www.ICGtesting.com
260214BV00001B/3/P